# Prophesies

# And War

Part II Betrayal

Book 12

Of The Warrior Series

By

Sandra J Yearman

**Seraphim Publishing LLC**

**We Will Bring Light To All The Dark Places**

Registered trademark-Sandra J Yearman

Seraphim Publishing
438 Water St
Cambridge, WI 53523
sandrajyearman@gmail.com

Library of Congress Catalog Number: 2016920861

ISBN: 978-0-9984057-0-4

First Edition

# About The Author

Sandra J Yearman is a native of Wisconsin, where she currently resides. She graduated from the University of Wisconsin with a Bachelor of Arts degree in Journalism. Sandra was a member of the United States Army Reserves for over twenty years. She retired from the Dane County Sheriff's Office in Madison Wisconsin as a sergeant.

Sandra is a cancer survivor. And it is on this journey that she says she found her voice and began to write. She established Seraphim Publishing LLC in 2008. Sandra has spent decades supporting and working with rescued domestic animals.

Books written by Sandra:

## <u>Novels</u>

Brother Kings
The Scroll And The Sword
Song Of The Second Son
The Faces Of The Damned
A Single Lion Roars
Stand Before The Children
Tyrants, Dictators And Kings

Politicians And Kings
Armada Of The Dead
The Eyes Below
Illusions And War
Prophesies And War

## Poetry

A Gathering Of Angels
I AM Who You Seek
A Celebration Of Angels
The Time Of Angels Is At Hand
The Warrior On Bended Knees
Celebration of God
On His Wings
The Voice Of An Angel
If I Had Wings
Souls On Fire
As Angels Hover Over
From The Mist The Angels Came
You Are The Song
Be Still
Walking With Angels
When Angels Smile
Angel Dreams
An Angel's Touch
Dancing With Angels

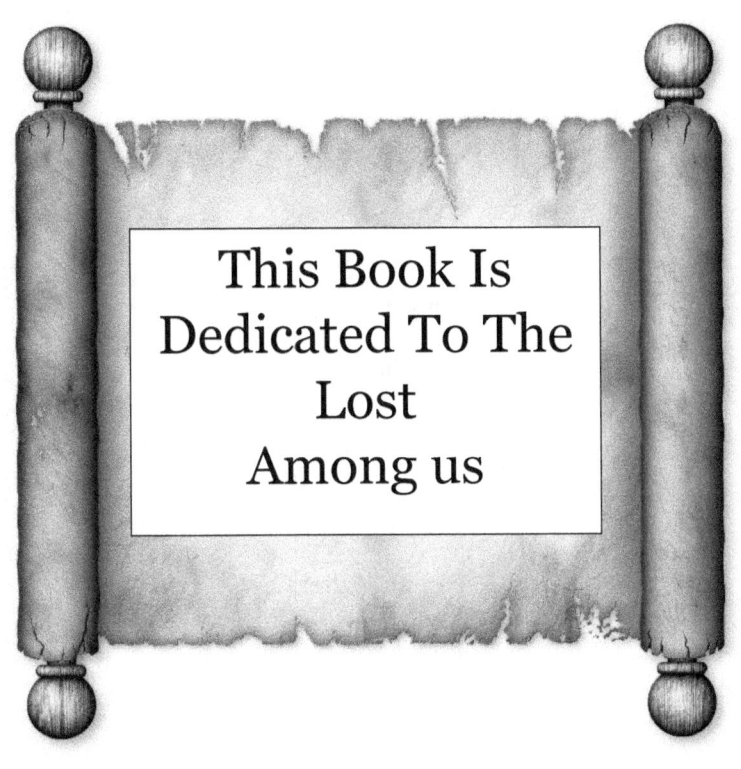

This Book Is
Dedicated To The
Lost
Among us

# Contents

# Contents

# <u>Contents</u>

# Chapter I
## Retribution

Retribution was swift although not just after the news circulated about the attacks on Prince Michael, Edward and Javier. Soldiers, team members, Nordes warriors, Ruala and Shettee warriors stormed the City of Langer. They dragged men and demons out of taverns and the Catacombs and hung them in the streets.

The fire at the Anchors Inn Tavern spread to entire city blocks because the battles prevented people from being able to put the flames out. Innocent citizens hid in terror. Dark lords and criminals unleashed their gangs.

No one thought to call the Angels in because rage, fear and hatred consumed the city.

The fighting was so intense that King Manu sent his warriors to the White Rose Restaurant to evacuate the people inside. It was then that many of the Ruala warriors learned that Prince Michael had been murdered.

The Sanuri had given his life force to Edward and Javier but both men were almost dead when he got to them. Hannah and the other healers prayed; for they felt there was little more that they could do for their friends.

When the wounded had been brought into the restaurant, the children were immediately ushered into a back room. The women now had the Ruala warriors transport the children first so they would not see the dead and wounded. Michael's sisters had no knowledge that their beloved brother was dead.

Sudfad and Renya were both crippled by their grief. They could not think, they could barely speak; Claudius and Rosa literally carried them.

Madeline was hysterical. She lost the love of her life and her cherished brother was dying. She clung to Emeral and sobbed.

The women who were working on the wounded were covered with blood and tears. Some would later have difficulty remembering those moments. Corsa alternated between praying and ordering Javier not to die.

Diana and Vivian held onto Kate; the woman who never faltered now could not stand without the help of her friends.

"Oh my god, please not now," gasped Vivian.

"What…"Diana did not finish her sentence as she realized Vivian's water had broken. "Iris, Batina, Rachel come here!" Diana yelled. "Vivian's water broke, she needs to be in the next group taken to the castle."

Fahron and his troops were in the city fighting with street thugs when a Ruala warrior flew over him and yelled, "Michael is dead. Those bastards murdered him. They attacked him from behind; he never had a chance."

Fahron never asked a question or even said a word. He felt as if he had a weight in his chest. He was consumed with grief, then anger, then rage. And all of these emotions flooded his being simultaneously. He grabbed a gang member who was fighting with one of the soldiers. Fahron threw the man to the ground and choked the life from his body.

It wasn't until the Ruala warriors brought the first group of women and children from the White Rose Restaurant to Mathas' castle that the King learned Michael was dead. Mathas put on his battle armor and led troops into the city. He bellowed orders, swore and cried as he led his men.

When the second group of Ruala warriors arrived at the restaurant to transport the women, Sasha ran up to them. "Vivian is in labor. She needs to go but she may fight you on this and someone needs to find Raphael."

Bella and Isadore returned to Mathas' castle with the second group of Ruala warriors so they could prepare chambers for Edward and Javier. These two pillars of strength were numbed by the brutality of the attacks on their friends and sickened by the riots and battles they saw in the streets of their beloved city.

When they entered the castle and learned that Mathas had joined the battle they took control. Isadore went to the kitchen with recipes for tonics. She told the cooks to prepare soups for the wounded and meals for those who would be arriving soon.

Bella made sure the children were taken care of and occupied. She told the nurses that under no circumstances were the children to leave the castle.

"Bella what is going on?" asked Nyla. "No one will tell us anything."

"We know it's bad," said Saran. "Everyone is crying."

Olivia was standing with her friends and the tears started to run down her face. "Olivia why are you crying?" asked Saran anxiously. Bella had not said a word. Nyla and Saran looked back and forth between Olivia and Bella. "You can read Bella's thoughts," Saran said accusingly to Olivia.

"Don't make me tell you," Olivia whispered.

"It's Michael isn't it?" asked Nyla frantically. "Is he hurt?"

Bella started to speak but choked up and tears were running down her cheeks. Both Nyla and Saran started crying. "He's dead isn't he?" Saran asked in a whisper. Bella couldn't answer the question and started to cry harder. She held out her arms and all three of the girls flew to her. They held each other and cried.

"Dagon, I'm not leaving," said Vivian. "I certainly won't have this baby before everyone leaves here. I don't want to leave Kate."

Kate had been staring at Edward in stunned silence. She now turned, looked at Vivian and started to sob.

"I'm not forcing her," Dagon said to Diana.

Diana pulled Dagon away from her friends and asked in a whisper, "Has anyone found Raphael?"

"We've got people looking for him but the city is wild; you'll see when we leave."

"Well, if he gets mad we are just going to have to tell him that we tried," Diana said.

"Is Bella or Isadore here?" yelled Misha as he ran into Mathas' castle. He had flown Ashley to the castle and now they both called the names of the women.

"I was making tonics," Isadore said as she ran out of the kitchen.

"Iris sent us," Misha said. "Vivian's water broke but she won't leave Kate and Hannah doesn't want us to move Edward or Javier yet."

It was obvious to Isadore that Misha and Ashley had been crying. "Are you two alright?" she asked.

"No," said Misha. "The stinking cowards shot them all in the back..." Misha stopped himself from saying anything else.

Isadore squeezed his hand and said, "I'll prepare a room for Vivian."

"I'll help you," Ashley said.

Isadore was about to leave when she turned back to Misha. "Are you going back to the restaurant?"

"Yes."

"I will let you decide if you want to tell Sudfad and Renya but Nyla and Saran figured out what happened. Bella and Olivia are with them. Nina and the other children don't know yet but they all understand that something awful happened."

"Honesty, I don't know if Renya and Sudfad are in any condition to deal with that now," Misha said.

"Well, Bella and I can tell the children but we thought more parents should be here."

"I'll talk to them," Misha said and left the castle.

Isadore and Bella had seen more than their share of grief and suffering in their lives. They were both married to military officers. Before there were hospitals in their kingdom, they would open their homes to the wounded. They had long ago lost count of how many military funerals they had attended.

The moment these women realized Mathas and Rosa were not in the castle, they put the staff to work. They had rooms prepared on the first floor of the center wing for the wounded and now an additional room for Vivian.

They had a chambers prepared on the second floor for Michael's body. This would be where the showings would take place.

Bella sent word of the death of Prince Michael to the Village of Tyger. In her letter she said she had chambers prepared for the team members and any villagers who wanted to stay at the castle. She said there would be a showing of the body this night for family and friends and the official showing would be the following afternoon. She sent the letters via Enrops.

Then she sent a second letter to Raul, Simon, Vitomas and Annabelle. Bella's tears so stained the first copy that she had to write a second.

Isadore sent messages to Claudius, Fahron, Mathas, King Manu, Sorren, Matthew, Thaos and Stephan with similar information.

Three hours after receiving the letters, women from the Village of Tyger, which included wedding guests, started to arrive at the castle.

Some brought the children of the team members, others brought flowers and candles for the showing and all of them brought food.

The battles were winding down in the city. As the fighting stopped people learned of Michael's death. The team members left the soldiers to finish in Langer and they returned to Mathas' castle.

Ratri ran into the dining room of the White Rose and said loudly, "Hannah, I know you don't want to move them but the fires are out of control and the wind is shifting. We need to get all of you out of here now! We will force you if we have to." As Ratri spoke, several dozen Ruala warriors entered the room.

Raphael and Joshua ran into the castle together. "Where is Vivian?" Raphael yelled.

"They are bringing her soon," Bella said. "She wouldn't leave Kate."

"What!" Raphael said and turned white. "What is she thinking?"

"Honey, Vivian is a strong girl and that baby isn't going to come for a while. I am sure she was thinking she would want her friends with her if that was you lying there. I will take you to the chambers we prepared for her."

As soon as the women from the village arrived at the castle they started working which was a welcomed relief for Bella and Isadore. Bella sent many of these women to help Ashley who was preparing medical supplies and rooms for the wounded.

Sudfad and Renya would not leave the restaurant before Michael's body, Edward and Javier were moved. Emeral and Maxwell flew the King and Queen to the castle. Rosa immediately ushered them all into a private parlor and handed them drinks.

"The first showing will be tonight and a chambers is prepared. Madeline and Angelina are cleaning his body and will dress him. Bella and Isadore have tried to keep the news from the children but Nyla and Saran figured it out on their own. Ryan and Olivia are with them. Bella didn't want to tell the other children until their parents arrived but everyone is returning and they will hear it soon," explained Rosa.

"Of course," Sudfad said and inadvertently touched his pocket. "Oh my god," he said then looked around in a confused manner. "Where...did anyone see that pouch I had?"

"Sudfad, I picked it up," said Emeral and took it out of a larger pouch that she always wore when she flew.

"I know that I am not thinking straight right now so before we bring the children in I need your advice," Sudfad said and took a small velvet box from his pocket. He opened it and handed it to Renya.

"Madeline's engagement ring," Renya gasped and started to cry again. "Sudfad, we have to give it to her. Now, so she..."

Sudfad put his arm around Renya and kissed her on top of her head. "Emeral would you please empty that pouch?" As Emeral placed assorted velvet boxes on top of a table Sudfad explained. "These are jewels for the wedding. There are necklaces and earrings for the girls and Margarit. There is jewelry for our other children, for you Renya and for Madeline. I don't know if we should give it to them but I...I don't want to get rid of it either."

"Sudfad give it to them. It will be their last gifts from him," Maxwell said. "At a time like this it might be a part of him that they can hold in their hands."

Sudfad looked at Renya who nodded but did not speak. "Rosa do you want to bring Margarit in with our girls?" Sudfad asked. Rosa nodded. "First let me find their things," he said but was having difficulty because of the tears in his eyes so Emeral helped him.

Rosa led Nyla, Saran and Ryan into the room first. Both girls ran to Sudfad and Renya; they all hugged and cried. A few minutes later Rosa walked back into the room with Nina and Margarit. As soon as Nina saw everyone's faces she let go of Rosa's hand and started to yell, "No! No!" She turned and ran out of the room. Ryan ran after her. She screamed as he carried her back into the room.

"Is Matthew dead?" Margarit asked as she started to cry.

"No Honey. It is your cousin Michael," Rosa said and hugged Margarit. Ryan was just entering the room with Nina when they heard Rosa. Nina started to sob.

"Ryan, I will take her," Renya said, Ryan handed Nina to Renya who carried the little girl to a sofa and sat down. Renya rocked back and forth as she hugged Nina. They both cried. Sudfad hugged Nyla and Saran.

After several minutes had passed Emeral said, "Sudfad, perhaps now would be a good time."

Sudfad took a deep breath and said, "Girls, I need you to listen to me. Nina will you look at me? Michael wanted you to be in his wedding and he bought these gifts for you today. I don't honestly know if these will make you feel better or worse." He handed each girl a red velvet box. "Margarit there is one for you too."

Nyla cried when she saw the diamond pendant necklace and earrings. "Were we supposed to wear these in the wedding?" Saran asked.

"Yes," Renya said.

"I'm putting on the necklace and I'm never taking it off," Saran said. "Nyla, Nina put yours on too." All three girls quickly grabbed their necklaces although they needed help clasping them.

"Nyla, Nina we make a pact," Saran said as she touched the diamond pendant. "We will never forget Michael. We will never forget Michael," each girl repeated.

"Me too," Margarit said as Rosa clasped her necklace. "I will never forget Michael." All of the adults cried.

Moments later there was loud noise in the hallway then a knock at the door. Rosa opened the door and Calen was standing in the doorway holding Christopher who was sobbing. Calen had tears in his eyes as he said, "Emeral, he wants you."

"Oh my baby," Emeral said as she took Christopher in her arms.

"Grandma, he was my friend," Christopher said but he was crying so hard that he could barely utter the words.

An hour later Maxwell escorted Madeline into the parlor where Renya and Sudfad were sitting. No one else was in the room. Maxwell kissed Madeline on the top of her head as she sat down and left the room.

"Would you like a glass of wine?" asked Sudfad.

"Yes," Madeline said. "I feel numb; I can't even cry anymore."

Madeline was sitting on a chair facing Sudfad and Renya who were seated on a small sofa. "People are starting to come for the showing," Madeline said as Sudfad handed her a glass of wine. Then in a dazed manner she looked down at her blood stained dress and said, "I need to change."

Renya squeezed her hand and said, "We wanted to speak with you first. Our son loved you and as far as we are concerned you are our daughter now. We would like you to move in with the family and we will take care of you and Javier."

Madeline's lip started trembling and tears ran down her cheeks as she listened to Renya. "I don't know what to say," she said in a whisper.

"Madeline, Michael and I went shopping today. If you don't want these we will understand." As Sudfad spoke he handed her a small velvet box.

Madeline started crying loudly as she opened the box and took out an engagement ring. It was a huge diamond in a silver setting. She put the ring on her finger and stared at it as the tears poured down her face.

"This he bought for you to wear with your wedding dress," Sudfad said. Madeline's hand was shaking as she took the red velvet box from him. The box contained a necklace with a large diamond pendant and matching earrings. She put her fingers to her lips and tried to talk but couldn't.

"You should know that he bought smaller versions of that necklace for the girls and we gave them their gifts to remember him by. He also bought jewelry for the rest of the family."

"He was so happy that you gave us your blessings," Madeline said in a whisper then put her face in her hands and cried.

Since this first showing was less formal there wasn't a receiving line. Sudfad, Renya, Madeline, Nyla, Saran and Nina walked into the room first. Michael's body was laid on a bed that was surrounded with flowers and candles. He was dressed in a suit.

Nina walked up to Michael and gently touched his hand. "He doesn't look dead. He just looks like he is sleeping. Michael thank you for the necklace," Nina whispered. "I brought you something too." She put a small stuffed bear in his arm. Suddenly she swung around and looked at the rest of her family with a smile on her face, "Is he with Mommy now?"

Sudfad, Renya and Madeline remained in the room. Gabriel, Hannah and their children were the next to enter the chambers. Gabriel was carrying Nicholas and set him down so he could pray over Michael. Nicholas stared at Michael then ran out of the room. Moments later he returned and set a stuffed toy on the bed next to Michael's body.

The showing lasted for hours and every child in Gabriel's household gave Michael a toy. "We are burying him with those," Madeline said to Renya and Sudfad. "He adored those children."

The showing was almost over when Mathas, Claudius, Fahron, Sorren, Matthew, Thaos and Stephan walked into the castle. They immediately walked up the stairs and into Michael's chambers.

"Did the children do that?" Stephan asked with a smile and nodded at the toys.

"Yes," Sudfad said. "We are going to bury him with them." Sudfad's comment brought brief smiles to the somber faces of the men.

The men left and Corsa walked into the room. "I am sorry, I am only going to stay a second; I don't want to leave Javier."

"Of course dear," Renya said.

"I will be down there in a little while," Madeline said. "I'm not ignoring him. How is he?"

Corsa walked around the bed and hugged Madeline. "He's the same. He's unconscious and...he's the same. So is Edward."

Mathas held a meeting after the showing that was not mandatory but most of the people in the castle attended. As soon as the door to the Great Hall was closed, Joshua, Micha and Thomas opened it and walked in. "Vivian kicked us out," Micha announced as they took seats.

Diana, Thor and Tanya sat with Kate in Edward's room. The four friends barely spoke.

Madeline walked into Javier's room and started to cry again. She sat down in one of the chairs near the bed. Corsa was the only other person in the room.

19

Within moments there was a knock at the door then Alex peeked his head into the room. "I wasn't sure this was the right chambers," he said as Corsa jumped out of her chair and flew into his arms. Alex hugged his sister tightly as Kent and George entered the room. She hugged all of them before she realized they were all wearing bandages.

"You're hurt," she gasped.

"That's why we are late," Kent said. "We were in Langer and Shara patched us up when we got here."

"I haven't seen you cry since mother died," Alex said to Corsa.

She did not respond to his comment but turned towards Madeline. "Madeline these are my brothers, Alex, Kent and George. And this is Javier's sister Madeline. Her fiancé was killed today too."

"We heard," said Alex and walked up to Madeline. She was sitting in a chair so he knelt down beside her. "Javier is our family which makes you family too. If you need anything at all please ask us." Madeline started to cry again and Alex put his arms around her.

She was able to compose herself after a few minutes and straightened herself in the chair. "Thank you for saying that," Madeline said to Alex then she looked at Corsa. "I didn't get a chance to tell you that Renya and Sudfad..." Madeline started to choke on her words so she paused for a moment. "They said they consider me their daughter now and they want us to move in with them so they can take care of Javier."

Fahron was the first to address the meeting. "The fires are out." He looked at Ashley and Ryan. "Neither of your places were burned but part of the shipyard was. That is where Gideon still is."

He paused then said, "Everyone in this room is filled with grief and anger but I have to tell you that when the fighting was over I was filled with horror too. Dozens upon dozens of men and demons were hung by the neck from trees all over the city."

"I don't even want to think about how many innocent people were hurt today on both sides. I am as guilty as anyone else but I think we lost control." No one in the room said a word.

Thaos walked to the front of the room. "Fahron, I am guilty and I agree with what you said but I am changing the subject for a moment. Stephan left to get Harlow and I want to discuss something before they get here."

"We still don't know who those bastards were that killed Michael or who was paying them. In case, some of you didn't know. We used the wedding groups as bait today and arrested close to ninety men who were hunting not only Javier and Madeline but Gabriel, Raphael, Stephan and me cuz we have bounties on us. Claudius and Fahron arrested three of the men who placed the bounties and General Amundsen will arrest the one in Port Friada. But who knows if we got them all."

"Stephan and I were talking and we think we should announce that Edward and Javier were killed too. That would keep the bounty hunters off them for at least a while. As far as I am concerned, any bastard who is such a coward as to attack a man from behind would attack them when they're laid up too."

"Regardless of what we vote here, Harlow will be writing something up about Michael. So what do you think?"

Sudfad stood up. "Madeline is family now and we want to take her and Javier home to take care of them. Of course that includes Corsa, Edward and Kate; they are already family. We can keep them all hidden in the castle for a while. I think it is a workable idea and I agree with Thaos."

Sorren stood up. "While I agree, I think we need to bring Kate, Corsa and Madeline in here. They should have a say in this."

"I agree," said Mathas. Koby and Joao were sitting the closest to the door. Mathas nodded at them and the two men left the room.

"While we wait, does anyone know where the Sanuri is?" asked Sudfad.

"We couldn't see the guys shooting at us," Matthew said. "That was when Michael, Javier and Edward got shot. I was trying to get Angelina and Shara inside a building. Erebus jumped behind a horse trough. He was mumbling something when I passed him. All of a sudden guys start jumping out of nowhere and burst into flames. He must have used magic. The Sanuri has been looking for him."

"If he used magic he could be in a really bad way," said Sorren. "I am going to look for him too." As Sorren stood up Madeline, Corsa, Kate, Koby and Joao entered the room.

"We already told them," said Koby. "Because they wouldn't leave the rooms."

"We just want to protect them," Thaos said. "What do you think about the idea?"

"Do it," said Kate.

"Madeline and I agree," said Corsa. "We need to get back."

It was almost three in the morning when the sounds of a baby crying woke many people on the first floor of the castle. Madeline and Corsa were sleeping in chairs near Javier's bed while Corsa's brothers were sleeping on the floor of the chambers. A knock on the door woke them all. Diana peeked her head in and announced, "Vivian just had a baby girl if you want to see her."

"I do," Corsa said. "Will someone stay here?"

"We will," said Kent.

"Then I will come with you," Madeline said and the two women walked into the hallway that was already filling with people.

Hannah walked into the hallway and announced, "Vivian and the baby are just fine. I am going to get her something to eat and Raphael will be out here in a moment with the baby."

A few minutes later Raphael, Joshua and Iris walked into the hallway and they were all beaming. Raphael was carrying a tiny baby that was wrapped in a pink blanket. "Meet Crystal Jillian," Raphael said proudly. Crystal is Iris' middle name and Jillian was my mother's name. I was on a mission when Robert was born so this has been such a blessing that I could be here for her birth. I know I am probably babbling, I am so excited but can you believe all of the black hair she has?"

The people in the hallway laughed and moved closer to see the baby.

# Chapter II
## Grief

"Zoya! Jared open up!" Gala yelled repeatedly as she pounded on the front door of their home.

The door flew open and Jared was standing in the doorway wearing only his trousers and holding a sword. He grabbed Gala and pulled her into the house then looked into the darkness for threats.

"I am sorry to wake you," Gala said as tears ran down her face. "I wasn't..."

"Gala, what happened?" asked Zoya.

"Raul just got a letter. Michael has been murdered and Edward and Javier might be dying. Raul and the family are in a really bad way. Jared someone needs to be there if they get attacked too."

"Who did it!" demanded Jared.

"They don't know. They were all shot in the back," Gala said. Both women stared at Jared as the rage that now filled him almost changed his appearance.

"You did the right thing coming here," Jared said through clenched teeth. "Zoya get dressed we will all go and get Archetenus and his family. I don't want any of you women staying home alone."

"Zoya, I'll help you," Gala said and the women quickly left the room. Jared went outside to saddle his horse. He punched the wall of the barn and kicked over a milking stool then he screamed to the heavens.

"Miranda! Miranda!"

Miranda appeared behind Jared and touched his shoulder; in that instant the anger left him and he started to cry. He turned around and faced her. "Jared right now your strength and your wisdom are needed not your hatred," Miranda said soothingly. "Tonight you and Archetenus need to be strong and take the controls of the kingdom."

24

"Michael's entire family is crippled with grief. You will be no help to them if you let your anger take control. Can you do this?"

"Yes," Jared said and nodded.

"I know you are upset but you need to listen to me now. You and Archetenus have a unique understanding of the men responsible for this slaughter."

Jared became angry again, "Do we know them?"

"Not personally. Are you going to be able to control your anger?"

"I am really trying."

"You will need to do more than try because the people in Langer are as broken as the people here. You and Archetenus have some choices to make."

"What do you mean?"

"The two of you have gone places that most of your friends will never understand. You may have to tread those roads again to stop this. Are you prepared to do that?"

"Hell ya. Wait, you don't mean we become Second Sons again do you?"

"The choice has always been yours as to who you let control you. Do you think you can walk in that world again and stay true to yourselves?" Miranda did not wait for him to answer. "Get Archetenus, you are needed at the castle," she said and disappeared.

Sleep came to few that night in the castle of Mathas. The birth of Crystal Jillian brought some relief from the grief and pain. People worked through the night to prepare for the public showing that would be held the following afternoon. Besides the normal procedures for such an event, the ruling families were greatly increasing security measures at the castle and all of their homes.

Gideon did not arrive at the King's castle until shortly before dawn. He was not surprised to find the Great Hall filled with people.

"You look awful, you need to get some sleep," growled Claudius.

Gideon looked around the room and said, "Apparently I am in good company. We lost two entire blocks of the shipyard and that huge area of lumber. Fortunately we didn't lose any men or any ships. We didn't have any attacks to deal with just the fire. Men are still working on that in the city. They think they put it out in an area then the wind fans the flames again. What have you found out?"

"We have the bodies of the archers," Mathas said. "But they are badly burned. The interesting thing is that they are all dressed alike. From what we can tell they are all men. They are all wearing white silk. Some strange type of pants and tunics."

"Did they have red sashes around their waists?" Gideon asked.

"Yes," said Stephan. "You know who they are?"

"No but I know who sent them. But why the hell would they be here? The Continent of Salszar lies west of Opots. It is huge with both large cities and areas with primitive tribes. There is a tribe in the southeastern tip of that continent that is ruled by a warlord named Zourlock. His armies are said to be unbeatable and they dress in the same clothing you described."

As Gideon spoke Matthew grabbed a map from the wall and brought it to him. "The area that Gideon just pointed to is northwest of Ryed and possibly the closest portion of Salszar to Opots," Matthew said.

"Could this have anything to do with our mission in Ryed?" Gabriel asked in amazement. "And if so why Javier, he wasn't with us?"

"If I had to guess," said Thaos. "I wouldn't be surprised if someone didn't pay Zourlock for some of his warriors. Gideon is Zourlock a dark lord too?"

"Not that I have heard. Why?"

"They were in plain sight yet our people couldn't see them until Erebus did some magic and exposed them," Thaos explained.

"I have heard a great deal about those fighters and I have never heard of them disguising their presence. Usually they fight in the open for all to see. They don't hide themselves. They have such bad reputations that when people see them they will just give up sometimes. What you describe is not their way."

"If they are such tough warriors why did they hide and shoot everyone in the back?" spat Misha. No one spoke although they all shared his anger.

"Then Thaos is probably right," said Fahron after a few moments.

"Wait," said Gideon. "I thought that Erebus couldn't control his magic once he started."

"I'm not really sure what the story is," said Claudius. "But the Sanuri, Sorren, Horace, Dagon and Rachel have been searching for him all night."

Archetenus, Jared, their families, a nurse and Gala arrived at the castle of Sudfad within thirty minutes of being notified about Michael's death. Jared told everyone Miranda's words as they traveled. Marie was sobbing as she opened the door. Gala put her arms around her and led everyone into the family parlor.

Raul, Simon, Vitomas, Annabelle, Laurel and Alexander looked shocked when their guests arrived.

"All of you are grieving," Gala said with a voice of authority. "You take care of everyone, let your friends take care of you now."

Raul stood up without speaking and handed a letter to Archetenus. Raul was shaking and crying.

"First, I am getting everyone here a drink and I mean everyone," Jared said. "Then you tell us what needs to be done."

Archetenus started to speak but stopped himself. His anger was written on his face. "Read this first," he said and handed the letter to Jared.

"We'll take you to a chambers so you can put the babies to bed," Annabelle said to Delilah and Zoya as she and Vitomas stood up.

"Perhaps, I will go with you and let the men talk," Laurel said. "We need more handkerchiefs anyways."

The women had only gotten a short distance down the hallway when they heard Archetenus yell, "Those stinking bastards! They couldn't take any of them in a fair fight."

Jared filled five large glasses with whiskey and handed them to the men. "Before anything else, let me tell you what Miranda said."

"Emeral are you up?" Maxwell asked in a low voice as he and Angus entered the chambers that Maxwell and Emeral shared in Mathas' castle.

Emeral quickly walked out of the bedroom and joined the men in the parlor. "Olivia and Joao are finally sleeping," she said in almost a whisper. "I don't want to wake them."

"Are they together?" Angus asked with obvious disapproval.

"Not like you are thinking," Maxwell said. "He guards her. Angus we have been watching over Olivia, we aren't allowing..."

"I know and that is why I wanted to speak with both of you," Angus said. "And I am sorry if I insinuated anything; my emotions are raw right now."

"Would you like some coffee or a little whiskey?" offered Emeral.

"Actually I could use both," Angus said and sat down on one of the overstuffed chairs. Emeral brought a tray with three cups of coffee into the parlor while Maxwell poured two small glasses of whiskey for the men.

"First, I want to apologize for the timing of this conversation but that will be made clear to you by time we finish," Angus said then gulped down his glass of whiskey. "As you know I have been spending time with Olivia because I want to adopt her. While I feel that we are building a good relationship there is something lacking. And honestly I think it is the two of you. Wait that didn't come out the way I wanted it to."

"What I meant to say is that you offer her something that I can't, at least not right now. I have been watching her with you. The girl has been an orphan for a number of years and although she doesn't say it I think she wants a family more than anything else. I think she wants a mother and a father and I believe she looks at both of you in that manner. Honestly, my relationship with her is more of an older brother."

"I don't mean to burden you, especially now. But if you would consider allowing her to stay with you I would pay you for your services. Please let me finish," Angus said as both Emeral and Maxwell were about to speak.

"Did you know that Edward's wounds broke open a short time ago? Hannah is working on him now. He is my friend in addition to being someone I have admired for a very long time." Angus stopped speaking for a moment as he composed himself. "I will not be returning to Wetpr for some time. I told Gabriel that I will be replacing Edward here in Langer, and by The Great Ruler I will get the people responsible for this."

Maxwell poured more whiskey into Angus' glass and said, "Emeral and I have seen the same things in Olivia that you have and honestly we both have become quite attached to the child. In fact, we have been considering adopting both of them?"

"Both? I don't understand."

"While Joao has lived in our house for a long time, we are seeing a very different side of him," Emeral said. "A more vulnerable side. He is rather lost right now. But back to Olivia. Maxwell and I were thinking about speaking with you about her."

"We will not accept any money from you," Maxwell said. "And you will always have a place in her life." Maxwell paused and looked at Emeral and they both smiled. "Our children and adopted children are grown and have families and while we are very involved with them; it is nice to have children who need us too."

"So then you will take care of her?"

"Yes," Maxwell said. "Now tell us about your plans."

"I have spoken with the members of Edward's team and they are going to work with me, which is fortunate because many of them are more experienced than my people. Kate of course will remain by Edward's side. We will be working closely with Dominic's team. I will tell you; as far as I am concerned we are at war."

Most of the women from the Village of Tyger had been up all night cooking for the public showing as serving a feast to honor the dead was traditional. The castle was filled with the smells of food baking and cooking. Pigs were being roasted in outdoor pits. Michael had been a liaison to the Nordes Tribe. He was both liked and respected by Sorren's people who mourned for him as if he was one of their own.

Breakfast was served in the Great Hall; although the room was filled, grief and exhaustion dampened conversations.

"How is he?" yelled Sol when Hannah walked into the hall.

"I stopped his bleeding," Hannah said wearily. "Is the Sanuri here?"

"Who was bleeding?" asked Lakin as he stood up from a table.

"Edward, he has lost so much blood. Can you help me?"

Lakin, Gael, Hadar and Ibula all jumped up from their seats. "Hannah don't hesitate to get us," Ibula said as all of the healers ran out of the hall. The room fell silent after they left.

"Corsa wake up; you're dreaming," George said as he gently shook his sister. She jumped out of her chair and looked disoriented for a moment.

"I was hoping this all was a nightmare," she said sadly.

"I only woke you because you started hitting the bed."

"Oh my god, I didn't disturb him did I?"

"No, I stopped you right away."

"Where is everyone?"

"Madeline left about ten minutes ago and Kent and Alex just left to bring us breakfast."

"George, I don't know what I am going to do if he dies," Corsa said with a trembling lip. Corsa had always been the pillar of strength in the family. George looked at her as he was trying to decide what he should do. He took her hand and the two stood by the bed and watched Javier in silence.

Madeline was unaware of Edward's condition. She walked to her chambers to bath and change her clothes. She wondered if she would ever feel that she got all of the blood off from her.

She had just entered the bathing room when she heard voices in her parlor. She didn't remember hearing anyone knocking on her door.

"I will be right there," Madeline yelled and put on a robe. When she walked into her parlor she saw Margarit, Nina, Nyla and Saran. All of the girls ran to her and hugged her.

"We are sorry to bother you but we have to talk to you," Saran said.

"It is never a bother," Madeline said wearily.

"We made a pact and we want you to join us," Nyla said.

"I don't understand," said Madeline.

"Madeline, you may not have seen these but Michael bought us all necklaces that are a smaller versions of yours," Nyla said soothingly. As she spoke all four of the girls showed Madeline the necklaces they were wearing.

"It was Saran's idea," said Margarit.

"What was Honey?"

"We are never taking our necklaces off and we swore never to forget Michael," Saran said and Madeline started to cry. The girls hugged her again.

"Renya said that you might have to take yours off sometimes because of the missions," said Nyla. "But we would like you to wear yours today."

"I am," Madeline said and opened the top of her robe enough to show them the necklace.

There was a knock on the door of Sudfad and Renya's chambers. When Sudfad opened the door he saw six soldiers holding traveling cases.

"My Lord, General Fahron had us bring your things from the cottage," said a young lieutenant.

"Thank you so much," Sudfad said and stepped aside so they could enter. "Just put them anywhere."

As the soldiers were leaving the lieutenant said, "My Lord, we all are truly sorry for what happened to your son."

"I know," Sudfad said sadly. "Thank you."

Diana and Jasmine were standing in a hallway with their arms around Kate. All three women were crying as they listened to the healers working on Edward.

"Wait! Wait!" shrieked Kate and ran into the bedroom. "Vivian told me that you used her to save Raphael. Use me now. Please. I beg of you."

Prince Hadar walked close to Kate and stared into her eyes for a few moments before he spoke. "This process could kill you. Would you give your life to save Edward?"

"Of course I will! Please, look at him. He is dying."

Hadar took Kate's hand and turned towards Edward's bed. "Please everyone leave us now," he said.

"May I watch?" Hannah asked. "I am learning your medicine."

Hadar looked at Kate who said anxiously. "I don't care who watches, please save him."

"We haven't told Petra yet," Annabelle said to Zoya and Delilah. "We thought we would wait until Kyra got here and tell both of them together." The tears were running down Annabelle's face as she spoke.

"Both of them were close with Michael," Vitomas said. "When he first got here, he seemed to be able to talk to the children better than the rest of us." She started to sob loudly; after a few moments she composed herself. "How do we tell our children? They all loved him so much."

The women had not yet joined Raul, Simon, Alexander, Archetenus and Jared in the parlor when Luca, Natalie, their children and Gala walked into the family parlor of the castle.

"We just heard," Luca said and the emotion was evident in his voice. "What can we do?"

"First drink this," Jared said and handed Luca a glass of whiskey."

"It's too early," said Luca.

"You are going to need it to read that letter," Jared said angrily.

"Gala, we really appreciate what you are doing," said Raul. "But you shouldn't be traveling by yourself in the middle of the night. Please, we don't want anything to happen to you too."

"Raul, I was just fine," Gala said. "Where is everyone?"

"The women left us because we are all so mad," Simon said. "They are setting up chambers for Zoya and Delilah. I will call to them."

Natalie was wearing a back carrier with Emma in it. She held baby Caleb and Luca was carrying Hunter. "Luca give him to me," Gala said. "We will find the others." Gala and Natalie left the room.

"Jared, tell him what Miranda said," said Raul. "I think we need some more whiskey."

Hannah had been allowed to remain in the room while Prince Hadar preformed the exchange of life force between Edward and Kate. Lakin and Gael stood near the bed. Ibula had been standing in the back of the room with Hannah explaining the procedures; now she too walked up to the bed. Her brothers had their eyes closed as they prayed.

"Hadar where is this blood coming from?" Ibula asked as she was examining Kate. "She shouldn't be bleeding. Hadar!"

# Chapter III
## Loss

Because of the circumstances and the numbers of people coming and going in the castle of Mathas, the breakfast meal was being served at three different times. Emeral decided they should wait until the last serving so that Joao and Olivia could get some sleep.

Maxwell, Emeral, Joao and Olivia had been up most of the night. Joao's emotions were still raw from losing his sister and now he lost a friend. Olivia hardly knew Michael but she was becoming close friends with his sisters and shared their pain.

When Emeral woke the two young people, Angus and Maxwell were waiting for them in the parlor of the chambers. "We need to talk with both of you," Maxwell said as soon as Emeral escorted them into the parlor.

"Angus, you are so angry," Olivia said. "Is anything wrong?"

"That is why I am here," Angus said. "Edward almost died this night and well...I won't get into all of that. I am going to stay in Langer and hunt the people behind the attacks. I've been talking with Maxwell and Emeral about your care." Angus now looked at Emeral and Maxwell.

"Emeral and I have been doing a lot of talking," Maxwell said. "We have not only enjoyed having the two of you staying with us but we have become very attached to you. Olivia, Joao we would like to adopt the both of you. Now, if you don't want us to adopt you we will still take care of you."

Both Joao and Olivia stared at all of the adults in the room with their shock showing on their faces. No one spoke for a few moments. "I can understand Olivia," Joao stammered. "But how can you adopt me? And why would you?"

"Honey, while Tina and Charles are alive they have not been parents to you for a very long time. You seem self-sufficient but everyone needs a family," Emeral said.

"And honestly, Maxwell and I are rather surprised at how attached we have become to both of you in such a short period of time. Joao, we've gotten to know you so much better and actually both of you feel like our children now. You don't have to make decisions right away."

"If we adopt you that doesn't mean that you can't still be girlfriend and boyfriend; you aren't related by blood," Maxwell said.

"Do you really mean this?" asked Olivia.

"Can't you hear our thoughts?" Emeral asked warmly.

"I think I am too emotional," Olivia said and started to cry. "I would love to be your daughter." She walked up to Emeral and hugged her then hugged Maxwell.

Joao hadn't moved; he just stared at everyone. "Joao say yes," said Olivia.

"If you are going to be protecting Olivia, you are going to be with us all of the time anyways," Maxwell said and smiled. "You might as well let us take care of you."

To everyone's surprise, Joao cried.

Sudfad and Renya had their breakfast served in their chambers. They were emotionally drained and wanted to compose themselves before they saw anyone else.

"I suddenly feel very old," Renya said. "I've never felt old before." Sudfad put his arm around her and the two sat in silence.

"Marie, we are going to tell the children now," Vitomas said. "Do you want to join us?"

Marie nodded and said, "Kyra hasn't really been close to anyone who died before. She really liked Michael."

"Marie, don't work today," said Annabelle.

"The boys told me that too," Marie said. "But I have to keep moving."

"Well, I have an idea then," said Vitomas. "None of us are thinking straight right now and we have to plan the funeral. Annabelle and I have never done that before, I mean planning a royal funeral. Let your staff take care of things and why don't you work with us. You know what Renya would want."

"We could really use your help," Annabelle said.

"Alright," Marie said in almost a whisper and took off her apron. "He never tasted chocolate cake before he came here. We should serve chocolate cake."

Petra and Kyra stared at Raul when he told them that Michael was dead. Simon, Annabelle, Vitomas and Marie were the only other people in the room. Moments went by and the children did not speak, they kept staring at everyone.

"Do you understand what Raul said?" Annabelle asked.

Tears started to form in Kyra's eyes but she shook her head from side to side to indicate 'no'.

"He's not coming back," Petra said to his friend. Then he grabbed Kyra's hand and said to the others, "We need to go."

"Do you think they understood?" Annabelle asked after the children left the room.

"They understood," Simon said. "I think they need to grieve differently."

Raul and Simon reluctantly let Luca, Archetenus and Jared take over their daily duties, so the family could work on the funeral arrangements. What the Princes didn't know was that their friends were working on plans of their own.

"Delilah didn't even yell when I told her," Archetenus said. "She just told me to be careful."

"Zoya never yells," Jared said. "But I can tell she is worried. She kept asking why she didn't have any visions about this. Of course I don't have the answers."

Archetenus looked across the desk at Luca. "You shouldn't come with us; you have so many babies. And besides it sounds like you have to be a Second Son to go where we are going."

"Our team is a family and three of our family members were attacked, I am going. But my role will have to be different from yours," Luca said angrily.

Soldiers filled the streets of Langer. Not because the ruling families were concerned with more terrorist attacks but the entire city had been traumatized by the destructive fires and the deaths. Wickfield's paper had come out early in the morning with a long story about Prince Michael. The paper also reported the deaths of Edward and Javier. Besides reporting their deaths, Harlow greatly changed the information about these men to protect them.

Langer was an old city. A city that had survived wars, destructive storms, fires and a host of other traumatic events. The people of Langer were fighters, they were resilient and on this day they were mourning. Never before had one of the members of their Royal Family been murdered in their streets. The citizens were filled with shame, with grief and with anger.

Noah and Lawrence were in Langer watching one of Javier's homes. The team members wondered if the houses would be ransacked after the news came out that he had been murdered. Soldiers too were watching the home but they were standing in the open, Lawrence and Noah were in an alley across the street.

"You're getting company," Adin called down from a roof top. "I am pretty sure they are the Elods that worked with Javier and Madeline.

"This could be a stroke of luck," Noah said to Lawrence. "Let's hear what they have to say."

Four men stormed into the alley. Two grabbed Noah and two grabbed Lawrence and threw them against the stone wall of one of the buildings. "What did you do with Madeline?" yelled one of the men angrily. "Where is she?" Six Ruala warriors watched the confrontation from roof tops.

"We are protecting her," Noah said.

"You lie!" yelled one of the men. Lawrence and Noah could see that the four Elods were clearly emotional.

"We know you were part of their team," Noah said. "And if we feel you aren't a threat to her, you can talk to her. Do you know who was behind the attacks?"

"There are bounties on her head as well," Lawrence said. "Do you know who is behind that?"

One of the four Elods appeared to be the leader. He stared at both Noah and Lawrence for a moment then said to his men, "Let them go."

"Why would you be protecting her?" the same man asked.

"It's a hell of a long story," said Noah. "Now as I see it, you don't trust us any more than we trust you but we may have the same enemies in common. What do you say we call a truce long enough to talk?"

"Turner, I don't trust them," said one of the men to the Elod leader.

"Hey, we've got you guys surrounded and we haven't attacked," Noah said and looked up. Now all of the Elods looked at the roof tops and saw the Ruala warriors with their bows. "Right now we are more interested in information than anything else. Have you been back to Inferus since the passageways opened?"

All four of the Elod men looked shocked, which was Noah's intent. "How do you know about that?" demanded Turner.

"Like I said, it's a long story. But Andrac put a bounty on Javier and had some of Hector's men after him. That's why a lot of us came to Langer."

"I don't understand any of this shit," said Turner. "And I don't know how you know these things."

"Well, before we get into that do any of you trust Andrac?" Noah asked.

Only Turner spoke, "No."

"Did you hear about the Credo escaping Inferus?" Noah asked. "The shock was evident on the faces of the four men. "Ok, I don't like to waste time. If you have been spying on us you know we work with Angels. And a couple of those Angels helped some of our teams rescue the Credo. We arrested Madeline and brought her with us. King Sudfad and King Mathas had bounties on both Madeline and Javier because we thought they committed a bunch of crimes. But it turns out Hector was setting them up. So that is how we know Madeline and Javier. So what is your story?"

"You are right, we are part of their team," said Turner. "They went back to Inferus to file their reports and no one heard from them for a long time. Then we hear stories that Madeline is romancing the prince from Wetpr, which we really didn't find suspicious. But we also heard that Javier was back in town looking for us and a bunch of Hector's men were following him. Then we heard that Madeline and some guys had to carry him out of a bar and he looked in bad shape."

"Well, that was us and he had been poisoned," Lawrence said. "I'm not saying this to scare you boys but could there be bounties on you too?"

"From Andrac?" asked Turner.

"We arrested a lot of, guess you could say bounty hunters and apparently because all of you spy on everyone you know a lot of dirty little secrets. Secrets that could ruin lives and careers. That is why some of the bounties were placed," Lawrence explained.

"Turner, I think we need to listen to them," one of the men said then looked at Noah. "But we want to make sure Madeline is alright."

"We can take you to her but understand she really was engaged to Prince Michael, it wasn't a con. She is understandably a mess right now. And...well...there is a lot more that we can tell you but I want to wait until Madeline say's you are alright. Now if we take you to her do you promise to play nice. Because after yesterday everyone's nerves are on edge."

"We are in the same boat," Turner said. "A few of the things you just told us, shall I say struck cords but we want to see if she is safe and if she too say's you are alright."

"That is understandable," Noah said. "But I've got to tell you that she is at the King's castle and everyone is in mourning so don't act like jerks."

"Not all Elods are barbarians," Turner said with indignation.

"Speaking of that, some of our people found the caves where your leaders do their experiments," Lawrence said. "Even the Angel was disgusted."

"So that really does exist," Turner said. "Wait, if an Angel saw it, does it still exist?"

"Let's just say that when they left the predators were the ones in the cages," Noah said and was surprised to see all of the Elods smile.

"Well, we may have some common ground to start with," Turner said. "Our horses are on the street."

Dack now flew down from a roof top. "I guess the question is do you want to be seen riding out of the city with our team or do you want us to fly you out?"

The four Elod men did not answer the question. "We aren't taking you prisoners unless Madeline says to. So, we will bring you back to your horses if that is a concern," Noah said. The four Elods stared at the team members.

"How's he doing?" asked Alex when he and Kent carried trays of breakfast food into Javier's room. Corsa and George were standing next to the bed looking at Javier. Corsa looked up at her older brothers and asked, "What is wrong? I can tell by the looks on your faces. What has happened?"

"We don't really know," said Kent. "But a lot of people ran to Edward's room and some of them were saying something about Kate."

"All of you stay here," Corsa said and ran out of the room.

Corsa pushed her way through the crowd that had gathered outside of Edward's chambers. As Corsa neared the door, Diana grabbed her arm. Diana was crying. "You can't go in there. All of the healers are with them."

"What is happening?" asked Corsa.

"Edward's wounds kept opening and they couldn't stop the bleeding so Kate demanded that the Ruala healers use her life force to save him and something is going wrong."

"I don't understand."

"The Sanuri taught the Ruala healers this, I don't know what to call it, ceremony or something but they can transfer life force. It is very dangerous but Vivian did that a while back when Raphael was dying and they both came out of it alright. I don't know what is happening now."

Corsa returned to Javier's room. "We were just coming for you," Kent said. "He started moaning."

Corsa ran to the bed and felt Javier for signs of a fever. "Javier, it's Corsa can you hear me?" He moaned again but did not open his eyes. "Javier if you can hear me squeeze my hand."

42

"Oh thank you god," Corsa said as Javier weakly squeezed her hand. "George find Madeline and bring her here." Corsa turned back to Javier. "I am not leaving you. You are safe here, we are in the castle of King Mathas."

"Who are you?" Saran asked accusingly when George knocked on the door to Madeline's chambers.

"I'm Corsa's brother. I need to talk to Madeline. Is she here?"

Nina, Margarit and Nyla all came to the door and stared at George. "Is she here?" he repeated.

"She's taking a bath," Nyla said.

"Well, tell her that Corsa was talking to Javier and he squeezed her hand."

"I'll tell her," said Margarit and turned and ran to the bathing room.

"What? Are all of you guarding her or something?" George asked with half a smile. "Cuz, you all look like you are going to attack me."

"She's really sad," Nina said. "We all are."

"Madeline said he should wait," Margarit yelled from the bathing room.

The girls moved so George could enter the parlor. "What's your name?" asked Saran in a harsh tone.

"I am George, I'm Corsa's brother and why are you acting like you are mad at me?"

"We aren't," said Nyla. "Michael was our brother. I'm Nyla, this is Saran and Nina and the other girl is Margarit; Michael was her cousin."

"She'll be right here," Margarit said as she joined the group.

"I'm real sorry about what happened to Michael," George said. "Alex and Kent are our other brothers and we were all going to Wetpr to the Learning Center to become priests but now we are going to stay with Madeline and Javier. So if you need anything just let us know."

"We live in Wetpr," said Saran. "Aren't they coming home with us?"

"Honestly, I don't know what is going on. But they are family and we aren't leaving them."

"George," Madeline said as she hurried to the front door. "I am sorry but I am not thinking straight. Tell me what you told Margarit."

"Javier hasn't moved or made a sound until a few minutes ago. Corsa left the room because something is going on with Edward and Kate and as soon as she left he started moaning. When she came back in she started talking to him. He didn't wake up but she says if you can hear me squeeze my hand and he did and she told me to get you." Madeline cried as she listened to him.

"Girls, you can come with us if you want," Madeline said and they all left the chambers.

"Javier, if you can hear me," Corsa said. "Alex and Kent are going to roll you on your side so I can check your bandages. Javier did not open his eyes or speak. Corsa quickly set all of the medical supplies and water she would need on a table next to the bed and nodded for her brothers to roll Javier on his side. Corsa cut the bandages off which exposed four wounds with crystals in them.

"Why are they black?" asked Alex.

"Because something evil was on those arrows," Corsa said. "Now be quiet because I have to pray."

As she removed the crystals Corsa said, "Great Ruler you know I am not as good at this as the Ruala healers but they are busy now. Would you cleanse this darkness from Javier and help him to heal. And please let me know what I can do for him. He's a good man and I ask that you save his life."

As Corsa was praying George walked into the room with the women. They all stopped so as not to interrupt Corsa, who was praying out loud. Corsa now looked at this group. "Madeline, hold his hand and talk to him. Say anything so he knows he's not alone. Nyla can you come here and help me and Saran find the Ruala healers and tell them that the crystals in his back turned black."

"I'll go with you," George said to Saran and they ran out of the room.

Madeline took Javier's hand but couldn't talk because she was crying so Margarit grabbed Nina's hand and the two girls walked up to the bed. "Javier, I'm Margarit and this is Nina and a lot of us are with you. Madeline is holding your hand but she is crying...."

"That's good, you girls keep talking to him," Corsa said to Margarit and Nina. "Nyla, that is blessed water in that bottle pour a little in each wound. Then hold the crystals in place while I bandage him." Javier moaned loudly when the blessed water was poured into his wounds. Corsa prayed over the crystals and kept praying as she bandaged his wounds.

Ratri knocked on the door to Javier's chambers then walked in. Corsa had just finished bandaging Javier's wounds. Madeline was crying and stroking Javier's hair.

"This might be a really bad time," Ratri said. "And I am sorry but Madeline we brought four men here who were part of your team. They attacked Noah and Lawrence to find out what happened to you. No one is hurt but they don't trust us and we don't know if they are really on your side."

"I will meet them," Madeline said as she stood up and wiped the tears from her face.

45

"Alex go with her. If those men aren't who they say they are she will need protection," said Corsa.

"I'll go with her," Nina said.

"No Honey, you stay here and keep talking to Javier," said Corsa.

Ratri led Madeline and Alex to a small meeting room. Dominic, Lawrence, Noah and Angus were in the room with the four men from Inferus. Both Alex and Ratri were amazed at how Madeline changed her demeanor as she entered the room. All four men were members of her team but she no longer knew if she could trust them.

"Madeline are you alright?" Turner asked and quickly walked up to her.

"That is not an easy answer to give right now," she said. "I am not hurt and I am not a prisoner if that is what you are asking. You don't need to save me." Then she turned to Dominic. "These men are members of the team we led. This is Louis, Turner, Bart and Garvis." No one else in the room spoke as Madeline walked up to each of her former teammates and stared boldly into their eyes. "We were betrayed. I don't know who I can trust anymore."

"Madeline, we did not betray you," said Bart. "And now that we know you are alright we are going after whoever killed Javier."

"So are we," said Angus. "Got any people in mind?"

Bart looked at Madeline. "Honestly, I am not up to telling you the entire long story," Madeline said wearily. "Javier and I defected and were given asylum by King Sudfad of Wetpr. We are working for him now. I know some of you have longed for that too and these are the people you can talk to. You can trust them. So very much has happened since I last saw you."

"You don't seem surprised by what she just told you," Dominic said. "Did you already know that?"

"We have continued to do our jobs while you were gone and we have heard many things," said Garvis to Madeline. "Things that we need to tell you. But first you said that you and Javier are working for King Sudfad. Is he still alive?"

"Barely. We are trying to protect him," Madeline said. "I lost Michael and Javier may be dying. I am sure you can understand that I am not up for talking business right now. But I would ask that you talk with these men." Madeline nodded at Dominic and Angus. Then she spoke to the team leaders.

"These men are members of our team of spies. As I told many of you before, many of the members of the Charto like this world and would desire asylum here but we could never escape the powers of Inferus before. These men have been good soldiers and good spies. They would be assets to us. I would suggest that all of you sit down and talk."

Madeline turned back to the four Elod men and said, "These are good men and as I said you can trust them. But if I find out that any of you or our other members helped with the attacks I will kill you myself."

"Did you know that you were pregnant?" Diana asked Kate as many of her friends were gathered around her bed.

"Yes," Kate said weakly. "I was going to make it special when I told Edward. He is going to be so upset."

"Kate, you saved his life," said Vivian.

"All I could think of, was that he was dying. I never thought it would hurt the baby," Kate said as the tears ran down her cheeks.

"How would you even have known?" asked Diana.

# Chapter IV
## Allies

After Madeline and Alex left the room, the members of the Charto team and the members of Dominic's and Angus' teams agreed to sit down and share information. Dominic sent for Gabriel and Raphael and had meals brought to the room.

"I was a little confused back there," Alex said as he escorted Madeline to Javier's chambers. "Those guys were from your team. Don't you trust them?"

"Inferus is a very different world than the one you are used to. It is a world of traitors and spies. Children are executed for their thoughts. The people in power rule with complete authority. I thought we were safe here because I thought the Angels would protect us. I guess we will never be safe."

"Oh my god did something happen?" Madeline screamed when she saw a group of people standing inside of Javier's room. Alex grabbed her hand and pushed through the crowd.

"Madeline," Corsa said and ran to her and hugged her.

Madeline stared in disbelief. Javier was very pale but he was sitting up in bed with Nina and Margarit sitting on either side of him. He smiled weakly at his sister who flew into his arms. "I thought you had died," she said and sobbed.

"Can one of you explain it?" asked Corsa as she looked at the Ruala healers.

"When Saran and George told us the crystals in Javier's wounds were black that told us there were still things in his wound that were poisoning him," explained Prince Hadar. "Everyone looks confused. Understand we have not completed our research but we believe the arrows that struck our friends had different poisons and dark magics attached to them. And the combination of all these things is what is making it so difficult to treat them."

"Michael had twice as many arrows in him as did Edward and Javier which is why we think he died so quickly. Edward's and Javier's symptoms have been very different."

"We came as soon as Corsa sent for us. She and Nyla had changed the crystals in Javier's wounds just minutes before we got here and they were already black. We cleaned out and scraped the wounds and found the tiniest shards which burst into flames when we threw them in blessed water."

"So it sounds like Michael was the main target?" Claudius asked as he had just entered the room. "And is this the first time that you have seen our enemies use a combination of different poisons like this?"

"Yes," said Hadar.

"Claudius what is it?" asked Ibula. "You look like you are going to explode."

"I just spoke with Mathas and I am not sure I can repeat everything correctly mainly because he is so upset. But hours before our men were attacked Erebus came to him. Erebus had been working on the riddles the Angels gave us, he had questions and called to them."

"Remember when we were in Ganz and the Angels told us to go home and clean up our backyards?" Claudius did not wait for anyone to answer his question. Well, they warned Erebus about all of our enemies and basically said they were frustrated because we don't heed their warnings. I think it was Adam who reminded Erebus about his statement when Erebus said that being with us was like watching children trying to touch a fire and the Angels were pulling our hands back. Adam said it looked to them like we were in the middle of a forest fire now."

Kent looked at the reactions of the people who were listening to Claudius. "I am Corsa's brother and I am sorry but I don't understand the significance of what you said."

"He said we possibly could have prevented this if we would have listened to the Angels," Misha said angrily.

"I don't understand," Madeline said as she wiped the tears from her face.

"The Angels say they can't always tell us things because it can influence our choices," said Jasmine. "So they give us hints to find the information and they have been telling us that we don't pay attention to what they say."

"Before we go into all that," Misha said. "Do we have any information about Erebus?"

"No," Claudius said. "We haven't received one message from him or the people searching for him. About an hour ago, Matthew, Stephan and Thaos got some men together and now they are searching for all of them."

"We just heard," Sudfad said as he and Renya walked into Edward's room. "How is he doing?"

"Hadar said he will sleep for possibly a couple of days," said Marina. "But that is good; it will help him heal. Kate gave up her life force and she will take longer to heal."

"We were told she lost the baby," Renya said. "Is that true?"

"Yes," said Bethany. "She wasn't far along and hadn't told Edward yet."

"She wanted to make it a special occasion when she told him," said Marina. "Understandably she is very emotional right now."

"Where are her chambers?" asked Renya.

"The door to the right of this one," Bethany said. "But I was just in there and she is sleeping. I would suggest you not wake her; she is very weak and needs her rest."

"We understand," said Sudfad. "Has there been any improvement with Javier?"

"Lakin asked us to watch over Edward and Kate because all of the other healers ran down to his room. We haven't heard yet what happened," Bethany explained.

"Sudfad, we should go there next," said Renya.

"It's at the end of this hallway," Marina said.

Sudfad and Renya walked through the crowd in Javier's room just as Claudius finished telling everyone about Erebus' meeting with the Angels.

"Claudius would you tell me what you just told them?" Sudfad asked.

"Certainly. Do you want to step in the hallway since it is so crowded in here?"

The two men left the room while Renya walked up to Javier's bed. To his surprised she bent down and kissed him on top of his head.

"Mama, we all helped," Nina said proudly.

Renya smiled. "And I want to hear all about it. But I would like to speak with Javier for a moment if he is up to it."

"Of course," he said weakly.

"Renya, he only woke up a few moments ago," said Madeline. "I haven't told him anything yet."

"What are you talking about?" Javier asked with concern.

"Michael died in the attack and Edward is only alive now because Kate gave her life force to save him but she lost their baby in the process," said Renya. "It seems that there is no end to the suffering from that attack."

"Harlow wrote stories saying that you and Edward were also killed. Sudfad and I are taking all of you back home. We will care for you until you are well. But we also spoke with Madeline. Michael loved her so much," Renya started to get emotional as she spoke so she paused for a moment.

"As I was saying, we consider Madeline our daughter now which makes you our family also. We are offering you a home and a family if you would like."

The shock was evident on Javier's face. "I...I don't know what to say," he stammered. "Thank you. I...really don't...you are most gracious."

"Are you going to live with us?" asked Nina.

"Yes," he said but it sounded like more of a question than a statement.

"Wait until you meet Milo; you will really like him." Most of the people in the room smiled as Nina spoke.

"Who is Milo?" asked Javier.

"He's our monkey," Nina said and Javier laughed loudly.

"Well, I am looking forward to meeting him," Javier said.

"I will be back," said Renya. "I am sure you need to speak with Madeline and Corsa."

As the Queen turned away from the bed, Javier said, "Renya, I promise you that I will find who killed Michael. He was a good man and I am so very sorry..."

Renya had tears in her eyes and nodded then walked out of the room. Corsa followed her into the hallway. "Would it be alright if I hugged you?" Corsa asked.

"Of course," Renya said and smiled.

After the two women embraced Corsa said, "Renya, I don't know if you realize what you just did. Madeline and Javier had horrible lives. They have been orphans since the age of ten and only survived because they had each other. Even when their parents were alive, they were all slaves. Sometime if you would like, I could tell you about their lives so you can understand them better."

"I would like that very much and I know Sudfad would also. Whenever you feel comfortable telling us." Renya paused. "Feel free to speak with us while we are still here too. Honestly it would be good to think about something else for a few moments."

The meeting with Turner and the other members of the Charto went on for several hours. Gabriel moved it to a larger room because so many team members kept joining them. The first hour little was accomplished because everyone was tense and prepared for attack. But as they ate and talked they started to share information and ease tensions.

Two hours before the public showing of Michael's body was scheduled there was a pounding on the door to the meeting room. Raphael stood up to open the door but it flew open as Tally and Drake threw a man onto the floor.

"This one's got information," Tally growled then he put his foot on the man to keep him on the floor as he and Drake stared at the four Elod men.

"Are you with them?" Turner asked Drake and Tally.

"These guys are in the dens all of the time," Drake said. "Our cover's gone now."

"They are members of Madeline's and Javier's old team," said Gabriel. "In a way we are starting to work together."

"Good!" said Tally then he looked at Turner. "You guys know this one on the floor?"

"I've seen him around," said Bart. "Did he have anything to do with the attacks?"

"He suddenly came into a lot of money," Drake said. "Was shooting his mouth off about being a guide of sorts to some strange looking fellas. We pulled him out of the Catacombs and thought you could give him that truth potion."

"You guys look like hell," said Angus. "Did he put up that much of a fight?"

Drake stared at Angus and for a moment; some people thought the monster of a man was going to cry. "Me and Tally owed Michael. We swore to protect him."

"We didn't do our jobs so we are making up for it. When we find the bastards who killed him we are going to skin them alive."

As Drake was talking, Tally pulled their prisoner up from the floor and set him on his feet. "I's told ya, I's didn't kill no body," the man said through swollen lips. He looked at the anger in the faces of the people in the room and started to tremble.

"Three good men died," Tally said. "Shot in the back by stinking cowards. And these cowards was dressed the same in strange clothing."

Gabriel looked at Turner and his men and said, "Our healers make a powerful potion that forces people to tell the truth. I am sorry to say that we used it on two of your people and they died. That had never happened before. You are welcome to observe the interrogation."

"Interrogation!" the man yelled. "Whats the hell yous guys gonna do to me? I'll gives ya information ifn yous stop these guys from hittin me. My damn mouth is so swollen I's can hardly talk."

"How do we know you would tell us the truth?" asked Raphael.

"Well's I's don't rightly know...let me's think. I could swear on sometin."

"Give him the damn potion," growled Drake. "We ain't got all day."

"Now just yous wait, I's don't want to die from that stuff. I's tell yous the truth. Whatcha want to know?"

Turner looked at Gabriel and said, "Since you are priests I doubt you know true torture techniques. We specialize in them. Then he looked at the man and said. "The men who died were our friends too, trust me it's not going to take a lot to get any of us to hurt you."

Nikki and Ingr were in the meeting filling in for their husbands and Claudius. The man looked at them and said. "Honey, yous ain't gonna let them hurt me are ya?"

54

In less than a second, Nikki threw a knife at the man and cut off the lobe of his ear. Both Tally and Drake jumped out of the way and laughed as the man screamed. "We're Nordes warriors," Nikki said loudly. "We'll torture you ourselves!"

Turner and his men laughed loudly. "I'm impressed," said Turner.

"You better tell the truth or we're handing you over to the ladies," Drake said and grinned.

"Ok," said the man as he pulled a filthy bandana from his pocket and pressed it against his bloody ear.

"His name is Clem and he is always mooching drinks off people," said Bart. "Of course it could be a cover?"

"Whatcha mean a cover? I's don't even know what the hell that means?" said Clem. "Ok, let's me explain. I's do odd jobs for people, yous might say I's am a freelancer of sorts. All's the barkeeps knows that and they get me jobs. So's I's in the dens the other night and I's go's in the one with the big ass cage for fighting."

Gabriel looked at Drake and Tally. "Do you know which one he is talking about?"

Both men nodded. "So do we," said Turner.

"Well's that old guy Ben was bartending and he asked me if'n I's wanted some work. Well's I's says hellya and he hands me a note. I's still got it in my pocket," as Clem spoke he reached into his back pants pocket and took out a piece of paper that had been folded many times. He handed it to Gabriel.

Everyone in the room was quiet as Gabriel read the note. "Have you done work for this Shepherd guy before?" Gabriel asked and handed the note to Raphael.

"Hellya and he pays good too. Usually he has me delivering things but this time he's wanted me to meet some men and show them the city."

"I's met them in the Excelsor Hotel but it gots kinda ugly cuz the damn staff wouldn't let me in cuz I's don't dress good enuf. So's I's yelling at this fancy pants guy who's standing in front of the dinin room and out walks this man kinda dressed like a woman and he asks if'n I's have the note. So's I's show's him the one yous holding. And damn the bastard slaps me across the face and tells me to stop making so much noise. Then he turns and talks to fancy pants and they let me in the dinin room."

"Well's there's four other guys sittin at the table and they's all dressed like women."

"Before you go any farther what do you mean they were dressed like women?"

"They's all had these fancy kinda robes on and lots of jewelry."

"Do you mean like priest's robes?" asked Gabriel.

"No, well kinda but they's was real fancy with stitchin and fur around the collars. And likes I's said they had on lots of jewels, yous know necklaces and rings. And damn if'n one of them didn't have a honkin diamond in the side of his nose."

"Slow down a little," said Ingr. "I'm trying to write all of this down."

"Sure's Honey."

"You call either of us Honey again and I will cut your tongue out," Ingr snapped.

"Man them girls is purty but they's sure is touchy."

A lot of the people in the room laughed at this comment. "Just keep your mouth shut about the women," said Tally.

Clem gave Tally a dirty look then continued with his story. "Well's they all talked to's me liken I's was their boy but they bought me a real good meal and some whiskey. Theys didn't tells me their names; they's weren't friendly fellars. All they wants was for me to show them the city."

"I's asked them if'n theys was interested in the bars or women and theys said just walk down the streets and points the places out. Damn if'n they didn't write down everything I's said."

"Clem this is important," said Gabriel. "Did they ask to see certain businesses or ask about certain people?"

"Likin I's said, theys wasn't real friendly. I's could understands them when theys talked to me but I's couldn't when they talks to each others. And theys wasn't makin no small talk with me. I's would stop in fronts of a building and tells em whats it was and one of the fellas was drawing a map and would write down what I's said."

"Give us an example of what you said," Gabriel said.

"Nutin fancy, well like I's stopped in front of Hanks Tack Shop and told thems the name but I's did have to explain what tack was."

"Did you take them around the entire city?" asked Gabriel.

"Well's not the homes. Theys was only interested in the shops but I's did show em the docks and where's theys building the navy."

"Did they ask to see that area?"

"No, I's was just running out of ideas. Theys really didn't talk much in front of me. I don't think theys liked me much."

"Can't imagine that," Nikki said sarcastically.

"Hey now that's hurt, Hon..." Clem was going to call Nikki 'Honey' until she gave him a look that gave him chills.

"Back to the story," said Gabriel. "How long were you with them?"

"Well's I's met them in the morning. We ate and got started about nine. We's didn't stop for lunch or nuting just kept walking till it was getting dark. Then theys wanted me to take them back to the Excelsor. I's asked them ifn they wanted to see the Catacombs and theys didn't."

57

"When we's get back to the hotel the guy that done slapped me gives me this big honking pouch of gold coins. I'll show yous." Clem pulled a pouch out of the inside of his shirt and handed it to Gabriel.

"Was this full?" Gabriel asked.

"Yes sir. I's did me a little drinkin."

"Did you see those men again after that night?" asked Raphael.

"Nope and I's asked them ifn they wanted my services more. Theys just says 'No' and walks into the hotel."

"Clem, I need you to think really hard because I want you to describe them. Were all of their robes alike?"

"Kinda. The guy whos slapped me, his was bright red and the others was kinda grey like. I's think the one in red was the boss man."

"You said they had stitching on the robes. Did the stitching form words or pictures?"

"Shapes kinda, but I's didn't knows what theys was."

"If I give you some paper could you draw them?"

"I's can try. Theys wore lots of necklaces but I's did see that theys all wore the same rings. Theys was gold with those pink diamonds, big ass diamonds they was."

"What did the men look like?"

"Regular guys."

"What color was their hair, did they have scars or tattoos, did they have facial hair?"

"Well's they's wasn't wearing hats or nuting. You knows now that you say that; they all kinda looked alike. Theys was all bald with a strange tattoo on their head, over the right ear. Some of them guys was wearing earrings, can yous believe that?"

58

Nikki rolled her eyes. "Theys was," Clem said defensively. Theys didn't have no hair on their faces but the guy that done slapped me had a droopy eye, lookin like it got cut in the corner. His right eye."

"Ingr will you go in the next room with Clem and help him draw those shapes?"

"I can't Gabriel, I'll kill him. I'll get Jasmine or Joao."

"Don't even say it," Tally said as he saw Clem starting to speak.

"Clem are you hungry?" asked Gabriel.

"Hellya."

"I'll get you a meal. Here's your money back but I am keeping the note. And here is another pouch of gold for your information."

"Gee thanks," Clem said with a big smile. "Let me know if'n yous need anything else."

"We're going to be watching you in the dens," Drake said. "If you have any new information tell us and we will pay you."

"You can include us in that too," said Turner.

"Wait," Gabriel said as Drake and Tally were taking Clem out of the room. "Clem what day did you give this tour?"

"Now lets me think," Clem said and took a very long pause.

"Oh my god!" said Ingr in frustration. "Just spit it out."

"Three days ago."

"Thank you," said Gabriel.

As Clem was being escorted from the room everyone heard him say, "Boy, those girls is touchy." When the door closed the room filled with laughter.

"Gabriel, all of you have the showing for your friend soon, we'll go to the Excelsor and nose around," said Turner. "If they are still in town we will follow them and leave messages with Drake and Tally."

There was a knock at the door then Alex entered the room. "Corsa sent me. Javier is awake again and wants to talk to his friends." Alex was looking at Gabriel when he spoke then he looked at Turner. "Madeline is getting things ready for the showing. She can't stop crying so she won't be talking to you."

Turner nodded, "Lead the way."

While Javier was sitting up in bed waiting for Turner and his men, Nina walked into the room. "Ashley brought these," Nina said and handed Corsa a black veil. Then Nina looked at Javier and said, "They're just for the girls."

He smiled and asked, "Are you alright?"

"No, I'm sad," Nina said and started to cry.

"Why don't you come up here and tell me about Milo."

"Ok," she said and smiled. Nina jumped on the bed and sat close to Javier. "Simon and Raul were fighting some bad men who hurt animals and brought home Milo and a bear. But we had to take the bear home after he ate." Both Javier and Corsa smiled as they listened to Nina. "Milo's home is far away and he is sick so he is living with us. Petra gets mad because I dress him in doll clothes but Milo likes it."

"I did meet Milo," said Javier. "I was with your brothers that day. Did they tell you about the sea creature? We saved her babies."

"No," said Nina as her eyes widened.

Alex led Turner and his men into the room. "Nina, I have to talk business with these men, why don't you come back and visit me later and I will tell you that story."

"Ok," Nina said and hugged Javier. She got off the bed and walked up to Turner and scowled at him. "Are you good or bad?" she asked.

"I'm not really sure how to answer that," he said and grinned.

"Nina why don't you draw a picture of Milo for Javier," said Corsa. Nina gave each of the Elod men a disapproving look as she walked out of the room.

"Cute kid," Turner said.

"Her brother was the one murdered," Corsa said to Turner. "Javier is still really weak and can only stay awake for short periods of time; so say your important things first." She turned to Javier. "Do you want me to leave?"

"No, the both of you can stay," Javier said. He looked at Turner and the other men. "This is Corsa, soon to be my wife and you have already met her brother Alex. This is Turner, Bart, Garvis and Louis." Each man walked up to Corsa and kissed her on the cheek and congratulated her.

"Are you a warrior too?" asked Bart. "We met Nikki and Ingr and they were something."

"Yes, we are from the same tribe," said Corsa. "I don't mean to be rude but Javier will need to sleep soon."

"We need to hear it from you," said Turner. "Are you working for King Sudfad now?"

"Yes, I was mad as hell when I found out that Madeline was but it is the best decisions we ever made. These are really good people and their Angels have protected us from Andrac and Gilder. Of course it is your choice but I would suggest you consider joining us. You certainly can't beat the pay."

Turner looked at his men who nodded then he turned back to Javier. "We will consider it. For the time being we have agreed to work with Gabriel and the others to find out who was behind these attacks. Is it true that Andrac put a bounty on you?"

61

"Yes, and the teams saved me from Hector's men. Did they tell you that Andrac murdered our father and I saw it? But I was too traumatized to remember because I was a kid. Now that he is in the Gefrey Games he is afraid for some reason that I would tell."

"Noah and Lawrence asked if we have bounties on us," said Garvis. "We really don't know. How did you find out?"

"The Angels told Madeline and the others."

"You are starting to look like you are going to pass out," Turner said. "So I will keep this short. We have agreed to share information and work with the teams to find out who is behind the attacks. After that we will not use the information we have against each other. But we will consider joining you. Gabriel said that he was going to offer you, your own team. If that happens look us up."

# Chapter V
## The Showing

After Turner and his men left Javier's room, Seth and George entered carrying all of Javier's and Corsa's belongings that had been in Dominic's house.

"Thank goodness," Corsa said. "Now I can bathe and change my clothes. Will one of you stay with Javier?"

"I will," said Alex.

Corsa picked up a large bag and walked into the bathing room.

"Don't any of you leave," said Javier. "I need you to do somethings for me."

Tally and Drake returned Clem to the City of Langer then they went back to Mathas' castle. They found Madeline and Renya in the room where the showing would take place.

"You two look awful," Madeline said. "Were you attacked?"

"No, and everyone's telling us that," Tally said.

"We are glad both of you are here," Drake said as they walked closer to the women. "We owed Michael and we swore to protect him. We didn't do our jobs and we won't rest until we catch the bastards responsible. We want you to know how very sorry we are."

Both women were surprised at the emotion in Drake's voice. "We appreciate that," said Renya. "But you won't be good for anything if you don't eat and get some sleep. This is long from over and you men are working in vital positions. I am ordering you to get some sleep. Do you have rooms here?"

"No," said Tally.

"Then come with me," said Renya and the men followed her out of the room. "When was the last time you ate?"

"Can't remember," said Drake.

The public showing of Prince Michael's body was a regal event. Earlier in the day Mathas had the body moved from the second floor chambers to the Great Hall. The room was filled with flowers in golden vases to match the golden candelabras that hung from the ceiling. Smaller versions of the candelabras were mounted all along the walls.

A deep purple carpet ran from the door where the public would enter, past the casket and to the door where people would exit. Musicians were set up on a platform in the corner of the room. The soldiers who lined the room were wearing their dress military uniforms. Two soldiers stood on either side of the casket as the family members stood behind the casket.

Tables were set up in the room and covered with purple tablecloths. Each table held a bouquet of flowers and a small golden candelabra with purple candles.

Soldiers wearing their dress uniforms formed lines on both sides of the hallway leading to the Great Hall. These lines went through the front doors of the castle, down the steps, along the courtyard, through the castle gate and five miles down the road.

Companies of soldiers patrolled the castle grounds. Since Michael was well respected by the Nordes Tribe, many warriors also volunteered to provide security for the ceremony.

Matthew, Thaos and Stephan had not returned to the castle by time the showing started. They were still searching for Erebus, the Sanuri, Sorren, Horace, Dagon and Rachel. Mathas, Rosa and Angelina stood behind the casket with Sudfad, Renya and Madeline. Neither of these families wanted their children close to the public as they felt there were many threats against them.

As the first members of the public were allowed entrance Corsa walked behind the casket and whispered to Angelina before taking her place near Madeline. Corsa had promised Javier that she would protect Madeline during the showing.

The Royal Family of Lentz was respected and loved by the majority of citizens in that kingdom. Mathas had not released word of the death of Isabella, so most of the citizens believed it had been decades since there was the death of a member of the Royal Family. When Juleta died she had been disowned by the King's family and there were no ceremonies.

Although complete strangers, people sobbed as they walked past the casket of the young Prince. People handed the members of the Royal Families so many flowers that countless vases were brought into the hall. Time and again, people expressed their rage and shame that the Prince had been murdered in their streets and countless people vowed to help find the people responsible for the murder.

Against the orders of their parents, Nyla and Saran implemented a plan. They went to the Great Hall with Olivia, Nina, Margarit, Joao and Dack. The girls covered their heads with black veils and they watched the crowd as Olivia listened to the many voices in the room.

Emeral and Maxwell spotted this group almost as soon as they sat down. The young people refused to leave so Emeral joined them at the table as Maxwell alerted other members of the teams. Jasmine and Batina quickly joined the table to help Joao sketch some of the visitors. Soon team members sat at the tables surrounding the young people, so they could assist if any terrorists were discovered.

No one at Olivia's table spoke so that she could concentrate on what she was hearing. Twenty minutes after the showing started she heard thoughts that concerned her. Olivia passed a note to Dack with the description of the person and he was escorted out of the line by the other team members. Within the first hour five men had been escorted from the room. Olivia would quickly write down what she heard and hand the paper to Dack who was now organizing the removal of people.

Angelina and Corsa were unaware of what this group of young people were doing. These two women had previously planned to protect the Royal Families who they believed were in so much pain and grief that they were not aware of their surroundings.

Both women wore black dresses with huge black shawls that covered small crossbows on their backs and small quivers of arrows. In addition to the many knives they had hidden on their bodies both women had poison darts braided into their hair.

The look of rage had not left Angus's face since the attacks on Edward, Michael and Javier. He now marched up to the table where the young people were sitting. He bent down because he could not tell which girl was Olivia because of the veils that covered their heads and faces.

"Angus, I am not leaving," Olivia said adamantly.

"I didn't come here to yell at you, although I probably should. I came to tell all of you how proud I am. Dominic's team is already interrogating the people you are pointing out."

"Wait!" There is something strange about that woman, she is third from Corsa. Joao go up there."

"I will," said Emeral.

"Emeral she might be a demon," Olivia whispered.

Angus now accompanied Emeral to the casket. Corsa saw this and quickly moved in front of the casket and blocked the woman from getting close to the Royal Families. Angelina grabbed the hilt of a knife that was under her shawl and watched the scene. The woman had her head and face covered with a black veil. Emeral had removed her crystal necklace and held it in her hand. The woman stiffened up and stared at Corsa then she turned around to leave the line but Emeral and Angus both grabbed her arms. Smoke rose from her arm where the holy crystal was touching it.

The woman did not resist nor did she speak as she was escorted to a small side room. Once the door was closed, Angus pulled the veil off from her head. "Bravo, how did you know?" said the woman who appeared haggard and very old.

"I find it curious that a demon would take on that appearance," said Emeral.

"That is because I am a witch," the woman said proudly. "The last time I spoke with Rualas they were traitors to their people."

"Why are you telling us this?" asked Emeral.

"You know of who I speak then?" the woman asked as she bolding looked into Emeral's eyes.

"Of course," said Emeral.

"And you believe you only had the three traitors among your people?"

"Miranda," Emeral called out loud. "Can I kill her?"

"Of course you can," said the witch. "But I don't think that is in your best interest. Your Angel has not answered you but I can feel the energy. I have not come to hurt you. Rather to sell you some information."

"I am listening," said Emeral skeptically.

"I have been in this world a very long time. I was here when the Originator first opened a door to this world. I was here when he killed the Venatores and by their deaths an incredible army was created. While you will not believe me, I like this world the way it is. I have traveled to other worlds and always come home."

"I am a maker of potions; that is my art and many of my customers are demons. Only the most wealthy can afford to pay my prices. I know your Angel is listening and I assume she will tell you if I am lying. In the last two weeks, I have had many orders for strong and dangerous potions. Some that I have not made in centuries."

"Wait a moment before you continue," Emeral said to the woman then she called out, "Miranda, why isn't she smoking because I too can feel your energy?"

"Keep asking her," said the Angel Adam although he did not appear.

Suddenly the woman started to shake. "I have heard his voice before. I visited Orantho and never in my nightmares would I wish that on any world." The woman looked up at the ceiling and said loudly, "Angel, you must know that although I have never killed anyone, I am sure that my potions have. I do not want this world turned into Orantho. I will give your people information but for payment I want Samael stopped. As an Angel, I am sure you can do that."

Adam appeared and the witch bowed before him. "Rise Risha," he said.

"I don't understand any of this," Emeral said. Risha was not acting at all as Emeral would have thought a witch would act.

"Like Hilgra, Risha was a healer of her people. She fled the horrors of the Originator and she is a maker of potions. And she has a great deal of information to tell you. She is right in that she has never directly hurt anyone. And while most of her potions are not used in murder, some are," explained Adam.

"I don't know why I am surprised that an Angel would know so much about a witch," Risha said. "But thank you for explaining that." She reached into a large pocket in her black skirt and took out a small journal and handed it to Emeral. "You have powerful healers working with you. Have them all make copies of these pages." Then she looked at Adam and asked. "Is it safe for them to read these?"

"Yes," Adam said and looked at Emeral and Angus. "Those are her recipes and the antidotes. Risha is known in many worlds for her potions and those recipes could be sold for fortunes. Your healers will not need to know magics to give the antidotes and if they have concerns they can call to us. But Edward and Javier both should be given antidotes."

"Why are you really doing this?" asked Angus.

"Samael is tearing holes in the walls that separate the hell worlds from others. He is doing this to get help in finding and freeing the Originator. That young Prince was suspected of being one of The Seven Sons of Prophesy," Risha replied.

"Whether he is or not, the dark worlds are now convinced that The Seven Sons can be killed. They will be hunting them all now and possibly using my potions."

"I live in a cave in the Rosu Mountains, I am not always aware of what happens in the world below me. Three days ago, two Rualas came to me with an order for potions of the darkest magics. I knew them for they had been customers of mine before."

"Two men, who bore the stink of hell. They said they would return in five days. They gave me two pouches of gold coins as a sign of good faith."

"She is talking about Morgan and Bruno," explained Adam. "They were being tortured in Ael's hell world. He was destroyed and many have fought over his territory. Samael assisted an Old One from the World of Planteen to conquer that region. The demon's name is Abrass. He has returned those Rualas to this world as he believes them to be valuable tools."

"Before that, two other Rualas came to me," said Risha. "A man and a woman. They had strange dark magics upon them, like I have never before seen. They told me they had been sent to buy a potion but they could not tell me who sent them so I made them leave."

"Tell them the rest," said Adam.

"I came here to see if that young Prince was killed with my potions. I don't know if he was. While I am not picky about my clientele, my purpose is not to put more weapons in the hands of the demons. I have sabotaged the potion that the demon Abrass ordered. When this is discovered, I will be killed. You have a few days to get information from me, I would suggest you use that time wisely."

"Adam is she telling the truth?" asked Angus.

"Yes."

"I am going to get some of the healers and bring them here," Angus said and left the room.

"Risha, we have a friend who was a powerful warlock. He turned away from the magic but used it again to help our people who were attacked. No one has seen him since. Can you help us find him?" asked Emeral.

"Are you talking about Erebus?" Risha asked.

"Yes. Do you know him?" asked Emeral.

"I know of him. Hecate had bounties on him but I heard they no longer exist. She might have him," Risha said then looked at Adam. "How would you not know where he is?"

"I didn't say I didn't know."

"What!" said Emeral. "How could..."

Risha held her hand up for Emeral to stop talking as the witch stared intently at Adam. The two stared at each other in silence for several moments.

"Are you two communicating somehow?" asked Emeral.

"I will do this thing," Risha said to Adam. "How much time do I have?"

"Speak with the healers and team members here. I will come for you tonight."

"What is going on?" asked Emeral.

"Adam showed me why Erebus lost his powers. He is a man to be admired. The demon Tobankto set up a trap for Erebus and when Erebus called to darkness instead of having a minor contact with it he was drenched so to speak." Risha looked at Adam. "Should I tell her the rest?"

"Please we have many searching for him," Emeral said with frustration.

"It appears that Erebus is fighting the magics from controlling him but he is also using this to his advantage to somehow help all of you. The others who are searching for him cannot be of help to him because they can't go where he is. I will go and help him."

70

"Where is he?" asked Emeral.

"Walking among the dead," Risha said.

After four hours Claudius announced that the Royal Families were exhausted and would be leaving the Great Hall. Soldiers would replace them behind the casket.

Raphael and Maxwell quickly walked up to the Royal Families, which included Madeline and Corsa and led them to Mathas' study where they told them about Risha.

"Where is she now?" asked Angelina.

"She is with the healers; they should be on this floor. They gave antidotes to Edward and Javier," said Raphael. Angelina quickly left the room.

"I am so exhausted I don't know whether to be shocked or enraged," said Sudfad. "Did her potions kill my son?"

"If they did, it was not intentional on her part. She basically put a bounty on her own head after she heard about Michael's death," said Maxwell. "And Adam is sending her on a mission to help Erebus."

"What!" said Sudfad.

"Let us tell you everything," Raphael said.

Ten minutes later Kent and George knocked on the door to the study. Maxwell opened the door and Corsa panicked and asked, "Is Javier alright?"

"Yes," said Kent. "But he would like you, Madeline, Sudfad and Renya to come to his room."

"You're smiling," said Madeline. "Why are you smiling?"

"Just come with us please," Kent said. George did not speak but his grin took over his face.

Alex was waiting in the hallway outside of Javier's room for Kent and the others. He opened the door for them and they saw that Javier was sitting up in bed. Gabriel, Gideon, Angus and Dominic were also in the room.

"What is going on?" asked Corsa as she quickly walked to the bed and started to examine Javier. "Did they give you the antidote?"

"Yes, it tasted horrible but I think I am starting to feel better. But we have other things to discuss now. Madeline and Corsa, I have some things to say and please don't yell or argue until I am done." Javier was smiling as he spoke.

"I have almost died twice now in a short period of time which makes a person think. Gabriel would you please hand out the copies."

"Gabriel helped me write a will. Corsa don't say anything yet, please. As you will read I have divided most of my assets between the two of you. If I live long enough to have children I will have to change the will. Since I am believed to be dead I have sold two of my homes to Gabriel who will use them for the teams. The sale of those homes will pay for the educations of Alex, Kent and George."

"What!" said Alex. "We can't let you do that."

"Please, I am not done," said Javier. "The cottage that Madeline and I called our home goes to her and the third house I am giving to Gideon for an Adam's Home. Now, I have many belongings and cash in those houses which the team members will get for me."

"After watching how distraught everyone has been after these attacks, I have made Alex the executor of my will. I know he will take care of both of the women in my life."

"Sudfad, in one of the houses that Gabriel bought I have a large suitcase of money that I won gambling. I am giving that to you to start Adam's Homes in Wetpr."

"You don't need to spend your money," Sudfad said. "I was going to start that project, I just haven't gotten around to it yet."

"Well, perhaps Madeline and Corsa can help me get them started," said Renya and smiled.

"Now, the last thing. While this may be a very inappropriate time, I honestly don't know if I will survive these injuries. George you're up."

George walked up to Corsa with a smile that his face could not contain. He handed her a small velvet box. "Javier, what is this?" she asked.

"Open it," Javier said. "Did you notice that in the will I referred to you as my wife?"

"Oh my," Corsa said when she saw the rings.

"I hope you aren't going to run out of the room again because I would like us to be married now. We can have another ceremony later."

"What?" Corsa asked in disbelief.

"Gabriel will perform the service. Madeline, will be standing up for you and Kent and George for me. Alex will walk you to the bed and Sudfad and Renya will you be our witnesses?"

"Of course," Sudfad said with a big smile.

The ceremony was short but everyone in the room was touched by happiness. "I hope at your next ceremony you wear a shirt," Madeline said kiddingly to Javier and kissed him on the cheek.

"I brought some wine so that we can have a toast," Dominic said.

"Javier, can you drink after taking that antidote?" asked Corsa.

"I told the healers about this and asked that question. The witch said I could but not to drink more than one glass."

"Have you seen her?" George asked then looked around the room as if he was afraid she was in there. "She is really scary looking."

"I am not sure scary is the word I would use," said Dominic. "But she was surprisingly nice. But first a toast." Alex handed out the glasses that Dominic was filling.

"To Corsa and Javier, may they have long and healthy lives," Dominic said and everyone repeated.

"I would like to say our family toast," said Sudfad. "To family, may our bonds never be broken." The King held up his glass and everyone repeated his words.

"I have one," said Madeline. "May there be peace in our lifetimes."

After everyone repeated the toast, Sudfad said, "Peace is almost too much to hope for."

Hilgra had opened a magic shop in the Catacombs so that she could work as a spy for the ruling families. She had decided to stay at work longer on this day because of some of the unusual things she was hearing people say. She arrived at the showing six hours after it started. She had just viewed Michael's body and was turning away from the casket when Thedes walked up to her.

"Ibula has had me looking for you," Thedes said. "A most remarkable thing has happened and the healers want you to join them." Hilgra didn't speak; she wiped the tears from her cheeks and followed Thedes into the hallway.

Once in the hallway and away from the public, Thedes told Hilgra about Risha. "She is going to help Erebus tonight so we only have her for a few more hours," Thedes said.

"That entire story is, well, unbelievable," Hilgra said as they hurried down the hallway and entered a chambers on the first floor. Ibula, Hadar, Lakin, Gael, Hannah, Shara and Angelina were sitting around a table with Risha.

Risha stared intently at Hilgra as Hadar introduced the women. "How did you lose your powers?" Risha asked.

"I let a dark lord take them as payment for changing my looks."

"You are lucky you are alive," Risha said. "I heard a great deal about that dark lord. She was trying to resurrect old and dangerous magics; there were reasons those magics were hidden. She was not a healer, physician or even a witch."

"She had little understanding of what she was doing. She sent people to me to find substitutions for some of the ingredients she needed. I did not help her."

"All of us at this table have been trying to translate the ledgers that dark lord used because we fear she killed people and put imposters in their places. Perhaps later we can speak with you about her magics," said Angelina.

"If we have time," Risha said.

"Are you saying that because you believe you will be killed?" asked Angelina. "Because we can protect you."

"My dear child, no one can protect me from what I did. I have lived a long life and I am not afraid to die."

"What exactly did you do?" asked Ibula.

"You might say that I cursed those who would use my potions for murder. Now we should resume our work. The Angel will be here soon."

After toasting Javier and Corsa's marriage, Dominic told everyone in the room what Olivia and her friends were doing in the Great Hall. "So far we are interrogating twenty-two men and that is how we discovered Risha."

"Are all of our daughters sitting at that table?" Sudfad asked with obvious disapproval.

"Yes, I was told the entire thing was their idea," Dominic said and smiled. "Why?"

"They were told to stay in their chambers," Renya said. "We couldn't bear to have anything happen to another child."

"So you understand," Angus said. "Emeral and Maxwell recognized them as soon as they entered the room and joined them. Within moments the team members sat in all of the tables around them. They aren't alone."

"They also disobeyed us," Sudfad said wearily.

"While I understand that you will need to correct them for disobeying you," said Gabriel. "I think we are all realizing those girls are becoming like the two of you. They weren't the fighters that they are now. I know they look up to both of you and I am beginning to wonder if they are trying to take after you."

"You aren't making this any easier," Sudfad said and smiled. "Are they still in there?"

"Yes," Angus said. "I would ask that you let them continue until the showing is over. Olivia has identified more potential threats than our men have."

Sudfad nodded, "But we still need to talk to them." His weariness was evident on his face.

"Before we go," Renya said. "Javier and Corsa we will have a celebration for your wedding when we return home. And I didn't realize your brothers would be attending the Learning Center. They are certainly welcome to live in the castle, we have plenty of room."

"Thank you," Alex said. "That is very generous of you. And I don't want to sound ungrateful but we should probably stay in the barracks so we don't get distracted from our work."

Renya smiled when she saw the disappointment on George's face. "Well, you can always stay with us for a couple of weeks and then decide if life in the castle would be too distracting."

Both Kent and Alex saw that Renya was looking at George as she spoke. "We will try that," said Alex. "But I have to warn you that we basically grew up in a shack. We have a great deal to learn."

"Sudfad and Renya treat everyone in their home like family," Gabriel said. "You will feel very comfortable there."

Sudfad and Renya entered the Great Hall and walked up to the table where their daughters were sitting. Dack and Joao quickly stood up and brought two more chairs to the table.

"Are we in trouble?" asked Saran. "Because this was Nyla's and my idea the others shouldn't be punished."

"Well, we weren't really thinking about punishing you," Sudfad said. "But Renya and I are both very disappointed that you disobeyed us. This is a dangerous situation and we don't want any of you to get hurt. We have already lost one child."

"I think I would feel better if you yelled at us," Margarit said.

"We deserve to be punished for disobeying you," Nyla said. "But please let us stay and finish this. We have found a lot of people."

"Angus and Dominic asked us to allow you to continue and we will. Mathas will soon be closing the doors to the public," said Sudfad.

"Where did you go?" asked Nina. "Were you looking for us?"

"We were in Javier's room," Sudfad said. "He and Corsa just got married."

"Married!" said Saran. "Why would they get married when he can't even get out of bed?" No one answered her. "Oh," she said seriously as she realized the answer to her own question.

"What are you saying?" asked Nina. "Something is wrong; I can tell."

"Nina, he has serious injuries," Nyla said. "They got married now in case he dies."

"No! He's my friend," Nina yelled as she jumped up from the table and ran out of the Great Hall. Sudfad and Renya followed her.

Javier's room was close to the Great Hall, Nina pushed the door open and ran inside. Everyone smiled at her because she still had the black veil over her head and face. "Javier are you going to die?" she asked frantically.

"I hope not," he said and smiled. "Why don't you sit up here?"

"Nyla said you got married now because you might die. You can't die too," Nina said and jumped onto the bed. "I don't want you to." She was crying as she spoke. Madeline too started to cry as she listened to the little girl.

"Let me take this off your head so I can look at you," Javier said and lifted up the veil. "That is what I told Corsa or she wouldn't marry me. It will be our secret."

"Secret! She just heard what you said." Everyone in the room smiled as Nina spoke. Sudfad and Renya were in the room now, although they had heard Nina speaking when they were in the hallway.

"It doesn't matter now because we are already married," Javier said and smiled warmly. "Are you ready for that story now? You know I think all of the men in this room saw that sea creature also."

"Really?" Nina said in awe. "Papa why didn't you tell us about the sea creature?"

"Honestly, I forgot," said Sudfad. "But she was already gone when I got there. "I would like to hear about her too."

"Then let me pour a little more wine into everyone's glass," said Dominic.

Nina now sat next to Javier so she was leaning against his pillow and looked at the people in the room. She started to giggle and whispered into his ear. "You should tell him," Javier said. Nina kept giggling and shook her head from side to side. "Can, I tell him?" she nodded.

"George, Saran thinks you are really cute," Javier said and laughed when George dropped his glass of wine on the floor.

"She does?" George asked and looked and sounded shocked. Everyone in the room laughed loudly. "Oh, I need to clean this up," he said and stared blankly at the floor.

Corsa laughed and cleaned up the wine with a towel.

"Well, that would be one distraction," Alex said and winked at Sudfad and Renya.

# Chapter VI
## Shame

Nana, Bethany and Marina were watching over all of the wounded in Mathas' castle as the more experienced healers were spending the afternoon and evening with Risha. Vivian and Diana had an additional bed moved into Kate's room as well as cradles and the two women stayed with their friend.

Joshua, Thor and Misha walked into Kate's room, where Vivian and Diana had been all day.

"What is the matter?" asked Vivian when she saw the serious looks on their faces. "Has something happened to Edward?"

"There is just so much to tell you," said Joshua. "But we don't have time for all the details right now. Olivia and her friends disguised themselves and sat in the Great Hall when the public was viewing the body. She found many suspicious people and the team members are interrogating them now. But she also identified a witch."

"What!" gasped Diana.

"Actually, it is not at all what any of us thought," Joshua said. "Apparently this woman is as old as time and was a healer but she fled to a cave in the Rosu Mountains when the Originator came here the first time. She lives an isolated life but she is a maker of potions and apparently is well known in many worlds. It sounds like only the rich can afford her."

"While she services demons she doesn't want her potions used to kill. She came here to see if her potions killed Michael. The Angel Adam came into the room when Risha, that's her name, was talking to Emeral and Angus. Now get this, the woman's skin smoked when Emeral touched her with a crystal but she knew Adam and agreed to go on a mission for him. We are going to see if we can go too which is why we are telling you this."

"What mission?" asked Diana.

"Please, just let me finish first," said Joshua. "Risha gave her book of potions and antidotes to our healers who have already used them on Edward and Javier. Adam said that book was worth entire fortunes. Risha said that she has received orders for very dangerous potions and after hearing about Michael she sabotaged the potions which will put bounties on her. She believes she will only be alive a few days and is offering to help us until then."

"Now for the really disturbing parts. The messengers that requested these potions were Bruno and Morgan. They had been in the demon Ale's hell world being tortured but one of Samael's buddies took over that world and released them back here. All Risha said was that they smelled of hell."

"Misha," Diana gasped.

"Honey, let him finish," said Misha. "There is a lot more and we will fill you in later."

"The demon who tried to take Matthew and Erebus into his hell world set up a trap for Erebus. When he used magic to expose the archers he was, Risha said drenched in it. He is trying to fight the magics from controlling him but somehow also trying to use the situation to help us," Joshua explained.

"Erebus is in a place that the people who are looking for him can't go so Adam asked Risha to help him. Adam will be coming for Risha soon and we want to go too."

"Where is he?" asked Diana. "And how does she know this?"

"Emeral said that Adam and Risha were staring at each other and then Risha said that Adam showed her how Erebus lost his powers and what he was trying to do. She said that Erebus was walking with the dead, we don't know what that means."

"There is one more thing," said Thor. "Risha said that many people suspected that Michael was one of The Seven Sons and now they believe they can all be killed and will come after them. She believes that is why she is getting orders for the potions and she will not assist them."

"Wait are you sure she is telling the truth?" Vivian asked.

"From what Emeral said a lot of what we told you came from Adam," said Joshua. "Emeral was confused because, well first you have to see Risha, she, well, let's just say she could scare the children. But she bowed before Adam and spoke with him like she knew him and she has been very helpful with our people."

"We are going to find her now because we don't know exactly when Adam is coming," Misha said and kissed Diana.

It was almost dark when Matthew, Thaos and Stephan found there friends in a large cave. "Quickly get in here," yelled the Sanuri. "There is enough room for all of you."

"Glad to see you boys," Sorren said as he watched for movement outside of the cave.

"Did you send the Enrops that brought us here?" asked Thaos. "And what are all of those bodies out there?"

"Are you alright?" asked Stephan as he could see that Horace and Dagon had bandages on them.

"This whole thing was an elaborate trap that the demon Tobankto set up," said the Sanuri. "They are trying to get Erebus and those of us who would rescue him."

"Where is he?" asked Matthew.

"We don't really know," said the Sanuri. "But Adam is sending someone else to get him. All I know is that we are supposed to stay here for a while."

"Well, certainly you didn't kill all of those whatever they are out there," said Thaos. "Are the Angels helping?"

"Oh, there are more than you can see," said the Sanuri. "And I suspect we are a diversion."

"So tell us what happened," Stephan said.

"Well, we started looking for Erebus," Sorren explained. "There wasn't a trail but the Sanuri was following some kind of energy and the next thing we know we are surrounded by demons."

"We fought them and all of us thought it was too damn easy. We knew something wasn't right. The Sanuri called to Miranda and she told us to go in this cave. We've been here for a while and haven't heard a peep from the Angels. What about you?"

"When none of us heard from you we got worried," said Matthew as he stood near Sorren at the mouth of the cave. We were traveling for hours. We asked the Angels for direction but didn't hear from them. Then about an hour ago some Enrops fly up to us and tell us they know where you are. We followed them here and didn't see any demons until we got to the cave."

"So should we take it that the Angels aren't talking to us because something is up?" asked Stephan as he picked up a burning piece of wood and examined the stone walls.

"What I want to know is who the Angels are sending to help Erebus," said Dagon. "I mean wouldn't you think it would be the Sanuri?"

To the surprise of all, Adam appeared in the room with the healers and Risha. "Adam," Angelina said as Risha stood up from her chair. "Risha is marked for death but she is helping us. Can we help her?"

"That would be up to her," Adam replied.

"I don't understand," said Angelina.

"I do," Risha said and walked up to the Angel.

"Wait!" yelled Misha as he, Thor and Joshua burst through the door. "We want to go too."

"You are fools," Risha said to the men.

"He is our friend," said Thor. "He would do the same for us."

"Tell them," Adam said to Risha.

83

"Erebus is in the world of nightmares, but it is not just his nightmares that he is living. It is a world of endless night. All of you would bring attention because you aren't from the dark worlds."

"Well, how can you be so bad if you know an Angel?" asked Thor angrily. "We are going. Adam can't you hide us or something?"

"Thor be quiet," said Joshua as he walked up to Risha and stared into her eyes. "What exactly are you going to do to help him?"

Risha looked at Adam who spoke, "Erebus has called to us to help him fight the magics until he can find the answers to many questions. But he cannot do this alone as he is being constantly attacked. Risha has offered to help him find the answers."

"And how are they going to get back?" asked Thor. "If they are being attacked, we should be there."

"Thor be quiet!" said Joshua. "There is more to this; I can feel it." He stepped closer to Risha. "What is it about you that seems familiar?" Risha did not speak as she and Joshua stared at each other. "Are you from our clan?" he asked. Risha did not answer. "How do you know about the Shadow Men and how is it that a powerful witch bows before an Angel?"

"Risha it is only fair that they know who they are risking their lives for," Adam said.

"They should not come," Risha said sternly. "They have no idea of what they are asking."

"Offering to take Erebus' place will do no one any good," said Adam. "Tell them."

Risha straightened up and held her head high but tears came to her eyes. "I became a member of your clan by marriage. I was a healer not a warrior but I followed my husband and the others when they went to Marba to fight the Originator. We could feel the evil for miles before we came to that opening in a cave but it was an opening in between the worlds and none of us realized that."

"Death was everywhere. There was not a blade of grass or an insect for miles. When we came to the cave we saw such horror that we wept. Sargei, he was my husband. He and the others overcame their fears. They prayed to the heavens and asked to fulfil their oaths to The Great Ruler even in death, for they all knew they would die."

"I stood by and watched as they ran into that cave. I heard the war cries and the screams. And I too ran but in a different direction. I was so afraid that I could not stop running until I collapsed from exhaustion. I lay on the ground and wept and that night Sargei came to me as the shadow you know of. He told me how they had been reborn in a way. He wanted me to join him. But I was too afraid."

"I prayed to have a long life so that I could join my husband and that was my curse. I turned to magics in the beginning to protect myself. Sargei would visit me until I allowed myself to be filled with darkness. I make no excuses, I called to the magics and welcomed them and I felt powerful. But that kind of power is addictive. I know better than any of you what Erebus is fighting. He must be a very strong man."

"I hid because of my fears. I lived the life of a recluse because of my fears and after a while the entire world looked different to me. I longed for death but my body would not die. It was Sargei who came to me and told me what the demons were going to use my potions for and he reminded me that I had once sworn and oath to The Great Ruler too. I was filled with shame..." Risha started to cry.

"Continue," Adam said. "They need to hear this."

It took Risha a few moments to compose herself and no one in the room spoke during that time. "I did something I had not done in a very long time. I prayed to The Great Ruler and asked Him to help me fulfil the oath I had sworn so long ago. And in that instance an old woman appeared in the cave with me and Sargei. She was an Angel and she told me many things. You see I had hidden from the world, not only out of fear but I didn't want to know the consequences of my potions."

85

"Her name is Ruth and she stayed with me for hours then she told me that I had many decisions to make. She didn't have to tell me because I already knew what I had to do. I took her through my caverns and showed her the fortunes I had acquired. I asked her to find a use for those riches. Then I sabotaged the kettles of potions and poured them into jars."

"I set the jars out but put spells on them so that the messengers would only see the jars intended for their masters. Then I told her that I needed to come here and asked her to help me with the journey."

"Risha how did you sabotage those potions?" asked Lakin.

Now the old woman grinned. "You have to understand that only the most powerful demons can afford to buy from me. The beings they send are just their minions. While minions can be hurt, it is difficult to hurt an Old One without the help of an Angel. I put in herbs that would stop the effects of the poisons and Ruth added some holiness. I only wish I could be there to see the show."

"Risha, I became a witch too because I was terrified," said Hilgra. "Adam, I am not a warrior and I guess I don't really know what I am anymore but can you use me to help Erebus and Risha?"

"And what would you do?" asked Adam.

"I have read a great deal about the world of the endless night. It is a world of illusions perpetuated by fright."

"Not so different from other worlds," Adam said. "So again how would you help?"

"The magics in that world reach into your minds and find what you are most terrified of. In Erebus' case he is probably reliving Sophie's murder. No matter how real things seem you have to remember it is like a dream. Perhaps I can help them all to remember that."

Micha, Bianca, Thomas and Sasha were standing in the open doorway of the room. "Do you really think you were going without us?" Micha asked and the four young people walked up to Joshua.

"Did you hear that she is of our clan?" asked Joshua.

"I think we heard it all," Micha said. "My question is are we going to be a diversion while Risha helps Erebus get the information and if so how much time do they need? And Adam can we ask you to touch us with holiness or would we stand out too much in the darkness?"

"Adam, I, well we may all have to ask you to help us overcome our fears," said Hilgra.

"It is facing your fears that make you strong," Thor said.

"While I won't disagree with what you said, I don't want to compromise this mission," said Hilgra.

Adam smiled and disappeared as did everyone who volunteered for the mission.

"I don't like the sounds of that," Thaos said as dirt and small rocks fell on top of him. "What could make the ground shake like that?" Everyone inside of the cave was being covered with debris.

After Risha and the others disappeared, Hannah left the room to tell Gabriel. Moments later Hannah returned to the room and announced that the public showing had ended.

"I would like to observe your ceremony," Hannah said to the Ruala healers.

"Of course, we will get you when we are ready," said Ibula. "Shara, Angelina would you care to join us?"

"What are you doing?" asked Angelina.

"Preparing Michael's body. He won't be buried until we reach Wetpr," Ibula said.

"I would like to see that but I have a feeling that we need to finish reviewing Risha's book," Shara said and looked at Angelina who nodded.

# Chapter VII
## Screams

A heavy, thick blackness enveloped Joshua and his family members as they found themselves transported into a nightmare world. "Is everyone here?" asked Joshua as he could not see the people standing with him. "Call out your names." Thor, Misha, Micha, Hilgra, Thomas and Bianca all said their names.

"Sasha," called Thomas frantically.

"I am here but I can hardly breathe," she said.

"Risha, Risha are you here?" asked Joshua but there was no answer.

"Erebus are you here?" asked Thor but there was silence. A thick and eerie silence.

"Adam will you help us to see?" Joshua asked in a whisper as he did not know if they were near enemies.

"Adam will you help me to breathe?" asked Sasha frantically and started to gasp for air.

"Sasha relax and breathe deeply," said Hilgra. "It is your nightmare."

Thomas reached into the darkness, "Sasha, I can't find you. Where are you?"

"She's right here," said Hilgra. "All of you listen. This is a world of nightmares. Whatever fears are in your minds will take life here. Control your thoughts and concentrate on helping Erebus."

"Well, I have never been afraid of the dark," said Thor with frustration. "And I can't see shit."

Hilgra had her arm around Sasha and kept telling her to relax and breathe. The others in the group were silent. After a few moments Sasha said, "I am better now, thanks."

"I find this ironic," said Hilgra. "Of all of us, I am the one who is always afraid. Adam must be using me to help you." Silence. "Is everyone still here? Call out your names." Silence.

89

A scream in the darkness. Misha listened intently as he tried to determine which direction it was coming from. Another scream. The thick darkness affected his senses. Another scream. He was trying to recognize the voice. Suddenly he started to run; it was his own voice that he heard screaming.

Risha found Erebus sitting on the ground with his arms wrapped around his knees. He was rocking back and forth and whimpering. He stared at Risha as she appeared before him.

"Erebus!" she said sharply. "I am Risha, I am a witch and the Angel Adam sent me to help you. Now stand up because we have work to do."

"How do I know you are real?"

"That is a good question. I don't know. Adam help us."

Erebus stood up and grasped Risha's hand and stared at her. She stood in silence for she felt that the Angel was giving Erebus information about her. After a few moments he said, "I have heard of you. Why are you helping me?"

"Now, that is a very long story, which we may not have time for now. Did he show you that your friends are here also? They are acting as diversions. And I don't know why but I feel we must hurry."

"Who is here?" gasped Erebus.

"Many have been looking for you but by normal means. When Adam asked me to come here, others volunteered. Hilgra, Joshua, Misha, Thor, Micha, Thomas and their wives. They are fools and have no idea what they did. We must hurry. I still have my dark powers. Now, what is it you seek?"

"Bianca! No!" screamed Micha.

Joshua was drenched with sweat and on his knees. "Great Ruler help us to do the job we came here to do."

"Adam how do I help them?" asked Hilgra.

Rocks and dirt rained down on the Sanuri and the warriors who had taken shelter in a cave.

"If I am going to die it will be fighting," said Sorren. "Not buried alive in a cave."

"They want us to run out," said Matthew.

"Well, they may be getting their wish," Sorren spat.

"Miranda what is going on here?" yelled Thaos.

Like many people, Thor channeled his fears into rage. He spun around in the thick darkness with his sword drawn. The images of his parents being murdered filled his head. "This is just a dream," he kept repeating. Tears ran down his cheeks as he continuously turned; he was prepared for an attack. "Adam, this is just bullshit," he screamed. "If we are being a distraction who is watching us?" Suddenly the images disappeared and he heard crying.

"Listen to me," Hilgra screamed into the darkness. "Don't let the nightmares take control. They aren't real. Nothing here is real."

"Miranda why aren't you answering us?" yelled Stephan. "Is this some kind of test?"

"Sanuri, what is going on?" demanded Thaos as he almost fell because of the shaking of the ground.

"Honestly, I don't know. I just feel that we are a distraction," the Sanuri replied.

"Well, if we are going to be a distraction, then let's give them a show," yelled Sorren as he ran to the mouth of the cave. "Miranda touch me with holiness or not but I am going to fight."

"I am not sure this is the smartest thing to do," yelled Thaos as he followed Sorren.

"Touch us all Miranda," yelled Dagon as he ran out of the cave.

"We could use some help down here," the Sanuri said to the heavens and followed his friends.

"Micha!" screamed Bianca as she stumbled in the darkness. She was crying hysterically which impeded her sight even more in the thick atmosphere. She screamed when she felt a hand grab her arm.

"It's Thor," a voice whispered and shook her. "Bianca get control, we aren't alone here."

"I love it," Risha said after Erebus revealed his plan to her. "I wasn't sure what you were going to do so I brought a few things." As she spoke, Risha poured the contents of a large pouch onto the ground. She created more balls of fire to illuminate their area as she arranged the items for a ceremony.

"I still don't understand why you are doing this," said Erebus as he sorted through the herbs and items that now lay on the ground.

"I forgot who I was for, well a very long time. If we live through this I will explain. Now we must hurry, I fear for your friends."

"Holy shit!" said Stephan as they all ran out of the cave. They had expected to see armies of demons but instead they saw images of themselves.

"Stop!" yelled the Sanuri. "These are illusions. There is an opening between worlds here, I can feel it."

"Was it here before?" asked Horace.

"No," the Sanuri said and started to hum.

"I don't know why you aren't answering us," Rachel called out to the Angels. "Can you at least give us a sign that you hear us?"

"I am your sign," said Thot as he appeared before the group. "You must all return to the cave. The Sanuri will be in that trance as long as I am here; it is hard to explain so just listen. There are points in time that are pivotal and this is one of those points. Beings have choices to make and depending on the choices, let's just say that there can be a variety of endings to the story."

"The demons know that the Sanuri will try to close that opening and that is the trap. If he continues he will be destroyed and I will assume all of his energy and come into your world. Go back into that cave. They have not been able to defeat you with might so they are using your fears against you. They will try to drive you into the open again. Stay in the cave."

"Are you Thot?" asked Sorren.

"Yes."

"What is your connection with the Sanuri?"

"You would not understand, even if I had time to explain it. But this I can tell you, I will remain here but outside of the cave. The Sanuri was right, we are creating a diversion and your friends need time. Now go back in that cave!"

Thor and Bianca held hands as they crept through the darkness. They had to concentrate on the information their senses were providing them. They both stopped because they smelled sweat. Suddenly a bolt of lightning flashed and illuminated the landscape. They saw a demon squatting next to a body. The light was gone. Both warriors ran to where they had seen the body. "Damn it, Adam can't you help us see?" asked Thor.

"This is a world of illusions of the mind," Adam's voice said into the ears of all the warriors and Hilgra. "Use the power of your mind. You can defeat all of this if you can overcome your fears."

"Let's concentrate on light," Bianca whispered. As both warriors focused on light the darkness around them started to recede. There was no demon and a log lay on the ground where they thought they had seen a body.

"Adam it worked," Thor said. "If we create enough light will eyes be focused on us?"

"Yes," Adam said. "But first concentrate on finding your friends."

Erebus and Risha sat on the ground and held hands as they chanted. Between them they had a pile of exotic herbs and bones. They focused on the words so they would not be frightened by the images that appeared around them. Images of hell beasts and lost loved ones.

Erebus had been a powerful warlock although he never sold his soul to a demon. Tobankto was trying to destroy Erebus' connection with the Angels and bring him back to the darkness. Tobankto gave Erebus more power than his human body could contain. Risha, a witch of extraordinary powers was now helping Erebus to channel his power. As Erebus was gaining control of his body and powers he and Risha were combining their powers and using the World of Illusions to their advantage.

"Misha, it's not real," said Thor as he and Bianca helped their friend to stand up. "Look at us, open your eyes and look at us." Misha whimpered but did not open his eyes. Thor slapped him across the face and Misha opened his eyes and was about to punch Thor. "Misha it's me. You aren't that victim any more. Come on, we have to find the others."

Hilgra was walking with Thomas and Sasha when they heard the sounds of fighting. Sasha pushed Hilgra behind her and readied her sword. They heard the war cry of the Venatores and ran towards the sound. As did Thor, Bianca and Misha.

A second war cry was heard. Thomas jumped into a thicket and joined Joshua and Micha who were fighting a group of demons. The war cries of the Nordes Tribe, the Ruala Tribe and the Venatores broke through the darkness; never had war cries pierced the World of Illusions before. Both Risha and Erebus smiled when they heard them.

Demons and monsters both real and imagined now ran towards the war cries. The Angel Adam gave a gift to the Sanuri and his group who were still standing in front of the cave with Thot. The war cries were carried through the opening between the worlds. Sorren and the others recognized the voices of their friends.

"Miranda, should we join them?" yelled Sorren.

"Your presence here is keeping more demons from them," her voice was heard by the entire group.

"Well can't we do more than hide in a cave?" Sorren yelled.

"And what would you do?" asked Miranda as she appeared next to Thot.

"We could fight...." Sorren was saying when he was interrupted by Thaos.

"Sorren, let me take this," Thaos said and walked closer to Miranda and Thot. "There are three emissaries here. Miranda what are our enemies seeing?"

"Actually little, because they are blinded by the light."

"And is that light drawing them away from other things?" asked Thaos. "Like when you and Adam were on the battlefield with us?"

"I wasn't sure you noticed that," she said and smiled.

"So would we be more help by asking you to touch as with holiness so we could shine too?"

95

"Thaos, you are learning your lessons well," Miranda said. "But we will wait a few moments and when you ask me, ask also that I surround all of your friends and family."

"What do you mean?" asked Stephan anxiously.

"I think this is a test of sorts," Thaos said. "Just do as she says."

One of the items that Risha had placed on the ground between her and Erebus was a small journal with blank pages. As the two powerful beings continued to chant, words appeared on the pages. And the pages moved as if a strong wind was blowing them.

"Adam, we could use some help!" Micha yelled as they fought the army that surrounded them.

"I thought you would never ask," Adam said and appeared in their midst. His holiness blinded the demons who momentarily stopped their assault. But when the masters of this demonic army realized an Angel had entered their territory new horrors were unleashed.

The World of Illusions was a game board of sorts that was observed by an audience of darkness. Now Old Ones and other powerful demons commanded their troops into that world. Troops that were being pulled from other arenas.

Demons from many worlds were exposing themselves to watch the battle for never before had an Angel entered this world.

"Thaos, now would be a good time to ask," said Miranda.

"Miranda..." he never completed his sentence for explosions shook the ground. The hole between the worlds was exposed for the humans to see as smoke and flames bellowed out. Screams and curses filled the air.

The Sanuri came out of his trance and Thot disappeared. "You had a lesson to learn today," Miranda said to the holy man.

Explosions after explosions shook the World of Illusions. The thick darkness was dispelled and the demons looked with horror at the armies of Shadow Men who were attacking their ranks.

When Joshua saw the Shadow Men he screamed the war cry of a proud people. A war cry that was repeated by the hundreds of thousands of voices of the Shadow Men.

Tears flowed down Risha's cheeks as she listened to the war cries of her people.

Suddenly Erebus and Risha felt a strong presence near them. "You can stop now," said the Angel Ruth. "You have what you came for."

"Do we?" asked Risha. "I had asked to be able to fulfill my oath." In that instant Risha's head dropped forward then her entire body fell to the side. Erebus stood up and ran to her.

"She is dead," he gasped. "Did you do that?"

"You should know better than to ask that question," Ruth said. "And she is not really dead."

"I don't understand. What did she come here for?"

"Redemption," said Ruth. "Now for you."

"Take this magic from me. And make these pages safe for us to read."

"Hello Hecate."

The demon swung around and saw her husband Sampson standing on a battlefield in northern Wetpr with her. His appearance was that of the powerful Venator she had once seduced.

"Sampson, I have searched for you..."

"I know your tricks," Sampson said and walked closer to her. He put his arms around her and kissed her passionately, then he grinned and as he grinned his face began to change in appearance. "My dear treacherous wife, you have been on the auction block and Visterle is the highest bidder." Hecate fought and screamed as Sampson dragged her to the World of Sidus.

# Chapter VIII
## The Long Road Home

"This isn't exactly how I thought we would spend our wedding night," Javier said as he was lying in bed.

"You over did it and you know it," Corsa scolded as she mopped his forehead with a cool wet cloth.

"But it was worth it," he said and smiled.

"You need to take this seriously," Corsa said and paused. "I don't want anything else to happen to you."

The bedroom door flew open and Kent stood in the doorway. "Corsa, I don't know what happened but they are bringing wounded in. I'll watch Javier. They are calling for you."

The wounded were not brought into the castle of Mathas, they simply appeared. Both the group that was in the World of Illusions as well as the group with the Sanuri materialized in the Great Hall. Every man and woman including the Sanuri was injured.

The public had recently left the Great Hall but the room was still filled with team members, family and friends of the Royal Families. All of these people now ran to the wounded soldiers and warriors.

Koby pounded on the door to the room where the Ruala healers and Hannah were preparing Michael's body. "The Great Hall is full of wounded," he yelled. Hannah, Ibula and Lakin ran out of the room. Gael and Hadar continued with the ancient ceremony.

"What happened?" was being asked over and over and most of the wounded gave the same answers, "Not really sure."

Corsa, Nana, Risa and Bethany ran into the Great Hall while Marina watched over Edward and Kate. Shara and Angelina were the first two healers to arrive and were separating the wounded by injuries. Hannah, Lakin and Ibula immediately went to the area with the most seriously wounded people.

Those who were not healers, were preparing rooms, bringing bandages and medical supplies and in some cases carrying wounded soldiers and team members.

"Why do you all have burns?" Hannah asked.

A soldier replied, "Because everything exploded."

"I'm not that bad," Stephan said as his father helped him to a bed. "Is Erebus here?"

"Yes, I saw him," said Claudius.

"We are going to have to ask the Angels what happened because I think it was something really big."

Erebus and Risha had been chanting powerful and complicated ceremonies. Ceremonies that had never before been combined and the powers of these two beings took these magics to new levels.

Suddenly demons, very powerful demons found themselves exposed. It was not the Angels these demons were hiding from but others of their kind. While Hecate had been commanding troops on the lands owned by Karzman she wore the guise of a man. Once that guise fell away Sampson found her. He had bartered greatly in the hell worlds and promised to bring them Hecate for a prize; for this, he would receive incredible rewards.

Zieman, the demon King of Stordt was in hiding after his minions learned that Sorphat, a lieutenant of Samael's had discovered that he was responsible for the curses that attacked Karzman.

Sorphat found Zieman and personally transported him to Samael. Then Sorphat returned to Stordt and stormed Zieman's castle.

Many demons were conspiring and competing in Samael's Gefrey Games. With their disguises removed these demons now attacked each other instead of continuing their search for the cave of the Originator.

Andrac and Gilder could no longer maintain their human appearances and the armies of humans they led ran in fear. These two powerful sorcerers were abandoned and surrounded by demons on Karzman's lands.

Karzman again lost the façade of a strong and healthy body, the body he had received for sacrificing his son to Samael. Karzman writhed in the dirt and screamed in pain.

But the demons involved with the Gefrey Games were not the only ones exposed. The streets and hell worlds of Nunc exploded in battles.

"No!" screamed Cabal and backed into the stone wall of his cell in the dungeons of Zieman's castle. Sorphat kicked the metal door open. "My boss wants to talk to you," Sorphat said and dragged Cabal to Samael's hell world.

"Erebus, where is Risha?" asked Angelina as she bandaged his wounds.

"Was that her name?" he asked in a dazed manner. "You are talking about the witch aren't you?"

"Yes, she was helping us. I haven't seen her."

"She's dead. At least she looked dead. Ruth said she really wasn't but I didn't understand what she meant."

Angelina smiled and said, "She became a Shadow Man. She is finally with her husband."

"I'm sorry, I don't understand," Erebus said. "I think having all that magic in me then having it removed did something to me."

"Or it could be this big gash in the back of your head," Shara said as she washed out the wound.

The explosions that resonated from the World of Illusions did more than to let the demons know that one of their worlds had been invaded. The powerful magics sent the horrors of that world back to those who had created it. Demons by nature have fear and paranoia gnawing at them always.

When Erebus and Risha blew up the World of Illusions the tiny particles of that explosion attached to all of the demons who had exposed themselves to watch the battles in that world. This act in conjunction with the magics that exposed many demons caused a frenzy in the dark worlds. The monsters turned on each other as never before.

Many of the Old Ones from different worlds knew that Tobankto was responsible for sending Erebus to the World of Illusions because the arrogant demon was bragging about his feats. Now many of these demons turned on Tobankto for exposing them to the magics created by Erebus and Risha.

Tobankto was an ally of Samael's. This collaboration only brought more enemies to his borders since many Old Ones were uniting in their war against Samael.

In the meantime, messengers of these powerful demons were arriving at the cave of Risha and picking up their merchandise. They did not suspect that anything was amiss when they did not see the witch. They simply left their payments and took the jars of potions.

Among these messengers were Bruno and Morgan. These two Ruala warriors had emerged from hell as shells of the men they once were. They had been tortured into submission by their demon captors. They remembered little of their lives before their time in hell; including doing business with Risha on a prior occasion.

As these men walked through the narrow and winding passageway to Risha's cavern they were overwhelmed with the putrid smells of her potions. Smells so strong that they touched the recesses of the minds of these two Rualas. Morgan and Bruno spoke little as they carried out their assignment but both of them were seized with great headaches and both of them started to remember.

Visterle was extremely pleased with Sampson for bringing him Hecate and showered riches and praises upon him. Visterle was known for many things which terrified others but like Hecate he had a reputation for paying well for services. Sampson had received little praise from his demon masters and allowed his ego to be filled with Visterle's words.

Visterle planned to execute Hecate in a public showing. He was sending out messages to the Old Ones and other powerful demons when word came to him that Morgan and Bruno had been released from their hell world. Visterle was infuriated for he would never trust Nada not to return to her former lovers.

Sampson had been given many gifts from Visterle, including a room filled with a variety of sexual partners. Visterle now sent his lieutenant to this building to get Sampson.

Visterle was successful and powerful because he thought deeply about every move he made. To him everything was like a chess game and he loved the calculating moves. Visterle knew about the Prophesies of The Seven Sons. He knew that the families of the Kings of Wetpr were suspected to be the Keepers of the Scrolls and he knew about the teams. He just didn't care. He knew what he wanted and he had seen too many demons lose control of their kingdoms by spreading themselves too thin.

Visterle also knew about Sampson's connections to all of these people which is why he saved Sampson from eternal torture. Sampson had been brutalized so long by the demons that he responded to praise and reward like a puppy; and this Visterle understood immediately. He knew that a man like Sampson could be tortured forever with little chances of submitting but under the right conditions he could be easily manipulated.

When Sampson was brought before Visterle, the demon was wearing the human mask that he wore for Nada. Sampson stared at him as he entered the Great Hall. "I have seen you before."

"Yes you have," said Visterle and laughed. "I like to visit worlds and see things for myself."

As he spoke Visterle poured two drinks and handed one to Sampson. "As you know I am very pleased with your work. And I have freed you of your contract. So tell me what are your plans now?"

"I don't know yet," said Sampson suspiciously.

"You have enough riches now to start a new life, really anywhere."

"Visterle, you don't strike me as a man, demon to make small talk. Why are you asking me these questions?"

Visterle laughed again. "I like your attitude. In fact, I like it so much I want to hire you to do special jobs for me. You have the experience of walking in many worlds and you understand the politics of demons and humans."

"I am listening."

"You know that I have taken the Ruala Nada for my wife. For years she had two Ruala lovers, men you have met."

"You mean Morgan and Bruno? I have to tell you I was on pain medications most of the time I was around them. So any information I could give you might not be accurate."

"I am not looking for information. The Ruala Misha killed them because they had raped and tortured him and his brothers and sisters for years. They were in Ale's world being tortured and I was pleased with that. A lot of new players are getting involved with the World of Nunc and the demon Abrass now rules over Ale's kingdom but you already know that. He has released Morgan and Bruno and returned them to Nunc as his minions. And that does not please me."

"Do you want me to kill them?"

Visterle smiled. "There is incredible turmoil in the hell regions of Nunc right now and I don't want to be sucked into those politics. I also don't want you in those hell worlds. Sampson, I believe you can be a very valuable soldier for me and as you know, I pay well for loyalty."

"For now I would like you to find those two and spy on them. I may want the pleasure of killing them myself."

Sampson stared at Visterle for several moments. "You think those two may be used against your family don't you? That is why you don't want me to kill them. And you would need to know who is behind such threats."

The demon smiled. "My assessment of you was correct."

"I will do this job but instead of gold I would like to be paid with information."

"I am listening."

"I too have a child. Hecate was pregnant when she left me. I know nothing about this child. I would like to get it. You have paid me well and I could afford to care for it now. Visterle, I will be loyal to you. Do you think you could help me unite with my family?"

The powerful demon was surprised at Sampson's request. At another time he might not have agreed but now that he was a father, Visterle had feelings which he did not understand. "In our own rights we are both monsters," said Visterle. "Yet, we both care for our families. You help me keep mine safe and I will help you find your child."

Twenty-four hours after Erebus and the others were returned to Mathas' castle, fifteen thousand soldiers from Lentz escorted the visitors from Wetpr home. Among this group were all of the wounded who had been involved with the rescue mission of Erebus as well as Edward, Kate and Javier. These last three patients rode in bocas with constant medical attention.

The soldiers from Lentz were given orders to remain in Wetpr until after the funeral ceremonies for Prince Michael, then they were to escort any team members who wanted to return to Lentz.

Alex, Kent and George rode to Wetpr with Corsa and Javier. Alex was torn as to whether he should go to Wetpr or stay in Langer and try to find his father but Sorren said that he would take over the search for Dirk. Sorren did not tell Alex and his family that Dirk was now a suspect in the attacks on Michael, Edward and Javier. Turner and his men had uncovered information that Dirk was seen in the Catacombs talking with demons just a day before the attacks.

Edward's team had now combined with Angus' team and remained in Langer to work with Dominic's team. They were going to investigate the attacks.

The emotions of the citizens of Langer were still raw and volatile. Many took the law into their own hands as they hunted the people responsible for the death of Prince Michael. In some cases these actions impeded the investigations, at other times they acted as diversions for the teams.

While Turner and his men and the team members did not trust each other they found that they worked remarkably well together. All of these people worked relentlessly to find the people behind the attacks.

During the twenty-four hours before the group left for Wetpr, the Angels explained many but not all of the consequences of Erebus's and Risha's actions. The group was told about Hecate, Sampson, Morgan and Bruno as well as the increased battles between the demons. They were also told about the fall of the demon Zieman and Samael's capture of Cabal which concerned many since Cabal knew the location of the cave of the Originator.

An hour before the group left for Wetpr they called to the Angels again. This time Adam told them about the effects of Risha's sabotaged potions, which attacked many of the Old Ones themselves. These powerful demons sent armies to Risha's cave to destroy the old woman but instead they found the cave filled with Shadow Men.

The Old Ones could not understand why their armies did not return from the witch's cave so they sent more soldiers to their deaths.

Madeline rode in a carriage with Renya and her daughters. All of the women were quiet, not only because of their grief over losing Michael but their sadness for leaving their friends in Lentz.

"I'm going to miss Margarit," Nyla announced.

"She may come for a visit soon," said Renya. "Rosa wants to bring her to Salar so they can visit the medical school at Cisero College."

"Can they stay for a while?" asked Saran.

"I certainly hope so," Renya said.

"Madeline what did Ashley give you this morning that made you cry?" asked Nyla. "Or shouldn't I ask?"

"No, that's alright," Madeline said and looked at Renya then at Nyla. "She gave me my wedding dress. She said she didn't know if I would want it or not."

"Are you keeping it?" asked Nyla.

"Yes," Madeline said. Her voice cracked with emotion.

"I'm glad," said Nyla. "I think I would want to keep it too."

"So do you ever plan on talking to the girl?" Kent asked George and winked at Alex.

"I don't know, what do you think?" George asked as the three brothers rode side by side on their horses.

"Well that depends," said Alex. "Do you think she is pretty?"

"Oh yeah," said George enthusiastically and his brothers laughed.

"Do you like her?" Kent asked.

"I don't really know her but I kinda do."

"Sounds like she kinda likes you too," said Kent. "So what is stopping you?"

"Her brother just died. I don't want to bother her."

"Well, she might really need a friend now," said Alex. "Look at Corsa and Madeline and they are both strong women."

"What should I say?" asked George.

"Well, you could go up and ask her and her sisters if they need anything. If they do, help them and if they just want to talk, then listen to them. That would be an appropriate way to break the ice. Or you could ask them questions about Wetpr and the Learning Center," suggested Alex.

"Thanks," George said with a big smile.

"She was hard to look at but there was something about Risha that I really liked," Erebus said as he sat next to the Sanuri in the front of his boca.

"She risked a lot to help you," said the Sanuri. "Did you ever find out why?"

"Ruth said it was for redemption. Don't you know her story?"

"No," said the Sanuri.

"Angelina told me and it's really interesting. She married into the Clan of Gesmal..."

Since Matthew was an adopted son of Sudfad and Renya, he and Angelina returned to Wetpr with the others. No other members of the Royal or ruling families were making the trip because of the political climate in Lentz. They had held a small private ceremony for Michael in Langer and the Sanuri officiated.

Matthew and Angelina were so concerned about attacks that they left their children with their grandparents. Shara, Sorren and their sons were staying in Matthew's and Angelina's home in Mathas' castle and all four grandparents were helping with the children.

Angelina rode up to the Sanuri's boca. "With everything that was going on, I don't know if anyone told you that Risha said for all of us healers to copy her journal. Corsa is riding in Javier's boca and making copies for both of you. I wish she would have lived longer. I found her fascinating."

"Erebus was just telling me her story," said the Sanuri. "He got pretty attached to her in a short time. I wish I would have met her now."

"When I first saw her, well I hate to say it but I thought she looked like a monster but then as I talked with her and learned her story, she didn't look scary to me anymore. Now I feel badly about how I judged her at first," Angelina said.

The Sanuri smiled. "I believe that is a common problem among people. Tonight when we camp, Erebus and I are going to read that book they created. You are welcome to join us if you want."

"Is it magics?"

"We asked for answers and the pages started to fill with words," said Erebus. "But you know how disoriented I was when I first came back. I didn't want to open it until I felt well. So, that is a long way of saying that I don't know what is written on those pages."

Instead of leading all of the troops, Sudfad led the delegation that transported his son's body. General Bishop was the ranking officer of the soldiers of Lentz and was leading the caravan. Mathas handpicked this General for that assignment. Bishop was supposed to protect Sudfad's family during the trip and during the funeral ceremonies; an assignment that made Bishop proud.

Kate and Edward were riding in the same boca. He had not regained consciousness since the ceremony where she gave him her life force. Although all of the Ruala healers told Kate this was expected she was scared.

She too was healing slowing but she was at least conscious. As badly as she wanted Edward to wake up she dreaded telling him about the baby. On this first day of their journey, Marina was watching over them.

"I haven't even asked," said Kate. "How is Javier doing?"

"Corsa said he has shown improvement after receiving Risha's antidotes which is also very hopeful for Edward. Did you know that Javier and Corsa got married a couple of nights ago because he was afraid that he would die and he wanted to make sure that she and her family were taken care of?"

"No," said Kate. "I thought he was too weak to get out of bed."

"He is. The ceremony was short and held at his bedside, but he was so excited that he invited people and they drank wine and talked. He should have been resting so now he is weaker since that."

"All of this has turned into such a nightmare," Kate said and started to cry. "We were all having such a wonderful day; how could everything go so wrong?"

# Chapter IX
## Michael's Star

The atmosphere at Mathas' castle was just as solemn as that of the group traveling to Wetpr. Mathas himself was filled with guilt because he felt that he did not heed the warnings that the Angels told Erebus. Mathas shared this information and his thoughts at the meeting he held after the guests left for Wetpr.

"Perhaps you should have taken them more seriously," Claudius said. "But you didn't learn of them in time to stop the attacks. We all are filled with guilt that Michael died in our streets, right under our noses. As far as I am concerned we are at war. In the past, some of these attacks seemed more like inconvenient disturbances...I don't feel we can ever view them in that same way anymore."

"And furthermore," Claudius was emotional and was standing at his place at the table and pounding his fist on the table. "Everyone is too damn scared to ask the question that all of us are thinking...he was one of The Seven Sons of prophesy, so what does this really mean now?"

"I prayed last night," Christopher said to Koby as they flew over the caravan traveling to Wetpr.

"Good, you should pray every night," said Koby.

"Well, this was kind of different," Christopher said. "All us kids are praying that the Angels will show us what Michael's star looks like so we can find it in the sky."

Bekka was flying next to Koby; the two of them looked at each other and Bekka started to cry.

Stephan, Thaos and Gideon joined Mathas' meeting almost an hour after it had started. "Sorry we are late," Stephan said. "But we just finished interrogating all of those guys that Olivia pointed out. I'll tell you I am impressed with her abilities."

As Stephan spoke, Thaos walked up to the front table and handed a fistful of papers to Mathas. "Those are the notes of the interrogations, we will have to make copies for the people in Wetpr."

"Most of those guys were just low level crooks...no loss to anyone if they got caught," Thaos said. "All of them had the same assignment, to see if Michael was really dead and to find out who was here. None of them were sent to hurt anyone. So the only thing of interest is who they were working for." As Thaos spoke he now turned to Turner and his men who were sitting with Tally and Drake. "You guys feel free to pipe in if you know any of these guys."

"The only name that really stood out to me was Tresdor, the Angels have warned us about him several times. He is out of hiding and someplace in the city." Thaos turned back to Turner and explained. "Tresdor is the nephew of Usman who was the leader of the Valdore Tribe."

"We know of him," Turner said. "Did you know that Usman and Deckor met on a fairly regular basis? We know this because when the meetings were near to or in Langer his men were in the dens and they couldn't get enough of anything. We bought them drinks and drugs on many occasions. As would be imagined Usman didn't share a lot of information with his soldiers. But we learned that these meetings were held about every two months and always in a different location."

"His men were afraid to talk about him other than to say he was praying to demons and very paranoid but they all talked about Tresdor. Now that guy sounds like a moron to me. They described him as all talk with a huge ego and no common sense. But he will do anything for recognition and praise, so that is his danger card."

"What do you mean danger card?" asked Sorren.

"Sorry, that is a term we use," Turner said. "Everyone has certain things whether it is emotions, fears whatever which will trigger them. So when we watch people that is one of the things that we try to figure out."

112

"For example those attacks against our friends were danger cards for all of us. I mean who would have thought we would all be working together like this?"

"From what I heard about Tresdor, I believe he is a coward and would hire his work done. But Gabriel told us that he is broke and desperate and has lost everything...that gentlemen makes him a rabid dog in my view."

Sudfad felt numb as he led the body of his son home. He was grateful that Mathas had put General Bishop in charge of the caravan. As he rode, Sudfad played over and over in his mind every moment that he had with Michael. Tears ran down his face as Sudfad realized that he and his son never really got to know each other.

"The other names that came up were Mattel, Iverson and Kantof," Thaos said. "Now, these three men sound like foremen; they hire and hand out assignments. None of the men knew who these three worked for. These three guys sent the majority of men so they must have guessed we would catch a few."

"Didn't Hector send anyone?" asked Fahron with surprise.

"Not in the group we've got," said Stephan. "And we used the truth potion on them all. We were surprised too, and you have to wonder why."

"Kantof is a name that me and Tally have heard," said Drake. "He's done a lot of work around the Ryed area. You are right he is a foreman and hires out."

"There is a guy that does a lot of work in Port Friada named Iverson," said Bart. "Same description. Now if this is the same guy he might work for that banker. Do we know if he was arrested yet?"

"I am still waiting for General Amundsen to get back to me," said Mathas. "The fact that he hasn't would lead me to believe he hasn't found Parker."

"Is that his name?" asked Turner.

"Yes, sorry we should have told you. Do you know him?" Mathas asked.

"No, but we have men in that city. We will make inquiries," Turner replied.

"That reminds me," said Gideon. "Where is Harlow?"

"Tracking down some leads," said Fahron. "But he didn't say what he was on to."

"That guy is good," Stephan said. "But we need to keep better track of him so we can protect him."

"And that reminds me," said Tally. "Did he ever go through all of his journals?"

"No, a group of them started, I think it was the day before the attacks," said Mathas. "Everything stopped after those attacks."

"You know that we was with Harlow when he got his notebooks and Michael got one of those weird stares he'd get when the Angels talked to him. He told Harlow it was important to take all of the journals because he might have information that he didn't realize was linked to Hector," Tally said. "If you ask me, I think someone needs to start going through those books."

Mathas looked at the faces in the room for a few moments before he spoke. "I am going to take a leap of faith here. I believe it greatly benefits us all to work together. I am forming a committee to review those journals. Sorren, Turner and Gideon are the core. Harlow should be involved if you can find him and Gideon, it might be wise to have Ashley work with you if someone can mind her business. All of you are familiar with the businesses and politics of Port Friada. Since Sorren is a ruling member he will head the committee."

"We have the journals here. Matthew locked them up so we can get them after the meeting. If you want more people on the committee that is fine but many of you have assignments that I don't want compromised."

"There are really a lot of journals," Nikki said. "Ingr and I will volunteer to take notes or make reports or anything you might need."

"You're on," said Sorren.

"I am surprised by this," Turner said. "We will work with you and not betray your trust."

Both Gabriel and Raphael felt unsettled about leaving Lentz. They wanted to get their families home and they had work and responsibilities in Salar but neither of them felt that they should leave the teams in Langer. As the day wore on these feelings became stronger which worried both men as they started to wonder if the Angels were trying to tell them something.

The caravan stopped for a midday meal. Since there were so many families, Bishop and Sudfad decided it should be a long break. Soldiers set up a perimeter to guard the group as they prepared meals and ate.

Hannah went to the boca that Javier was riding in. She told Corsa she would watch Javier for a while. Corsa took the journals she was working on and walked to the Sanuri's campsite.

"I am copying Risha's journal for you," she said to Erebus and the Sanuri. "I have one done and the other about half done. I should have that ready for you tonight." As she spoke she handed one of the journals to Erebus since the Sanuri was preparing food.

"How is Javier?" asked the Sanuri.

"He is so weak that it scares me. He has been sleeping since we left Langer. He just doesn't look good."

"I will stop over to see him after our meal," the Sanuri said. "You are welcome to join us."

"I would appreciate you looking at him. And thank you but I should get back. Hannah is watching him."

"I have made a lot more food than Erebus and I can eat. Have some and take some back for Javier and Hannah."

"He's a pretty good cook," Erebus said and smiled. "Of course, I am just paging through this but these potions are fascinating."

"I know," Corsa said. "And she came up with them herself. Did anyone tell you that Juleta sent messengers to Risha to buy potions for the transformations and Risha refused to sell them?"

"The more I hear about her the more I wish I could have met her," said the Sanuri.

"I didn't meet her either but after reading her journal I think she was rather brilliant," Corsa said. "And it sounds like everyone who did meet her was, I'm not sure of the right word. First, she wasn't anything like they expected and they all liked her but it was more than that."

"You sound like Angelina," said the Sanuri as he handed Corsa and Erebus plates of food. "She is joining us tonight on a little project and you are welcome to come too."

"Risha and I performed a number of ceremonies. She put a journal with blank pages on the ground between us and as we asked for answers the pages filled with words," explained Erebus. "I was so disoriented when I first came back that I didn't want to open the book until my head cleared. So that is what we are going to do tonight."

"Oh, I would love to help with that," Corsa said. "But it will depend on how Javier is."

"Sudfad is a much better cook than I am," Renya said to Madeline as they sat in their campsite.

"And she is not just saying that to be polite," Sudfad said as he and his daughters were preparing the meal. "I can't think of a thing that Renya doesn't excel at except for cooking." Both women laughed at this comment. "I actually like to cook."

"That surprises me for a king," said Madeline.

"I was a soldier long before I became a king. Sometimes a good meal is the only thing that brightens a soldier's day. It got to the point where I would cook for a lot of the men. I'll tell you I never felt so appreciated." All of the adults laughed.

"George, is anything wrong with Javier?" Madeline asked with fear in her voice as the young man walked into the campsite.

"No, he is still sleeping. I just came by because, well me, Kent and Alex were talking and if any of you need anything just let us know. We want to help but we don't want to bother you at a time like this."

"That is very sweet," said Renya. "Why don't you sit down and join us. Sudfad is a great cook."

"The King is cooking?" George asked with astonishment.

"Long story," Sudfad said and chuckled. "We have more than enough food."

Renya, Sudfad and Madeline all noticed how quiet Saran, Nyla and Nina became when George joined them. "Thank you, I will," he said shyly. "It sure smells good."

Sudfad glanced at his daughters then said, "So George tell us about yourself. I am sorry to say we don't know much about your family. Corsa never talked about you."

"That's because of our father. We all hate him because we think he killed our mother."

"What!" said Renya.

"Well, not directly, at least I don't think so but the others don't always tell me everything. Our father, Dirk is his name, drinks too much and gets really mean. He would beat all of us until we were old enough to fight back." George grinned. "Corsa was the meanest of us; they used to get into some fights. But she was doing everything after mother died and going to school and warrior training and Father drank away every cent he earned. She started taking care of us when she was seven, but I don't ever remember her acting like a kid."

117

"Even before mother died, Alex was working to get us food and he was just a little kid. In a way he has always been more of a father to us than our real father."

"Alex and Kent never left home cuz they were afraid of what would happen to me and Corsa. She was the first to leave. She went to the Village of Tyger and trained to be a healer and to get on the teams. Sorren just told us that she didn't have a cent to her name and worked every odd job she could get and studied. He said that was all she did. She's so pretty and Sorren said a lot of guys were interested in her but she knew what she wanted."

"That made us all feel real bad because Corsa sends us almost all the money that she makes. Alex takes care of the money or Father would spend it on whiskey."

"It's strange, Javier and Alex are the same age but Javier almost acts like our father. We would do anything for him; he has been so good to us. We talked to Sorren and he said the best thing we could do was to study real hard and get our educations." As George spoke he was devouring the plate of food that Sudfad had given him. "Boy, this is really good." George was looking at his plate as he talked and didn't realize how everyone was staring at him.

Nyla sat down next to George and said, "Our real father was a monster too. He used to beat all of us. But everything is so different now that Sudfad and Renya adopted us. We are really happy. I think all of you will be happy too when we get home."

"As long as Javier gets better," George said. "Corsa told me she didn't know what she would do if he died. I didn't even know what to say to her."

The hundreds of Ruala warriors who had gone to Lentz to attend the wedding of Ratri and Batina now traveled to Wetpr with the caravan. They would honor Sudfad's family by attending Michael's funeral.

Because of the attacks and all of the work they found themselves involved in, Thedes and Ibula hired nurses for their four children.

This change in life style was more difficult for Thedes to get used to than it was for Ibula, who had immersed herself in the study of Risha's journal.

"Mind if I join you?" Thedes asked as he walked into the campsite shared by Gabriel's and Raphael's families.

"Hannah is checking on her patients, if you need to see her," Gabriel said as he held his toddler son.

"No, I came to see the two of you," Thedes said and sat down near Raphael and Gabriel. "I can't get rid of this bad feeling I have about leaving Langer," Thedes said in a low voice. "I just feel like the teams are in danger."

"That does it," said Gabriel. "Raphael and I have had the same feelings all day. Iris would you take Daniel?" After Gabriel handed his son to Iris, he walked out of the campsite and Raphael and Thedes walked with him.

"Are any of the Angels giving us these feelings?" Gabriel asked when the three men were alone.

"You are learning," said Ruth as she appeared to them.

"Thank you for coming," said Gabriel. "Are the teams in danger?"

"All of you are always in danger," said Ruth. "While all of you grieve, your friends and family in Langer are consumed with guilt over Michael's death. So consumed that they are not noticing our nudges, so to speak. You will need to send them a message. Samael has been so pleased with the performance of Sorphat that he has allowed him to declare war on Stordt. If Sorphat wins he will become King of that dark kingdom."

"Zieman has been destroyed by Samael, thus the bounties he placed on all of you have disappeared. Because of the work of Risha and Erebus the infighting between the demons is taking on tremendous proportions. For the moment at least their concerns are war and they are not searching for the Originator."

"Andrac and Gilder have fled Wetpr and returned to Inferus. One of the ceremonies that Erebus and Risha preformed destroyed the disguises of many demons, sorcerers and dark lords. Those two were leading armies of human men who left them to the demons when their true appearances were exposed. While these two sorcerers are powerful they could not fight armies of demons. But expect them to return at some time."

"The Gefrey Games are in a sort of stasis because of all the mounted attacks against Samael. His enemies gather against him, those who would be afraid to stand alone are finding great courage in numbers."

"The message you need to send to Sorren and the others is that Tony has become Sorphat's lover and fights at his side. She will seek revenge against those she feels betrayed her. And I hope now, when an Angel warns any of you of a threat you will take it to heart. We warned you over and over about Tresdor and no one paid attention. He was the one who paid for Michael's murder and he is still in Langer and a great threat to all of you."

"Now, I have others to speak to and I would like the three of you to accompany me. First, gather the children of your home." The four walked in silence because the men were consumed with guilt and shame for not heeding the Angel's warnings about Tresdor. When they reached the campsite of Gabriel's and Raphael's families the children flocked to Ruth.

"I will gather the others," Raphael said solemnly and left the campsite. He returned within minutes with the rest of the families who lived in Gabriel's home.

Ruth spoke only to the children who were overjoyed to see her. "We have heard your prayers. Tommy will draw Michael's star. You will be able to recognize it in the heavens. Now I must speak with Sudfad's family."

Tommy ran and got paper and charcoal and the children gathered around him as Gabriel, Raphael and Thedes escorted Ruth to Sudfad's campsite.

"Our Angel!" screamed Nina as she and her sisters jumped up and ran to Ruth and hugged her. George was so shocked by their words that he fell backwards from the log he was sitting on.

"My time here is short," Ruth said to Sudfad, Renya and Madeline. "I have given a great deal of information to Gabriel, Raphael and Thedes which they will share with all of you. You must send messages to the people in Langer before you proceed on your journey. It is Nyla, Saran and Nina who I want to speak with."

Ruth looked at the young girls and said, "We have heard your prayers. If you are serious about protecting your families and helping with their struggles, it would benefit many if you translated the scrolls that Michael was working on. You know where they are."

"We will do that," Nyla said proudly. "Will you help us if we need it?"

"Of course my child."

Renya started to speak but Ruth interrupted her. "They will not be harmed doing this work and it will be a great contribution." Then Ruth paused and looked at the faces of everyone in the campsite.

"As you know, Javier gave the children a great gift so they could look at the stars. All of the children in your homes have been praying that we will tell them how to recognize Michael's star. Although his body is dead, his spirit lives and he requested that an image be sent to the children. Tommy is drawing it as we speak."

"The image is that of a broken star because Michael says that is how he was here. He wants all of you to know that he is no longer broken."

Both Madeline and Renya began to cry as Ruth disappeared.

# Chapter X
## Family Matters

When Gabriel, Raphael and Thedes escorted the Angel Ruth to Sudfad's campsite they had to travel the width of the perimeter that was set up for the caravan. While many felt the heavenly presence, she and the men with her looked so intent on what they were doing that no one stopped them to talk.

"Come on George," Saran yelled and all of the young people ran to find Tommy after Ruth disappeared.

Gabriel repeated her words to Sudfad, Renya and Madeline and the shame and guilt were evident in his voice and mannerisms. As a group they sat down and started letters to their families and friends in Langer.

"Hannah, I brought lunch," Corsa said as she walked to the back of the boca that Javier was being transported in. "The Sanuri made it. I didn't realize he was such a good cook."

"Great, I am starving," said a male voice and Corsa started to cry. She set the two plates on the back rim of the boca and climbed inside. Javier was sitting up with a big smile on his face. Hannah was sitting next to him and also smiling.

"I don't know what happened," Hannah said. "He just woke up and looks so much better."

Corsa flew to Javier and hugged and kissed him. She was crying and laughing. "Ruth just walked through the camps with Gabriel, Raphael and Thedes. I am sure she did this," Corsa said as she wiped the tears from her cheeks. "Thank you Ruth," she said loudly and kissed Javier again.

Edward too, was touched by the Angel's presence as were all of the wounded within the camps. Edward was still weak but he was conscious and sitting up. Kate cried as Marina examined him.

"I will get him some food," Marina said to Kate. "How much time will you need?"

"I don't know," Kate said haltingly. "But he needs to eat."

"What are you talking about?" asked Edward and Kate started to cry.

The children from Gabriel's and Sudfad's homes were excitedly showing everyone the picture that Tommy drew of Michael's star.

"You can come with us," Saran said to George.

"Ok," he said shyly.

"Are you shy?" she asked him and George smiled broadly.

"Not sure," he replied.

"Well, she isn't," Nyla said kiddingly. "I'd watch out if I was you George." Nina laughed hysterically at her sister's words and the shocked look on George's face.

Marina deliberately stalled for time before returning to Edward's boca.

"It's Marina, I have a tray of food."

"Come in," Kate said.

When Marina climbed into the back of the boca it was obvious to her that both Edward and Kate had been crying. "There is food here for both of you," she said. "I'll come back later."

"Marina, tell Gabriel that I'm awake," Edward said weakly.

"Mama look," said Nicholas as a large group of children ran up to Hannah, who was just leaving Javier's boca. "Ruth said they heard our prayers and they showed Tommy what Michael's star looks like."

"Oh Honey," Hannah said sadly when she saw the drawing of the broken star.

"I'd like to see that too," Javier called out from the boca.

"Is that Javier?" yelled Christopher.

"He's awake but weak so you will have to take turns going in there," Hannah said and started to lift children into the boca.

The excitement of the children brought smiles to the faces of Javier, Corsa and Hannah. They were hugging Javier and all talking at once.

"We can't understand when you all talk at the same time," Corsa said as she laughed. "One of you tell us."

"Paul you tell," said Joey.

"We've all been praying that the Angels show us Michael's star so we can find it in the sky," Paul explained. "The Angel Ruth visited us and said they heard our prayers and that Tommy would see the image."

"Did she say anything else?" asked Javier.

"That she had to talk to Sudfad's family," said Adrone.

Nyla, her sisters and George pushed through the crowd of children until they got to the back of the boca. "Put me in, put me in," Nina said excitedly. George picked her up and put her into the boca. Nina ran to Javier and hugged him tightly.

"Ruth told our parents that she told a lot to Gabriel, Raphael and Thedes and that they had to send letters to the people in Lentz," Nyla said. "Then she said they had heard our prayers and if we really wanted to help that we should translate the scrolls that Michael was working on. She said she would help us."

"Hannah would you tell Gabriel that I would like to hear what was said?" asked Javier.

After letters were sent to people in both Lentz and Wetpr, Gabriel held a meeting and repeated Ruth's words. The people were solemn as they now shared in the guilt for not taking heed of the warnings of the Angels.

Once the caravan resumed its journey, Madeline rode in the boca with Javier and Corsa and briefed him on the many things he had missed. Thor rode in the boca with Edward and Kate so that he could brief them on the same issues.

Only the adults had attended the meeting, their guilt now mixed with their grief and few spoke. The children on the other hand were very excited that Ruth had visited them and shown them Michael's star; the children couldn't stop talking.

Saran and Nyla were sitting in the carriage across from Renya and Nina. Saran looked at Renya and asked, "Would it be alright with you and Papa if I liked George?"

Renya smiled while Nyla and Nina giggled. "He seems like a very nice boy," Renya said. "Sudfad and I like him."

"Well, I don't know if he likes me or even how much I like him," Saran said. "I thought he was really handsome but then after he told us about his family, I just liked him more."

"I think we all did," said Renya. "I don't know him well but I think he might like you too."

"Really?" Saran said with a big smile. "How can you tell?"

"He is considerably more quiet and self-conscious around you then he is normally. And I've seen the way he looks at you."

"So what do you think I should do?" asked Saran.

"Well, if you want to get to know him better, you are probably going to have to start the conversations at first because he is really shy around you. But, and I am not saying this to discourage you; he will be attending the Learning Center and will be busy with his studies."

"We'll be busy with the scrolls too but I would think we could still see each other wouldn't you?"

"Yes," Renya said and smiled warmly.

"You're so quiet," Emeral said as she was flying with Olivia in her arms.

"I can hear everyone's thoughts and they are so sad that they make me sad," Olivia said.

"It will get better, it always does," Emeral said although she had sadness in her voice.

"Emeral, when we get home can I enroll at the Learning Center?"

"Why, I think that is a wonderful idea. Do you know what you want to study?"

"No, maybe you could help me figure that out but I like to learn."

"Tonight why don't you, Maxwell and I go and visit Raphael. He is responsible for the Center and can tell us about the courses."

"Emeral, I am really glad that you and Maxwell adopted me."

"We are too dear, we are too."

"I have to admit that this has been a little difficult for me," Madeline said after she and Corsa briefed Javier on the information from the meetings he had missed.

"What do you mean?" asked Corsa.

"Well," Madeline said and smiled. "Javier and I have taken care of each other our entire lives. It is difficult for me not to just take over because you two are married now but at the same time I don't want you to think that I am not constantly thinking about you."

126

Javier started to speak but Corsa interrupted him so he took Madeline's hand in his. "Madeline, you are family. Don't ever think you have to stay away for any reason. Actually, I have been feeling guilty because I haven't been there for you." Then Corsa got a big smile on her face. "If you want to help take care of him you are more than welcomed to but I have to warn you he doesn't listen." They all laughed.

"Oh, I will tell you stories," Madeline said. "But I want to change the subject for a moment. Javier, you have been so sick that I don't know if you remember that Sudfad and Renya have taken us, all of us in as family. Honestly, I thought it was just words at first but they really mean it. I have been spending a great deal of time with them and the more I get to know them they are wonderful people."

"But all of us have choices to make now. If we become part of their family we will have responsibilities as their other children. And while part of this terrifies and excites me at that same time; that kind of exposure could greatly compromise our working on the teams if we still want to. I just want you to think about this."

Javier stared at his sister for several moments as he tried to digest her words. "I remember Renya offering us a home but honestly I thought it was until I was on my feet again. Are you saying they are literally offering to take us in as family?"

"Yes. And Gabriel is still thinking about offering us our own teams but he wants to wait until everyone has healed and has had time to think. So you could be the head of a team or a prince in Wetpr. The same for me and Corsa. Renya already wants us to work on establishing Adam's Homes, which of course I think is a wonderful idea."

"I am as shocked at this as Javier," said Corsa. "But I have worked with the teams longer and Simon and Raul worked on missions and still performed their responsibilities as princes. It can be done, you don't have to look at this like you have to make choices between one life or the other."

"But I will tell you also that they all work really hard and that surprised me. I guess I thought that kings and queens just sat around and had people wait on them."

"Some do," Javier said. "I am not kidding; this is making my head spin."

"Or that could be the medicine," Corsa said jokingly. "I know you two spent a lot of time spying on everyone so you may already know this. Emeral told me that Sudfad and Renya are both soldiers at heart. She said that almost as soon as they married there were wars and Sudfad was gone all of the time. Renya was from Lentz and didn't really know anyone in Wetpr."

"She and their cook Marie, have an unusual relationship because Marie was basically the closest thing to family that Renya had in the beginning and she helped raise Raul and Simon. Sudfad and Renya always wanted a big family but he was gone more than he was in Salar so she was basically running the kingdom and taking care of a baby. Emeral said that Renya was very lonely so now that they have a castle full of family they are both really happy."

"I didn't know any of that," Javier said then looked at his sister who shook her head from side to side to indicate 'no'. I would like to speak with them. And I think that both of you should be there when I do."

"What are you going to say?" asked Corsa. "If you are turning down their offer, be kind because I really like them."

"I was thinking more of thanking them and asking them what they needed us to do," said Javier.

"Corsa, you know that once Michael was taken into Sudfad's family that he spent most of his time on missions. He was trying so hard to adjust to his place in the world that I wish he would have taken more time to get to know his family for all their sakes. I am telling you this because there is a lot I don't know about them so don't assume that Michael told me things," Madeline said.

"I can tell you what I know, but most of that is what I have heard from Sorren and the team members," Corsa said. "I need to speak with them too because...is she saying that you and I would kind of be like daughters?"

"Javier, perhaps if you are up to it we can all meet with them tonight," Madeline said. "But I must tell you also that now that I know who is behind Michael's death I am going back to Langer and kill him."

"You aren't going back there without me," Javier said. "You know you are too emotional now."

Madeline stared at her brother for a few moments then said, "I am going to change the subject to something more pleasant. Corsa your little brother and Saran have crushes on each other. They are so very cute. George is so shy and awkward around her."

"They are princesses," Corsa gasped. "How do Sudfad and Renya feel about that?"

"They invited George to lunch then told him to bring all of your brothers back for dinner. Renya told Saran that she and Sudfad like him and that she may have to start the conversations because he is shy," said Madeline with a warm smile.

"I don't know why that surprises me," Corsa said. "He's never had a girlfriend. I hope he doesn't do anything stupid." Javier laughed loudly.

The caravan had not traveled very far from the border of Lentz when they sent letters containing Ruth's words to the teams and ruling families in Langer. Mathas' morning meeting had gotten a late start and was running into the early afternoon when Enrops arrived with the letters.

The reactions of the men and women in the meeting were the same as those in the caravan for they had all dismissed the Angels' warnings about Tresdor.

After Mathas read his letter to the group Turner stood up and said, "There is more to this. The looks on your faces speak volumes, what is going on?"

"All of us feel like shit because the Angels warned us over and over about Tresdor and we really didn't pay much attention because compared to our other enemies he didn't seem like much of a threat. I think I need one of you guys to punch me because I deserve it," Stephan said emotionally.

"We all do," said Claudius. "Turner if the Angels start appearing to you, know that they tend to greatly understate things. And they can't affect the choices we make so they really make us think things through. They don't give a lot of warnings normally. Stephan is right, we heard their words but dismissed them. I will tell you now that will never happen again."

Thaos shot out of his seat, "Ok we all feel like shit and we are all guilty as hell. But are we going to sit in here all day and beat ourselves up or are we going to get the bastard?"

"Now just wait a damn minute," said Gideon and stood up. "You guys know me as the emotional one so it's kind of funny that I am telling you that you are too emotional. You know that Tresdor is a whinny piss ass of a coward without a friend or a cent to his name. So how the hell did he import mercenaries? Tresdor is the bait and I sure as hell want to kill him too but I'm not going to lose any more friends. So we think this out before we charge out those doors."

Turner stood up again, "Gideon is right. Let me and the boys dig up some information on him. From everything I have heard, I don't think he is smart enough to have pulled those attacks off by himself. We will be back tonight to brief you on whatever we hear." Turner's men stood up to leave.

"We're coming with you," Drake said.

"Are all of you going to the Catacombs?" asked Dominic.

"For something like this, that is the best place to find information," said Turner.

"How about if a few of us go in there in disguise. If nothing else we can be back-ups for you if you need help," Dominic said.

Jasmine stood up and said, "First, Angus you can't go because you are the most emotional. You can just be mad at me for saying that. And secondly, Madeline gave Lana and me a bunch of wigs and taught us how to change our appearances with makeup and things. So Lana and I should go to the Catacombs too."

"You're in," said Dominic then he looked at Raven. "Since you don't want to take part in the training I can't let you work with us."

"Fine," she said belligerently.

Sorren now stared at both Raven and Dominic. "What do you mean she won't take part in the training?"

"She thinks it's beneath her," Noah said with disgust.

"Raven, pack your gear you are off the team. These are coveted positions and I am not going to let you earn the pay and prestige with an attitude like that." Raven did not say a word as Sorren spoke but her face turned red with anger.

"Dominic, I will have another healer for you by tonight," Sorren said angrily.

That evening, Sudfad made his family's campsite near the boca that Javier traveled in. Alex and Kent helped Javier out of the boca so he could join everyone around the campfire for the dinner meal.

As Corsa helped Sudfad prepare the food she said in a low voice, "Madeline told me that George and Saran like each other. He's a good boy but he's never had a girlfriend so if he does anything stupid you let me know."

Sudfad laughed loudly, "I would be more worried about him. Saran isn't shy at all."

"This is nice, having everyone together," Renya said.

"Actually could we talk about that?" asked Javier. "After speaking with Madeline, I am not sure if I misunderstood something you said the night of our wedding."

131

"Renya, when you offered us your home did you mean until I was back on my feet?"

"No," Renya said. "We really do consider Madeline our daughter now. Granted we haven't spent as much time with you but that would make you a son and Corsa a daughter. You look embarrassed. I don't mean to make you feel uncomfortable and we certainly aren't going to force any of you into changing your lives."

"I don't think that I am embarrassed but shocked," Javier said. "Why would you open your home to us?"

"Because you are family now," Sudfad said. "Trust me son, when you get to be my age you realize that family really is the most important thing. I spent most of my life in battle and missed so much. Guess in a way Renya and I are making up for that now."

"Is he our brother now?" Nina asked with a big smile.

"If he wants to be," Sudfad said to Nina then he turned back to Javier. "While we live a life of privilege it is a life of hard work and many responsibilities. Michael had a great deal of trouble adjusting. I wish I would have helped him more," he said sadly then paused and joked. "Once you see what our lives are like you may not want to be a part of them."

"I don't know if you know about our lives," Javier said. "Our father was murdered when we were small and our mother committed suicide shortly afterwards. We were bred to be sex slaves and Madeline and I did everything we could to survive and claw our way out of that life. We have done a lot of things that I am sure you would not approve of and you should know that. We are so honored by your offer but we don't want to bring shame to your family either."

"From what we have heard about your lives they were nightmares as were the lives of our daughters here and Vitomas and Annabelle. What matters is the person you are now," said Sudfad.

"Both Renya and I come from long lines of royalty and honestly we found many of those people shallow and well, I will leave it at that," Sudfad said. "We look for different things in people than their breeding. I will admit that Madeline and I got off to a rough start because I didn't see her for who she really is and I am sorry for that. But we have seen the kindness, courage and integrity in, well everyone sitting here. That is what is important to us."

Corsa and her brothers as well as Javier and Madeline all stared at Sudfad as they were touched by his words. "Corsa, Madeline and I accept your offer with great pride. Now, what do you need us to do?"

Sudfad and Renya both laughed. "You are going to be so sorry you asked that," he said.

"They said that to us too," said Nyla. "But we like the things we are working on, you will too."

"There's a lot of paperwork and politics," Sudfad said as he handed out plates of food.

"Actually, Madeline and I might be very good at the politics," Javier said. "But what about us working on teams?"

"That is certainly up to you. I guess we just assumed you would. We have ruling families now to share the responsibilities but everyone works on teams. We try to alternate assignments so that the kingdom is taken care of as well as the missions. We will train you in the duties so don't worry about that, but son, I don't think that either you or Madeline are in any shape to hunt Tresdor now."

"How did you know?" asked Madeline with great surprise.

"Because I am planning the same thing," Sudfad said solemnly.

# Chapter XI
## Prophesies and Oaths

The group having dinner at the Royal Family's campsite talked and laughed for two hours. "Javier would you mind if I helped the Sanuri and Erebus with a project?" Corsa asked. "They asked me and Angelina because we are healers."

"That is fine with me but what is the project?"

"When Erebus and Risha were performing those ceremonies they asked for answers. Risha put a blank journal on the ground and it filled with words. Erebus was really disoriented when he was brought back and didn't want to open the book until his head cleared so they are doing that tonight."

"I think we would all like to see that book," Sudfad said.

"I didn't ask them why they are opening it in a small group; there might be a reason," Corsa said. "But I will tell you everything when I come back. Madeline will you watch Javier?"

"Of course. If we are sleeping when you come back, wake me because I would like to hear about that book too," Madeline said.

"You know, this has been so nice being together like this," Renya said. "Why don't we move our campsites together for the rest of the trip?"

"That sounds great to us," said Alex and grinned. "You're a better cook than we are."

"Of course," said Javier.

Saran stood up and walked up to Renya and whispered into her ear. Renya smiled and said, "It's fine, no one is related by blood."

Saran quickly turned around and asked, "George do you want to go for a walk with Nyla, Nina and me?"

"Sure," he said with a big smile and stood up.

As they walked out of the campsite Nina asked loudly, "I'm getting confused. Are you our brother too?"

"She is so cute," Madeline said of Nina.

When Saran and the others were out of sight Corsa said, "Alex if he does anything stupid..."

"Corsa, he can't even talk around her. All he does is smile. What do you think he is going to do anyways?"

"Well, those girls act normal but they had really horrible lives. I don't want him to do anything that will scare them."

"Corsa, we are finding out that probably like the rest of you here, they never had childhoods. They are very old for their ages," Sudfad said. "And Nyla and Saran are turning into little warriors in my opinion. As far as I am concerned if he is with all three of them, he doesn't stand a chance."

"I agree," said Madeline and laughed.

The teams and ruling families in Langer weren't laughing about anything. The knowledge that Tresdor was behind Michael's murder only intensified their feelings of guilt. During the dinner meal Stephan and Thaos announced that they were going to join the team members at the Catacombs.

"I don't think that is a good idea," said Ingr. "You both are too emotional."

"And I agree," said Claudius. "Boys, you know I believe you can do anything but this is not the time for you to join them. You will put all of their lives in danger. Why don't you help Gideon and me after dinner?"

"He's not just saying that for busy work," Gideon said. "Starting my first day here I have had my sailors document every ship that pulls into dock. I have some of my men sailing up and down your coastline documenting the ships. Today I collected all of those reports and as you can imagine there is quite the stack."

"If those assassins were from the Continent of Salszar they would have to sail to Opots so it would be logical that they sailed around the continent and docked here instead of docking in Ryed and traveling across land."

"Now, all seafaring captains have some kind of record of their journey, if for no other reason than business. My men are checking these records also. Of course, we don't have lists of names but I believe we have enough to try and figure out when and where those assassins came from. Now, how Tresdor contacted them is another matter."

"I was not at all of the meetings when the Angels talked about Tresdor and I think it is important to review the notes from those meetings and establish a timeline. From what you tell me that demon was punishing Tresdor and making him stay in the diamond mines. The guy didn't have any money so just how did he hire assassins from another continent? Claudius said that at one of the meetings the Angels told us when Tresdor came to Langer. I think that if we put all of this information together we can get an idea of who is really behind this."

"Gideon, I would like to help," said Ashley.

"We would too," Nikki said. "But we have to put the babies to bed first."

"Alright," Stephan said reluctantly.

"You two just want to hit someone," Nikki said. "Sounds like we have a better chance of getting information helping Gideon."

Lana and Jasmine had significantly changed their appearances with wigs and makeup. Jasmine was Noah's escort and Lana was Dominic's. They entered the Catacombs and stopped at the magic shop to check on Hilgra then they went to a den that featured sex acts.

"I will never get used to these acts," Jasmine said with disgust.

"This is my first time here," said Lana. "Yes the show is disgusting but this is rather fascinating. I mean look at the people who come here. You have people of means standing with men who look like hired fighters, drunks and demons. The sailors seem like visitors here. You would never see these people socializing together in other places."

"Javier said that the first time he brought Isabella here she knew a lot of people but it was her first time in the Catacombs," said Jasmine. "Is it possible there was another place where all of these people socialized before the Catacombs were opened?"

"I have been thinking about that same thing," said Dominic. "These dens were first opened just a couple of years ago. I wonder if Deckor had some kind of place going before that."

"Let's finish these drinks and move to another den," said Noah.

"Heads up," said Dominic as one of the doormen of the den walked up to their table.

"There is a witch outside who said you left this in her shop. She doesn't want to pay the cover to walk it in herself," said the man and handed Dominic a small book.

Noah looked at the doorway of the den and saw Hilgra watching them. She turned away when Dominic took the book. "Thank you," Dominic said and handed the man several gold coins.

"Hilgra was making sure you got it," Noah said in a low voice.

Dominic opened the book and found a note. "Time to go," he said. "Some of Hector's men are following Turner and his crew. Hilgra says they are really outnumbered. She said they are in the den next door, on the right."

The line was long in front of this den. Dominic walked to the front of the line and handed a pouch filled with gold coins to the doormen who allowed the group to enter next. The den was smoky and smelled of sweat. It also smelled of demon but that smell permeated all of the dens.

"Cage fighting," Noah said as he looked at the crowd. "There's a hell of a lot of black hats with red feathers in here, wonder what is going on. Does Turner's team have bounties on them?"

"There they are," said Jasmine. "They're sitting at a table near the east wall."

As soon as Dominic's group walked up to Turner's table, Jasmine said loudly. "We have been looking all over for you. Where have you been?"

"We saved you some seats," Garvis said loudly. "We've been looking for you too."

Dominic sat next to Turner and asked, "So what is up with all of Hector's guys?"

Turner smiled, "We've been busy since we left the meeting. Not all of Usman's soldiers were killed in those battles. We recognized one drinking in Drake and Tally's den. Bart knew him and had drank with him on a couple of occasions. Bart bought him a bottle of whiskey but the guy was already drunk. We asked him to join our table. Once he said he had seen Tresdor and talked to him, we motioned to Tally."

"Tally came to the table and dropped something in his drink, while he brought us another bottle. Don't know what it was but the guy started puking. Tally helped him to the toilet and then he and Drake handed him off to Angus who was outside with a bunch of men. They're taking him to the castle."

"After about twenty minutes one of the black hats goes looking for him, when they find out he isn't in the toilet they start searching the place. They talked to Tally who gave them shit then they turned their attention to us."

"So were they watching him in that den?" asked Dominic.

"Yeah and we saw that right away," Turner said. "Makes you wonder why that many black hats are watching him, doesn't it? So I guess you could say that we are the diversion right now."

"I didn't know that this many of Hector's guys were in Langer," Jasmine said.

"Oh, I am sure there are a lot more than we have been aware of," said Dominic. "So does anyone want another drink?"

Corsa arrived at the Sanuri's boca just moments before Angelina. Both women were excited to be allowed to read the book.

"I put another pot of coffee on the fire," said the Sanuri as Erebus took a couple of chairs from the back of the boca and set them near the fire. "I see you both brought paper and pens, that is a good idea," the Sanuri said to the women.

When everyone was seated, the Sanuri said a protection prayer over the book and was starting to open it when Adam appeared. "Mind if I join you?" he asked.

"I was just thinking about calling to you," said the Sanuri.

"I know," said Adam. "Before you open that book I would like Erebus to tell us about his experience. He hasn't told anyone yet. And I am sure that he has questions."

"Honestly, I don't remember a lot of it clearly," Erebus said. "I remember you saving us from that demon in the tavern then I woke up on the street and in minutes arrows were flying through the air. I could hear the soldiers yelling and no one could see where the arrows where coming from. Then I heard screaming and saw Michael, Edward and Javier lying in pools of blood and I was just so angry. I jumped behind a horse trough and before I realized it I was using magic, powerful dark magic."

"At the same time that I saw those assassins burst into flames I heard that demon laugh and I knew I had been set up. Suddenly I got sick, my head was spinning and I was puking. Later I realized he had given me too much magic."

"I don't understand," said Angelina.

"Think of it as a drug addict who took a lethal dose," Erebus said. "I started running away from the city because I was afraid of what I might do because I didn't feel in control of myself. Some of this I am blurry on, I know I was running because I was afraid I would hurt the wrong people and Adam did I call to Ruth or did she call to me?"

"You actually were screaming her name over and over as you ran from the city. Do you remember talking to her?"

"I remember she stopped me from running and I think I asked her to help me, to get rid of the magics and..."

"And she started to," Adam said. "Then as your head cleared you asked her to stop then you asked her if you could use your situation to find the answers all of you needed."

"Yes, I remember that now," Erebus said as he tried to recall his memories. "She told me that demon set a trap for me and in a short time I would be in the World of Illusions. She told me it was a nightmare world but I had already heard of it."

"I am going to stop you here," said Adam. "Because it is important that everyone understand what really happened. The demon Tobankto is the one who set the trap in the Anchors Inn as well as the trap with the magics. He is as powerful in the World of Filsum as Samael is here. Samael has few friends but Tobankto is one and that is because Samael has promised him many great things."

"You already know that many demons and dark lords suspect the line of kings that rule Wetpr are the Keeper of the Scrolls as well as being somehow associated with The Seven Sons. Since that prophesy predicts great blows against the dark worlds, demons and dark lords have been trying to determine who The Seven Sons are and destroy them so they can't fulfil the prophesy. So this is what you need to share with the others. All of the men on the teams are possible candidates for being The Seven Sons in the eyes of many. They all have targets on their backs."

"Since the dark worlds believe they killed Edward and Javier as well as Michael, they are ecstatic that they can stop the prophesy but we will get back to that. Erebus, Tobankto was trying to bring you to their side. You are that powerful that the Old Ones want you."

"I thought it was because I had a bounty on my head," Erebus gasped.

"No and that bounty no longer exists. You never sold your soul yet you are or were perhaps the most powerful warlock in Opots, if not in Nunc," Adam explained.

"He sent you to the World of Illusions to force you to use your magic to escape and that would have sealed your fate, at least in his eyes. Instead, you asked us to help you control it for a short period of time so that you could use it against the demons and get answers that others could not."

"I do remember that but once I got there it was so horrible that I was losing control," said Erebus. "When Risha found me I was basically in a ball, crying. Tell me, what happened to her?"

"She was a Venator and made an oath to serve The Great Ruler, then when her people saw the horrors of the Originator she made an oath with them to continue to serve Him after their deaths," Adam said.

"I asked her why she was with me and she said she didn't have time to explain other than to say that she had forgotten who she was for a very long time. She almost seemed happy."

"I don't know why that is making me cry," said Angelina. "She looked like a monster but there was something about her that I really took to."

"She was a beautiful woman once," said Adam. "She hated herself for running away from her people and denying her oaths. She hated herself for letting her fears take control. She thought of herself as a monster and her body became what her mind saw."

"Even though she tried to forget her past because the guilt weighed so heavily upon her, she could not. She knew of the Prophesy of The Seven Sons and when she found out that one of her potions could have been used to kill one of them she was torn apart. She prayed to be forgiven, to correct what she may have put into place and to renew her oaths."

"Ruth stayed with her for a long time and told her of the world she had run away from. Ruth told her about all of you and your struggles to stop this world from becoming like Orantho."

"And she told Risha how your resistance and faith was giving hope and strength to other worlds. Risha made a plan and asked the heavens to help her execute it. She hoped to die in the process."

"As much as she tried to be absorbed in the world of darkness she still had integrity, which all of you have now realized. She sabotaged the potions and set traps for the demons, thus putting bounties on her head. She asked Ruth to transport her to Langer so that she could spend her remaining days helping all of you."

"Emeral asked her to help them find you, Erebus. I showed Risha the man you were and the choices you had made. She admired you for what you did in Ryed. Then I showed her where you were and why. She was proud to help you and volunteered. She said that she would do everything she could to help all of you and she gave you her book which people and demons would kill for and she told me for payment she wanted me to stop Samael. Now, that isn't really how the heavens work," Adam said with a broad smile. "But I am certainly working on her request."

"So that I know you understand; what is important about what I have told you so far?"

"That Erebus is highly sought after by the demons which puts him in great danger," said the Sanuri. "But some of us already knew that."

Erebus swung around and stared at the Sanuri. "You knew that?" he asked.

"Erebus, didn't you question why a holy man spends so much time with you?" Adam asked.

"At first I thought he was trying to change me but we are friends now."

"You are friends but he has also been protecting you," said Adam. "You see, like us he saw the goodness and potential in you when you could not. And what else did you learn?"

"That basically there are bounties on all of the men we work with," said Angelina. "Adam, with Michael dead will that stop the prophesy from coming true?"

"No, but his death affected many things and now all of you need to be even more careful."

"Adam, I well, you know I am not a shy person but I just get so choked up around all of you; so please don't laugh at me," Corsa said. "Can someone else become one of The Seven Sons? I ask because Renya and Sudfad just adopted Javier."

Everyone in the group now stared at Corsa. "I didn't even think about that," said the Sanuri. "But do you realize that Sudfad's family now consists of Elods, Rualas and Shettees besides humans? Did he plan that or was that a coincidence?"

"You forget that you also are part of his family. While Sudfad and Renya adopted these people because of their personalities and conditions they both were very aware that they were uniting these different peoples," Adam said.

"Corsa, to answer your question, the prophesies don't just have beings waiting as backup but choices can be made and not just for Javier. And not just for men, even though the prophesy refers to them as sons they are the children of The Great Ruler. But before anyone prays to fill Michael's spot they need to read that prophesy because it is a dangerous road to travel. Battles will be lost and people will betray you and many will die before the battles are over."

# Chapter XII
## Answers and Fears

Angus marched into Mathas' morning meeting. "The bastard passed out, I think it was because he drank his body weight in whiskey before we grabbed him. We gave him aplewort and plan to interrogate him again."

"What are you talking about?" asked Fahron.

"Sorry," Angus said. "Since I was late I thought you knew."

"We got some rather disturbing letters from the Sanuri that we were reading. The Angel Adam helped the Enrops to deliver them. First, tell us about Usman's soldier," said Mathas.

"What!" Claudius yelled.

"Is Turner here?" asked Angus. "They're the ones who found him."

"There was a fight between our people and a bunch of Hector's men. Shara and the Court Physician are patching our people up now. None of them had really serious wounds," Mathas replied.

"Damn! Me and Thaos wanted to go last night and get into a fight," Stephan said with frustration.

"We've got Hector's men in the dungeons so you still might have your chance," Mathas said with a grin. "It was a busy night. Angus you have the floor."

"Turner and his crew were working the dens and saw a guy they knew to be one of Usman's soldiers. Bart had gotten drunk with the guy a couple of times so it didn't seem suspicious when he bought the guy a bottle and asked him to join their table. The guy, whose name is Tucker was already drunk when Turner's men found him and apparently he was oblivious to a small army of Hector's guys who were watching him. Why? We don't know yet."

"The advantage for us was that the guy was drinking in Tally and Drake's den. Tally slipped something into the guy's drink and when he started to puke, Tally pretended he was taking the guy to the toilet but gave him to us. I was waiting outside with some men. The bastard puked all the way to the castle."

"We can fill you in on what happened after you left with him," Mathas said. "But tell us about the interrogation."

"Tucker said that he and some other soldiers ran when they realized Tresdor was losing all the battles in the Nordes lands. He said he knew of about twenty other guys and they all escaped when they got their asses kicked in Minges. As far as he knows the other nineteen are still in the area but they don't get together."

"Tucker hates Tresdor and would go on tirades cursing him. He said that Tresdor has always been a coward and if anyone said shit to him, Tresdor would run to Usman and he would punish or kill the guy, while Tresdor grinned like a kid."

"He said that after your armies defeated Usman that Tresdor was drunk with power. None of the soldiers thought that Tresdor's attack plans would work but they were afraid to say anything because he was working with a demon. I asked him how they knew that and they said he changed. They said his eyes became black and he had sort of a cloud around him."

"Tucker said he barely got out of Minges with his life and he wasn't going to die for Tresdor. Basically Tucker has been in Langer getting drunk ever since. He has been robbing people to get drinking money. I asked him why he would stay in Lentz and he said he didn't have any place to go. So that's that background."

"Tucker said that about three or four weeks ago he was sitting in one of the dens and see's Tresdor walk in, only he didn't recognize him at first. He said Tresdor was never a big guy but he had lost a lot of weight and looked like he aged ten years. He said that Tresdor is in his twenties and when Tucker saw him in that den, Tresdor had grey in his hair."

"Tucker said that he wasn't drunk yet when he saw Tresdor and was curious about the physical changes. He said that Tresdor looked scared when he walked into the den."

"Tucker said that he thought about walking up and killing Tresdor but his curiosity got the better of him. Tucker had just robbed a couple of guys and had a pouch of gold in his pocket. So he called Tresdor over. He said that Tresdor actually looked happy to see him and they had never gotten along."

"Tucker said that Tresdor was telling him some wild story about living in the diamond mines and being too afraid to sleep for fear Rogetts would get him. Tucker asked him why he was in the mines and he says Tresdor looked around like he thought he was being watched and said that the demon Bertuck was punishing him for losing the battles of the Nordes lands. Tucker said that instead of being his normal cocky and obnoxious self, Tresdor acted like he was glad to have someone to talk to and told of how scared he was and how he was bargaining with that demon."

"Tresdor told Tucker that Bertuck sent him to Langer and told him he better not fail him again. At this first meeting Tresdor was scared of finding out what Bertuck wanted him to do. Then not three days later, Tresdor finds Tucker in one of the dens and wanted to buy him a drink. Tucker said that Tresdor was acting more like his old self. Tucker said that he was just damn curious about Tresdor and had a few drinks with him. Tresdor said he was acting as a kind of middle man and connecting people together."

"Tresdor said that a guy had approached him with a message, to go the Bottom Barrel Tavern and sit at a table and someone would contact him. He does and a guy gives him a large pouch of money for him to keep and another pouch to pay for bribes. They wanted information about what was going on in Sorren's Village; that's when they were getting ready for the celebrations. He said the guy wanted details, drawings and maps. Tresdor thought Bertuck was going to attack Sorren's village again and was glad to provide the information."

Sorren was tensing up as he listened to Angus and Angus saw that. "Sorren, Tresdor said that he had a couple of spies in your tribe and I've sent men after both of them. Dirk has been selling information to Usman's men for years and so has Raven."

"What!" screamed Sorren and jumped out of his chair. Sorren pounded his fist on the table several times. "I brought Raven into the castle and on the teams. She knew what was going on here!" Sorren pounded his fist on the table several more times. "Mathas when we catch them, I get to kill the traitors." Thaos poured Sorren a big glass of whiskey and handed it to him.

"Angus keep talking," Thaos said and returned to his seat.

"Tucker ran into Tresdor three more times in the den over the next four weeks. He said Tresdor had a lot of money to spend. Tucker didn't ask him about his work but Tresdor would volunteer information. He said a group of dark lords came here from Salszar and Tresdor was going on about how strange looking they were. They were bald, wearing robes and lots of jewelry and tattoos. Tresdor said he didn't want to be seen with those guys so he paid for someone to show them the city."

"Then a couple of days before the attacks, Tresdor sees Tucker in a den and is acting nervous. He told Tucker this might be the last time they have a drink together because all hell was going to break loose in Langer. He told Tucker to leave the city but he didn't tell him why."

"Just before Tucker passed out he said that Tresdor once said the guy he always met was named Iverson. And he was pretty sure they always met at the Bottom Barrel Tavern."

The Angel Adam stayed with the Sanuri, Erebus, Angelina and Corsa the entire night as they reviewed the small journal. The answers in that book came from the magics of the dark worlds and at times were vague and disconnected. The words were also written in different languages and Adam helped with the translations. During the night, the Sanuri sent messages to Mathas, Simon and Raul. With the morning light, Adam left and the four held a meeting with the team members.

The Sanuri started out the meeting by repeating Adam's words about what had happened to Erebus and the threats against him. Then he repeated the Angel's words about the Prophesy of The Seven Sons.

While no one in the group was surprised to find out they had targets on their backs they were all shocked to find out that they could petition the heavens to replace Michael in the role of the prophesy.

"I don't understand," said Madeline. "I have heard some about that prophesy but how does it involve all of you?"

No one wanted to answer Madeline's question; they all looked at the Sanuri to speak. "Actually Madeline and Javier, it very much involves you now also. For centuries the Kings of Wetpr have been the Keepers of The Scrolls. Have you ever heard that term?"

"Yes," said Javier with a look of both fear and awe on his face. "But I am not sure what it really means."

"The demons and dark lords would weaken the children of The Great Ruler by destroying their connections with Him. The Keepers of the Scrolls guard many of The Great Ruler's gifts until His children are ready to receive them. Also, the dark worlds seek to obtain these items so they can use them for their power. In addition to this, there is an ancient prophesy about Seven Sons who lead armies to stand against the darkness. All of the men in Sudfad's family are one of these sons. Michael was also and that is probably why he was murdered."

"This is what we have really been fighting and sacrificing for. Javier, Corsa asked what your role would be in all of this since Sudfad and Renya just adopted you and Madeline. I don't have an answer to her question at this time. I can tell you that nothing is forced on anyone. If you and Madeline have questions, Sudfad, Renya and I can meet with you. You must understand that all the members of his family have been given a choice as to whether they will uphold these oaths. Michael's sisters know nothing about this yet."

"I don't know if you will be asked to take the oaths but you should know about all of this since your new family is always under attack."

Javier turned to Corsa and asked, "Did you know about this?"

"Yes but I was sworn to secrecy."

"Then how come we are being allowed to hear this?" asked Alex.

"Because the dark worlds have been trying to predict for centuries who The Seven Sons are so they can stop the prophesy from being fulfilled. Every person here has a target on them and that is the reason. If any of you don't want to be involved with us anymore, that is understandable," said the Sanuri.

"Actually Madeline and I would like to hear much more about this," said Javier. "Both of us are truly in shock right now. But now it makes sense why so many demons are watching all of you."

"We are kind of distant family because of Corsa and Javier," said Alex. "Would it be alright if we heard it too?"

"Of course," said the Sanuri.

Kent looked at George and said, "You can't tell Saran and her sisters about this."

"I know," he said. "I don't really understand it but I can tell it is really important."

"Perhaps we should meet tonight," said the Sanuri. "Anyone is welcomed to join us. Now we need to talk about that journal. As I told you the information came from the dark worlds and for a variety of reasons it was difficult to understand, which is why Adam stayed with us."

"I am not really sure where to begin with this," he paused for a moment. "You know that Samael came here to stop all of us from stopping the demons but he also knows that the Originator has a doorway in this world and he wants to find it."

"Because of his arrogance he continues to accumulate enemies among the demons so he is offering great things to other demons to come to his side. And one of these things is the Angel Miranda." Many in the group gasped at this statement.

"The demons of Filsum as well as Andrac have declared war against her. She was seen by the Elods on the shores of Lentz during the armada attack and in Inferus when we freed the Elods. As well as our battles in Ganz."

"Miranda would not allow others to see her unless she had a reason but I don't know what those reasons are. I do know that the demon Tobankto is an Old One from Filsum."

"There are also bounties on me, Thot and other emissaries that you are not familiar with. While this is part of the territory so to speak, Samael is using us as tests for his Gefrey Games. So being in our presence is now dangerous."

"What exactly does that mean?" asked Kent.

"To score points in the Games they have to bring the emissaries to Samael," explained Gabriel.

The Sanuri continued, "Samael is planning on turning our world into anther Orantho so all of you must understand what we are fighting for. We also learned that Visterle saved Sampson from eternal torture. Sampson brought Visterle Hecate and garnered great favors from the demon who freed his soul and has hired him. At this point Visterle has no interest in any of us. He has his hands full with other things although he is still trying to get Molach's hell domain in this world."

"Sanuri what about Bruno and Morgan?" asked Diana.

"I was just getting to them," he said. "During the course of our conversations last night, it was apparent that both Angelina and Erebus became bonded to Risha on some level. They both have been concerned about her and asked Adam about her welfare. Actually when I am done I will let Angelina tell you what Adam told us about Risha's history. But to answer Diana's question, Risha not only sabotaged the potions but set up traps for the messengers and armies of demons that would be sent to kill her."

"Risha's cave is filled with Shadow Men who have been battling the demons. It was her understanding that Morgan and Bruno would return to get the potions, if they did they have been killed."

"She too is a shadow now and according to Adam she felt a kinship to many of you here. Adam told us that we can ask the heavens to send us Shadow Men like we do the Hengers and Enrops. But, and these are just my old bones talking, I have a feeling we will hear from Risha again in some form."

"We were already told that the Gefrey Games were interrupted by the demon wars. There was no clear favorite in that competition. Hector is working with both Andrac and Gilder but apparently those dark lords don't realize he is using both of them. I have sent letters to Mathas, Raul and Simon with this information," said the Sanuri.

"Wait!" said Madeline. "Is that it? Wasn't there any information about the attacks? The more that Javier and I discussed it the more we believe Tresdor was the front man in all of this. Who was really behind the attacks?"

The team members who had fought Hector's men as well as Turner and his men walked into Mathas' study as Angus was speaking. All of these people wore bandages and or splints.

"Good fight?" Thaos asked.

"Yeah," said Lawrence and grinned.

"Angus can catch all of you up on the interrogation as soon as we are done here," Mathas said. "I want to share a series of letters that I received from the Sanuri last night. But before I get into that, Wickfield do you have any idea where Harlow is?"

"No, just that he is working on a lead."

"Well, we have thirty-six of Hector's men in the dungeons. We need to keep track of him. Angus send some of your people to find him," said Mathas.

"Stephan and I can do that," Thaos said. "Everyone else was up all night."

Mathas looked at the letters before him then at the faces in the room. "Mathas," Nikki said and jumped up from her chair. "Miranda just said to call to her before you say whatever you are thinking."

The King smiled and shook his head. "I too have lessons to learn," he said to the group then he said out loud. "Miranda can I share all of the content of these letters with everyone in this room?" Only Mathas heard the Angel's answer. He now addressed the men and women in the room.

"I have been told to give you a choice about what you want to hear," Mathas said and paused. I am trying to determine how to say this because it is complicated not because I want to withhold information. Wickfield and Turner you know that we worship The Great Ruler and try to work on His behalf but there is much more to us as a group. There are things which have been secrets for centuries and by telling you these secrets we are putting targets on your backs."

"Miranda said that the demons and dark lords have been trying to learn these secrets for a long time and that is behind many of the attacks that we are experiencing. If you continue to fight with us it is only fair for you to know what you are fighting for. But I will be honest, that information may also change your lives. Turner, you should speak with your men individually and not speak for them."

"Before any of you in this room make a decision, I will be able to share most of the information in these letters with you if you choose not to hear the, for lack of a better word, secrets. But if you want to be told everything, we have some explaining to do before I read the letters."

"While they are thinking," Stephan said and turned in his chair so he could look at Nikki and Ingr. "Why is Miranda always talking to the two of you?"

Both women laughed, "You're not going to like the answer," Nikki said.

152

"But we are waiting," said Thaos.

"Ok but Stephan better not divorce me over this," Ingr said and stood up. "All of you men are the same in here. You are all leaders but you are also kind of pigheaded." Sorren laughed as Ingr spoke. "We have Angels, real Angels that walk among us and talk to us and sometimes all of you forget what a miracle that is. And god forbid any of you ask them for help or information."

"So Nikki and I told them that we would always be open to listening to them and to let us know when you were too stubborn to talk to them. You can all just be mad at me now," Ingr said and sat down.

"The girls are right," Sorren said. "So don't anyone get mad at them. I know I have had to change a lot."

"Are you telling us that you actually talk to Angels?" Wickfield asked in utter disbelief.

"That is part of the secret," Mathas said. "We can take a short break while you think about your choices."

"Wait Mathas," Wickfield said. "Do you really think you can say something like that in front of an old newspaper man and I would walk away? I want to hear everything."

"As do we," Turner said.

"Is there anyone in this room who does not want to hear the information?" Mathas asked. No one responded. "Then I do not need to tell you that what you hear in here is not for the public and you will understand why as we tell you. Dominic, you are a priest do you want to come up here and explain the prophesy?"

153

# Chapter XIII
## Prophets, Poets and Kings

Many of the people who attended Mathas' meeting as well as the Sanuri's meeting with the caravan wondered greatly that information about the Keepers of The Scrolls and the Prophesy of The Seven Sons had been shared so freely. Most of these people came to the same conclusions although they did not speak of them. They all believed that these acts were signs of significant changes to come and they all felt fear.

"What is going on?" asked Ashley as she joined many of her employees at the front windows of her shop. The streets were filled with soldiers. "Is there a battle someplace? I'm going out to..."

"Ashley stay here," said Matilda, one of the seamstresses from the Nordes Tribe. "A couple of the men already went out there to find out what is happening."

Within moments two of the Nordes warriors who were assigned to protect Ashley and her shop reentered the building. Both men had solemn looks on their faces.

"Cal what did you find out?" asked Ashley.

"We need to gather everyone," Cal said. "This is about our tribe. Several of the women who were standing at the windows now turned and scattered throughout the building. In less than five minutes all of the people working in the shop were gathered around Cal and Sven.

"Last night one of Usman's soldiers was captured and interrogated," Cal explained. "I don't know all of the details but two members of our tribe have been selling information to Usman's men for years. The soldiers as well as members of our tribe are searching for them." Cal paused, "It was Dirk from the Village of Minges and Raven from our village. Sorren and Hugo are each leading search parties."

"I don't know if all of you know this," said Sven. "But Sorren put Raven on one of the teams. He will want to kill the traitors himself."

Ten minutes later Gideon entered Ashley's store and announced, "We are closing for business today."

"Gideon, what on earth are you talking about?" demanded Ashley.

"Do you know that the soldiers here are searching all of the buildings for two Nordes traitors?" As Gideon spoke both customers and employees now gathered around him. "Well, all kinds of criminals are running and a couple of them have taken hostages in some of the businesses. I have soldiers with me to escort all of you home."

Ashley looked at the faces of several of her female customers and they looked terrified. "We'll make sure that you get home safely," Ashley said soothingly.

On this particular day there were many additional members of the Nordes Tribe in the building as they were working as carpenters on the new expansion. "Once we get everyone home," said Cal. "I think we should join the search."

"Well, this is nice; having my wife sleeping with me instead of watching over me," Javier said as he and Corsa cuddled under the blankets in the back of the boca that Kent was driving.

"I am so tired but I don't think I will be able to sleep," Corsa said. "Javier do you think it is possible that all of us were brought together to fulfil a prophesy?"

"I have no idea and I am only vaguely familiar with the prophesy you are talking about. I have many questions for our meeting tonight"

"I know that so much has to be explained to you and Madeline but what are your thoughts about this so far? The Sanuri was right, no one will force you to do anything."

"I don't have enough information to make any decisions but so many things that Madeline and I saw and heard make sense now. I just keep playing things over in my mind. I have to admit that I find all of this exciting too. In Inferus there is no hope to stand up to the monsters but here…"

"You're going to do it, aren't you?"

"Do what?"

"Take the oaths."

"Honey, I don't even know what they entail. But I am staying on the teams and we are now members of Sudfad's and Renya's family. Even if I don't take any oaths I believe our lives have changed greatly."

"Well, since we can't sleep I will tell you as much as I know. Gabriel told us that there were several times when Sudfad was gone that armies of men and demons stormed the castle because they believed them to be the Keepers of the Scrolls and thought the castle would be defenseless. And this was when Raul and Simon were children and had no idea what their parent's lives were really like. Each time Renya led the soldiers who protected the castle."

"Gabriel said that before Raul and Simon were to marry that the Sanuri met with them and Matthew and explained all of the duties of the Keepers of the Scrolls and they were each asked if they would honor the covenant that their forefathers had made with The Great Ruler. Then after the weddings all of their wives were asked the same things."

"But for centuries it was only the emissaries of The Great Ruler and the King and Queen of Wetpr who knew these secrets but now the Angels are telling so many more people that everyone thinks that is a bad sign."

"A sign of what?"

"That the battles will get worse and," Corsa paused for a moment. "And that the Royal Family will be killed."

After Sorren removed Raven from Dominic's team, she packed her belongings and left the Village of Tyger. She didn't leave because she thought they would discover her treachery, she left because she would not endure the humiliation. Being on the teams was an incredible honor for a Nordes warrior and never had anyone from her tribe been taken off a team.

She traveled north and planned to visit several of the villages of her people before deciding where to make her home. Raven had no idea that she had been exposed as a traitor and she had no knowledge of the hundreds of soldiers and warriors who were searching for her and Dirk.

"What the hell is going on!" yelled Dirk as he was stepped on by people who were running through the alley where he was sleeping. He jumped to his feet only to be knocked down by a group of men who were running from the soldiers.

A dozen soldiers ran past Dirk as they chased the gang of criminals. "Just what the hell!" he yelled again as he stood up then staggered back into the wall of a tavern. "Can't a guy get any sleep...," Dirk heard movement behind him and turned to see a fist coming towards his face...then darkness.

Edward and Kate also cuddled together in the back of a boca. Because Kate had given him her life force and that combined with healing energy from both the Angel Ruth and the Sanuri, Edward was improving rapidly. Like Javier, Edward's body had been infected with half a dozen poisons besides the injuries caused by the arrows that were lodged in his body.

Kate would take longer to heal both physically and emotionally. Almost losing Edward and losing their baby took more of a toll on her than she imagined. She was filled with guilt about losing the baby and thought that Edward would hate her but he just kept telling her that he loved her.

As Kate was falling asleep, Edward's mind was racing as he thought about everything the Sanuri said during the meeting. He had lost his friend, his unborn baby and he almost lost Kate and his own life. Edward was not yet sure of what he was going to do, he just knew he was going to make some major changes.

Madeline rode in the royal carriage with Renya, Nyla, Saran and Nina. Madeline's mind was filled with questions about the Keepers of The Scrolls and the Prophesy of The Seven Sons but she could not speak about these things in front of the girls.

"Is something wrong?" asked Nyla. "You are both so quiet."

"We just have a lot to think about after that meeting," Renya said. "And I am sure that Madeline has many questions."

"Maybe we can answer them," Nina said and both women smiled.

"Not these questions," Madeline said and smiled warmly. "I thought you were drawing pictures but now I realize you are writing. Letters to Ryan?"

"No but I need to write to him," Nyla said. "We promised our Angel that we would translate the scrolls that Michael was working on. We started last night and worked on them while you were in the meeting. We are translating the words but Cerfic is a tedious language. It is like walking in the forest, you can get lost so we are writing down everything as we translate it then we have to go back and look for a hidden code. But Ruth said she would help us."

"We are just making copies for everyone of what we have so far," said Saran. "Michael had several scrolls in his room but our Angel told us to start with this one. She said she had told him lots of times to translate it and he didn't. So we are starting with that one."

"I think that is wonderful that you girls are doing that," Renya said. "But I don't remember Ruth telling you that she told Michael to translate that particular one and where did you get the scroll? Did Michael bring it to Langer?"

"Well first we asked Ruth to give us the right one," said Saran. "Because he had a lot of them."

"Then she visited us again last night," Nyla said. "We were nervous because we don't want to make any mistakes but she will help us. And I think she already is because we have translated a lot so far."

"May we see what you are writing?" asked Madeline.

"We are copying them in sections, so they won't make sense until we put them together. You know, like the pictures that our Angel had us draw," Saran explained. Both Madeline and Renya suddenly felt a sense of urgency and neither of them understood why.

"Girls, it sounds like what you are working on is very important," Renya said. "I think we can postpone all of your studies until you are done with that scroll."

"Good," Nina said. "Our Angel told us it was important. We love her. She is so nice."

"Well, this may take us a while," Saran explained. "That scroll is really long. But we can do both."

"I will speak with Sudfad," Renya said with concern.

Like many large cities, the streets of Langer boasted musicians, poets and self-proclaimed prophets on many of its busiest corners. While the criminals were running from the soldiers these trademarks of the city refused to leave their corners. The criminals and soldiers simply fought and ran around them. Even though some of these people were considered crazy and many more were considered irritating they were tolerated with a welcoming grace.

Thaos and Stephan had brought soldiers into the city to replace the team members who had been working all night. But many, Angus included, refused to stop working and continued searching for the people who had betrayed an entire nation of their brethren.

Stephan and Thaos were walking down one of the main business streets. They had just sent Ryan, Artis and Ralph to their castle with a military escort. Now they were going to check on Ashley's shop. They crossed a street and were passing a filthy man whose clothes were torn and tattered. He was a regular sight on this particular corner. They never took the time to listen to what the man was always yelling; they simply threw money into his hat that was lying on the walkway, whenever they passed him.

"You are looking in the wrong places," the man said with such a clarity and commanding voice that both of Claudius' sons stopped walking and turned to the man.

"What did you say?" asked Thaos.

"If you want to find people on these streets you need to talk to the people who live on the streets," said the man. "The real demons in this city don't hide, they are in plain sight and watch you always."

"Who are you?" asked Stephan as he walked closer to the man and stared into his eyes.

"A friend. A friend who loves this city and the Royal Family. Now gentlemen, I pose a question to you. All of the women in your families do all of their shopping at Ashley's shop now. Wouldn't you agree they spend a great deal of time there without drawing suspicion?"

"Yes," Thaos said. "Are they in danger?"

"I believe all of you are always in danger," the man said. "And it certainly is not from me. Perhaps you should be asking where Isabella and Juleta spent all of their time without drawing suspicion. I believe the women in your families as well as Madeline can provide you with those answers."

Both Thaos and Stephan felt the man was telling them the truth and they were surprised by his words and demeanor which seemed in stark contrast to his physical appearance. "What is your name?" asked Stephan as he now took a handful of gold coins out of his pocket and put them in the hat.

160

"My name is Cyril, and I do not tell you this information for money. Much, much more is at stake here. Now I have one last question for you my sons. Which came first the chicken or the egg?"

Both Thaos and Stephan could not contain the shock on their faces. Thaos stepped closer to the man and whispered, "Are you an Angel?"

Cyril laughed, "That Thaos is an insult to the heavens. I am simply a man who pays attention, which I may say is more than the two of you do."

"What do you mean?" asked Stephan.

The man did not turn his body but only his head and nodded at a building on the other side of the street. "How many times can you walk past that?" asked Cyril.

"Well, I'll be damned," said Thaos.

"We may all be damned if you don't clean this place out," said Cyril.

"Cyril can you come to the castle and speak with us?" Thaos asked.

"Then I am lost as a faceless set of eyes and ears. But every morning and evening Artis and Ralph bring me food. I would think they could pass information."

"Well, I'll be damned," Thaos said again.

"If the two of you are thinking about charging in there and busting heads I would advise against it," said Cyril. "I can promise you that we are being watched. Those people are not amateurs. You will need to be creative."

Stephan now pointed farther down the street and acted as if he was asking Cyril directions. "We appreciate this," Stephan said and he and Thaos walked down the street in the direction he had been pointing. Both men barely glanced at the large purple building with the sign *The Chicken and The Egg*.

When Hugo learned that Raven had been seen riding north of the Village of Tyger the previous day, he organized several search parties of Nordes warriors to go after her. Sorren on the other hand, led search parties in the City of Langer. He was convinced that Dirk was in the city.

"Sorren, I have a present for you," Angus yelled and dumped the limp body of Dirk at the feet of the Chief of the Nordes Tribe. "Found the bastard in an alley, looks like that is where he was living. I know you are going to kill him but we should give him the truth potion first."

"I was planning on it," Sorren said as he picked Dirk up and dropped him in a horse trough.

"What the hell!" yelled Dirk as the cold water forced him into consciousness. "Sorren, what the...,"

"I know you sold us out to Usman," Sorren yelled and grabbed Dirk's head and pushed it under the water. After several moments he pulled Dirk's head out of the water and yelled, "You sold out your own people for money to buy whiskey." Sorren again pushed Dirk's head under the water and moments later pulled his entire body out of the horse trough. "Dirk, before I kill you I am going to find out every word you said to Usman's men."

The Nordes warriors were exceptional trackers. It did not take long before one of the search parties found Raven's trail. This group of warriors was led by a man named Grant who had lost two of his son's in Tresdor's attack on the Village of Tyger.

Grant led twenty-five male and female warriors. He now sent three to tell the other search parties of the location of Raven's trail. Never in the history of that tribe had there been a traitor among them, now there were two. Grant led his people with focused determination.

Raven had deviated from her original northern course when she changed her plans of going to the Village of Absal. She decided to travel to the Village of Minges instead since it was becoming a bustling city. Minges was a port city on the shore of the Sea of Grevdt. She changed to a northeasterly course and rode south of the Village of Devor.

Sorren and Angus sent out word that Dirk had been captured. The soldiers remained in the city since their building searches were exposing many of the criminals and demons in Langer. None of these men had yet received word that Raven's trail was found. While Sorren did not believe she was in the city he had his warriors continue the search.

Dinner was served late at Claudius' home because the family members were straggling in. Thaos and Stephan were the last to come home and Bella immediately had the meal served.

"We met a friend of yours today," Stephan said as he looked across the table at Artis and Ralph.

"Is something wrong?" asked Artist because of the tone of Stephan's voice.

"No, the guy may have given us great information," Stephan said. "We will all have a meeting after the kids go to bed."

"In fact, we were so impressed with his information that we asked him to come here," Thaos said. "But he said that would render him useless as a faceless set of eyes and ears. He said you brought him food every morning and night and that you could pass messages."

"We give food to a lot of people," Ralph said. "Did you get his name?"

"Cyril," Stephan said. "He was filthy but the way he spoke, we thought he might be an Angel in disguise."

"He is a prophet," Artis said. "Of course, we don't know if what he says is true. He's dirty but he's a real smart guy. He says he was a teacher and one day he just knew he was meant to be a prophet and he gave up everything and preaches on the street corners."

"Well, he might be the real deal because he knew one of the riddles Miranda gave us. In fact, he gave us the answer," Thaos said. "We already told Mathas and will repeat everything at the morning meeting but we need to talk to all of you about it."

"Why?" asked Bella.

"Because you might know things that you didn't even know were important," Stephan said. "But we will discuss everything at that meeting."

"I know that all of this is important," Ashley said. "But I want to go back to what Ralph said. Who do you give food to?"

"Well, me and Artis couldn't find work for a long time and we didn't have money to buy food or a place to stay. That's how we started going to Ryan's shop cuz Bella sets out all that food. We know there's a lot of people in the same boat but then some of them don't want to work none either. We know what it's like to be hungry so we fix food every day and take it to a lot of the people we know."

Bella and Ashely stared at each other. "Ok, I know exactly what you two are thinking," Gideon said. "I have a huge empty building by the docks. It won't take much to fix it up." Ashley smiled and kissed Gideon on the cheek.

"What are you talking about?" asked Cassidy as all of the children looked confused.

"Bella and Ashley are going to start feeding the hungry," Claudius said with a smile. Then he addressed Bella and Ashley. "Wait until we are out of the meeting tomorrow then I will go with you and we can hire people and buy everything."

"Artis and Ralph, when we are set up, you two take a day off from work and go around and tell all of these people," Bella said. "Of course you will be paid for this."

"We sure will," Ralph said with a big smile.

After all of the children had been put to bed the adults in Claudius' household met in his study. Stephan and Thaos repeated every word of their encounter with Cyril.

"I'll be damned," said Gideon.

"That's what I kept saying too," Thaos said. "So ladies, do you know what that shop is?"

"It's a woman's clothing store," said Bella. "It is very nice but nothing compared to what Ashley has. Honesty, I never paid that much attention to Isabella and Juleta but I certainly wouldn't be surprised that they shopped there. Rosa should know."

"Well, that is what we thought too," said Stephan. "But she pretty much said the same as you."

"Ashley, Rosa and Mathas have always used their personal seamstresses until you opened your store," explained Bella. "I would imagine those women also made clothing for Juleta and Isabella."

"Well, we need to get in there and even Cyril knew that all of you are loyal customers of Ashley's. We need some new faces," said Thaos.

"How about Drake's girlfriend?" suggested Gideon.

"She's been at the castle. I think we need some really new faces and they can't be members of the Nordes Tribe because everyone knows they are associated with Ashley and us," Stephan said.

"Was Madeline the only woman who worked with Turner's men?" asked Ingr. "I mean Madeline may have been the only Elod woman but they may have used others in their schemes."

"We can ask them tomorrow at the meeting," Claudius said. "I also want to see if Wickfield knows anything about that shop."

"I can go to the Land Office and find out who owns it," said Ryan.

"I don't think anyone from our families should be seen doing that," said Thaos. "We need to write to Madeline."

"I've already started a letter," Nikki said. "As soon as you said Cyril said that Madeline might have information."

"Well, what exactly do you think goes on in that place?" asked Bella.

"Who knows," said Stephan. "But it was important enough for the Angels to tell us about it. And both Juleta and Isabella were such horrible people, it could be anything. That is why Thaos and I don't want to take any chances of scaring them off."

# Chapter XIV
## Tessa

Tessa was a woman of extraordinary beauty, a card shark and a con artist. She based herself out of the City of Port Friada, which is where she met Madeline and Javier. While she did not know they were Elods, or even what that word meant she did know that they paid well and always had interesting assignments.

The news that a prince and heir to the throne of Wetpr had been murdered by terrorists spread through all of the kingdoms of Opots and beyond. Since there were few women in the fields of spies and con artists, Madeline and Tessa became friends and wrote to each other on a regular basis. Madeline never revealed that she was from the Kingdom of Inferus but she did tell Tessa that she was changing her life and had finally fallen in love.

It took several letters before Madeline disclosed the name of the man she loved. When she finally did, Tessa paid considerably more attention to the news in Wetpr and Lentz. Tessa was both happy for her friend and intrigued that Madeline would give up the life she knew, for a man.

Tessa had thick black hair and brown eyes. On more than one job she passed for family with Madeline, Javier or both. It was on one such job in Port Friada that she and Javier had a brief but torrid affair. Neither of them were emotionally invested and remained professionals after the affair ended.

A good con artist stays current on the politics and events in various places. Tessa was familiar with Harlow, Ashley and Gideon from meeting them all at social events. Madeline did reveal that all of these people had now moved to Langer and that she and Javier were involved with them. Tessa was no fool, she realized that Madeline and Javier were working a job, she just didn't know what they were doing.

When Tessa heard that both Michael and Javier had been killed, she packed her bags and took a ship to Langer. She wasn't really sure what she was going to do once she got there, she just knew that Madeline and Javier were the closest people she had to family. Like them, she had been orphaned at a young age and survived on the streets.

There was nothing shy or even conventional about Tessa. Before she boarded the ship she sent a letter to Harlow.

"Harlow where the hell have you been?" growled Claudius as the newspaper reporter joined Mathas' morning meeting. "We've got a small army of Hector's men in the dungeons and they have bounties on you. We can't protect you if you don't tell us where the hell you are."

Claudius sounded frustrated and angry and Harlow was smart enough to realize those emotions probably had nothing to do with him. "I do apologize but too it is difficult for an old dog to learn new tricks. I have been in Zorta and I will share my news with you but perhaps you should catch me up on what I missed."

"We are putting a damn bell around your neck," Stephan said kiddingly then gave Harlow a quick summery of the events which included the revelation that Tresdor was behind the attacks, the traitors and Cyril's words.

"The Chicken and The Egg, isn't that where Elizabeth and Maggie shop?" Harlow asked Wickfield.

"Yes and I am not happy about that one damn bit," Wickfield growled. "We need someone in disguise in there and I know both women will volunteer but...well...damn...I don't want my wife doing that."

"I may have a solution," Harlow said and walked to the front of the room. "Turner, you are going to be interested in this. Before I talk about Zorta, I want to read a letter that was waiting for me when I returned."

*Mr. Harlow,*

*We have met on several social occasions in Port Friada, although I have to admit every time I portrayed myself as a different person. My real name is Tessa Demont.*

Turner and his men started to grin. Harlow saw this and stopped reading the letter. "Do you know her?" Harlow asked.

"Oh yes and perhaps you should finish reading that letter before I say anything," Turner said.

Harlow resumed reading the letter to the group:

*I am not the type of person to beat around the bush, I have many talents which include being a con artist. In my line of work I have few friends as you can imagine. Madeline and Javier were my family. Madeline and I write often. She told me she was giving up her life as a con artist because she had finally fallen in love.*

*But, she also told me that you, Admiral Gideon and that lovely store owner Ashley not only moved to Langer but somehow were working with her and Javier. I am no fool. I don't know what all of you are working on but it must have been important for two good men to be murdered. And this sir is why I am writing to you.*

*I will be boarding a ship named Hell's Wrath. It will dock in Langer. I will contact you upon my arrival. I have not yet worked out a plan but I intend to seek revenge for Madeline and Javier. I know well of your work and am sure that we can collaborate on something. I do pay well.*

*Tessa*

Gideon jumped up from his seat, "That is a passenger ship although you wouldn't guess by the name. It is scheduled to arrive here sometime this morning. Any idea what the woman looks like?"

"Enough like Madeline to pass for her sister," Turner said. "Bart, you're in charge, I am going with Gideon." Then Turner looked at the ruling members.

"Tessa was an orphan who grew up on the streets of Port Friada. So you know she is a survivor. She is smart as a whip and a real firecracker. If she wants revenge, trust me she will get it. I would strongly suggest we involve her in all of this. If we don't she will be working on her own."

"I think I will tag along," Thaos said and stood up.

Turner was walking out of the study then turned back to the group and smiled, "I would also suggest that none of you play cards with her." Turner's men roared with laughter.

"Wait Thaos, you can't be seen with her until we know what role she is going to play," said Stephan.

"I agree," said Turner. "She knows me. I will get her into a hotel and we can plan a meeting later."

"The reason I went to Zorta," Harlow continued after Gideon and Turner left the room. "Was this." Harlow took a piece of paper out of his pocket and handed it to Mathas but continued to address the group. "We all know that the man who said he was Zane was murdered in Port Friada. He was running the Lazy J Tavern which was paid for my Juleta. The tavern is still in operations."

"One of my contacts went in there basically to see if the place had changed. He said he was playing cards with three other men when a group of really mean guys walked in. He said they looked like professionals. He said that one of the guys started to walk into the back room and when the bartender tried to stop him the guy said that he was Zane and that was his place. He said the bartender tried to argue and the man punched him then walked into the back room, which my guy thought was probably an office, and stayed in there for an hour."

"This happened during the day and most of the guys in the tavern weren't drunk but everyone was watching this new gang. Well, the guy who claims to be Zane walks out of the back room with several books and tells the bartender he will be back, then they left."

"I disguised myself and went to Zorta and kept hearing the same story. I hung around in the Lazy J and never saw this guy but I sure heard about him. Now, what I found curious is this guy didn't look that much like the other Zane. We believed that Juleta made several copies of Zane and the Sanuri had a vision of something similar."

"This new Zane is big and muscular with dark hair but apparently his face does not look the same. I started thinking that it would be really hard to explain two identical guys in the same place, so if this is one of the original Zanes did someone change his appearance again? And if so, who?"

Gideon and Turner didn't have to wait long for Hell's Wrath to pull into dock. Gideon stood back and watched for trouble as Turner walked towards the ship. The sailors were helping the passengers onto the boardwalk. Turner called Tessa's name and she looked around suspiciously then smiled when she saw him. He had brought a carriage and loaded her luggage.

As Turner helped her into the carriage she saw Gideon watching them and nodded to him. "This is a very dangerous place right now," Turner said in a low voice once they were both seated in the carriage. "We are being watched always. But I am damn glad you are here, we could use your help. And you will never believe what we are working on."

"I just had a feeling it was bad," Tessa said. "I assume Harlow showed you my letter."

"He read it at a meeting this morning in the King's study," Turner said and grinned then he laughed at the shocked look on Tessa's face. "I told you, you wouldn't believe it. Everyone in that meeting wants to meet you but first we have to figure out what role you will play here."

"Is Madeline here?"

"No, she is on her way to Salar for the Prince's funeral. I never saw her fall apart before. Too bad you weren't here then, she could have used a good friend. Don't get me wrong, everyone was good to her but they don't know her like you do."

"Do you know who is behind the attacks?"

"Not yet but we are making headway but that is kind of where things get complicated. This isn't anything like the kind of work that we normally do and when you find out what it is all about, you may want to change your mind about helping us."

"Turner do you really think I am going to do that?"

"Let's put it this way, I will bet you a bottle of fine wine that you don't believe half of what I am going to tell you. I don't want to really talk until we are in your hotel room."

"There are a lot of crazy stories going around Port Friada," Tessa said. "One is that an Angel saved Harlow and a bunch of people from a ship of demons. It was said that the ship bore the same marks that are seen on Hector's ships. And he, by the way, left Port Friada after those huge battles. He has a small home in the Village of Hafsfat. He stayed there for a while after the battles."

"Apparently he hired a bunch of the villagers to get jobs at the monastery and the fort. You know those villagers are isolated and rather backwards. Apparently they had no idea he was a dark lord until some soldiers came with wanted posters of him and that Clev. From what I heard the entire village told the soldiers about every word he ever said."

"Are you sure your information was accurate?"

"I was dating one of the majors from the fort," she said and smiled. "Have you heard about those stories of the Shadow Men?"

"Yes and I can explain that when we get to your room," Turner said as the carriage stopped in front of the Excelsor Hotel.

Once inside of the Excelsor, Turner paid for Tessa's chambers and explained to the clerk that while he would not be staying there, Tessa was in the city to visit him and he didn't want her paying for a thing. The clerk smiled and nodded.

Turner requested a chambers with the balcony facing the back of the hotel and he requested that a bottle of their finest wine be delivered to her room as soon as possible. Tessa did not speak but smiled and kissed Turner on his cheek. Once they were in the room she asked, "Why a balcony in back?"

"Because we work with Ruala warriors and talking messenger birds called Enrops," he said then answered the door. "Three young men carried her luggage into the room and a waiter carried in a small tray which contained a bottle of wine and two glasses.

Both Turner and Tessa checked her rooms and her luggage for anything unusual before they sat down in the parlor. It took over an hour for him to explain many things. He did not tell her about the Kingdom of Inferus, the Keepers of The Scrolls or the Prophesy of The Seven Sons. She listened intently but asked few questions which surprised him

"I will be honest, there is more but at this point that additional information will only put you into more danger," Turner said. "Now, that you know that Madeline and Javier were working for these kings who are at war with the demons, I can tell you. Javier is not dead although he still may not survive his wounds. That was the second attempt on his life in a matter of weeks and his friends though it would be safer to say that all three men had been murdered, the other man, Edward, is also alive but not doing well."

"And Tessa, Javier is married now and really happy. He married a young warrior from the Nordes Tribe and she works on the teams that I spoke of. I have never seen him happy before."

"This may surprise you but I am happy for him. We had a meaningless affair, it was nothing more. Madeline also sounded happy in her letters before Michael was murdered."

"And it also may surprise you that I have heard of some of the things you were talking about. Did you know that when those two sects of the Insidiae were fighting, the one group butchered people in Joy City to get back at Hector for killing their lieutenant? It was a blood bath. But, you know how that city is."

173

"New people have taken over the businesses and Joy City is open again. And there is a great improvement in the businesses. There are actually nice restaurants and shops alongside the demon dens. I spent a great deal of time there after the attacks. I heard about these people who were at war with the demons and dark lords. There was a huge battle in Ganz and all of the demons were talking about it for weeks. So these are the people all of you are working with now?"

"Madeline and Javier were working with them, me and the boys got involved after the attacks and gotta say they are good people. They're all warriors even the women but they have so many enemies that it makes your head spin," Turner said.

"I heard a lot of talk in Joy City that Samael wants to turn this world into Orantho and everyone, even the demons are scared to death. And I heard that because your friends are trying to stop him that Angels fight with you. Is this true?"

"Well now, that was some of the things that I didn't think you were ready to hear."

"Have you actually seen an Angel? Do they really exist?"

"From a distance I have. And I will tell you my knees wouldn't hold me up. The Angels don't just appear to everyone but they did Madeline and Javier almost from the beginning. And they appear and talk to the people we are working with."

"You said King Mathas would pay me but I would do this just to see a real Angel. My mother used to tell me about them before she died. Then after that I just couldn't believe they existed with all of the horrible things in the world. My mother never really saw an Angel but she sure believed in them."

"I am the last person to try and explain this but I was told that people have free will and the Angels can't affect that. So they give those people hints a lot and they have to try and figure things out like that riddle I told you about with the chicken and the egg."

"We could talk all day but you understand now how dangerous it is here. If you choose to help us we need a new face to go into places like that dress shop."

"The people we work with now have had two situations, well actually three, where they were running a con and found out that innocent people, mostly children were kidnapped. Hector has a business where his men steal kids, kills their parents and sells them at auction. So they want to be careful with this shop because we don't know what is going on."

"Did they save them?"

"Yes and the stories are really bad."

"Then my old friend, I think it is time that we saw the sights. That shop shouldn't be the first place we enter."

As they were walking out of the room Tessa asked, "So Turner, did you ever think that you would be one of the good guys?" He shook his head and laughed.

Turner and Tessa walked the streets of Langer arm in arm, they laughed and kissed; but their roles did not prevent them from noticing the many eyes upon them. They entered every shop in the main business district. By the time they entered The Chicken and The Egg their arms were filled with packages.

This store, like many others that catered to the wealthy, was furnished luxuriously. A well-dressed woman immediately walked up to them and offered to take some of their packages. They continued their story of being lovers and Turner acted proud to show off Tessa.

They both walked through the store picking out items for Tessa to try on as well as asking questions. They deliberately were keeping the two clerks busy as they looked around the building for anything suspicious.

Neither of the clerks acted or looked suspicious. One was an old woman and the other a young girl. They were both friendly and accommodating. Tessa and Turner did not see any demonic items or writing in the shop. Tessa was looking for hidden doors when she was in the changing area. She bought many items including six articles of clothing which needed to be altered. She was told that she could return for the items in two days.

Turner and Tessa gathered their packages and resumed their shopping trip. An hour later they entered Ashley's shop which was filled with people. Ingr and Nikki were also in the shop since their husbands had told them about Tessa and the team members and Patronus priests who were watching Turner and Tessa reported that they were shopping.

"I know you!" Tessa said loudly and quickly walked up to Ashley and hugged her. "When Turner told me a woman from Port Friada opened a shop here, I just knew it had to be you. I will tell you a lot of us miss your designs."

Ashley recognized Tessa and played along. "Yes, I fell in love and came here with Gideon. I hope you will be in the city long enough to attend our wedding."

Tessa smiled and batted her eyes at Turner, "I don't know yet how long I will be here," she said with an excited voice.

"Well, let me show you around," Ashley said then turned and called Nikki and Ingr. "These are two of my close friends, Nikki and Ingr. Nikki's mother is my manager and Gideon and I are staying with their family until our home is done. And this is..."

"Tessa." As she spoke Tessa hugged both of the young women.

"Honey, I am just going to sit here and have a cup of coffee," Turner called to Tessa as she disappeared in the store with Ashley, Ingr and Nikki. He sat down at a table and wrote the name of Tessa's hotel and room number on a piece of paper. He folded the note inside of a newspaper then set the paper on Harlow's table as he poured himself some coffee. After Turner poured his coffee he picked up a different newspaper from Harlow's table and walked to a table closer to the windows.

Nikki and Ingr looked around the back changing area to make sure no one could listen to them talk as Ashley and Tessa picked out a dress for her to try on. When they got to the changing area Tessa spoke in a low voice but very fast.

"We went to that shop and there was nothing out of the ordinary and we looked for trap doors and everything. There wasn't a feeling of evil there or actually anything that seemed unusual. We were the only customers and there were two female clerks. One was old and the second could be her granddaughter. Do they have meetings or anything in there?"

"I will have to think about this," said Ashley. "Do you know what I really did in Port Friada?"

"Oh yes, and I heard about Moses going after you too. We should get together some time and chat."

Ingr walked up to Tessa with a beautiful blouse. "It is dangerous here," Ingr whispered. "Nikki and I are warriors, if you ever need any help."

Tessa smiled and nodded. "I believe I will try this on," she said and took the blouse.

# Chapter XV
## Raven

For over twenty-four hours the only break that Sorren took from interrogating Dirk was to attend Mathas' morning meeting. Several team members were helping him by taking notes and stopping him from killing Dirk before all the questions were asked.

Dirk had been selling information to Usman's men since before he was married. Dirk, himself was not a warrior and never lived in Sorren's village, yet he seemed to hear a great deal about the tribe from others and everything he heard he sold to the enemy.

Sorren was systematically asking Dirk everything he had told Usman's men, who often asked for specific information. Seth was taking notes and had to jump up and restrain Sorren when Dirk said that Usman wanted information about Angelina since he wanted her for one of his wives.

It was almost dinner time when Sorren walked into Mathas' castle, where he and his family were staying as they cared for Matthew's and Angelina's children. Noah was with him and both men had blood on their clothing.

"What happened?" asked Shara who was in the parlor with Rosa.

"Wait, let me get Mathas," Rosa said and quickly left the room.

Noah poured two glasses of whiskey and handed one to Sorren. Then he poured a third glass when Mathas entered the room.

Sorren looked enraged and exhausted at the same time. "That bastard was selling his people out for over forty years. Minges is a great fishing area and people from all our villages go there to fish. Apparently Dirk gathered as much information as he could and sold every bit of it to Usman's men. Dirk never talked to Usman himself but did talk to Tresdor a couple of times."

"Mathas do you remember that time when Angelina and I came here after she had met Matthew?" Mathas nodded. "And she told him that Usman had talked to her a couple of times and wanted her to be his wife." Mathas, Rosa and Shara stared at Sorren in silence. "Well, that damn Dirk is the one who passed information about my baby."

Sorren stopped talking momentarily as he took control of his emotions. "Noah's got all the notes. I just killed the bastard and we dumped the body in the forest so the animals can tear it apart." Sorren paused again and drank down his entire glass of whiskey. "Now I have to write a letter to Dirk's kids. They are going to be so ashamed."

Raven was a well-trained warrior and had no fear of traveling alone. But the past two nights she felt uneasy as she camped. She rarely felt uneasy and had no idea why. Now as she prepared another campsite, those feelings crept into her again. She dropped the armload of firewood that she had gathered and searched the area around the outside of her campsite for some distance. Nothing was out of the ordinary.

As Raven was returning to her camp she suddenly stopped and crouched down because she smelled wood burning. Her senses were heightened but she neither saw nor heard anything unusual so she crept towards her campsite which was only yards away. She peered at her campsite through some bushes and saw that the wood she had gathered was piled and burning.

The sun had not yet set so Raven could clearly see her camp. She saw no foot prints or any sign of disturbance other than the roaring fire. She waited twenty minutes then pulled one of her knives out of its sheath and walked into her camp. "Ok, what the hell is going on?" she asked loudly and searched the brush with her eyes. She turned suddenly as she felt a presence behind her.

"Toni!" Raven gasped as she stared at her old friend and her male companion. "Toni what happened to you?" Something was very different about Toni but Raven could not initially determine what it was.

179

"We have a proposition for you," said the man. "Your tribe has learned that you betrayed them and they are close behind. You know they will kill you. You can come with us."

"Who are you?" asked Raven as she walked closer to the two. Every sense in her body was telling her to run. It was when she got closer to Toni that she saw that Toni's eyes were black. "Toni are you a demon?" Raven gasped then her eyes widened with the realization of the situation. "You must be Sorphat!"

"Toni, you were right she is a smart girl," Sorphat said. Toni had not yet said a word. Sorphat was wearing the guise of a human man, richly dressed and handsome.

"And what would happen if I went with you?" asked Raven. "Would you turn me into a demon too?"

Sorphat smiled. "You are a beautiful woman; I would be willing to negotiate."

"I thought you had taken Toni as your mate," Raven said as she stared boldly at the powerful demon.

"I am actually surprised that you know that and know my name. I am interested in hearing how you came by that information."

Raven kept looking back and forth between Sorphat who was calm and Toni who appeared to be in a trance. "What have you done to her?"

"She needed a little correction but she should not be your concern now," said Sorphat. "Your people are but minutes away. Do you choose certain death or a new life?"

"I will not be the puppet of a demon," Raven spat and started to scream the war cry of her people. She and Toni threw knives at each other simultaneously and they both jumped to avoid the paths of the oncoming blades. Both women were impaled by the weapons. Sorphat grabbed Toni and disappeared as Grant and his warriors raced into the campsite.

Grant was in the lead and jumped from his horse while it was still moving. Raven was lying on the ground with a knife in her chest. She knew she was dying and grabbed Grant's arm as he picked her up.

Raven choked on her own blood as she tried to talk, "Toni and her demon are he..."

The warriors scattered when they heard Raven's words and searched for Toni and her demon lover. All they found was a large pool of Toni's blood.

Tessa and Turner were sitting in the dining room of the Excelsor Hotel. Both were dressed for an extravagant night on the town. They laughed and kissed as they ate a fine meal and drank wine. After almost two hours she kissed him on the cheek and whispered, "The hair on the back of my neck is raising. Do you see anything?"

"I am feeling the same," he said. "And no."

Although the two pretended to be focused on each other they were watching everything in the dining room and the front entrance of the hotel.

"Something isn't right," she whispered.

He nodded then motioned for a waiter to come to the table. Turner purchased another bottle of wine and paid their dinner bill then the two walked up the two flights of stairs to her chambers on the third floor. As soon as they entered the chambers they both searched the rooms again without finding anything suspicious.

"I am staying here with you tonight," Turner said as he looked out the balcony door. "I'll take the sofa."

"Honestly, I don't think I am going to get much sleep," she said and poured two glasses of wine. "Now you can finish telling me about what is going on here."

"I might have to tell you something else," he said as he continued to look out the door. "I think I know why we were feeling like that."

"What are you looking at?"

"I can't see anything, I just have a feeling," Turner said. He closed and locked the balcony door and turned to Tessa. "If anything happens to me you go to the King's castle as quickly as you can. It is just outside of the city."

"Turner what are you talking about?" asked Tessa. When she saw the look of fear on his face she opened one of her traveling cases and took out two knives and a small crossbow. "Turner, I have never seen you look scared before, just what the hell is going on?"

"Tessa, I am going to tell you something that you probably won't believe and I don't want to but I need to explain why we are feeling this energy."

"I am listening," she said and sat down on one of the overstuffed chairs. "Turner, you are turning white, what is that bad?"

"You have known me and Madeline and Javier for a really long time. And we have been keeping something from you. We did it to protect you but now..."

After dinner the Sanuri and Erebus walked to Sudfad's campsite. They were surprised to see how many people were there and waiting for them. Almost all of the team members were there including Edward and Kate. Javier, Corsa and her brothers were there as well as Thedes, Ibula, her brothers and father. There were no children in the campsite.

"Sanuri, some of us may have to leave to take care of babies," Diana said.

"I understand and I can certainly repeat the information here. Are you all here because Adam said that you could petition the heavens to take Michael's place?"

"That and a lot of us really don't understand that prophesy," said Misha.

"We may need to make some coffee, this may be a long night," the Sanuri said.

"Already working on it," Maxwell said as he and Emeral each walked towards the campfire holding two pots of coffee.

Grant and his warriors buried Raven's body. They packed her belongings and took her horse to return to her family. Then they left the campsite and traveled south. They had only traveled a few minutes before Grant told everyone to stop and they searched her things. They found a large pouch of gold coins and a cryptic note that merely stated a time and had a simple drawing.

"She was supposed to meet someone tomorrow at those caves west of Minges," Grant announced to his warriors. Then he looked at the faces in the group. Alicia come up here. Grant stared at the young warrior who had long black hair. "I think you could pass for Raven from a distance. Will you find out who she is meeting?"

"Of course," Alicia said and beamed with pride at being asked.

"We are turning around and heading for Minges," Grant told the group.

Tessa drank three glasses of wine as she listened to Turner. He told her about the Kingdom of Inferus, about the Charto being spies and that Javier and Madeline were bred as Etos. He told her about the team members rescuing the Credo and how Madeline and Javier really became involved with the Royal Families of Wetpr and Lentz.

Then Turner explained about Andrac and Gilder and that those sorcerers had possibly placed bounties on all of his team members. Tessa never said a word, she just kept pouring wine into her glass and staring at him. When he finished speaking she got out of her chair, walked up to him and touched his face.

"I really don't understand how you can't be human," she said.

"That is the part you are focusing on?" he asked with frustration. "Did you hear me when I said I think the energy we were feeling was the presence of Andrac?"

"I heard you. I may be shocked but I am not drunk. Honestly this explains a lot. All your secret meetings and trips and your tattoos. And Javier and Madeline are the two sexiest people I have ever met. Are you sure you aren't human?"

"Tessa, listen to me. You have no idea how evil and powerful the sorcerers are in my world. They are nothing like the dark lords here. If I felt Andrac he is looking for me and that puts us both in a great deal of danger."

"What are you going to do about it?" Tessa asked as she poured more wine into his glass.

"What do you mean?"

"You just told me this really long story about Angels saving this kingdom and the Credo and Madeline and Javier. You told me what that Angel did to Andrac. So call to her."

"What! Are you crazy?"

"Actually, I am excited. I would really, really like to believe that something, anything good exists in this world. Turner, I dare you."

"Even if I did, they probably wouldn't show up."

"Are you scared?"

"You better believe it."

"Well, how do your friends call to them?"

"By their names."

"Well, what are their names?"

"Why?"

"Just tell me."

"Miranda, Adam, Daniel and Ruth."

Tessa looked up at the ceiling and said loudly, "Angels, I don't know if you are listening to us or even if you care but if we are in danger from the sorcerers would you please help us? And I will help your people but would it be possible for me to meet one of you? My mother talked so much about Angels. She even drew pictures of you."

"You stopped calling to us after your mother died," Miranda said as she and Adam appeared in the room. Turner dropped his glass of wine.

"Oh my god, oh my god," Tessa kept repeating and curtsied to both of them. Then she ran out of the room and ran back in. "Please stay here there is something I have to show you. She curtsied again and ran to the bedroom. She ran back into the parlor with several pieces of yellow, tattered paper in her hand and tears were running down her face. She showed the pictures to Turner and he turned white again.

"My mother drew these," Tessa said and handed the pictures to Adam and Miranda. "She said she never saw an Angel but she must have because she drew these pictures of you."

"And you held on to them and never called to us," said Miranda. "Why?"

"I don't know," Tessa said.

"Yes you do," said Miranda.

Suddenly Tessa became angry. "She believed in you so much but she died and I was all alone. How could Angels let that happen?"

"Your mother knew she was dying for a long time. That is why she told you about us and drew those pictures for you. She wanted you to remember your faith so you would be safe. But instead you cursed the heavens for what happened in your life. We have protected you but we could have done so much more if you would have let us in," Miranda explained.

"Tell us Tessa, why do you call to us now?" asked Adam.

"I just really wanted to know if you existed," she said as she cried. "And Turner has been talking about you."

"The Great Ruler and Angels have been whispering to you your entire life," Adam said. "You didn't realize it but you started to listen to us several months ago. That is really why you came here."

"Really? Why do you want me here?"

"Many reasons," Miranda said. "And some are for your own safety."

Tessa straightened her posture and stared at the Angels. "It's because of that Chicken and Egg place isn't it? What do you need me to do?"

"Finally, someone asks us," Miranda said and looked at Adam.

"Become a regular customer," Miranda said to Tessa. "And go in alone."

"Will she be safe?" Turner asked.

"She knows our names now," Miranda said and smiled. "And Andrac feels our presence and will not bother you again tonight. He has placed bounties on all of you and you too know our names."

"Why?" asked Turner.

"All of you are so good at your jobs," Adam said. "You see and hear things but don't always understand the significance." The two Angels disappeared.

The Sanuri's meeting continued for hours. The people asked many questions and even though some of them had been told about or read the Prophesy of The Seven Sons they were now getting new understandings.

"Well, this is kind of sad," said Diana. "It sounds like we get betrayed all along the way."

"It is a prophesy but you must all remember that everyone of us has freedom of choice which means we can ask the heavens to help us change many things," said the Sanuri. "For the core members here, just how many times have the Angels told us to read this prophesy?"

"A lot," said Koby.

"Even The Lion told us," the Sanuri said. "The Angels don't just say things to make conversation. And you know they can't always come out and tell us things. We are all filled with guilt because we believe we could have prevented Michael's murder and the attacks on Javier and Edward if we would have heeded their warnings about Tresdor. Well, let me tell you that perhaps we couldn't have but we did learn a major lesson here."

"I am just throwing this out there as a suggestion, I have no insight from the heavens but maybe we should sit down and rethink our strategies. We have more enemies than we can count and they seem to understand us better than we understand them. While we have suffered loss, we have won our battles but the prophesy predicts great losses for us..."

"Now, wait a minute," interrupted Misha. "Didn't you just say that we had freedom of choice and could ask the heavens for help?"

"Yes, now tell me how many of you actually pray to The Great Ruler or ask the Angels to help you before you run into a fight or battle?" The Sanuri looked around the group. "Few hands have been raised. From what Miranda told me the prayers of your children protect all of you more than your own prayers."

"Some of you were in Ganz when Adam showed us the horrors of the World of Orantho and told us that Samael planned the same for this world. This fight is for so very more besides us and not one of us can forget that."

Corsa raised her hand and the Sanuri smiled and nodded at her. "Do you think we were all brought together because of that prophesy? I mean...well...don't you think it is strange how we have all gotten together?"

"A lot of us have wondered about that," Vivian said.

"What do all of you have in common?" asked the Sanuri. "You come from different tribes and even different worlds. I'll tell you. Every man and woman here is defined by their courage, their integrity and their faith. I believe that is what is bringing us all together but it also makes our behavior predictable."

# Chapter XVI
## Predictable

While the people traveling in the caravan felt as if they were moving slowly in a dream, the family and friends in Wetpr felt that time was racing away from them. Because so many of them were burdened by their grief, Gala took control of many of the functions at Sudfad's castle.

Archetenus and Jared had moved their families into the castle temporarily. Besides helping with the duties of the kingdom, these two men were putting together a plan to get revenge for Michael's murder. Delilah and Zoya were helping Vitomas, Annabelle and Laurel plan a funeral befitting the eldest son of a king.

Luca had taken over the security measures for the funeral and Royal Family. Luca and his family had not moved into the castle but they went there every day to help.

Alexander channeled his grief into making an exquisite coffin for Michael. Vitomas, Annabelle, Laurel and Marie couldn't stop crying and Raul and Simon walked around as if they were dazed.

Gala hired two more of Marie's sisters as temporary nurses for everyone's children and she took it upon herself to meet with the mayor of Salar to prepare for the homecoming of the Royal Family and the funeral.

Enrops and Florines continuously filled the skies as they carried letters between the people in Wetpr, Lentz and the caravan. Raul and Simon had read the letter from their parents that told that Madeline and Javier had been adopted into the family. Neither of these Princes could wrap their heads around this move and wondered if their parents had been taken advantage of.

Vitomas and Annabelle were considerably more understanding although they too did not understand the motivations behind the adoptions.

While Michael's sisters were rarely seen crying by the people in the caravan, the letters they sent to their family in Wetpr always brought tears to the eyes of those who read them.

Amidst all of the grief and preparations, Petra and Kyra had become afterthoughts. These children basically withdrew from the family circle after they had been told about Michael's death. The adults knew that the children were at the castle but little more.

Turner and Tessa had gotten little sleep; they sat up and talked most of the night until he had to leave for Mathas' morning meeting. "I don't feel good about leaving you alone," he repeated as he washed up.

"And when did you become my protector?" she asked kiddingly. "I will make a grand appearance in the dining room then go shopping. If anything is off, I will leave a note for you at Ashley's."

Turner had left the door open to the bathing room so they could talk. "I don't know how you can be so excited about the Angels; they scare me for some reason."

"It is like my mother is alive again," she said and walked into the bathing room as he shaved and placed a cup of coffee on a stand.

"Where did you get that?"

"What do you think? I ordered it."

"You don't really know who was bringing that to the room."

"Turner, listen to you. We've known each other for years and I have never seen you like this. For a long time I thought you never gave a shit about anything. Now you are a bundle of nerves. What is really going on?"

"I wish I could tell you and I am being honest about that. I just started having this feeling...can't explain it."

"Did it have to do with feeling Andrac's presence last night?"

"I am sure that is part of it but it started before that. I really don't know and the fact that I am feeling like this is unnerving me."

"The man of steel is unnerved," she said kiddingly. "I am going to have to write this down in my diary."

"It's not funny," he said and gulped down his coffee. "Do you really keep a diary?"

"No, you fool. Do you think I would keep something that could be used against me?"

"Tessa, I just thought of something...but even in my head it sounds strange. Last night I told you about Isabella and Juleta. Everyone who is trying to figure them out is a warrior, whether they are a man or a woman. Maybe that is what we are doing wrong. I have certainly found out since we started collaborating with the teams that despite all of our differences we are really very much alike and think alike."

"You need a normal girl to try and get into their heads," she said thoughtfully. "Can't say that I am normal and they certainly weren't...but we all had to have been at some point. Turner, I think you are onto something. Let me work on this." She was quiet for several moments.

"Ok, this is the plan. I am going to be Miss Charming and spend lots of money in the shops. I am going to tell people that I am expecting you to propose to me and I want to know everything about this city. Women always get excited about proposals and weddings...that story will open doors. I'll bet that I can find out more from the women here than you can in the dens."

Turner walked out of the bathing room and into the parlor. He took a pouch of gold coins from his jacket pocket and tossed it to her. "I like your plan. I am going to tell them about it at the meeting. A lot of people will be watching you don't assume they are all the good guys."

191

"Why would I?" she asked and laughed. "I don't know many good guys. Don't forget to tell them what I told you about Hector and the villagers of Hafsfat." As Tessa spoke she straightened Turner's tie.

"After we get these bastards, I would like to visit Madeline and Javier. Do I need someone to make those arrangements for me?"

"I am sure that King Sudfad will greatly increase the security in his city, so I will tell King Mathas to give them a heads up then I will take you there. I would like to see them too." Turner paused. "The last time I saw Javier he looked like hell. He was too weak to carry on a conversation. I hope to hell he lives long enough for us to visit them."

"Is there a special way we send letters to them now?"

"Yes, the birds. I don't know how you call to them so give me your letters and I will give them to Mathas to send."

"Wait," Tessa said as he started to walk out the door. "Let me look at you." Tessa stared at him as she was trying to determine the size of clothing he wore. "A real perspective bride would be buying things for her man."

"I could use some shirts," he said and chuckled.

"Oh trust me, you could use some new ties," she said and smiled.

He turned and again she said, "Wait. If I am going to be singing your praises what is your cover story here?"

"I work for the Port Friada Bank and I am here looking into investments."

"Oh that is good," she said. "I'll bet that opens doors."

When Turner entered Mathas' study he was going to tell his men about the bounties on their heads when Mathas called him to the front of the room.

"I would like to start with you today," Mathas said then paused. "You look like hell did something happen?"

"Yes and I have a lot more to tell you than about our trip to that shop. But would you mind if I pour a cup of coffee first, I was up all night."

"Having fun?" Bart asked kiddingly.

"No, being chased by Andrac and talking to Angels and I am not sure which scared me more," Turner said as he got a cup of coffee then returned to the front of the room. "I am just going to start at the beginning."

Turner told the group everything from the moment he met Tessa at the shipyard. He told of their search of The Chicken and The Egg, of their contact with Ashley and Harlow. He told of their feelings of danger during dinner. Then he paused for a few moments and told of their visit from the Angels Miranda and Adam.

Turner looked at his men who were sitting together, "So obviously we have something on Andrac and don't realize it. Think gentlemen, our lives may depend on it." Then he looked at the ruling members. "You might get pissed about this but...well just let me tell you."

"I had this really bad feeling even after the Angels left and a lot of it was for Tessa's safety. She on the other hand was elated about meeting Angels...so we sat up all night and I told her everything. About Inferus, the work you do, Juleta and Isabella. The only things I didn't tell her were about the Keepers of the Scrolls and the prophesy."

"Now, I need to explain something before I go into the plan she is hatching. Tessa is an incredibly smart woman. She thinks quickly on her feet and her mind is always going so she stays three steps ahead of everyone else. She could charm the pants of the devil himself and probably has," Turner said and chuckled.

"But until I met your women, I thought of her as a warrior. She is nothing like the women on your teams. Do not expect her to be able to fight hired killers. She may trick them or charm them but she does not have the skills of your warriors. But that may work in our favor."

"In Inferus we are taught to hate everyone and to see them as enemies. Since we have been collaborating with all of you I have been surprised that we have more similarities than differences and we all think alike because we are warriors. Tessa isn't a normal woman but she isn't a warrior either. She believes that at some point both Juleta and Isabella had to have been what we consider normal. It is possible we can't figure them out because we can't think like them."

"So this is her plan; she is going to charm the business people in the city. She is going to say that she expects me to propose and she wants to learn everything about the city. And instead of infiltrating the taverns and dens, she is going to infiltrate the women's groups."

"That would make sense after what Cyril told us," said Stephan.

"She also wants me to explain something to you. She is by profession a con artist. She said that it sounds like your teams go into areas, shake things up and then get into fights."

"That's pretty much it," Thaos said and laughed.

"She says the real cons take time and detailed planning. She said it might be months before she gets what we need but she will get it. I told her about the situations you had when you discovered hostages and she too wants to take this job carefully."

"Now that I have told you that, there are a couple of other things. First, Tessa would like to visit Madeline and Javier after this job. I would assume that King Sudfad will increase his security. King Mathas would you make arrangements for such a visit?"

"Of course. And after the meeting I will give you money for this job. I don't want you spending your own money."

194

"Thank you," Turner said. "And the second thing, am I the only one who thinks it is strange that the Angels sent Tessa here and that she had pictures of them? I will tell you I was unnerved and she acted like an excited child."

"She's not the only one who was sent to us," said Claudius. "And, well, just a lot of damn strange things happen and after a while you kind of get used to them."

"But, I am getting concerned about her safety also. I will have men watching over her. They will be in civilian clothing, so let her know."

"If she is going to work the women and shopkeepers then she will have more of an excuse to talk to Ashley," said Thaos. "It would be good if we could organize something so she could at least see us so she knows who we are."

"Anything like a private dinner would be too dangerous at this point," Turner said. "A big social event would work."

"Well, Bella is planning an engagement party for Gideon and Ashley," Claudius said and grinned. "And she doesn't know how to plan anything small."

"That would work but wait a few weeks. That prophet said that we are not dealing with amateurs. It would be expected that you find some way to contact her. No, for the most part she is working this on her own. But she needs to ask Madeline questions. How do you call your birds?"

"You pray for the birds to come. But if she is being watched, the Enrops can't come to her," said Mathas. "Bring the letters here and we will send them."

Grant and his warriors slept for a few hours then resumed their journey towards Minges. There were a series of caves to the west of the village and Raven's note included a primitive map of a small cave on the western side of this group of caves.

Grant's plan was to get to the caves early and search the area before sending Alicia in to meet the unknown person. The previous night, he had sent two riders back to the Village of Tyger with the warning that Toni and Sorphat were in the area.

Sorren was standing before the group in Mathas' study and talking about his interrogation of Dirk when there was a knock on the door then Rosa immediately walked into the room. "I am sorry to interrupt but one of the men from Sorren's village is here and he has something really important to tell you."

Sorren could see the warrior standing behind Rosa. "Eric come in," Sorren called. "You can tell us all."

"Grant sent me back. You know we were following Raven's trail. Last evening before it got dark we were riding and heard a female voice screaming our war cry but it stopped before it was completed. We were only minutes from the area and found Raven's campsite. She was on the ground with a knife in her chest. She said that Toni and her demon were here then she died. We searched the area and found another big pool of blood, which we assume is Toni's."

"After we buried Raven we started back then Grant stopped us and searched her things. He found a large pouch of coins and a note that had a map. Raven was supposed to meet someone at those caves just west of Minges at noon. Grant is headed there and Alicia is going to pretend to be Raven."

"I am sorry Mathas but I don't like the sound of any of this," Sorren said. "I need to leave."

"You want us to come with you?" asked Stephan.

"No, I'll take my people. You have enough to deal with here."

Simon knocked on the door to one of the chambers in the central wing of the castle. Jared opened the door and Raul and Simon entered the room where Luca and Archetenus were sitting at a table that was covered with maps, papers and cups of coffee.

"We know what you are doing," Simon said. "We want to help. Maybe we can get our heads on straight if we strategize."

"Right now we are just throwing out ideas," Jared said. "We haven't called to the Angels yet because we want to work some things out; of course once we talk to them everything may change."

"Tell us again what Miranda said to you," Raul said. "You told us but that was right after we found out about Michael."

"Well, I was too damn mad to remember the exact words but she said that Archetenus and I had walked in places that none of you could and we might have to go back there to stop all of this," Jared said.

"Now, you could take that two ways," Luca said. "They were both criminals but we are thinking that she meant about them both being Second Sons.

"Then we started looking at the places we had both been before we hooked up with all of you," Archetenus said. "Except that Jared never got to Port Friada, we've spent a lot of time in the same areas."

"They were both involved with Roch and the Insidiae," Luca said. "But what we have been really talking about is how to make a good cover that they aren't part of our group anymore because you know spies have seen them."

"Yeah, it's not like we blend in a crowd," Jared said and grinned.

"This is really Gabriel's expertise," said Raul. "But we could have you act normal then something happens to you once you get some place. Like you can pretend you are bewitched or something."

"Actually we thought about that," Archetenus said.

"You know the Angels want the Sanuri and Erebus to go to Ryed," Simon said. "Maybe you start out guarding them."

197

"Of course we have both been pulled into hell; hope that's not where we have to go," said Jared and laughed.

"You don't have enough information here," Raul said as he was looking at the maps. "We need to call to Miranda."

"I agree," she said and materialized in the room.

"We wanted to have a plan together before we bothered you," said Archetenus.

"Before we talk about those plans there are many letters you have not yet received from Lentz and the caravan. I am not going to repeat everything in those letters but all of you are getting help from unexpected people."

"The witch who made the potions that were used to kill Michael was so devastated when she learned what her potions were used for, that she prayed to The Great Ruler. She set up traps for the demons and asked Ruth to take her to Langer. She gave the healers her priceless book of potions and antidotes then she sacrificed herself to help Erebus escape from a trap. But before they escaped these two used their powers to shake up the dark worlds."

"The Elods who made up Javier's and Madeline's team are now working closely with your people in Langer and it is a good collaboration. And probably the best con artist in your continent went to Langer to help. She grew up on the streets and her only friends were Madeline and Javier. She has many skills and different views of things."

"The citizens of Langer are filled with rage and grief and have declared war against the demons and dark lords like the people in Port Friada. But while this will not keep the dark ones out it will make things considerably more difficult for them."

"Luca, hold up that map you have of the Insidiae regions," Miranda said. "While highly organized, the Insidiae is made up of numerous independent groups. And the secrecy of the organization can prevent members from finding out many things."

"The Discedo Sect broke away from the many body of the Insidiae and saw this splintering of groups as a weakness. Their new organization works together as one group and that is giving them strength."

As Miranda spoke little lights appeared on the map. "Now, besides the Insidiae, there are thousands upon thousands of criminals, dark lords and witches who have things in progress. The vast majority of these plans and crimes have nothing to do with any of you or the prophesies. But because of the battles you have won all of you are becoming famous. And people are starting to look at you like you are the law. Which means they could fear that you will interfere with their schemes."

"Know that most of those people will never raise a hand against you but groups are uniting for what they believe is their own protection against the law."

"So what you are really saying is that someone could tell a bunch of crap to crooks and send them against us as diversions," Archetenus said. "So we could be chasing all of these low level nothings around while the big guys go scot-free."

"That has already been happening," Miranda said. "Last night the Sanuri had a meeting with the members of the caravan and told them what I am telling you. First, every one of you is overwhelmed. You are trying to do too much. There are too many battles. Archetenus remember when you would spend countless hours planning how to save Vitomas from Roch?"

Archetenus turned red and glanced at Raul. "Yeah."

"When was the last time any of you thought anything out that completely? I will tell you if you had; there would have been less battles. Raul, Simon remember how you used to play chess? What do you do now?"

"We make one move then have to take care of a baby or business," Raul said.

"You are The Seven Sons of Prophesy and while you realize it or not every single person you are involved with is a gift. Erebus knows the dark worlds like no other. In your lifetimes none of you could ever gain that experience."

"And the two men you sit with were notorious criminals. How best do you think you can use their expertise?"

"You want us to take those lawman jobs don't you?" Archetenus asked Miranda.

"Name me anyone you think would be better? Except perhaps for members of the Charto who know both the dark worlds and the criminal worlds," Miranda said. "Now while you think about that question I am going to tell you something just once. Raul and Simon your parents are not fools and while you want to protect them you should be applauding their brilliance."

"You are the family of The Seven Sons. Who now makes up your family?"

"Rualas, Shettees, Elods and humans," Luca said. "Were the adoptions a political move?"

"That was part of it. But Renya and Sudfad now see Madeline and Javier for who they really are and all of you should take the time to look too. Their childhoods were no different from Vitomas', Annabelle's, Delilah's, and Michael's sisters among others. Raul what one thing did both Vitomas and Nyla say?"

"That they thought they were in dreams and were afraid they would wake up."

"And what else?" asked Miranda.

"That this family and way of life are worth fighting for," Simon said.

"And those are the thoughts of Javier and Madeline," Miranda said. "Part of the reason you two feel so guilty is that you never took the time to really get to know Michael, even though your wives harped at you to do so. Don't make that mistake again."

200

"You have two children here who really took the time to get to know him. They made him feel loved and welcomed and he was their friend. Where are they? When did you last see them?"

"Are you talking about Petra and Kyra?" Raul asked anxiously. "Are they alright?"

"Perhaps you should find out the answer to that question yourself. Now back to the question I posed to Archetenus."

"Jared and I have been discussing that with each other and our wives," Archetenus said.

"Oh hell, we'll do it," Jared said. "So you are saying that the Charto would help us?"

"I believe you would find that a prosperous collaboration. The members of Javier's group are trying to find out who is behind the attacks but they also plan to come here and visit their friends and they will bring their new helper with them. I would suggest you take advantage of that visit."

"The dark worlds now believe The Seven Sons can be killed and since they don't know who they are, every one of you is considered a possible candidate. And I hope that this is a warning you will actually pay attention to."

# Chapter XVII
## A Home

After Miranda disappeared, Raul and Simon left the room and started to search the castle and grounds for Petra and Kyra. After an hour Vitomas and Annabelle joined their husbands. After another hour Laurel and Marie also joined in the search.

"Father have you seen Petra and Kyra?" Annabelle asked anxiously as she ran into Alexander's workshop.

"Yeah, they are in the barn next door. Why what is wrong?"

"Miranda told us to look for them," Annabelle said and ran out of the workshop. Alexander followed her.

"They're in that barn," Annabelle yelled and pointed to one of seven barns in the area.

"What's wrong?" asked Petra as he and Kyra jumped when their family ran into the barn.

"We haven't seen you for a while," said Simon. "What are you doing?"

The children were standing at a table that had boards and papers on it. "You'll just think it is stupid," Petra said and turned back to the table.

"No we won't," said Vitomas. "Show us. Please."

Petra and Kyra looked at each other for several moments then Petra nodded at her. "I can't draw as well as Annabelle," Kyra said and started to arrange the papers on the table. "When Michael was in that cage he used to always dream of having a home and it always looked the same." Kyra moved as the adults gathered around the table.

"It wasn't anything like a castle," Petra said. "He said he used to really think about the house when he was cold and hungry and it would help him. He described it to us a couple of times." Petra stopped talking and looked like he was going to cry. "You will just think it is stupid," he said dejectedly.

"No we won't," said Raul. He could hear Vitomas crying behind him. "Are you drawing him a picture?"

"No, we're going to make him his house and put it on this grave, so he will finally have it. Of course it will be small," said Petra with enthusiasm.

Annabelle quickly left the barn so the children wouldn't see her crying.

"Mind if we help," Simon asked and picked up one of Kyra's drawings.

"That's fine," said Petra. "We still need to find stuff."

"Laurel, looks like we need blue curtains for the windows," Simon said. "And stones for this fireplace."

"First we need to figure out how big we are going to make this," Alexander said as he looked at one of the drawings. "I know you don't want to go in my workshop because of the coffin, so let me bring a few things in here."

"Marie, you know how to braid rugs," Simon said. "Think you can make one this small?" He showed her one of the drawings. Marie couldn't talk, she nodded as the tears ran down her face.

"We aren't as good of carpenters as Alexander but we can help," said Raul as he rolled up his sleeves.

Grant and his warriors arrived at the caves midmorning. They spread out and watched the area. They did not see any people in the area before noon, which concerned them all. Whoever Raven was supposed to meet could have seen them or they were already in the cave. The worst scenario would be Alicia finding a demon in that cave. All of the warriors knew there was a high likelihood that she was walking into a trap.

Alicia rode Raven's horse up to the cave. She rode in from the direction that Raven would have taken on her route. It was a bright and sunny day and Alicia knew that her sight would be momentary affected when she entered the darkness of the cave. She carefully studied her surroundings before dismounting.

She slowly entered the cave and a pungent smell instantly filled her nostrils.

"You're not Raven," said a frail woman's voice. "What have you done to Raven?"

"I am a friend of hers, my name is Alicia. Who are you?"

"She didn't tell you?"

Alicia's eyes were slowly becoming accustomed to the darkness. She heard no other sounds besides the voice of the old woman. Alicia didn't know if she had walked into a trap. Her mind raced as she decided whether she should throw her knife or tell the truth.

"Raven got into a fight last night with a criminal and a demon. She was killed. We found a note in her things telling her to come here." Alicia said. "If you are really Toni or Sorphat come out of the shadows and fight like warriors." Alicia tightened her grip on the hilt of her knife as she heard movement. Then she realized the movement was slow and unsteady.

"I don't know who you think I am," said the woman as she walked towards Alicia. The woman was crying. "I left that note for her." As the woman got closer to Alicia, the smell became stronger.

"What is all of this about? Do you need help?"

"You will understand when we walk into the light," the woman said and walked past Alicia and outside of the cave. The woman wore a tattered black dress with a black scarf over her head. She walked slowly and was bent forward. Alicia followed the woman. Grant and the other warriors tensed up as they watched the scene.

The woman removed the scarf from her head and Alicia gasped. "We are lepers, we were cast out of our homes in the Valdore Lands. Raven found us one day and helped us move to these caves so that we would be closer to her village. She brings us medical supplies and food. But I wanted to warn her."

"Warn her about what?"

"That monster Tresdor was here. We hid and when he left we found a demon altar."

"What is your name?"

"Martiz."

"Martiz, I am going to call to my friends so don't be afraid." Alicia made the sound of a yellow bird. Grant and the other warriors rode to the cave.

"Don't be afraid," Alicia said again to the old woman as the Nordes warriors surrounded them. "This is Martiz. She and other lepers live in these caves. They are from the Valdore Tribe. Raven would bring them medical supplies and food. Martiz left that note for Raven to warn her that Tresdor built an unholy altar here."

"Miranda is she a demon?" Grant asked loudly.

"She tells the truth." Miranda's voice was heard only by Grant.

Grant dismounted and walked up to Martiz. "Take me to your people. We will not hurt anyone." Most of the Nordes warriors dismounted and followed the old woman into the cave. The rest stood guard, in case of attack.

Martiz led them through several narrow tunnels. Putrid smells filled the dank air as they walked farther into the ground. Light could be seen in the distance and five minutes later they entered a huge cavern that was lit by torches and several small fires.

"Oh my god," said Alicia and tears filled her eyes as she looked at dozens of terrified and diseased people.

"Do not be afraid," yelled Grant. "We mean you no harm." Then he turned to Martiz. "What is this hell you live in?"

"We were cast out of our villages. Many of us have died. Raven and her lover found us one day. He was one of us and sought to leave but Raven would not. She helped us move to these caves and she comes every few weeks with food and medicines. She is very good to us."

"Grant, we can't leave these people here," Alicia said.

"I have no intention of it," he said then he turned to several of the men who were standing behind him. "Go to Minges and get bocas, food and water. If they do not give these things to you, tell them Sorren will make sure they get paid."

"Get blankets too," said Alicia.

Grant was a strong and tough man who had seen too much death in his life. His heart broke after his wife died. What was left of his heart shattered after his sons were killed by the Valdore soldiers. Grant stopped feeling after those deaths. Not until this moment did he realize he had emotions again. He felt pain as he looked upon these pitiful people.

He now talked loudly to the terrified remnants of the Valdore Tribe. "I don't know how long you have been here but Usman and Tresdor attacked our tribe. Usman was defeated and Tresdor is in hiding. There are no borders anymore. All of these lands are open to everyone. We are one people now. There is a hospital north of Minges, we are going to take all of you there. I promise you that you are safe now."

"Usman was an animal to treat his people like this," Grant said in a lower voice more to himself than to anyone else. Then he turned to the old woman. "Martiz where is that altar you found?"

"As you face this cave opening it is the cave to the right. You will see it as soon as you enter. Take one of the torches."

"Alicia, organize the others into getting these people out of here," Grant said and grabbed a torch from its holder and turned and quickly walked towards the entrance of the cave. Grant was a close friend of Sorren's and had been with the Chief on many occasions when he called to the Angel Miranda. Grant had never seen Miranda but he had heard her voice many times.

"Miranda are these people in danger?"

"All of you are."

"Will you help me destroy that altar?"

"It is not just the altar that poses a threat. Tresdor was not the only beast in there. And yes, I will help you."

"Then will you also protect these people?"

"You would pray to protect people from the tribe that killed your sons?"

"These poor people did not kill my sons, the monsters who sent them here did." Grant suddenly felt dizzy and light headed. "Miranda what is happening?" he yelled and clutched his head.

"You are being healed," she said as she appeared before him. "It is a gift for the courage and mercy you have shown. My brother is in that other cave, we will take care of the demon and the army of Rogetts that are gathering. You concentrate on getting these people to safety." Grant was overwhelmed and could not speak, he simply nodded. Then he turned and ran back towards the cavern.

Most of the people suffering from leprosy were too weak to walk and were being carried by the Nordes warriors, who placed them on the ground outside of the cave then ran back in to get others. By the time all of the people had been carried out of the cave, the five warriors who had ridden to Minges returned and they were not alone.

Dozens of people from Minges followed these warriors to the cave. People jumped out of bocas and off their horses and gave food and water to the emaciated people on the ground. People put blankets around the sick and carefully put them in the bocas. Most of the people being rescued were crying as were many of the people from Minges.

"Take them to the hospital and I will catch up with you," yelled Grant. When everyone was out of sight he walked to the entrance of the cave which contained the altar. He heard growling and snarling and pulled his sword. He entered the cave which suddenly became filled with light. Thousands of Rogetts screamed and shielded their eyes from the light created by Adam and Miranda.

"Was Tresdor setting these monsters loose on Minges?" asked Grant as the horror of the situation grasped him.

"Yes, and why Minges?" asked Miranda.

"I have no idea unless it is a diversion," Grant said.

"He ran from Langer when he saw all of the soldiers and search parties because he thought they were after him. The demon he serves did not want him to leave the city so Tresdor stopped in this cave to pray to Bertuck who is irate with him. To save himself Tresdor offered the souls of the people of Minges but they are not his to give," explained Adam.

"Where is he?" growled Grant.

"He is going back to the lands of his tribe. That was the only place he ever felt safe and in control," said Miranda. "He will continue to spread his poison unless he is stopped."

"Do you need me here?" Grant asked.

"Not anymore," Miranda said. "He is heading to Isador."

"Thanks," Grant said and ran to his horse.

Tessa was still so exhilarated from meeting Adam and Miranda that the fact that she had not slept the previous night had no effect on her. She started working the shops as soon as they opened. She was now walking back to the Excelsor Hotel to meet Turner for lunch. She smiled and spoke to most of the people who she passed on the street.

After just one morning she was already on a first name basis with many of the shop owners and clerks, who she waved at as she passed the windows of their businesses.

"Now that is one good looking woman," Noah said to Seth as they watched Tessa from the opposite side of the street.

Seth grinned. "You better watch where you are walking or you're going to trip."

Noah laughed. "It sounds like she and Turner just have a working relationship but I'm going to ask him. I haven't seen a woman in a long time who set me on fire."

Seth laughed loudly and slapped his friend on the back. The men walked passed Cyril and put money into his hat. He nodded and winked at them.

"I really wanted to talk with him," Seth said as they continued down the street. "I've never met a real prophet before."

"Who knows if he is real but stop..." Both men now stared at the two men who had just stepped out of a tavern and were deliberately blocking Tessa's way.

"Need help with those packages, little lady?" asked one of the drunken men.

"No thank you," Tessa said and tried to walk around them but the two men moved to block her again.

"You sure are a pretty little thing," said the second man and spit a wad of tobacco on the walkway.

Tessa smiled sweetly and said in a low voice, "And you are disgusting, drunken fools. Now get the hell out of my way."

Noah and Seth laughed as they heard her words. They had crossed the street and now stood in between Tessa and the men from the tavern. Since these men had been standing close to Tessa, Seth and Noah were almost leaning against them so the drunken men backed up.

"Leave the lady alone," Noah said. "Or her fiancé won't take it kindly." Noah deliberately said these words so Tessa would know that they were working with her.

"Are you the fiancé?" asked one of the men.

Noah grinned, "No, wish I was."

While the two drunken men were large, they were not hired fighters. Noah and Seth clearly looked like professionals. The two drunken men turned and walked away without saying another word.

"Well, we may have blown our disguise," Noah said is a low voice as he helped Seth take Tessa's packages. "Where are you heading?"

"The Excelsor, to meet my fiancé," she said and smiled. "You two come in pretty handy. What are your names?"

"Noah and that's Seth," Noah said as he and Tessa stared admiringly at each other.

Seth laughed, "Come on you two."

"I know who you are," Tessa said in almost a whisper as they walked down the street. "Madeline has written to me about all of you. You were freedom fighters in Ryed weren't you?"

"That's us," Noah said.

"And you are going to be priests?"

"Why did you say it like that?" asked Seth.

"I didn't mean to insult you. I've just never seen such cute priests before."

Noah laughed and Seth turned bright red.

Once they approached the Excelsor, Seth asked, "Should we come in?"

"Yes, just follow my lead," Tessa said with a smile while Noah held the door open for her.

Turner was already seated in the dining room. He had requested a table that gave him a good view of the front entrance of the hotel. He stood up and got a concerned look on his face when he saw that Seth and Noah were with Tessa. She immediately ran to him and hugged him. Then she said loudly, "Honey, the most horrible men were bothering me and these two nice men stopped them." She turned and smiled at Seth and Noah.

"Please won't you join us," Turner said loud enough for others to hear.

Noah and Seth piled Tessa's packages onto a chair and they each shook hands with Turner and told him their names.

"Tell me what happened," Turner said after everyone sat down at the table.

"You tell him," Tessa said. "I am still too upset."

"A couple of drunks came out of the Double T Tavern and wouldn't let her walk down the street," Noah said. "They didn't even try to fight us."

Turner waved a waiter to the table and said loudly, "These two men just saved my Tessa. Give them whatever they want."

"Are you alright?" the waiter asked Tessa with genuine concern.

"Yes and thank you for asking."

"A couple of glasses of whiskey," Noah said to the waiter.

"Then your finest steaks all around," Turner said.

"You bought a lot of things," Seth said shyly to Tessa as he stopped several packages from falling off the pile.

"I had a very worthwhile morning," she said in a business tone of voice. "I must say people certainly are friendly here."

It did not take Grant long to find the trail of a single rider traveling north. He wondered why Tresdor didn't make an attempt to hide his trail. Then Grant wondered if he was riding into a trap. But the more he considered this idea the more he believed the Angels would have warned him.

Grant scrutinized his surroundings as he rode. But something was gnawing at him which he couldn't put his finger on. Finally, he realized what it was. Martiz could barely walk yet she said that she had left that note for Raven but Raven was hours east of the caves when they found her. So who really left the note? None of them asked her who Raven's lover was. And Martiz was one of the only people who could walk although she appeared considerably older than most of the people in that cavern.

211

And they had found the note the previous night yet Tresdor had been in the cave just a matter of hours before. Nothing about the timing made sense. Suddenly fear gripped him and he called out loud, "Miranda is Martiz a demon or any kind of threat to my people?"

"No," was the only word the Angel said.

Turner, Tessa, Noah and Seth ate and talked for almost two hours. They weren't able to talk about business because the restaurant was very crowded that time of day.

"Well, this has been very enjoyable," Turner said to Noah and Seth as everyone stood up to leave the table. The men shook hands a second time. "I hope we cross paths again."

"Thanks for the meal," Noah said to Turner then smiled and nodded at Tessa. He and Seth left the restaurant.

Turner picked up all of Tessa's packages and the two slowly walked out of the dining room and up the two flights of stairs to her chambers. As soon as they entered the chambers they both searched the rooms before they spoke.

"Oh they are really cute," Tessa said with a grin when they both entered the parlor.

Turner laughed loudly. "You never change. Afraid I don't know them well, so I can't tell you much."

"Oh I do," Tessa said. "Madeline has written to me about all the people. They were the freedom fighters that we used to hear about in Ryed. We thought there were a lot of them but Madeline said there was just a handful and some of them were children when they started. They lived in caves to avoid Teivel's demons. She didn't tell me how they got here but they are all studying to be priests. And that is a shame, boy are they good looking."

Turner laughed again. "They are going to become Patronus priests; they are warrior priests. Their existence is kind of a secret in the Church. But a lot of the men on the teams and a lot who are watching you are Patronus priests."

"Really, I have never heard of them. You will have to tell me."

"I saw the way that Noah was looking at you," Turner said and grinned. "Perhaps I should let him explain."

Tessa laughed and started opening her packages as she spoke. "I only made it to about a quarter of the shops because I spent a lot of time talking with people. I wasn't kidding when I said that people were friendly here. The family that owns that jewelry shop with the big clock in the window, invited us to their home for dinner. And two different ladies asked me to join some kind of Ladies Society. It meets tomorrow night at the home of Elizabeth Wickfield. It's held at different places every week."

"A couple of things about that, first, Isabella belonged to at least one club like that and secondly, Elizabeth's husband owns the largest newspaper in the kingdom and he works with us. I will take you to the house and pick you up."

"I can hire a carriage."

"Tessa, besides that we are playing these roles, I keep telling you that I have a bad feeling."

"You're just being paranoid. Now here are shirts I bought you and the ties. Try them on. I'll return them if they don't fit or you don't like them. Then I got you this." She handed him a velvet pouch.

Turner took the golden pocket watch from the pouch, "Tessa this is really beautiful. Thank you."

"I had it engraved inside but you can always change that after the job."

"I might just want to keep it the way it is," he said and smiled. "Did you go into The Chicken and The Egg?"

"No, I am going to go there this afternoon, I didn't want to seem too eager."

"I am going to try these on," Turner said as he picked up his shirts and ties. He walked out of the parlor and immediately returned. "I forgot all about these," he said and handed Tessa a stack of papers.

"There are several artists in the group and they are drawing pictures of the members so you will recognize them if you see them. You should burn those when you are done."

Turner stood near Tessa and told her the name of each person and their connection to the group as she studied the drawings. "Thaos is an unusual name," Tessa said as she stared at his picture. "Is he the one that Harlow wrote about?"

"Yeah, those stories were printed in the paper here too. Just so you know Wickfield and Harlow are old friends."

"I cut those stories out. Turner every time I read them I cry. Not because it is like reliving a nightmare but because people cared enough to actually help those kids. I want to meet this Thaos."

"You met his wife Nikki yesterday and you're working now with the people who saved those kids."

"Really? Are you kidding me?"

"Why would I kid about something like that?"

"Turner, these people are heroes."

"About that. I was part of an interesting conversation this morning. First, you have to understand that the teams are made up of all kinds of people, royalty, warriors, ex criminals, priests, demon hunters, a holy man and even an ex warlock. Apparently the Angels have said that all of their behavior is too predictable because as soon as they hear about anyone who needs help they run in and save the day. A lot of traps have been set for them."

"Well, that does make sense but it is kind of damn sad too. Start a fire in the hearth so I can burn these." Tessa was still studying the drawings as she spoke. "I hope that when this job is done that I can meet these people."

"Actually Claudius' wife, do you remember who he is?"

"Yes."

"She is going to throw a big celebration for Ashely's and Gideon's engagement. I told them to wait a couple of weeks so they won't blow your disguise. Just so you know they all want to meet you too."

"Really? Why?"

"Mostly because you are a stranger who is risking her life to help them and I told them you are a con artist and a card shark." Both Tessa and Turner laughed.

# Chapter XVIII
## Suspicions

By the time that Sorren and the group of warriors he led arrived at the caves near Minges, the warriors who had ridden with Grant returned from the hospital.

Since Alicia had spent more time talking with Martiz than anyone else, she explained the entire story of finding the note that led to finding the people in the cave. She described how people from Minges helped to transport the sick to the new hospital.

"Grant told us he would catch up but he never did," Alicia said. "We need to find that cave with the altar; he might still be in there."

It only took a few minutes for one of the warriors to find the cave with the remnants of the unholy altar and thousands of dead red snakes on the floor of the cave. "Miranda! Miranda!" Sorren yelled when he saw the snakes. He was one of the few in the group who understood the significance of the scene before them.

"What happened here?" asked Sorren when Adam and Miranda materialized outside of the cave.

"Tresdor thought your search parties were after him," explained Miranda. "So he ran but his demon didn't want him to leave Langer so that tells you that things are still in the works there. Tresdor stopped here and built an altar and bartered the souls of everyone in Minges for his life. Of course, Tresdor did not have the power to offer those souls to the demon. But Bertuck decided to cause fear and a distraction with the Rogetts."

"Eric take half the warriors and go back to Langer and tell them what Miranda said," ordered Sorren.

"Grant is following Tresdor to Isador," said Adam. "Know that while Tresdor has no special powers now, his demon may not easily give him up."

"We will call to you," Sorren said and mounted his horse.

Tresdor had an eight hour head start on Grant and was running for his life. He was not paying attention to his environment because he believed that all of his problems were behind him.

"You disappoint me again," said a loud voice.

Tresdor started to whimper. "But Bertuck, I gave you all those souls in Minges." Tresdor stopped his horse and stared at the cloud of black mist that was forming in front of him.

"We both know that you had no power to barter away those souls but I thought the distraction would be beneficial. The distraction never happened."

"What! Why?"

"Angels destroyed my pets. So now it is back on you to cause a distraction."

"But Bertuck, please, they will catch me."

"And you fear them more than you fear me?" the demon yelled.

"No, no Bertuck. I fear you much more."

"Then turn around and go back to Langer."

"Isn't there someone else...?" Tresdor fell screaming to the ground. He rolled around in excruciating pain for minutes before Bertuck stopped the punishment.

"That is just a small taste of my wrath," Bertuck sneered and the demonic cloud disappeared. The only value that Tresdor held for Bertuck anymore was that there were bounties on him. These bounties would provide a small fortune for whoever brought Tresdor to the King. Bertuck knew that Tresdor's appearance in the right place would cause havoc.

Tresdor lay on the ground and cried for several minutes. He was vomiting and had soiled himself. He slowly stood up and mounted his horse. He continued to cry as he rode south to Langer.

Tessa spent the afternoon shopping and talking with people; it was late afternoon before she entered The Chicken and The Egg. On this day the store was filled with women who Tessa followed around and listened to their conversations. She also initiated conversations with many of the customers as well as the store clerks.

It wasn't until Tessa was in one of the changing areas that she heard anything of interest. The changing areas consisted of a large room that was divided into small cubicles by heavy red drapes. The drapes hung from the ceiling to the floor. Two women to the left of Tessa's cubical were talking in whispers. It sounded to Tessa like both women were in the same cubicle.

"I never thought it would be like that," one of the women said. "It was horrible. You didn't tell me it would be horrible."

"You didn't go in with the right mindset. You were scared from the beginning. But lots of women are like that at first."

"I don't want to do it again."

"You swore an oath; you have to."

There was a long pause before the first voice spoke again and Tessa could hear the fear in the woman's voice. "But what if someone finds out."

"We have been doing this for a very long time and no one has ever found out. I mean look at us; mothers and wives and some of the most powerful women in the city. Do you really think anyone would believe someone if they told?"

"I just..."

"Be quiet, someone is coming."

Tessa heard the voices of several women entering the changing areas. She also heard one of the clerks talking. Tessa quickly changed into the gown she had brought into the cubicle and walked out to see if she could find the women she had been listening to. The cubicle was empty.

Tessa left the store and walked into two others before she entered Ashley's shop, which was filled with people. She glanced around the front of the store then sat down at one of the tables.

"Can I get you anything?" Nikki asked. "Ashley isn't here now and I am helping Mother." Nikki knew that Tessa might need help or want to pass information.

"Would it be possible to get some paper and a pen? And I believe I will have a cup of coffee."

"You can help yourself to the coffee and pastries over there, they are all free and I will get you some paper. Do you need a large sheet?"

"Oh yes, thank you," Tessa said as she stood up and walked over to a long side table that was filled with delicacies and fine dishes. "This is absolutely wonderful," Tessa announced although she wasn't speaking to anyone in particular.

"Here is some paper, let me know if you need more," Nikki said and started to walk away.

"I am making a list," Tessa said excitedly. "I suspect that I may be moving here and I have heard about so many wonderful places that I want to write them down before I forget. Turner, he is my boyfriend, is always telling me how absent minded I am. And I know but part of that is just being excited." As Tessa spoke, her eyes carefully searched the dress shop.

Nikki saw how Tessa was looking around and wondered if there was someone in the shop that Tessa was suspicious of. "If you have any questions, I am from this area and would be glad to help you."

"Why, thank you. Just this afternoon I was telling Turner how friendly everyone is here."

"Nikki can you help me a minute?" Gladys called.

"I'll be back to check on you," Nikki said and Tessa smiled.

Tessa leisurely drank her coffee and wrote on the paper as she watched the people in the street. She poured herself a second cup of coffee and smiled when she saw Bart and Louis walk past the window of the shop and look at her.

She waited another twenty minutes then walked into the back of the shop where she picked out three dresses and carried them to the changing area.

"Do you need any help?" Nikki asked and followed her into the changing area.

"This is the wrong size," Tessa said. "Would you mind putting it back?" As Nikki reached for the dress, Tessa slipped a piece of paper into her pocket. Tessa left the shop after purchasing a dress and a pair of shoes. She bought some flowers then returned to her chambers at the Excelsor Hotel.

Tresdor now walked his horse. He was in no hurry to reach Langer. He cursed himself for ever selling his soul to Bertuck then he became fearful that the demon could hear his thoughts.

Grant on the other hand was riding fast and hard as were Sorren and the warriors he led. Tresdor had no idea of what he was riding into.

"It's me," yelled Turner as he knocked on the door to Tessa's chambers. She was wearing a robe when she answered the door. He grabbed her and kissed her in the hallway then they both entered the chambers.

As soon as the door closed Tessa said, "Damn Turner, I think your paranoia is rubbing off on me."

"What do you mean?" he asked as he looked out of the back balcony door.

"I heard an interesting conversation when I was in the changing area of that chicken egg store. This is your copy; I slipped another copy into Nikki's pocket, in case something happened to me before I saw you. And I can't even believe I just said that."

"That was smart and this is interesting," Turner said as he read the note. "You can get mad at me but I am going to be spending nights here. I will tell you; something just isn't right." He paused. "What no argument?"

"I figured as much so I bought you some more clothes and some whiskey."

"Damn you're good to me," he said and chuckled. "Now I have something for you. I saw Noah in the Catacombs. He wanted to know what our relationship was. I told him that you were like my little sister and that you couldn't stop talking about how cute he is."

"You didn't! Did you?"

"I sure did," Turner said with a big grin. "And he said you make his blood boil. So I am thinking that the two of you should stay apart until after this job is done or you won't be able to focus on work."

"Did he really say that?"

"Gee, could you grin more?"

"Well, did he?"

"Yes and I told him too that the two of you shouldn't get together until after we are done here."

"You are right," she said with a big smile. "Will you button the back of my dress?"

Eric and the other Nordes warriors who rode with him went straight to the castle of King Mathas and told him what they had witnessed at the caves near Minges and the words that Miranda spoke.

Mathas asked the warriors to stay while he sent messages to the ruling members. Then he called one of his generals to the castle and ordered him to fill the city with soldiers and to be prepared for anything.

"What the hell!" growled Grant as he dismounted and searched the ground. Tresdor had been leaving a clear trial and now there was nothing. Grant carefully searched the area. There were no rocks or bodies of water that Tresdor could use to help hide his trail. There wasn't a broken branch or a bent blade of grass to be seen.

"That bastard isn't that good," he said out loud. Grant stood up and looked up to the sky. "Miranda, I just got a really bad feeling. How do I stop him?"

"For that you will have to return to Langer."

"How did he get past me?"

"In a sense he didn't; it was the work of his demon. Sorren and others are a few hours behind you. All of you should turn around."

"Thank you," Grant said and mounted his horse. "Miranda how dangerous is he?"

"Very but Mathas has been warned; the city is filled with soldiers."

"Then what do you need me to do?"

"Take that gold that Raven had and give it to the people you had taken to the hospital; that was its original purpose."

Grant did not want to deviate from his course of searching for Tresdor but he would not disobey an Angel. He mounted his horse and started to travel south. "Miranda, was Raven good or bad?"

"Like many people, she was both."

Turner and Tessa were walking down a street in the business district of Langer when hundreds of soldiers filled the area. Turner took her hand and walked up to a soldier and asked, "What is happening?"

"The King said for us to prepare for an attack," the soldier replied.

"By who?"

"I don't know, My Lord."

"I am taking you back to the hotel," Turner said to Tessa. They walked quickly and paid attention to everything they saw.

"Wait," said Tessa. "I know him." She stopped walking.

"Who?" asked Turner.

"You know him too; from Port Friada. He's standing in that window." Tessa nodded at a building across the street. A large, heavy set bald man was standing at the window watching the soldiers. "What is that building?"

"I don't know, there isn't a sign. It might be a home. Let's keep going, we can check that out later. Where do you know him from?"

"He owns merchant ships. He has a lot of money, but I've seen him most in Joy City. He has a lot of dirty little secrets."

"Do you remember his name?"

"Frankwich,"

"Doesn't sound familiar," Turner said as he held the door so she could enter the Excelsor Hotel. "Sorry but we are eating here again."

"That's fine. Do you still have that bad feeling?"

"Oh yeah."

The following morning Madeline and Renya were helping Nyla, Saran and Nina to dress before the caravan started out.

"Now, when we get just outside of Salar all of us will move to the front of the caravan and we will lead Michael's body home," explained Renya.

"I don't want to have to smile and wave at all of those people again," Saran said.

"In this case you don't have to," said Renya.

"Do we have to ride can't we just stay in the carriage?" Nina asked.

"We are honoring Michael this way," Nyla scolded. "We are all going to do it. Is everyone wearing their necklaces?" Saran and Nina nodded while Madeline and Renya both said, "Yes."

Even at that time of the morning, the scene at Sudfad's castle was chaotic. Raul and Simon had ridden into the city to check on the preparations for the arrival of the caravan.

The women in the household planned a feast to be held at the castle that afternoon for those returning from Langer. The public showing of Michael's body would be the following day and evening in the chapel at the Learning Center. Delilah, Zoya, Gala and Marie were helping Vitomas, Annabelle and Laurel and all of the women were busy.

Luca had sent soldiers and Enrops into Salar the previous day to search for terrorists. He also had soldiers and the students studying to become Patronus priests searching the castle grounds and the areas in and around the Learning Center and the chapel. Everyone realized this would be an optimal opportunity for an attack. Classes had been canceled for the Patronus priests for one week so they could assist with the duties of the royal funeral.

As with any big event in the city, the merchants imported flowers and delicacies but this time they also imported thousands of bolts of black cloth and ribbon.

The flags in the kingdom had been flying at half-mast after the announcement of Michael's death. In addition, every tree, post and balcony in the city displayed black ribbons. It was the only way the people could think of to show their support of their royal family and to pay respect to the fallen. People from all over Wetpr as well as other kingdoms flocked to Salar for the funeral.

While many of the citizens of Salar had never met Michael, they loved their royal family. Sudfad and Renya were generous and loving people who always included the citizens of their kingdom in the special events of their lives. Many of the citizens took the death personally and felt as if they had lost a family member. The bustling city was filled with grief and anger.

Thousands of men from all over the kingdom enlisted in the military after the news of Michael's murder. The commanders at each fort had to build additional buildings to accommodate this influx of recruits. But by far it was Fort Nora, the only beacon of safety and freedom in the Kingdom of Stordt; that drew the most recruits.

The people of the City of Nora had led lives filled with terror until King Sudfad bought the majority of land and businesses in that city. Under his leadership a fort, schools, a monastery and a temple were built. For the first time in their lives these people felt safe and hopeful and they were filled with gratitude to the Royal Family of Wetpr.

After Sudfad bought the controlling interests of that city the citizens built a display in the center of the city. This display included a huge statue of a Ruala warrior as well as two flag poles. One flag pole held the flag of the Kingdom of Wetpr and the second the flag of the City of Nora. This display had grown over time and contained bushes, plants, trees and benches. It now also contained thousands of bouquets of flowers and black ribbons.

There were no attacks on the streets of Langer the previous night but the soldiers remained at their posts. Because of the threat of attack, Turner told Tessa to remain in her chambers until he returned from the King's morning meeting.

"Turner, again I would like you to speak first," said Mathas as the meeting started.

"Thank you," Turner said as he walked to the front of the room. "I have a few subjects to bring up. I told Tessa to stay in her chambers until after this meeting because I don't want her working until I know more about the threats."

"As I expected she is gathering information and I will discuss that in a moment. Only my men in this room know Tessa so I want to tell you a little about her. She is twenty-one and was orphaned at the age of seven. While Madeline and Javier are only a couple of years older they saved her when she was being attacked on the streets of Port Friada. You might say we all grew up together and except for a brief and meaningless affair that she and Javier had, we all regard her as our little sister."

"Thaos knows what life is like on the streets of that city and you can only imagine what it was like for a beautiful little girl. She does not trust easily. In some ways she seems so much older than her years and in other ways she is like an impressionable child and this brings me to what I want to share with you."

"Madeline has written about all of you, as friends would. She has not revealed secrets. But between those letters and Harlow's newspaper stories Tessa rather idolizes all of you now that she realizes who you really are. And she has developed quite the crush on Noah."

Turner now looked at Noah and said with a big grin, "I am sorry but if I hear one more time about how cute you are, I am going to puke." The people in the study roared with laughter.

"I think you all understand why I am telling you this. These emotions could be used as weaknesses. She is aware of that and we discussed the matter at length last night. She is a professional and I would expect her to act like one but you should be aware of these things."

"I have told all of you that I have been consumed with prevailing feelings that something is very wrong here. And because of these feelings I plan to sleep on the sofa in Tessa's chambers every night. Not only does that play well into our disguises but for some reason I am really worried about her safety. She has been scolding me for feeling paranoid until yesterday evening."

"Thaos did Nikki give you the note that Tessa slipped into her pocket?"

"Yes, our entire family read it as have Mathas and Fahron."

"I will read that note in a moment," Turner said. "But first you have to understand that Tessa is rather fearless. She prefers to look at things as an adventure or challenge. She told me that after overhearing that conversation that she felt very paranoid and decided to give that note to Nikki in case something happened to her before she could tell me about it."

Bart stood up. "We are new to your group but as members of the Charto our group and I am including Tessa have worked together for years. We often kiddingly refer to Turner as the man of steel. Neither he or Tessa are fearful or paranoid people. If they are feeling like this, there is some kind of reason."

"We have found that sometimes the Angels give us strange feelings as warnings," Dominic said. "You might want to ask them if they are making you feel this way."

Jasmine and Lana quickly stood up before Dominic was done speaking. "I am sorry," Jasmine said. "But we have a person basically working by herself in a city that is filled with threats and she doesn't know hardly anyone or the city. I know that is how she may work cons but we are looking for murderers and demons. Madeline gave Lana and me all kinds of wigs and makeup and taught us how to change our looks. Let us contact her or at least go into the same places with her."

"That is more than fine with me," Turner said. "Let's talk after the meeting." After Lana and Jasmine sat down Turner continued. "Wickfield, your wife is hosting some kind of women's club tonight. Two different store owners invited Tessa and she plans to attend. I plan to take her to your home and pick her up."

"Do you think there is something suspicious about that meeting?" Wickfield asked.

"Let me read you the conversation that Tessa overheard in the changing room of The Chicken and The Egg and all of you can decide." After Turner read the note the room was silent for several moments.

"I don't know why but that made me shudder," Harlow said. "Wickfield when we get done here I am going back to the office and look up everything I can find on women's groups, witches and anything else I can think of."

"I usually don't pay much attention to those things," Wickfield said. "Let me find out if they keep attendance records or any kind of records and I believe I will stay at home tonight."

"We had a meeting after dinner last night," Claudius said. "After Nikki read that note to us, of course the women in our family and that includes Ashley want to help. Bella, Isadore and Rosa haven't been ones to go to those kind of clubs. Bella said it was just a bunch of bored women who gossip but now they are going to look into some of them."

"We can't make it too obvious," said Angus.

"They were thinking of starting out by talking to some of their friends who belong to these clubs," Claudius said.

"What the hell can these women be involved in that is so dangerous that the Angels warn us?" asked Fahron.

# Chapter XIX
## Clear Sight

It was with extreme sadness that King Sudfad and Queen Renya led their family members into the streets of Salar. The King and Queen rode side by side, behind them rode Madeline, Nyla, Saran and Nina. Behind these women was the boca which carried Michael's body. Two Wetprian soldiers were in the front seat of the boca. A company of soldiers rode behind it.

For the rest of the caravan, General Bishop alternated large groups of soldiers between the carriages, bocas and civilian riders. He did this so the soldiers could provide the highest level of security in case they were attacked.

Simon and Raul were wearing their dress uniforms and waited for the caravan at the eastern edge of the city. The Princes took their places behind their parents. When Nina saw her brothers she started to sob.

Everyone in the caravan was shocked except for Raul and Simon as they rode down the streets. There was no shouting or applause. The streets were filled with people, as were every doorway and balcony. Everyone was silent and the vast majority of citizens wore black clothing. Flowers were everywhere to be seen as were thousands of black ribbons. Soldiers lined the streets; they wore their finest uniforms and stood at attention.

"This is almost worse," Nyla said and started to cry.

The lines of spectators spread from the city to the castle gates. Crowds swarmed around the castle and they all stood in silence. Trumpets were blown to announce the arrival of the caravan. Vitomas and Annabelle represented the Royal Family and they stood on the platform at the top of the steps of the castle where Sudfad and Renya traditionally stood to welcome their guests. Both princesses wore black dresses and black veils.

Many people in the caravan were crying by time they entered the courtyard of the castle. Sudfad dismounted then helped Renya from her horse. They walked up the stairs and stood on the platform with Vitomas and Annabelle.

"The sadness in our hearts is lightened by all of you," Sudfad announced to the crowd. Those who were closest could see that the King was crying. Raul and Simon now dismounted and ran up the steps to the platform. Raul addressed the crowd.

"Our family is overwhelmed with grief. We cannot thank you enough for your kindness during this time. Because we are so emotional we do not have the normal musicians and refreshments set up on the castle grounds but we have provided them in the city. There are signs announcing the areas; please enjoy yourselves."

"The showing will start at dawn tomorrow. It will be held in the chapel at the Learning Center. All are welcome. The funeral will be the following day but that will be for family and close friends only. Thank you all again."

As soon as Raul finished speaking he and Simon walked back down the steps and helped their sisters and Madeline from their horses. Everyone was crying. Raul carried Nina and put his other arm around Madeline. Nyla and Saran were holding hands with Simon. Vitomas and Annabelle led Sudfad and Renya into the castle.

Once the Royal Family entered the castle, Archetenus and Jared worked with the commanding officers in the caravan to assign barracks and duties to the soldiers. Delilah, Zoya and Gala directed guests to their chambers.

King Manu ordered the army of Ruala warriors who had been flying over the caravan to fly over the city and castle grounds before going to their chambers.

Alexander and Laurel directed the soldiers who removed Michael's body from the boca and carried it into the castle. The body was placed in the exquisite coffin which Alexander had built. The coffin was placed upon strong supports in the chambers that had been prepared.

The chambers were filled with flowers and candles and on a table next to the casket sat a miniature house, complete with furnishings.

Edward, Kate and Javier were all brought into the castle and put into temporary chambers on the first floor of the center wing. The castle was filled with members of the Credo who were helping with all of the duties. None of them had ever witnessed the ceremonies involved with a royal funeral but they wanted desperately to help.

"Javier, I don't think this is a good idea," scolded Corsa as Alex and Kent helped their brother-in-law to walk to Edward's chambers. Even though Edward and Javier had been riding inside of bocas they could see out of the open doors of the wagons. Both men were touched by the love and respect the citizens of Salar showed to Sudfad's family.

The Royal Family was gathered in their family parlor with close friends. Luca and Natalie had previously brought all of the family pets to the castle so that the children of Gabriel's household would be content to stay at the castle after their trip. Now the hallways were filled with laughing children and barking dogs. The adults welcomed the sound of laugher.

"Javier what are you doing?" asked Madeline and quickly ran to her brother as Kent and Alex were helping him into the parlor. Maxwell and Calen grabbed chairs as Gabriel and Raphael helped Edward into the room and George helped Kate.

"I told them to stay in bed," Corsa announced with frustration. "None of them should be walking around."

"This may not be the best time but we want to talk with you," Edward said as he sat down. "We want to attend the funeral but since we are supposed to be dead we want to make sure that our appearances don't put anyone in danger."

Gabriel looked at Raul and Simon and said, "We put out word that they were dead to protect them from more assaults until they were on their feet."

"We know," said Simon. "While we understand the sentiment, neither of you look like you could stand that long."

"We'll help them," Nina said and climbed onto Javier's lap.

"It's the three of you I would worry about," Sudfad said as he walked up to them.

"He was family and a friend," Javier said. "It is the very least we can do."

"Matthew send someone for our tailor, Javier and Edward will need uniforms. Kate do you want a new dress made?"

"No but thank you," Kate said.

As Matthew started to walk out of the parlor Sudfad said, "Wait. Does anyone else need a uniform or outfit?" Alex, you and your brothers will need something. You can choose if you want suits or the uniforms of our military."

"But we aren't even enrolled in school yet," said Kent.

"That doesn't matter, you are family now," Sudfad said. "For those of you who may not know each other, these are Corsa's brothers Alex, Kent and George and this is Raul and his lovely wife Vitomas, Simon and his lovely wife Annabelle, her parents Laurel and Alexander. This is our son Petra and his friend Kyra."

After everyone was done shaking hands, Raul said. "Matthew before you leave why don't we all go to the chambers that we prepared for Michael, we have something to show you."

The chambers were two doors down the hallway from the parlor. Petra and Kyra ran ahead of everyone else. Once everyone from the parlor was in the chambers Simon closed the door and said, "Alexander built that beautiful coffin."

"There are Angels carved on it," Saran said excitedly.

"He did a wonderful job but this is what we want to show you," Raul said and pointed to the miniature house that Petra and Kyra were standing next to. "Simon and I had lessons to learn."

"Look," Nina said with awe and walked up to the house.

"I don't understand," Renya said as Madeline started to cry loudly. Javier put his arms around his sister.

"Miranda paid us a visit," Raul explained. "She told Simon and me that we were filled with guilt because we never took the time to get to know Michael even though our wives kept telling us to. She told us not to make the same mistakes again. Then she said that Petra and Kyra made Michael feel loved and welcomed and she asked us where they were."

"Simon and I got scared because we hadn't remembered seeing them since we told them about Michael days earlier. When we found them they were in a barn starting to build this house. You two tell the rest," Raul said and looked at Petra and Kyra.

"We spent a lot of time with Michael and he would help us with our pets," Petra said proudly. "He told us that when he was in that cage that he would dream about a home so he didn't have to think about being hurt and cold and hungry. He told us a lot of times what that home looked like. So we finally wanted him to have it. We're going to put it on his grave."

Every adult in that room was crying or had tears in their eyes as they walked up to the house to look at it. "Renya, Sudfad there is a reason that Madeline is crying so hard," Javier said as he continued to hold his sister. "While we have many mansions as part of our disguises, our real home is a little cottage we share by the Sea of Grevdt. Our cottage resembles this house greatly. We were going to take Michael there but he never saw it."

Sorren and his warriors found Grant that previous evening. After learning that Tresdor was back in Langer they decided to make camp. While they were eating Grant told them everything he had seen and heard since leaving the Village of Tyger. He also told them about Miranda healing him and his questions and concerns about the note and Martiz.

Sorren started to chuckle. "What is so funny?" asked Grant as he could not see the humor in anything he had said.

"I think I am beginning to understand," said Sorren.

"Understand what?"

"How the Angels work. Think about it. You went to those caves because of that note, then you called to the Angels and look at all the people who were saved. It's like when we went to Port Friada. We did it because of a letter that the real Harlow didn't even write and we saved a lot of people. I'll bet you a bottle of whiskey that when we get to that hospital tomorrow we find out that Martiz doesn't even exist."

"What! I saw her."

"I'll bet that was the Angel Ruth. Just you wait."

The following morning as Sudfad and Renya were leading the caravan into Salar, Grant and Sorren were walking into the newly built hospital north of Minges.

"We need to see the lepers who were brought in yesterday," Sorren told a healer who led the men to one huge room that had rows of beds on both sides of the rooms. Long white drapes separated the beds.

Sorren and Grant walked around the room and spoke to each patient. They had previously counted out the coins in Raven's pouch and handed five coins to each patient.

"I swear all of you are looking better already," Grant said with a huge smile. "Where is Martiz?" As Grant asked this question Sorren looked at him and grinned.

"Martiz died," said one of the women emotionally.

"What! When? This morning?" Grant asked.

"My Lord may I ask how you know Martiz?" asked one of the male patients.

"She wrote the note that led us to finding you. She took us to you and that altar," Grant said.

"When was this?" asked the same man.

"Yesterday. I talked to her myself."

"My Lord, Martiz died three days ago," one of the female patients said.

Tresdor did not initially realize that Bertuck had transported him and his horse back to Langer. All Tresdor knew was that he was riding south and suddenly felt really sick and when he felt better, he was riding down a street in Langer. As if this transition didn't fill him with fear, he became terrified when he saw all of the soldiers in the streets. Tresdor knew that he could clearly be seen by all of them.

The morning of the public showing, the Royal Family took Michael's body to the chapel. The Sanuri led a small service then the family left. Since this showing was scheduled to be so much longer than the one in Lentz, the Royal Family was not going to be standing behind the casket. Instead, the casket was surrounded by an honor guard of soldiers. The miniature house was not on display.

"You are never going to make it through that service, you're going to pass out," Corsa said angrily.

"Then I will pass out," Javier said as two tailors were measuring him. A team of tailors and seamstresses were at the castle making suits, uniforms and dresses. Instead of complaining because they were called in at the last minute, most felt good that they could do something to help the Royal Family.

Ibula and Thedes relieved Raul, Simon, Vitomas and Annabelle of many of their duties so they could spend more time with their parents.

After the family returned from the chapel, Sudfad handed out the remainder of the jewelry that Michael had purchased for the family members in his wedding. The women, including Kyra received necklaces and the men received cufflinks and tie bars.

Saran told everyone about the pact that was made concerning the necklaces. All of the women now put on their necklaces and promised never to forget Michael.

Thousands of people from all over the continent attended the showing. The line outside of the castle gates had started to form almost immediately after the caravan arrived the previous day. It extended for miles.

Raul and Simon had tables of refreshments set up in and outside of the castle wall. They were concerned that the people would need sustenance.

Soldiers directed the visitors to the chapel then later out of the back gate of the castle wall. The soldiers hastily set up tables when they realized that the majority of visitors had brought flowers, candles or gifts. Ruala warriors, Enrops and Florines constantly flew over the castle grounds and the City of Salar. All of the students who were studying to become Patronus priests infiltrated the crowds to look for threats.

"Are you sure the King said that?" Alex asked the tailors repeatedly.

"My Lord, you may ask him yourself if you don't believe me," said one of the tailors.

"I am sorry, I didn't mean to insult you," Alex said. "We just didn't expect anything like this."

Simon and Raul walked into the room that the tailors were using for the fittings. "Ask them," said the tailor.

"Did Sudfad really tell them to make us entire wardrobes?" Alex asked.

"Well, you are part of the family now and we have a lot of ceremonies and responsibilities where you need to wear certain outfits. Other than those you can dress however you want. We decided that we want all of you in the military dress uniforms for the funeral. And that includes everyone not just the three of you."

"I'm kind of nervous," George said as he was being measured.

"You don't need to do anything but follow the casket out of the chapel and stand near Edward and Javier. We have bets on which one of them passes out first," Simon said with a grin.

"Do you really?" asked George.

"If you do, I'm putting money on Javier," Kent said and chuckled.

Corsa suddenly appeared in the open doorway of the room, she was crying and couldn't speak. "Is Javier alright?" asked Alex. Corsa nodded and handed the letter in her hand to Raul who was standing the closest to her. He quickly read the words and asked everyone but Corsa's brothers and Simon to leave the room.

"Corsa, what is it?" asked Kent.

"I can't even say it," Corsa said in a whisper. Raul handed the letter to Alex who turned pale then bright red as he read Sorren's words about how their father had been a traitor to their people.

"Is Father dead?" asked George.

"Yes, but that is the only good news," Alex said and handed the letter to Kent.

"Will someone tell us," George said with frustration.

"Raul you say it," whispered Corsa.

"That letter is from Sorren. They have been searching for the people behind the attacks. Some of Javier's old gang found a soldier of Usman who told of two traitors in the Nordes Tribe. Your father and a woman named Raven have been selling information to Usman's soldiers for years. You can read the rest," said Raul then turned to Corsa, "Did you show Father, Matthew or Angelina this?"

"Not yet," she said as tears ran down her cheeks.

"We need to show them," Raul said. "Simon and I will go with you."

George started crying. "I'm not crying because Dirk is dead," he said defensively.

"We know," said Alex. "We are all filled with shame."

"Has Javier seen this?" asked Kent.

"No, he just fell asleep and I don't want to wake him," Corsa said as she walked up to her brothers and hugged each one of them.

Kent looked at Simon and Raul and said, "Corsa brought Javier home and he had wonderful gifts for all of us. He talked to each one of us and it was like he could see into our minds. He's the one that saw the real evil in Dirk and he predicted that Dirk would sell us all out. But everyone was thinking he would betray the mission. We never realized he had been selling out our people for years."

"People have died because of him," Alex said angrily.

Simon was the last one in the room to read the letter. "I hope all of you read the ending," Simon said. "Sorren says several times that Dirk's actions will not reflect on any of you. That everyone in the tribe knows you are all warriors and people of honor."

"We read that but it doesn't really help," said Alex.

Within the next hour, Corsa, her brothers, Raul and Simon talked with many people in the castle about the letter. Raul sent a soldier to Gabriel's home to get him since everyone realized that Dirk could have compromised more than what Sorren had written about.

Corsa, Alex and Kent were filled with shame and repeatedly apologized to everyone. George didn't say a word, he just cried. Renya found her daughters and Madeline in the chambers that had been set up for Michael; they were all looking at the miniature house.

"Girls, Corsa and her brothers just received some devastating news. Madeline, they are in the Great Hall; you should go in there and read the letter that Sorren sent to them."

"Saran, Nyla and Nina, George is very upset and could use a friend right now. He might be too ashamed to tell you what happened but he might really appreciate the company."

"Is it alright if we take him to our chambers?" asked Nyla. "Because there are just so many people everywhere."

"That is fine and thank you for asking," Renya said. "I am sure that you could find some milk and cookies in the kitchen to take to your chambers too."

"Is he in the Great Hall?" asked Saran.

"Yes," said Renya.

"I'll get the milk and cookies," Nyla said. "You get George and I will meet you in our rooms."

Madeline, Renya, Saran and Nina walked to the Great Hall. The women stood in the doorway and watched Saran and Nina walk up to George. None of the children spoke. Saran and Nina each took one of his hands and the three walked out of the room.

"Is their father dead?" asked Madeline.

"Yes, but that is not why they are all crying," Renya said and took Madeline's hand and they walked up to the group of people. Matthew handed the letter to Madeline to read.

Angelina had her arms around Corsa who was crying. "We never knew," Corsa repeated.

"Of course you didn't," said Angelina. "All of you would have stopped him. We know that. Father didn't just say those words in the letter. The entire tribe knows that none of you are like Dirk. They tolerated him because they respect all of you."

"I am so sorry," Madeline said after she finished reading the letter.

"We haven't shown it to Javier yet," said Kent. "He is the only one who saw that in him. Javier said he would betray us."

# Chapter XX
## Diversions

Few people in the castle of Sudfad slept that night. Tailors and seamstresses worked through the night to create the uniforms to be worn at the funeral. The kitchen was filled with people who were preparing food for the feast that would be held after the funeral.

Soldiers and warriors were constantly searching the areas for any signs of threats. Friends and family members talked with and comforted each other.

At one point in the night, Renya, Sudfad and Alex went to the chambers of Nyla, Saran and Nina to check on the children. Dogs whined and wagged their tails when Sudfad opened the door. Petra and Kyra were also in the parlor of the chambers which was filled with plates, glasses and dogs. All of the children were sleeping either in chairs or on the floor.

George was sleeping in a chair with a puppy snuggled beside him. Alex started to enter the room to wake him. "Leave him," Sudfad whispered. "He is alright."

Tresdor was terrified and didn't know where to hide so he went to the Catacombs. Turner and Tessa were frequenting establishments in the City of Langer while the rest of his team worked in the dens that were underneath the city.

Earlier in the evening Tessa had gone to the meeting at Wickfield's home. Hours before the meeting started Wickfield had shared Tessa's note with his wife Elizabeth who was horrified at what she read. Elizabeth immediately contacted her close friend Maggie, who was the wife of Mayor Tetly and these two women decided to help with the mission.

The meeting started out as Tessa had imagined it would. Most of the women talked about their families and little else of interest to her. Elizabeth personally took Tessa around the room and made introductions. "Watch their faces when I stand up and talk," Elizabeth whispered to Tessa.

Once the business portion of the meeting started, Elizabeth and Maggie walked to the front of the room.

"We have a surprise for you and we hope that all of you will be as excited as Maggie and I are. You all know how my husband loves to buy things," Elizabeth said with a big smile. "Well, he out did himself this time. He bought me a building and said I could turn it into whatever I wanted. Well, as you can imagine I made lists of all sorts of ideas. Then I told Maggie and she of course came up with the perfect idea."

"I am turning it into a museum. And the first area we are going to put together will be a history of the women of this city. There are many exhibits that showcase the men but nothing about our mothers, grandmothers and others who worked and died to make this great city what it is." The women were clapping before Elizabeth finished speaking.

"And of course part of the display will be our societies that have donated so much to this city and made it strong. So we will need donations of items for the displays. Maggie put some sheets on the front table and I would ask you to sign up for the different committees."

"I will start on the administrative part which I assume will be boring but I also believe it to be crucial to the accuracy of the museum. Please bring me any and all paperwork and ledgers from the societies. And we will need names of members. If you can remember if your grandmother belonged to a particular society please write it down and give it to me because I want to honor them all." The women clapped loudly again and many stood up to show their approval of Elizabeth's ideas.

Maggie now spoke, "We want this museum to be a reflection of all of us and our ancestors. And in order to provide accuracy Elizabeth and I believe we will need the help of women who do not belong to our societies. So please bring your friends, family and neighbors to the meetings and ask them for things for the museum. Even if the people don't want the items displayed, if they will just show them to us it will help immensely."

Tessa watched the faces in the room and did not see anything that she felt was suspicious.

As Tessa and Turner had a drink at the White Rose Restaurant she told him about the meeting. "Actually, I was very surprised at their ingenuity," Tessa said. "But it will take some time for them to gather things."

"Yes but now Claudius' and Fahron's families and others can attend those meetings without raising suspicions. It is a clever idea. Speaking of which, where do you want to meet up with Jasmine and Lana?"

"Do they have to go to the meeting first?"

"I don't know but at least the first day they probably will because I didn't tell them where to meet you."

"How about that bakery on Ninth Street at say, ten o'clock."

"They are going to draw rose tattoos on their arms so that you recognize them."

"This might be fun," Tessa said and took a sip of her wine. "Did you mail my letters today?"

"I gave them to the King."

"Now that all of you have bounties on your heads," Tessa said in a whisper. "What are you going to do when this job is over?"

"Well, Mathas has already offered to hire us. And before Javier was shot, Gabriel was going to offer him and Madeline their own teams. Of course we would prefer to work with them. You are welcome to stay and work with us."

"I will have to think about that. I would like to visit Madeline and Javier before I make any decisions."

"You know that this is the city that Noah's team is assigned to," Turner said with a grin. "I can't believe you are blushing. I can't remember the last time I saw you blush." Tessa laughed and took another sip of her wine.

Tresdor was walking through the Catacombs in his soiled clothing. It was one of the few environments where people did not take notice.

While the streets above were filled with soldiers, the Catacombs were not. But they were filled with sailors and Patronus priests who were all dressed like civilians. Bart was the second in charge of what was now, a small group of the Charto. Since they had bounties on them, Bart wanted to keep his men together as they worked in the dens. Their assignment was to find out any information about threats to the city and, or the Royal Family.

Almost as soon as Bart and his men sat down in the den run by Tally and Drake, Tally walked up to the table with a bottle of whiskey and glasses.

"Can we buy you one?" Bart asked loudly.

"Don't mind if I do," Tally said and sat down at the table. "Things are too damn quiet," he whispered. "We've been checking with our people and no one has heard a thing. And we haven't seen even one of Hector's men in the place. I've beginning to wonder if people are getting out of here."

"I think it is the soldiers keeping them out," said Garvis. "Before the armada attack these dens were damn near empty. So what you've got down here now are guys who are hiding from the soldiers and people who don't have anything to hide."

"Do me a favor will ya?" asked Tally.

"Sure," said Bart.

"Just stop in and check on Hilgra at some point. Her shop is so far from the rest of us."

"We'll do that next."

Drake walked up to the table and said loudly, "If your socializing is over I could use some help."

"Sure," said Tally and stood up. All the men at the table understood that Drake really didn't come to the table to make Tally work.

"Finish my whiskey then, you damn bastard," Tally said and left the table.

Drake sat in Tally's chair. "One of my informants said that Tresdor is walking around down here. He looks like hell and is filthy. All I know is he is a little guy with dark hair and a red shirt."

"Well, the red shirt should help us," Bart said.

Drake gulped down Tally's drink and left the table. Bart and his men had another drink and left the den ten minutes later. Once they left the den they walked the length of the Catacombs to Hilgra's shop. Since the shop was filled with people, Bart bought some herbs and whispered to Hilgra about Tresdor. The group left and proceeded to search the dens.

Tessa and Turner left the White Rose Restaurant and leisurely walked down the streets to the Excelsor Hotel. They walked arm in arm and laughed frequently but nothing missed their gazes.

"Doesn't it seem awfully quiet to you?" he asked. "And I don't think it is because of the soldiers."

Tessa didn't say anything, she kept looking at their surroundings. After a few moments she whispered, "This is like the calm before the storm. I don't like it."

As they continued to walk Turner realized, "Tessa all of the street people are gone."

"What?"

"You know the musicians and people who stand on the corners. They are always out here no matter what time it is."

They walked another two blocks when Turner heard someone call his name. He looked down an alley and saw Sol and Ralf standing on the ground and motioning to him. He and Tessa looked around to see if anyone was watching them and walked into the alley.

Bart and his men were just leaving the eighth den they had searched when they heard what sounded like a fight. They followed the sounds which led them off the main street of the Catacombs.

"Help me! Help me!" a voice was screaming. Bart and his men pushed through a small crowd who were looking at a man who was standing in the alley and screaming. It appeared that the man's body was breaking open and green snakes were coming out. The man was wearing a red shirt. The crowd stared at him in horror. The snakes were slithering down his body and crawling on the ground. Then the man's body started to smoke.

"Miranda," Bart uttered but it didn't seem like his voice calling to her.

"Tresdor is the diversion," Bart heard in his ear. The ground started to shake. "Get everyone out of the Catacombs!"

"Out of here now!" yelled Bart. "Everyone out of here! Louis get Hilgra. Garvis get Tally and Drake."

"What the hell are you saying?" asked Louis.

"I don't know but an Angel just talked to me," Bart said then ran down the streets yelling.

"What is going on?" asked Turner.

"We'll tell you on the way," said Sol. "We're taking you to the castle. At that moment the ground shook with tremendous force. Ralf grabbed Tessa and ascended into the night sky. Sol and Turner were right behind them."

"Oh my god this is incredible," gasped Tessa. She paused then screamed, "Turner look!"

"What the hell is that?" asked Turner as he looked down at a form in the darkness.

"The reason we are taking you to the castle," said Sol. "We aren't really sure."

245

The people and demons ran out of the Catacombs. The exodus was hysterical and chaotic, people were hurt and trampled in the process. The ground was shaking with such force now that parts of the Catacombs were crumbling.

When Garvis told Tally and Drake that an Angel told Bart to get everyone out of the Catacombs they too, ran to the dens and yelled for people to leave. Drake ran to the den where his girlfriend, Abigale worked. The den was still filled with people and demons. "Everyone get the hell out of here now!" he yelled and grabbed Abigale's arm and ran out of the den.

As the people entered the streets of Langer they found the same hysteria as people were pouring out of taverns and restaurants and running down the streets.

Claudius and Fahron were riding through the streets yelling to the soldiers to hold their positions.

"You know, Adam, now would be a damn good time to tell us what the hell is going on!" Claudius shouted.

Louis and Hilgra were waiting for their friends near the entrance to the Catacombs. Drake and Abigale found them first. The four pushed through the crowds and yelled for the others. Bart, followed the sounds of their voices and found them. "We're missing Tally and Garvis," Louis said. "I'm giving them five minutes then I am going back in."

"I don't think that is a good idea," Hilgra said fearfully. "Does anyone know what is happening?"

"I am sure we are under some kind of attack," said Bart. "Just don't know what the hell it is."

Cage and Gad, two of the Ruala warriors on Dominic's team landed next to the group. "We need to get all of you back to the castle," said Gad.

246

"Why? What is going on?" asked Bart.

"Wait!" yelled Tally as he and Gravis pushed a demon through the crowd. They had seen the Ruala warriors land and ran to that location. The demon was bleeding and battered. He had obvious burn marks on him. "Finally found a good use for these crystals," Tally said to the group then he yelled at the demon, "Tell them!"

The demon started to laugh. "Miranda," yelled Bart. Suddenly the demon's skin started to smoke.

"What is happening?" asked Abigale as she clung to Drake's arm.

"An Angel is here," said Hilgra. "Her holiness is affecting the demon."

"Bertuck is getting his revenge," the demon said and tried to smirk.

"For what?" yelled Drake.

"Usman promised him the souls of this kingdom."

"Oh there is a lot more to this," Bart said. "You tell us and we will let you go. Tell us!" The demon was a low level demon who did not have the power to change his appearance or to fight against the holy energy in the crystals from the Ice Caves that many in the group were wearing. And he certainly did not have the power to stand against an Angel.

"Ok, ok, I'll tell you. But you've got to move me back before I burst into flames," said the demon frantically. Tally and Garvis pulled the demon backwards several feet. "Bertuck has entered the Gefrey Games. Samael is changing the rules since so many are trying to enter. He is making them pay to play. Bertuck has made promises but each time he has been humiliated by humans and their Angels."

"So what is he after?" asked Bart. Before the demon spoke, Bart's eyes widened. "Who does Bertuck think are The Seven Sons?"

"Seriously pull me back some more," the demon yelled. Garvis and Tally moved him backwards a few more feet.

"Who!" yelled Bart.

"The sons of Claudius," the demon said.

"You two take Hilgra and Abigale and tell Mathas," said Drake to Cage and Gad. "Miranda where are Thaos and Stephan?"

"What would be a better question?" Miranda asked although she did not appear.

"Hell if I know," Drake spat.

"You're talking to an Angel you moron!" Tally yelled. "He didn't mean to talk to you like that," Tally said to Miranda as he looked around for any sign of her. "You know we aren't so good at these things. Maybe you could help us with the words."

"I apologize," said Drake. "What do you need us to do?"

"Tell Claudius and Fahron; they are but blocks north of you." Miranda said. Immediately the group started to run.

"Anything else?" Bart yelled.

"For now, just find them," said Miranda.

"Angels, Angels," shrieked Tessa. "What is that monster?"

Ralf, Sol, Turner and Tessa all heard Adam's voice, "A diversion."

"For what?" yelled Turner. Adam didn't answer.

"Why aren't you answering him?" yelled Tessa. "You better not be leaving me again Adam. What are we supposed to do?" Adam still did not answer. "Is Noah in danger?"

"You're all in danger," Adam said.

Tessa looked at Turner and asked angrily, "Do Angels always talk like that?"

"You think I know?" he replied.

"Adam are you playing games with us because this isn't funny," shrieked Tessa.

"You're talking to an Angel," Sol scolded.

"Well, you've got to be holier than me," Tessa snapped at Sol. "You ask him."

"Ask him what? Besides you know he can hear you," Sol said.

"Ask him what he wants us to do," said Tessa with frustration. "Why is it so hard to get him to talk to us? And they scolded me because I didn't call to them. They don't answer!"

"The demons are going after The Seven Sons," Turner said. "But, they aren't here so who do they think..."

"Stephan and Thaos," Ralf said and he and Sol sped up.

"You talked to him and not me!" Tessa screamed at Adam. "We are having a talk when this is all over."

"Do you really understand you are yelling at an Angel?" asked Ralf.

"Oh, all of you damn men are the same," Tessa said angrily and folded her arms across her chest.

"Claudius! Claudius!" Drake yelled as the General was riding through the congested streets of the city. "Claudius!" Claudius stopped his horse and looked around when he heard his name called. "Claudius!" Drake yelled again and waved his arms. Claudius saw him and rode to the group.

"We don't have time to tell you everything," Drake said. "But the demon Bertuck is going after Thaos and Stephan, he thinks they are The Seven Sons. All the rest of this is diversions."

"Adam protect my sons!" Claudius yelled. The crowd parted as Claudius charged his horse through the people.

"Adam, Miranda will someone tell us where Stephan and Thaos are so we can help them?" Tally yelled.

"Others need your help right now," Miranda said. "But you will have to run towards the monster."

"Fine," said Tally "Which way?"

"Keep going north."

"What are we looking for?" asked Bart.

"Trust me, you will know when you see it."

Ralf and Sol landed in the courtyard of Mathas' castle, they set Tessa and Turner on their feet and all four ran inside. They ran to the study which was empty then they turned and ran towards the Great Hall.

"Mathas! Mathas!" yelled Turner as they ran.

Soldiers ran into the hallway. "Where is the King?" yelled Sol.

"In the Great Hall," one of the soldiers replied. Sol and his companions never slowed down they sped past the soldiers and ran into the Great Hall which was filled with people.

Mathas had heard them screaming his name and was walking towards the doorway. "Mathas, the demons are after Thaos and Stephan; they think they are The Seven Sons," Turner yelled.

"Damn it! I just sent them out," Mathas said then turned to one of the soldiers. "Lieutenant, find them and tell them." The Lieutenant ran out of the castle.

"Everything that is happening in the city are diversions," Turner told the King.

"What is happening? Do you know?"

"There is some kind of monster on the loose but Adam won't tell us what the hell it is," barked Tessa then she paused. "I didn't mean to yell at you, My Lord. I am sorry."

"Mathas if you have a map of the city we can show you what we saw," Turner said.

"Holy Shit!" said Louis and the group slowed down.

"That kind of looks like that snake we fought in Inferus," Tally said. "Only bigger."

The men looked at the monster that was moving down the street then they quickly looked around the area they were in.

"Damn it!" Drake said. "This whole damn block is Adam's Homes."

"What are Adam's Homes?" asked Garvis.

"Orphans," Tally said. "Why don't Drake and me be a diversion while the rest of you get all of those kids out of here."

"And just where are we supposed to take them?" Louis asked. "That thing will be here before we get them all out anyways."

"Miranda how do we save those little kids?" Tally asked.

"For your courage you will receive a gift this night," Miranda said as she appeared among the men. The men were filled with both fear and awe. "What in your world kills snakes?"

"Eagles," Drake said meekly. He was considerably more intimidated by seeing Miranda than he was by merely hearing her voice.

"These are Blue Hengers, the ancient war birds of the heavens," Miranda explained. The men watched as the sky filled with giant blue eagles that attacked the snake. "There are other such monsters in these streets and the Hengers will destroy them."

Miranda was looking at the Hengers and now turned and stared at the men who became weak from her gaze. "I am real sorry for yelling at you before," Drake said.

Miranda did not acknowledge his comment. "Why do you think an Angel stands before you this night?" she asked and the men shook with fear.

251

After what seemed to the men like a very log moment Drake said, "I know. It's what Ingr and Nikki said. It's cuz we were doing the right thing."

"And what else did they say to you that night?" asked Miranda sternly.

"That if I betrayed them or acted like a criminal they would kill me."

"All of you have led the lives of criminals. Until recently you have ignored the voices of the Angels and The Great Ruler when we have tried to talk to you. Why are you calling to us now?"

"Because we're working with the teams?" Tally said as more of a question than a comment.

"Every one of you has been making some good choices lately but don't let your rage and hatred because of the attacks turn you into monsters again. If you allow yourselves to be filled with darkness then the demons have won."

"The people you work with have many long and horrible battles ahead of them to keep the demons from conquering this world. And while none of you believe it, they need you. You all possess skills and knowledge that are essential for these missions. But you can't help them or anyone else if you allow yourselves to turn into monsters. You have choices to make and I would suggest that you make them quickly."

Miranda swung around so quickly and looked at Louis that he fell backwards. "Say what you are thinking so the others can hear."

"The Angels and The Great Ruler aren't in our world..." Louis did not complete his sentence.

"We are in every world but the people of your world turn us away. When a child called us in, look at the miracles that happened. Tally, Drake later you tell all of this group about your time in Inferus."

"I am not making excuses," Louis said defensively. "We don't know you."

"And yet you fight alongside priests," Miranda said. "Perhaps it is time for all of you to talk about more than the current mission."

"I am confused," said Bart. "Do we need to have those talks before we make choices?"

"It would help. But now you need to return to Mathas' castle. You have one more choice to make this night. You can return to the castle safely or you can take the old country road that Thaos and Stephan are traveling."

"Our horses are on the other side of the city; do we have time to get them?" asked Bart.

"I believe your faithful companions followed you here," Miranda said and disappeared. The men turned around and saw their horses standing in the middle of the road. They quickly mounted and rode towards the old country road.

"She was so beautiful but she just scared the hell out of me," Garvis said. No one else said a word.

# Chapter XXI
## Ambush

Thaos and Stephan were leading troops into the City of Langer as reinforcements for Claudius and Fahron. Dominic's team also rode with the sons of Claudius.

Claudius jumped from his horse before it stopped and ran into the Great Hall of Mathas' castle. "Where are Thaos and Stephan?" he bellowed as he entered the room.

"I sent them in as reinforcements," Mathas said. "You should have passed them."

"What! The demons are after them, they think they are The Seven Sons. How long ago did they leave?"

"Maybe twenty minutes," Mathas said. "Turner told us the same thing so I sent Lieutenant Anderson after them."

"They must have taken the old country road," Claudius said and ran out of the hall.

"It's too quiet," Jasmine said. "Something isn't right."

"I was just thinking the same thing," Noah said as they rode in the back of the formation. "I am going to ride to the front and find out if anything is going on."

"Noah!" screamed Jasmine as she watched her friend fall forward in his saddle with an arrow in his right shoulder blade. She screamed the Nordes war cry as she pulled her sword from its sheath on her saddle.

"Form a circle! Form a circle!" Stephan yelled as his horse was rearing up because it was frightened by the barrage of Huta arrows that were being shot at the soldiers.

Huta war cries filled the air as hundreds of Huta soldiers charged the troops. The ambush happened so quickly that Thaos and Stephan did not have time to get their archers into position.

The soldiers of Lentz grabbed their swords and battle axes as the army of Hutas was upon them.

Ralf, Sol and the majority of Ruala warriors who were assigned to Dominic's, Edward's and Angus's teams were riding with Lieutenant Anderson and the five hundred troops that he led. Sol was flying a considerable distance in front of the rest. When he heard the war cries he yelled the war cry of his people and sped ahead. The other Ruala warriors followed him.

When Anderson heard the Rualas scream their war cry he knew there must be a battle ahead. He ordered the Horn of Shana to be blown then Anderson yelled, "Charge!"

Drake, Tally, Bart, Louis and Garvis too, heard the war cries and charged towards the sounds of battle. But because they were coming from the City of Langer and not the castle they saw something the others did not. There was a great chasm that now ran horizontally across the road. A pungent, grayish fog was coming out and covering the land. Drake dismounted and crept to the edge of the chasm because they were all hearing sounds from below.

Tally held Drake's horse. He and his companions had their weapons pulled but sat motionless as they watched Drake. The sounds of drums and voices were floating upwards from out of the chasm. Drake was now crawling on his stomach. He expected to see a hell world when he looked into the chasm but what he saw surprised him more.

Drake was looking downwards into a huge cavern. There was a giant fire in the middle of the cavern and hundreds of Huta soldiers dancing around it. They screamed and hit each other as they were trying to work themselves into a frenzy. There were giant shadows on the stone walls. Drake gasped when he realized that the shadows were not moving but the Hutas were.

Suddenly some of the smoke cleared and Drake realized that people were shackled to the walls. He blinked and looked again and the shackles hung empty from the walls. The Hutas stopped dancing and became eerily quiet. Drake did not understand why fear shot through his body at that moment.

The army of Hutas parted as people wearing dark robes walked through the throng and to the huge fire. Five people wore the robes. When they reached the fire they all turned and faced the Hutas. One of them stepped forward a few steps and was holding a book. Drake couldn't hear what was being said but it looked to him like the person was reading to the Hutas.

One by one, the four people standing behind the reader removed their robes and let them drop to the ground. Four naked women now stood behind the reader and in front of an army of Hutas. The Hutas remained silent, which surprised Drake.

The reader raised his arms into the air and yelled then he quickly turned and faced the women who in sequence jumped into the fire. The Hutas started to scream and yell their war cries. Suddenly the reader looked upwards at Drake. Drake threw himself backwards and the chasm closed.

"Damn!" Drake kept repeating as he ran to his horse.

"What did you see?" asked Tally.

"I'm not really sure but it scared the hell out of me," Drake said. The five men rode forward and checked the ground where they had seen the chasm. Bart crossed the area first and the rest followed. They sped towards the sounds of battle.

Claudius was riding alone as he raced to find his sons. "Angels protect them," he repeated until it became a fearful mantra.

"Whoa," he yelled and pulled the reigns tight as he saw the image of Usman in the road. The image did not speak, it simply glared at him.

"You're a damn illusion," Claudius yelled and rode his horse through the image which now disappeared.

"Why would Bertuck try to keep me separate from my sons?" Claudius asked himself out loud. As he realized the answer to his question he resumed his mantra.

Seth found Jasmine in the melee and fought at her side. Chaez and Lana fought back to back. Fennel, Dominic and Lawrence formed a triangle around Noah and kept the Hutas off from him.

Stephan and Thaos thought they were imagining the fact that the Hutas were not charging at them. Neither man realized the reason; they were both embroiled in battle.

The Ruala warriors were the first reinforcements to arrive. They launched their aerial assaults on the rear of the Huta army because both sides were on the ground and fighting hand to hand. The Ruala warriors were afraid they would shoot their comrades if they aimed at the Hutas in the front of the battle.

Drake and his group arrived on the scene shortly after the Ruala warriors; all five of these men stayed together and looked for Thaos and Stephen.

"Get behind us," yelled Tally as he and his group surrounded Thaos and Stephan, who were on foot. "Where are your horses?"

"What are you doing?" yelled Thaos.

"This whole damn thing is a plot to get you two," Bart yelled. "Some demon thinks you are some of The Seven Sons."

Garvis left the group and returned a few minutes later leading two horses by their reins. "Mount up!" he yelled.

"Those aren't our horses," yelled Stephan.

"Don't really give a shit," yelled Garvis, "Get on the damn things!"

"That must be why the Hutas aren't coming after us," Thaos said as he mounted one of the horses.

"That just means something else is," Drake said. "And we've seen our share of monsters tonight. The Horn of Shana was heard announcing the arrival of more troops. "We'll let them other guys fight," Drake yelled. "We're protecting you two assholes." Stephan laughed.

257

Noah had fallen from his horse when he was shot. He hit his head on a rock and lost consciousness for several minutes. The sounds of battle forced him awake. He tried to jump up but grabbed his head because everything was spinning and he felt like he would puke. Noah felt the warm and sticky blood on the left side of his head.

"Stay down," yelled Fennel.

"No," snapped Noah but he didn't stand up. "As soon as I can see I am going to fight."

Dominic grinned at the comment and thrust his sword through the chest of a Huta soldier.

The citizens of Langer ran and hid as the loud screeches of the Hengers and the bellowing of the demonic snakes terrified them. No one sought to fight with the soldiers guarding the streets. Fahron had not heard the information about the threats to Thaos and Stephan. He did not know that Claudius had left the city and he certainly didn't know that his eldest son was fighting for his life just a few miles away.

Fahron did know that someone must have called to the Angels for the Hengers to be battling the snakes. As he rode through the streets he was overwhelmed with a sense of uneasiness. Then he realized the snakes were not the real threat but a diversion. "Miranda, Miranda what is really being attacked?"

"Your family and friends just a few miles outside of the city on the old country road." Fahron took two companies of soldiers and they raced down the old country road. They did not travel far before they heard the sounds of battle. "Blow the Horn," Fahron ordered.

In less than three minutes Fahron came upon the battle scene. He ordered his men to surround the Hutas and to attack them from the rear. With these additional troops, the Ruala warriors now landed and fought the Hutas with their hands and knives.

Moments later Claudius rode into the bloody scene. He hacked and stabbed Hutas as he rode through the battleground looking for his sons. What he saw confused him. Thaos and Stephan were on horseback and surrounded by Bart, Tally, Louis, Garvis and Drake. The Hutas seemed oblivious to these men. Claudius now searched the area with his eyes for the real threats.

"Miranda what am I not seeing?" Claudius asked with fear in his voice.

"Bertuck wants to give The Seven Sons to Samael as payment to get into the Gefrey Games. He wants them alive."

"That did not answer my question."

"You have been praying for us to protect your sons and we have."

"I appreciate that but you still haven't answered my question."

"How would you get them off this battlefield?"

Claudius instantly looked up but saw nothing but a starry night sky. "Does the threat come from below?"

"No, it comes from the streets of your city and the homes of your friends."

"I don't understand," Claudius said with great frustration.

"Bertuck knows he lost this battle but that will not stop him from trying again. He is called here by those you know."

"Can I kill him?"

"Not even if I touch you with holiness."

"Who are these people you speak of?"

"When you return to the castle have Gideon help Drake understand what he saw tonight."

"I know there is more to this."

"While there are demons everywhere there are those who walk among you who actively call the demons into your city. And the demons are answering the calls."

"Can't you give us more information?"

"We've already given you a great deal. Have Gideon help Drake remember what he saw."

Although Claudius' conversation with Miranda was brief, by time it ended so had the battle. The soldiers were killing the last of the Hutas and helping their wounded.

"Chaez!" screamed Fahron with such anguish that Claudius looked for them on the battlefield. Lana was covered with blood, her own and Chaez's. She was trying to stop the bleeding from one of Chaez's many knife wounds when Fahron found them. Fahron tore off his uniform shirt and then the lighter shirt he wore underneath. This second shirt he tore into strips for bandages.

Claudius jumped from his horse and immediately tore off his uniform shirt too. He and Fahron never said a word to each other as Fahron and Lana were trying to bandage Chaez's wounds. Claudius ripped the shirt he wore under his uniform into strips and was handing them to Lana when he saw the blood running down her side. "Lana, you're wounded too!" he said sharply.

At that moment Fahron looked up and saw how pale Lana was. "Claudius help her while I finish with him," Fahron said. Claudius gently pulled Lana away from Chaez.

"I just have the one," she said weakly and lifted her left arm exposing a knife wound. Claudius helped her to lie down and he used his shirt to apply pressure to and bandage her wound.

Noah was on his feet before the battle ended. He was guarding Dominic and Fennel who were removing an arrow from Lawrence's right leg.

"It's over," Noah announced to his friends. He was talking about the battle. He was looking over the scene for several minutes. "I don't see Seth or Jasmine," he said with fear in his voice.

Five hours later Noah opened his eyes. He instantly felt sharp pains in his head and shoulder. It took him several moments before the dizziness passed. He knew he was in a bed, but he didn't know where the bed was. He closed his eyes and opened them two more times before he could see clearly. He heard movement and started to jump up.

"Don't!" yelled Tessa who was entering the room with two cups of coffee. "Just lay back down." She set the cups on a table and ran to Noah.

"You fool," she scolded but gently checked his bandages. He didn't say anything but stared at her.

"Are you dizzy?" she asked.

"Are you real?"

Tessa laughed loudly. "If I was a dream, I probably wouldn't be yelling at you. Do you want me to help you sit up?"

"Yeah. Where am I?"

"The King's castle. Everyone is here. Apparently a lot of crazy things happened last night and Mathas isn't letting any of us leave until we have a meeting. Are you hungry?"

"Not yet but that coffee sure smells good."

"I pictured you as a coffee guy," she said as she was piling pillows behind his back. She brought both cups to the bed and handed him one. "You are as white as a sheet. So don't spend a lot of needless energy. I can guess the questions you are going to ask so here goes: Dominic and Fennel have minor wounds, basically nothing. Lawrence was shot in the leg. He will be fine if he doesn't develop infection but the Court Physician wants him in bed for at least two weeks."

"Chaez got stabbed a bunch of times and Lana once but it was pretty bad. Fahron took them to his house. A Huta tried to cut Jasmine's throat, she is fine but Seth hit the guy so hard he broke his right hand. Then Jasmine killed the Huta." She paused.

261

"I am trying to remember the other members of your team. Basically everyone in that battle had some kind of injury. Eighteen soldiers were killed."

"Thank you for that but how do you know so much about my team?"

"I've been sitting with you all night, figured you would want to know. Now, you just drink that coffee and let me tell you the rest. I don't know everything but it sounds like some demon sent giant snakes into the city at the same time that Tresdor exploded into flames with green snakes coming out of him. That happened in the Catacombs where my team and Tally and Drake saw everything."

"Turner and I were in the city and saw the giant snakes, apparently we all called to the Angels about the same time and they told us that everything were diversions. The demon Bertuck thinks Stephen and Thaos are some kind of sons and was going to kidnap them to give to the demon Samael so he could play in some demon Gefrey Games."

"So, now understand there is a whole lot I don't know, mostly because I was in here taking care of you but everyone started going wild looking for Thaos and Stephan. The guys on my team were with Drake and Tally and they somehow stopped one of the snakes from destroying a bunch of homes with orphans. The Angel Miranda helped them then she told them to help all of you because you were fighting the Hutas."

"Now, this part is going to sound really crazy but this is what Turner told me. Bart, Louis, Garvis, Tally and Drake were racing towards the battle on some old country road. They were coming from Langer and all of a sudden the ground opens up before them, like when there is an earthquake. Smoke and the sound of drums were coming out of the opening. So Drake crawled up to it. He was looking in the opening for a while then jumped back and it closed. He hasn't told anyone what he saw but later Claudius talked to Miranda who told him twice to have Gideon help Drake remember. He is going to do that at the meeting."

"I'm going to that meeting. Do you know when it starts?"

"The hell you are. The Physician said you're staying in bed for a week."

Noah grinned. "You're kind of bossy."

"You haven't even started to hear me yet," she said and giggled.

Tessa was sitting in a chair next to Noah's bed and the two looked at each other smiling for several moments before Noah asked, "So why did you stay with me?"

"You're hurt pretty bad."

"Is that the only reason?" he asked then grinned.

"Damn it; what did Turner say to you?"

"Don't get all mad now. He told me you were attracted to me which is great because I am really attracted to you. I just wanted you to know what he told me."

Tessa sat back in her chair and stared at Noah while she sipped her coffee. He was smiling at her because of the look on her face. "Ok, I have a lot of questions," she said. "Until I came here, I've never really talked to any priests before. So can priests go out with girls?"

"So you want to go out with me?"

"Just answer the question."

"First, I am not a priest yet. I am studying to become one and yes. Many of the priests we work with are married and have families. Will you go out with me?"

Tessa set her cup of coffee down and started talking really fast. "I am so glad you said that. All night I have been sitting here looking at you without your shirt on and thinking I was going to hell for having impure thoughts about a priest. Now, I have probably done a lot of things that I will go to hell for but I've never had impure thoughts about a priest before."

Noah laughed so hard that the movement hurt his wounds. "So you had impure thoughts about me?"

"Well, maybe they weren't impure; let's just say thoughts," she said and smiled at him.

He laughed again. "You are really funny. I don't know why I didn't expect that. But you didn't answer my question. Will you go out with me?"

"We'll see," she said and smiled. "But I don't think you are going anyplace for a while."

"We would have to wait until the mission is over anyways since you are pretending to be with Turner."

"Well, from what Turner said, at this meeting we may find out if the mission is over or at least changed."

There was a knock on the door then Turner walked in. He looked at Noah and said, "Good, you're awake. Do you feel as bad as you look?"

"Pretty much. I'm trying to see if Tessa will go out with me."

"She will," Turner said and grinned.

"Turner!" Tessa scolded.

"Don't tease the man, he's wounded. The meeting is going to start."

"I'm going," Noah said and set his cup of coffee down. Then he started to pull the blankets off from him.

"No you aren't," Tessa said loudly.

Noah grinned at her but continued to get out of bed. "Turner help me; if he falls I can't pick him up," Tessa said with frustration as she ran to Noah who was out of bed. He was wearing only his trousers.

"I don't think I am going to try to put my boots on," Noah said. "Where is my shirt?"

"Torn up and bloody and you are really pigheaded," Tessa said as she held onto one of Noah's arms and Turner the other. They helped Noah walk down the hallway to the Great Hall. Dominic saw them as soon as they entered the meeting.

"Should you be out of bed?" Dominic asked Noah.

"No," Tessa said angrily.

Dominic quickly pulled a chair out for Noah to sit on. He stared at Noah then yelled, "Fennel, I'm putting money that Noah passes out before the meeting is half over." Noah laughed.

# Chapter XXII
## Visions

While Mathas was preparing for his morning meeting, Sudfad was leading his family into the chapel at the Learning Center. They wanted a few minutes alone to say goodbye to Michael before others arrived.

Madeline and Renya carefully placed all of the stuffed toys that children had given to Michael around his body. Raul and Simon set the miniature house near the coffin.

The Sanuri, Gabriel and Raphael were already in the chapel setting things up for the service. High Priest Othnial had offered to come and help with the services but with all of the threats no one wanted him traveling from Langer.

Only Michael's immediate family initially arrived at the chapel. Thedes, Ibula and their children, Javier, Corsa and her brothers arrived as a second group thirty minutes later. The rest of the people started arriving thirty minutes after that. Only family, friends and team members attended the funeral service which lasted for over an hour.

After the service, the casket was closed and a Wetprian flag was draped over it. The casket was carried out of the chapel and placed in the back of an open topped boca. A team of eight white horses pulled the boca. Soldiers in dress military uniforms riding matching black horses rode in front and behind the boca. Fine carriages transported the mourners from the chapel to the gravesite.

Javier was trying to holdup Madeline but he became so weak that Kent and Corsa had to help him stand and Alex held onto Madeline as she wept. Matthew and Angelina held onto Michael's sisters. Calen, Luca and Dagon where helping Edward and Kate to stand.

While everyone in attendance had been grieving, they had also been busy with preparations for the funeral ceremonies as well as against another attack.

Now, as they watched Michael's body lowered into the ground the reality of the situation overwhelmed many of them again.

Sudfad, Renya, Raul, Simon, Vitomas and Annabelle basically held each other up. Laurel, Alexander and Marie comforted Petra and Kyra.

The Sanuri had to keep raising his voice as he spoke over the grave because the cries of the mourners were so loud.

A feast was held in the Great Hall of Sudfad's castle after the funeral service. Many of the Elod women helped to prepare and to serve the meal. They wanted desperately to help the family who had delivered them from hell.

Sorren had arrived at Mathas' castle during the night but after the battle ended. He helped with the wounded and was briefed on the events that had occurred while he was searching for Tresdor.

Mathas was standing as he started the meeting. "We have a great deal to cover because many different things occurred yesterday and last night. So many of you here are wounded; know that if you need to leave please do so and we will fill you in on what you missed."

"After speaking with many of you I have tried to put together a timeline in an effort to better understand what happened. I will call the speakers as they appear in the sequence of events. Sorren, you are the first up."

Sorren explained how Grant and other warriors found Raven dying and her words that Toni and Sorphat were in the area. He then told about the note which led to them meeting Martiz and rescuing the people in the cave.

Sorren explained how Tresdor bartered for his life with the souls of the people of Minges and how the Angels stopped an army of Rogetts from attacking that village.

Sorren repeated Miranda's words that Bertuck wanted Tresdor in Langer because more plans were in the works. Then Sorren retold Grant's story of suddenly losing Tresdor's trail and Miranda telling him to turn back. Sorren finished by telling how he and Grant went to the hospital and was told that the woman who helped save her people was a ghost.

When Sorren finished speaking Tessa said, "That story was scary and I didn't see anyone in here even blink or laugh. Has this happened before?"

"Tessa, so many bizarre things happen that after a while you kind of expect them," Claudius said.

Mathas had Bart, Garvis, Louis, Tally and Drake talk about what they saw and heard in the Catacombs and when they found the monster snake. He was going to have them talk about the chasm that opened in the road last.

Next Turner was called to the front of the room to explain what he and Tessa observed and did. Before he sat down he looked at Noah and grinned. "Noah, your girl bitched out an Angel last night, you may need to know that." Noah turned and looked at Tessa who turned red and slid down in her chair. Many of the people laughed.

"Actually, we may need to talk about that later," Mathas said. "But I want to continue with the timeline. Claudius your next."

"Great," Tessa said under her breath and Noah grinned.

Stephan and Thaos spoke after Claudius. Dominic and others added to what Thaos and Stephan said about the battle as many people got different views of what they saw. Lastly Fahron spoke.

Mathas again addressed the group. "I think we are all getting a good idea of what happened. The next speakers may give us some answers but Gideon will need to put Drake into a trance. We are taking a ten minute break now. Refreshments will be brought in momentarily."

"Do you need to go back to bed?" Tessa asked Noah.

"Yes, but I'm not missing this. So which Angel did you bitch out?"

"Adam, he made me mad." Tessa wanted to change the subject. "I'll tell you about it later, I'm going to get you some food." She started to walk away from the table then returned. "You know just because Turner said I was your girl, doesn't mean that I am." Noah and Dominic laughed as she walked away again.

"She is going to be a handful," Noah said with a broad smile.

When the meeting resumed Gideon walked up to the front of the room with Drake, Tally, Bart, Louis and Garvis. Gideon had already placed a chair at the front of the room and Claudius was going to take notes.

Both Bart and Tally told how and why they left the city and were racing down the old country road, then they explained about the chasm, the smoke and the sound of drums.

"Don't know why I am kind of nervous about this," Drake said as he took a seat in the chair.

"Before we get started, does anyone have questions for Drake?" Gideon asked.

"I heard a little about this last night," Tessa said. "I know he didn't have a lot of time but any kind of description about the women would help."

Drake explained in great detail what he saw inside of the cave. He described the shadows that didn't look like they came from any of the Hutas. He talked about seeing people shackled to the wall then blinking and the shackles were empty.

He described how the Hutas suddenly became quiet when the five people walked to the fire. He explained about one of the people appearing to read from a book while the women disrobed and jumped into the fire. Up until this point of the story Gideon had only asked one question and that was for Drake to describe what he saw.

Gideon stopped Drake and told him to concentrate on the book and to describe it. "Now that I think, the person was carrying it when they walked up to the fire but it was closed. She didn't open it until she turned and stepped towards the Hutas.

"Why did you call the person a she?" asked Gideon.

"Don't know, cuz the others were; I guess."

"I need you to really concentrate on the book."

As Drake sat in the chair he was squinting his eyes like he was looking at something. "It was big for a book. Maybe a foot high and ten, eleven inches across. It was black but I could see gold on it."

"Was it gold writing?"

"No, fancy decorations. Like a lot of swirls. I can't see the pages or the words but for some reason I think the book is really old. I couldn't hear what she was reading. All of a sudden the four people standing behind the reader all take off their robes and drop them on the ground. And they were all naked women. I couldn't believe that the Hutas didn't make a sound or go after them. The one just kept reading then all of a sudden like she raises her hands into the air."

"She must have dropped the book cuz it wasn't in her hands then she turns around real quick like and those ladies jumped into the fire one by one. They screamed then all the Hutas went crazy screaming."

"Can you describe the women?"

"I couldn't get a good look at their faces. They all had long hair. Two had dark hair and two had blonde hair. Their bodies looked good so I suspect they were fairly young."

"Really look at the women."

"Well, the blonde closest to me was kinda short." Drake paused. "None of them have any muscles like our women warriors. They can't be warriors. I mean they look good they just don't look like warriors."

"Do you see any marks or tattoos?"

"No," Drake said as he was squinting to see the images in his mind. "Now just wait a gal darn minute. Guess I was too busy looking at their bodies." Everyone in the room laughed. "All those gals have long hair. One of the dark haired gals has curly hair all the rest has straight but they is wearing these jewels in their hair."

"Like a crown?"

"No, like what Ashley always wears."

"Now just wait." Drake moved to the edge of his chair as if he was trying to get a closer look at something. "They're all wearing necklaces; the same necklaces." Tessa was sitting next to Noah and squeezed his arm.

"Describe the necklaces."

"They are long gold chains with three squares hanging one below the other. The squares aren't gold," Drake paused as he squinted harder.

"Are they brown stones with strange inscriptions?" Tessa asked as she stood up.

"Yeah, yeah that's what they are."

Gideon looked at Tessa and asked, "Do you want to say anything?"

"Afterwards," she said but continued to stand.

"Can you tell us anything else about the women?" Gideon asked Drake.

"Just that they each just jumped in that damn big fire but as soon as they did they screamed bloody murder. I wondered if they was drunk or in a trance or something."

"Do you need us to slow down?" Gideon asked Claudius because he was taking notes.

"Just give me a second," Claudius said then moments later nodded at Gideon to continue.

271

"What else did you see?" asked Gideon.

"I was staring at those poor gals burning and all of a sudden the one who was reading looked up at me like he knew I was there. He stared right at me. And it weren't no woman at all but a man. His eyes was real evil, that's why I jumped back then the opening closed."

"Would you recognize him again?"

"Oh, I know him, I just don't know what his name is."

"Was it Hector?" asked Fahron.

"No this guy was a lot older and it weren't that picture of his daddy neither. Let me think. I've seen him since I joined up with all of you."

As Drake was trying to remember the face he saw in his mind the people in the room were becoming anxious. "Miranda will you help him remember?" Thaos yelled.

"Tell him to look at the hands," Miranda said for all to hear, including Drake.

"Damn she's right," Drake said. "He has real old looking hands. Lots of wrinkles and brown spots and his fingers are real fat. He has this huge ring on his left hand. I don't know how I could have missed that. It's a really wide band, like I've never seen before. It's gold with all kinds of engraving and four of the biggest diamonds I have ever seen."

"Can you describe the engravings?"

Not only did Drake squint but he turned his head from side to side. "Well, on the left side of the ring it looks like a damn building. I think it's a castle and on the right side its words. Drake started to spell out the letters as he saw them. "M, A, L..."

"Malga," said Angus. "That is a ring that the highest order of priests wear at the monastery at Malga."

"Noah!" Tessa screamed.

Dominic and Fennel jumped forward and grabbed their friend as he fell out of his chair. Turner and Garvis helped Dominic and Fennel carry Noah back to his room.

"I'll be back," Tessa yelled to the group as she followed the men out of the room.

Fahron walked out into the hallway and told one of the soldiers to get the Court Physician. "We'll take a short break here," Mathas announced and quickly left the room. Gideon brought Drake out of his trance.

"Damn he's a heavy guy," Garvis said as they carried Noah down the hallway.

Mathas practically ran past them and said, "We sent for the Physician."

The four men tried carefully to put Noah in bed without reopening his wounds but they were not successful. Tessa was taking off the bloody bandages when the Physician ran into the room and took over.

"What happened?" demanded the Physician.

"He passed out in a meeting," Dominic said. "He knew he wasn't supposed to get out of bed."

"I need a couple of you guys to roll him over," the Physician said.

Tessa helped the Physician to stop the bleeding from the wound in Noah's shoulder and to bandage it.

"Someone is going to need to stay with him to keep him in bed," said the Physician as he walked out of the room.

"I would but I need to get back to work," Tessa said.

"We'll work something out," said Dominic. "He's out cold now so we can all go back to the meeting."

"He needs someone to make sure he stays in bed," Dominic announced about Noah as the group took their seats in the Great Hall.

"Is he alone now?" asked Fahron.

"Yeah but he is out cold," Fennel said.

"If everyone is here now we are going to resume," Mathas said. "During the break I went to a locked storage room where I keep all the notes from our meetings as well as the letters and notes that I receive from the people in Wetpr and other kingdoms."

"Several years ago, before Gabriel's team even met Sudfad they were working a mission in Stordt. Several priests at the monastery at Malga were members of the Insidiae and were trying to free the demon Omnibus from his prison in the Abyss. That was a long mission in which the Sanuri, Raul and Simon became involved. These books on my desk are their reports."

"First, the scene that Drake witnessed is similar to scenes they described in their reports and secondly, I remember reading something about a ring similar to the one Drake described. I am going to reread these reports. Any of you are welcome to read them also. Claudius is copying his notes to send to Sudfad and Gabriel. I would not be surprised if Gabriel doesn't return after he reads them."

"Tessa did you have something to tell us?" Mathas asked.

"Yes My Lord," she said and stood up. "As part of my disguise I have been basically doing nothing but shopping and talking with people. Besides the shops, I have been frequenting the street vendors so I can say with certainty that the necklaces that Drake described are only sold in The Chicken and The Egg."

"Also the jeweled combs are a specialty of Ashley's shop. She has a jeweler from Port Friada make them. And there is something else although it may be totally unrelated. Every night Turner and I walk around the streets and watch everything. Two nights ago I saw a man standing in the window of a building and watching the soldiers. I recognized him from Port Friada."

"He wasn't doing anything suspicious but he kind of fits the description that Drake gave." Tessa was standing near her chair as she spoke.

"Tessa come up front so everyone can hear you better," said Mathas.

"I didn't want to be in front of the group," Tessa said as she grabbed Turner's hand and pulled him to the front of the room with her. Turner laughed.

"The man's name is Frankwich and he owns a fleet of merchant ships. He is filthy rich and while he acts like a pillar of society he is in Joy City almost every night and not just to watch. He has a lot of fetishes. We need to contact Madeline and Javier because they will know him," explained Turner.

"I recognize the name," said Garvis. "He is old, heavy set and bald and wears more jewelry than you normally see on men."

"Drake said he has seen him with us but I don't recognize that name," said Claudius.

"I know who she is talking about," said Gideon and so will Ashley. Drake probably saw him at our engagement party in Port Friada. He is an intense man. While his physical appearance isn't anything that would make him stand out in a crowd, his intensity does. It's like you can feel it coming off him. Where was he?"

Tessa now looked at Turner who spoke. "We were in the business district. You know how some of those buildings don't have any signs in front of them? Well, this was one of them. It was about two blocks south of the Excelsor Hotel on the opposite side of the street. There was nothing outstanding about the building. It had a stone front with gray trim and large windows. If there were porches or balconies they weren't in the front of the house."

"We saw him, just as the streets were filling with soldiers so I was trying to get Tessa so a safe place so we didn't investigate the building."

"We will," said Thaos.

"Son, a lot of people got hurt because that damn demon wants the two of you. I don't want you working until we figure all this out," said Claudius.

"We don't want anyone to get hurt but we aren't sitting on our butts either," said Stephan.

"Claudius is right," Mathas said to Stephan and Thaos. "Yet I understand your feelings. You two read these reports. Trust me you won't be bored."

"Miranda," Stephan yelled. "Miranda are we a threat to our families?"

It was Adam who appeared in the room and when he did Tessa turned red from embarrassment. "Most of you in this room are marked men because the dark worlds are speculating as to who The Seven Sons are."

"Well, we can't do our work if we are in hiding," said Stephan.

"And I agree," Adam said. "And don't discount that the demons are trying to disable you through fear."

"It's getting others hurt that we are afraid of," Thaos said.

"Your concerns are legitimate but instead of focusing on them, let's focus on the vision the heavens allowed Drake to see. Tell me what you believe at this point of your investigation."

"That the Insidiae is involved and possibly a priest from the monastery at Malga," Thaos said then paused. "Juleta belonged to the same sect that was trying to free Omnibus and Mathas said there are similarities with the mission that Gabriel was on. And Juleta was involved with people in Port Friada."

"See where you go when you don't let your fears block you," Adam said. "Remember we have told you more than once that many criminals and groups are paying attention to all of you simply because they fear you may stop their plans that have nothing to do with the prophesies."

"All of you are always asking us what you should do but you know we can't tell you what choices to make," when Adam said this he turned and looked at Tessa.

"But today I will offer some suggestions based on what you just told me. You know there are connections between Langer and Port Friada. You know actually more than you realize and once you start reading those reports and Harlow's notes you will start connecting the dots. Most of you saw that elaborate map that Michael's sisters drew of Karzman's lands. You are not children and I am not going to help you draw pictures but if you were wise you would start one yourself and give yourselves plenty of room for drawing."

"You have a number of people in this room who are very familiar with both cities, do you believe that to be an accident? That vision was part of a key and your time would be better spent working on that then having the sons of Claudius tracking down a building."

"Now, I am going to tell you something that you don't know yet. When Raul received the letter about Michael's death his family collapsed. This family that has always been the pillar of strength for everyone else was paralyzed which allowed their friends to be strong and many, many of them called to us. Archetenus and Jared will be sending you a letter soon."

"They have accepted new positions within Sudfad's government. Archetenus is the head lawman in that kingdom and he and Jared decided to run their positions like Gabriel does his teams. But this aside they have been strong for Sudfad's family. They have both called to Miranda because they want to avenge Michael's death."

"While revenge is never a positive thing, the feeling did cause them to ask many questions of the heavens. They are in a unique positon to investigate the attacks because of their backgrounds. They have spoken with their wives and will be heading to Port Friada after things settle from Michael's funeral. If enough of you have done your research by then you may want to have them come here first or you may want to accompany them to Port Friada."

Several people stood up to speak but Adam turned and looked at Tessa and Turner. "I believe you wanted to have a talk with me," he said.

"Yes," said Tessa. "And I am sorry I was yelling at you but..."

"But what?"

"I don't understand how to talk to any of you. You want us to call to you but then you don't answer and that was kind of an emergency. And then you talk to Turner instead of me, is that because I am a girl? That's not right because I was the one asking the questions."

Adam smiled at Tessa then turned to Louis and asked, "What did Miranda tell you?"

Louis stood up and it was obvious that he was intimidated by the Angel. "I...I told her kind of the same thing that Tessa said. We never heard of The Great Ruler or Angels until we came here. I told her that you didn't exist in our world and," he paused. "Oh yeah, she told Drake and Tally to tell us about their mission in Inferus and she said there was a reason we were working with priests."

"Dominic, Fennel this is your assignment," said Adam. "How can you be priests and not seek every opportunity to teach about The Great Ruler and the heavens?"

"You are right; we are sorry," said Dominic.

"You don't need to apologize, you need to teach," said Adam then he looked back at Tessa. "Join them and no I am not leaving you again and no I am not a typical guy." Adam smiled when he said this and many laughed. "But there is much you need to understand and you will continue to be frustrated until you do."

"If all of you were wise you would make everything I just suggested a priority for today. I normally don't make such suggestions but even the heavens can see that all of you are exhausted and overwhelmed. Turner what were you told about the reasons that your team, Javier and Madeline have bounties on them?"

"That we are so good at our jobs that we notice many things without realizing what we are really seeing and hearing. That is the second time in a couple of days that you brought that up. That is connected to all of this isn't it?"

278

"You are starting to learn," Adam said. "All of you have been given a treasure chest now open it and look inside."

Claudius stood up and looked emotional which was uncharacteristic for him. His voice quivered as he spoke, "Adam, I want to thank all of you for saving my sons last night. I have never prayed that desperately. Is there some way that I can pay you back? I am serious?"

"Earlier this morning you listened with horror as Sorren described the people that his warriors found in that cave. Do all of you lead such privileged lives that you do not see the world around you? That is not an isolated case. The Great Ruler creates children and others hide and discard them because they are flawed in their eyes. You are an exceptionally intelligent man, I believe you will figure something out." Adam disappeared.

# Chapter XXIII
## The Chicken and the Egg

"I think we all learned our lessons after Michael," Mathas said. "At least I did. Thaos and Stephan you have the right side of the room, set it up however you want. Dominic you have the left. Let's get to work."

"Is it just our team that you need to teach?" Tessa asked Dominic. "Because if it is can we move this into Noah's room so we can watch him at the same time?"

"Wait a moment," said Claudius loudly. "First, Fahron go home. We will get you if we discover anything. Secondly, I see that most of you moved to the right side of the room. I don't mean to embarrass anyone but it might be a hell of a lot more efficient if we read these reports and notes out loud. We need maps, paper and pens. And let's hang everything on the walls."

"When we are done we want to join you," Dominic yelled over to the other group.

"When we are done I need to change my clothes and get back out on the streets," said Tessa. "Turner and I can find that house and I want to buy one of those necklaces from the chicken, egg store."

"We might need to wait on that," Turner said as his team, Drake, Tally, Dominic and Fennel walked into Noah's room.

Soldiers remained on the streets of Langer to provide security and to help clean up the destruction caused by the giant snakes. The snakes had been killed by the Hengers, now citizens and soldiers were cutting up the bodies and burning them. Smoke and a putrid smell permeated the city.

Crews of people and demons were fixing the damage in the Catacombs. The remnants of Tresdor's body were unrecognizable and thrown on a burn pile. While his body was destroyed his soul was being tortured in Bertuck's hell region.

Companies of soldiers from Fort Langer cleaned up the battlefield on the old country road. The bodies of the Huta soldiers were burned. The bodies of the soldiers from Langer had already been taken to the fort for burial.

Gideon left Mathas' castle and went to Ashley's shop. Ingr and Nikki were spending more time helping in the shop because they wanted to be available if Tessa needed help. Gideon asked Ashley, Nikki and Ingr to go into the office and he repeated everything from the morning meeting. Much of what Gideon said both surprised and horrified the women.

"Gideon, I am sorry but I don't take the names of people that I sell small items too. I can go through my records and tell you how many of those combs I buy and sell. I have to tell you that they are a very popular item. But do you understand that they are also quite expensive. They certainly aren't something that just anyone can afford."

"You have them specially made don't you?" Gideon asked.

"Yes, and I know for a fact that the people who make them don't sell them to anyone else," Ashley said.

"How can you be so sure of that?" asked Gideon.

"Because they are made by a small group of women who I have helped. We have a contract. This is how they support their families."

"Understand that I am not accusing them of wrong doing, we need to find out how those women got them. The fact that all four were wearing them in a ceremony is significant."

"Two of the women who make them were beaten so severely by their husbands that they are crippled now. I am their only source of income but I will contact them to make sure."

"Ashley go with Gideon. I am sure you can be a lot of help to them," said Nikki. "Ingr and I will speak with the staff. From now on we all will pay more attention to who buys those combs."

After Tally and Drake told of the mission in Inferus, Dominic and Fennel taught their first class on The Great Ruler. To their surprise everyone, including Drake and Tally asked questions. Noah woke up during this time and both listened and added to the class.

"All of you are students," said Tessa. "How do you know so much?"

"We spent a good part of our lives hiding in the monastery at Rubar," Fennel said. "Now, I have a question for all of you. I speak for both Dominic and me when I say we are really surprised by your questions and interest. We just covered the basics with you. It will take more than three hours for you to really understand. Would any of you like more classes?"

"Sure," said Tessa.

"Are you just saying that because your boyfriend is a priest?" Turner asked kiddingly.

"First of all he isn't my boyfriend..." Tessa started to say.

"Yet..."Bart said and grinned. "We're already placing bets." Noah laughed.

"Well, that really has nothing to do with what I was going to say," Tessa continued. "You know we are going to keep working with these people whether Mathas hires everyone or Gabriel. And from just the little that we heard it sounds like we need to know this for the missions. I mean, isn't everything we are doing right now...well, I guess it just all seems tied together to me."

"I mean we are talking to Angels almost every day and I don't know about the rest of you but I need to know what I am doing. We prepare for every other mission and that's what this is. They aren't asking you to become priests or anything."

"I'm with Tessa," said Bart. "But I don't want to do a second lesson now. Tessa needs to get on the streets and I have a feeling that we need to get to the Catacombs. Maybe later tonight?"

"That is fine with us," said Dominic. "You're the first class we've ever taught and I'm enjoying it."

"Well, we certainly wouldn't guess we were your first class. You are both very good," Tessa said. "And I am not just saying that. My only question is not related at all to the lessons though. For my disguise I have not been seen with any of these people. So do I go back to that role?"

"That's a really good question," Noah said. "If spies see her here then she goes back into those shops she could be in a lot of danger. And on the other hand it may not be safe for any of you to stay in the city any longer."

"Our house is near here," said Dominic. "You would be safe there but it is still on some of Mathas' land."

"Let's think about this," said Turner. "We should all check on our places and if we believe someone has been in them then we should move in with Dominic's team but I am not so sure that our disguises have been compromised. I'll go with Tessa today and we will feel things out."

"I, at the very least want to buy one of those necklaces," Tessa said.

"So if we feel we are in danger we will just come back to the castle," Turner continued. If not let's meet in the dining room of the Excelsor Hotel at seven and we can compare notes. I'll get a private dining room and say that I am making a pitch to prospective investors. So ask for me when you get there."

As everyone stood up to leave the room, Tessa said, "Turner, I will catch up with you in a couple of minutes." She waited until all of the men left the room then she closed the door. Tessa turned and smiled sweetly at Noah then said.

"You scared the hell out of all of us! You're staying in bed for a week if I have to tie you down. Do you understand me mister?"

Noah laughed so hard that he grabbed his head because the movement was causing him pain. Tessa had been walking towards the bed as she scolded him. Noah was sitting up in bed and held his hand out to her.

"Come here," he said.

"You just keep laughing like that," Tessa said as she sat down on the edge of the bed. "You think I am kidding."

Noah took Tessa's hand and said, "I am worried about you."

"Don't change the subject."

"Tessa, listen to me. This isn't my first mission either. I have a bad feeling about all this. I know you are smart but we don't know really who we are fighting against yet, so be careful. If I wasn't laid up I would go with you."

"Noah, you know you couldn't. I know what I am doing but I would like to come back and see you and I don't know if that is possible."

"We'll think of something. You just keep your head in the game."

Tessa smiled and leaned forward and softly kissed Noah on the lips. She started to stand up when he pulled her back to him. Tessa laughed until Noah kissed her. His kiss was intense and passionate. She put her arms around his neck as they embraced. Then she moved closer to him. They lost track of time.

Turner knocked on the door and yelled, "Tessa are you coming?"

"Oh my god," Tessa said. "Oh my god. I knew you would be a good kisser. Oh my god. I am coming back." She quickly left the room.

Turner was in the hallway waiting for her and laughed loudly. "Gee, can't imagine what you were doing."

"Just kissing but he is a great kisser."

"Well, you might want to straighten your hair and dress before we go any farther."

They both stopped in the hallway. As Tessa was putting the loose strands of her hair back into a bun she smiled and said, "He wants me to be his girl."

Turner threw his head back and laughed loudly again. "What? Have you known each other a whole thirty seconds?"

Tessa looked angry for a moment then she laughed too. "I will admit it is pretty fast and even he said so. But he said we are at war and he doesn't want to waste any time."

"Tessa, you know that I want the best for you but..."

"But what? Don't you like him?"

"I like him fine for what I know of him. No, I was going to say that sometimes your love life seems like a game to you and I don't think you should look at it that way with him. Those guys, and I mean the freedom fighters had a hell of an existence, don't break his heart on top of that."

Tessa looked at Turner for a moment before she spoke. "I am not going to disagree with anything you said but I do like him."

"And how long is that going to last before the next guy comes along? I'm not saying this to be mean. Besides we may be signing up to work with these guys and I don't want us starting off on the wrong foot. In case you haven't noticed they are pretty much a family."

"You mean the freedom fighters?"

"Well yeah, but all of them. Tessa, you don't have to make any decisions right away; just be honest with the guy. And it wouldn't hurt for you to find out a little more about all of them."

"Oh trust me, I was already planning on it," she said and smiled.

Tessa had barely left Noah's room when Fennel walked back in. "Are you sweating?" Fennel asked and roared with laughter.

"She just makes my blood boil," Noah said and laughed too.

"Want us to follow her?"

"Yeah, I have a really bad feeling. She could be walking into a trap."

"Dominic and I are thinking the same thing."

Because of the attacks on her sons, Bella made Ryan close the shop and return home. She kept Amy, Cassidy, Logan and Marty from their Nordes training. Neither the children nor Ryan were happy about being forced to stay inside of the castle. Bella had the cooks fix treats but this act did not appease their temperaments so Bella thought she would try a new approach.

She had Ryan and the children meet with her in Claudius' study. "While I understand that none of you are happy with me, you have all lived here long enough to know I would not do something like this without a reason. What I am trying to decide is if you are ready to hear that reason. All of you have had horrible lives and seen more than children your ages should have."

"So I have decided to treat all of you as grown-ups; no offence Ryan." He laughed. "Some bad things are happening; do you want to hear about them? You don't have to but you do have to understand that we are in a war and there are times when that fact will cause us to be inconvenienced at times."

"I want to hear," Ryan said. "But we can talk later."

"Is Papa, Grandpa and Uncle Stephan alright?" asked Amy. "Because they didn't come home last night?"

"Yes, thank god but Chaez and Lana are seriously wounded."

"Tell us," said Cassidy.

"Understand that there is a lot that I can't tell you. But the bad men who killed Michael went after Thaos and Stephan last night. And a lot of people got hurt protecting them."

"Why did they do that?" asked Amy as tears came to her eyes.

"Because they are fighting all the bad men, like the ones who stole Logan and Marty," Cassidy said. "And Mama is afraid they will steal us to get Papa, Thaos and Stephan to come to them."

"Cassidy, I am both shocked and impressed," said Bella.

"I was on the streets for a long time and I saw a lot of things," Cassidy said proudly.

"So children by staying here you are actually protecting everyone in the family right now. Do you understand that?"

"Yes," said Logan. "We're sorry."

"You don't have to apologize. But you do need to understand that I am not trying to punish you. I am trying to protect our families."

Isadore was beside herself with worry because of Chaez and Lana. She had sent a soldier into Langer to hire a physician and a nurse to stay at the castle. Sally and April did not attend their warrior's training instead they stayed at home to help care for their brother and Lana.

"Why are you home so early?" Isadore asked Fahron with concern.

"They don't need me. Later I will tell you about the meeting," Fahron said. "How are they doing?"

"Better," Isadore said and started crying. Fahron put his arms around her and hugged her tightly.

Turner and Tessa were working out different stories they could use to explain their absence but there was so much chaos on the streets of Langer and in the hotel that no one appeared to take notice that they just got out of a royal carriage.

They immediately went to Tessa's chambers which appeared untouched. They carefully searched the rooms. Then they changed their clothing and went to the dining room for a late lunch.

The dining room at the Excelsor Hotel was always busy and on this afternoon everyone was talking about the events of the previous night. Tessa and Turner listened carefully to the stories. They heard little that really peaked their interests.

Turner rented a small dining room for the evening and told the host that he was going to hold a business presentation in it. He told the host what items he would need and that he had invited a number of people but wasn't sure who would actually attend. Tessa and Turner left the hotel to work the shops.

"Oh my god that stinks," Tessa said as she covered her nose. "What is that?"

"If I had to guess they are burning those demons snakes," he said. "All this smoke might be a good thing." They decided to first walk past the building where they had seen Frankwich.

Tessa and Turner slowly walked down the street. They found the building and made note of the landmarks. They didn't see anyone in the windows or around the building. They didn't want to linger around the building in case they were being watched so they went shopping.

They walked into all of the shops in the business district. Because they got a later start than Tessa normally did, they did not spend as much time talking with people but they were listening to everything they could. People could not stop talking about the giant snakes and everyone had a theory about them.

Both Tessa and Turner had their arms filled with packages when they entered The Chicken and The Egg. There were considerably fewer customers than usual. Turner walked to the jewelry section while Tessa checked on some articles of clothing that she had previously bought but they needed alterations. She met Turner in the jewelry area where the clerk had already prepared several pieces to show her.

"I just love this shop," Tessa gushed. "Are you the owner?"

The woman showing them jewelry laughed and said, "Oh my no. But I have been asked that before because I have been here so long."

"Joanna Franks owns this business but she doesn't work here. She comes from a long line of old money, if you know what I mean. But she is a wonderful boss; I certainly can't complain. We only see her on Wednesday afternoons."

"She comes in to look at the books and check on things. She even has lunch catered for us."

"She sounds like a wonderful person," Tessa said. "But how can she keep up such a magnificent business if she is only here one day a week?"

"Oh, Teresa is the one who does the ordering and runs everything. She has been the manager for about two years. We go through a lot of managers and I don't understand why."

"What is your name?" asked Turner.

"Suzette."

"Well Suzette, my Tessa here tells me about all of her adventures in the city every night at dinner. And I will be honest, until she came to visit I didn't even realize this store was here. I don't know why because I must have passed it a hundred times. Did it have a different name?"

"Oh my no," Suzette said and laughed again. "We've had this name since we opened. It has to be almost ten years now. But Joanna did recently have the building painted and that may be the reason. It was white before. I think more people notice it now that it is purple. But we have always done a great business."

"Have you worked here for ten years?" asked Tessa.

"Yes. My husband Phil died just around the time Joanna opened this shop. I needed work but I had never done anything like this before. I make a nice living here and like I said I can't complain about anything."

"I hope I don't insult you but honestly how did Joanna pick this name? You have to admit it is a bit unusual," Turner asked.

"Now there is a story," Suzette said. "Neither of you folks are from around here are you?"

"I work for the Port Friada Bank and was sent here almost five years ago now," Turner said. "I find investment businesses and properties. I never guessed I would still be here five years later. I met Tessa in Port Friada a few months ago and we really hit it off so she came here to get a taste of my life."

"And I love this city," Tessa said with exuberance.

"The reason I asked is because we have an absolutely wonderful King and Queen. But in the past few years their family has had some difficulties. You know now that I am saying this, the King's sister Isabella used to shop here every week. I just realized I haven't seen her in a while. She would come in on Wednesdays and talk with Joanna, apparently they were old friends. I will have to ask Joanna if Isabella moved."

"But back to the name. First, you have to understand that Joanna is a very friendly person and will go out of her way to make anyone feel welcomed here."

"Well, what some of the other clerks told me; Joanna met King Mathas' daughter at a function and felt sorry for her because no one wanted to speak with the woman. Honestly, every time Juleta came in here the hair would raise on the back of my neck. No one can tell me that woman was normal. But I keep getting side tracked. Juleta and Joanna started spending a lot of time together and often Isabella would join them."

"That of course was before Joanna opened this place. You see her family is very wealthy so they socialize with the higher ups. Well, Joanna decides to open this shop and hired all kinds of people to help her design it and fix it up because she had never run a business before. So one day Juleta marches in here and she and Joanna go into the office and they are arguing so loudly that people stop working and listen."

"Apparently Juleta demanded in no uncertain terms that Joanna name this place The Chicken and The Egg. Honestly, the entire thing just sounded absurd to me. I mean why would a princess even care about the name of a store and what an incredibly strange name."

"That is a strange story," said Tessa. "Do you think this Juleta was part owner?"

"I never thought about that but I don't see why Joanna would need investors. She comes from the Franks family. They own most of the ships that dock here."

"Did Juleta own any businesses herself?" Turner asked. "I mean it sounds to me like she was trying to sabotage Joanna's shop."

"Now that is an interesting idea," Suzette said. "I was always hearing stories about Juleta but who knows if any of them were true. No, I don't know about any businesses here. I did hear that after her father banished her from the kingdom that she started several businesses in Zorta."

"Dress shops?" asked Tessa.

"No, Joanna's father loaned Juleta money to start a shipping business. But she doesn't have anything as grand as the Franks. She owns a couple of ships and some warehouses, I think in Cadia."

"Suzette did you say the King banished her from the kingdom?" Turner gasped. "I have never heard such a thing."

"Everyone said it was because she was a dark lord. Which I think is silly because has anyone ever heard of a woman dark lord? Personally I just think she was insane."

"Suzette, you are absolutely intriguing," Turner said and Suzette blushed. "Unfortunately, I have a business meeting I must get to but trust me we will be back to visit you." He turned to Tessa. "Darling, did you decide what you wanted?"

"I was so captivated by that story I forgot," Tessa said and laughed. "I will take the ruby earrings but I kind of like unusual things. Give me just another moment to look." After a moment Tessa pointed to a necklace with a gold chain and three square stones hanging from it. "I really like that. Do you know what those markings are?"

"I don't really know if they mean anything," Suzette said as she handed a necklace to Tessa. But we do sell a lot of those. They are one of the few items that Joanna procures for the shop."

Turner and Tessa quickly returned to the Excelsor Hotel. They had less than an hour before the bogus business meeting started.

Tessa went to her chambers and started to write down everything they had learned from Suzette. She also added the location and a description of the house where she had previously seen Frankwich.

Turner checked on the final preparations for his meeting with the host. Then joined Tessa in the chambers. "Help me make copies," she said as soon as he entered the parlor.

"I think we are going to have to go to the castle tonight, if for no other reason than to explain all of this," Turner said as he was reading her notes.

"Well, then we need to take some things," Tessa said. "It is going to be impossible to explain that we keep arriving in the hotel wearing the same clothing we wore the night before. If we played single people it wouldn't be hard to explain but for a couple."

"It will take you longer," Turner said. "Pack some things and I will work on these."

Tessa and Turner walked down to the dining room forty minutes later. Dominic and Fennel were already sitting at the bar of the main dining room having a drink. They walked up to the couple and shook hands with Turner then the four walked into the private dining room that Turner had rented.

"I must say you two look really nice," Tessa said as she closed the door. "I was surprised to see you in suits."

"Playing the part," Dominic said. "Just so you know, Noah asked us to keep an eye on both of you today. He's getting paranoid too. You were in The Chicken and The Egg so long that we were getting worried. We were just about to go in when you came out."

"We hit the jackpot," Turner said as Tessa handed each man a copy of her notes.

There was a knock at the door. Turner started to talk loudly about investments while Dominic and Fennel hid their papers. Tessa opened the door and three waiters walked in carrying trays of delicacies, a bottle of wine and a bottle of whiskey.

Immediately behind the waiters were Louis, Bart and Garvis. All three of these men were also wearing suits. Turner continued to talk about investments for several minutes after the waiters left the room. Tessa handed all of the men copies of her notes.

"You did well," Garvis said to Turner and Tessa.

After the men finished reading the notes, Tessa passed around the necklace they had purchased. "Does anyone recognize those inscriptions?" asked Turner.

"I wish Erebus was here," said Fennel.

There was another knock on the door and to the surprise of all Angus walked into the dining room. He too was dressed in a business suit. "Is anything wrong?" asked Turner as he handed a glass of whiskey to Angus.

"Just about everyone at the castle thinks you are going to walk into a trap. I've got people outside. Mathas wants you to come back."

"Actually we expected that," Turner said as Tessa handed Angus a copy of her notes and the necklace.

"Holy shit!" Angus said and sat down at the table as he continued reading.

"While we have a great deal of information we still don't know where that cavern is or who the man was that Drake saw. Tessa and I have talked about it and think we are still in a position to get more information; which means we can't give up these disguises just yet."

"If we go to the castle we will need the Rualas to get us. It is unwise for us to keep returning to the hotel in the same clothing we wore the previous night so we've packed a few things to either keep at the castle or Dominic's team's house."

"I'll have some warriors get you as soon as it gets dark," Angus said then reread the notes.

"We have to stay in here for at least an hour since this is supposed to be a business meeting so please help yourselves to the food and I will order more if you want," Turner said.

# Chapter XXIV
## The Franks Family

Turner's meeting lasted for almost two hours because his group was waiting for it to get dark. After the men left the restaurant, Turner and Tessa returned to her chambers. Twenty minutes later Ralf and Sol landed on the back balcony.

"You aren't going to yell at any Angels are you?" Ralf asked Tessa kiddingly as they entered the chambers.

"Are you afraid to fly with me?" she teased.

"We both are," said Sol and they all laughed. "Angus told us that you were going to start moving things to the castle. You know we have these huge backpacks; we can carry more than those two little cases."

"That might be a good idea," Turner said to Tessa. "We might be leaving here really fast."

"Read these," Tessa said and handed Sol and Ralf copies of her notes while Turner poured two glasses of whiskey for the men. Then Turner and Tessa quickly started packing.

"My disguise is that I have to get to know the store owners," Tessa explained so I have been buying a lot of stuff. If you two are hungry that box on the table is full of baked goods."

"Thanks," said Ralf as he grabbed a handful of cookies from the box. "Boy, you guys really got a lot of good information."

"But there is still so much that we don't know," said Turner. "We want to keep up these disguises as long as we can."

Angus and the other men who had been in Turner's meeting were at the castle and briefing everyone when Turner and Tessa arrived. Sol and Ralf set the belongings on the floor in the Great Hall and everyone joined the meeting.

"I have more copies of the notes," Tessa said as she walked to the front of the room. "And here is one of those necklaces." She handed the notes and necklace to Mathas.

"All of us have been worried about you two," Claudius said after he finished reading the notes. "Angus said you want to keep this up but we may have to talk about that."

"What Drake saw was a vision," Turner said. "We don't know where that cavern is or who that man was and even with all of this information we haven't really tied anyone to the attacks. Tessa and I want to play this out."

Mathas read the notes, then reread them and each time his face became redder. "Mathas, we don't have enough copies for everyone, why don't I read this one out loud," Claudius said and the King nodded.

"Are you shitting me?" Stephan repeated loudly as his father read the notes. As soon as Claudius was done speaking Stephan said, "Tomorrow I am going to the land office and find out who really owns that business and if there is a cavern or tunnel under that store like at Ashley's."

"Let me," said Dominic. "I'll pretend that I am researching properties to purchase or invest in."

"Obviously those names mean something to all of you," Turner said.

"Everything that store clerk told you is true," Stephan explained. "The Franks family is one of the original families in this city. They have lots of money. All of us kids used to play together and when I say all of us that includes Hector. His parents are friends of theirs too. They have Joanna and a son who is two years older named Jack. Now that I think of it, I haven't seen either of them for a long time."

"The father's name is Otto," said Mathas. "While we were all friends we weren't close enough for him to finance my daughter's business. Which he must have done after I banished her."

"I haven't seen Joanna in a number of years," said Stephan. "But I always remembered her as a nice person. While I could see her being nice to Juleta and Isabella, I certainly couldn't see her being good friends with them."

"We've got a guy of interest named Frankwich and now the Franks family...those names are just too similar to be a coincidence to me," said Bart.

"I think we are all thinking the same things," said Thaos. "But finding out that Juleta owns ships and warehouses in Zorta does help explain a few things. Some of us need to take another trip there."

"For those of you who left the building today. Our group has been reading the reports that Sudfad and Gabriel sent when they were trying to stop the Insidiae from raising the demon Omnibus. So far we have learned a great deal about the Insidiae but nothing in particular concerning Juleta or Isabella. But I've got to tell you those reports are damn interesting. I think all of you might want to read them. We've got a bunch of charts and maps if you want to see them."

"But the one thing we have found that may really affect us was in some letters that the Sanuri sent to Mathas. Apparently the Sanuri is often tested so he can, I don't know the right word...become holier or something. Well, while Gabriel's team is in the middle of this mission The Lion pulls the Sanuri out and tests him. For those of you who don't know, the Angels take on different forms because we aren't holy enough to see what they really look like. The most powerful warrior Angel always looks like a lion."

"Well, during these tests the Sanuri has a bunch of visions that include priests that have become members of the Insidiae. Anyways in one vision he sees a murder but he can't see the face of the murderer, only his robe and hands. And the guy is wearing the same ring that Drake saw in his vision."

"Are you awake?" Tessa asked as she opened the door to Noah's room.

He was sitting up in bed but he had his eyes closed. "Yes, I was hoping you would come back. I've been worried about you. Dominic told me a little about what you did today."

"Mind if I move a few things in?"

"Does this mean you are my girl?"

"Still thinking about it," she said and winked at him. "Here read this while I unpack a few things." Tessa handed Noah a copy of her notes. "I'll show you the necklace when the others are done looking at it."

Instead of reading the notes, Noah was watching Tessa make several trips into the hallway to get cases and packages. He laughed. "If you are moving all of that in here you are my girl."

"Some of this is for you, just read that while I work." Tessa handed him a package. "That bakery on Ninth Street makes the best cookies." A moment later she put a bottle of whiskey and a bottle of wine on the table next to his bed. He kept grinning at her. Tessa unpacked her clothing and put them either in a dresser drawer or the large armoire in the room.

"These I got for you. I had to guess at the size but with all of those muscles you have to be an extra, extra large." She set a stack of folded shirts on the bed.

"Thank you but why..."

"I have to shop to keep up my disguise and you needed them. Besides I am spending the King's money. If they don't fit I will get you some others. Now, when was the last time you took your pain medicine?"

"I didn't take any today because I wanted to have a clear head."

"Well, you are a fool. Want some whiskey then? Should go good with those cookies."

"Yes," he said and laughed. "I haven't read all of this yet because you are so distracting but you guys really got some great information."

"We'll, talk about that after you finish reading it." Tessa poured a glass of whiskey for Noah and a glass of wine for herself. She moved the stack of shirts to the dresser then sat down on the side of the bed. "Before you say anything, Turner and I still need to get more information and our disguises are strong. We're not coming in yet."

"You know I am not the only one who thinks you are walking into a trap."

"I know, everyone does but we still don't know where that cavern is or who that guy is. What if those girls were drugged and really didn't want to be sacrifices for demons? Someone could be stealing women off the streets."

"I understand what you are saying and you and Turner are doing a great job but be careful."

"I like it that you worry about me," she said with a coy smile.

"Tessa, we've been kidding around but I really do want you to be my girl. I don't want you to think this is just about sex."

"If we had sex now it would probably kill you," she said with a big grin. "Besides I know you aren't one of those kind of guys."

"Really? And how do you know that?"

"I have my ways."

"Who told you?"

"Fennel. You know everyone heard about the freedom fighters in Ryed but it always sounded like there was an army instead of a handful. Your lives sounded awful. But even now you are spending more time saving people than you are dating."

"So you checked me out?" he asked with a broad grin.

"I wasn't going to move in with just anybody." Tessa paused. "We don't really know each other and who the hell knows what the future holds. Noah, I don't know if I am going to stay in Langer."

"Turner told me he asked you to stay and work on the team."

"I am not making any decisions on that until after I talk to Madeline and Javier. Turner is taking me to Wetpr to visit them after this job is done."

"Want some company?"

Tessa smiled brightly. "Would they let you go with us?"

"Don't see why not."

"I would really like that."

There was a knock on the door and Seth walked in. He had a huge bandage on his right hand and wrist. "Sorry to interrupt. I didn't realize Tessa was here."

"Come on in," Noah said. "Want some cookies and whiskey?"

"Sure," Seth said. "But I can't pour."

Seth sat in a chair next to the bed and Tessa handed him a glass of whiskey. "The reason I came in was that Lawrence is wondering if you want a roommate."

"I've already got one," Noah said with a big grin.

"Did you move in here?" Seth asked Tessa.

"You don't have to act so shocked," she said and laughed.

"I'm not shocked. I won the bet," Seth said. They all laughed.

Jasmine copied the markings on the necklace that Tessa bought at The Chicken and The Egg. Mathas wanted to include the drawings with the fourth letter he sent to Sudfad that day.

Claudius, Thaos, Stephan, Gideon and Ashley left Mathas' castle with six hundred soldiers. They rode into Langer and picked up Ingr and Nikki from Ashley's shop before they rode the two hours to Claudius' castle.

This was the first time that Thaos and Stephan would be home in almost forty-eight hours. And even now they were wondering if they should have stayed at Mathas' castle. These two warriors were not afraid that they would be attacked again. They knew they were being watched and were afraid they would lead demons or Hutas to their home and families.

Bella was so grateful that her husband and sons were alive that she had a special meal prepared. After Stephan made arrangements for the soldiers to have barracks he joined the rest of the family in the parlor and immediately picked up his oldest son. "God, it smells good in here," he said.

"Bella fixed special treats for us," Thaos said and nodded at a side table that was filled with candles and delicacies.

"Where did she go?" asked Stephan.

"She and Claudius went into his study," said Gideon. "And our boys said that Cassidy is with them."

"Is he alright?" Ingr gasped.

"Yes, it's because of what he told her," said Marty.

"What do you mean?" Ashley asked.

Before Marty could answer the question, Bella and Claudius walked into the room. He was carrying Cassidy.

"I have something to tell all of you," said Bella. "And you might get mad at me." At that moment Ryan walked into the parlor with a roll of paper. He grabbed a plate of food and sat down. "Ryan and the children were all quite cross with me today because I made them all stay home. I tried to find ways to entertain them but their moods got worse so I told them the truth. All of these children have seen more of life than some adults. I thought they would understand."

"I said that the bad men who killed Michael tried to hurt Stephan and Thaos. Then Cassidy tells everyone that I am afraid that those bad men will take all of them as a way to lure the rest of you into a trap. Well, you can imagine my amazement."

"I told him I was impressed and he told me that he had lived on the streets for a long time and knew a lot of things. Then all of the boys started talking. Boys tell them what you told Ryan and me."

"Cassidy was living on the streets longer than me and Marty so he saw more," said Logan. "But when we were put in those cages we would listen to the other kids. You know there were a lot more people stealing kids than the ones who got us. And other people were getting stole too, grown-ups. Well we were all scared so we paid a lot of attention to what people looked like."

"The men who stole me and Marty were the guys wearing those black hats with the little red feathers. Sailors would steal people and sometimes priests. That's why some of the kids were scared when we were at the monastery."

"How do you know they were priests?" asked Thaos.

"Their robes," said Marty. "Me and Logan never talked to any but Cassidy did."

Claudius set Cassidy down. "When I was in Port Friada, one day these three priests walk up to me and some other kids. They asked us if we was hungry and we all said, 'yeah' cuz we was starving. They told us to come with them and we didn't think anything bad would happen because it was the middle of the day and they was priests."

"So we followed them for a bunch of blocks. We thought they would take us to a priest place or a kitchen but they take us in this gal darn tunnel under the docks. Well, me and some of the other kids started to get real nervous. Then we hear a lady screaming like she is getting killed. Well, we all turned and ran but one of the girls fell and a priest grabbed her so we all ran back and kicked him until he let her go. He kept calling us damn little bastards. One of the kids said real priests can't talk like that."

"Ryan before you go ahead, I just want to say something," said Bella. "I hope it is alright but I didn't know when any of you would come home and I couldn't stand to think about any more children in danger so I sent letters to High Priest Barnabas and General Amundsen. Claudius, I told them I was your wife and what the boys said."

"Bella you did a great job with all of this," Claudius said and put his arm around her. She nodded at Ryan.

"On that last mission Stephan and Thaos brought all kinds of maps home. I found one of the City of Port Friada and the boys showed me places where people were taken, that cave under the docks and other areas. I have them indicated on this map. The boys can tell you more. As he spoke, Ryan unrolled the map and spread it out on a table.

The majority of people who had been meeting in the Great Hall of Mathas' castle as well as the team members had gone without sleep for over thirty-six hours. Mathas ended the meeting after the dinner meal was served. Tessa had been going back and forth between the Great Hall and Noah's room as she brought him things to read and to look at.

"Well, it's over," Tessa said as she walked into Noah's room again.

"You look really tired."

"I am and it just hit me all at once. Do you want anything?"

"No, why don't you just come to bed? Actually, I like the sound of that," he said with a grin.

Tessa gave him an exhausted smile as she took off her blouse, skirt, shoes and stockings. She walked up to the bed wearing a light pink lace slip. "You look so beautiful, Tessa." She smiled and got under the covers. She cuddled close to him and he put his arm around her. "You should wear your hair down more, it is really pretty."

"It kind of depends on the role I am playing." She paused. "This is really nice."

"Yes it is," he said and kissed her on top of her head.

She suddenly sat up and looked at him. "I'm kind of afraid to kiss you because we can't get carried away with you the way you are now."

He laughed. "Well, let's say we will stop when it gets too intense."

"Oh, and you really think we will," she said sarcastically and put her arms around his neck. He pulled her close to him.

# Chapter XXV
## A Plan

Turner knocked loudly on the door to Noah's room. "Tessa get up! They have to get us back before its light. I'll be back in ten minutes." Turner laughed when he heard a loud thud in the room.

Tessa jumped out of bed although she was not awake. She immediately tripped over Noah's trousers that were lying on the floor.

"Are you alright?" Noah asked and shot up to a sitting position.

"Yes. I need to light a candle. I tripped on something." She lit the candle next to the bed and looked on the floor. "Our clothes," she said and started picking them up.

"I'll get that, you just get dressed."

"You aren't getting out of bed to clean this room. We're just lucky your wounds didn't break open."

"It was worth it," he said and smiled.

Tessa was holding up Noah's trousers and looking at them. "I'll buy you some more today. Is this your only pair?"

"The only ones I have at the castle so don't take them. And you don't need to buy me clothes."

She smiled mischievously. "Well, if I took them that would guarantee you'd stay in bed."

"Tessa, if you take them I am getting up right now." Both of them were laughing as they talked.

"Ok," she said and folded his trousers and put them at the foot of the bed.

"What are you going to do today?"

"Dominic is going to the Land Office and look up the paperwork on Joanna's shop. I was thinking of visiting Elizabeth to see if she got any information on the women's groups. We need to go about this differently now. We've made the connections to Juleta and Isabella, now we need to find out about the group or person behind this. Joanna might be the lead."

"I am having people follow you and Turner," Noah said as he pulled the covers off and sat on the side of the bed.

"Noah the physician doesn't want you up."

"Well, I feel a lot better; think it's because of you."

"Think it's because we made love all night," she said and smiled at him. "Since you are up can you button the back of my dress?"

"I am sure you are aware of this sort of thing. But in Ryed all of the really secret societies didn't advertise themselves. They didn't announce meetings and do things publically like Elizabeth's group does. There was this one group in Ryed; they were soldiers who were against Teivel. Well, the only way they communicated in public was to draw a symbol on the ground or a wall. They were the only ones who understood what that symbol meant." Noah was buttoning Tessa's dress as he spoke.

Now she sat down on the bed beside him. "Noah, I think you are on to something. Madeline and Javier do the same thing with their group. And that prophet said 'If you want to catch people in the streets talk to the street people'. That is where I am headed today." She kissed him on the cheek and stood up.

He grasped her hand, "Not by yourself you aren't."

"You don't understand, I can dress like a street person. I've played that role before."

"Tessa are you ready?" Turner yelled through the door.

"Turner get in here," yelled Noah.

"Sick of her already?" Turner asked kiddingly as he entered the room.

306

"She wants to dress like one of the street people and get information that way," Noah said with frustration.

"Actually that is a great idea," Turner said.

"It's too dangerous," said Noah.

"Turner, Noah said that in Ryed the really secret groups would communicate by leaving a symbol someplace, like all of you do. And remember what that prophet said."

"We spend a lot of time in the tunnels under this city and we have seen symbols that weren't ours. Let me think about this a minute," Turner said and started to pace back and forth across the room. After a minute he stopped in front of Tessa and Noah, who were both sitting on the bed.

"I don't want to give up the disguises we have been using because I think they are still strong. We are going back to the hotel and announce that you are moving here and we are going to take a couple of days and look at properties. We can get some more of our stuff out of that room and move it here or Dominic's house. Then we all start working the streets."

"Gideon was saying that he cleaned up a building by the docks and Ashley and Bella hired people to set up a kitchen and feed the hungry. Gideon said he has his sailors cleaning out a second building and making benches because the first place is filled every day. That is where we will start to make contacts. We'll need to leave now. Noah can you tell the others what we are doing? We still need to make an appearance but we will be back."

Tessa stood up and kissed Noah. "You two make a good team," Turner said and grinned.

"What are you doing out of bed?" Dominic asked loudly as Noah walked into the Great Hall of Mathas' castle. The morning meeting hadn't started yet.

"Tessa and Turner have a new plan going and I need to tell everyone."

"Is that a new shirt?" Seth asked with a grin.

Noah smiled warmly. "She bought me a dozen shirts. If any of you need a clean one help yourselves." Jasmine stood up from the table and walked over to Noah and hugged him. "What was that for?" he asked.

"Just because," Jasmine said and returned to her seat because Mathas, Claudius, Fahron and Sorren entered the room.

"Mathas, Noah has some things to tell us," Dominic said. "Can he talk first since he's not supposed to be out of bed?"

"Of course," Mathas said. "Is anything wrong?"

"Tessa and Turner changed their plans," Noah said. "Can I just talk from here, instead of the front of the room?" Everyone could see how pale Noah was.

"Actually why don't you sit back down," said Mathas. "You aren't looking good."

"Thanks," said Noah. "This morning Tessa and I were talking about how they were going to find out the rest of the information we need. I told her about the secret societies in Ryed. Those people only communicated with a symbol. Apparently Turner's group does the same thing. Tessa remembered what that prophet said and decided she was going to play the role of a street person to get information."

"That is really good," said Claudius.

"But dangerous," Noah said. "Turner joined us and after we all talked he's changing their plans. They should be back at the hotel now. He is going to make a big deal about how Tessa is going to move here and the two of them will be looking at properties for a couple of days. They are going to pack more of their things and bring them here. He really thinks that once their first disguises are uncovered they will need to move fast."

"Turner said that his team travels the underground tunnels a lot and has seen symbols that weren't theirs. When they return, Turner wants his entire team working the streets and they are going to start at that soup kitchen that Ashley and Bella run."

"The Angels said that Turner's men have seen and heard things that they didn't know the significance of," Sorren said. "I wonder if this is part of that."

"I think it sounds like a really good plan," Mathas said.

"We can draw you some of the symbols we've seen," said Bart. "Then we need to dirty ourselves up." He grinned.

Claudius stood up and retold the story that Cassidy had told them the previous night. "Ryan had the children point out a lot of different places on a map of the City of Port Friada. I am going to pass that around. Thaos and Stephan are going to be late."

"Do they need help?" asked Angus.

Claudius smiled, "They might when Bella and Ashley find out they are getting the kids puppies."

Ingr and Nikki did not go to work in Ashley's shop this morning because they knew their husbands would be returning with puppies. The two women were preparing food and beds for the dogs in their own homes. They met in the dining room of Claudius' and Bella's portion of the castle.

"Why are we here Mama?" Amy asked Nikki.

"We fixed treats," Nikki said and smiled. All of the children were seated at the table eating pie when Thaos and Stephan walked into the room; each man was carrying a large puppy. The children yelled so loudly that Bella and Ryan ran out of Claudius' study.

"What happened?" Bella yelled as she ran into the room. Then she stopped and stared at the children who were on the floor playing with the pups. Both Thaos and Stephan laughed loudly at the disapproving look on her face.

"Listen up," Thaos said to the excited children. "We are starting out with two and if you can prove to us that you can take care of them, well there just might be more in your future. Thaos and Stephan laughed again at Bella's reaction.

"One pup is for Marty and Logan and the other for Amy and Cassidy. You need to feed and water them and train them. We will help," Stephan said. "Do you want to pick your pups out or do you want us to do it?"

"We love them both," Marty said excitedly.

"We should pick them out so there is no fighting," Nikki said and looked at Thaos.

"Now let me look," Thaos said kiddingly. "Amy the one you are holding is for you and Cassidy and the one Logan has is for his family."

Bella had not said a word but stared at her sons. "We need to leave now," Stephan said and grinned. "Ryan, you are coming with us."

"Why?" Ryan asked with genuine shock.

"Because we realize you have a skill that we don't," Thaos said. "We are trying to put all of these pieces of a puzzle together and you do that all of the time in your head when you create things."

Turner and Tessa were at the Excelsor Hotel playing up their roles as the happy couple who were planning a life together. Turner explained to the desk clerk that they would be gone a couple of days and asked for maps of the area and ideas of properties for sale. Soon the clerk had other patrons in the dining room joining the conversation.

In the meantime Tessa was in her chambers packing most of her and Turner's things. She had decided to only leave one outfit each at the hotel. When she was done, she joined Turner in the dining room for breakfast. "I am going to need to buy us a few things," she whispered to him. "And I have an idea."

A waiter walked up to their table with a pot of coffee. Tessa said to him excitedly, "I am going to spread my good fortune today. Would you have the kitchen make up a couple of dozen sandwiches and wrap them?"

"Why?" asked Turner.

"Honey, every day I walk past all of these poor people on the streets. Today I'm giving them sandwiches."

"That's my darling," he said proudly and kissed her on the cheek. "Want me to come along?" he whispered.

"I have a feeling I can get more done by myself. Why don't you work that other angle and we can meet back here at noon."

Tessa decided to hand out the sandwiches before she went shopping. She walked down the street with a large basket and stopped at every corner. She engaged the people of the streets in conversation as she handed out sandwiches and put coins in their hats. She learned little of value but she wasn't discouraged because she was working her way to Cyril.

When she found Cyril he was standing on his usual corner preaching. A man and a woman were listening to him so Tessa stood beside them. Ten minutes later the couple left, as they were leaving Tessa asked loudly "Are you really a prophet?"

In a low voice Cyril said, "Tessa are any of us who we say we are?"

Tessa stepped closer to him and handed him a sandwich. "Good, you know who I am. I am trying to find the real demons here and their cavern. Are people being stolen to be used as sacrifices?"

"Let me look through your basket child." Tessa handed him the basket of sandwiches which he set on the ground. He squatted by the basket and she did the same. "You have been looking in the right places but eyes have been upon you. Not because they suspect who you work with but because you are a beautiful young woman. And sometimes beauty draws the eyes of darkness."

"Are you saying only beautiful women are sacrificed?"

"A sacrifice has to be worthy of the beneficiary. But many have dark appetites. There is a men's clothing store on Seventh Avenue."

"A lot of people go in there and leave without buying anything. Wealthy people who one would think would have their clothing made by tailors."

"Thanks," Tessa said and dropped a handful of coins in his hat.

Cyril examined two different sandwiches. "I'm not done. Be in there by ten and you will see someone you recognize. I'm taking two," he said and stood up with the sandwiches.

"Thanks again," Tessa said.

"Child, you travel a dangerous road doing this. Remember your mother's drawings."

Tessa got close to Cyril and stared into his eyes. "Are you Adam?" she whispered.

"No, I am a typical guy," Cyril said and grinned. Tessa stared at him for several moments as she was trying to determine if he was an Angel or a prophet. She smiled and walked away without saying anything else.

Tessa quickly finished handing out sandwiches and returned to the Excelsor Hotel. She returned the basket to the kitchen staff and left a note for Turner at the front desk. Then she left for the men's shop on Seventh Avenue.

Turner returned to the castle to join Mathas' meeting. Noah had gone back to bed and did not realize that Turner returned alone. Dominic handed Turner his notes of the meeting when Mathas said, "Deborah is something wrong you look terrified?" She was standing in the doorway of the Great Hall.

"I need to speak with Gideon for a moment My Lord." Gideon knew how shy Deborah was so he left the meeting and they walked into the hallway. "I am sorry to bother you."

"Deborah, you can always speak with me. Is something wrong with Lawrence?"

"No. You know that I have taken off from my duties at Ashley's shop to take care of him. Well, he was telling me a lot that was covered in your meetings. Master, I mean Gideon. I sold three dozen of those jeweled combs to a woman about two weeks ago. I didn't get her name but as I was wrapping them another woman walked up to the counter and said, 'Joanna are you spying on the competition?' Both women laughed and she paid for the combs and left."

Gideon put both of his hands on her shoulders and said, "Deborah that is very important information. Thank you for telling me and don't ever feel like you can't join us. You always have good observations." Deborah smiled proudly at the praise and Gideon returned to the meeting and repeated the information.

He paused and said. "For those of you who don't know Deborah, she joined us in Port Friada. She is a smart and sweet girl but she has been so beaten down in life that she doesn't think that anything she says or does matters. I am telling you this because if she wants to talk to any of you, don't dismiss her. It will probably be something important."

"She's doing much better since she is dating Lawrence," Fennel said.

"Oh, I did not mean to imply that he treats her badly. I apologize if anyone got that idea," said Gideon.

There was only one men's clothing store on Seventh Avenue. It was named *The Rooster*. "What the hell is with these names?" Tessa said to herself and entered the shop. Immediately after she walked through the door a well-dressed man passed her as he was leaving. His face was flushed and he wasn't carrying any packages.

She walked over to a cupboard that was filled with piles of folded trousers. She held a pair up to examine them and saw another man walk out of a back room and leave the store without purchasing anything.

"May I help you, My Lady?" asked an older man.

"Actually yes. Is this your store?"

"No, I merely work here. How can I assist you?"

As they were speaking a man walked into the shop and entered the back room. "Well, you are probably going to think that I am crazy she said and smiled at the man. I am getting engaged and my fiancé is wealthy. We've invited our families to join us and well, my family isn't wealthy. I have five brothers and I want to dress them so they don't embarrass Turner and his family."

"I understand my dear. Why would I think that is crazy?"

"Because I haven't seen my brothers in a while and I am not sure of their sizes so I am going to buy a variety of things." Tessa was hoping that story would allow her to spend a great deal of time in the store.

She walked around the store and watched everything. Unlike the stores for women, the male customers in this store did not talk to each other, which Tessa found surprising. She was in the store for almost twenty minutes when Frankwich walked in. He stared boldly at Tessa as he walked past her and entered the back room. She wondered if he recognized her from Port Friada.

Tessa was stacking clothing, jackets and boots on a counter. "Where are the belts?" she asked the clerk and was happy when he pointed to the back of the shop. She heard loud and angry voices in the back room but she couldn't make out what they were saying. She had just taken another armload of items to the counter when Frankwich walked out of the back room and directly up to her.

"Excuse me," Frankwich said. "Where do I know you from? It is driving me crazy."

"I just hate it when that happens," she said and smiled sweetly at him. "My name is Tessa and I am from Port Friada but I am moving here."

"Well, that solves the mystery," he said and laughed. "I too am from Port Friada. I come here often on business, so often that I have a home here."

"Really, how fascinating. This is my first time in Langer and I must say that I have fallen in love with this city. Then she laughed. "And the clerks are falling in love with me." As she spoke she nodded at the many packages the clerk was filling for her.

"My dear are you dressing an army?"

"No," she said and laughed. "My family is coming to meet my boyfriend and I don't want them to embarrass him."

"Boyfriend, my heart is broken. I was just going to ask you to join me for dinner tonight."

As Frankwich was speaking, Turner walked into the shop and immediately recognized him. Turner walked up to Tessa and kissed her on the cheek.

"Turner this is. I am sorry I didn't get your name," Tessa said.

"Frankwich," he said and shook hands with Turner. "Both Tessa and I are from Port Friada. I walked past her and for the life of me could not remember where I had seen her before. Would you allow me to take the two of you out to dinner tonight?"

"Actually there is more than two of us," Tessa said. "Turner's sister is also with us. But she is a lovely woman."

"Well, then may I take the three of you out for dinner?"

"That would be very nice," said Turner. "Where should we meet you?"

"The White Rose Restaurant at say seven."

"That would be perfect. Until then," Turner said and Frankwich left the store. "I have a carriage outside," he said to Tessa.

"Good because you will never believe what I bought for my brothers."

315

# Chapter XXVI
## Band of Brothers

Turner and Tessa arrived at Mathas' castle in a carriage that was driven by two Patronus priests. Jasmine ran out of the castle and up to them as soon as they got out of the carriage.

"Is something wrong?" asked Turner.

"Is Noah alright?" Tessa asked fearfully.

"Yes, but listen to me," Jasmine said. "We have a female warrior in our village named Elexas. She is beautiful and believe me she uses her looks. She screws every guy she meets and thinks it is a challenge if the guy is spoken for. She and Noah had sex once when they first got here from Ryed. Now don't get mad; she practically attacked him. Well, she heard he got hurt and is in his room now."

"What!" Tessa said.

"Tessa, I heard Noah tell her that he had a girlfriend and she said she wanted to meet you. He told me to have the other guys come in. She visited Lawrence earlier and I don't know what she did and said but she had Deborah crying."

"Now don't start anything you can't finish," Turner said to Tessa sternly. Then he said to the priests, "We are going to need help with all of these packages."

A few moments later Turner, Tessa, Jasmine and the two Patronus priests all walked into Noah's room with their arms full of packages.

"Just throw them anywhere," Turner said.

Noah was sitting up in bed and Elexas was sitting on the bed next to him. Noah looked uncomfortable which made Tessa smile. Seth, Dominic and Fennel were sitting in chairs and they were all grinning.

Tessa walked up to Noah and kissed him on the lips. "Tessa this is..." Noah didn't finish his sentence.

"Elexas, I know. I have heard so much about her," Tessa was smiling sweetly as she stared at Elexas who seemed to be enjoying the moment.

"Elexas, you know all these guys are sitting here because they think we are going to fight and perhaps we will but not tonight. I have a proposition for you. We are working on a very dangerous mission and Turner and I just made arrangements to meet a man who may be a dark lord as well as the person behind Prince Michael's murder and the attacks on Javier, Edward, Stephan and Thaos. We also suspect he is having young women stolen to sacrifice to demons."

"Want to flirt with an old, ugly guy while we have his house searched? You would be playing the part of Turner's sister. This is Turner, he is in charge of all this tonight." Tessa turned and nodded at Turner as she spoke. She turned back to Elexas. We will pay you but I have to warn you this is really dangerous. But, you are so beautiful that I am sure you can keep him distracted."

Everyone in the room was watching Elexas' face. When Tessa first started talking Elexas looked angry but now she jumped off the bed and said excitedly, "Are you kidding me? Seriously you are asking if I will help with a mission?"

"I am very serious," Tessa said. "And believe me if you could get him to tell us a few things all the better."

"You don't have to pay me, I'll do it! This is so exciting."

"Turn around," Tessa said. "I need to figure out your size." Elexas turned completely around.

"Jasmine, she looks closer to your dress size but I think my shoes will fit her. And I have lots of jewelry here," Tessa said to Jasmine then looked at Elexas. "You will look like a princess when we get done with you." Elexas smiled brightly.

"There might be a problem," Jasmine said. "She might have problems walking in those kind of shoes."

"That case next to the dresser is all shoes, do you want to help her practice?"

Elexas ran up to Jasmine and said, "This is going to be so much fun."

"Well, we all lost our bets," Dominic said kiddingly after Jasmine and Elexas left the room.

"Who are you having dinner with?" asked Noah.

"Frankwich," Turner said. "And we have a lot to tell you. But in the meantime your girl had to find a reason to be in a men's clothing store so happy birthday to all of you."

"What!" said Seth.

"I bought every size they had. There's boots, jackets, trousers, shirts, you name it. What doesn't fit all of you, just give to someone else," Tessa said.

"Let me touch base with Mathas and the others," Turner said. "Then I will be back. We don't have to meet Frankwich until seven."

After Turner left the room Noah asked, "Are you mad at me?"

"No, Jasmine explained everything. But if she touches you I will break her arm," Tessa said and smiled. "But she is perfect for the part. I was going to ask Jasmine to play it but I was afraid she has been seen on the teams. Now, let's open these packages so we can get all of this stuff picked up."

Tessa quickly organized the items she had bought while the men tried them on. She didn't talk about Elexas or much of anything which Noah noticed.

"It's amazing how you just happened to buy things in our sizes," Dominic said. "This wasn't random. Why did you buy all of this for us?"

"I was going to buy things for Noah and well, all of you are such a band of brothers that it kind of didn't seem right to buy for just one. Besides, it wasn't my money I was spending," she said and smiled.

"Well, thank you," Fennel said and kissed her on the cheek. Dominic and Seth kissed her also.

"I can't get over how you knew our sizes?" Seth said. "You've hardly seen Lawrence and I bet all of his stuff fits too."

"To be a con artist you have to be really observant," she replied.

"Guys, can you leave Tessa and me alone for a little while?" Noah asked.

Tessa was picking up the room and putting Noah's new clothing away as the men left.

"That was a really nice thing you did," he said.

"I like all of them. They are good men."

Tessa was standing at the armoire, hanging up some of Noah's clothing when he walked behind her and started to unbutton the back of her dress. "You shouldn't be out of bed," she said.

"I can walk, I am just weak from losing blood. I can tell that you are upset. Elexas and I had sex once a long time ago. She doesn't mean anything to me. I'll bet it's been over a year since I even saw her anyplace. I have no idea why she just showed up here. Tessa, you do mean a great deal to me and I don't want her to come between us."

Tessa started to turn around and Noah said, "Wait, I have a couple more buttons." She laughed. "I'll tell you I was damn impressed with how you handled everything."

"Well, don't be too impressed. When Jasmine first told me that she was in your room, I wanted to pull her hair out. Go ahead and laugh," Tessa said but she started to laugh too. "What you don't understand is that I am not the jealous type of girl so that shocked me. But honestly once I saw her, she really is perfect for the role tonight. She's sexy and beautiful. Jasmine said she is a warrior so she can defend herself. But I don't know how smart she is and I am not saying that to be mean. This is a dangerous role for her."

"I know she is very manipulative and," he paused and chuckled. "Let's say determined. She is not a fool, but I honestly don't know if she has what it takes for playing a role. I'm done," he said referring to the buttons. Tessa took off her dress and hung it up in the armoire. "Do you have to be any place before dinner?"

"I am sure we will have a meeting of some kind and I really want to take a bath, why?"

"I want to spend a little time with my girl," Noah said and bent down and kissed her. Then he grinned broadly. "I would carry you to the bed but we would both end up on the floor." They both laughed loudly and walked to the bed hand in hand.

Turner briefed Mathas and the people who were in the Great Hall studying reports. "You two aren't going in there alone," Claudius said. "We'll have some priests in disguise."

"I have to say," Thaos said and grinned. "You and Tessa are really impressive. I hope you take Mathas up on his offer and stay here. We could really use you."

"Tessa reminds me of Natasha," Stephan said then turned to Turner. "That's Gabriel's little sister. She is just like that, a spit fire and can charm the pants off anyone. But she's married now and having babies so she's not working on the front lines anymore."

"Dominic asked my team to move into their place, since we have bounties on us. I think we will take him up on the offer. And Tessa is a lot more likely to stay if things work out between her and Noah," Turner said and winked.

"I am still mulling over the idea of Elexas helping you," Sorren said. "She is smart enough but she always has her own agenda."

"She'll be crawling into your bed before this is over," Thaos said to Turner and laughed.

"Well, if she does I'm not kicking her out. She's a beauty."

"Is she the reason Ryan left?" Sorren asked.

"No, we gave him our notes and he wants to catch up on what he missed," said Stephan. "He's in that side room." Stephan nodded at a closed door on the west wall.

"Stephan and I had been talking and while Ryan is not a warrior he is brilliant at putting things together in his mind. So we brought him along," said Thaos.

"He's a good kid," Sorren said to Thaos and Stephan. "You can see how proud he is that you included him." Sorren looked at Turner and chuckled. "Elexas is always after him and he is so shy he can barely talk to a girl."

"Well, speak of the devil," Thaos said as Ryan walked into the Great Hall. "We were just talking about you."

"Why?"

"Elexas is here?"

Ryan's eyes grew wide, "Where?" The others laughed.

"Don't worry, they're keeping her busy so she won't bother you," Stephan said. "She's going to help on the mission tonight."

"She's just scary," Ryan said. "And she doesn't take no for an answer." The men grinned. "I came out here because I need some paper. But I want like a roll, is there anything like that here?"

"Let's ask Mathas," Thaos said.

"Also, can I have some charcoal instead of a pen?"

"I can see the wheels turning in your head," Stephan said. "What are you doing?"

"I am still working that out. And I hope you don't think that I am rude, I just need it to be more quiet so I can concentrate."

When Dominic, Seth and Fennel left Noah's room, they went to Lawrence's room to give him his gifts from Tessa. Lawrence was sitting up in bed and talking with Deborah. It was apparent to the men that Deborah had been crying. Fennel closed the door to the room, after everyone had entered.

"We come bearing gifts," Dominic said as the men started to pile packages on the bed.

"What is all of this?" asked Lawrence.

"Tessa found out about a men's clothing store that is a front for something. She was snooping around and had to make it look good so she bought us all a lot of stuff," Fennel said. "And really nice stuff. Open the packages."

"That was so nice of her," Deborah said and started to open packages. "Oh Lawrence, look at this jacket; this is going to look great on you."

"So what did Elexas do to make you cry?" Dominic asked Deborah who did not answer his question.

"She was just being a bitch," Lawrence said angrily. "She is flirting with me and insinuating that we had something going on which isn't true. She doesn't come out and really say things, she makes these snide remarks and was making Deborah feel bad. I kicked her out of here."

"Well, she went straight to Noah's room afterwards," Fennel said. "Jasmine found out and went in there. Noah asked her to get the rest of us because he didn't want Tessa walking in and finding him alone with her. Jasmine told Tessa and Turner about her when they got here. When Tessa walked into the room we thought for sure we were going to have a cat fight but then Tessa asks her to help with the mission tonight."

"Turner and Tessa are having dinner with Frankwich and Tessa asked Elexas to help be a distraction. She is going to pretend to be Turner's sister. Elexas is so damn excited she is acting like a little kid."

"Didn't Tessa care that Elexas was after Noah?" Deborah asked in disbelief.

"Oh, we could tell she was upset," Dominic said. "In fact, Noah asked us to leave so they could talk. But she's a professional and saw that Elexas could help. I give Tessa a lot of credit."

"We don't know if Frankwich is a demon or dark lord or what," Seth said with a grin. "Maybe Tessa is just trying to get rid of Elexas for good." Everyone laughed.

"Tessa wake up," Noah said.

"Oh my god, what time is it?"

"You've been sleeping for an hour. I hated to wake you but you have to get ready for tonight."

"Didn't you sleep?" Tessa asked as she got out of bed.

"No. I got you something."

"What? Are you telling me you left the room and I didn't wake up?"

"You're exhausted. A long time ago, the Ruala Tribe was almost wiped out by the Hutas. The Sanuri took the Rualas to the Ice Caves of Mordv to heal. I haven't been there but there are huge crystals bigger than trees that grow all over in the caves and they are filled with healing energy and blessed by The Great Ruler. The Rualas make necklaces out of slivers of those crystals." As Noah spoke he handed Tessa a necklace.

"Even a sliver is powerful enough to heal a wound. If you get hurt just put the crystal inside of the wound. And there is so much holiness in the crystals that if you touch one against a demon or dark lord their skin will begin to smoke. We all wear them. I got one for you and I want you to wear it tonight."

Angus decided to lead the group of warriors who would search Frankwich's home. Immediately after being briefed by Turner, Angus had men watching the house.

Tessa was taking a bath and Noah stood in the doorway talking to her. "Dominic asked Turner and his group to move into our house here, mostly for their own safety," Noah explained.

"I am going to start moving your things in when I am feeling a little better."

"A lot better," she said sarcastically.

Noah grinned at her remark. "Our house is an old mansion. Wait until you see it. Everything is made out of marble and gold. And King Sudfad bought us a huge house in Salar; it's really nice but nothing like our place here." He paused.

"Dominic and Fennel had a little brother named Asher. He was killed in our last battle in Ryed, so were a lot of our friends," he paused again. "Asher and Seth were just little kids when we decided to fight Teivel. I mean we all were kids but they were just little boys."

"You know we spent most of our lives hiding in caves, well, Asher always dreamed of living in a house someday. He would talk about that so much. We have two houses now and he never got to see either one of them."

Tessa could hear the sadness in his voice. "I know you had horrible lives but I think all of you are heroes and to hear that you were just kids and were the only ones with enough guts to take a stand; well, I am just proud to know all of you." She could see that her words touched Noah, who was too emotional to speak.

"Meeting all of you and I mean everyone here has been a good thing for me. After a while when all you see is the bad in people you start thinking everyone is like that." Tessa was now putting on a robe and walked up to Noah. "You've restored my faith in people again." She stretched up and kissed him on the cheek.

There was a knock at the door. "It's Jasmine and Elexas," Jasmine said loudly through the door. "We have Tessa's shoes and we need some help with our hair."

"Well, don't you two look pretty," Noah said when he opened the door. Both women were wearing gowns.

"Dominic and I are going to be in the restaurant when they get there," Jasmine explained. "And there will be priests in there too."

"Good," Noah said then he lowered his voice. "I don't have a good feeling about this."

"I heard that," Tessa said as she walked out of the bathing room. "You both look great." She walked to the armoire and took a small carrying case out of it. "This is all jewelry. Pick out anything you want," Tessa said and handed the case to Jasmine. Tessa chose a few articles of clothing and returned to the bathing room.

"Oh my god!" Elexas said. "I have never seen such beautiful things."

"Turner talked with us about this mission," Jasmine said. "So, we know what to look for."

"Elexas, I am glad that you are helping," Noah said in a stern voice. "But if you want to work with us again we will need to have a talk. We have to have each other's backs and can't afford to play the games you like to play."

Elexas looked at him sheepishly. "Dominic and the others already told me the same things. I am sorry about all of that and I really am excited to work on this." Noah didn't say anything but walked over to the closed door to the bathing room and called in, "Do you need me to button your dress?"

"Yes," Tessa said with a big smile and walked out of the bathing room.

"You look really nice," Elexas said sincerely.

As Noah was buttoning her dress, Tessa stared at the two women. "The place we are going is really fancy so we will have to wear our hair up a little. I've got some ideas for you and I have some hair jewelry in that case."

Noah was not the only person to have a bad feeling about Tessa, Turner and Elexas having dinner with Frankwich.

Dominic and Angus had team members and Patronus priests take positions near Frankwich's home, the White Rose Restaurant and various areas along the streets.

Ruala warriors had been spying on Frankwich since Tessa and Turner made contact with him earlier that morning. Frankwich appeared to have a busy day, he entered multiple businesses and had lunch with a group of men. He returned to his home late afternoon. One of the warriors went to the castle before the planned dinner meeting and gave Mathas Frankwich's itinerary from the day.

Claudius, Gideon, Thaos, Ryan and Stephan did not go to their home; they stayed at Mathas' castle in case there were problems. Thaos and Stephan were men of action and did not like doing research although they did find the reports from Gabriel's team fascinating. These two men wanted to be on the streets when their people met with Frankwich but they knew their appearances could put Tessa, Turner and Elexas in danger.

The group that was doing research read the reports and other documents from Gabriel's mission out loud. They took notes and made charts and maps. They were learning a great deal about the clandestine group called the Insidiae and the heinous crimes of some of the priests at the monastery at Malga. And for the first time most of them were learning about Sophie, the wife of Erebus.

"When I first met Erebus I couldn't believe he was allowed to be with us," Sorren told the group. "His eyes were as black as night and he gave off this presence of evil that you could feel from across the room. But I will say he always acted like a perfect gentlemen which really confused me. I would have thought that a powerful warlock would act crazy or like a criminal. But I'll tell you, now that I know the guy I can't believe he could love someone like Sophie. In my mind she was the monster."

Harlow and Wickfield were part of this group and both men were fascinated with everything they were learning. Not only about the mission itself but the roles and lives of the team members. Since Gabriel considered everything relevant his reports read more like diaries of the team.

"You know everyone gives Calen so much crap for being protective of Natasha," Stephan said. "Now I understand why and damn I would be the same way. In fact, I would probably be a whole lot worse."

"These people are more than friends, they are family," said Thaos and with all we've been through, I didn't know a lot of this. Of course I am reading between the lines but am I the only one who thinks Gabriel was the loneliest man alive until he met Hannah?"

# Chapter XXVII
## A Glimpse into Hell

Life in the castle of Sudfad was considerably calmer than in the castle of Mathas. Once the funeral services were over and the guests left, exhaustion and grief consumed everyone. The ruling members as well as Archetenus and Jared temporarily took over many of the duties of the Royal Family.

Matthew and Angelina decided to extend their visit. While greatly upset over the death of Michael they were not as crippled as other members of their family. After the funeral Matthew worked for hours in Sudfad's office addressing paperwork and matters of the kingdom.

Corsa and her brothers were devastated by the actions of their father. They wrote numerous letters to Sorren and other members of their tribe and apologized over and over for not realizing what Dirk was doing and for not stopping him.

Madeline had not come out of her chambers since the funeral. She was isolating herself partly because of her grief and partly because she felt as if she had lost herself. Renya understood what Madeline was going through and was having her meals served to her in her room. It was almost time for the dinner meal to be served when Madeline heard a knock on her door.

"Renya, you're bringing my tray," Madeline said with embarrassment. "Please let me take that."

"Honey, I can carry a tray," Renya said as she placed the tray on a table. "I came for a couple of reasons. One, I wanted to see how you are?"

"Would you like a glass of wine?"

"That would be lovely."

The two women walked onto the balcony and sat down at the ornate table. "I don't mean to be so rude," Madeline said. "One of the first times that I talked with Michael he told me that his anger was the only thing that kept him alive and as soon as you told him he was home, that anger left him."

"He said after that he felt so lost at times that he didn't even recognize himself in the mirror. Now I understand what he was talking about. I don't know if I am like this because of grief or something else."

"Michael saw the world through his anger and that included his own image. We all understood that and thought the best thing we could do was to give him time to heal," Renya said. "But now we wonder if that was the right thing to do. We should have spent more time with him." She paused for a few moments to control her emotions.

"Now I am not an expert but I think you are feeling like that for entirely different reasons. You lost Michael and you almost lost Javier but my dear your life has also been turned upside down. You need some time to get your bearings. But we don't want to make the same mistakes with you. We don't want to push ourselves on you but know that we care about you and are here for you."

Madeline started to cry and got out of her chair and hugged Renya. "All of you are so wonderful. Thank you."

After Madeline returned to her chair Renya took an envelope out of her pocket. "A few moments ago a large flock of Enrops delivered letters and they were mostly for Sudfad. The birds said he needed to read them right away and that other birds were delivering similar letters to Gabriel's home. The letters came from Lentz. I don't yet know what they say but I suspect they have to do with the attacks. One also came for you. I just want you to be prepared if it is unsettling news."

Madeline was hesitant to take the envelope but as soon as she saw the handwriting she smiled. She tore the envelope open and quickly read Tessa's letter. She smiled, laughed then frowned and put the letter on the table.

"I want you to read that but first I have to tell you about the person who wrote it. You know that Javier and I were orphaned at the age of ten. As soon as our mother killed herself we joined the Charto because some of the Abuckto were going to auction us off as sex slaves." Renya gasped as she listened to Madeline speak.

"Like with any job, some people perform better than others and the life expectancies of members in the Charto were not usually long because they made so many mistakes in their work. There really wasn't any training and our work is very dangerous. We were assigned to a relatively small team which had recently lost several members. All of the replacements were very young, although Javier and I were the youngest."

"The older members of the team didn't like working with kids and we believed they were setting us up at times to get rid of us. So we kind of formed our own group. We trained ourselves and learned as we went. And we were determined to learn from every mistake. There are four men, still alive from that group. They visited Javier and me at Mathas' castle. Now, you have to understand how untrusting we all are. Although we are friends we...well let's just say we were all looking at each other with new eyes."

"Anyways these men are working with our teams now and apparently are getting along so well with everyone that Mathas has offered them jobs. Their names are Turner, Bart, Garvis and Louis. So these four men and Javier and I basically grew up together."

"One of our first assignments was in Port Friada and you read Thaos' story. The lives of children on the streets there is horrible. One evening Javier and I were walking down a street and heard someone screaming. We ran towards the screams and found two men raping this little girl. Javier and I both carried weapons and we killed the men and brought her back to where we were staying. She was seven and an orphan. Her name is Tessa and she joined our group."

"She didn't know we were Elods so she didn't know we were spies. She thought we were con artists which is what she became. She is like our little sister. She is so much fun and bright and adventurous. This letter is from her. She read about the attacks in a newspaper in Port Friada. The story said that Javier and Edward had been killed also. She packed her bags and went to Langer to find the people responsible. She is now working with the teams. She swore to get revenge for the attacks."

"You will read that Turner won't let her stay by herself. Turner would only act like that if Tessa was in extreme danger. Then she goes on to say that Turner told her about Inferus. I can only guess that Andrac or Gilder went after them for Turner to tell her that information. After the job there is done she wants to come here and visit me and Javier." Madeline handed the letter to Renya.

Renya laughed several times as she read the letter. "Sometimes she almost sounds like a child and in the next sentence she sounds like a warrior."

"That is Tessa," Madeline said proudly of her friend.

"Madeline, you have to show this to Javier but would you feel up to going with me to Sudfad's study to find out what the other letters contain?"

So as to not draw unnecessary attention, Patronus priests and some team members started to arrive at the White Rose Restaurant well in advance of the meeting with Frankwich. Bart and Mallory, a female Venator from Dominic's team arrived as a couple as did Dominic and Jasmine. Simultaneously, other team members were preparing to search Frankwich's home.

In an unprecedented act, High Priest Othnial announced that he was going with the group to Frankwich's house and that he wanted to be the first to enter the building in case there was a demonic presence.

The warriors who were spying on the house had not seen any sign of life other than Frankwich entering the building. This in itself made them curious as they expected a man of his means to have staff.

In addition to having the White Rose Restaurant and Frankwich's home watched, Claudius had soldiers spying on The Rooster clothing store. These soldiers were dressed as civilians. The plan was for one of the members of Turner's team to try and gain access to the back room of that store the following day.

"Well, you two should definitely keep Frankwich distracted," Turner said to Tessa and Elexas as they rode in a carriage to the White Rose Restaurant. Two Patronus priests dressed in civilian clothing were driving the carriage.

"Elexas, I know I have already said this," Turner explained. "But this is definitely not the type of job I would start someone off in. It is imperative that you follow our lead in this."

"I know," she said defensively.

"Elexas, I don't know how much you pay attention to the work the teams do but there have been at least three situations that I know of where the teams discovered hostages while they were investigating other things," said Tessa. "And that is one of our concerns with Frankwich. We suspect he may be involved with many things and we don't want him getting suspicious and leaving the restaurant early."

"We weren't working with the teams then but on one of the missions they discovered children kept in cages in the ground," said Turner. "So we are taking this seriously."

"I did hear a little about that," said Elexas with embarrassment because she had not paid attention when her tribe was involved with helping those children.

"Also, we don't know a lot about Frankwich as Turner already told you," Tessa said. "Now, from one woman to another I would initially peg him for a dirty old man. He doesn't come across as being highly intelligent but I believe that is all a ruse so keep your guard up."

Zander, one of the Nordes warriors on Angus' team, crept closer to Frankwich's house. His curiosity was getting the better of him because he could not understand why they were not seeing anyone in or around the building; other than Frankwich who was still inside.

Since the teams suspected that Frankwich might be a dark lord, the warriors spying on the house had been told not to touch anything until High Priest Othnial prayed over the building.

Zander looked in two windows in the back of the house. He did not see anyone but all of the furniture was covered with sheets. He crept to the side of the house and looked into another window. He saw a huge parlor that was furnished but the furniture was also covered with sheets. He crawled back to his hiding spot and called to several Enrops to take messages to Mathas and Angus. Moments after the birds left the area a carriage stopped in front of the house. Frankwich left the house and got into the carriage.

Angus, High Priest Othnial, Garvis and Louis were riding towards Langer when Angus received his message from Zander. "The warriors have been watching the house all day and there has been no sign of anyone other than Frankwich entering the building. Zander looked in some of the windows and all of the furniture was covered with sheets. He thinks this may be a trap."

A few minutes later Mathas received the same message. "That does it," Stephan said. "We're going in."

"It may be a trap to draw you and Thaos out and you know that," scolded Sorren. "I'll go in and see what is going on."

The group in the Great Hall of Mathas' castle had finished reviewing Gabriel's reports and now they started on Harlow's notebooks. While the task initially looked daunting to the group, Harlow was a meticulous note taker and categorized the sections by both subject and date.

"I am handing out the books that have tabs with either Frankwich's name or shipping or something similar highlighted. I can't guarantee we will find anything of interest but it is a good place to start," said Harlow.

"Do you have anything on the Franks family?" asked Claudius.

"Not that I saw in my tabs but I might have failed to tab something properly," Harlow said.

Turner, Tessa and Elexas did not see Frankwich when they entered the restaurant so they asked for him by name.

"Mister Frankwich has not yet arrived," said the host. "But he did reserve a table." The host led the group to a table overlooking the ocean. Within moments Frankwich joined them.

The first thing Turner did was to look at Frankwich's hands. He wore two rings but neither of them were from the monastery of Malga. "You have met my Tessa," Turner said and Frankwich kissed her hand. "And this is my lovely sister Elexas."

"I must say you took my breath away," Frankwich said to Elexas then kissed her hand. She smiled and batted her eyes at him.

Angus and his group continued traveling to Frankwich's house. He sent an Enrop back to his team telling them not to go near the house again until he arrived.

To the surprise of both Tessa and Turner, Frankwich was a charming man who spoke intelligently about many subjects. In fact, he was doing most of the talking as the four drank wine. It was apparent that he was quite attracted to Elexas who was not shy about flirting with him.

Angus and the others gathered in the back of Frankwich's house. High Priest Othnial prayed to remove the darkness in the building, to protect the warriors and to reveal any evil in the home. Then Angus led them into the building. He broke the lock on the back door and told Othnial to stay behind him. As soon as the door was opened Ruala and Nordes warriors, Venatores, soldiers and Patronus Priests swarmed into the house.

Sorren decided to go to the White Rose Restaurant instead of Frankwich's home. He was not dressed in the manor for such an establishment but he didn't care. He entered the restaurant, walked through the dining room so his people would see him then sat down at the bar.

All of the team members realized something was wrong when they saw him. Frankwich watched Sorren also but continued telling his story without hesitation.

Tessa studied Frankwich, his clothing, jewelry, demeanor, the way he pronounced words. She was looking for a sign of something more than what he was presenting. Suddenly she remembered Noah's words. Tessa was wearing the necklace made of a sliver of crystal from the Ice Caves. She wore this necklace in addition to others as Noah had warned that Frankwich might recognize it if he was a dark lord. Now she was thinking of how she could discretely take her crystal necklace off and touch Frankwich with it.

Renya, Javier, Madeline and Corsa were walking to Sudfad's study. Javier had just read Tessa's letter and agreed they all needed to find out the information in the stack of letters Sudfad had recently received.

Madeline suddenly stopped walking and leaned against the hallway wall and grabbed her head.

"Honey what is the matter?" asked Renya. "Are you dizzy?"

"No," Madeline stammered. "I just had a vision. I haven't had one in years." She stopped speaking as she tried to recall the fleeting images in her mind. "It was so fast. There was a cave and I was overwhelmed with the feeling of evil. Renya, I don't know why but I think we need to gather everyone together."

"Something is wrong here," Angus growled. "Search everything again. Look for hidden doors. Tell the others." Nana and Enzo turned and left the room.

Angus and High Priest Othnial were standing in a room on the third floor of the house. It was a bedroom and the only room in the house that looked as if it had been used in years. The bed was unmade. There were several suits and shirts in an armoire. There was an open suitcase on the floor that contained shoes and socks. There was little else in the room.

"He's not living in this house," Othnial said. "This is all a ruse. We need to send someone to the restaurant."

When Renya, Javier, Madeline and Corsa entered Sudfad's study they found that Raul, Simon and Matthew were with Sudfad and they all were reading letters.

"We are joining you because of a letter that Madeline received," Renya said.

"Good," Sudfad said. "I'll tell you we haven't gotten through all of these yet."

"Let's do this differently," Simon said. "These are not social letters and each one contains a great deal of information. Instead of us individually reading each one, let's move to the other side of the room and one person read the letters out loud and someone else make notes."

"Whoever takes the notes, put the paper on the wall so we can all see it," Matthew said. "I think we are going to have to connect the dots on a lot of this."

"We have a problem," Thaos said and stood up. He handed the journal that he was reading to Claudius and pointed out a particular passage. "Harlow, you have notes about the shipping magnate Frankwich who died during a boat race eleven years ago. It says he fell overboard and his body was never found. His wife Matilda and his son Olin inherited his fortune. It's time we found out who this guy really is." Thaos and Stephan quickly left the room.

"Mathas, I'm taking some troops into the city," Claudius said as he stood up. Mathas nodded.

"What a wonderful story," Elexas said to Frankwich as she stared into his eyes. "So is that why you started your business…"

"Excuse us Elexas," Stephan said and he and Thaos set down chairs on either side of Frankwich and sat on them. Frankwich was now pinned between the two men who grabbed his arms and pulled up his sleeves, exposing his wrists. "Well, you aren't one of Juleta's concoctions so just who the hell are you?"

"My name is Frankwich and you..."

"Then do you want to explain the newspaper articles about Frankwich dying eleven years ago?" Thaos asked.

As the men were talking Tessa took off her crystal necklace. "Here Thaos," she said and handed him the necklace.

Thaos touched the crystal to Frankwich's arm and nothing happened. "Now that is a damn surprise. So you aren't a demon or dark lord, guessing maybe con man? Hired killer?"

Before Frankwich could speak Angus marched up to the table. "He's not living in that house he is squatting. Who the hell are you?" Angus growled at Frankwich.

"We were just trying to find that out," said Stephan.

"I find it interesting that he isn't that shocked by all of this," Turner said. "Go through his pockets."

Thaos and Stephan emptied the contents of Frankwich's pockets onto the table. Turner searched the wallet while Tessa and Elexas unfolded several pieces of paper. Elexas handed her paper to Turner.

"What is this?" asked Turner as he looked at a series of numbers written on the paper. Frankwich didn't answer the question.

"My paper is blank," Tessa said. "But I wouldn't be surprised if there isn't a hidden message. Let me work on this."

As this was taking place at Frankwich's table the other team members and Patronus priests were watching the crowd. The busy restaurant fell silent as staff and customers watched the scene. Everyone recognized Sorren, Thaos and Stephan as being ruling families of the kingdom. For them to be in an exclusive restaurant and interrogating someone drew the curiosity of all.

"You're coming with us," Thaos said as he and Stephan stood up and pulled Frankwich to a standing position. It was at that moment that Sorren saw Frankwich look at a man at another table. Sorren quickly stood up and yelled "Knife!" But his warning came too late to save Frankwich who had a knife impaled in his chest. Two Patronus priests tackled the man who had thrown the knife and had him pinned against the floor.

Thaos and Stephan were lowering Frankwich to the floor. "Why?" asked Stephan.

"The heel of my..."Frankwich said and died. Both Thaos and Stephan heard these words but they didn't want to search his shoes in front of the crowd.

"Let's get them both back to the castle," Thaos said as he suspiciously looked around the room.

Turner and Tessa realized their disguises had been compromised so they and Elexas left with Thaos and the others. But the team members and priests who had not approached the table remained in the restaurant to watch the crowd because they all believed there were probably more terrorists in the room.

Angus still had people watching Frankwich's house and now he sent word to them about the murder and told them to stay in place.

"So what now?" Elexas asked Turner while they rode back to the castle in a carriage.

"Well, our disguises have been exposed so we can't use them anymore. I need to hear what that prisoner says before I make the next move."

"If I can still help, I would like to," Elexas said.

"This is going to be a long night. Stay at the castle tonight while we figure things out," Turner said and looked at Tessa. "Do you have any thoughts?"

"I'm working on that. I am beginning to wonder if he was a ploy to expose us. He looked like he expected to get caught. Now I am wondering who the hell these people are really after."

Turner now looked at Elexas and said, "Honestly, I don't know how much we can trust you. You have to know that you are not respected as a warrior or even a person for that matter." Elexas turned white as Turner spoke. "And we have already seen that you like to cause dissention among the group. But you did play your part very well tonight."

"Are you beginning to understand that people's lives are affected by every move we make?" Elexas clearly looked upset and didn't answer. "If you truly want to work with us you are going to have to prove that we can trust you and screwing everyone on the team doesn't do it."

"Now that we have that in the open, you are a natural actress and game player. We can teach you a lot. But you play by our rules. This is very dangerous work and you need to understand what you are asking to get involved with. Almost every one of us has bounties placed on us by demons and dark lords. And why is that? Because we are all damn good at what we do. We take pride in our work."

"Elexas, you wanted to screw with Tessa and she was the only one who saw what you are capable of. No one else wanted you involved with anything. We have to be able to trust each other. If you work with us and get someone killed because you chose to disregard our rules or you betray us, trust me I will kill you myself and it will not be a pretty death." No one spoke for the remainder of the journey.

As soon as they entered the castle, Tessa walked straight to Noah's room which was empty so she went to the Great Hall. Turner was briefing Mathas and the others in the room about what had happened at the restaurant. Noah and Lawrence were sitting with the group who were reviewing Harlow's notes. Tessa sat down next to Noah and gave him such a disapproving look that several people grinned, including Noah.

"She's going to keep you in line," Lawrence whispered.

"You shouldn't be out of bed either, I'm about ready to tie you both up," she said in a low voice and everyone laughed.

"Turner, sorry for the interruption," Noah said with a grin. "We're getting scolded."

"Tessa before you hurt those boys why don't you come up here and explain the theory you are working on," Turner said and grinned.

As Tessa stood up she gave Noah and Lawrence another angry look and they both laughed loudly. "As Turner said, I am working on this. I am trying to go over every step I've taken since I started working this job and look at things with new eyes. I really think that guy was a set-up to expose us, which he did. If anyone else was in that restaurant they now know that we are all working together and what we are looking at. We exposed a lot tonight in my opinion."

"Before you ask, the reason I am thinking this is because Frankwich, or whatever his name is was not a dark lord or demon. We know this because we touched him with the crystal. And he certainly wasn't a fighter and no weapons were found on him. Yet, he didn't look scared or even surprised when he was confronted. He looked like he expected it."

"All of you are always saying that you are being spied on which makes sense. I am starting to wonder if this Frankwich isn't involved with the attacks at all but some other criminal job and his people want to know our involvement. I keep thinking about what Cyril told Stephan and Thaos. He said if we want to know what is going on we need to speak with the people who live on the streets. That leads me to believe that there are a lot of people watching everything."

"There are always soldiers in the streets now and team members. Thaos and Stephan were probably noticeably absent. And maybe someone recognized me or Turner. Frankwich did ask me where he knew me from. This may have been a set-up to find out what kind of job we were working and who the players are."

"I am not sure that I understand what you are saying," Deborah said shyly. She was more intimidated to speak in front of Elexas than the rest of the group.

Elexas was sitting in the back of the room by herself. No one had spoken to her or even acknowledged her since she entered the castle.

"Ok, let's say there is a group of men who are planning on robbing a bank or pulling a big con on someone. So they are starting to put their plans into motion. Most criminals and con men who are worth their salt do a lot of preparation and research before they make a move. So, let's say these people are doing research and they see that suddenly there is an entire army in the streets. They are going to wonder if that army is there to stop them from the job they are planning. They may know nothing about the threats to the ruling families."

"And on top of it, if they recognize one of us or they are watching the streets and wondering why so many people are watching me and Turner, they will suspect something is going on. I know if I was setting up a big con I would certainly want to know what other games were going on and who the players are."

Turner had returned to his seat when Tessa spoke; now he stood up again. "Mathas, something has been gnawing at me all night and I can't put my finger on it. But I believe we need to reread the notes from the meeting where Gideon put Drake into a trance. I think I missed something important tonight."

While the group in Sudfad's study were reviewing the letters they had recently received, more Enrops flew into the room with letters. This time everyone but Corsa received at least one letter. One of the giant birds spoke. "The people in Langer have been working around the clock. Claudius told me to tell you that they are sending the same letters to Gabriel as they are to Sudfad. Claudius said that so much is happening that they can barely make time to write but it's important you read all of the letters right away."

341

"Do you know why?" Renya asked.

"Because they think their mission is somehow involved with the one we worked on in Nora," said the Sanuri as he entered the study with a handful of letters.

"The one to raise Omnibus?" Raul asked with amazement. "Don't tell me the Insidiae are trying to do that again."

"Obviously we need to read all of these," said Simon. "But why do they think that?"

"Because Drake was shown a vision that was similar to events that had happened in Nora. A man dressed like a priest and wearing the ring of the monastery at Malga was in a cave sacrificing people before an army of Hutas."

"Oh my god!" Corsa said as Renya and Javier now looked at Madeline. "Madeline, tell them about the vision you had."

"Sanuri, you may need to look in my mind again," Madeline said emotionally. "I haven't had a vision in so long that I thought that sense had been bred out of me. As we were walking here I had a vision but it was so fast that I am not sure of what I saw. I saw a huge cavern filled with people. There was a giant fire in the middle and a priest near it and I was filled with the feeling of evil."

# Chapter XXVIII
## Clues

Elexas was a woman who enjoyed feeling powerful. She used her beauty and her body to manipulate others and that gave her a sense of power. She was an intelligent woman, so intelligent that she was bored living in the Village of Tyger. She combated her boredom by creating havoc whenever she could. Like many people, Elexas felt empowered when she was able to hurt and humiliate other others. She was self-absorbed and never gave a though to the feelings of others until this moment.

She sat in the back of the Great Hall. No one wanted to sit with her or to speak with her. Elexas was used to being the center of attention and in this room full of powerful men, no one even glanced at her.

Turner's words had both shocked her and hurt her. But at the same time she felt like he could see inside of her, she felt exposed. Sorren entered the room and did not speak to her, he walked to the front with the others.

Elexas was going to walk out of the room until Tessa spoke to the group. Elexas had been sitting at the same table in the restaurant yet Tessa saw so much more than she did. Elexas prided herself on being a trained warrior and to her knowledge Tessa was not yet she had superior observation skills and knowledge of a world that Elexas never paid attention to.

As she listened to the meeting, part of Elexas was intrigued by what she heard and yet another part of her wanted to get back at all of them for shunning her.

Mathas had left the room to retrieve the notes that Turner requested. When the King returned he stood in front of the room and read the notes. They contained information about Raven's death and the people who were rescued from the cave near Minges. The notes covered the occurrences that had happened the night that Bertuck attacked Thaos and Stephan.

343

Mathas read Drakes description of the vision he saw and Tessa's information about the jewelry on the women who were sacrificed as well as her observations of Frankwich. Gideon's observations of the man were included in the notes as well as the words of the Angel Adam.

"Thank you," Turner said and stood up. "Elexas, Tessa I want your observations here. Gideon said that Frankwich was so intense that one could feel it coming from him. Did either of you get that impression of the man we met?"

"Not at all," said Tessa. "And I forgot about that. Elexas come up here," she said in an almost scolding manner.

Elexas did not speak until she was next to Tessa. "I felt just the opposite. He reminded me of a grandfather type." Elexas said then hesitated. "But while I am a trained warrior, I didn't see a lot of the same things that Tessa saw so maybe I am off on this. But I have something to say about another thing that was in those notes."

"Hold that thought for a moment," Turner said to Elexas then addressed the group. "Elexas did a very good job tonight, especially being so inexperienced and just thrown into things. She asked me if she could continue to help us. I had a talk with her that hurt her feelings. While she has many qualities that we can work with she also has choices to make. I am considering letting her stay on this mission. If any of you do not trust her or have other issues, take that up with her yourselves."

"Elexas if you continue to work with us, we routinely ask everyone's observations after a situation because people see and hear different things. You are certainly not at the level of Tessa but you are a smart woman and well trained. What were your observations tonight?"

"I thought he had a gentle presence about him. But the thing that stuck out to me were his hands." She now looked at the others in the room. "My role was to flirt with him so I was touching him a lot. He had a lot of calluses on his hands which I would not expect for a man who is that wealthy."

"Now, that is an excellent observation," Turner said. "Tessa and I were wondering if he was a con man but it is unlikely he would have calluses on his hands. I am now wondering if he was a, let's say normal person who was paid or blackmailed to fill a role. Anything else Elexas?"

"His smell," she said thoughtfully. "The people of my tribe don't normally wear fragrances so I always notice them on others. Whatever he was wearing I have smelled before and Claudius I think it was when I was at your castle for Stephan and Ingr's wedding."

"Elexas, you are doing really good," Tessa said. "Anything else?"

"I was watching him more than I was you and Turner but I thought that a couple of times he looked intimidated by Turner but maybe it was the guy who threw the knife. He was sitting behind Turner."

"You did really well," Turner said to Elexas. "So we may possibly have had a man being forced into that role. Now, for the rest of those notes. Thaos said that there were newspaper reports that Frankwich had died eleven years ago. He was a prominent man in Port Friada. So who was making appearances at parties and in Joy City? As well-known as he was you would think people would question all of that."

"Let me look into that," said Harlow. "But you are absolutely right."

"I think it was us who was conned tonight," Turner said. "Now we need to find out by whom and why." He turned to Elexas. "I am done talking about Frankwich, what else did you have to say?"

"Actually a couple of things," Elexas said.

"Elexas come to the front of the room so we can hear you better," said Sorren.

The woman who thrived on attention looked humiliated standing before this group of warriors. "The part where you were talking about Raven. I knew she had a boyfriend who wasn't from our tribe but I didn't know he worked for Usman. His name is Kinsman. She was with him for a couple of years and when I asked why she never brought him around she said it was because he was married and they were trying to keep their relationship a secret. She really loved him."

"She never told me about the people in the cave but she did go riding every day and sometimes she would be gone for really long times."

"Wait a moment," Sorren said. "Elexas, I didn't realize that you and Raven were close friends."

"I had a problem that she helped me with and she never told anyone else and she knew the man I was seeing was married. After that we became close. But before you ask, I had no idea she was a traitor and in fact it is really hard for me to believe."

"Honestly, it was hard for all of us to believe," said Sorren. "But she had a lot of gold in her saddlebags. Do you have any idea where she got it? And apparently she brought food and supplies to those people every couple of weeks."

"Sorren, she never told me about any money and she sure didn't live like she had any. But wherever she was going she would comeback hurt. I thought that her boyfriend was beating her. A couple of times she asked me to help her with wounds on her back. When I would ask her about them, she always said she didn't want to talk about it."

"Could she have been fighting?" asked Claudius.

"I don't know," said Elexas. "I guess I never questioned anything besides that it was probably her boyfriend."

"Thank you," said Mathas.

"There was one more thing," Elexas said. "And this may be nothing but after Toni was put into the dungeons a lot of us would visit her, at least in the beginning. Everyone thought she was going insane being locked up and I know that Hugo talked to some of the healers about ways to help her."

"One day I was visiting her. I had brought her a basket of food and sat outside of the cell and talked with her while she ate. She had been in prison maybe three or four months at that time. We had a normal conversation. She told me that she hated being locked up but no one was hurting her. She threatened to kill Edward for choosing Kate over her and the rest of the conversation she asked about people in the tribe. But in a normal way not like she was going to hurt anyone."

"We must have been talking for an hour when Hugo comes in with Edna. Edna is a powerful healer in our tribe. I was sitting on the floor with my back to them. Toni leans towards me and whispers that they are coming and tells me not to tell them about the drums."

"I asked her what drums and she looked at me like I was crazy and said the ones that are beating. I said where? And she said they were coming from below. Well, I didn't know if there was anything below the level we were on in the dungeons. I asked her why they were beating and she said 'that is how he sends messages'. Hugo and Edna walked up to us so I stopped asking questions."

"Now that is interesting," Sorren said and looked at the others in the room. "In case you didn't know, one of the warriors from our tribe fell for Edward and viciously attacked him and Kate. Edward never led Toni on but she developed this entire relationship in her head. Our village isn't large and we all know each other well. Until Toni attacked Edward none of us had any idea that something was wrong with her."

"Then, she is put into the dungeons and we saw her changing before our eyes. She turned into a monster. I don't think saying she was insane even explains it. We were wondering if somehow she was communicating with demons. Elexas was there anything else?"

"It was probably three or four weeks before I visited her again. Honestly, I really didn't like going into that place. She acted like she didn't know me. At first I thought it was an act because I hadn't been there for a while until I saw the blank look in her eyes."

Stephan walked into the Great Hall. He walked directly to the front of the room and stood next to Elexas. "When you are done..."

"I'm done," she said and sat down.

"Thaos and Angus are interrogating the man who killed Frankwich. We searched him and other than a bunch of weapons we didn't find anything but some money."

"When Frankwich was dying he started to say the heel of...we tore his boots apart and sent a couple of men back to his house to get his other shoes. We tore them all apart. We got two pieces of paper from his pockets before he was killed. One has a bunch of numbers and the other is blank but Tessa said she is going to find out if there is a secret message."

"In the left heel of the boots he was wearing tonight we found two pieces of paper folded into tiny squares. One was actually a news story from a paper. It was a story about Frankwich. Harlow look at this and see if there is anything strange about it or if you can figure out what paper it is from."

"The second was a letter which all of you can read. *It says Sam, I hope this information will help you. Please let me know if you need anything else. And be careful. Matilda.* That is the name of Frankwich's wife."

"Since the guy is dead, Sol and Adin tore his clothing apart. In the lining of a jacket they found a couple of maps. One is the City of Langer. One is the City of Cadia and the third is Port Friada. Before I pass these around I want you to notice the dots marked on the dock areas of all three cities."

"Now for the kicker. In the heel of one of the shoes he had at his place we found a contract. It appears that Matilda Frankwich hired Sam Endleson to do some kind of job for her."

348

"It doesn't say exactly what that job is but he gets bonuses for the information he provides her. She is paying all of his expenses and a good salary. We didn't find much money on him or in that house he was staying in so we may want to hit the banks tomorrow."

"Mathas, we will need you to write one of those letters giving us permission to search safety boxes. I would put the names of Frankwich and his wife as well as Sam Endleson on it."

"So it appears this guy was investigating something where he needed to present himself as Frankwich. We read in Harlow's notes that Frankwich's body was never found. So I have three thoughts right now. The wife is trying to find her husband, or trying to determine how he died or now that she is in charge of the businesses she discovered something that didn't seem right."

"That would make sense," Turner said. "We were discussing our observations. He certainly didn't seem scared when he was confronted by all of you and we reviewed the notes from the meeting the other day. Sam did not fit Gideon's description of Frankwich at all. Then Elexas said his hands were all callouses like a working man. And he was wearing an unusual fragrance that she remembered someone wearing at your wedding."

"While we have answers we just have more questions," Sorren said. "And we need to talk to Matilda." As Sorren spoke Stephan handed him one of the maps. "I wonder if these dots on the docks of Cadia are Juleta's ships."

As much as Ryan did not want to talk in front of Elexas his curiosity was getting the better of him. "I am new to some of this but it certainly sounds like Frankwich might have faked his own death and still has some businesses going on. I mean why would his wife's investigator impersonate him eleven years later? My question is why would someone that wealthy and well-known fake his death?"

"Ryan those are the hundred dollar questions," Stephan said. "You know we put out stories that Edward and Javier were dead to protect them. This guy may have gotten involved with criminals or the Insidiae or something and couldn't think of another way to protect his family and himself."

"Or he wanted another life," said Turner. "He may have met another woman or if that was Frankwich who Tessa saw in Joy City he had a life that he couldn't disclose to others."

"In both those cases he would still need money. That's what we have to be able to track," Ryan said. "Who knows, maybe Matilda found a secret bank account that he had and that is why she hired the investigator. But how does that bring him to Langer?"

Stephan smiled proudly at Ryan. "That's it, you're working with us all the time," Stephan said. "Now I have a question. Was Dominic able to get to the Land Office to look into the deed to Joanna's shop?"

"As you know it has been a busy couple of days for everybody," Lawrence said. "Dominic and Fennel did go to the Land Office but the clerk couldn't find any information about that store. Dominic said he didn't think the clerk was lying to them. The clerk was going to see if the paperwork was misplaced. He told them to come back but they didn't have time."

"When they go back they will have to check on that men's store now too," Stephan said.

The team members and priests who had remained in the White Rose Restaurant did not see anyone who they considered suspicious. But everyone, customers and staff talked about the murder the rest of the night. Dominic was intently watching one particular waiter who looked more distressed than the other people in the room.

"We need to talk to that waiter," Dominic said in a low voice to Jasmine. "Do you think you can get him to come to this table?"

"Give me some money. I'll tell him you lost something of value when he was your waiter and you would like to ask him some questions."

Dominic smiled and nodded. He handed Jasmine a small pouch of gold coins. She waited until the waiter had stopped talking with some people then she approached him. After a few moments she turned and pointed to Dominic."

"The waiter shook his head from side to side and looked worried. Jasmine handed him the bag of coins as sign of good faith then they walked up to Dominic.

"Have a seat," Dominic said.

"My Lord, we are not allowed to sit with the customers. Would you please describe what it is you lost?"

"What is your name?"

"Aldo, My Lord."

"Aldo, I didn't lose anything but I will give you another bag of gold if you can answer a few questions," Dominic said.

"I will try, My Lord."

"You look really upset, is that because of what happened here tonight?" Aldo nodded. "Did you know either of those men?" Dominic asked.

"I've waited on Mister Frankwich fifteen maybe twenty or more times now. He is a very nice man and always tips well. One day I was late getting here because my wife was sick and he gave me extra money for her."

"When did he start coming here?"

"He always comes for lunch. Tonight I was surprised to see him here for dinner. Let me think. Maybe two months ago. I think he had just come to the city because he was asking me all the typical questions."

"Like what?"

"Where is the best place to buy clothes and get your hair cut? Things like that. He liked to talk a lot. I would tell him about the city."

"Did he ever ask you questions that weren't typical?"

Aldo's face turned white. "Oh my god! Now Aldo leaned closer to Dominic. About two weeks ago he came in here and asked me if he could lock some things up in our safe."

"I spoke to the host who said that he could. I told that to Mister Frankwich and also said that there were safety boxes at the banks. He said he was carrying a lot of money and thought some men were following him. I asked him if he wanted me to talk to the soldiers outside and he said no that he just wanted to lock up some of the money for a while. But he didn't act scared so I didn't really think any more about it."

"Did you see or hear anything else that was strange?"

"Well, it's not really strange but tonight is the first time that he came here that he didn't ask the host to be seated at my tables."

"Do you think it is because he wanted to be closer to the windows?"

"I have tables in that area too. I hope that I didn't do something to offend him because I really liked him."

"Aldo, he might have been trying to protect you," Dominic said and handed him a napkin that had a pouch of gold coins inside. "I am sorry you lost your friend."

"Thank you," Aldo said emotionally and walked away.

"Stay here," Dominic said to Jasmine and walked up to the host who led him to the office of the restaurant. When Dominic returned to his table Bart and Mallory were sitting with Jasmine.

"What have you got going?" asked Bart in a low voice.

"Frankwich was a regular customer for lunch and he always asked for that waiter. Two weeks ago he said he was being followed and wanted to put something in the safe here. That waiter made arrangements for him to do so. There is a package in the safe with his name on it but understandably the host can't give it to me. He said he could give it to family or since Frankwich was murdered here to one of the ruling members."

"We'll take care of that. You keep your eye on that safe," Bart said. He and Mallory stood up and the men shook hands and Jasmine and Mallory hugged each other as if they were old friends. Bart and Mallory left the restaurant.

Twenty minutes later Claudius entered the restaurant. He did not look at any of the people seated at tables. He walked directly to the host who took him to the office. A few minutes later Claudius left the restaurant. As he was exiting he looked into the dining room and nodded at Dominic.

# Chapter XXIX
## The Rooster

It was almost dawn when Tessa crawled under the covers next to Noah. Both he and Lawrence were still weak and had to leave the meeting earlier than the others. She propped her head on her hand and watched him sleep. Since the first moment that she saw him she felt weak inside every time she was near him. He was a ruggedly handsome man, muscular with thick black hair and the largest brown eyes she had ever seen.

She thought he was probably ten years older than her but she never asked because it didn't matter. In fact, she had always felt so very much older than her years.

She had heard about the freedom fighters of Ryed for years. She never knew if they were real or just hopeful stories of an oppressed people. And now to be with them. They weren't anything like she had imagined but then as she thought about it she wasn't really sure what she imagined them to be. They were clearly good men and heroes in her eyes but there was a deep sadness in all of them that touched her heart. She kissed Noah on the cheek and cuddled against him.

In Salar the homes of Gabriel and Sudfad were busy as they continued to receive letters from people in Lentz throughout the night. Sudfad sent a messenger to Gabriel's home announcing that it was time to put grief aside and return to the business of the kingdom. Sudfad had scheduled his first morning meeting since before his son was murdered.

Hours before the meeting was to start Sudfad sent soldiers to Erebus' home to escort him to the castle. Both Erebus and the Sanuri spent the majority of the evening and night in Sudfad's study with his family members as they read and charted the information in the letters. Bart had sent two envelopes containing drawings of symbols Turner's team had seen written on walls and in underground tunnels.

Mathas had also sent drawings of the strange markings on the necklace that Tessa had bought in The Chicken and The Egg. Mathas' thoughts were that if four victims of sacrifices were wearing the same necklace the markings had to be significant; no one disagreed with him.

While the majority of letters came from Mathas, Claudius, Sorren, Dominic and Angus, the letters that Madeline and Javier received were from Tessa and Turner. These letters gave different prospectives to many of the subjects. All of the letters were read out loud as a group.

The letters not only contained a great deal of information about people and events but there were many questions that the people in Lentz were asking. Matthew wrote all of the questions on a huge sheet of paper that was hung on the wall. There were so many questions that a second sheet had to be used. After the questions were written down they were divided by subject then assigned to the individuals in the room.

"Corsa, I am not trying to push anything on your brothers, especially at such an emotional time for them," said Sudfad. "But do you think they would be interested in attending the meetings and helping with this?"

"I think it would be just what they need," Corsa said. "At least Alex and Kent. They are humiliated and angry but George is broken hearted. I can't say if he will want to be a part of this."

"We will have them all here for the meeting," Javier said. "Then they can decide what they want to do but I agree this would be good for them."

"This is changing the subject for a moment," Renya said. "But I am bringing this up because of Tessa's letters. While some of you are new members to the family, you are family and this is your home. And Corsa I hope you realize I am talking about your brothers too. I hope you feel enough at home here to have family and friends visit. Tessa said they would stay in Dominic's house. There is no reason they can't stay here."

"Thank you. I was going to speak with you about that," Madeline said. "You'll like Tessa and Turner."

"I already like her from her letters," said Renya. "And honestly, I am pleased that she and Noah are having a relationship. He is a good man and all of them just seemed so lost when they got here."

"What are you talking about?" asked Javier.

"Dominic, Fennel, Seth, Lawrence and Noah are the last of the freedom fighters of Ryed," said Raul. "There was only a hand full of them to begin with and half of them died in the last battle we fought there. They were kids when they started to fight Teivel's demons. He hunted them like animals most of their lives. High Priest Othnial was hiding them in the monastery in Rubar when Gabriel found them."

"It was kind of like with Michael, they had such bad lives that they didn't know how to adjust when they got here. But they are doing much better."

"Would I offend them if I asked them to tell their stories?" asked Javier. "I know we heard about them but I don't know if half of what we heard was true. I think it would be fascinating."

"They will tell you about it," said Simon. "The only subject they don't seem to want to talk about is Asher. He was Fennel's and Dominic's little brother and he was killed in that battle that Raul mentioned. I don't think any of them have gotten over his death."

Most of the people in Mathas' castle slept through breakfast since they had again been up all night. There was only a handful who were working in the early morning hours, among them were Louis and Garvis. These men and those who were going to guard them this morning had slept the previous night so they would be prepared for their mission.

Garvis and Louis rode into Langer to meet with the soldiers who had been watching the store named The Rooster all night. The soldiers said the store appeared to have closed around seven the previous night and they had not seen any activity after the clerks left.

The store was not scheduled to open for another two hours. Ruala warriors flew around the area to make sure there weren't people watching the soldiers who were watching the store. When Garvis and Louis felt that it was safe, they walked down the street and into an alley behind the store. There was a back door and several windows but the windows were boarded over.

A new crew of both soldiers and warriors were watching the store and the surrounding streets. Louis and Garvis initially planned to enter the store after it was opened and try to gain access to the back room. But they realized they might need a password or at the very least an idea of what was in that room, so they decided to start the mission earlier and break into the store. They knew it was likely there were guards inside.

Ruala warriors landed on the rooftops of the alley while Garvis picked the lock to the back door. He slowly opened it and listened for sounds. He didn't hear anything so he and Louis entered the shop, four Ruala warriors were with them. They walked into a huge storage room, which they expected.

The sun was up and providing filtered light through the spaces between the boards covering the windows. The men quickly searched the store. After a few minutes Louis said. "Well, the storage area is the back room and the windows are boarded, something is back here. Be careful."

Angus couldn't sleep and rode into Langer. He arrived at the shop just after the men had entered. He did not go inside but spoke with the soldiers who were watching the store.

All of the men inside of the shop realized there could be traps. They carefully checked for hidden compartments and moved shelves and clothing items.

"Does anyone smell that?" asked Ethan who was one of the Ruala warriors assigned to Angus' team.

Garvis and Tony another Ruala warrior from Angus' team walked to the corner of the storeroom where Ethan was standing. It was the only area of the huge room that wasn't cluttered with items. There was a large area that was clean and free of furniture.

"I know that smell," said Garvis and started to examine the floor.

"Watch out," said Tony who moved a shelf slightly and found a lever on the wall. When Tony said this all of the men in the room now walked to this corner.

Garvis jumped as the portion of floor that he was standing on started to recede. It moved towards the middle of the room. The strong smell of the drug shartish filled the room as did light from the room below. As that portion of the floor moved it exposed a wooden staircase. Tony stayed in the storeroom as a guard while the other men descended into the room below.

Garvis was the first to set foot on the floor of the shartish den which was not occupied. The room was filled with mattresses and sofas. There were tables containing bottles of whiskey and wine and drug paraphernalia. He held his hand up for the men coming down the stairs to stop. "Tessa would have smelled this; there is more going on down here," Garvis said in little more than a whisper. All of the men had swords drawn as they silently moved through the den.

Louis was feeling along one of the walls when it started to move. All of the men heard the groaning of the rusty hinges. They heard movement and prepared for attack. As they rushed into the room they heard two feeble screams and found two young women shackled to the wall. The women appeared drugged.

"You're safe," Garvis said as he and Louis picked the locks of the shackles.

"I don't think they have been down here that long," said Louis. "There clothes are relatively clean and they look normal weight."

"What is this writing on the wall?" asked Ethan.

After Louis freed one of the women he walked over to Ethan as Reese, one of the Ruala warriors carried the woman out of the store.

"We've seen this before," Louis said. "Those were the symbols that Bart drew."

"Let's get the hell out of here," said Garvis as he picked up the second woman. Just as he was about to walk up the stairs, Angus led a group of soldiers down the stairs into the shartish den.

"I'll take her," Ethan said and took the woman who Garvis was carrying. "You explain all of this."

Angus had a couple of the soldiers draw the layouts of the rooms as well as the symbols on the walls. The rest of the soldiers searched the shartish den. Besides drugs and weapons they found little of interest.

"Go back to the castle," Angus said to Garvis and Louis. "I don't want your disguises exposed. I'll take care of this."

Louis and Garvis quickly left the area. They rode back to the castle, initially taking back streets in the city. Two Ruala warriors flew over them for protection.

Angus had his men take positions within the shop and they waited for the staff to open the store.

"We need help!" yelled Reese as he ran into the castle with one of the young women. A housekeeper was the first to run to him. "We need a physician and another girl is coming too."

A soldier went for the Court Physician while the housekeeper led Reese to a room. Within minutes Ethan arrived with the second woman.

The women were placed in separate rooms. Reese and Ethan stayed with them. Both women would have moments of consciousness then pass out again.

Queen Rosa ran into the room where the Court Physician was examining the woman who Reese had brought to the castle. "Do you want me to wake Mathas?" she asked.

"I don't know," said Reese. "I know he was up all night. We went to that men's store and found a shartish den in the cellar and a room with two women shackled to the wall. Ethan is with the other woman, she is in the room next door."

"I haven't seen the other woman yet," said the Court Physician. "Other than a few bruises, I can't find any significant injuries. She's been drugged and now that he said a shartish den, I would suspect that is what she was given."

"I'm getting Mathas," Rosa said and quickly left the room.

The male store clerk who unlocked the front door to The Rooster clothing store had no idea he was being watched or that the store had been entered. He went through his normal morning routine. He hung his hat on a hook then walked into a tiny kitchen area. He started a fire in the hearth and put a pot of coffee on the flames. He turned around to enter the main part of the store and screamed when he saw Angus standing behind him.

"I don't know the combination to the safe. The manager does that. If you want clothing just take it but please don't hurt me."

Angus stared at the man who looked terrified. "I'm not here to hurt you," Angus said. "What is your name?"

"Hors, my name is Hors," stammered the man.

"Hors we need to talk. My name is Angus and I work for King Mathas and the ruling families. We've heard some things about this place and have been watching it."

"A couple of hours ago we broke in the back door and found a shartish den and two women shackled to the wall in the cellar. Can you explain that?"

"My Lord, you must be mistaken, we don't have a cellar."

"Look for yourself," Angus said and took hold of Hors' arm. He led the terrified man through the store, into the storage room and to the corner where the floor was still open to expose the stairs.

"What is that smell?" asked Hors as the color drained from his face.

Angus stared intently at the man as he was trying to determine if Hors' behavior was an act. "That is what shartish smells like. Walk down the stairs."

Hors looked fearfully at Angus and at that moment he realized there were soldiers and Ruala warriors in the room. He looked at the men fearfully. "I really never saw this before. You have to believe me."

"Walk down the stairs," Angus repeated.

Hors tripped and almost fell down the stairs. The den and the room where the women had been imprisoned were filled with soldiers. Hors looked like he was going to cry as he looked around. Angus led him to the back room. "Oh my god!" gasped Hors when he saw the shackles attached to the walls.

"I want you to look around before I ask you any questions," Angus said.

Hors walked up to two soldiers who were copying the symbols that were written on the wall. Hors looked shocked and was noticeably trembling. "What are these?" he asked in almost a whisper.

"We were hoping you could tell us," said Angus. "You recognize them don't you?"

"Just the one," Hors said and walked close to the wall and pointed at a symbol that looked like five swords intertwined. "You should too My Lord. It is on our sign in front and all of the paperwork for this store."

"Hors if you really are innocent, nothing will happen to you. And we can protect you if that is a concern. But we suspect some murders are linked to this store. I really need you to talk to me."

"Murders," Hors gasped and tears came to his eyes then he looked at the ceiling and said, "Great Ruler help me." He turned back to Angus. "I am afraid to ask but who was murdered?"

"Four young women like the two we found in here."

"My Lord, I have only worked here a few months. I have a wife and five children. I will help you as I can but we might need protection."

"You have my word that we will protect you," said Angus. "Let's go upstairs and have a cup of that coffee."

By time the King was awakened and dressed, the Court Physician was examining the second woman. "Rosa told me," Mathas said to Ethan as he entered the room.

"She appears to be in the same shape as the other woman," the Court Physician said. "Both women have bruises on their necks and wrists. The ones on the wrists are from the shackles. Young Ethan here told me where they were found. I suspect both of these poor creatures were attacked and abducted."

"Reese and Ethan pointed out that neither woman looks starved and their clothing is relatively clean for the place they were found. And these bruises on their necks are not old. If I had to guess, I would say they were taken in the last day or two."

"Reese is in the next room with the other lady," Ethan said to Mathas. "We're supposed to stay with them in case they wake up."

"Here you are," Garvis said as he and Louis entered the room. "Angus told us to leave so our disguises wouldn't be compromised. He's waiting for the staff to get there."

"Rosa would you make sure that Ethan and Reese get something to eat?" Mathas said. "I need to talk with Garvis and Louis."

"What time do the others get here?" Angus asked Hors who was pouring coffee into two cups.

"I am the only one here for the first two hours. I stock the shelves and make everything presentable. Hugh, that's our manager comes in around ten. He gives me money so that I can make change for the customers. He handles the ordering and the billing. He is the second manager we've had since I have been here and that has been for three months and three weeks. Hugh is a lot younger than me and not real friendly so we don't talk much."

"Is he coming in today?"

"Yes. There is a small office here. I will take you in there."

"Actually we already searched the place before you got here," said Angus. "I saw the office. I have had spies in here who tell me about men walking into the back room, which turns out to be the storage room. Then those same men are seen leaving without buying anything."

"I just knew this was too good to be true," Hors said sadly. "We are paid very well here. Much more than in other stores. On the days that I work I am the only clerk and I am always busy. But some of our customers come in and walk directly into the back. My first day here I tried to stop a man from going back there and Hugh told me that if I ever did that again he would fire me. Great Ruler forgive me. I knew something was going on but I didn't want to lose my job."

"Did you ever see or hear anything suspicious?"

"Besides what you described, very little. The men are always well-dressed, they look like businessmen. Wait, the other day Mister Frankwich came in and I could hear loud voices coming from the back room. I was helping a young lady who was buying a great deal so I didn't walk to the back of the store."

"Who owns this place?"

"Honestly, I don't know. I asked the first manager that. His name was Randolph. He told me that he didn't know, which I found strange. Did you find any paperwork when you searched the office?"

363

"The desk drawers are locked and I didn't want to break into them yet."

"Well, I have the key here in my cash box. We, there are other clerks besides me. We need to go back there if someone wants to pay a bill or has a question about one." As he spoke Hors opened a small metal box, which contained a few coins and a key. He and Angus walked into the office. "The same key opens all of the drawers," Hors explained and unlocked all of the drawers in the huge wooden desk.

All of the drawers were filled with papers. Angus told one of the soldiers to put all of the papers into a crate and to take them to Mathas.

"While we wait for Hugh, what can you tell me about Frankwich?"

"I first met him, let me see. I think it was two months ago. Nice man and very talkative. He would come in here and shop. In fact, the other day was the first time I saw him go in that back room. I remember being a little surprised but like I said I was really busy. This young woman was buying clothing for her five brothers. In fact, Frankwich came out and talked with her. I heard him invite her and her fiancé to dinner at the White Rose. A nice couple they were; they looked so happy."

"Hors, this is important. Did anyone else overhear them talk or did you tell anyone they were going to that restaurant?"

"I certainly didn't tell anyone; I had no reason to. But there were other customers in here."

"Can you describe them?"

"I can give you their names," said Hors. "One was Jack Franks and his brother-in-law Mister Wilchess. I don't know his first name. They were the only other people in here at that time." Suddenly Hors looked scared again. "Something happened didn't it or you wouldn't be asking these questions?"

"Frankwich was murdered in the dining room of the White Rose last night."

"Oh my god, oh my god. Great Ruler help us."

A soldier stepped into the room and said, "Someone is walking up to the door."

"If that is Hugh, he is early," Hors said nervously. "What do you want me to do?"

"Just act normal," Angus said and walked into the back room. But Angus knew that Hors was too scared to play a role. Hors quickly hid Angus' coffee cup and started to dust one of the shelves.

Two men entered the store, "Good Morning," Hors said. "Hugh you are so early."

"Business," Hugh said and led the other man into the office. The second man closed the office door as Hugh opened the safe. "He's in the dungeons, they want him dead before he can say anything."

"Too late for that," Angus said and walked into the office. The six soldiers behind him quickly grabbed the two men in the office. Angus looked inside of the safe which was filled with money. "This is a lot of money for a clothing store. You must sell a lot of trousers," he said sarcastically and rummaged through the safe. "I need a couple of crates in here!" Angus yelled to the soldiers outside of the office.

Angus was piling bags of gold coins on the floor. "Well, this looks more interesting," he said and took a book out of the safe. "The money and the men go to the castle," he said to the soldiers. As soon as the two men had been taken out of the store Angus walked up to Hors, who was still in the front of the shop.

"This place is closed for business," Angus said. "Some of my men will take you home and stay with you at least until we have this sorted out. But if you want, I can have men watching over you for some time."

"I would appreciate that," Hors said.

"Here, I am sure this is what you would have earned if the place stayed open," Angus said and handed Hors a large bag of gold coins.

# Chapter XXX
## Dungeons

Fahron had not attended any meetings for a couple of days so that he could be home with Chaez and Lana while they healed from their wounds. Since their conditions were improving, Fahron decided to attend Mathas' morning meeting, which on this day had been postponed. Fahron arrived at Mathas' castle as the King was meeting with Garvis and Louis.

Mathas quickly briefed Fahron on the overall events that had occurred and explained that almost everyone in the castle had been up all night and he wanted to let them get a couple of hours of sleep. Then he gave Fahron a small stack of documents.

Fahron gathered two hundred soldiers and they rode into the City of Langer.

Claudius and his sons were all in the same chambers in Mathas' castle. This particular chambers had four bedrooms, a parlor and a bathing room. Mathas had told them to get some sleep. Instead, Stephan, Thaos, Ryan and Claudius sat around the table in the parlor and reviewed the paperwork that Claudius had gotten from the safe in the White Rose Restaurant.

The large envelope that Sam Endleson had put into the safe included several letters from Matilda Frankwich and his personal notes from his investigation.

"I just thought of something," Thaos said. "First, he wouldn't be carrying all of this on him unless he was afraid someone would search where he was staying. He sounds like a really smart and observant guy. It could be a possibility that he set that thing up in the White Rose so he could get to us."

"I don't understand," said Ryan.

"When we get through all of this we may find more," said Thaos. "But already he writes about a half a dozen times that he is being followed."

"And the way he describes the guys they sound like professionals. He recognized Tessa from Port Friada. He might have known she was working with us. If we arrested him that would be a way to communicate with us and be protected while maintaining his disguise."

"I think you might be on to something," said Stephan. "We need to meet with Mathas as soon as we finish these papers."

Fahron and a dozen soldiers entered every bank in the City of Langer. They had decrees from the King ordering the bank managers to open the safety boxes of a list of people. Fahron confiscated all of the paperwork in the boxes they found.

By ten o clock in the morning everyone in Mathas' castle was awake and in the Great Hall. Rosa was having a late breakfast served as Garvis and Louis started the meeting by telling about their experiences at The Rooster clothing store. The two women who had been rescued had not yet regained consciousness.

Mathas announced that he had sent Fahron into the city to get the contents of safety boxes of people they suspected were involved with either the murder of Michael or Sam Endleson. Mathas then turned the meeting over to Claudius and his sons. But before any of them could speak two soldiers entered the room.

"Come forward," Mathas said. "Were you with Angus?"

"Yes, My Lord. This crate contains the papers he took from the office of the shop. Others will be in shortly with all of the gold but he wanted us to tell you that they arrested two men and will be interrogating them in the dungeons."

"Think I will join him when I am done here," Thaos said. "Hope you don't mind if I eat while we talk. I'm starving and we have a lot to cover." Several people in the room laughed.

"First thing I am going to talk about is my interrogation of the guy who murdered Sam Endleson. We gave him the truth potion, which you know works if you ask the right questions. The guy is still alive if any of you need to talk to him."

"The guy is a professional named Haris. He travels all over but was in Port Friada when he received a letter that offered him work here. The letter wasn't signed, which he said wasn't abnormal. He was supposed to contact the manager at The Rooster clothing store for instructions. This was about two months ago."

"He said he met a man named Hugh who was his only contact. Hugh said that a man claiming to be Frankwich was in town nosing around. Hugh said his bosses knew the real Frankwich and wanted to find out what this guy was up to. At first Haris was ordered to just follow Endleson around."

"Haris said that after the first three weeks he started to wonder if Hugh was telling him the truth. He said that all Endleson did was to walk around the streets, shop and eat in restaurants. He said, now mind you he didn't know what Endleson's name was so he called him Frankwich. He said that Endleson seemed like a really friendly guy who liked to talk to people. He said Endleson was always giving money to the street people and just talking with people in general."

"He said that Endleson went into a lot of the shops and a lot of them women's shops including Ashley's and The Chicken and The Egg. He said he never saw Endleson buy anything. Haris said that he didn't have any prior knowledge of the attacks on Michael and the others. But he said that between the fighting and the fires he lost sight of Endleson for almost three days."

"He said he finally sees Endleson after three days and the guy is walking into the Excelsor Hotel for lunch. Haris follows him in and sees him watching a group of men at a table."

"Haris didn't know who these guys were but they all wore suits. He said that Endleson was writing stuff down while he watched the men."

"Haris said that when he saw Endleson again after the three days that he changed his routine. Instead of spending so much time in the stores he was going to the banks and the Land Office and the Catacombs. Haris said he didn't even know the Catacombs existed until he followed Endleson there."

"That's the exact same things we've been doing." Tessa gasped. "But I don't remember seeing him."

"We'll cover some of that when we go through his papers," Claudius said.

"Well to finish up," continued Thaos. "Haris said it was getting harder for him to keep track of Endleson. He was sure that Endleson realized he was being followed and would try and lose him. But Haris also said that after Michael was murdered that the soldiers and just normal people would stop him in the street because he was a stranger, then he would lose Endleson in the crowds."

"He said that a couple of days ago, before the giant snake attack that Hugh tells him to kill Endleson if he sees him talking to any soldiers or anyone who works for the King. Haris hadn't been in Langer for some time and doesn't know a lot of people here. He said that Endleson liked to talk but was always talking with waiters, store clerks and normal people on the streets; he never saw him with anyone suspicious."

"So we got the poor bastard killed," Sorren said and shook his head.

"Thaos, you and Stephan help Angus," Claudius said. "Ryan and I will go over the notes." Claudius and Ryan walked to the front of the room. "Last night Dominic discovered that Endleson had hidden some paperwork in the safe of the White Rose Restaurant when he was being followed. Ryan is passing all of that around now."

"There were a couple of letters from Matilda and a couple of hundred pages of notes. I am just going to tell you what we found to be important. First, Endleson sounded like a professional."

"We all got the impression that he was an intelligent man. We also got the impression that he was very calculated in what he did which made Thaos wonder if he was deliberately trying to get arrested by us because he knew he was in danger. If we arrested him he could maintain his cover."

"Matilda was married to her husband for almost thirty years and fell apart after his supposed death. She was in bed for months then became a recluse. Their son Olin took over the family businesses. Now this part is speculation but she claims she lost her memory for a long time and we are wondering if she was drugged. Apparently during this time there were sightings of Frankwich in the city but no one told her."

"To shorten this up, about a year ago some of her lady friends visited her and asked her about all of the sightings. They had been telling Olin and wondered what he found out. Matilda didn't know anything about them. There were a bunch of medicine bottles in her room and her friends started looking at them and asking why she was taking them. Well, after a few hours the women determined that Olin and his father were involved in some scheme and that she should stop taking the medicine."

"Now, the lady isn't stupid. She pretended she was still taking the drugs and started to spy on her son and her lady friends helped. She hired an accountant to go through their books without telling Olin, who sounds like he was gone from the house a lot. The accountant found all kinds of secret accounts and large sums of money going to people and businesses she had never heard of."

"From what we read, Endleson was following the money trail. Before he came to Langer, he was in Port Friada and verified the sightings. He also looked up every old newspaper article he could find on Frankwich. Harlow look at this," Claudius handed him a yellowed piece of newspaper. It talks about the death of his step-father a Norbert Franks from Langer."

"It names the surviving family members. Otto Franks is Frankwich's step brother. This article is old and neither man was married at the time."

"But the article then talks about the history of the family. Many of the family ancestors were priests. Now the thing that we missed the first time is the age of Frankwich and Otto Franks."

"They are the exact same age according to this," Harlow said in disbelief.

"So Norbert either had two wives at the same time or that is another family mystery," Claudius said. Now, we didn't find a lot of really interesting stuff in most of his notes. As Tessa said he was doing the same thing she was but not finding out as much information until the day of the attacks on Michael, Javier and Edward."

"He had been watching the streets that day because everyone was talking about the shopping trips of the royal wedding couple. He saw men who looked like hired killers watching the people in the wedding parties and he saw our team members and Patronus priests arresting them. This got his curiosity up so he followed Sudfad and Michael from a distance."

"Endleson later saw a group of four men who he refers to as criminals watching Sudfad and Michael too. Then he and the four men saw our people grab some guys who were following Sudfad and Michael. The four men turned and left the area quickly so damn if Endleson doesn't follow these guys and that's when the story gets interesting."

"He follows them into the Black Bear Tavern. He tried to sit as close as he could. He said the men looked worried and made comments like 'he is going to be real pissed.' But then one of the men says, 'He's bad but his daughter scares the shit out of me.' Then one of the men tells them all to watch what they are saying in public and the group leaves the tavern. Endleson followed the men and they went into an underground tunnel near the docks."

"I'll bet that is the one we use," said Turner.

"Endleson said the men disappeared in a cave and he heard voices. He said there wasn't many places to hide so he curled up it a kind of crevice. He couldn't understand what was being said but he heard loud voices and one of them was a woman's."

"The men walked out of the cave and back into the tunnel," continued Claudius. "They walked out the same way they came in."

"Endleson watched a well-dressed blonde haired woman leave the cave and walk the opposite way in the tunnel. He followed the men and heard one of them yell, 'Holy shit what happened?' Then another said, 'I think they started and we weren't ready. She is going to skin us alive. Everyone meet in the Catacombs in two hours'."

"Endleson said that when he got out of the tunnel the streets were filled with soldiers and buildings were burning. He lost sight of the men and asked some people on the street what had happened. He went to the Catacombs and didn't find the men he had been following but was planning on spending time in there asking questions. That's where his notes end."

A woman's scream caused everyone to jump out of their seats and run out of the Great Hall. Rosa was running towards the people. "One of the girls woke up. No one is getting hurt," Rosa said and the group slowed down.

Mathas, Claudius and Sorren walked into the chambers and found Reese sitting on the side of the bed holding a sobbing woman. "Do you need a woman in here?" Tessa asked as she ran into the room.

"She just started screaming as soon as she woke up," Reese said.

"Young lady, I am King Mathas can you tell us what happened to you? You are in my castle. You are safe here."

The woman nodded but continued to cry for several moments, then she pulled away from Reese and tried to compose herself. "How did you find us?" she asked.

"We will answer all of your questions but first we need you to answer ours because we don't know how many people are in danger," said Mathas. "What is your name?"

373

"Daisy, I work at Martin's Grocery Store. We always close around ten and I was walking home and I don't know what happened."

"The next thing I remember is waking up in..." she started to cry. After a few moment's she composed herself again. "It was a dungeon I think, we were shackled to the walls. Some of the girls were crying and others were unconscious."

"Daisy, how many women were there in that room?" asked Mathas.

"There were nine of us. The looks on your faces. Oh my god are the others dead?"

"We only found two of you in there," Mathas said. "The other woman is still unconscious."

"Can you remember anything else?" asked Mathas.

"No," Daisy said and started to cry again.

"Let me talk to her," Tessa said and sat down on the bed. "Daisy, my name is Tessa and we have been watching that place because we heard there were strange things going on there. Can I ask you some questions?"

"Yes," Daisy said softly. "What place? Where did you find us?"

"In the cellar of The Rooster clothing store."

Daisy stared at Tessa for a few moments then said, "That can't be right because we could smell the ocean and hear the waves. One of the women even said we must be close to the ships." Claudius ran out of the chambers.

"Daisy, I want you to close your eyes and describe the room where you heard the waves." Tessa said. Daisy closed her eyes and started to cry again. Tessa held her hand.

"I think it was a dungeon. It was cold and filthy. There was one tiny window by the ceiling and it had steel bars. That was the only way that we could tell when it was night or day."

"You are doing really good," Tessa said. "How many times did the sun come up?"

"Two, I'm pretty sure it was two."

"Daisy, keep your eyes closed. Now look around that room in your mind. What is on the ceiling?"

"Spider webs."

"Is anything drawn or painted on the ceiling?"

"No."

"Now look around the walls, what do you see?"

"There are young women shackled to the walls." Daisy paused and the tears ran down her face. "There are blood stains on the walls but nothing is drawn or written."

"That is really good Daisy, now look at the floor."

"Oh my god there are rats in there with us!"

"What else do you see?"

"All of the women are sitting on the floor so I see their shoes."

"Is there any furniture or writing on the floor?"

"No."

"Did you know any of the women?"

"No. But we all kept passing out and sometimes we would talk a little but everyone was afraid the guards would hear us."

"How do you know there were guards?"

"We could hear men's voices on the other side of the door."

"Could you hear what they were saying?"

"It sounded like they were playing cards."

"Did you ever hear a woman's voice on the other side of the door?"

Daisy didn't speak for a few moments. "I remember, but it may have been a dream. I think I woke up because I heard a woman yelling, she was yelling at the men like she was their boss."

Daisy paused again. "She said they better do better because her father wasn't paying them to sit on their asses. Oh my god," Daisy turned pale. "One of the men said something like he never told us we couldn't taste the merchandize. Then she yelled really loud and said 'Those girls are for the Master. If you want to keep that tongue in your head you will keep your hands off from them'. Then she must have walked away because I just heard the men talking."

"One man called the woman a bitch. And the other said something like 'yes but you can't beat the pay'. Then the first one says 'I would like to beat her.' And the second one says to be careful because she is a witch. I forgot that. Oh my god a witch had us." Daisy was squeezing Tessa's hand tightly.

"Daisy, did you ever see the men?"

"I never saw anyone but the other girls."

"What did they look like?"

"Regular girls. In their teens and twenties. Some were beaten up more than others but they were all pretty."

"Was there anything alike about them? Their clothes or jewelry? The color of their hair."

Daisy was quiet as she searched her memories. She started to shake her head from side to side then stopped. "Wait," she said and paused again. "I thought it was dirt but four of the women have marks on their foreheads. They look like a dark thumb print."

"What color is the hair of those girls?"

"They are all blonde."

"Daisy do you remember them moving you to another building?"

"No but I couldn't stay awake."

"Daisy, you did a really good job. If you remember anything, no matter how small it might be, please tell us. Are you hungry?"

"Yes," Daisy said in a whisper.

"We'll get you something to eat and let you rest."

"Don't leave me alone," she said anxiously.

"I'll stay with her," said Reese.

Everyone from the meeting was standing in the hallway listening to Tessa and Daisy. "That does it," Dominic said to Tessa. "You are on our team."

Noah put his arm around Tessa and kissed her on top of her head, "You did a great job."

"Thanks, but I have to write this down before I forget it," Tessa said and suddenly her demeanor changed and she looked angrily at Noah. "You were running! You aren't even supposed to be out of bed and you were running!"

"Lawrence tried too," Deborah said.

Tessa stared at both men as her face became red. Everyone could see how angry she was. When she spoke it was calmly but through gritted teeth. "If I could spank the both of you I would." Then she turned to the King. "Mathas will you lock them in your dungeons?" Everyone was trying not to laugh since they were outside of Daisy's room.

"I will think about it," Mathas said with a grin. "But seriously you did a great job. When we get back to the Great Hall I want to talk to all of you in Turner's group."

It only took them a few minutes to walk back to the Great Hall. Once everyone was seated Mathas said, "Turner, Tessa, Bart, Louis and Garvis. All of you have impressed us over and again with your work and your professionalism. I have been told that as a group you want to speak with Javier and Madeline before you make any decisions about working for us."

"I would like to make a suggestion. Why don't you let me put you on the payroll from the time you first came here? You will be assigned to Dominic's team until Gabriel, Javier and Madeline make some decisions about other teams. And you can always transfer between teams. At least you would be paid for risking your lives every day. And you know we will protect you and can certainly use your help."

"That is a generous offer," said Turner. "Can we talk among ourselves first?"

"Of course," said Mathas to Turner then looked at all of the people in the room. "Even those of you who got some sleep only got a couple of hours. Let's take a break and meet again after the midday meal."

"Come on," Noah said and took Tessa's hand. The two walked out of the Great Hall.

"Do you want Tessa here to talk?" Bart asked Turner.

"Leave them be," Turner said with a grin. "I suspect he is going to talk her into staying."

"So are you going to yell at me for yelling at you?" Tessa asked kiddingly as they walked into the room they shared.

Noah shut the door then took her in his arms and kissed her passionately. "I like it when you are feisty," he said after a few moments. She didn't say anything but kissed him again. They kissed hungrily as they lost themselves in each other. "I also like how weak you get when I kiss you," he said softly.

Tessa laughed. "Noah, you really scared me that day you passed out. You know that I just want you to get better."

"I know and I like it that you worry about me," he said and kissed her again. "I have to laugh, you know how shy Deborah is. I think she wants to yell at Lawrence but she won't, so she tells you."

"Yeah, I can yell for both of us," Tessa said and giggled. "She is so sweet but she acts like she was abused. What is her story?"

"I'll tell you later," Noah said as he kissed the side of her neck.

## Chapter XXXI
## The Letter

Michael's death had a significant effect on the people in Gabriel's home; more than the loss of a friend. While the children could find release in their tears the adults tried to be stoic but the deaths of Melinda, Jason and Michael in a short period of time brought them all to their knees. The finalization of seeing Michael's casket lowered into the ground forced their emotions forward.

After the frenzy of the funeral preparations, many of these people felt numb. Sudfad sent them a note stating that he was done grieving and had to focus on the security of the kingdom, thus there would be a meeting the following morning. While Sudfad was talking about his own emotions, his words helped Gabriel's family to relinquish their grief. In a way his words gave them permission to resume their lives.

And this permission came just when it was needed. As in Sudfad's home, the members of Gabriel's team had stayed up most of the night to review the many letters they received from their friends in Langer. The letter in which King Mathas wrote that there were similarities between the vision Drake was shown and details from a mission where Gabriel's team tried to stop a heinous crime, shook them all.

Besides reviewing the letters, Gabriel's team reviewed their copious notes on the mission where they tried to stop members of the Insidiae from helping the demon Omnibus to escape his prison in the Abyss.

Although exhausted, the members of Gabriel's team and family arrived at Sudfad's castle before the scheduled meeting. Because the mission concerning Omnibus had such an impact on them as a group, all of the adults in the household wanted to attend the meeting.

"I am both surprised and pleased with this turnout," Sudfad said to the group, which also included all of the adults in his family as well as Archetenus, Jared, Edward and Kate. General Bishop had planned to return to Lentz that morning with the army that Mathas had assigned to escort Sudfad's family home. But Sudfad asked him to stay for the meeting.

"I expect this is going to be a very long day for all of us. Renya has made arrangements for refreshments and meals in addition to a small celebration to keep all of the children occupied."

"Some of you are new to my meetings and I want to explain a few things before we get started. These meetings are very informal because I want people to feel comfortable making comments and asking questions. Don't let your fears stop you from asking questions because you might see something that the rest of us don't."

"Alex, Kent and George, this is your first meeting and we are glad to have you. I have meetings every morning although todays' will run longer than normal. While you are now part of this family, you are also dealing with another issue so if you don't want to be here or decide to leave later, that is fine. But there will be a time when I expect all of you to attend on a regular basis. And the same goes for the two of you," Sudfad looked at Nyla and Saran when he spoke.

"We're staying," Nyla said with such conviction that others smiled.

"We are honored to be here and will certainly do what we can," said Alex.

"General Bishop," continued Sudfad, "I want to thank you for delaying your plans. You have to know I would not have made such a request unless it was important. Last night, Gabriel's household as well as mine received basically stacks of letters from Mathas and others in Langer. Not only do these letters contain information about the investigation into the attacks against Michael, Javier and Edward but also other security concerns for both of our kingdoms."

"Since we received so many letters from different people, I want to start the meeting off by having these read out loud to the group. Besides that some of you have not read them, they may not all contain the same information. Gabriel, while the letters that you and I received will be similar, Madeline and Javier received letters from their friends who are now helping in the investigations. These letters contain different insights and also need to be shared."

"Madeline and Javier, you should read your letters to the group. Since they are personal, feel free to omit anything you don't think is relevant."

"Actually," said Renya. "Javier and Madeline of course the choice is yours. But none of us have met your friends who are now risking their lives to help us. I would suggest that you do read some of the personal parts. They aren't revealing in an embarrassing way but I certainly feel like I know Tessa and the others after reading them. And Gabriel, if Mathas didn't tell you, he wants to hire all of them for the teams."

After a brief discussion, Raul was going to be the first to read some of the letters. As he was walking to the front of the study there was a knock on the door. Erebus and the Sanuri had arrived late and were still standing near the door, Erebus opened it. Olivia was standing in the hallway looking embarrassed.

"Are you alright?" Joao asked.

As she spoke she blushed deeply, "Miranda said I should be here too. I am sorry to interrupt."

"Sit with us," Nyla said and George walked to the back of the room and got a chair.

"That is fine," Sudfad said. "Actually any of you are welcome to attend. We just didn't think you would be interested."

Olivia was still walking with crutches and Joao stood up and moved a few things out of her way. "Miranda didn't tell me why I should be here. I probably should have asked."

Joao and Dack now moved and sat at the small table with Nyla, Saran, George and Olivia. Corsa smiled that her brother seemed to be making friends.

"You can talk and ask questions and there is paper to write on," Saran explained to Olivia. Sudfad smiled as he listened to his daughter.

"I am arranging these letters in the sequence of the time they occurred in Lentz, not the time that we received them. Madeline, that means you should read your letter from Tessa third and tell about your vision at that time," explained Raul. "Matthew and Angelina are in the process of making a timeline which they will show you later. Also, the letters that we received had a lot of questions. Matthew wrote all of them down and we grouped them by subject. Then Father assigned them to us. Now that more of you are here we might ask some of you to help."

"We'll help," Saran said enthusiastically.

"You are going to be sorry you said that," Simon said kiddingly. As Raul started to read the first letter, Simon and Annabelle were handing out copies she had made of the drawings that were sent in the letters. The drawings of symbols that Turner's group had seen and the drawings of the markings on the necklaces of the four young women who were sacrificed in Drake's vision.

After Mathas announced that there would be a break in between meetings, Turner, Bart, Louis and Garvis went to the Excelsor Hotel. Turner believed that his and Tessa's disguises had been exposed so he wanted to get their things and sign out of the hotel.

Bart, Garvis and Louis entered the hotel first and got a table in the dining room that gave them a good view of the front desk and foyer.

Five minutes later, Turner entered the hotel and walked up the front stairs to Tessa's chambers. As soon as he touched the doorknob the door opened slightly. He knew they had locked it when they left. He now kicked the door open with great force so it would hit anyone who might be standing behind it.

He quickly entered the room and as he did he pulled a knife from its sheath on his belt.

The parlor was empty but it clearly had been searched. Whoever was in the room made no attempt to cover up their activity. Things were thrown everywhere. He entered the bedrooms and bathing room and they were all in the same condition. Tessa had previously packed all of their things except for one outfit each and a small empty suitcase. The clothing was in place but the suitcase was open and thrown on the bed.

Turner, packed the rest of their belongings in the suitcase and again looked through the rooms for any clues that might have been left by the intruders. He went down the stairs and to the front desk. He acted as if he was upset and said loudly. "Someone has been in our rooms. Everything is gone except for this." He set the small suitcase on the counter of the desk. He was talking loudly so his men could hear. "They tore the rooms apart. Come, see for yourself."

The desk clerk looked frantic. He quickly ran up the stairs with Turner behind him. Turner showed him the items in the suitcase after the men looked through the rooms. They returned to the front desk. The clerk notified his manager who also looked at the room.

During all of this commotion, Bart, Garvis and Louis were watching the faces of the people in the dining room. They were not surprised that someone had been in Tessa's room. In fact, they all expected it after the disguises were exposed. Now they had to find out who had searched the rooms.

Both Turner and the clerk had been talking loudly so both patrons of the hotel as well as the restaurant were aware of what had happened. The hotel manager reported the incident to soldiers who were patrolling the street.

Afterwards Turner attempted to pay his bill but the manager dismissed it because of the crime. As Turner was leaving the hotel the manager called to him. "There is an envelope here for you. I am sorry, with all of this I didn't see it before."

The manager handed Turner a large envelope and he left the hotel. Bart, Garvis and Louis left a few moments later and the four men met across the street from the hotel. "This looks like the same kind of envelope that Endleson used," Turner said. "I suspect this is why our rooms were searched. I don't want to read it here."

After Claudius heard Daisy describe her prison, he led over one thousand soldiers to the docks. While the soldiers searched for underground dungeons, Claudius rode to the naval yard. He told Gideon about everything that had occurred that morning and gave him notes from the previous night's meeting.

Because Claudius, Thaos and Stephan had spent the night at Mathas' castle, Gideon remained in Claudius' castle with the families. As he was leaving in the morning a sailor came to the castle to tell Gideon that some dangerous looking men had threatened people in the kitchen on the naval yard. The sailor explained that one of the women who cooked in the kitchen left to get the sailors but by time they returned the men were gone.

Claudius briefed Gideon about the information that Thaos had gotten during an interrogation and the information in Endleson's paperwork. Both of these sources of information indicated that Endleson routinely spoke with the people living on the streets. "You can't tell me this is a coincidence," Gideon said. "I'm going to that kitchen and find out what those thugs were looking for."

"Claudius, I had my men thoroughly search this area of the coastline when we were drawing up the plans for the naval yard. We didn't find any dungeons but I will send some sailors to help your men search."

"It's up to you. I have a lot of men searching," said Claudius. "I hope we find the bastards who stole those girls."

After Claudius left the naval yard, Gideon walked to the building that Bella and Ashely had turned into a kitchen for the poor. The building was huge and a second one was being prepared for the same purpose.

Gideon had signs posted in the building offering work. He was not surprised when dozens of people wanted to work in the kitchens and preparing the second building. Gideon hired whoever came to him.

People were already lining up to be fed the midday meal. This line was forming outside of the building because the kitchen staff were not yet ready to serve. "Can I have your attention!" Gideon bellowed. "During the breakfast meal some men came in here and roughed up some people. First, I want you to know that I will have men assigned here to protect you every day. And secondly, I want to find out why those men were here. If anyone knows or overheard anything they said would you please step out of line and tell me. Your places in line will be saved."

No one moved. A man was standing towards the front of the line and staring intently at Gideon. "A better question might be to ask if anyone knows about women being abducted," the man said. The man was filthy but spoke and carried himself as a nobleman. Gideon walked close to the man and asked in a low voice, "Are you Cyril?"

"At your service Admiral," Cyril said with a twinkle in his eye.

"Do you have that information or others here?"

"Admiral, you are a man known for your fearlessness. Look at these people. They don't even have a door to shut to keep the criminals out. If they felt protected you might be surprised what they will tell you."

Gideon stared into Cyril's eyes then smiled. "You know everyone who meets you believes you to be an Angel."

"Their expectations are high," Cyril said with a grin.

Gideon stepped back and really looked at the people who were standing in line. Many of them were women with children. "Look into their eyes," Cyril said.

Gideon walked up and down the line and spoke with the people. He saw the fear in their eyes and heard the hopelessness in their voices and his heart was overwhelmed.

"I have an announcement to make," Gideon said loudly. "All those buildings behind me are going to be barracks for the sailors we will hire. I haven't hired those men yet. They are modest dwellings but they are dwellings."

"After you eat if anyone would like to live in them until we can find you something better come back out here and I will have some of my men make the arrangements." The people in line started talking excitedly. A woman ran up to Gideon and kissed his hand. This act humiliated him because he realized he had never really looked at these people; he should have known.

Gideon walked back to Cyril who could see how emotional he was. "Admiral, when you are at sea you notice the tiniest change in the wind and the waters and yet on land you can walk through a sea of people who are invisible to you."

Gideon suddenly felt overwhelmed like he always did when Miranda spoke to him. He nodded at Cyril because he couldn't speak. After he composed himself Gideon said, "We are trying to save some young women can you help us?"

"The ones who would be sacrificed against their wills will be found today. But there are many who have been sold illusions and do not understand who they follow. You have been doing well but you should know that I warned Tessa that her beauty has attracted attention by those with dark souls." Then Cyril smiled. "She understood my words but for her that was a challenge. Noah doesn't understand why he has been so worried about her. He will one day."

"I will take care of that," Gideon said. "Is there anything else you can tell me? Or help me ask the right questions?"

Cyril stepped out of line. "Much of this land is unused, which is why you chose this location for the naval yard. I believe you can find room to build a little neighborhood. The people who live there can provide support for your navy. Think of all the services they have in Port Friada, why, there is just one street of seamstresses and tailors. You need people to cook, do laundry and build things. When your men assign housing have them ask the people their names and skills. This can be a win, win situation for everyone."

As Cyril spoke he was leading Gideon away from the line of people and pointing at the landscape. "That is a great idea," Gideon said. "Thank you."

"I have always been amazed that while the concept of betrayal is so completely foreign for some it is second nature for others. Elexas is not a spy but she may betray you before this is over. But like anyone else she has choices to make. Speak with the others about what you want to do about her. Now my good man I need to get back into line."

Elexas had been given a room in the castle but with everything that was happening most of the team members forgot about her.

"Ryan, what are you doing?" asked Elexas as she entered a small room that was off from the Great Hall. This was the room where Ryan went so he could concentrate on the paperwork he was reading. Never before had Claudius, Thaos and Stephan included him in their work on the missions and he didn't want to disappoint them.

"You'll laugh if I tell you," he said uncomfortably.

"No I won't," she said and walked around the room looking at all the pieces of paper he had affixed to the walls. "What is this?"

"Seriously Elexas don't laugh because I don't know how to explain it to you. You know I am a carpenter?"

"Yes and I have heard you are excellent at your craft."

Ryan stared at her because she actually sounded sincere to him. "Well, before I make anything, especially the first time I keep working the plans over in my head. Sometimes the tiniest detail can make or break a project. All of the people here are concentrating on the big things because they are warriors. Stephan and Thaos asked me to help specifically because I am not a warrior. I am looking for the little things and trying to build a picture."

"Ryan, that sounds really smart. Can I help you?"

"I think you would get bored."

"I am bored now. I think everyone forgot I was here. I was supposed to have a meeting with Turner but he is gone. Ryan, I know you don't trust me but I promise not to flirt with you. Honestly, I find all of this fascinating and the other night when I was playing a role I felt really alive. I would like to work on the teams."

"Ok, but if you do anything...well...you know; you'll have to leave."

"I understand. So what are you doing?"

"The wall behind you is Frankwich's family and the opposite wall is the Franks family. The west wall is information about Endleson and the other wall is divided in half, everything on the right is the unknowns and on the left is general information. These are Harlow's notebooks. You know he is a famous reporter from Port Friada? Well, he documents everything but he assumes that people lie to him so he doesn't print things until he can get it from multiple people."

"See here, I've found three references about Frankwich being the stepson of Franks but no mention of the mother, which I find surprising considering the amount of detail in some of these stories. If you want to help you can start with this notebook but don't mark in them."

Gideon wrote a letter to Mathas that contained every word that Cyril said to him. He sealed the envelope with wax and had a sailor deliver it to the King.

When Turner and his men returned to the castle they found the Great Hall empty. They sat at a table and Turner opened the envelope that had been left for him at the hotel. It was a large envelope that contained many sheets of paper and a necklace like the one that Tessa had bought at The Chicken and The Egg.

On the top of the stack was a letter written to Turner.

*Mister Turner,*

*I know you have been watching me as I have been watching you and your people. I have seen you in Port Friada as well as Langer on several occasions. I will admit I haven't always been sure if you were investigators, as I am, or con men. But, since your people are following the same trail of bread crumbs that I am, I am assuming you are investigators and if not I hope you have enough conscious to get these papers to the right people.*

*I am leaving these with you because I am in great danger here. I will probably be dead when you read these. Over a year ago I was hired by a woman named Matilda Frankwich. Her wealthy husband was said to have died in a boating accident but his body was never found. In her grief, Matilda took to her bed and was not aware of the many appearances her husband was making in Port Friada. I saw one of your men talking with a reporter named Harlow the other day. He would be a good contact for information about the Frankwich family.*

*Matilda was being drugged by her son Olin who is now in charge of the family fortunes. And this is where the story gets interesting. Matilda provided me with all of the ledgers and papers of the family and the businesses, copies of many of the pages are in this envelope.*

*Before her husband disappeared he opened accounts in banks in every kingdom. His son routinely transfers money into these accounts and I am assuming it is Frankwich who is withdrawing the money.*

*Matilda told me that her husband and now her son would leave for long periods of time without really explaining to her where they were going. She wants to think the best of them and is afraid they are the victims of some criminal activity.*

*My investigations are finding that they are creating victims wherever they go. I have been following the money. Wherever either of these men are, no matter how large or small the village or city, young women start disappearing from the streets during the time those men are in those locations.*

Of course, with cities as large as Port Friada and Langer it is more difficult to have exact time frames.

While I have followed these men as far west as the City of Nora, they do seem to prefer the cities on the east coast. You will find newspaper reports of women missing in Port Friada, Leven, Hafsfat, Cadia, Castor and Langer in this envelope.

As you, I haunt the seedier businesses in any community to gather information. One evening about a year ago I was in Joy City in Port Friada when two extremely well-dressed and beautiful women got into an argument that eventually caused them to be kicked out of the den.

You have been to those dens so you know how bad that argument must have been. I watched them with curiosity until I concentrated on their words. Apparently both women were lovers with the Princess Juleta, who is alleged to be a dark lord.

The one woman was accusing the other woman of leaving her for Juleta. Apparently the first woman had just found out some information that the other woman's father provided Juleta with money to start a shipping business. The second woman tells the first woman that their relationship was over before she met Juleta and to keep her voice down. They were yelling some of the typical things like 'you never really loved me.' Then the second woman yells, 'I'm going to tell Hector.' Well that got the attention of everyone in the place.

The second woman yells, 'Isabella keep your damn mouth shut or I will shut it for you and you know I can do it.' Hector is a notorious dark lord and his men basically own Joy City. When Isabella mentioned his name, several of Hector's men got up from their table and escorted the women out of the den.

I was sitting at the bar between a demon and a drunk and the three of us were buying rounds. I said, 'I would like to have those two fighting over me.' The demon said, 'Hector won't like it. But that is what he gets for screwing women in the same family.' I said 'were those two women related?' He said that Isabella was Juleta's aunt. He said Juleta was the dark lord who turned Hector.

*I asked who the other woman was and the demon says she is Joanna Franks and that Juleta turned her into a witch. Since this event I have discovered a relationship between the Franks family in Langer and Frankwich. So this led me to Langer.*

*I cannot prove that Franks had anything to do with the murder of Prince Michael but I had heard that Otto Franks owed his family's fortune to some kind of demon and that he had to pay heavily for that. And that for some reason demons were collecting on debts now.*

*The dark worlds believe in prophesies and there is one that scares the shit out of them. I have not read it but it has to do with seven sons. I overheard some demons in the Catacombs making bets on who the Seven Sons were and Prince Michael was one of the men mentioned.*

*Shortly after I arrived in Langer I started to be followed by men who look like hired killers. I have some papers hidden in the safe at the White Rose Restaurant as well as in the heels of some of my boots. I implore you as a gentlemen. If you are reading these papers, please take them to King Mathas.*

*And one final note; this is last but very important. Olin and his father do not travel together. When Olin is in an area the missing women all have the same descriptions. They are beautiful young women with dark hair. Olin is in Langer and I have seen him watching the girl on your team.*

*Sam Endleson*

"Bart, find Mathas and tell him we need to meet at once. I am going to find Tessa," Turner said.

# Chapter XXXII
## Olin

"Noah, where is Tessa?" asked Turner as he barged into Noah's room. Noah was sleeping and jumped to a sitting position.

"She was sleeping with me. I don't know. Is something wrong?"

"Here you read this and I will be right back. I am going to check the rooms of your team members."

Noah quickly read Endleson's letter to Turner, then he jumped out of bed and ran into the bathing room, hoping that Tessa was taking a bath. He quickly dressed. "Did you find her?" Noah yelled as he saw Turner walking down the hallway towards him.

"She's in the city. Think you can ride a horse?"

"I will."

"Good because Garvis is saddling them. We have to drop that letter off with Mathas," Turner said.

Noah and Turner almost ran into the King's study. "This is the letter that Bart told you about. Did he tell you the part about Tessa?" Turner asked.

"Yes," Mathas said. "Is she gone?"

"She's in the city. We didn't take the time to look at the other stuff in that envelope," Turner said.

"I have it just go," said Mathas.

As soon as Tessa walked out of a jewelry shop a handsome young man approached her. "Mind if I walk with you?"

"That is up to you," Tessa said. She was smiling but staring at him.

"I saw you a while back," said the man. "You have to be the prettiest girl I've ever seen."

"Why, thank you. That is very sweet. So have you been following me?"

He hesitated. "I guess you could say that but I didn't think of it like that. I just wanted to talk to you."

Tessa smiled although the hair on the back of her neck was raising. "What did you want to talk about?"

"I guess, I don't know."

"You don't know?"

"This is sounding bad isn't it? I am sorry. I usually don't come up to girls like this but you are just so darn pretty."

"What is your name?"

"Amos."

"Well, Amos I am Tessa. Do you live in Langer?"

"No, we live in Castor. We have a little farm outside of the city. Pa sent me here today to pick up some things he ordered. I haven't yet cuz I saw you as I was going to the store."

"Well, Amos this is all very sweet but I have a boyfriend. In fact, I was buying him a gift in that jewelry store."

"Well, I should have known," Amos said with disappointment in his voice. "A girl as pretty as you would be taken. But do you mind if I walk with you a little more. I like talking to you."

"That is quite alright but I am going to a woman's store next. You can come in if you want."

"I'll just walk you to the door so I make sure you get there alright."

"Excuse me My Lady, is this man bothering you?" Olin asked as he suddenly appeared in front of Tessa. She saw the way he looked at the crystal hanging around her neck.

"No, Amos is my friend. And thank you but I know you."

"Oh, I think I would remember you."

"Unless you were distracted in Joy City." Tessa was staring at him in a challenging manner.

"Now, that poses several questions. Were you watching me? And why were you there?"

"I watch everyone; you might say it is in my nature." She turned to Amos and said sweetly, "See that man standing on the corner."

"You mean the one preaching?"

"Yes, he is a friend and I promised to buy him a sandwich today. If I give you the money will you ask him what he wants and buy it for him?"

"Sure, but will you be alright here?"

"Yes, thank you."

She watched Amos walk away then she stepped closer to Olin, "I know you are a dark lord. What the hell do you want?"

"You are just more amazing all of the time. I would think you would be frightened."

"Then you think wrong. Women have been stolen from these streets, tell me dark lord would you know anything about that?" Olin smiled at her as she stared at him. "And demons have been behind attacks on a lot of good men in this city. Would you know why?"

"One doesn't often meet a beautiful woman who is so knowledgeable of the crime in a city. How is that?"

"I've seen you watching me before, why is that?"

"I'm not going to answer your questions if you don't answer mine," Olin said.

Tessa took a step back and looked at his hands. He wore several rings but none with the markings of the monastery at Malga. "You knew that boy was no problem. So why did you stop me?"

"A chance to talk to you. You are right I have watched you before."

"Why?"

"Because you are very beautiful."

"I don't believe that, what do you really want?"

"I told you."

"Ok, I will answer one of your questions if you answer one of mine."

Olin liked the cat and mouse game that Tessa was playing with him. "Deal."

"Who's the old priest wearing the monastery of Malga ring who is sacrificing women?"

The color drained from Olin's face. He stopped grinning and looked shocked. "How do you know of these things?"

"I talk to Angels and if you don't believe me I can show you. But of course you will burst into flames. So this is the deal, you start talking or I call the Angels in."

"You have no idea what you are doing," Olin said. "The Master is stronger than Angels. He can see and hear everything. He will punish you greatly for this."

"No, he will punish you because you just verified he exists. You might need an Angel to protect you. And I am laying bets that mine is tougher than yours. So spit it out."

Olin was a man who was used to feeling powerful and in control of every situation. He didn't know if Tessa was crazy or telling the truth but the fact that she knew about the Master terrified him.

"Adam, I might need some help here."

"Woman, you are crazy. Who are you talking to?"

"Well, it's not me making your neck smoke. Can your Master do that?"

Olin turned around and started to run. Tessa ran after him. Olin started to mumble incantations but he felt like his power was gone. He pushed people out of his way, knocking a man to the ground. Tessa only lifted her skirt higher and jumped over the things he was throwing in her way.

"What the hell!" yelled Garvis. "There she is chasing a guy." Turner, Noah and the others now raced down the street on their horses.

Olin was becoming terrified that the Master had taken his powers. He kept chanting and nothing was happening. He ran into the road and crossed the street. Tessa's legs were not as long as his but she was fast. Olin was now running on the opposite side of the street in the opposite direction.

"Tessa!" yelled Amos as he was crossing the street to give Cyril his sandwich.

Cyril watched as Olin and Tessa ran towards him. Olin looked behind him and suddenly tripped. He fell face first onto the walk way. Tessa was completely out of breath but she jumped on his back and at the same time she tore her crystal necklace off and pressed the crystal against Olin's neck.

Suddenly she flew off from him as Noah grabbed the back of her dress and lifted her up. Turner and Bart grabbed Olin's arms and lifted him to his feet. "He's a dark lord and knows about the Master and the abductions," Tessa said haltingly as she tried to breathe.

"Why didn't you use your magics against her?" Turner asked.

"Believe me I tried," said Olin.

"Are you Olin?" barked Noah as he stood with his arm around Tessa.

"Yes he is. Why are all of you here anyways?" Tessa asked.

"Because we found out that he has been responsible for missing women and they all look like you. He's been watching you," Turner said.

"I know, I just didn't know how he figures in all of this. Adam helped me or Cyril."

"Don't look at me," Cyril said with a grin.

"Adam help us to get him to the dungeons," Tessa said loudly. "He says that Master sees everything."

"We are having a talk when we get home," Noah said sternly but he was smiling.

"Oh no! I lost my package. I have to find it."

"Tessa, I'll get it. I think I see it," Amos said and ran across the street.

"Now who is he?" asked Noah.

"A friend," Tessa said and smiled.

"Amos this is my boyfriend Noah, this is my friend Amos and these are my other friends. You've met Cyril, Turner, Garvis, Bart and Louis." As she made introductions, Tessa opened the package that Amos had handed her.

"Nice to meet all of you," Amos said. "Is he really a dark lord?"

"Yep," said Bart.

"And Tessa was chasing him?"

"Yep," said Bart and all of the men grinned.

"Oh good, it's not broken," Tessa said and handed Noah a golden pocket watch.

"This is why you came into the city?" he asked in disbelief."

"We need to get going," Turner said and laughed. "You two can argue or kiss later. Tessa do you have a carriage here?"

"It's down the street."

"Tessa," Cyril said. "Thanks for the sandwich. And you did my heart good today."

Tessa, Noah and Turner rode inside of the carriage with Olin, who had his hands tied behind his back. "You've been awfully quiet," Turner said to Olin. "I would have expected you to curse us or something."

"He is terrified of his Master," Tessa said as she stared at Olin. "He believes that Master can see and hear everything and since he has already told me that the Master exists he is probably on the old boy's shit list."

"You need to watch your mouth," Olin said. "He will not be taunted like that."

"So what do you do, give him young girls so he won't hurt you?" Noah asked.

"You are all fools. You will see."

"And what will we see?" asked Turner. "That he is going to unleash an army of Hutas on the city."

Olin turned white as he stared at Turner. "How do you know these things?"

"I told him but he doesn't believe me," Tessa said. "So when is this attack supposed to take place?"

"The Master has his own time," Olin said hauntingly.

"So how is this related to The Seven Sons?" Noah asked. Olin didn't answer. "Is the Master the one responsible for Franks' fortune? The one he owes?" Olin started to squirm in his seat and to sweat. "Where is your father?"

"What I want to know is was Joanna really screwing both Juleta and Isabella?" asked Turner. "I would have thought she had better taste than that."

"How do you know all of this? Who is the traitor among us?" demanded Olin.

"Well, you are going to be soon," Tessa said.

"I will not tell you anything."

Noah looked at Olin and smiled.

"Look out the windows, you've got to see this!" yelled the driver as he maneuvered the team of horses around an army of dead Hutas. "Look at them. They all look like they are terrified and there's not a mark on them."

"I asked Adam to help us get you to the dungeons," Tessa said to Olin. "He's the one who took your powers. Still think your demons are stronger than Angels?"

"The Master isn't a demon."

"Then what is he?" asked Turner. "A dark lord or warlock?"

"It's kind of hard to explain."

"Well, try us, you would be surprised what we believe," said Noah.

"Do you think your Angel will protect me?" Olin asked. The fear was evident in his voice.

"We can't speak for him, you will have to ask him yourself," said Noah. "I'll tell you that if I was you I sure would."

"How do I say it?"

"They can hear and see everything so say it out loud or in your head," said Noah.

Olin looked at the floor of the carriage. "Angel Adam will you protect me from the Master?" he asked in a whisper. Then he started to weep uncontrollably.

"What is happening? Is Adam punishing him?" asked Turner.

"I think he is touching him with holiness," Noah said. "He might not be a dark lord after this but I'm not really sure how that works."

"Take him into the Great Hall instead of the dungeons," Adam's voice said to Turner, Tessa and Noah.

"We're going to the castle," Noah yelled out of the window to the driver. Within minutes the carriage stopped.

"Bart run in and tell them what we have," yelled Turner.

In less than two minutes, Thaos, Stephan, Dominic, Fennel and Angus ran out of the castle and up to the carriage. "Adam said to take him to the Great Hall," Noah said. "Don't know why."

"We heard," said Thaos who grabbed Olin and pulled him out of the carriage.

Olin was led to the front of the room. Angus closed the doors to the Great Hall.

"I feel like we need to get right to this," Tessa said. "And I don't know why. I'll tell you later how I met him but I asked him who the old priest was, who was wearing the ring from the monastery at Malga and sacrificing girls. He turned white and called him the Master. He is a dark lord and he is so terrified that the Master will punish him that he asked Adam to protect him."

"The Master plans to send an army of Hutas on the city but we don't know when and he was just starting to tell us who the Master is."

"Tessa asked Adam to help us get him to the dungeons and we passed an army of dead Hutas on the road," said Noah.

"Olin tell us who the Master is?" said Turner.

"Like I said, he isn't a demon but I don't think any of us really know what he is. Hundreds maybe thousands of years ago when the monasteries were first built the priests who were in charge were called Holy Lords instead of High Priests. The Master was the first Holy Lord at the monastery in Malga. He was also the first priest to change sides so the demons really rewarded him. I have heard that they took him to some demon they worship and that demon did something to the Master. Gave him powers and long life."

"But most of the time when someone sells their soul they always look the age they were when that happened but the Master doesn't even look human any more. His skin is nothing but wrinkles and it looks like leather."

"So you've see him?" asked Mathas.

Olin nodded. "I saw him once a long time ago. In Port Friada but I heard he is here now. He travels around. Don't ask me why because I don't know and trust me you don't make conversation with him."

"Where did you see him?" asked Claudius.

"In a cave that was south of the city. There was a huge celebration of some kind. My father took me there and all I really remember was dozens of people being thrown into a huge fire. I never smelled anything like that before. I was young and all of it scared me."

"So is your father a dark lord too?" asked Claudius.

"No, he is a warlock. My Uncle Otto is a dark lord."

"And your mother?" Turner asked.

"Oh she doesn't know anything about this, it would kill her if she found out."

"So why did your father fake his own death or did he die and someone impersonated him?" asked Claudius.

"All of you seem to really know a lot so you may already know this but when people sell their souls it is like a contract. The person does certain things for a specified time and the demon gives him a specified reward. I don't know how many generations back that one of my grandfathers sold his soul but in exchange for power and wealth he had to give the souls of his sons to the demons."

"When my father and Uncle Otto sold their souls they didn't have to do anything big for a really long time. They agreed to do whatever the demons wanted when they asked them to pay up. Now, my father is a warlock but that he did on his own."

"Eleven years ago some demon came to him and said it was time to pay his dues. Father never told me what he had to do but he travels all of the time. We arranged the boating accident and had bank accounts and homes set up. I don't see him much but I know he is taking money from the accounts."

"And what does Otto have to do?" Claudius asked.

"I don't know. Honest. All of you are looking at me like I am lying. I think it is some kind of secret."

"What do you have to do?" asked Turner.

"There is kind of a hierarchy. Ok, think of it as like a business. The Master would be like a really rich man who owns a lot of big businesses. Each one of those businesses is run by a head boss with a series of underbosses and managers, then workers. Father and Uncle Otto are like the head bosses, I am more like a worker."

"Why is that?" Turner asked.

"Well, if you listen to my father it's because I am lazy. I have money and like to enjoy life."

"Ok, but you haven't told us what you have to do," said Turner.

"I am kind of more like their boy, I do whatever they tell me."

"And you are satisfied with that?" asked Claudius.

"I'm not always happy with the jobs but it hasn't been bad. The way you are all looking at me. Ok, I'm not a real ambitious person."

"What I want to know is why are you telling us all this?" asked Thaos.

"Because your Angel told me I had to tell the truth."

"So why are you in Langer?" Claudius asked.

"Because Mother hired an investigator to find Father and the guy has been digging up a lot of crap. Father sent me a letter and told me to shut him up."

"So are you the one who had him killed?" Thaos asked.

"No, one of Uncle Otto's men did that."

"So why is the Master in Langer?" asked Claudius.

"I don't know if he is in the city but he has been in contact with Otto and his family and they are all nervous wrecks. Before you ask, yes they are my family but remember the hierarchy. Joanna is a witch and a really powerful one. Jack is a dark lord and high up in the hierarchy. And Andre, that is Joanna's husband, is a dark lord but he isn't as high up. I am way beneath all of them. I don't think there are things they could tell me if they wanted to."

"Do you have any suspicions why the Master has contacted them?" asked Tessa. "You must have overheard something."

"A really powerful demon is holding Gefrey Games. And apparently the prizes are incredible. Well, at first he just charged some money for entering the games but there are people and demons from all over who want in so now the entrance fees are really high. It sounds like whoever can bring him the best prize is in. But he is fighting a bunch of wars now so the games have been put on hold which just gives everyone more time to work on their entrance fees."

"So is your family behind the murder of Prince Michael?" asked Mathas.

"No, that wasn't us. And Uncle Otto was really pissed because he thought that prince was some important guy in a prophesy and he was going to kidnap him."

"Is Otto entering the games?" asked Claudius.

"No, for the Master. He wants to enter the games."

"Tell us about the women who are sacrificed," said Claudius. "And what is your role in that?"

"Yeah, I have to grab women sometimes but sometimes I just do it for myself too. Women are grabbed but a lot volunteer." Olin looked sheepishly at Mathas when he said this.

"You know you are going to have to explain that," Claudius said.

"I am telling you right now that the King is going to get really pissed."

"I will be a hell of a lot more pissed if you don't say anything," Mathas said so sternly that it scared Olin.

"Uncle Otto likes sex, I mean we all do but he is in an entirely different category and for an old guy he really gets the women. I don't know how he does it but he, I don't know; charms them. He has this group of people and they all have orgies all of the time. Joanna, Jack and Andre are part of that. In fact, Joanna brings a lot of the women. Well, some of these people will agree to be sacrifices but apparently the Master mostly wants young girls."

"So how does that affect me?" demanded Mathas.

"Your sister and daughter were part of that. I was told your sister got involved a long time ago then brought your daughter to the gatherings. Don't get mad at me, I'm just telling you the truth. Otto had affairs with both of them for a long time and so did Joanna. In fact, Juleta and Isabella apparently weren't jealous when they were both screwing Uncle Otto but they got real jealous when they were both with Joanna."

"So how is Hector and his family involved with all of this?" asked Claudius.

"Well you know that Hector was screwing all of them, I mean Joanna, Juleta, Isabella and god knows who else. But, he married Juleta because she promised him a lot of power and money."

"What about his parents?" asked Mathas.

"I've never heard anything about them being involved in anything. As far as I know they are regular people. But Hector has so many enemies that Joanna said he has his family hidden some place. People really hate him, and I mean all kinds of people, good and bad and demons too. I mean people hated Juleta but they really hate him."

"Do you know about any threats against any of us or the Royal Family in Wetpr?" asked Mathas.

"Most of what I know I've heard in the dens and taverns. I don't know of any direct threats. But there are a couple of things going on. Have you ever heard of the Insidiae?"

"Yes and I know that Juleta was a member," Mathas said.

"I don't belong but that group is all over and they have all these little groups. Well, there was this big, huge project going on where they were trying to breed people to be bodies for demons. The Master played a big part in that according to my father. Well, there were a lot of problems with the guys they were breeding so Juleta and another dark lord named Dieter presented this really wild plan to the Insidiae and demons and dark lords. They got investors and made big promises but then they both got killed so a lot of those investors are going after Hector to either get their money back or for him to fulfill the promises."

"I know all kinds of people are worried that some of you are going to screw those plans up. Don't bother to ask me because I am telling you what I know. Then there is some badass prophesy called The Seven Sons and everyone is trying to figure out who those guys are."

"Demons are always trying to figure stuff like that out but now it is a frenzy and my guess is that people and demons want to give them as entrance prizes for those Gefrey Games."

"Does anyone else have any questions?" asked Mathas.

"Yes, where are those orgies held?" Jasmine asked.

Olin laughed. "The location changes. But if you go into Joanna's store you can find out."

"I think we can all use a break," Mathas said as he was having difficulty controlling his anger and everyone could see that. He looked at Olin. "And what do you want for giving us this information?"

"I want protection from the Master but none of you can do that. I would be happy with you just letting me go."

"While I am not opposed to that," said Mathas. "I can't allow you to abduct young women. I am going to put you under house arrest in one of the chambers for a couple of hours while we discuss this. We may have more questions. Do you want a meal?"

"Sure." Olin said.

"We'll take him," said Stephan.

As Thaos and Stephan were walking Olin through the Great Hall, Ryan and Elexas walked out of the side room with their arms full of paperwork. "Olin," Elexas said in surprise. "What are you doing here?"

# Chapter XXXIII
## Collaborators

Stephan and Thaos stopped walking and stared at Elexas when they heard her words. For just a moment the room became silent as everyone stared at her.

"Bring him back," growled Claudius. "Elexas up here now!"

"What is going on?" asked Elexas as she set her stack of papers on a table.

"Now!" yelled Claudius, whose face was becoming redder every moment.

"Really, what is going on?" she asked again as she saw the way people were looking at her as she walked to the front of the room.

"She is my responsibility," said Sorren, who had already read Gideon's letter about Elexas betraying the group. "I'll question her. Thaos move Olin so they can't look at each other."

"Elexas how do you know Olin?" asked Sorren.

"Why?"

"Answer the question!"

"I would really rather not say."

"Then it's the truth potion and that stuff will make you really sick so I suggest that you speak now."

"Leave her alone," Olin said. "She goes to the orgies that's why she doesn't want to tell you. That's how we know each other."

"Is this true?" asked Sorren through clenched teeth.

Elexas was bright red now and clearly intimidated by Sorren. "Yes," she said in a loud whisper.

"So you know the Frank's family and you didn't say anything?"

"Yes."

"Who in that family have you had sex with?"

"I don't..."

"Elexas this is important," said Tessa. "We'll tell you why."

"Well, all of them. Except for Otto's wife she doesn't take part." Olin laughed at Elexas' comment.

"Why are you laughing?" demanded Sorren.

"Just the idea of Aunt Ruthie taking part, that's all."

"How long have you been doing this?" Sorren returned his attention to Elexas.

"I don't know, maybe seven years."

Sorren stepped closer to her. "Did you know they were dark lords and witches?" She didn't say a word. "Did you know they were going to kidnap Prince Michael?"

"I didn't know anything about that."

"Did you see Isabella or Juleta at those things?" asked Mathas.

"Yes, all of the time."

"And Hector?"

"I never met anyone who said his name was Hector, but we really don't give names."

"Do you know about the women being sacrificed?"

"I've never seen anything like that and only heard stories. Sorren these things are huge celebrations. They are fancy with musicians and dancing. Otto always has the best food and wines. And a lot of people are there."

"Why do you go?" asked Mathas.

"What?"

"Why do you go?" The King repeated.

"They are fun and I meet a lot of wealthy people that way. I don't always want to live in that tribe."

"So you would rather socialize with dark lords, witches and murderers than your own people?" Sorren spat.

"What murderers?"

"Well your boy Olin here for one," said Stephan. "We can't take any chances; we need to give her the truth potion."

"Stephan! I am telling you the truth. I was looking at all kinds of things that I couldn't afford to buy in The Chicken and The Egg. Joanna started talking to me and invited me to a party. She gave me things to wear. I went there with her and it was fun and exciting. All of you have money; what you take for granted is a dream for the rest of us. Yes, I liked dressing up and having wealthy men flirt with me."

"All of you are so angry," said Dominic. "Let me ask the questions for a while. Elexas what was your relationship with Juleta?"

"Not much, she was such a bitch. She would get really jealous when any of the other women got more attention than she did. In fact, one time Joanna told me to stop coming for a while because she didn't trust Juleta."

"What was your relationship with Isabella?"

"Mathas, I am sorry but all of you hate me already so I am just going to say it. First, I couldn't stand Isabella or Juleta. And second," she hesitated.

"You were all competing for attention weren't you?" asked Tessa.

"Yes. I want a rich husband some day and that is why I started going. How else was I going to meet anyone? They both already had lots of money and they were like needy little kids. They would pout and throw tantrums if they didn't get what they wanted. And they always competed for the same lovers whether they were men or women. Don't you understand; they were my competition."

410

"I stopped going for a little while after Angelina, Ingr and Nikki married into your families because I thought that might be another way for me to meet wealthy men but that didn't work."

"That's because you scared everyone off," Stephan said. "And you were trying to compete with our wives." Elexas didn't say anything but looked like she was going to cry.

"Yes, I heard all of the stories about the threats to your families but honestly I didn't care. I was going to those parties for a reason. And I hope you don't think people were just talking about that stuff in front of everyone. These were parties that you went to, to meet people and have sex. People kind of had other things on their minds."

"Well, that is probably true," Thaos said and sneered.

"What was your relationship with Otto?" asked Dominic.

"Every woman who first comes to a party must have sex with him before she can meet anyone else. Sometimes he has sex with a dozen women in the same night. So I have had sex with him; actually a lot but we never talked about any of you or politics."

"Did you ever hear of or take part in any threats against the royal or ruling families of Lentz or Wetpr, the Sanuri or the teams?" Dominic asked.

"She's been telling you the truth so far and you know that I have to," Olin said. "These parties are huge social galas. When your families throw them, I am sure that all the important stuff is talked about behind closed doors by a selected few. Otto invites a lot of people to these things so he can black mail them later. That's what they are all about. He's not going to invite the prominent people of the city and talk about attacking any of you."

"Elexas is a whore; she will never be anything more than an horderve that Uncle Otto serves to others. She isn't privy to information."

"Screw you Olin!" Elexas yelled.

"Well, you know it's true. You tell me one time you were asked into any of the meetings? Or to socialize with any of them outside of the parties."

"I did hear something once," Elexas said defiantly to Olin. "It was kind of a long time ago. I did hear the name Hector, honestly if I met the guy I wouldn't know but Isabella and Juleta got into another of their spats. Honestly it happened so often that most people stopped paying attention. But this time they got into a physical fight which was kind of funny because neither of them can fight. They were fighting over Mayor Deckor."

"Isabella yells that she followed him and Juleta to his lodge and saw some men carrying a body out. Juleta went wild and started putting a curse or some witch thing on Isabella. Well, Otto himself jumps between the two of them, now remember this is in front of a room full of people. He says he made them and he could break them and they better start acting like adults. Well, both women immediately stopped and apologized to him. Then they each kissed his ring which shocked me."

"Can you describe the ring?" asked Dominic.

"A really wide gold band and the biggest diamond I have ever seen. On both sides of the band there were five swords interwoven and made out of silver."

"Is there anything else you can remember?" Dominic asked.

"No," she said meekly as she looked at the hostile stares she was receiving.

"Olin and Elexas what did Otto mean that he made Juleta and Isabella?" asked Dominic.

"I know he helped Juleta get her powers but Isabella wasn't a witch or anything," Olin said and paused for a few moments. "Isabella started to go to the parties as Otto calls them first and she brought Juleta; maybe she received something for that but I don't really know."

"We need to take a break," said Claudius. "Elexas, you are under house arrest too until we figure this out."

412

"Me! What did I do?"

"You consorted with the enemies of this kingdom. Innocent people have died who we probably could have saved if you would have come forward with this information," Claudius said.

"And I will be determining whether you have a place among your people anymore," Sorren snapped. "You prefer the company of dark lords and witches perhaps that is where you should go, if they don't put you in the dungeons."

"What?" gasped Elexas and started to cry.

"Can I say something?" asked Ryan.

"You have the floor," Mathas said.

"I understand that you are all angry and I am not making excuses for what Elexas has done but she has been helping me all day and we found some things; besides that, I have some questions for Olin. Do you want to hear this now?"

"Go ahead," snapped Mathas.

"First, Olin how can your father and your uncle be the same ages yet supposedly be born to different mothers and we have found no information about your father's mother," asked Ryan.

"That is a family secret. The men in the family have been dark lords for generations. Joanna is the first woman to work with them. My great grandfather Norbert had his wife Tomina who was Uncle Otto's mother but he was screwing other women. My father's mother was named Nami and was a witch from the Kingdom of Stordt. Norbert paid her a great deal of money to keep her mouth shut and set her up in Port Friada."

"So he basically had two families but Uncle Otto's family got all of the privileges. As far as I know Nami suddenly disappeared. That was when I was a boy but Father told me she was always really pissed about being in second position so I don't know if Norbert had her killed or what. He was trying to protect the family name."

"So was there competition between your father and Otto?" Ryan asked.

413

"Hell ya, they hated each other when they were younger now they are all friends."

"Why?"

"Don't really know."

"Don't you question why your father spends so much time in Stordt?"

"How do you know that?" asked Olin.

"Just answer Ryan's question," Claudius said.

"I already told you that he travels a lot and I am not high enough on the ladder to be included in things."

"But what does your gut tell you?" asked Thaos.

"I suspect that my grandmother is alive, either that or she has family there. If she was killed, I would expect Father to avenge her, he's that kind of guy. I will tell you, I was curious when he and Otto buried the axe but so far, I mean it has seemed like a normal family." Olin laughed. "Ok, normal for our family."

"Your father seems to spend most of his time around Taperia," Ryan said. "But several years ago he spent a lot of money in the City of Nora," Ryan said to Olin then looked at the others in the room. "That was around the time of Gabriel's mission."

"Is your father in the Insidiae?" asked Mathas.

"No," Olin said.

Elexas screamed, "Your neck is starting to smoke."

"That is because an Angel is making sure he keeps his word to tell the truth," Tessa said.

"What!" shrieked Elexas but no one explained it to her.

"I'm not really lying. There are other organizations besides the Insidiae. He belongs to one called The Tempest. From what I have heard it has similarities to the Insidiae but it is make up of primarily witches and warlocks as opposed to dark lords."

414

"I don't know if you understand but everything has hierarchies. Dark lords look down on the witches and warlocks."

"Let me understand this," said Stephan. "Your grandmother was a witch and your father is a warlock and you are a dark lord. Why?"

"I didn't want to work that hard. Otto helped me to become a dark lord because every man in the family has to be but I'm kind of the black sheep because I would rather be playing."

"Tell us what you know about the Tempest," said Claudius.

"Most of the members are in Ryed and Stordt. They don't do the big business with other continents so they don't have to be in the coastal cities like the Insidiae. They also don't flaunt their wealth like the Insidiae. My father used to say that the Insidiae was all show and ego. He said the serious magics happen in the Tempest."

"So why didn't you join?" asked Claudius.

"I'm not good enough, that's what I keep telling you. I may have family money but I am basically an errand boy on a leash. Both my father and Uncle Otto are afraid that I will expose the family and apparently they were right because that is exactly what I am doing."

"We know an ex warlock and he has never mentioned the Tempest," said Sorren.

"But I will bet you anything that he heard about it," Olin said. "Look at Langer. How many clubs, committees, organizations and other groups do you want to guess exist here? You can't because there are so many. Why don't you realize it's the same for the underworld? The only time anyone really hears about these groups is when they are fighting among each other or when they do something really crazy like trying to create bodies for demons."

"And just like other groups there are all kinds of reasons they get together. Everyone thinks that witches and warlocks live in caves like the old days. They blend in with everyone else."

415

"But they can't talk about what they do or ask questions about magic with normal people. That's one reason Joy City and the Catacombs are so popular; well besides the acts," Olin said and laughed.

"Olin, so basically you are a spoiled rich kid that the family doesn't know what to do with," said Thaos.

"And that is what I have been trying to tell you."

"So they probably don't tell you anything important and may even give you bad information to see if you tell." Thaos continued. "And they probably have you watched."

"I am not stupid you know. I would probably know if they gave me bad information to set me up. But yeah, you are probably right."

"So then their spies probably know you are here?"

"Tessa chased him down the middle of the business district and jumped him," Turner said. "You can't tell me everyone isn't talking about that." Many people now looked at Tessa and laughed.

"I'm thinking if we let this fool go he is dead before nightfall," said Thaos.

"That really isn't our concern," said Claudius.

"Hey, you were going to protect me," Olin yelled.

"You asked the Angel Adam to protect you from the Master," said Tessa.

"Give us a reason not to kick you out the door," said Thaos. "I was thinking we could use you as a spy but I think you are pretty worthless."

"Let me think about that," said Olin. "Seriously, I will come up with something."

"How do you communicate with your father?" asked Ryan.

"We really don't. Like I said we set up all kinds of bank accounts and homes before he faked his death. I usually get the paperwork from the banks which is what you must have to know some of these things."

"Why doesn't he do his own paperwork?" asked Claudius.

"Because he uses different names now but the money all comes from the family businesses."

"If you really needed to contact him how would you?" Thaos asked.

"I would send letters to his banks so he would get them when he picked up the money. He didn't want anything sent to his homes."

"It sounds more like he is on the run," said Thaos. "Who is after him?"

"Honestly, I have wondered that myself. Father may be a lot of things but he really loved Mother. I have considered the idea that he disappeared to protect her. And I am just going to tell you all something. I'm not close to him and I'm not big in the dark lord business but I never heard my father talk about any of you or The Seven Sons or really anything else that you've been asking about. Maybe he is involved with all of that but he never talked about it around me."

"Could he be hiding from Otto?" asked Turner.

"Anything is possible. Like I said they were rivals until just a few years ago."

"Write down all of the names, banks and homes your father has," said Claudius. "And that will be a start."

"I have a couple of more questions," said Ryan. "Otto is in the Insidiae but your father isn't. Is that what you are saying?"

"Yes," Olin said. "Now that I think about it, he got Juleta in."

"And there are conflicts within that organization now. How about these other organizations you were talking about?" asked Ryan.

"I would expect so but I don't know a lot about that. Like I said from what Father told me a long time ago all of this stuff is handled as he said, 'in the back room'. Most people only hear about things when they get out of control like with Hector in Port Friada. That's why I am here, I didn't want to get caught up in that crap. I don't know if you heard but the group that was fighting Hector slaughtered the people in Joy City. More people were killed there than in Port Friada."

"Why?" asked Stephan.

"Because Hector was extorting protection money from those businesses. And he was making a lot of money off them."

"Could it be a possibility that your Father would start a war against Otto?" asked Ryan.

"I don't think you would ask that question without a reason. What is it?"

"Can I have Elexas help because she is the one who saw this," Ryan asked. "I am not sure of what all she is guilty of but she has been working with me." Elexas looked at Claudius who nodded. "Give us a few minutes to hang these things on the wall," Ryan continued to talk as he and Elexas sorted through papers.

"First, we were looking for all of the little things that you don't have time to look for. We set up the walls in that room and one was all information about the Franks family and the other Olin's family. Then we were documenting things on maps and charts. This map is big so I think you can see things better with it on the wall. If all of you want to come up here. Olin should too."

"This is the continent and all of those stars are banks where accounts are set up from the Frankwich fortune. Now what I questioned were the locations, some are remote places where I wouldn't even think there would be banks."

"And if he is trying to keep hidden, well that much money would make him a prominent citizen. And other areas are large cities. Elexas saw that all of these areas are near waterways. Elexas you tell them the rest."

"I haven't been to these places but looking at the map, most of these areas have mountains or caves very close to them. To me it looks like they are defensible positions and of course the waterways could be used in defenses or launching attacks. It also looks like a lot of these caves are used for mining. I first thought that was to get money for whatever Frankwich is doing. But then Ryan told me about those priests using mines for raising a demon and other things. Some of you who have been to those areas should look at this."

"You might be redeeming yourself girl," Sorren said as he walked closer to the huge map.

"Elexas, I don't want to embarrass you but I hope you realize you have a lot more worth than just for sex and you should think about that," Tessa said in a scolding tone. "This is very good work." Elexas looked embarrassed by Tessa's words.

"Look at all the stars in Ryed and Stordt," Dominic said. "We really need to study this."

"We aren't done," Ryan said. "Because you know how much stuff there is to read but come into our room." Ryan led the group into the side meeting room where he and Elexas had been working. The walls were covered in charts and writing. "I would like Olin to look at some of this stuff," Ryan said. "We've been going through Harlow's notes. Is he here?"

"No but when he comes back you really have to show him all of this," Thaos said.

"So you know he is a reporter, so a lot of his notes were things you would expect to read about like who was at social events. We've been charting where and when members of either of those families have been seen as well as Juleta, Isabella and any other names that we recognized."

"I can't tell you how proud I am of you son," Claudius said.

Ryan was clearly touched by Claudius' words. "We still have a lot of paperwork to go through yet but I wanted you to get an idea of what we are doing," Ryan said.

"Can Elexas keep working with me because we have kind of a system going here? Of course if she tries to escape she could probably kick my butt."

"I won't try to escape," she said. "Honestly, I don't have any place to go and I don't want to go to the dungeons."

"I think we are going to need to study all of this too," said Turner. "Some of these areas are near where there are windows."

"Windows?" Elexas repeated.

"Sorry Honey, but you aren't ready to hear about that yet," Turner said to Elexas but he was looking at one of the smaller maps on the wall of the room.

"Olin will you look at the two walls where I have information about your families and tell me if anything is wrong or missing?"

"What is your name again?" asked Olin.

"Ryan."

"Well Ryan, I don't know you and I am damned impressed. What, are you some kind of genius?"

"I tend to agree," said Mathas. "But you clearly need a bigger room. Claudius, I am thinking that we make some kind of office in here that is separate from the Great Hall and my study. A place where Ryan and others can work because I don't want to pack any of this information away. In fact, we need to send copies of everything to Wetpr."

"You might want to consider a chambers," Stephan said. "So they can have a place to eat and a bathing room. And more workspace."

"Actually I am thinking about remodeling an area just for this but in the meantime a chambers would work," Mathas said.

"Ryan is clearly out of wall space in here," said Fennel. "Why don't we fix up an area near the Great Hall and all of our chambers are on this floor too. We can help move everything."

"We have to keep it in order," Ryan said nervously.

"We will," said Dominic. "Ryan and Elexas this is pretty incredible; the work you've done here."

"We didn't know what was going to be important," Elexas said. "So we have these other lists that we are working on. So if we keep coming across the same name of a person or location in the different papers we are keeping track of where we saw that because we don't want to mark in the books."

"Do you want some help?" Jasmine asked.

"Sure," Ryan said. "We still have a lot of stuff to go through."

"Elexas, you can stay here and help Ryan," Mathas said. "I don't know what your future holds but you have to realize that if you betray us and our work I will have you executed."

"I understand," she said emotionally.

"I'll help too," Olin said as he was reading a chart. "This is really fascinating. Ryan, I don't know if you want to add this here but Joanna's marriage to Andre was arranged by Otto. That happened when our fathers were feuding so I don't know much about it but we did come to Langer to attend the ceremony."

"So they aren't in love?" asked Jasmine.

"They barely tolerate each other, which is kind of strange that Otto would force her into that kind of marriage since she is the apple of his eye."

"Olin, you can stay with the same conditions as Elexas," said Mathas.

"I'm not going to escape, hell I am a lot safer with all of you besides that Angel will probably get mad. He kinda scares me," Olin said. "But could we have something to eat? I am starving."

"A lot of people are still out of the castle," Mathas said. "So I need to meet with everyone except for Olin, Elexas and Ryan right now. Then Dominic and Turner have your people find a location that all of you like and start moving this work in there. Stephan you know this castle like the back of your hand, so pick out a place for an office and Ryan you tell me what you will need in there."

"And the rest of you we, well we will discuss that later," Mathas said as he decided not to finish his sentence in front of Olin and Elexas.

"King Mathas, if I may make a suggestion," said Olin. "I don't think any of you realize how powerful the Master is or even Otto. I never knew Angels existed before today and honestly I don't even understand what Adam is but he was strong enough to take away my powers. If I were you I wouldn't consider going after any of them without him. All of you will be slaughtered."

# Chapter XXXIV
## Fears

"I think we all have more questions for Olin," Thaos said to Mathas. "Was there a reason you pulled us out of the room?"

"I got a letter from Gideon earlier," Mathas said. "He is convinced that Cyril is an Angel..."

"We all are," said Tessa. "Sorry to interrupt."

"I want all of you to read this letter in case you see something I didn't but Cyril says that Elexas may betray us then he says she has choices to make. So I don't know if she will betray us or not and I am very concerned with the information we allow her to have access to," Mathas said and handed the letter to Thaos.

"Then there is the subject of Olin..."

"King Mathas, I am really sorry to interrupt you," said Tessa as she stood up. "But before any of you make decisions you need to hear how this all started because Adam needs to be part of this."

"Come up front," Mathas said.

"You know that every day I have been going shopping in Langer. I not only talk with the people in the stores but on the streets especially after what Cyril told Thaos and Stephan. I often buy food for the street people now and I do that so they will trust me. I don't know if any of you take the time to talk to them but most of them look really scared. This is a beautiful city with soldiers everywhere so why should these people look so scared? I don't have an answer to that question yet but I will bet you anything it has to do with what we are working on."

Tessa looked at Noah and said, "Don't yell at me."

"I can already tell I am going to get mad," he said.

"Some of the street people, Cyril included have warned me that I am being watched by bad people. Cyril says the eyes of darkness. Which is kind of what I am working on since girls are being abducted."

"I've seen Olin before and I knew he was watching me. But there are men watching him too and I don't know if he realizes that."

"Today a farm boy came up to talk to me. That was Amos, who I introduced some of you to. He was harmless but as we talked the hair was raising on the back of my neck and I saw Olin watching us from a store window. Well, moments later Olin is suddenly in front of us and we were walking down a straight street so I don't know how he did that. But as soon as he saw my crystal necklace he looked scared. He wanted to know if Amos was bothering me."

"I just knew Olin was a dark lord so I gave Amos money and told him to buy Cyril a sandwich because I thought he would be safe with Cyril. So right away I tell Olin I know he is a dark lord and I ask him what he wants. You know how some men word everything to make it sound like you should be afraid of them? Well he was doing that with such a cocky look on his face that I wanted to slap him."

"So anyways, he and I are both asking each other questions but neither of us are answering them. So I said, I will answer yours if you answer one of mine and he agreed to that. So I ask him who the old priest is who wears the ring from the monastery of Malga and sacrifices girls. Honesty, he started to sweat and asked me how I knew that, so that was my confirmation. We played word games for a few more minutes and I yelled to Adam that I might need some help. Sure enough just as Olin is going to mumble something Adam came because his holiness caused Olin's skin to smoke."

"He tried to use his magics on me and Adam took his power so Olin ran away."

"Sorry, I've got to tell this," said Bart as he and his team laughed. "We see her running like a deer chasing this guy down the street. He keeps looking over his shoulder like he is scared. He's knocking people down and pushing them at her."

"He is knocking stuff over to block her and she pulls her skirt up higher and jumps over them. Then I am sure that Cyril tripped him but as soon as he's on the ground she's on his back and sticking her crystal in him. It was the funniest damn sight; wish all of you could have seen it."

424

"That is true," said Tessa and laughed. "But the important thing that I have to tell you is. At one point Olin says I have to be careful because the Master can hear and see everything and he will punish me. And I say, he's going to punish Olin for telling me that he exists. So while we are in the carriage, Olin looks really scared. Turner asks why and I told him. So Olin gets so scared he asks if our Angel will protect him from the Master."

"Noah told Olin to ask and suddenly he starts crying like a baby. Then Adam tells us to take him to the Great Hall instead of the dungeons. Well, you know he did that so Olin and Elexas would run into each other, and maybe to help Ryan too. I'm not holy like the rest of you but Adam is in this up to his elbows so we need to include him."

"First, none of us are holy," said Stephan. "We've just talked to the Angels more than you have. And I agree. Also, damn I wish I could have seen you going after him." Others laughed.

Tessa looked at Noah, "So how mad are you?"

"I am not sure. I am proud of you and want to spank you at the same time. But this might be a good time to bring something up. Turner, your whole group is top notched. We all respect you and like working with you. But all of you, and that includes Tessa are kind of used to working alone. I know that sometimes it seems like all we do is have meetings but we all have to talk so we can have each other's backs. If Adam wouldn't have taken Olin's powers away Tessa could be in a lot of trouble now."

"You aren't getting any argument from me," Turner said. "She usually at least tells me where she is going."

"I thought you two would stop me which is why I didn't tell you about the warnings. But don't you see; I am in the best position to get that information."

"Not anymore," said Garvis. "Believe me, everyone on the streets was watching you chase down a dark lord. That disguise is useless now."

"We all agree that we need to talk to each other and we all agree that we sure wish we could have seen that," Claudius said and grinned. "But something that Tessa just said is really bothering me. Gideon's letter is being passed around. But basically, Gideon walks up to a line of street people and asks if any of them know why men were harassing them earlier. Cyril says a better question would be to ask about the missing women. Gideon realizes the man is Cyril and they talk in private."

"Cyril says that if the people felt safe, Gideon would be surprised at what they would tell him. Then Cyril tells him to look into their eyes. Gideon is a tough bastard and when you read his letter you can tell how emotional he was. He saw fear and heard the hopelessness in their voices. What the hell is terrifying all of these people that we don't see?"

"Let me go back on the streets," said Tessa. "I'll change my disguise. I can do this."

"You can't go without telling us and I am going to be watching you," said Noah sternly.

"Agreed," Tessa said. "Now we need to call Adam."

"Tessa, the Angels don't always make appearances and he might not with Elexas and Olin in the next room but he can still talk to us," said Dominic.

"They cannot hear or see us," said Miranda as she and Adam appeared. Miranda looked towards the room that Olin and Elexas were in as she said this. "First, Tessa do you realize that your encounter with Olin was as much a test of faith as it was you apprehending a criminal?"

"And a criminal he is. He is also a pompous fool who has never had to be accountable for his actions. He was telling you the truth though. And Elexas has a lifetime of bad choices. It is difficult for people to change their behavior but Tessa might just help her to see herself differently. Both Elexas and Olin can be of great help to you right now. They both possess information that seems insignificant to them but will be important."

"You want us to tell you what to do with them and we will not. But I would advise that you wait on making decisions. While they are extremely different types of people, the two of them and Ryan are forming a good team. They will not turn him but he is in a way awakening things inside of them."

"Miranda, Elexas is my responsibility," said Sorren. "Has she too been a traitor?"

"She is too self-centered for that. Even if she has over heard things she dismissed them if they did not play into her plans to get a rich husband. Understand I am not saying she isn't intelligent, I am saying she only cares about herself."

"Tessa, you did well today," said Adam. "Why did you call to me?"

"Because you said you wouldn't leave me. Even though I get mad at you; I believe you."

"All of you need to remember that. You have uncovered knowledge of a monster beyond your comprehension and who calls us in? A dark lord and a girl who didn't believe in the heavens until a couple of weeks ago. No matter how well you prepare you cannot go against the abomination call the Master without us. Even the dark lord realized that," said Adam.

"Well, now we feel like... you know what I am getting at," said Stephan.

"Lesson learned," Adam said. "And here is another lesson that will help to answer Claudius' question. What did Ryan say that he and Elexas were doing?"

"Working on the details that we didn't have time for," said Fennel."

"You can fill the streets with soldiers but if they act as Gideon did. If those people became invisible because the soldiers only see the giant monsters they will miss the details," said Adam. "And now a different prospective. Children are often afraid of the dark. They think there is something under their bed or in a closet. The father looks but see's nothing. Is the threat real?"

427

"Can the child see or feel things that the father can't?" asked Dominic.

"Or are you suggesting that imagined fears are as real to that person as a real threat?" Turner asked.

"Very good questions now keep those in mind and send more people on the streets with Tessa. Perhaps you need to walk in their shoes, so to speak," said Adam. "All of you are always running into the fire to save people. Sometimes you need to step back and look at the fire itself."

"In Ryed, Teivel could control entire communities through intimidation," said Seth. "Is that what you are talking about?"

"Another good question," said Adam.

"I am going to change the subject because I don't want you leaving before we get to this," said Thaos. "That vision of the Master that Drake had; is he in Lentz?"

"He does not travel as you do. He can be in a lot of places very quickly. What we showed you was not in this kingdom. So what should you be asking?" said Adam.

"How did those girls get those necklaces?" Tessa asked.

"Another good question." Adam said. "And I know all of you are feeling frustrated. Claudius what does that usually mean when we leave you like that?"

"That we have more work to do or we aren't seeing things right."

Adam nodded. "And since we are talking about fears. Claudius what have you come up with since our last conversation?"

Claudius looked embarrassed, something his sons had never seen before. "I have been thinking about it but with so much going on it has been in the corner of my mind. But, I will do it."

"I know you will and I didn't say that to embarrass you. Actually, I am giving you an answer. You read Gideon's letter, don't you believe Cyril's words could apply to many things?"

"Father!" Jack yelled as he burst into Otto's office in the Bank of Lentz. Jack stopped talking when he saw that his father was in a meeting. "I apologize," Jack said. "But we have a family emergency."

"Gentlemen, I believe we have covered everything for today," Otto said. "Same time next week."

Otto was sitting at his desk, Jack remained standing and watched the men as they walked out of the bank then he closed the door. "We have a big problem." As Jack spoke he walked to a table in his father's office and poured two glasses of whiskey. "Trust me you are going to need this," he said as he handed his father a glass.

"I have had multiple reports that a couple of hours ago Olin was seen running in the business district with a small dark haired woman chasing him. I am told he looked scared and was throwing people and things between him and the girl. She jumped him and had him on the ground when a group of men took him away."

"The girl and one of the men were with Endleson the night we killed him. Now you tell me what girl has more power than a dark lord?"

"I do know that he has been watching her because she is his type. There is a possibility he tried to grab her and she too is a dark lord and went after him. But the fact that she was with Endleson...I have a bad feeling."

"I know he is a pussy but the fool does have powers," said Otto. "Why the hell didn't he use them?"

"I have no idea but it is all over the city because she was chasing him for a while. And like I said people said he looked scared."

There was a loud pounding knock at the door. "It's Dillion," a deep voice yelled.

"Come in," yelled Jack.

Dillon quickly entered the office and closed the door. "Boss, we might have a problem."

"Are more women beating up our men?" asked Otto sarcastically.

Dillion looked confused. "I don't know what you are talking about but there has to be two hundred dead Hutas outside of town. And, well you should see this for yourself. Not a drop of blood anywhere and no one else is dead. But those damn Hutas all look terrified. Now what in hell can scare a Huta?"

"This isn't a coincidence. I wonder if the Master was trying to stop those people from taking Olin. Jack get those damn Hutas moved; I'm going to my altar," Otto said and gulped his glass of whiskey.

"Why would the Master try to save Olin, he is a nothing?" asked Jack.

"I know, that's why I'm worried," Otto said and pulled a lever in the book case that opened a door in the wall behind his desk.

After Miranda and Adam left the meeting, the people in the Great Hall walked into the room where Ryan and the others were working. The table was now filled with plates of food as well as papers. "We have more questions," said Mathas and Ryan, Olin and Elexas all grinned.

"We aren't laughing," said Ryan. "We knew you would so we have been trying to guess what you would ask and Olin's been writing down the answers." Olin handed Mathas two sheets of paper.

"I am sure you want to know about the girls. There is a bunch of us who grab them and we are told where to take them. In Langer there is an underground prison near Otto's bank. It's next to the docks. Then…"

"I just searched that area," said Claudius. We didn't find anything."

430

"I'll draw you a map but Uncle Otto must have it blocked with magics. You won't be able to see it without your Angel." Olin grabbed a piece of paper and was making a map as he spoke. "Otto chooses which girls will be taken to the Master and those girls are then transferred to The Rooster. It's a men's shop. But in every city there is a different place for this."

"Before you ask anything there are some things I have to explain. The Master in the dark worlds is a god. So there are special ceremonies for all kinds of things and these ceremonies are secrets to everyone but the highest priests, of which Otto is one."

"The chosen girls are prepared so they are perfect for him and in Langer that is done below Joanna's shop. Only the highest people can even help with the ceremonies so in Langer that is Otto and his immediate family. No one but Otto, Jack and Joanna know anything about the preparations and ceremonies. I have no clue how they get the girls to him. I wouldn't be surprised if he didn't screw them first before he kills them, but that is just my guess. I have never seen any of the ceremonies."

"I honestly don't know if anyone sees them. What I do know, I have basically overheard in Otto's house. Andre, Joanna's husband isn't allowed to be part of any of this. Now, he is a dark lord but he isn't high enough in the hierarchy to help."

"Before you ask, I would really doubt that Otto has those girls taken to his home for any reason because he is so concerned about his public image. I don't know how often the ceremonies occur. I just know that I will get a note that says how many to grab and it might say a specific hair color...so I would assume that has more to do with the ritual instead of the Master's taste in women."

"I have to admit you did a good job of guessing our questions," said Dominic. "But I went to the Land Office and they can't find any paperwork on either The Rooster or The Chicken and The Egg. Who owns those buildings?"

"Juleta did. I don't know if Joanna or Otto bought them from her. And I am not surprised that the paperwork disappeared," said Olin.

"Why did Juleta buy them?" asked Claudius.

"Otto used to just keep the women under the docks. Juleta always wanted power and was basically kissing up to the Master. She came up with the idea of the shops. Because a lot of the customers are chosen from those shops. So it is like they come to us. And yes, men are sacrificed too but I think that is for certain ceremonies."

"King Mathas don't get mad at me, but you have to know that Juleta was anything but discrete. Uncle Otto liked her ideas but he was afraid that she would bring attention to all of them because she and Isabella were always trying to get attention. So he may have bought them from her."

"So what's with the names?" asked Thaos.

"I know they sound stupid but it has to do with some ancient texts. I don't know what texts but those names have significant meanings."

"We heard that Juleta and Joanna got into a screaming match in front of a bunch of people about the name of that store," said Turner. "Why would that be?"

"Ok, I am not a good person, in fact you would call me a criminal but I am a lousy dark lord. I don't read any of that stuff but I do know that specific words will have some kind of significance. I will bet that Juleta did a lot of research and picked those names to give herself standing in the eyes of the Master. Otto, Jack and Joanna may have had their own agendas."

"So you tried to grab my girl," said Noah. "Just what were you planning on doing with her?"

Noah's stare was intimidating Olin. "I was going to keep her for myself."

Tessa jumped between Noah and Olin. "I know you are full of yourself," she said to Olin. "But did you know that all those days you were watching me some men were watching you?"

"No, were they Otto's men?" Olin asked.

432

"Now how would I know that?" asked Tessa. "But it wasn't always the same guys. And remember a week ago when you were standing in the doorway of that bank, there were six men in different alley's watching you."

"That is Uncle Otto's bank and I never saw them. And you are sure they were watching me?"

"As sure as I was that you were a dark lord when we first met. What? Were you too busy staring at women or too self-absorbed to realize you were being followed?" asked Tessa.

"While I would not be surprised that Otto had me watched he would never send that many men to one area because he wants everything to be discrete and why would he need that many men?"

"Can't imagine you would have any enemies," Thaos said sarcastically.

"It might be important to know," said Dominic. "Would your father have you followed?"

"I can't imagine he would waste the energy," said Olin. "I am going to have to think about this. Tessa what did they look like?"

"Hired killers that's why I noticed them."

Angus had not spoken a word since Olin was brought to the castle. Angus was an intense man and he was studying both Olin and Elexas. Now as he looked at the maps and charts in Ryan's workroom he had an idea.

"Ryan, here are the notes from the interrogations of those men from The Rooster. I was going to brief everyone but Olin basically told us the same information. And Mathas after seeing the quality of this work, I think we should just give Ryan all of the paperwork we collected."

"I agree," said Mathas.

"Jasmine and I will help with that," Seth said because he didn't think that Olin should read those papers. Seth didn't realize that Angus was trying to get a reaction from Olin.

"What guys from The Rooster?" asked Olin.

"We closed that place down this morning and got two of the girls you were going to sacrifice," Angus said and carefully watched Olin's reaction.

"Does Uncle Otto know?" Olin asked. "Seriously you don't want to get on his bad side, he is not a normal man."

"We'll he's going to have a bad day then," said Claudius. "Besides our soldiers searching the docks for Otto's victims, Fahron is taking soldiers into every bank in the city and going through safety boxes. He was going to save Otto's bank for last."

"Are you trying to push him into a move or reacting to information as you get it?" asked Olin.

"Why?" Mathas asked suspiciously.

"Those girls were already the property of the Master, they have just not been prepared. He will not let you take what is his. I don't even want to know where those girls are but he will definitely go after them," Olin said. "And he will punish Otto for losing his prizes. Otto puts on the show of the mild mannered businessman but he is a real bastard and he's scared shitless of the Master. You guys better be prepared for some kind of an attack and I am not kidding."

Claudius nodded at Stephan and Thaos and both men left the room.

"I am trying to think of a way to explain this so you understand how serious this is," Olin continued. "I know that you call your god The Great Ruler. What if you promised Him something or one of the Angels then you didn't do it?"

"Actually, I think that happens all of the time with people," said Dominic.

"Well, it doesn't with the Master. I will be honest, I am more worried about my hide than yours but you are protecting me. They will hit you and hit you hard."

"Yes My Lord, I know it has the seal of the King but Mister Franks always wants to approve things himself," said the nervous bank teller. "I don't know where he is. I never saw him leave his office but it is empty."

"I know you have a job to do," said Fahron. "But I don't need his permission for one and two I am not waiting around. Take me to these safety boxes now or I will have you taken to the dungeons."

"Very well but Mister Franks is going to be really mad."

# Chapter XXXV
## Messages

"Damn this isn't good," said Jack as he and Dillon stopped their horses and watched several companies of soldiers piling up the bodies of the Hutas. "They aren't fools. They will notice this wasn't a battle. Well, we don't have any place to hide, let's see what they know."

"What the hell happened here?" Jack asked some soldiers as he and Dillon rode up to them.

"Damndest thing I ever saw," said a soldier and spit tobacco on the ground. "Look for yourselves. Not a mark on any of these monsters. No blood and no other bodies. Can't figure it out."

"Are you going to burn them?" Jack asked.

"You betcha."

"Did you just come up on these Hutas or did they attack something else?" asked Jack.

"Don't rightly know if they attacked anything. Didn't see nothing. General Claudius sent us out here to burn the bodies."

"Don't envy your job," Jack said and he and Dillon started down the road. "So the General already knew about them; interesting."

"I tore my dress chasing that jerk," Tessa said as she and Noah entered their room. "It won't take me long to change."

"Take all of the time you need," Noah said and started to unbutton her dress. "I haven't had a chance to really look at my watch yet; with everything going on. I want to do that now."

Tessa took off her dress and took it into the bathing room to try and clean off some dirt stains.

When she returned to the bedroom she saw Noah sitting in a chair reading the inscription in his watch. "Do you mean this?" he asked.

"Yes," she said and walked up to him and sat on his lap.

"Tessa, I've never had anything this nice before in my whole life. Thank you." They kissed softly then he said. "Remember that first day that Elexas showed up and you said you were shocked that you got jealous?"

"Oh yeah," she said and smiled.

"Well, I am trying to get used to all of the feelings I have for you. And one of them is that I am so worried about you. I know how capable and smart you are but, I just can't explain it. I want you to promise me right now that you won't just take off without telling me again."

"I promise but you have to understand too that I am used to being independent."

"I know, I really can't explain it. You know how it is when you can't remember something but it is on the tip of your tongue? I know it sounds crazy but it's like that. Like I know why I am worried about you but I can't remember."

"So this is from a specific threat and not just general worrying?"

"Yes and it's really bothering me. I'm thinking about talking to Gideon. He does this thing where he kind of put's people to sleep and he can make them remember things and tell the truth."

"You really are worried about this."

"Yes, so humor me for a while."

While Tessa and Noah were in their room, Claudius walked into the Great Hall.

"Adam, Miranda I need to find those girls. Will you help me?"

"And what would you like us to do?" asked Miranda as she and Adam materialized.

"Olin said that Otto has done something with magics so we can't see the prison. Will you remove the magics?"

"We need you to think this through first," said Miranda. "You are going against possibly the most powerful dark lord you have ever met and steal the women who are marked for the Master. What Olin just told you is true. Do you think there might be more in place than magic blocking the entrance? And you are going to show your hand and you are not ready to do that yet."

"So what do you suggest? We certainly can't leave them there."

"We have no intention of doing that," said Adam. "But he saw your troops searching that area earlier. He now knows about Tessa going after Olin and believes her to be a stronger dark lord than Olin. Otto's son is riding back to him, as we speak, to tell him that you were aware of that army of Hutas. Both Otto and Jack will suspect that you have knowledge of the deaths of that army from hell."

"He has not yet learned that you attacked The Rooster or that Fahron is in his bank now, searching safety boxes. When he realizes all that has happened he will consider this war."

"If he wants a war, he has it!"

"Claudius, you aren't listening to us. Now is not the time," said Adam. "Otto is praying at his unholy altar now but I am blocking the communication with the Master. Otto will get scared and move the women; that is when you get them."

"Where is he moving them to?"

"Joanna's shop. He will put them in a carriage. Have your soldiers on the streets." Adam and Miranda disappeared.

Stephan and Thaos contacted the commanders at Fort Langer and Fort Castor and put them on alert for an attack.

They did the same for the commanders of the troops at the homes of Mathas, Claudius, Fahron and Gideon's home which his family had not yet moved into. Soldiers were sent into Langer to alert the soldiers on patrol there. And a company of soldiers was sent into the city to find Fahron.

During this time, Claudius was preparing troops and team members for the mission of saving the captive women who Otto would be transporting.

The members of both Turner's and Dominic's teams quickly designated a chambers on the first floor of Mathas' castle for the temporary office. Members of both of these teams had a short meeting and decided to help Ryan compile information. They made this decision for two reasons; one, they all felt an urgency to find out what they were dealing with and two, no one trusted Elexas and Olin.

To Ryan's relief the team members quickly and efficiently moved all of the charts, maps and paperwork. Ryan was in charge of determining the locations for these items in the huge chambers the office was moved to.

Dominic entered Mathas' office to tell him about the plans of the teams. Angus and Sorren were meeting with Mathas at the time.

"Excellent," said Mathas. "We were just talking about that. This is a ledger that Angus took from The Rooster, I don't want Olin or Elexas to look at this. And these are the notes from the interrogation of the man who killed Endleson."

"When you read Angus' notes from the interrogations of the men from The Rooster you will learn that Hugh was hiring the second man to kill our assassin. That leads us to believe they all may have more information than we got from them. So Sorren and Angus are going to do more interrogations."

"While Ryan is in charge of putting everything together I want you and Turner to oversee the security of the work. I know the Angels said that those two derelicts have information for us and I don't doubt that but no one should trust them."

"We agree," said Dominic. "Anything else?"

"The second woman finally regained consciousness. Send Tessa to talk with her. Both those women are terrified. I was going to send them home but after what Olin said I will keep them here for a little while. I don't want him to go near them."

"There is also the matter of the two notes that were found on Endleson, we need to figure out what they are. And tell Turner that everyone on his team is getting paid from the day they joined us. I am putting them on your team and if they want to change that after this mission they certainly can. If they want to argue send them to me. They are risking their lives for us and should be paid."

"I think they will be pleased with that," Dominic said. "Do you want us to review the things that Fahron brings back?"

"I am not sure yet because you have your hands full now," Mathas said. "How are things going in there?"

"Well, with all of us working, the office is basically set up. Ryan, Olin and Elexas have some kind of system and they don't want us interfering. So Seth, Lawrence, Deborah and Jasmine are in one of the bedrooms reviewing the papers from The Rooster. Everyone is getting along well considering the trust issues."

"Actually it is kind of interesting to watch. Olin is as enthusiastic as Ryan because he says he loves puzzles and I think this may be the first time anyone has ever complimented Elexas on her brains. She is all fired up. It's kind of like watching three kids working on a game. And I may be really off base on this but I will bet you a bottle of whiskey that neither Olin or Elexas have a lot of friends."

"Well, I can tell you that Elexas doesn't," said Sorren. "Mathas, I feel like you did when you learned about Juleta and Isabella. Three people from my tribe and two of them from my own village are traitors right under my nose. I will never forgive myself."

"Well, we don't know if Elexas is really a traitor," said Angus. "And Dominic may have just hit on something. I was watching those two and they are rather similar."

"They are both self-centered little snots. But when you listen closely to what they say I think they are both lonely. Olin doesn't think that anyone in his family gives a crap about him so he doesn't care about them. And Elexas just seems lost to me."

"Understand, I am not making excuses for them, I am identifying weaknesses. They are both loners and I will bet anything they really want to be a part of a group, any group. They know we don't trust them but look how they are responding to Ryan. I think we give them a little rope and see what happens."

"You're thinking that is the best way to get information from them?" asked Mathas.

"Yes, I mean it's worth a try. If it doesn't work, what have we lost?" Angus said.

"I'll talk to Turner and we will make them feel more included without giving them too much information," Dominic said. "Actually, I like that idea and I think it has merit. When I left the room to come here, Olin was chatting away about his family. I got the impression that he has never been able to talk about them before."

"My only concern is Ryan. He is such a good kid. He sees the good in everyone," said Mathas. "I don't want him getting hurt somehow."

"That is exactly why Ryan is perfect for this," said Angus. "He isn't judgmental, he is enjoying the company. And he certainly isn't stupid."

"Everyone is already watching out for him," Dominic said.

"Speaking of Ryan," said Sorren. "What he is doing is, well, impressive doesn't come close. And you know he is working this hard because he always feels like an outsider because he isn't a warrior. Which now that I said it, that is probably why he is connecting with those other two. But Mathas when things settle down perhaps we should talk about offering him a position or giving him a title; that would mean a lot to him."

"Already been thinking about that," Mathas said and winked at Sorren.

After Claudius had everyone in place for the rescue mission, he, Thaos and Stephan rode to the naval yard to brief Gideon on the day's events.

It was late afternoon when the men walked out of Gideon's office. "This has been the damndest day," Gideon said. "Besides all the stuff that has happened, I've just had a bad feeling so I had Ashley close the store early and had soldiers escort all of our wives home."

"Thanks, that was going to be our next stop," said Thaos.

"Before you go I want to show you something," Gideon said. "Did you all get a chance to read the letter I sent to Mathas?'

"Yes," said Claudius.

As the men were talking, Gideon was leading them to the barracks that now housed the homeless. "That entire stretch of land over there," Gideon pointed out the area as he spoke. "I am going to build a neighborhood. I am going to have to talk to Mathas and see if he will let me annex more of this land."

"It's vacant, just tell us where you want the boundaries," said Claudius. "Adam told me I should consider doing the same thing for the cast outs. We should put our heads together on this when things settle down a little."

"All but two of these barracks are filled now," Gideon said and shook his head as they entered one of the buildings. "I had no idea this many people were homeless. And from what my men said, they all want to work. I've sent my men to every store in the city, buying supplies for these people."

"I hope you plan on giving the bills to Mathas. You aren't paying for all of this," said Claudius.

"Look at all of these little kids," said Stephan with both horror and amazement.

"I know," said Gideon solemnly. "I can't believe that I never saw them."

"Neither did we," said Thaos and walked up to a woman. "Excuse me My Lady but I have probably an incredibly stupid question."

"No one has called me My Lady in a long time," she said and smiled. "I want to thank you for all of this."

Claudius, Stephan and Gideon walked up to Thaos and the woman. "We will build you homes," said Claudius. "What my son wants to ask you is the same question that all of us are thinking. Why didn't we know that so many people were homeless? We are on these streets every day. Honestly we are both shocked and ashamed."

"My Lord, there is a good reason for that," said the woman. "Most of us don't live on the streets of the city, we live underneath them. That is why you don't see us. It took us a while to get used to it but it is safer if we stay in groups."

"What do you mean underneath the city?" asked Thaos. "We know of a few tunnels but..."

"Oh My Lord there is very much more than a few tunnels. I was told, and mind you I don't know if this is true but before Langer was built this area was inhabited by other people who were killed during a horrible storm that started at sea. The storm was so devastating that it buried their village. Then later Langer was built on top of it. I used to be a teacher before my husband died and there were a couple of different tribes that are said to have lived in this area, so the story may be true."

"What is your name?" asked Claudius.

"Argail."

"Argail, would you or someone else here take us to that place? We would like to see it, besides we want to help anyone else who is there," Claudius said.

"Oh, there are still people down there. I have my children to watch but wait just a moment and I will be right back," Argail said and walked down a hallway. She returned several minutes later with a man. "My Lords, this is Tom. He will take you."

"Hello Tom, I am..."

"Oh, I know who all of you are," Tom said. "And thanks for the buildings. Argail said you are going to build homes?"

"That is true," said Claudius. "It is no excuse but we just never knew so many people needed homes."

"I will be building businesses here to support the navy," said Gideon. "So there will be jobs too."

"Well, I am a shoemaker," Tom said happily. "If your navy needs shoes, I am your man."

"Oh, they will need shoes," Gideon said and laughed. "Tom and Argail can I ask you to do something and feel free to say no? This is going to be an enormous project with building the naval yard, the businesses and the homes. And I can see already we will need a school. Can you talk with the people here and perhaps organize the tradesmen so I know what trades are represented and what they will need to open their businesses?"

Argail started to cry. "You just say it and it's done Admiral Gideon," Tom said emotionally.

"Tom, we have something going on in the city that we need to attend to now," Claudius said. "If we return say midmorning tomorrow will you take us underneath the city?"

"Where should I meet you?"

"Do you know where my office is?" asked Gideon.

"I sure do," said Tom.

"Meet there and if you are early we can talk about these businesses," Gideon said.

"Her name is Julie and she remembers less than Daisy does," Tessa told Turner. "She was walking home from a society meeting when she was attacked. I did ask both of the women if they had been in The Chicken and The Egg shop recently and they both had been within the last two weeks."

"Since they are both awake now, we moved them into the same room. That will give Reese and Ethan a little break. I told them we were investigating what happened to them and want to keep them here a little longer for their safety."

"They are both so scared they were glad to hear that. But they worry about their families. I told them I will check with the King as to when we will notify them."

"Good job, I will brief Mathas," said Turner. "I want you to work on those notes that we got off from Endleson. Mathas wants all of you to stay in the castle tonight because he isn't sure what will happen after Claudius gets those women."

Turner's and Dominic's teams were in the chambers set up for an office. Ryan, Elexas and Olin set their work area up in the parlor. Dominic's and Turner's teams each set up work areas in different bedrooms.

"Hey Olin, got a question for you," Fennel said and walked into the parlor. What does that symbol mean with the five swords because it is on all of the paperwork from The Rooster?"

"Every big shot in the Insidiae has to come up with a symbol that represents them. It has to be unique to them so I heard there is a committee that approves the symbols. It is like a Trades Card for any business. As far as I know that doesn't have any special meaning, it's just what Uncle Otto chose." As Olin spoke members of the teams came out of their work areas.

"Olin, look at these will you?" asked Bart and showed him drawings of symbols. "We see these in the underground tunnels can you tell us what they mean?"

"Sure," said Olin who was flattered that these warriors where coming to him with their questions. "But first I have to give you some background. I already told you that there are lots of different groups in what you call the dark worlds. And there are lots of different criminal groups that have absolutely nothing to do with demons and magics."

"Every group that I know of marks out a territory. For example part of Hector's territory is Joy City. Hector forces the people in that area to pay protection money which is a common practice."

"Most of the groups that I have heard of, have some kind of racket like that going. So they mark their territory, you know like a dog pissing on bushes. And if you go in that territory to do business you usually get the shit beat out of you."

"Uncle Otto, Deckor, Juleta, they all did the same thing. But you know how secretive the Insidiae is; they use the symbols for communication too. That one with the eye with the lightning bolts is the Master. That one with the four sets of eyes was Juleta's."

"Hector's is the four swords with the dots underneath them but that used to belong to the Grand Masters Emeric and his sister Banaka. I heard that Juleta bought it from them for Hector and you know that had to cost her."

"Why would she do that?" asked Jasmine.

"There is probably some kind of power connected to it," Olin said then continued to explain the symbols. "The four J's with the diamonds is Joanna's and Jack's is the upside down J. My father's is three bolts of lightning and a sword, which isn't on here. That one that looks like a soldier is a warning that soldiers are in the area," as Olin was talking he was writing on the sheet of paper that Bart had handed him. "Now these two I haven't seen before. Where did you see these?"

"In one of the tunnels under the docks," said Bart.

"Are they old or new?" asked Olin.

Bart looked at Louis and Garvis, "What do you guys think?"

446

"We've been seeing them for at least a few months," Garvis said.

"Ok, you know that I am such a loser that I don't have a symbol and I am certainly not an expert. But, look at the detail in these. If I had to bet I would say that there are some new players in the city. And when I say that I mean in the Insidiae or one of its offshoot groups."

"I think these are big players; maybe that is one reason that Uncle Otto has been nervous. Maybe his competition increased for kissing up to the Master."

"I heard that the guys that actually killed Prince Michael and those others were assassins from Salszar. I wonder if this is their symbol."

"But there are two," said Jasmine.

"You see that a lot with assassins," Olin explained. "One is for the group they are a part of and the other for who hired them to do the job in that area."

"Thanks, you've been a lot of help," said Bart. "I'll owe you a whiskey."

"I'll take you up on that," Olin said.

"When we found those girls in The Rooster there are the same marks over and over on the walls," said Garvis. "What does that mean?"

"That is like an assignment sheet. For example there were probably a lot of ones for the Master in groupings and that means that on that day he ordered let's just say four girls. Then underneath that might be Otto's symbol to indicate he fulfilled the order."

"Now, if Hugh or whoever just sees the marks for the Master he knows that order still needs to be filled. As far as I know, Otto, Jack and Joanna are the only ones who write those orders."

"Do you ever see anything like this?" Noah asked and showed Olin the note they took off from Endleson which was all numbers.

"I was going to say these are accounts but look they are divided in groups of four; it's hard to see at first. I'll bet these are locations on maps," Olin said.

"We may all be buying you whiskey," Fennel said and grabbed the note with the numbers.

"I'll have to drink it here," Olin said. "I'm pretty sure that if I walk out of this castle I'm a dead man."

"You think the Master?" asked Elexas.

"And Uncle Otto. He is going to think I gave you the information for the attacks today. And trust me that is exactly how he is going to view those things."

"I'm going to show you something," Tessa said as she carried a small tray into the office. "I have a blank piece of paper which might be a secret note. Now, don't ask me what it was written with but for some reason this works. I made a pot of tea. Pretty much any tea will do but you have to let the water really boil then pour it over the leaves and let that cool. Then I am pouring a little in this bowl. The note is made of paper so you can't leave it in the tea long."

"Oh my god!" said Elexas as images started to appear on the piece of paper covered with tea.

"I've never seen that either," said Olin.

"I don't think any of us have," Jasmine said.

"Javier taught us this," Tessa said. "I don't know how he learned it." Tessa was gently blowing on the paper. "It's a map but I have no idea of what."

"Olin figured out that the note with numbers were probably map coordinates," said Fennel.

"Can I see that?" asked Seth. After he studied the small map for several moments he said, "Jasmine, doesn't this look like one of the maps we found in that folder that Isabella hid in Javier's house?"

"What are you talking about?" asked Olin.

"Isabella was pissed because one of her boyfriends broke it off with her so she hid a folder of papers in his house; probably to set him up," said Seth.

"Can I see that map?" Olin asked.

"Careful, it's still wet," said Jasmine as she handed it to him.

"Honestly, I don't know what this is a map to but maybe six months ago Uncle Otto said some of his papers were stolen during one of his celebrations. If she stole his things he will kill her."

"She's already dead," said Dominic. "She sold her soul to a demon who was turning her into one. An Angel helped some of our people destroy her."

"And you are sure about this?" Olin asked. "Because that doesn't make any sense."

"What are you talking about?" asked Dominic.

"I thought for sure that; hell I know they did. Uncle Otto and Joanna said they were getting letters from Isabella. She is in Port Friada and they wanted to know if I knew anything about that."

"How long ago was this?" asked Fennel.

"I don't know how long she has been sending letters but they asked me when I first got here which was a little over a month ago," Olin said. "Those papers she stole, do you know what they were?"

"Before we get into that, do you know what Isabella wrote in those letters?" Turner asked.

"No, they didn't show them to me or tell me anything," said Olin.

"We couldn't read the language those papers were written in," said Seth. "What languages can Otto read?"

"I don't really know," Olin said thoughtfully. "I am just throwing out an idea here. You think she was setting up one of her boyfriends but she could have been trying to set up Uncle Otto. I don't know any other languages so I can't guess about those papers but I do know that really important information is often written in other languages so that if someone finds it they can't read the message."

"How do you think she would be setting up Otto?" asked Jasmine.

"Well, if those papers were really important and now he lost them and who knows if he read them; I am just saying he could be in hot water."

"The people and demons who Uncle Otto deals with aren't exactly forgiving. They punish you if you screw up, which is why I don't deal with them."

# Chapter XXXVI
## Victims

"Actually, I didn't get that much," said Fahron as he handed Mathas the contents from the safety boxes he had searched. "It took longer to verify the names than it did for me to grab the stuff. Juleta didn't have any boxes under her name and neither did Endleson. There weren't any under the name Frankwich. But Isabella had boxes in every damn bank. All of that stuff is hers."

As Fahron spoke Mathas dumped the contents of a huge pouch onto his desk. Besides papers and books there were six pouches of gold coins and a considerable amount of jewelry. "I did wonder why she was hiding her jewels unless those aren't hers," Fahron said. "Or maybe they have spells on them."

Mathas picked up a necklace from the pile of jewels. "I am sure this is Rosa's. Don't tell me she was stealing from her own family."

"Remember her diary, she did a lot of things for excitement."

"I am going to get Rosa; pour yourself a drink. You might want to stay here for a while. We think Otto will move those girls as soon as it gets dark."

"I don't have a damn clue what is going on," Sorren said to Angus. They had been interrogating Hugh for the second time when he slumped over. "He is breathing," Sorren said and slapped Hugh across the face. Hugh jumped as he regained consciousness. His eyes were red and green foam was coming out of his mouth. The sounds he was making were that of a swine.

"Miranda!" Sorren yelled. "Is he turning into a demon?"

"No," said Miranda and appeared in the small room. Hugh was tied to a chair and now became wild when he saw the Angel. "He sold his soul to the Master who just collected his debt. There is no humanity left in that vessel."

"So then the Master knows that he is here?" asked Angus.

"You have not dealt with anything like the betrayer known as the Master before and all of you must keep that in mind. He knows that his pawn was taken and he assumes he is in the dungeons. The two hired killers you arrested own their souls, you will be able to question them but they probably won't be able to give you more information."

"Does the Master own Olin's soul?" asked Angus.

"He did until Olin prayed to Adam. The Master would have been able to see through Olin's eyes. He knows he lost a soul and he is irate."

"Well, if he is so powerful why didn't he attack us too?" asked Angus.

"Because of the Angels," Sorren said. "I'll bet he can sense them."

"You have learned well," said Miranda. "But it isn't like he knows our exact locations. He feels us when he looks at all of you. While you are all courageous you are not prepared to go to war with him, not yet anyways. But every action that your group has taken today was considered an act of war by both Otto and the Master."

"Are you saying that we should have consulted with you first?" asked Sorren.

"Some things you never learn," Miranda said but she smiled. "There are few who will challenge them. The Master heard Tessa's taunts when she first met Olin and we allowed that because now he knows the heavens are watching. Tessa proudly told Olin that she talks with Angels then bet him that we were tougher than his Master. We protected her but in her words she also told the Master that humans who know of his existence will stand against him."

"Demons and abominations such as he are empowered by the fears of humans. They are fed by the souls they own. If enough people knew of him and refused to bow before him that would weaken him greatly. Now, do you understand why a little band of seemingly normal humans is under attack by so many demons?"

"Your faith and courage are slowly inspiring epidemics of resistance in many worlds. If the children of The Great Ruler ever realized the power they possess there would be no more darkness."

"While Hugh's body still breathes he will be dead soon. A body cannot exist without the soul. You will need to burn his body."

"But, now that you say that," asked Sorren. "How does that work when someone sells their soul?"

"It remains in the body until the demon wants the debt paid."

Claudius, Stephan and Thaos were sitting in a small restaurant eating dinner. Aunt Maries Restaurant was across the street from The Chicken and The Egg and one building to the north. They had a clear view of the streets and the clothing store from their table near the front window.

Several hours earlier Claudius ordered his soldiers to search carriages and bocas in the city. They were supposed to tell the story that they were looking for some dangerous criminals. So far the ruse was working. The citizens of Langer were still shaken from the recent murders and riots and felt safe that the soldiers were guarding the streets. The soldiers were ordered to be respectful of the citizens and their property. The soldiers also knew they were really looking for kidnapped women.

Claudius knew it would look suspicious if he and his sons remained on the street. He was afraid that Otto would suspect something was wrong and perhaps kill the women.

"Joanna just put the closed sign on the door but all of the candles are lit in the store," Stephan said in a low voice. Neither Claudius nor Thaos commented since the restaurant was filled with people.

The Lieutenant running the operation on the streets was the only soldier who knew all of the information. He also knew where Claudius and his sons were. Lieutenant Strauss was watching the docks near Otto's bank when an elegant carriage seemed to appear out of nowhere. The Lieutenant told one of his men to ride forward and tell the other soldiers the location where he wanted the carriage stopped. Strauss followed the carriage down the busy street.

Because of the time of night, there weren't as many carriages and bocas on the street. Most people had finished their shopping and work. Suddenly a carriage pulled out of an alley and in front of the one that Strauss was following. His men let it travel a block before they stopped it and searched it.

Strauss was close enough to the elegant carriage to see the driver looking around nervously. Within moments this driver drove around the carriage in front of him and sped down the street. Strauss quickly rode to the driver's side of the carriage and ordered the driver to stop. The driver did not and soldiers surrounded the carriage; two soldiers grabbed the reigns on the horses forcing it to stop. The carriage was a block south of The Chicken and The Egg.

"I'm just the driver," yelled the man nervously.

Soldiers jumped from their horses and opened the doors to the carriage. "Strauss, it's full of women and they might be dead!" yelled a soldier so loudly that citizens on the street heard him.

"Stay back we don't know what we have here," yelled another soldier to the citizens who were running up to the carriage.

One of the soldiers had climbed into the carriage and now yelled at the top of his voice, "They're alive but we need a physician. Someone get a physician!"

Strauss sent a soldier to get Claudius and his sons. He remained on his horse as he was watching for any sign of attack but Strauss had moved so he could see into the carriage.

"There's seven," yelled the soldier who was still in the carriage. "They all look beat up and I think they are drugged." People were running down the streets and coming out of buildings to see what was happening. People who were closest to the carriage were repeating the words of the soldiers and yelling them to the rest of the crowd.

Claudius, Thaos and Stephan ran down the street. They reached the carriage at the same time a physician did. "Arrest the driver," ordered Claudius.

It was very cramped but the soldier remained in the carriage with the physician.

"I need your attention!" yelled Stephan.

The soldiers were yelling for the crowd to be quiet.

Stephan walked to the walkway and stood on a chair that was outside of a store. "We have been hearing rumors that innocent women are being abducted off the streets of our city; that is the real reason the soldiers were searching carriages and bocas. We have seven young women in this carriage who are drugged and may have been beaten."

"We are taking them to the King's castle for their own protection. If you know of anyone who has a missing family member or friend please come up here. And if you know anything at all, even a rumor please speak with us. We have no reason to believe that these poor girls are the only ones."

"Hang that damn driver!" yelled someone in the crowd.

"We need to question him first," Thaos yelled.

Soldiers had already pulled the driver off the carriage and tied his hands. They set him on a horse while two other soldiers climbed into the front seat of the carriage.

Lieutenant Strauss was to remain in Langer with two companies of soldiers. Their assignments now were to keep the peace and to obtain information from the citizens.

Many people surrounded Claudius and were asking him questions. Thaos and Stephan left the area and walked back to the restaurant to get their horses.

"Stephan! Stephan!" yelled Joanna as she ran down the street. "Stephan do you know what is going on?"

"Thaos meet Joanna Franks, she is Otto's daughter and over the years has been very close to members of Mathas' family," Stephan said with a sneer. Joanna looked stunned, she turned white then red. "Joanna, this is my brother Thaos."

Thaos took her hand and kissed it. "My Lady," he said and smiled. Joanna had never been that close to Thaos but she certainly knew all about him and his relationship to Juleta and Hector. "My Lady, you look as if you have seen a ghost."

"I am sorry for staring, forgive me I don't know what happened to my manners," Joanna said but continued to stare at Thaos who was still holding her hand.

"Joanna, we've received a lot of reports about young women being abducted and we just found seven of them," Stephan said. "Would you know anything?"

"Why would I know anything?" she asked sharply.

"You own a woman's store. Don't the women talk about things like that? I mean if you had any idea of the number of people who have come to us, I can't believe you haven't heard anything. So if you do, tell us and be careful. Do you want us to take you home?"

"No, no I will be alright but thank you. So there have been a lot of reports?" she asked.

"People are still stirred up from the murders and the riots," said Thaos. "A bunch of them were starting their own little army and they were going to storm every business and home in the city. We stopped that. But Claudius is down there because that mob wants to lynch the driver."

Joanna became pale again, "This is all so very awful."

"Seriously Joanna, we can wait with you until you close up and take you home," said Stephan.

"No but thank you again," she said then turned to Thaos and smiled. "It was very nice to meet you."

He smiled and the two men walked to their horses. "Yep, she had it bad for Hector," Thaos said under his breath. "We might be able to use that."

Every word and action taken by Claudius, Stephan and Thaos was planned. The Angels had warned Claudius that they were not ready to go against the Master and Otto. And Olin had said several times how worried Otto was about his public image.

The plan was to make Otto believe that the citizens of Langer were aware of the abductions and watching for suspicious behavior. And these same citizens were ready to take matters into their own hands. Claudius hoped that Otto would be worried enough to stop the abductions, for at least a while, and perhaps expose himself and his organization.

"Where's Olin?" barked Claudius as he walked into the temporary office.

"I'm right here," Olin said as he turned around from writing on a chart on wall. "Is something wrong?"

The members of Dominic's and Turner's teams walked out of their work areas and joined Claudius and Olin in the parlor. "I am really trying to decide if I should tell you any of this you little piss ant." It was clear to everyone that Olin was intimidated by Claudius who towered over him.

"We've rescued nine of the women. Joanna has been told that the citizens are up in arms and going to bust down doors. That story wasn't hard to sell since they wanted to hang Otto's driver." Olin looked as if he was shaking as he listened to Claudius.

"First, I don't want you near any of them. Everyone has orders to kill you on the spot if you go near those girls. And secondly, we spread that story for a couple of reasons and one was so Otto didn't think information was coming from you. Now tell me boy, what do you think his next move will be?"

"Here," said Fennel and handed a glass of whiskey to Olin. "You look like you are going to pass out."

"I might. Do you have any idea of what you have done?"

"Saved nine young women," Claudius said as Fennel handed him a glass of whiskey also.

"Can I sit down my legs are shaking?" Olin asked Claudius. "In some ways you are scarier than Uncle Otto. First, no one defies the Master. He will punish Uncle Otto and maybe his family then he will make an example out of all of you. He might go after the women in your families."

"Well, you haven't met the women in our families," said Claudius. "But what you are saying makes sense. So how would he punish Otto?"

"Think of the most powerful demon you know of and the Master is worse," said Olin. "There are so many ways but it will be something big because he needs to prove a point and keep his people in line. Otto is really powerful so if I had to guess, the Master won't kill him but might kill everyone else he cares about."

"Joanna is really smart. She is probably trying to figure out a way to appease the Master. Otto has a really bad temper and is scared shitless of the Master. In my mind you just made him a cornered animal. He will strike out but how and when I don't know."

Olin paused during which time he gulped down his whiskey. "I am sorry I am trying to think. Did you make it sound like the citizens reported it to you or you told them?"

"That the citizens were giving us reports of missing women," said Claudius.

"That was smart. Is that how you found out? No, don't tell me I don't want to know. Otto is paranoid and always worried about his public image." Suddenly Olin grinned. "I'll bet he is going crazy right now." The grin left Olin's face quickly. "You better ask your Angel to help those girls because the Master will be in their heads. They were already given to him."

"What do you mean?" asked Claudius.

"When they are first taken, there is a ceremony that Otto does. I wouldn't be surprised if Joanna and Jack don't help. But, they basically give him the offering but he doesn't sacrifice them until later." Dominic stood up and quickly left the room; he didn't want to pray to the Angels in front of Olin.

Claudius stared at Olin as he was trying to read him. "The Master doesn't own your soul anymore. Adam took it back when you prayed to him. Of course you will probably sell it back."

"What did you say! I never sold it to him in the first place," Olin shrieked.

"Well son, the Angels don't lie. In fact, I don't know if they can," said Claudius. "So if you didn't offer it up who did? Otto or your father?"

"I don't know; they are both pricks!" Olin was so upset that he started to cry. "I'm crying because I am that mad," he said defensively. "Angel Adam thank you," yelled Olin as he looked at the ceiling. "I owe you one."

Olin now looked at the faces of the people in the room. "You are all looking at me like I am crazy but that is because you really don't know what you are involved with. There is a big difference between working for someone, or even worshipping him and having him own your soul."

"How could you not tell?" asked Elexas.

"I couldn't." Olin said. "Why do you look so scared?"

"I've spent a lot of time with Otto and the others. Can you look at my eyes or something and tell?" Elexas looked terrified.

"Elexas ask Adam to help you," said Tessa.

"I don't know how," Elexas said as she became panicked.

"Come on," said Fennel and held out his hand. The two walked into the hallway.

Claudius kept staring at Olin. "You look too upset to talk anymore. If you think of anything let me know?" Olin nodded. "Ryan, you and I are staying here tonight. Stephan and Thaos will bring us some fresh clothes in the morning."

"Good, then I can keep working," Ryan said to Claudius but was staring at Olin. Ryan didn't understand Olin but for that moment in time he wouldn't have traded places with him for the world.

Claudius walked into the hallway and saw Elexas and Fennel holding hands and praying. She was crying. He marched into Mathas' office and poured himself a whiskey. Mathas, Fahron, Sorren and Angus were reading the things that Fahron had gotten out of Isabella's safety boxes.

"What's the matter?" asked Sorren.

"Olin and Elexas, I just can't figure them out. One minute I think they should be executed and the next they seem like victims. They're both crying and talking to Adam, he didn't show. But damn, I thought Ryan was going to start crying too. Olin didn't sell his soul to the Master, either his father or Otto did. The kid is scared shitless to say nothing about feeling betrayed. And since he didn't even know the Master owned his soul, Elexas is practically hysterical thinking that Otto may have sold hers too."

"Olin said that Otto does some kind of ceremony over the women as soon as they are abducted to give them to the Master. He said the Master will be in their heads and to ask the Angels to help them. That little piss ant dark lord says that. I thought I was going to fall out of my chair. Dominic is doing that now."

"Well, bring that bottle over here," Fahron said. "We can all use some more. We've found more of Isabella's diaries. Everyone in here is so pissed at her that if she wasn't dead they would kill her; don't know if I am going soft but she seems kind of pathetic to me."

# Chapter XXXVII
## Strategies

Soldiers stationed at all of the forts in Lentz as well as the homes of the ruling families were prepared for an attack. Sorren had sent word to his villages and they too prepared for an attack. The headquarters of the Patronus priests was also prepared for attack, although most of them were in Langer watching the homes and businesses of Otto, Joanna and Jack.

The sailors at the naval yard were also on alert but their primary assignment was to protect the people taking shelter there.

Although Ashley had closed her shop early, the building was filled with Nordes warriors and Patronus priests since it was a prime location to observe the business district and because of the underground tunnel to the docks.

Thaos, Stephan and Gideon were traveling to Claudius' castle with two companies of soldiers. The men wanted to see their families as well as to brief their wives about everything that had happened and been learned in the past twenty-four hours. They knew their children were not happy about being confined inside of the castle so each man carried toys and candy in his saddlebags.

Mathas had asked the ruling members to assist him in documenting the official notes and writing letters to Sudfad and Gabriel. This in itself was becoming a daunting task.

The members of Dominic's team, which now included Turner's group felt an overwhelming need to get through the piles of paperwork and books that had been confiscated. While none of them liked or trusted Olin and Elexas they did feel sorry for them as they were realizing how broken these two people were.

The group learned that both the stores The Rooster and The Chicken and The Egg were used to launder money as well as the other criminal activities. Ryan started a new chart to help them learn the size and complexity of Otto's operation.

Otto was at his unholy altar for almost two hours. When he returned to his office he found Jack, Joanna and Andre sitting in the room looking anxious.

"Why were you gone so long and what happened to you?" demanded Jack.

"The Master was not accepting my offerings. I didn't get any information and everything sort of exploded in there," Otto said as he wiped the dirt from his face with a towel. "All of you look scared shitless what is going on?"

"A lot and you better take this," Joanna said and handed her father a large glass of whiskey.

"First, early this morning men broke into The Rooster. They grabbed the two women and everything in the safe. All of the employees are missing and there is a big sign that says the place has been closed by order of the King," Jack explained.

Otto swore and threw his glass of whiskey against the wall. "Father, this is just the beginning," said Joanna. "Listen to Jack."

"You already know about Olin and the dead army of Hutas," Jack said. "We saw them and you wouldn't believe it. Not a mark on them and they all looked terrified, just like Dillion said. Then Fahron went to every bank in the city with papers from Mathas ordering the banks to turn over safety boxes for a list of people. The clerk here tried to stall but you were gone so long. The only thing they got from here were boxes that belonged to Isabella. Here is the decree."

Otto became pale as he read the list of names. "There is more," Joanna said. "You know that Claudius was searching the docks. Well, all afternoon soldiers have been searching every carriage and boca traveling through the city. They got our girls and arrested the driver." Otto started pounding his fist on the desk and swearing.

"Father let me finish. I saw it. Claudius and his sons were eating in a restaurant and the soldiers got them because a huge crowd had formed around the carriage and they wanted to hang the driver. I heard part of what Stephan was saying to the crowd so I stopped him and Thaos."

"At first, I thought they knew about us because Stephan makes this snide remark about me being really close with some of Mathas' family. But I think that was just his normal smart ass self because then he acted really worried about me. He said lots of people have gone to the King and reported about the abductions and suspicious things they have seen."

"Thaos said that everyone is still so upset after the murders and riots that they are wild and formed groups to break into every home and business. He said that they talked the people out of doing that. But they made it sound like people are watching every move in the city. Stephan asked several times if I wanted them to wait with me then take me home. He really did act worried about my safety."

"I waited until the soldiers took the carriage then I walked down the street and they were right. You should have heard what the people were saying. They were talking about burning places down."

"Ok, we are all pissed," said Jack. "But the one thing we have all been thinking is how the hell did they find out about all of these things. They closed The Rooster before Olin disappeared. You know Joanna isn't a pushover and she really believed Stephan and Thaos. We thought they planted spies but now we are wondering if the whole damn city isn't spying on everyone."

"It actually makes sense," said Andre. "Everyone is still really pissed about Prince Michael. But that doesn't explain the Hutas."

Otto calmed down and sat back in his chair and stared at the others. "We don't trust Olin but even if he did give them information, they haven't had him long," Jack said.

"Wait," said Otto. "You know where Olin is?"

"Well no," Jack said. "But with all of this going on I am assuming that Mathas has him."

"We may be looking at this all wrong," said Otto. "You know Mathas, if he was receiving those complaints from the people, of course he would look into them. And that story about that little woman scaring the hell out of Olin and chasing him through the streets. You can't tell me she wasn't a powerful dark lord or witch. And who knows who those men were who helped her; they may have just been regular people helping a young woman."

"How do you explain The Rooster?" asked Andre.

"If citizens are spying they are going to see the people walking in and out without buying anything. That store has a lot of traffic. The thing that I can't explain is the safety boxes. But, and this may go with that insinuation that Stephan made. You know that Isabella and Juleta were like two spoiled brats and when they were fighting they didn't care what they said or who heard them."

"As jealous as those two bitches were, I wouldn't be surprised if they didn't talk about their love lives once in a while," Otto continued. "I think we need to also consider that we have competition in the area. The underworlds are going crazy because of those damn Gefrey Games. I still haven't found out who was behind the giant snakes and the attacks on Stephan and Thaos. And I am still trying to find out who killed Prince Michael."

"We aren't going to dismiss the ruling families but I think they aren't our primary threats. If I was trying to take over someone else's territory I would certainly incite the citizens against him. I mean look at what has happened in Port Friada. The more I think about this, I think we have rivals in the area who are using the people and the King against us. Which leads me to believe they are powerful and well organized."

"Joanna send a note to Stephan and Thaos thanking them for being such gentlemen and being concerned about your welfare. Offer their wives gifts from the store and you be there. Make sure they are so impressed with what they see that they drop any suspicions they have."

"Jack and Andre you get our men on the streets and have them listen to everything. In fact, we might need to hire some more who don't look so much like professionals so that people will talk in front of them. And I may need to pay a visit to Mathas."

"I still don't understand how we explain the Hutas," said Jack.

"Well, whoever went after Stephan and Thaos used Hutas. Maybe it was the same thing and the Master stopped them. He would certainly scare the shit out of them. And if you see that girl who was chasing Olin, I want to talk to her. Don't force anything. I am thinking more of an invitation. She is probably working for our rival and I want to know what we are up against before we do anything drastic."

"What about the driver?" asked Joanna.

"Make sure he dies tonight," Otto said. "And Andre and Joanna come up with some scheme to make us look good to the citizens. Give away some crap, I don't care what it is just make sure they know it came from us. The bigger the better."

"I have the perfect idea," Joanna said. "Mathas is building hospitals and that giant orphanage and the people love that. Let's give money to both and set up an account to pay for the training of healers and nurses. That way we will look like we aren't against women."

"You really need to become a politician," Otto said proudly.

After the children were put to bed, Stephan, Thaos and Gideon met with their wives and Bella in Claudius' study to tell them about the day's events as well as the information they had learned. After the first ten minutes, Ingr told everyone to stop talking so that she could get some paper and take notes. After that the women sat in relative silence for hours listening to the men talk.

"Ok, it really isn't like any of you to be quiet," said Thaos. "I can see the wheels turning. What are you thinking?"

"First, that all of you have to start calling to the Angels more," Nikki said sternly. "And there is more going on here, I can just feel it."

"I come from Port Friada which is hometown to dark lords. Dieter ruled there for a long time and whenever something happened that could make him look bad he threw a lavish party and gave money to charities to make his image look better. I will bet you money right now that Otto does that," said Ashley. "And you gave Joanna just enough information to make her curious. She will reach out to you or us to try and find out what we know. If I had to guess we either get an invitation to a party or her store."

"Then there is Tessa," said Ingr. "And yes we all thought it was funny too but you told us that she asked Adam for help. But for another dark lord, they are going to think that she is either a demon or a stronger dark lord. And you said you told these stories to play on Otto's paranoia about rivals. He is going to think that Tessa is the rival or is working for them. She's in a lot of danger. Send her a message now, telling her not to leave the castle until you talk to her."

"Ingr is right," said Nikki. "If you set anyone up it should be Elexas. Sorry but I hate her and everything you just told us is disgusting."

"Mother of all the women here you certainly are never without words," Stephan said sarcastically.

"I'm thinking about Ruth. I don't care what Olin said, you can't tell me that she can be married to Otto that long and not at least have suspicions. For all we know she may be a captive in that house. I need to reach out to her but I can't do it this soon. I will tell you before I do anything."

"Ladies, you do us proud," said Gideon. "They told me you would have different views of everything; which is good. So let's discuss them. If anyone is invited to a party or anything else do you think we should go?"

"Yes," said Ingr. "And we all should go because all of us do see things differently. Remember Bella and Isadore were suspicious of Isabella long before anyone else."

"Would it be suspicious if we invited them to something?" asked Gideon.

"Yes, if we do it this soon," said Bella. "We need to wait for the right time. But, the more that I think about what Ingr said I too feel Tessa is really in danger. Let's stop right now and send a note."

The following morning Mathas held his meeting in the Great Hall. "We have much to discuss this morning," Mathas said as he stood in front of the room. "A little after midnight the driver of the carriage that held the girls was found hanging in his cell. The guards said they didn't see or hear anything suspicious and had checked on him just thirty minutes earlier."

"But when Angus went to the dungeons he talked with some of the other prisoners. The driver was in a cell by himself. But several other prisoners swear they heard him talking to someone just before the guards found him hanging. They said he kept repeating, 'I didn't say anything.' They said they couldn't really make out the words that the other man said but they all said he had a really deep voice."

"So, Angus is talking with all the guards and prisoners to find out who the guy was talking to. Now for the next subject, I have just been told that the members of Dominic's team basically stayed up all night again working with Ryan and the others. If any of you need to leave, you may but we are covering some important things. The first speaker will be High Priest Othnial."

Dominic and Fennel both jumped to their feet to escort the old priest to the front of the room. He carried a stack of papers. "First, I would like to thank you for allowing me to speak," Othnial said to the King and the ruling members. "Although I do not attend many meetings, King Mathas provides me with copies of the notes and of course Dominic and my other sons tell me what is discussed."

468

"As all of you know I was the senior High Priest at the monastery at Rubar for most of my life. A kingdom of great darkness and many monsters. One might say, I specialize in monsters which brings me before you this day. The Angel Daniel saved the priests of my monastery and when he did he said The Great Ruler had other assignments for us. He told me to go to the house of Gabriel and to wait for word of when I was needed someplace else."

"I was given many important assignments in Salar and wondered if that was where I would end my days. Every day when I pray I ask The Great Ruler to show me where I am needed. I knew I needed to come to Langer but I thought it was to provide an education for my sons."

"As soon as I arrived here I was overwhelmed with the sense of evil, a feeling I am more than familiar with. The feeling was so strong that I called to the Angel Daniel. He told me that soon all of you would uncover the identity of the worst monster of mankind. He told me that I needed to go to the monastery at Malga to research this monster in the Hall of Antiquities. He told me I should leave after I found out who this monster was."

"Dominic and Fennel will you please hand out these letters for everyone to read. I immediately wrote to the Sanuri, Gabriel and Raphael."

"I did little more than to tell them the words that Daniel said but apparently that was enough. You will read that within the week I should expect an army of Patronus priests to escort me to Malga. They are bringing with them the two priests who were instrumental in uncovering the identities of the dark lords who were hiding in that monastery."

"I have not met Padre Bartholomew and Padre Thomas but they are special friends of the Sanuri's. They have temporarily given up their positions at the monastery at Nora, the only monastery in the Kingdom of Stordt, to help me with the research. I am honored to be in such company and to have such an important assignment."

"High Priest Fredrick from the headquarters here in Langer will be taking over the duties of your educations," Othnial said to Dominic and Fennel who were still standing near him.

"We want to go with you," said Dominic.

The old priest smiled, "Daniel said you would say that but you are needed here. This is my journey to take."

Mathas called a short break because he could see how emotional Dominic, Fennel, Seth, Lawrence and Noah were. Tessa was sitting with these men and was surprised by their emotions. Noah had previously told her that they considered Othnial a father and that he had saved their lives but she did not expect these tough men to be so affected by his leaving. She whispered into Noah's ear.

"That would be nice, ask Dominic first," he said.

Tessa pulled Dominic aside and spoke with him for a few moments and he nodded.

When the meeting resumed, Thaos, Stephan and Gideon repeated the words of the women in their household at the previous night's meeting. "Tessa, did you get our message last night?" Stephan asked.

"Yes and thank you. Since we were all up we had a meeting and think we can use this to our advantage."

"The problem is that a dark lord or witch will see that she has no powers," said Noah.

"We are still exploring ideas," Tessa said.

"What she is really saying is she is trying to figure out how she can impersonate a dark lord," Noah said. "It is too dangerous."

There was a knock on the door to the Great Hall. People were still standing in the back of the room speaking with High Priest Othnial. Risa opened the door. Ryan, Elexas and Olin were standing in the doorway. "You all look like little kids who think you're going to get yelled at," Risa said and laughed. "Come on in."

"Claudius is it alright if we come in?" Ryan asked loudly.

"Why wouldn't it be?" asked Claudius.

"He doesn't want to say it but because of me and Elexas," Olin said. "We aren't trying to hear anything; we have some things for you."

As the three entered the room they saw the group of people standing around Othnial. Olin stared at the High Priest and dropped his papers. "Ryan that is him. I don't believe it," Olin said in amazement.

"I'll get it," Elexas said and ran out of the room.

"Ryan, what is going on?" asked Claudius.

"First, who are you?" Olin asked Othnial.

"This is High Priest Othnial. He was the head High Priest at the monastery at Rubar in Ryed before it was destroyed," said Dominic. "Olin what is it? You look like you've seen a ghost."

"I've got it," Elexas said loudly as she ran back into the hall.

"Ryan you start," said Olin.

"A lot of us in here..."

"Ryan come up here so we can all hear you," said Mathas.

Ryan ran to the front of the room. "Last night a lot of us here worked on all that paperwork because we all feel like we need to get it done quickly. Nobody slept all night but people would sleep for an hour or two. Olin fell asleep at the table and it was strange. One second he was reading and the next we hear this thud. Elexas even checked him to make sure he was alright."

"Then he starts moaning and making these strange sounds. And he did that for a couple of minutes. I was about to get one of the priests when he woke up. He looked dazed and said that he had the strangest dream. Then he grabbed some paper and started drawing. He just kept drawing and didn't talk so we got up and looked over his shoulders. He said he was supposed to give the drawing to a priest."

"Wait!" said Dominic. "Adam, Miranda, anyone, was that dream sent from you or a demon?"

"Why don't you look at the drawing and decide," said Miranda as she appeared in the room.

"What is happening?" asked Elexas. "You are all looking so strange."

"An Angel is here," said Fennel.

"How come I'm not smoking?" asked Olin frantically as he looked at his body.

"She said I should look at the drawing," Dominic said. "And I don't know why you aren't smoking." Dominic didn't want Olin near Othnial so he deliberately stood in front of the priest and took the paper that Elexas had handed to Olin. "What is this?" asked Dominic.

"Well, the voice in my dream said it was underneath the monastery at Malga. She said that someone named Raphael and other priests had found all these underground chambers before but there are still more. I don't draw so good so those big squares are where there are unholy altars. She said a priest would need that for his journey then she showed me his face."

"Dominic that boy is no threat to me," said Othnial.

"He is a dark lord," Dominic said.

"I am not so sure about that," Othnial said kindly and took the drawing. "Son, come closer and explain this to me." Olin looked at Dominic who nodded.

"Like I said I don't draw very good. What she showed me was better. These kind of squares are the doors and these lines here are stairs. The circles are pits, now I am guessing those are fire pits but I felt evil when I was drawing this. I saw your robe before I saw your face and I expected to see the face of the Master."

"I don't know what kind of journey you are on or even if I understood that dream but I think the Master has something to do with that drawing. You have no idea how powerful he is. I have heard that he is more powerful than a lot of demons."

472

"I hope you don't plan on fighting him by yourself." Othnial smiled and patted Olin's shoulder.

"Olin the Angel said you should tell Othnial about the ring," said Dominic.

"Honestly I don't even know if this is true," said Olin. "I saw him once when I was small and I was so scared I don't remember a lot. But my father told me that the Master still wears the ring of the monastery at Malga. It is supposed to have huge diamonds in it and somehow they help him. I think like those crystals you wear help all of you."

"What do you mean?" asked Othnial.

"I have always been told that The Master was the first Holy Lord at the monastery at Malga and he was the first priest who the demons corrupted. He was considered a really big prize and the demons took him to a demon god or something that they worship and that demon god gave the Master incredible powers."

"The Master isn't a demon and he doesn't look like someone who sold their soul," Olin paused as he saw the confused look on Othnial's face. "When someone sells their soul they always look the same age that they did when they sold it. Even the Grand Masters are said to look the ages they were when they sold their souls and they are thousands of years old. He looks powerful but he is all wrinkles like a piece of old fruit and his skin is like leather, so I don't know what he is."

"But, I don't think the story is saying that all of his powers are in the ring, I think maybe that ring connects him to that demon god somehow."

"Olin, Miranda said you should give Othnial that necklace your uncle gave you," Dominic said. "She said you don't need it anymore."

"I don't even know what it is," said Olin as he unbuttoned his shirt. He was wearing a large medallion that hung from braided rope. The medallion was made of a dark metal with engravings. He took it off and handed it to the priest. As soon as Othnial touched it, the medallion started to smoke. "Holy shit!" said Olin.

473

Othnial did not drop the necklace but prayed over it and the smoke disappeared.

"How long have you had this," Othnial asked Olin.

"I don't know, since I was a kid. I thought my father gave it to me but that Angel said Uncle Otto. Do you know what it is?"

"Olin, your uncle is the one who sold your soul to the Master and that was like you wearing his brand," said Claudius who had walked up to the group. "Perhaps that is why your father and uncle were feuding."

"Ask the Angel..." Olin started to say.

"She is gone," said Claudius as he looked at the necklace. "What did you want to ask her?"

"Am I still a dark lord? I don't even know anymore."

"I don't think so," said Dominic. "Why?"

"Because I want to kick Otto's ass," Olin said angrily then he paused. "But I was never that strong to begin with."

"So help us," said Tessa. "Because that is what we plan to do. He thinks I am a dark lord because his men saw me chasing you. How can I pretend to be?"

"You can't. For one he would be able to feel how powerful you are. The more power that a witch or dark lord has the more they can see about others. You could just tell him the truth, I am sure the Angels would scare the hell out of him. Or you could pretend you are one of the Overseer's from the Insidiae. They aren't all dark lords and witches. But you would have to really get your story down good and you would work in groups."

"Tell us about the Overseer's," said Turner.

"Ok, you know the Insidiae is all about ego and secrecy. Well, they didn't really pay a lot of attention to what their members were doing until that sect tries to raise Omnibus and destroy the world."

"Since then there are different levels of people who investigate the members of the Insidiae and they apparently aren't happy with what they are finding, Like the Discedo group that is warring with Hector. And Hector scares the shit out of a lot of people and I don't really know why."

"In the notes from Gabriel's mission in Nora, one of those Overseer groups was called to Nora to investigate the priests who were trying to raise Omnibus and the demon Ahriman killed them. I would have to go back to that report to get the name of that group," said Thaos.

"Are the groups divided up by geographical areas?" Turner asked.

"No by levels of, I guess you could call it clearance. See there are hierarchies in everything in that group. Someone wouldn't have to have much clearance to investigate someone like me but for Uncle Otto they would have their top team."

"So say someone was investigating you and that led them to Otto would they then turn their notes over to someone higher in the hierarchy?"

"Yes, but remember I don't belong to that organization so I don't really know the ins and outs. Joanna and Jack do and they would know a lot. That's what you should do first Tessa, is play up to Jack. I'm sure you could get him to tell you a lot."

"She's not doing that," said Noah.

Tessa was standing next to Noah and quickly swung around and looked at him. The stern look he gave her stopped her from arguing with him. Turner was watching them and laughed.

"Joanna was looking at Thaos like he was an old love," Stephan said. "Olin, how bad did she have it for Hector?"

"I don't know. What I was told is that Hector, Juleta, Isabella and others all got to know each other at Otto's parties. King Mathas, I am just repeating what I was told," Olin said and looked at Mathas as if he expected to get yelled at. "Isabella started going to the parties right after she got married."

"Having a princess there, well you can imagine the attention she got and you know how she was. I never heard anything about her wanting more than to go to the parties. But not too long after she starts going, she brings Juleta who was still a kid. Otto saw something in Juleta and took her under his wing. I don't know if she was already practicing dark magics but Joanna told me it was like Juleta came to the parties with a purpose and that was to absorb everything she could about the dark worlds."

"I don't remember who first brought Hector. You see you have to be brought by someone to get in. But Jack said that all the women wanted him. It sounded like he started going because all the women were lining up to have sex with him."

"I know that Juleta made him a lot of promises to win him from the other women but he wasn't an innocent. I just don't know a lot about him. I know, hell the entire world knows she changed him to look like Thaos; after that people talked about them a lot more. I don't know if this makes a difference but Hector, at least in the beginning always liked blondes. He really had a thing about them."

"Olin, after the meeting let's talk," said Thaos.

"I want to talk with him too," Turner said.

"Ryan, what did you come in here for to begin with?" asked Mathas.

"Olin wrote down all of the names his father uses and the locations of all of the homes. We matched those up with his bank accounts and how much money he has taken out of each account. Then, well this is Elexas' idea. She looked for the kind of land that surrounded these areas and she thinks he is either arming groups or buying a lot of weapons to have ready for a war."

# Chapter XXXVIII
## Advice

Because the people in Langer were uncovering so much information so quickly, their comrades in Salar were also working around the clock to process the information and to find answers to questions.

So focused were they on the copious amount of letters they were receiving that they paid attention to little else. It was quite by accident that Simon walked past the huge table in Sudfad's study that held the maps of Karzman's village and noticed a change. A meeting was being held at the time.

"Everyone!" Simon said loudly and the people in the room stopped talking. "Either I am crazy or this map is different. Girls come up here." Nyla and Saran quickly walked to the table.

"It is different," Saran said. "Ruth had to have done that."

Now everyone got out of their seats to look at the map. There appeared to be a dark haze over the map that resembled smoke. Areas of the map were difficult to see because of the haze.

"It's like this thing is alive," said Corsa. "I don't think anyone should touch it until we talk to the Angels."

"Wait just a moment," said the Sanuri. "In fact, everyone back away from the table." He walked to the table and stretched out his hands and began to hum. Everyone in the room stared at him in silence. After a few moments he said. "That darkness has nothing to do with this room or anyone who is in it. I think Corsa is right. I think we are seeing what is happening in the village. Ruth would you explain this to us?"

Nyla and Saran ran up to Ruth and hugged her as soon as she appeared in the room. "Ruth, did you change the map?" asked Nyla.

"Yes," Ruth said. "And I did it to get your attention. Your teams in Langer are doing an exceptional job right now. All of their attention is on their work."

"You are at a time now where you cannot afford to have everyone's attention focused on the same dot on the wall."

"You want us to go back to working on the scrolls, don't you?" asked Saran.

"Yes child," Ruth said and smiled.

"Can we bring Nina in to see you?" Saran asked. "She will be mad if we don't."

"I would like that but why don't you wait a few moments," Ruth said to Saran then she turned to Maxwell and Emeral. "Why have you not told Olivia about her people?"

"We were hoping the soldiers would find more information first," said Maxwell. "The child has already been through so much."

"As have all of the children in this room," said Ruth. "Olivia, shortly after you arrived here Sudfad sent troops to get your people and take them to safety. When the soldiers went to the farms that your people lived in, they found no one. They have been searching ever since."

"Were the animals gone too?" asked Olivia.

"Yes, child."

"Then they are in the Forest of Tobar," said Olivia. "Do you know who went after them?"

"Actually no one did but the voices of the demons on the lands owned by Karzman became so strong that they knew it was a matter of time before the demons found them. Tell Sudfad where they are."

"That has long been the plan of my people because there was so much darkness on the lands north of us. They already built cabins and barns in the forest. They had everything ready because they knew that once they had to move it would be quickly. They are just north of the monastery at Philiste on the western edge of the forest."

"Sudfad have your soldiers go for them today," said Ruth. "Andrac has returned to that area. While he is in no position to fight the armies of demons he did sense the energies of Olivia's people. He is trying to find them and figure out what they are. He of course would like to use them as a weapon of sorts."

"I caused the distraction with the map so we could talk about a few things. One, Olivia's people need help. They are not warriors, they cannot defend themselves from those who would find them. Sudfad have the soldiers take them to the monastery and tell the priests what they face."

"And there is another reason we need to talk about this. Everyone in this room, even the children want to protect everyone else. Nikki, Angelina and Vivian have scolded all of you numerous times about this. You are not normal people and these are not normal times. Every child in this room has seen more of life than many adults. Withholding information, even for the kindest of reasons should no longer be considered an option."

"Andrac and his monsters would have captured those innocent people and none of you would ever have known. The time for secrets is past."

"Now I need to speak with Joao, Alex, Kent and George. It is not a fluke of fate that all of you are here. You are right where you are needed. All of you are allowing yourselves to be crippled by the darkness in your parents. You cannot allow this to happen. Grieving for their poor choices is one thing but all of you are past that. If you cannot help yourselves then pray to The Great Ruler to help you. And you can always call to us."

"And Kate, you are so protective of those who you love. Even finding out that Toni is the lover of a powerful demon has not deterred your plans of revenge. You too are needed here. For now at least, your focus should be on other things."

"I know that I am sounding like a scolding mother but you face powerful enemies and you must as Michael always said, 'have your head on right.' Every person in this room has experienced life changing events in the past few months. But look at you, you have all come together as a family."

479

"All of you who are new to this group may not have been told what we have said to the others many times. It is no coincidence that any one of you are here. All of you have more skills, power and information than you realize. And as a family your strength knows no limits."

"And with that I am going to speak directly to Sudfad's family. I will tell you now that none of you will ever get over Michael's loss but you cannot let that cripple you. Raul and Simon, as would be expected you had difficulties accepting Michael at times. But you are not a normal family. You cannot give in to the emotions of a normal family. Javier, Madeline, Corsa, Alex, Kent, George and of course Michael's sisters are all part of your family now. And they each have parts to play before this is over."

"Nyla, Saran and Nina flew into the arms of the family of their dreams and never looked back. They have accepted this new life with everything they have and have stepped up for enormous responsibilities. And they are little more than children."

"Like these girls, Sudfad and Renya have given the rest of you the family you have always dreamed about. But as adults you feel humbled and out of place to step up to some of these responsibilities. Madeline, Javier get over your feelings that everyone looks at you as criminals. This family and these teams need you for so many reasons."

"Corsa, Alex, Kent and George. I am smiling because George just can't believe that he has anything to offer. You feel humiliated because you grew up poor and because of Dirk."

"It is time to let go of those feelings because you are holding yourselves back. All of you have very important things to offer and once all of you actually start to feel like a family everyone will realize that."

"Sudfad, you and the men in your family are The Seven Sons and your entire family are The Keepers of the Scrolls. Ah, some of you did not know this, I am hearing your thoughts. It's time all of you knew because the demons are figuring it out. The destinies of these men, this family will consume more and more of their lives. They need every family member to be actively involved with the running of the kingdom as well as the missions."

480

"Sudfad, it was wise for you to appoint ruling families to help govern and protect the kingdom but they too have many roles to play. I know you are still grieving but when you are ready you should all sit down and learn about each other. Your strengths and weaknesses, your skills and experiences because you will need to form a chain and you want it to be strong."

"Sudfad and Renya if you have not already realized this, Javier and Madeline are well versed in politics from their experiences as being spies. They understand and see things that others will not and they would never have thought to tell you that."

"Mother is done scolding her children now," Ruth said with a warm smile. "It is time for me to visit Nina."

"Ruth, before you go can you tell Jared and me more about our mission?" asked Archetenus.

"You certainly aren't ready to leave here. You know now that the Master was involved with the diabolic undertaking of the Second Sons. If you are asking me for advice, I would suggest that you two spend time in Erebus' library. There are still books and journals that Sophie and Meekos left that Erebus has not yet found."

"You are intelligent men. You are beginning to understand that this mission is not one where you are going to win by busting heads. You must be prepared and you certainly need to have us with you."

"In case you don't know, High Priest Othnial, Padre Thomas and Padre Bartholomew are going to Malga to uncover the secrets of the Master. He is an abomination in this world. These three faithful priests are prepared to do battle with the first of their kind to sell out to the demons."

"But they are all old men," said Jared. "They will get slaughtered."

"Jared, they are very faithful old men," Ruth said. "That makes all the difference. I know this will be difficult for many to understand but sometimes you earn your battles."

481

Mathas' meeting lasted until noon. Instead of eating the midday meal Noah took Tessa by the hand and led her to their room. "So what is going on? Are you mad about something?" she asked.

Noah did not say anything until they entered the room and closed the door. "Tessa, we need to set some ground rules. I have heard so many of the team members say how difficult it is to date another team member and I am beginning to realize why."

"I am listening," she said as she stiffened up.

"First, pretending to be a dark lord around powerful dark lords is insane. I know you are very good at what you do but this is not a normal disguise. We will think of something else."

"Well, Olin did," she said challengingly.

"And that is what I wanted to talk about next. Tessa, I understand that flirting is part of the disguise but I don't want you kissing other guys or anything else. We've listened to both Elexas and Olin talking about Otto and his family. You know that if you tried to get close to Jack that he would probably force you to have sex with Otto or rape you or god knows what else. I admire how fearless and passionate you are about things but I don't think you are thinking clearly about any of this. Why is that?"

"Before we get into my thinking process, I want to address some of the other things you just said. You don't want me kissing other guys..."

"Tessa, how would you like it if I walked in the other room and started kissing Elexas?"

"I wouldn't at all and that is why I want to clarify this. So you don't want me going out with anyone else either?"

"What! Of course not. I can't believe you even asked that."

"Well, then these rules; do they apply to both of us?"

"Of course they do. I have no intention of going out with anyone else."

"Then when you say ground rules what you are really saying is that you want a committed relationship instead of just dating?"

"Honestly, I didn't think of it like that but yes. I know we haven't known each other long. So you are going to tell me you aren't ready for that aren't you?"

"No. I agree to your ground rules."

"Ok, something else is going on here; what is it?"

"What do you mean?"

"I expected a big fight because you are the independent and free woman of the world."

"You don't have to be an ass. I said I agree."

"Seriously Tessa, what aren't you saying?"

"You want to know what I am not saying. I'll tell you what I'm not saying. I think you've lived in caves too damn long. Last night when we were all working Elexas rubbed up against you three times. She has done nothing but flirt with you since she came here. Do you even realize what she is doing? If I have to play by the rules so do you. You tell her to stop because if I do there will be a fight."

"First of all that is just Elexas. I don't think she knows how not to act like that. But you are really jealous," he said with a huge grin. "Honey, you don't have any reason to be jealous of Elexas or anyone else. I only care about you. But I have to admit I kind of like it."

"Well, you aren't going to like it if I pull her hair out."

"I'll tell you I wasn't expecting this at all." Noah pulled her close to him as he spoke and kissed her.

"Noah, I have to tell you that I have been feeling frustrated. I don't think you understand anything about women. If you did you wouldn't be surprised by this. You are a gorgeous man. Do you have any idea how women stare at you? I'm not talking about on the team, I mean when we are in Langer. It's like you don't even notice."

"You are right. We spent all of our time fighting and trying to survive. I missed all the social training so you might have to help me with that."

"You don't even understand. I never get jealous."

"So what are you saying? You better not be telling me you want to break up because I won't."

"Damn it Noah, I don't know what I am saying. I'm realizing that I care for you a lot more than I thought I did. You are wondering where my head is at. It's with you. I can't stop thinking about you."

"While I love hearing that, Tessa, you can't be working on the frontlines anymore. You have to realize that."

"Actually, I just did. Noah, what am I going to do? I can't think straight." Tessa sat down on the bed as she spoke.

Noah sat down next to her. "I can't stop thinking about you either. You know maybe we should go to Salar sooner than we planned. Maybe a break would help."

"I don't think we should leave now. Something about that just doesn't feel right. I need to talk to Turner."

"We both will. Let's do it now." Noah stood up and held out his hand to her. She took it and they walked back to the Great Hall where the midday meal was being served.

Turner was sitting at one of the long tables next to Dominic and Fennel. Garvis, Bart and Louis were sitting across the table from him. All of the men started grinning as they watched Tessa and Noah walk up to them.

484

"Turner, wait, why is everyone grinning?" asked Tessa.

"Because we've placed bets on what you are going to say."

"All of you are a bunch of asses," Tessa said with a grin.

"So what do you want to talk about?" asked Turner.

"We can wait until you are done eating."

"Oh no, we've got money riding on this," said Bart. "Spit it out."

"What the hell did you guys bet on?" asked Tessa as Noah laughed.

"We aren't telling you because we have money riding on what is going to come out of that pretty little mouth of yours," said Bart. "Just say it, we're all family."

"I realize I care about Noah more than I thought I did. I can't think about anything but him so I don't have my head in a good place for this mission."

"For the girl who prides herself on reading people you are the last one in this entire room to realize that," said Turner. "Do you think anyone was going to let you try and fake being a dark lord?"

"Are you telling me the truth?"

"Ask anyone here," said Dominic. "And I hope you talked about Elexas because I thought you were going to slit her throat if she touched Noah one more time."

"See, I told you," Tessa said as she quickly swung around and looked at Noah. "He doesn't even realize what is going on."

"I'll talk to her," Noah said and laughed.

"Actually Dominic already did," said Fennel. "We all saw the death look in Tessa's eyes last night."

"Why didn't I see that?" asked Noah.

"Because you are both so in love you can't see straight," said Garvis. "Maybe if you just admit that, you will get your emotions in check."

Neither Tessa nor Noah spoke for a few moments. "You guys know me," Tessa said. "I am always serious about my work. And this is such an important mission. We don't want to screw anything up or get anyone hurt. So what do we do so we can think again?" Everyone at the table laughed loudly.

"Hey, Thaos, Stephan come here," yelled Dominic. "Tessa, we aren't in that position to give you first hand advice but they can."

Both Thaos and Stephan were grinning when they walked up to the table. "Tessa, ask them your question," said Turner.

"All of these guys are asses," Tessa said again and everyone laughed. "This is a serious question although, I guess it is kind of funny. Noah and I can't think straight anymore. So how do we get our heads on straight for this mission? We don't want to get anyone hurt."

"Honestly time helps but both Stephan and I are still like that when our wives are on a mission with us. If there is an easy answer, I don't know it," Thaos said.

"Just get married now and get it over with," said Stephan. "Don't look at me like that, I'm serious. You asked for our opinions. I was so crazy about Ingr but I didn't want to give up my life. I was going nuts for months and driving everyone else crazy. Ask Father if you don't believe me. Then Juleta sent demons after her and we fought back to back then she was almost killed. When I realized I almost lost her. I don't know it was like something snapped in me and my head cleared after that."

"That story is kind of horrible and romantic at the same time," said Tessa.

"You could just take a break from the mission," said Louis.

"Hell, this room is filled with priests. You could be married in five minutes and get it out of your system," Stephan said with a huge grin.

"I don't know if any of these suggestions are good," said Tessa. "Noah why aren't you saying anything?" Before he had a chance to answer she turned to the next table. "Jasmine what do you and Seth do?"

"Tessa, we've been together for a long time and that helps," said Jasmine. "I don't know what to tell you. But I understand how you feel."

"We didn't start dating until after a mission," Seth said. "And we were both really injured so we couldn't go on any other missions for a while so we didn't have that to be concerned with."

"You know they're married don't you?" asked Dominic.

"Are you? But you don't wear rings," asked Tessa

"We hadn't been together that long before we got married," said Jasmine. "We really didn't want people to know. I guess we thought they would tell us we were making a mistake."

"I feel like my head is spinning," Tessa said and looked at Noah. "What do you think?"

"I think that if we get married I would like Othnial to perform the ceremony. I don't know if we will see him again."

"So you think we should get married?"

"Tessa, I knew I wanted to marry you after our first night together. But I realized that was expecting a lot from you. You're a lot younger than me and pretty wild."

"I'm not that much younger than you."

"Tessa, I don't think that getting married will be a quick fix for us being able to concentrate better," said Noah. "And that shouldn't be the reason to get married."

"I'm walking you down the aisle," said Turner.

"Shut up, I can't think. I need a glass of wine and a hot bath," Tessa said. "Noah, you stay here. I need to think." Tessa left the room.

# Chapter XXXIX
## Rage

Noah entered the room that he shared with Tessa and saw her lying across the bed on her stomach. She had her back turned to him. "I know you want to be alone but I need to tell you a couple of things then you can be with your thoughts."

She rolled over and sat up. "I feel so confused. I am never like this. I'm beginning to wonder if it's because I am so tired."

"Well, I am sure that is part of it," he said and sat down on the bed. "None of us have had a decent night's sleep for some time. Tessa, you asked why I was so quiet in there and that is because I was watching your reaction to things. I will say you have surprised me today but before I get into that."

"Tessa, if we get married it should be because we love each other and want that kind of commitment; not because our friends are pressuring us or we need to clear our heads. I want to marry you but neither of us are ready for that now so don't even worry about it."

"I am so glad you said that," she said and kissed him on the cheek. "Everything is happening so fast that my head is spinning. But you want Othnial to do the service."

"Don't worry about that. And I have to tell you I planned to propose the right way, on one knee with a ring. Stephan basically proposed for me."

"No he didn't," she said and laughed. "So you have been thinking about this? I do have to tell you that if we get married, I can't cook very well."

Noah laughed. "That doesn't matter but we should talk about what our lives would be like. You are seeing my life. I don't own a house or property and while I make a good salary I will never be wealthy. I work on the team and I am studying to become a priest, both of these take up a lot of my time."

"We might be living in the team's house; how would you feel about that?"

"See, in a way that is why we are perfect for each other because that is my life too. Well, not studying to be a priest." She laughed. "Madeline and I write to each other all the time and she was telling me about Gabriel's home. She was amazed that all of these families live in a mansion and they are really happy together. She said that she and Javier have their own chambers in the house and they enjoyed living there."

"All of that is true and they have a lot of kids. Most of them are adopted but over time some of the parents of the team members have come to live with them and they help a lot."

"So it could work. Noah, I haven't made any big decisions but if we do get married I want Madeline there."

"Then that is settled, we aren't making any major decisions today. I really didn't want to get married in a lunch room." They both laughed loudly.

"So how did I surprise you?"

"I thought I was a lot more serious about our relationship than you were. I never expected you to want a committed relationship or even consider marriage."

"See, I told you, you don't know anything about women," she said and smiled. Then she kissed him.

"Well, I'll let you be with your thoughts."

"I have a better idea," Tessa said and started unbuttoning his shirt.

"Sorry that we had to reschedule this," Claudius said to Gideon and Tom when he, Thaos and Stephan entered Gideon's office. "There was a lot of serious business at the meeting. Gideon we will catch you up."

"Actually Tom and I have gotten a hell of a lot of work done," said Gideon with a big smile. "Look at these lists. We have everyone's names and skills. Argail got lists of all the children and their ages and will help put together a school."

"I already have lists of supplies. And I had to explain that I am a man of the sea so they are going to plan out the neighborhood."

"It sounds like a good thing that we were late," Stephan said as he looked over some of the lists. "Isadore has her hands full with Chaez and Lana but Mother would certainly help; especially with the school supplies."

"Everything is falling into place," Gideon said. "I suppose we should go now. Are we walking or taking the horses?"

"Walking would be best," said Tom. "I think you are going to be surprised, I know I was. It's an entire village with streets and everything but of course things are in ruins but we make do."

The men followed Tom out of the naval yard and along the docks. Tom walked under a pier and up to a small rock wall. He opened a thick wooden door that exposed a tunnel.

"My men searched this area and they didn't talk about this," said Gideon.

"It's dark under this pier so they probably didn't see the door," said Tom as he grabbed one of the lit torches that hung on the stone wall of the tunnel. "Before you ask, we built the door and this is not the only opening but the openings are all near the shoreline. There are two others."

"How long have people been living down here?" asked Claudius as they followed Tom through the narrow and winding tunnel.

"Don't really know, but think it's been for a while," Tom said. "I'm from Zorta myself. I had a little place and the Hutas got it, thank The Great Ruler that me and the family were gone at the time."

"We come here because we heard is was a great city but then I couldn't find work and I didn't have enough money to start my own business. Then one of the kids got real sick, so mostly what I make pays the physician."

"This all just makes me sick," said Claudius. "How could we not have known? We'll hire a physician for your neighborhood. I'm going to talk to Mathas, we have to do something better. I don't know what it is yet but we need to make some changes."

"I smell food," said Thaos. "Are we close?"

"Right around the bend here. I've already told them you were coming so people wouldn't hide."

"Tom stop!" said Claudius. "So many of the people we've seen look afraid what are they afraid of?"

"A lot of things. Because we don't have homes a lot of thugs think we don't matter. They beat and kill us for sport. They rape the women folk and a lot of us get stolen. Once someone's taken we never see them again..." A woman's scream stopped Tom from talking. Claudius pushed him aside and ran past him. The other men followed.

Other voices were heard, some cursing, some screaming for help. The bend as Tom called it was a ninety degree angle in a very narrow tunnel. Claudius was in the lead and could not see what was ahead until he ran into the ruins of an underground village.

"Help us! Help us!" screamed a woman.

"Where are they?" asked Claudius and the woman pointed north. Claudius, Thaos, Stephan and Gideon didn't have to run far before they came upon a group of men who were beating others.

"You want to fight?" yelled Stephan as he kicked the back of one man's knee. When the thug next to him turned around Stephan ran his sword through him then stabbed the man he had kicked.

Thaos punched the first thug he came up to so hard that he broke the man's jaw. Claudius and Gideon were both huge men and fighters. The group of ten men who were brutalizing the homeless were no match for these warriors.

491

"Why are you down here?" yelled Claudius as he held a man by the throat and punched him several times in the face. "You'll die here if you don't start talking!"

"They're looking for someone," yelled one of the bloody men who had been beaten. Gideon, slammed a man's head against the side of a stone wall and the man fell unconscious to the ground. "Who's next?" Gideon yelled.

"They work for Franks," yelled Thaos as he pushed a bloody man towards Claudius.

"What the hell are you doing down here?" growled Claudius.

"We're looking for Frank's nephew," the hired fighter said.

"And why the hell do you think he would be down here?" yelled Claudius.

"Cuz we've looked every place else."

"Tom, there is a company of soldiers just outside of Gideon's office bring them down here," said Claudius who was so enraged that he punched the thug who was talking. The man fell unconscious to the ground.

"I am Claudius. I am one of the ruling members of this kingdom," he yelled to the people who were living in the ruins. "These are my sons Stephan and Thaos and this is Admiral Gideon. Pack your things. We will take you to a safe place until we can build you homes."

Stephan helped one of the victims of the attack to his feet. "They come down here and steal us too," said the old man.

"Not after today," said Claudius as he looked around at the families who were living in the ruins. Most of them were dressed in rags and looked malnourished. Claudius was overwhelmed with rage that Otto would send his hired killers after these people.

Soldiers started running into the ruins. "Half of you take these ten and hang them in the business district. Put signs up that this is what we do to those who victimize our people," yelled Claudius. "The rest of you move these families to the barracks in the naval yard then watch over them. I'll meet you there."

Claudius didn't say another word as he stomped out of the tunnels and mounted one of the horses that belonged to a soldier. Thaos, Stephan and Gideon also mounted horses.

"You are going to need help," said Cyril who was standing with many of the homeless people who had left the barracks to help their friends who were still in the ruins.

"So will he," said Claudius. "You're welcome to ride along."

"Want a horse?" Stephan asked with a grin.

"I'm not really a rider," Cyril said.

"Suit yourself," said Claudius.

Claudius shattered the door to Otto's office with one powerful kick. "Anyone who isn't a damn dark lord get the hell out now!" yelled Claudius and he ran across the room and punched Otto in the face as he was getting out of his chair. The other men in the meeting sat motionless.

"Otto is a dark lord," Stephan said loudly so that people in the bank could hear him. "He's been sacrificing our people to his Master." Stephan grinned when he heard people running out of the bank.

Otto was not a fighter. Every time he started to mumble his magics Claudius punched him. "We're decorating the streets with your men," yelled Claudius. "You filthy piece of shit! Who do you think you are to victimize our people! Your people! You piece of shit!"

"Boss!" yelled Dillion as he ran into the bank. "They've hung..." Thaos hit Dillion in the stomach then hit him with an uppercut to the face. Dillon punched Thaos in the jaw.

Thaos jumped on Dillion, knocking him to the ground. As the two men rolled around punching and gouging each other the six men who had been in the meeting sat fearfully in their chairs.

Suddenly one of the men jumped up. "Just as we got here they were dragging some kid behind that wall." The man yelled and pointed to the wall behind Otto's desk. "He said it was a back door, the whole wall was open."

"Where's the lever?" yelled Claudius as he punched Otto again.

Gideon and Stephan quickly searched the wall and bookcases for a lever. "Found it!" Stephan yelled but as he pulled the lever, the wall exploded with such force that all the men in the room were blown off from their feet. Otto tried to get up but Claudius grabbed him again. Gideon and Stephan charged into the smoke. Thaos threw Dillon out of a large window, the glass had already shattered because of the explosion. Dillion lay on the walkway, unconscious. Thaos quickly turned to help the others.

Suddenly Otto started screaming as if he was in pain. "Claudius let go of him," said Cyril. "Help them bring the others up. They were sacrificing Olin when he called the Angels in." Claudius jumped to his feet and ran into the thick smoke that was pouring out of the opening that once was a wall.

"You should leave," Cyril said to the six men in the room but they were so frightened they couldn't move. Otto too could not move. His skin was cracking and smoking and green foam was coming out of his eyes, ears, nose and mouth.

"Master help me," Otto cried.

"I hope he tries to," said Cyril.

"What is happening?" asked one of the men.

"That is what happens when a dark lord is in the presence of an Angel," Stephen said as he set Olin on the floor and disappeared into the smoke. Gideon carried an unconscious woman into the office.

"If you are going to stay in here then help us," Gideon said to the men. "There's people down there." Gideon's words broke through their wall of fear and the men ran into the smoke.

Twenty-three people were helped to escape the torture room in back of Otto's office. The injured were placed on the floor of the bank's lobby as physicians ran into the building.

"Is that him?" Thaos asked of the smoking pile of clothing on the floor of Otto's office.

"Yes but Jack got away," said Cyril.

Now that all of the victims were being helped, Claudius, Gideon and Stephan walked up to Thaos and Cyril. "What happened here?" asked Gideon.

"Olin come here," said Cyril who was still dressed as a street person. "Tell them what you did."

"Are you really an Angel?" Olin asked.

Cyril smiled and repeated, "Tell them."

"I came here and told Otto that I was going to kill him for selling me to the Master..."

The earth shook violently and the men grabbed onto furniture to keep from falling. It was as if multiple explosions were happening underground. "What is that?" asked Stephan.

"A war," said Cyril. "Now, Olin finish your story."

"I knew he would sacrifice me," Olin said. "Jack and another guy grabbed me and pulled me into the back room. Otto puts his sacrifices on the altar then kills them. I waited until Jack called to the Master then I called to Adam and I don't know what happened after that."

"Did you plan that?" asked Claudius with astonishment.

"I couldn't think of any other way to destroy Uncle Otto. You have no idea how powerful he was."

"That shaking is that Adam fighting?" asked Stephan as he pulled his sword out of its sheath.

"Trust me, Adam is not alone," said Cyril. "That shaking was the Master's temper tantrum. He sent his demons after the Angels then escaped. You will fight him but not today."

"Olin why did you wait until Jack called to the Master before you called to Adam?"

"I am not really sure. It seemed like a good idea."

Cyril smiled. "When Jack called to the Master it was like opening a window. The Master opened, well let's just say a window so that he could receive Olin's soul. Only it wasn't the soul of a victim that was transported it was an army of Angels."

"Olin what you did took faith and courage," Cyril said. "You have a lot of choices to make. I cannot tell you what decisions to make but I will tell you don't ever forget today."

"You used to dream of having courage. With the right choices you can be the man you've always wanted to be."

"How did Jack get away?" asked Thaos.

"He was holding the sacrificial knife when Olin called to us. Holy energy struck Jack and he ran from the room," Cyril explained.

"Ok, what aren't you telling us?" asked Stephan.

"Like Olin, Otto sold his children's souls to the Master when they were babies. Otto has controlled them all their lives. Now we will see what choices they make."

"What do you want us to do then?" asked Claudius.

"You keep on with what you are doing. Like Juleta, Otto had spun a web. Now others will try to take his territory. This is long from over. But a lot of good has come from all of this. A lot of prayers have been answered."

"What do you mean?" Claudius asked.

"Sometimes people pray just to be seen."

"I don't understand what you are saying," said Stephan.

"How can people walk through this world and not see their brethren, not hear their cries, not hear the screams in the night? This is a question that has long perplexed me, which is why I disguise myself as I do."

"Seriously, we will do better," said Gideon.

"You have done well," Cyril said. "Stephan why are you smiling?"

"If only people knew. I think everyone thinks Angels should look like Miranda and Adam did that day we did battle in Ganz. I wonder what people would do if they knew that Angels walked around them like regular people."

"And demons walk among them," said Thaos.

"Oh, I think people could believe about the demons pretty easily. But, think of the guy who is looking down his nose on someone wearing rags, only that someone is an Angel. I know I think twice now." Stephan said.

# Chapter XXXL
## Freedom

When Claudius, Thaos, Gideon, Stephan, Cyril and Olin walked out of Otto's office and into the lobby of the bank they saw Harlow and Wickfield talking to the victims who had been saved.

"We have a story for you," Claudius shouted. The crowd became quiet. "Otto Franks was a dark lord, he is dead now. He was going to sacrifice these people at his unholy altar. We saved nine women last night who were going to be sacrificed and who knows how many people there were before we found out about him."

"He was using the businesses The Rooster and The Chicken and The Egg to abduct people and for other criminal acts. But he was not responsible for the death of Prince Michael. We are still investigating that. When you write your story you say that the good citizens of Langer will not fall victims to dark lords and demons. If they want to come here they will have a fight on their hands." People in the lobby clapped and yelled then some of them ran into the streets and repeated Claudius' words.

"You know you just drew a line in the sand," Cyril said with a smile.

"I know," said Claudius.

"So Cyril are you sticking around for a while or is your mission done?" asked Thaos.

"I might just stick around for the fireworks," Cyril said then turned to Gideon. "You have not attended Mathas' meetings the past few days. Go to the castle now. Noah will ask you to help him remember why he is so worried about Tessa."

Both Joanna and Jack felt the great loss of power that was destroyed when Otto died. They had been bonded to him their entire lives and they now felt weak and disoriented. Jack had been thrown out of the bank by the power of the explosions. He did not understand what had happened; he just ran.

Jack ran almost a mile before he realized how badly burned his right arm was. But even the excruciating pain did not stop him; he was overwhelmed with terror.

Joanna's knees were weak and she clung to a desk in her parents' home to keep from falling. "Dear are you alright?" asked Ruthie as she ran to her daughter.

"Mother, I think something awful has happened to Father," Joanna said weakly.

"I know," Ruthie said and smiled. "And it's about time."

"Mother, what are you saying?"

"You all think that I am a fool and that I don't know what is going on here. I have been so ashamed of all of you. Where did I go wrong? I live in a house filled with monsters. Now that he has been exposed all of you will be. If I were you, my darling daughter I would run and take your brother and husband with you. I will no longer stand in silence."

"Mother, what on earth has gotten into you?" shrieked Joanna.

"I have lived in fear since I married your father. Today I found out I have friends," as Ruthie said this Bella, Isadore, Ashley, Nikki and Ingr walked out of the parlor and stood beside her.

"Miranda!" called Ingr. "What should we do with her?"

Miranda's voice was heard by all of the women. "What are her choices?"

"You heard her," Nikki said to Joanna. Both Nikki and Ingr walked closer to Joanna. "Tell your mother how you abduct people to sacrifice to the Master. Tell her you are a murderer and a witch. I am sure the list goes on," Nikki said with disgust.

Joanna straightened herself up and stared at the two women walking towards her. She knew that Nikki and Ingr were warriors.

"Are you going to change your ways?" asked Ingr.

"Who is Miranda?" asked Joanna.

"An Angel," Ingr said.

"Girls stop!" yelled Isadore. The women stared in horror as Joanna's face changed over and over. Not only were other faces shown but also scenes. The changes were happening quickly and the women were trying to understand what they were seeing. Suddenly one image took control and that was the face of the Master.

A feeling of evil overwhelmed the women. "Miranda can we kill him?" asked Nikki.

"No, but you can weaken him. You know the words."

Nikki and Ingr slowly walked towards the illusion. "We know you exist and we will not bow before you. You have no power here, you have no power here; you have no power here."

The room shook violently; the women could barely stay on their feet. Joanna screamed and fell lifeless on the floor.

"What did you girls do?" asked Bella.

"Gabriel taught us the words." Nikki said. "Don't anyone go near her body. Miranda, what happened?"

"She made her choice and the Master took her soul."

Now, Miranda's voice was only heard by Nikki and Ingr. The other women watched as they spoke with the Angel. The two women turned and quickly walked to the others.

"Ruthie, that was the voice of an Angel that you heard," explained Ingr. "She said you should have called to them long before this. Many lives could have been saved. But she said it is no longer safe for you to live here. People know about Otto and they have set the bank and both the stores on fire."

"They hung Andre and Jack was on his way here but he is running for his life. She said that even if the people forgive you this building has been given to demons, it will never be safe for you."

"What was that Angel's name again?" Ruthie asked.

"Miranda," said Bella.

"May I call on her?"

"She would like that," said Nikki. "But we need to get you out of here."

"I should be frightened but I have been frightened my entire life," Ruthie said. "I did plan to run away. I have accounts set up in Port Friada and a home there. Do you think I have time to get a carriage?"

"We will get you on one," said Nikki. "You should pack now."

"Bella, Isadore the house and everything in it is yours. We have a great deal of money in the bank if it isn't burned. Use it for whatever you want. I am sure you will want to search this place before you burn it down. I really don't know where he hid everything."

"Ruthie pack!" said Ingr. "People are coming."

"Miranda, we could use some help," Nikki said as they watched a crowd walking up to the house. Both women opened the door and walked outside. They stood on the top step of the porch shoulder to shoulder. "Listen to us!" yelled Nikki. "Ruthie was a prisoner here. Joanna is dead. We don't know where Jack is. You are going to allow Ruthie to leave this city. She has been terrified by monsters her entire life, she deserves a chance."

"She is leaving us the house to search so you can't burn it yet. We need to find out if there are more victims stashed any place. Go home all of you!" yelled Ingr.

"You heard my wife!" yelled Stephan as he, Thaos, Gideon and Claudius rode through the crowd.

"Enough people have been hurt this day," Claudius shouted. "Go to your homes and families. We will take care of this."

The men rode up to the house but remained on their horses. The people in the crowd grumbled and swore but they slowly walked away.

"Boy, are we glad to see you," said Nikki. "Did Miranda send you?"

"We were talking with Cyril and he told us to get here right away," said Thaos. "We heard everything you said. Did you kill Joanna?"

"The Master took her soul," Ingr said. "But before she died her face kept changing and we saw all these different faces and scenes like we were watching a play."

"Damn, that is the same thing that happened to Teivel when he died," Stephan said. "I wonder what that means."

Jack had been running towards his parent's home when he saw a huge crowd walking towards it. Suddenly he heard his name called and men ran towards him. Jack turned and cried out to the Master as he ran.

News of the explosions and fires in Langer reached Mathas shortly after they occurred. He sent soldiers into the city. The team members started to leave also.

"Dominic," yelled Ryan. "I have to tell you something before you go."

Dominic was running past the office and now stopped and turned around. Ryan and Elexas were standing in the doorway and they both looked frightened. "Olin went to the bank to confront his uncle. He made us promise not to tell."

"Sometimes keeping a promise is not a good thing. Hopefully he is still alive," Dominic said and ran out of the castle.

Noah and Tessa heard the commotion in the hallway and jumped out of bed. Noah was pulling on his trousers as he opened the door. "What is going on?" he yelled.

"Don't know yet. But there were explosions and fires in the city," Seth said then continued down the hallway.

"Tessa stay here," Noah said as he grabbed his shirt and boots. "I mean it. You stay here; this could be a trap. In fact, you should check on those women."

"Oh my god you could be right," she said and quickly dressed.

While fear and hatred spurred some citizens to set fires there were many others who refused to let their beloved city go up in flames as had happened but weeks before. Citizens and soldiers were working together to put out the fires at the bank and both of the clothing stores.

Soldiers from Fort Langer were sent into the city to help their comrades control the crowds that had gathered in the streets.

"We are so glad to see you," Bella said and hugged Claudius as the men entered Otto's house. "Ruthie was a victim as I thought. Isadore and Ashley are helping her pack. Miranda told her she would never be safe here so she is leaving for Port Friada. Hopefully there is a carriage leaving soon."

"I will make sure of it," said Thaos and quickly left the house.

"She is giving us the house but she says she doesn't know where Otto hid things," Bella continued. "And any money in the bank here. She has accounts and a home in Port Friada because she was planning an escape."

"If the money doesn't burn we should use it for the homeless," said Gideon. "What did Miranda say about this house?"

"That it has been surrendered to demons," Bella said. "Why?"

"I have several hundred people who have never seen furniture this nice. I could put all of this to good use but not if it is cursed or something."

"Miranda," called Stephan. "Or anyone, can we talk to you a moment?"

"Miranda has joined her brother in battle," said the Angel Ruth as she appeared. "Yes, you can give these things to the homeless but not the house that should be burned after you search it. And no you cannot search it without our help. I am ready when you are."

"You're better at reading my mind than my wife is," Stephan said kiddingly. "Should we wait for Ruthie to leave first?"

"That is not necessary. Bella, she told you the truth but she also learned a great lesson today. If she would have called us in or even told someone else what her family was doing, so very many lives could have been saved. She will bear that guilt the rest of her life if she does not pray to The Great Ruler. You will want to tell her that."

"Ruth, if there is anything that isn't destroyed in those stores can we give it to the poor?" Gideon asked.

"You are seeing things with new eyes. That is good. Citizens are putting out the flames as quickly as they were set. Search Joanna's shop before you allow others in to get the clothing. You will need us to go with you."

"Claudius, good you are here," said Ruthie as she, Isadore and Ashley walked down the staircase carrying suitcases. "Everything we have I am turning over to you. Ashley was just telling me about the neighborhood you will be building for the homeless. Take everything. I will be moving in with Matilda in Port Friada. We share the same shame."

"Here are the keys he carried. I don't know why he left them home today. I know some are for his desk drawers. There are two safes, one in his study and one in our bedroom. These are the combinations." Ruthie handed Claudius several pieces of paper. "I don't know what he keeps in them. Isadore suggested you ask the Angels before you open them."

"The Angel Miranda said this house was cursed. Otto owned eight ships, they are yours now. This is the address to Matilda's home. If you need me to sign any paperwork just send it there. Otto shared little with me. If we own other properties they too are yours but I don't know what has been cursed."

504

"Are you sure you want to give everything away?" asked Nikki.

"Everything has blood on it," said Ruthie.

"Otto sold the souls of your children and Olin when they were babies," Claudius said and Ruthie started to cry. "Olin has been with us. He didn't know what Otto did and he confronted him today and called the Angels in. He is no longer a dark lord and he seems lost."

"Do you want me to wait for him? He will have a home with us."

"She should leave now," the Angel Ruth said although Ruthie did not hear her voice.

"Thaos is getting you a carriage. We will tell Olin what you said and I am sure it will make him feel better," said Claudius.

"While we wait, perhaps we should look through Otto's study," said Ruthie. "In case there are papers I need to sign over to you."

"Start in the desk," said the Angel who appeared to all except for Ruthie.

"Otto had an extensive library," Ruthie said as she led the group into Otto's huge study. The walls of the room were lined with huge oak bookshelves. "The safe in here is behind that picture of the ship and in our bedroom the safe is behind the portrait of our family."

Ingr and Nikki walked into the room. "Ruthie were you serious about giving everything away?" asked Ingr.

"Yes, take what you want."

"Your kitchen is huge and full of food. We were going to get some of the soldiers to help us take it to the homeless," Ingr said.

"By all means child. But you should talk to your Angels because I don't know what is cursed in this house. In fact, I wanted to give all of you things for being my friends but I don't know if they are safe to give."

505

"Tell her that is fine as well as the food," said Ruth.

"An Angel is here and she said it is fine," said Nikki.

"Is she standing in here?"

"Yes," Nikki said. "She is next to the desk and her name is Ruth."

"Can she hear me?"

"Oh yeah," said Stephan.

Ruthie walked up to the desk. "Look to your left," said Ingr.

"Angel, I am sorry I never prayed to any of you. I guess I didn't know if you existed. I promise you that I will change that. My family brought so much pain into this world that I would like to make up for it. Perhaps you can let me know how to do that." Ruthie suddenly started to sob.

Fahron was directing the soldiers who were trying to disperse the crowds. Angus was helping to put out the fires. Olin was sitting on the walkway across the street from the bank when Dominic found him. It was obvious to Dominic that Olin had been crying. Dominic sat down next to him, "Ryan said you were going to confront Otto. What happened?"

"I did because I knew that he would sacrifice me. I waited until they had me tied to the altar and as Jack lifted the knife he called to The Master and I called to Adam. Then everything blew up and I don't know what all happened." Olin's eyes now grew wide. "Dominic there was another Angel here and he was dressed in rags. He killed Otto and he said because I waited until Jack called to the Master that it opened a window and an army of Angels went after him. I wish I could have seen that."

"Olin that took a lot of courage. Why didn't you tell us what you were planning?"

"I didn't want to get you hurt but some of you were here already which was good because there were a lot more people than me that were going to be sacrificed."

"Who was here?"

"Claudius, Gideon, Stephan and Thaos."

"Where are they now?"

"The Angel in rags told them to go to Uncle Otto's house."

"So what are you going to do now?"

"What do you mean?"

"Well, I would really doubt you still are a prisoner after what you did. And you're not under Otto's control anymore. You have your life back."

"I hadn't thought about that. I don't know. Do you think King Mathas would let me back in the castle? I want to help Ryan finish his project."

"Come on, I'll take you back there and we can talk to Mathas," Dominic said as he stood up. He didn't want to tell Olin that he might still be in danger from Otto's family and the Master. "Where's your horse?'

"I didn't have one so I walked."

"You walked this far to be sacrificed?" Dominic asked kiddingly. "Come on."

They walked through the streets and saw that the stores had been set on fire. Both buildings were burnt but the fires had been put out quickly. The crowds in the streets were dispersing. "I see our people over there," Dominic said and nodded to Jasmine, Seth, Noah and Fennel who were standing across the street. Dominic and Olin walked up to the group.

"Olin here walked into town to confront Otto. They had him on the altar to sacrifice him and when Jack called to the Master, Olin called to Adam and the bank blew up. He said Cyril said a window opened and Adam led an army of Angels after the Master."

"Good job Olin!" said Seth. "That took guts."

"I asked him what he wants to do with his life now and he wants to help Ryan finish the project." As Dominic spoke the members of his team were looking at Olin who looked lost and disoriented. And they too realized he was probably in danger. "Jasmine, I was wondering if you and Seth could ride together so Olin could ride your horse. I want to take him back to the castle."

"We should probably all get back now," said Noah. "Olin, I would like to hear the whole story if you don't mind telling it again."

Thaos walked into Otto's house and found everyone in the study. "Ruthie, there is a carriage outside and I have a platoon of soldiers who will escort you to the border of the kingdom."

"Thank you. All of you have been so kind."

"I'll help you with your things." Thaos said as he could see that the other men were engrossed in the paperwork they were reading. "Where is Nikki?"

"The girls are in the kitchen packing up the food to give to the homeless. Do I have time to say goodbye to them?" asked Ruthie.

"Of course. I will put your things in the carriage."

"You certainly work fast," Ruthie said when she walked into the kitchen. "My carriage is here and I just wanted to thank all of you again and to say goodbye."

"Write and let us know that you got there safely," said Bella as she hugged Ruthie. All of the women walked up to Ruthie and hugged her.

"Go up to my bedroom. On the dresser I have gifts for all of you to thank you for your kindness and your courage. No one else ever realized I was a prisoner here."

# Chapter XLI
## Aftermath

"I don't know what is happening," Tessa said to Mathas as he and Rosa ran into the chambers where the rescued women were staying. "They all started screaming and crying. I asked Adam to protect them."

"Were they all in the same room when you found them?" asked Mathas.

"No, I put them together so I could watch them. Noah told me to come here in case what was happening in the city was a trap."

"Do you know why they are crying?" asked Rosa.

"They are crying too hard to tell me," said Tessa. "My Lady, perhaps we could have some tea made for them."

"Of course," said Rosa.

"I think some whiskey might be in order," said Mathas then walked further into the parlor where the nine women were. "We want to help you; can you tell us what is wrong? Please we want to help."

One of the women tried to compose herself. "I think Tessa did help us. I was in my room and I woke up because I felt this horrible evil then I felt like I was being dragged, I don't know how to explain it. Then it was like whatever was dragging me suddenly let go."

"Is that what happened to all of you?" asked Mathas.

The women either nodded or said yes. "Mathas, we have to tell them," said Tessa.

"Tell us what?" asked one of the women.

"You were stolen to be sacrificed to a monster," Tessa said. "I called to the Angel Adam to protect you. Whenever you get scared again call to the Angels and you will be alright."

"Oh my god!" shrieked one of the women and they all started to cry again.

"I'll get some tea," Rosa said and left the chambers.

"Sorren help us," said Ingr when she saw him ride up to Otto's house.

"Is everyone alright here?" he asked and dismounted.

"Joanna is dead and Bella was right; Ruthie was a prisoner here. She just left for Port Friada and gave us everything. Miranda said the house is cursed but we can give the things inside to the homeless."

"The men are in Otto's study," Nikki said as she carried a crate of food out of the house and put it into a boca.

"I'll be right back with help," said Sorren. "Things are really quieting down in the streets."

Sorren only rode two blocks before he found Fahron and told him what Ingr and Nikki said. Fahron ordered two platoons of soldiers to follow him and they rode to Otto's house.

"Here's your help," said Sorren.

"We need more bocas," Nikki said.

"What do you need done?" asked Fahron.

"We are taking everything out of the house and taking it to the naval yard to give to the homeless," said Ingr. "Claudius and the others are inside going through papers. Actually some of this stuff can't go to the homeless now that I think about it."

"Sergeant Jackwitz, work with the women on this project," Fahron said. "Ingr, Nikki, you tell the men what they can take out of the house."

"Thanks," said Ingr as Sorren and Fahron dismounted and walked into the mansion.

510

"Does anyone know what the hell happened?" asked Fahron. "Isadore what are you doing here?"

"We have a lot to tell you," said Claudius. "But first, Miranda said this house isn't safe because it's been given to demons. The Angel Ruth was here for a while. She said we are going to need the Angels when we search some areas. And she wants us to take all of these books and put them in our new office. She said they are safe for us to move now."

"The girls are separating the things for the homeless. Ashley is sorting through the extravagant things. She plans to sell them at auction to raise money for the Adam's Homes. And the rest of us are going through the papers because we all feel like we need to get the hell out of here. We will tell you what we know while we work."

"I'm going to get more soldiers," said Fahron and walked outside to talk to Sergeant Jackwitz.

"All of the stuff on the desk and that table is from the desk drawers," said Thaos. The table that Mother and Isadore are at; well those things came from the safe in here. There is another safe upstairs that we haven't opened yet."

"We're organizing the stuff and quickly looking it over for information about more victims or attacks. Gideon gets everything about the shipping business."

"Where do you want us to start?" asked Sorren as Fahron entered the room.

"Here's the combination for the safe upstairs," said Claudius. "It's in their bedroom behind the family portrait. Ashley can point you to the room. We don't know what is in there so you will have to call to the Angels."

"Mathas we need to talk with you," Dominic said as he led Olin and some of his team members into the King's study.

"Of course," said Mathas. "Olin what happened to you?"

"You tell it," Olin said to Dominic.

"He's in a daze," Dominic explained. "He walked into Langer. Threatened Otto so that Otto would try and kill him. He was tied to an altar and Jack was going to sacrifice him. As Jack called to the Master, Olin called to Adam and things started exploding. Otto is dead and an army of Angels is fighting the Master."

"There were a lot of other people who were going to be sacrificed. Claudius, his sons and Gideon were in the bank and got all of those people out. When the citizens heard what was happening they set the stores and bank on fire but all of the fires have been put out and the soldiers made the crowds break up."

"But, what we want to talk to you about is Olin. Is he still under arrest?"

"Considering the circumstances, no. But Olin don't you dare commit any more crimes," said Mathas.

"I won't. Can I stay here and help Ryan finish his project?"

"Yes."

"Can I go there now?"

"Yes," said Mathas. As soon as Olin left the room Mathas asked. "Is he alright?"

"I think he is just dazed but he doesn't seem to realize that the Master and others may be after him for what he did," Dominic explained. "We haven't told him that yet. I told him he was free now and he has no idea what he wants to do besides help Ryan. We would like him to stay here for a little while, while we sort all of this out."

"That is fine," said Mathas as he leaned back in his chair. "Actually I am really surprised by what he did."

"We all are but Ryan told me what Olin was planning to do so I searched for him," Dominic said. "He didn't tell the rest of us because he didn't want to get anyone hurt."

"I can tell you have more on your mind," said Mathas. "What is it?"

"I still have to talk this over with my team," said Dominic. "When I found the kid he was sitting in the street crying. He really doesn't have anyone and he is making good choices and talking to the Angels. I'm, don't anyone yell until I am done. I'm thinking about adding him to the team as a resource like Erebus is. If it doesn't work out he can always leave. But right now I think Ryan is his only friend and Ryan is a good influence on him. I think he is better off with us."

"You aren't going to get an argument from me," said Fennel. "You could have knocked me over when you told us what he did. I think the question that we all have is how much of what he did in the past was because the Master owned his soul and how much was his own choices."

"I agree with Dominic," said Noah. "The kid is at a crossroads right now and I think he could take two sharply different paths. I say we take him under our wing for a while and if it doesn't work, well, we gave it a shot."

"That is fine by me but I would like to run it past the ruling members before we make it official," said Mathas.

"Maybe someone should ask him if that is even what he wants," said Jasmine.

"Ruth, we're ready to start searching the house," said Stephan. "Will you join us?"

"I am pleased with the choices you have made for distributing this property. I would suggest that you go to the bank before the end of this day and take all of Otto's money. Take it to Mathas' castle. Jack is still on the run and the anxiousness that you feel is caused by the eyes of Otto's rivals who desire his kingdom. Burn this house when it is empty."

"I'll take some soldiers and we will transport the money," said Fahron.

"You will need a boca," Ruth said.

"So we should get everything out today?" asked Sorren.

"Yes."

"I'll send more soldiers here," Fahron said and left the study.

"Stephan, remove that second row of books on the shelf near that red chair," said Ruth.

"Bella, Isadore you should stay here," said Claudius.

"What are you going to see?" asked Bella.

"I am sure an unholy altar," Stephan said.

"Well, I have never seen one," said Bella and stood up. Both Stephan and Thaos grinned at the look on Claudius' face. "Ruth is here and the girls taught us how to weaken a demon today. With the way our lives are going we should know what these things look like. What if we come upon one?"

Claudius didn't speak as Isadore stood up with Bella. He just shook his head.

"Mother stay behind us," said Stephan. "There might be victims down there or some of Otto's men."

"We understand," said Bella with determination. Stephan couldn't stop grinning.

Stephan removed the books as Ruth had directed and found a lever on the wall; he pulled it and one of the walls in the study started to move. It only moved far enough to expose a door.

"Do we need to ask you to touch us with holiness?" Claudius asked as he tried Otto's keys in the lock of the door.

"Actually, I will go down first," Ruth said.

Claudius opened the door which revealed a stair case. There were lit torches on the walls. The stairs were narrow so everyone had to walk in single file. No one spoke but all of the men had swords drawn. At the bottom of the stairs were three rooms. "Stay here," said Ruth and walked into one of the rooms. After a few moments she called out, "You may enter."

They walked into a large chamber with an unholy altar and a huge fire pit. The shackles attached to the walls were empty. "Mother, Isadore, since you want to learn. Ruth went in first because there were demons in here. It you ever happen upon one of these things assume there are demons present and call to the Angels right away. These types of altars are usually covered with demon snakes too," said Stephan.

"This is horrifying," said Isadore as she looked around the room. "Do people get thrown into the fire?"

"Sometimes," said Ruth. "And sometimes the dark lords dance around it."

"Ruth where does that door lead to?" asked Sorren.

"See for yourself." The group walked into a tunnel that was lit by torches. Stephan pushed his mother and Isadore behind him. They walked in silence for several hundred yards before they came upon a door. The lock clicked open, then Claudius kicked the door open. Two men who were playing cards jumped to their feet and pulled their swords. The men had been sitting in front of a cell. When these men saw who was entering their area they turned and ran.

"Let them go," said Ruth. "They are running to the tunnel that opens into the bank which is full of soldiers. This is where Otto kept those women you rescued. Follow me." Ruth turned and walked the way they had come.

When they reached the stairs she opened the door to another room. "This was being prepared for more victims," Ruth explained. "Otto was terrified of the Master and thought he could incur favors by increasing the numbers of people who he slaughtered. Now for the last room."

Ruth opened the door to the third room and the sound of a rushing wind was heard. "What is this?" asked Claudius as they entered a large room with a golden throne sitting in the middle of it. The walls, ceiling and floors were covered with strange writings and drawings. There was a thick, rich carpet under the throne and golden candelabras in the room.

"This is the reason you will be burning this house. This is the Master's room."

"What was that wind we heard?" asked Bella. "There aren't any windows in here."

"That was evil fleeing."

"Ruth, I am new at this but we saw what Ingr and Nikki did. Does something like that need to be done here?" asked Bella.

"Demons and monsters are fed by the fears of others."

"So that is why the girls kept repeating that he had no power," said Isadore.

"You didn't answer my question," said Bella.

"Since this room is surrendered to the Master he has a window into it."

"Come on Isadore, we need to learn how to do this," said Bella and took her friend's hand.

"Bella, just what the hell are you thinking?" asked Claudius.

"I am thinking that we should not let our children fight battles that we are not willing to fight ourselves," Bella said to Claudius and the two women marched up to the golden throne. "We have seen your face. We feel your evil and we know who you are yet we will never bow before you," said Bella.

In unison both women repeated, "You have no power here, you have no power here..."

The ground began to shake and Claudius and Gideon lunged towards the women. "Leave them," said Ruth.

The women continued to repeat their mantra. The ground shook harder and things fell in the room. Suddenly screams were heard but everyone in the room stood their ground. The men readied their swords for battle as the women continued to speak. The throne started to move a little at first then more and more until it was shaking violently.

"Bella and Isadore you should come back here now," said Ruth. The women continued their mantra as they walked back to the doorway. The floor in the room was cracking and groaning. "All of you should leave now."

"If you are fighting demons we're staying with you," said Sorren.

The cracking and groaning sounds became louder and louder. The floor underneath the throne gave way and the throne fell into nothingness. The women continued their mantra. The men stood ready to fight but no monsters appeared.

"He is gone," said Ruth. "But you will still need to burn the building. Bella and Isadore, your husbands and children do not always tell you what they experience and learn on the missions because they do not want to distress you. You have now learned the power of faith. And you are right you will need to know that."

When Dominic's group left Mathas' study they walked into the office where they found Ryan, Elexas and Olin sitting around a table talking.

"Are we interrupting?" asked Fennel.

"No, he was telling us what he did," said Ryan.

"Well, we have some things to discuss," said Dominic. "Nothing is set in stone yet because Mathas wants to talk to all of the ruling members. Ryan, everyone is so impressed with your work that Mathas is thinking about offering you a special positon but he also knows that you love being a carpenter so you might want to think about that and discuss it with your family. I am sure you could arrange the hours so you could do both if you wanted."

"Really?" Ryan said with a big smile.

"Ryan once we get caught up on all this paperwork, there might not be a lot to do in here for a while," said Fennel. "I can't imagine it will always be as intense as it has been."

"Olin, we have other teams and one of them in Salar has an ex-warlock on it. He has helped us in so many ways and been a resource about the dark worlds. Today is probably not the day for you to make any decisions but we want you to consider a position like that on our team. But like I said, Mathas wants to talk all of this over with the ruling members."

"Would I be able to keep working with Ryan?"

"Yes," said Dominic.

"I think I would like that." Olin said. "Thanks."

"What about me?" asked Elexas. "I would like to be on the teams."

"We haven't figured out what to do with you yet," said Dominic. "While you have many good qualities and you certainly are doing a good job on all of this, you don't play well with others. It is like you are self-destructive. You can't start wars among the members. You had Deborah crying, Tessa has to stay away from you so you two don't fight and you've made many of the men here feel uncomfortable. Elexas, Tessa was the only one who wanted to give you a chance so what are you trying to do by flirting with Noah?"

"I don't know," said Elexas in almost a whisper. Tears were flowing down her cheeks.

"We can't have you on the teams if we can't trust you," Dominic continued. "People want to trust you but you don't make it easy. So I am giving you an assignment right now. You think about all of this and if you decide that you really want to be on the teams you come up with ways that you can fit in. Then you tell us your plan. And don't think you are going to pull anything over any one here."

"Elexas, you are going to get pissed at what I say but I am saying it to help you," said Seth. "You seem very self-centered and full of yourself but the past few days as I've been watching you; sometimes I think you hate yourself. Maybe that is where you should start when you are thinking about these things."

"Noah, I am sorry," said Elexas.

"You are a beautiful woman but I love Tessa and plan to marry her. You aren't going to change that. And if you apologize to anyone it should be her because she really stood up for you with Turner."

"Now, I feel really awful."

"You should," scolded Jasmine. "But Dominic is right you have proven yourself in some ways. But you and I were trained together and you know you can't go into war with people you can't trust and we are at war."

When Fahron brought an entire boca filled with bags of gold to Mathas' castle he briefed the King and Dominic's team about what he had been told by Claudius and the Angel Ruth.

"I'm going into Langer and make sure none of the team members try going into those shops without calling to the Angels," said Dominic.

"We'll come with you," said Fennel.

"Noah, you and Tessa should stay here. Gideon said he was coming to talk to both of you after something that Cyril said to him," Fahron said. "It sounded like he was leaving after I was. I am surprised he isn't here."

"Do you know what it was?" asked Noah.

"No, sorry. A lot was going on and he yelled to me as I was leaving. Where is Tessa anyways?"

"With those girls we rescued," said Mathas. "They all felt like something evil was trying to get them. Tessa called to Adam and they are all safe now. From what you said it was probably the Master."

"I am going back to Otto's house to help. It sounded like Ruth wanted us to have everything out by tonight," said Fahron.

After Fahron left the castle, Noah walked to the chambers where the nine women were gathered to talk to Tessa. He heard loud voices and quickened his pace.

"Are you two fighting?" Noah asked as he walked up to Tessa and Elexas who were standing in the hallway outside of the girls' chambers.

"Kind of," said Tessa. "She is apologizing."

"Well, I hope the two of you work it out," said Noah. "Elexas if they don't allow you on the teams you can't blame anyone but yourself and you know that."

"I know," she said softly.

"She told me what everyone said. And if she stays she is basically going to have to change her personality," said Tessa. "I told her she could do it but it's going to be hard. But worth it."

"Elexas, you put on a good show but you never really seem happy. Maybe this is just what you need," said Noah. "And Tessa may need you to watch the girls here. Fahron told me that we had to stay in the castle because Gideon is coming to talk to us about something Cyril told him."

"Sure, I can do that," said Elexas.

"I just got them to stop crying so don't stir them up," Tessa said. "I was about ready to pour whiskey into their tea. If they feel like something evil is coming for them call to Adam."

"Gideon is looking for you," Rosa said as she walked up to the young people. "He's in Mathas' study."

# Chapter XLII
## Dreams

"Noah, I am sorry but I don't trust her," said Tessa.

"No one does," he replied.

"Are you talking about Elexas?" asked Rosa as the three were walking to Mathas' study.

"Yes, she wants to be on the team but it's like she sabotages everything," Noah said.

"You know maybe you should have Gideon put her in a trance and see what she says. That's what he did with Tally and Drake and they are working out fine as far as I know."

"Rosa that is a really good idea," said Noah then knocked on the closed door to Mathas' study.

Gideon opened the door then stood to the side so everyone could enter. "Have a seat," he said. "I am sorry that I haven't been around but so much has been going on. I think it was yesterday or maybe the day before I spoke with Cyril at the naval yard. We were basically talking about the missing women and the homeless but before he left he said something to the effect that Noah would remember why he was so worried about Tessa then today he told me to meet with you this afternoon."

"He told me you wanted me to help you remember something and he said I shouldn't wait. Tessa, he had already warned us that you were being watched and I think most of us thought that was Olin but especially after today I don't think that is the case. Three times now an Angel has warned us about you. We need to take that seriously."

"Noah, you have seen me put people into trances before. Do you want us to be alone?"

"No but for some reason I think that Turner should be here. Is he in the building?"

"Yes, he is in the office. I will get him," said Rosa. "Noah would you mind if I watched."

"No, it is really interesting what he does."

After Rosa left the room Noah looked at Gideon. "Since Cyril has been warning us will you ask the Angels to help you with the questions?"

"Already planned on it," said Gideon.

"I will take notes," Mathas said. "Tessa, you are so quiet."

"I'm not really sure what to make of all this. Will what Gideon does hurt Noah?"

"No, it is like putting him to sleep," Gideon said as he rearranged some of the furniture. "Tessa, I want you to sit at that table. Once I start just let me ask him questions. Noah this is your chair."

"I explained everything to him on the way here," Rosa said as she and Turner entered the room.

"Rosa and Turner would you sit with Tessa? Mathas is taking notes. Once I start please don't talk unless it is really important. I don't want Tessa talking at all because I think she can influence what Noah is thinking."

When everyone was seated Gideon pulled out his pocket watch and began to move it slowly in front of Noah's eyes. He spoke softly and within moments Noah's head fell forward.

"Noah when I snap my fingers you will sit up and answer my questions truthfully. If you attempt to lie your right eye will twitch." Gideon snapped his fingers and Noah's head quickly shot up.

"You have been worried about Tessa why?"

"The dreams."

"Before we talk about the dreams are there other reasons you worry about her?"

"What she does is dangerous and she takes too many chances. She doesn't tell us where she is going or what she is doing."

"Are there other reasons?"

522

"No."

"When did you have these dreams about Tessa?"

"The first one was a long time ago. When Othnial was hiding us in the monastery. I dreamt about this beautiful girl. I was watching her walking down a street then she starts screaming then the next thing I see is an unholy altar. But she isn't on it but I can hear her screams. Then I woke up."

"Do you know where that altar was?"

"No but it looked like a cave and it was covered with snakes."

"Did you see her get attacked or grabbed from the street?"

"No."

"Do you have different dreams about Tessa or the same one?"

"The same one."

"Is it exactly the same?"

"No, now every time I have it I feel a strong evil."

"How many times have you had this dream?"

Noah didn't speak for a few moments. "Ten times."

"Were they all before you met her?"

"Yes."

"Are you sure it is Tessa in the dreams?"

"Yes, I can see her face clearly. She is always wearing a blue dress. She has that dress in our room."

"Have you ever had other dreams like this, without Tessa in them?"

"I used to dream a lot about Teivel's demons attacking villagers but that was different."

"In the dreams do you know why you are watching her?"

"Because she is so beautiful."

"Now tell me about the street she is on. Do you recognize it?"

Noah didn't answer. He started to squint as if he was staring at something. "Noah what do you see?"

"The dream is changing. The woman's face is changing back and forth between Madeline and Tessa. Whoever is after them knows them both. They are both wearing blue dresses. I don't know where that street is. It's really busy like in a big city."

"Gideon! Now I see that day that Moses attacked Ashley's store and I see Ashley in a blue dress but it is a different dress but she is walking down the same street."

"Noah, I want you to concentrate. Are all the women walking in front of the same buildings?"

"Yes."

"Can you see any signs?"

"I couldn't before but now I can. It is a huge sign and it says Isabella but how can that be...wait the sign is changing. It says Red Moon Shipping. There are men standing in front of the door who look liked hired fighters. They are watching the women but they don't say anything or move. I am feeling evil again but I don't know why."

"Is it sunny or nightfall?"

"It's real sunny like the middle of the day. The women are walking like they don't realize they are in danger. I don't see anyone following them. I just see them in front of that building then I hear screams."

Tessa raised her arm in the air and Gideon nodded at her. "Is it our screams he hears?"

"I don't know, I hear a woman screaming for help. She says 'help' twice then silence."

"Adam help him!" Tessa said loudly.

524

"This isn't my dream any more. I see Tessa, Madeline and Ashley all standing next to each other wearing blue dresses and they resemble each other. Now I see a triangle with words on each corner. One is Isabella. The second is Moses and the third is Hector. Now I see a ship and I hear a lot of people screaming. I can't see the markings on the ship." Noah stopped talking.

"Adam spit it out will you," Tessa said.

"You have got to stop talking to him like that," scolded Turner.

Gideon scowled at Tessa and Turner then looked at Noah. "Noah what are you seeing?"

"A lot of things from that mission we were on in Port Friada. I see the men that were hanging in your yard and I keep seeing the attack on Ashley's store. Gideon, I see you in the street talking to Moses. I see the docks there."

Suddenly Noah was awake but Gideon didn't wake him from the trance. "I remember those dreams now. Tessa the three of you know something and you might have something too. But Adam told me that people are afraid of what you know. But there was more too."

"Olin told us that Otto and Joanna had gotten letters from Isabella who said she was in Port Friada. I think that is Hector sending those letters or he knows who is. I think this is separate from the information you know."

"And I don't know what I was seeing with the screaming people on the ship. But I kept seeing Ashley, Tessa and Madeline and every time I did I remembered a mission that Gabriel's team was on in Stordt."

"I know which one you are talking about," said Mathas. "Roch was turning into a powerful demon. But he was in disguise so Gabriel devised this elaborate plan to drive him crazy, thinking he would expose himself and it worked. In part of the plan Vitomas, Hannah and Ibula all wore blue dresses and Roch would get glimpses of them then the Rualas would grab them off the streets. Roch thought he was seeing ghosts."

"So what does that mean?" asked Tessa.

"I don't really know," Mathas said.

"This is so frustrating," Tessa said. "I expected him to say that the Master wanted me for a sacrifice. I don't know what any of this means. But that Red Moon Shipping is in Port Friada. Also I highly doubt that it was me, Madeline or Ashley screaming because we are all fighters and carry weapons. We would be fighting before we would be screaming."

"Noah, I can't believe you dreamt about me before we even met."

"I know and I don't know why I couldn't remember them."

"I think it was so the Angels could show you more things," said Gideon. "And I don't mind telling you that I am really unsettled by this. I am going to ask Ashley if I can put her in a trance and ask her about this."

"Tessa, you and Noah need to send Madeline and Javier a letter and include all of the details. They may see something that we didn't. Do that as soon as we leave here," said Turner then he looked at Mathas and Gideon.

"Our teams have been working in Port Friada for years. Madeline and Javier did steal some things from Hector but they gave them to Gabriel and the others. Off the top of my head I can't think of anything we stole from a person but I am sure we've seen and overheard more than we can remember."

"Deborah stole a ledger from Moses and gave it to Ashley. He attacked her house and shop to get it back," said Gideon. "Sudfad has it locked up but Moses is dead. Hector's men killed him. I would think that if those dreams were about that book that Noah would have seen Deborah."

"Now the last I heard, Hector's men were in Wetpr on Karzman's land," said Turner. "But we know the Gefrey Games are on hold so I would assume he left there. But would he go back to Port Friada? There are wanted posters of him everywhere. With all of his enemies I am sure that he has a lot of hideouts. I think that is one thing that we have to figure out."

"And so much of what has happened here since and possibly including Prince Michael's murder is linked between Langer and Port Friada. I think we need to finish going through all of that paperwork and look at things with different eyes."

"When I was in the office, Ryan told me that Dominic wanted Olin on the team as a resource. I think that is a good idea. And even if you don't end up making him a team member we need to keep him around for a while. Because he too is a link between these cities."

"Turner our teams have questioned why so many dark lords go to Port Friada when the people there are actively fighting them. Do you have any idea?" asked Noah.

"I don't know but that is a good question. Maybe it's because it is close to Marba but there are probably a bunch of reasons."

"Mathas could I copy your notes so I make sure I include everything in my letter?" asked Tessa.

"Yes but so you know I will be sending a copy of the notes to Sudfad and Gabriel; we do that with everything. I don't know if I am reading too much into all of this but this is the second time that the Angels have shown us visions with similarities to missions that Gabriel's team was on. I am beginning to suspect they have some unfinished business."

The following morning Mathas rescheduled his meeting from early to late morning. Claudius started the meeting by telling of the previous day's events that he was involved with.

"We didn't get everything out of that house until after midnight and we had a lot of help, so you can imagine the crap that was in there. I put crates of papers and books in the office that have to be sorted through. We quickly looked at them for information about victims or attacks. There are two bocas here filled with expensive stuff that our wives are going to auction off for the Adam's Homes so if anyone wants to help you can talk to Rosa."

"Everything else went to the naval yard for the homeless. All of the money we got from Otto's bank account will go for building that neighborhood. After we were sure that everything was cleared out we called to Ruth. She stood by while we burned the place down and let me tell you I've never seen anything like that. Different colors and I guess images would appear in the flames. I have no idea what the hell was going on."

"Needless to say most of us haven't had a wink of sleep so after the meeting my family and Gideon's family are going home. Angus you're up."

"We found out it was Otto's hired man Dillion who hung the carriage driver in the dungeons. The bastard killed one of our soldiers for his uniform and just walked into the dungeons easy as pie," said Angus. "Sorren is still interrogating him, which is why he isn't here. Dillion worked for Otto for about a year and was giving us a list of crimes they were involved with when I left to come here."

"Otto and Joanna are dead and Ruthie is on her way to Port Friada but Jack is still unaccounted for. A mob was chasing him and some of them said he just disappeared which makes me think magics or demons were involved. Sorren spent a lot of time asking Dillion questions about Jack which he will present later. From the little I heard, I believe that Jack is a genuine threat and will try to regain his father's empire."

"Now, what I found interesting from the men we have interrogated so far, is it doesn't sound like Otto or his family had any back up plans. They were so arrogant they never thought they would be caught by us. The wife had set things up as she was planning to escape from her family but the crooks had nothing. They apparently weren't worried about us."

"But Otto was really worried about rivals and had his men constantly looking for the types of symbols that Olin told us about and watching the streets. Dillion said that Otto was always paranoid but he started to get really bad a couple of months before Prince Michael was killed."

"Dillion said that he always had men watching all of us and knew that Otto was particularly interested in Michael. But Dillion said that Otto was adamant that none of us should be hurt."

"He said that Otto went nuts after Michael was killed and ordered Dillion to find out who was behind the attacks, then again after Thaos and Stephan were attacked. I'm thinking the old boy was right to be paranoid. Otto's men knew as much as we do; that the assassins sounded like that tribe from Salszar. And Dillion said they didn't find out squat about who was behind the giant snakes or the attacks on Thaos and Stephan."

"Now, another thing I found interesting is apparently Otto kept going to his altar to get answers from his demons and no one was telling him shit. That even made me wonder if he was on a black list especially after Olin told us how powerful he was. We really may have a new boss moving in the area."

"This afternoon, I am taking the teams into both of those shops. We couldn't search them yesterday because everything was too damn hot from the fires. And I know I need to have an Angel with us."

Stephan was the next speaker. He walked to the front of the room and did not have his normal grin or swagger. He paused before he spoke. "I am so damn pissed I can barely talk. After we saved those girls who were in the carriage, I made an announcement that citizens should tell our soldiers about missing people and things they thought were suspicious."

"Well, we are still getting reports. So far the suspicious stuff really isn't anything we don't already know. But as of this morning there are over thirty young women missing from Langer besides the nine here. There are also twenty-seven men."

"I am having soldiers make posters and hang them everywhere telling people to report missing people to our soldiers at once. Wickfield is also putting a big thing in the paper about that. He and Harlow aren't here because they are writing up a storm about Otto and everything that has happened. We are putting it out to the dark lords that they aren't welcome here. Of course Cyril said we were drawing a line in the sand and yes we are."

"I am going home to get some sleep because I just want to punch something. Oh, I almost forgot. The families of the nine girls will be coming here today to pick up their daughters if any of you want to talk to them."

"Claudius and everyone who was working all night. I gave you the notes about Noah's dreams so you don't have to sit through that part but I want you to stay just a few minutes longer," said Mathas. "Sol will you open the door?"

Sol was standing near the main door to the Great Hall and now opened it. Ryan, Elexas and Olin were standing in the hallway looking sheepish.

"Come up here, the three of you," Mathas said. "Dominic and Turner you come up here too. Hell, Claudius, Stephan and Thaos get up here."

"Are we in trouble?" asked Elexas.

"Not yet," said Turner.

"I am not telling you anything new," said Mathas to the room full of people. "That the last week has been overwhelming for us all. I don't think there is a person here who has had an entire night's sleep. The ruling members and I are very proud of all of you. We will be giving you all bonuses and other signs of our appreciation next week at the celebration that we are having for High Priest Othnial. I apologize but we just haven't had time to put everything together for today."

"As you know, I put Turner's group on Dominic's team so that I could pay them. These two groups will continue to work as one until Gabriel, Javier and Madeline make some decisions about teams. But with everything that is going on don't forget that all of Turner's people and some of you still have bounties on your heads."

"Now for the three of you," Mathas said and smiled. "What an unusual group you started out as. Two prisoners and a carpenter and you turned out an extraordinary product. Ryan, many of us here now realize how brilliant you are. I am bestowing the title of Information Minister on you."

As Mathas spoke Rosa handed Claudius paperwork, a sash and a plaque to give to Ryan. Claudius proudly presented these items to his son.

"We know that you have a thriving business and I am not asking you to give that up. But I would also like you to oversee the information we get in, as it is necessary for the safety of our teams and our kingdom. One of those papers tells you what your salary will be."

"Olin, Dominic and Turner want to offer you a position on their team as an adviser. They envision you filling a role much as Erebus does on Gabriel's team. You too will be paid for your work." Rosa handed Dominic paperwork that he handed to Olin.

"Elexas, you surprised everyone with your abilities on this project. Turner is taking you under his wing for the next six months to work with you on the teams. But in the meantime I would like you to continue working with Ryan and Olin on the current project." Rosa handed Turner paperwork which he gave to Elexas.

Rosa handed items to Claudius, Dominic and Turner as Mathas spoke to the group. "For their extraordinary work on compiling the mountains of paperwork that we have obtained and forming pictures for us to understand what we are up against they are all receiving medals of honor." Claudius pinned a medal on Ryan, Dominic on Olin and Turner on Elexas. The three young people where both shocked and proud.

"And lastly, we are paying you for the work you did." As Mathas spoke Rosa handed small pouches of gold coins to Claudius, Dominic and Turner, who in turned presented the money to the three young people. Everyone in the room applauded and some yelled war cries.

"Turn around and face your teammates," Mathas said. Ryan, Elexas and Olin turned and faced the applauding warriors. It was clear to everyone that the three young people were overwhelmed with emotions. They could not speak but looked humbly at the people who now called them peers.

# Chapter XLIII
## Preparations

The Sanuri spent the night praying for clarification for the shards of visions he had been seeing. He did not attend Sudfad's meeting but continued to pray. Midmorning he was visited by The Lion.

"Thank you for coming old friend," said the Sanuri. "What is it that the heavens are trying to tell me?"

"It is not just the heavens that you are sensing," said The Lion. "Your friends in Langer have stirred up a hornet's nest, which you may want to tell them. You have not yet received the letters but Otto Franks and his daughter have been destroyed. Jack is on the run but when he makes his next appearance in Langer it will be one of power and revenge."

"All of these people were hand puppets of the Master. The reason he prefers female sacrifices is because of his disdain for women. He spent his life being rejected by them. After he became a monster he is making all women pay for his ill-fated love life. In the last few days Tessa, Ingr, Nikki, Bella and Isadore; daughters and mothers, have taunted and defied him. They have called to the Angels and they have repeated the words that would disempower him. His rage is uncontrollable. He will seek revenge."

"The dark lord boy Olin set Otto up. Olin had no friends. He and Adam have developed an unusual relationship. Olin set himself up to be sacrificed and as soon as Jack raised the knife and called to the Master, Olin called to Adam. Because of the timing Adam was able to jump through the window that was opened and he did not jump alone. A heavenly army is still fighting with the beasts of the Master."

"Did Olin and Adam set that up?" the Sanuri asked in surprise.

"No but Adam was reading Olin's thoughts. The boy went through his life feeling scared and unprotected by his family which caused him to cling to the dark magics."

"Adam is the only one who has ever made him feel safe. So the creation of monsters, the dark lord child turns out to have more faith than many of The Great Ruler's children. I would call that a miracle for the day."

"Wickfield and Harlow are doing a series of stories exposing Otto's empire and they talk about the Master. Claudius was quoted as challenging dark lords to enter that city. These stories are being sent to newspapers all over the continent. The editors in Salar will receive them soon. Cyril has decided to stay in Langer for the firestorm that will ensue. And other Angels are begging to be assigned to the handful of humans from a small world who are shaking up the dark worlds."

"You are enjoying this aren't you?"

"It is about time people rose above their fears and realized their powers. But the battles to come will not be easy. And in some ways it doesn't matter if the teams win or lose the battles; their courage to challenge the demons is infectious."

"There is more to this, I can feel it."

"Of course there is. The Master wanted to join the Gefrey Games and he too wants to free his master, the Originator. But all of these seemingly insignificant humans are drawing the eyes and the wrath of many. Without realizing it, Claudius and the others have distracted the monsters from searching for the Originator."

"With all of this going on do you still want Erebus and me to go to Ryed? Shouldn't I go to the monastery at Malga?"

"Ryed is where you need to go now but you are correct, you may be needed in Malga. Perhaps you and Erebus should consider leaving soon, very soon."

"Ruth wants Erebus to go through his library with Archetenus and Jared. Should that wait?"

"No. When we are done here go to Sudfad's meeting and tell them my words. Tell Erebus, Jared and Archetenus to go directly to his library and they will know the books they must take."

"They are safe for Archetenus and Jared to read. If either of these men have difficulty understanding what they are reading they should call to us. You and Erebus leave tomorrow morning."

After the Angel Ruth had talked to Sudfad and those in his meeting, committees were formed. Gabriel, Raul, Simon and Javier were in charge of organizing and analyzing the information they were receiving.

Joshua and Vivian were going to work with Nyla and Saran on the mountain of scrolls that were written in the Cerfic language. The plan was for Nyla and Saran to teach the language to Joshua and Vivian as they worked.

With two of the ruling members on committees, Raphael and Maxwell had to take on more duties. Madeline and Corsa were tasked with setting up a system to provide Adam's Homes in the kingdom. Alex, George and Kent wanted to be on committees but everyone agreed it was time for them to start their educations. Olivia too was going to the Learning Center. Raphael was working with all of these young people to get their educations scheduled.

Nyla, Saran and Nina decided they wanted to go to the Learning Center with their friends and didn't need private tutors any longer.

The core group who made up Gabriel's original team were tasked with reviewing the copious notes from prior missions since like Mathas they realized similarities with things on the Langer mission. This group consisted of Natasha, Calen, Luca, Koby and Dagon.

Team members who were not specifically assigned to committees were working on various projects such as research, taking notes and writing letters.

After The Lion left the Sanuri's chambers he went to Sudfad's meeting and repeated the words of the Angel.

"So he still didn't tell you why you are going to Ryed?" asked Jared.

"No. Only that we must visit the Clan of Gesmal then go to Erebus's castle. I know it is short notice but if any of you want to send gifts or letters along I will take them."

"Perhaps we should end the meeting," Sudfad said.

"I will take Archetenus and Jared to my home now," said Erebus. "But while I am gone, Gala will be staying at the house, so she can let any of you in if you need to use my library. Also, I would appreciate it if someone would check on her."

"We can do that," said Micha. "Don't worry about anything."

With all of the information coming from Langer, Matthew told General Bishop to stay in Salar a few more days as Matthew and Angelina now planned to return to Langer with those troops.

King Mathas' plan for establishing hospitals in the Kingdom of Lentz was designed to be implemented in phases. And this project had been turned over to Matthew and Angelina. The first phase was near completion. Six hospitals were built along the eastern coastline where there was a higher likelihood of attack.

The first group of healers had been trained at the Learning Center in Salar and a number of physicians and nurses had been hired from the medical school at Cisero College.

With the recent attacks in Langer, Matthew decided to start the second phase of the project sooner than originally planned. He asked Bishop to help him. The men went to Cisero College and interviewed an entire class of physicians and nurses who would be graduating within the year. Contracts were drawn up and most of these students were hired.

Angelina worked with Hannah and Gala to prepare for another class of healers that would be taught in Langer. Matthew was paying Calen to draw building plans for a considerably smaller version of the Learning Center for Langer. Only medial classes were going to be taught at this school.

Calen had previously drawn up the building plans for the hospitals in Lentz. Sudfad was now using the same plans to build more hospitals in the Kingdom of Wetpr. Because of these hospital programs in the two kingdoms, Cisero College was building onto its medical buildings and sending announcements to every city and village in the continent in an effort to recruit students.

Although Mathas had told the team members to get some sleep few of them did. The majority went to Langer and helped Angus as he searched The Rooster then The Chicken and The Egg. Ruth was the Angel who answered Angus' call as he started at The Rooster.

"Before you say a word," said Ruth. "Yes the clothing is safe for you to give to the homeless and I would prefer you have the soldiers take that now. There were things that you did not see the first time you searched this building because stacks of clothing were concealing them."

Angus had several large bocas parked outside of the store. It did not take long for the soldiers and the team members to empty the store. "Now let me take the lead," said Ruth. "And don't touch things until I tell you. Jasmine, I will need you to draw a few things. There is paper and pens in the office."

Ruth led the group to the front of the store. "Please move those two sets of shelves." As soon as the shelves were moved a small door was exposed. Ruth looked at the door and the paddle lock opened and fell to the ground then the door swung open.

There wasn't a room behind the door but a small cupboard. The shelves had been removed and on the back of the cupboard were hung various bones and feathers.

"This is an altar of sorts," explained Ruth. "It is primitive and is rarely used any more but Otto was a paranoid man and was covering his bases. These bones are human as are those scalps."

"Oh my god!" said Jasmine.

"Jasmine, I would like you to draw this so please come to the front," said Ruth. "Centuries ago, before mankind developed the unholy altars that they use now they set up altars like these. Sometimes they were locked away and other times displayed in the open. The victims may or may not be killed at the same time. The altar can be added to."

"Obviously the goat's head in the center is not human but it is very significant as it represents the demon that the offerings are given to. When the person is making such an altar, the goat's head is placed first. Then each bone or body part is prayed over and placed starting south, west, north then east. This ritual is believed to give the person performing it power."

"Although Otto had sold his soul to the Master he created this altar to worship the demon Ahriman. This was his backup plan. Ahriman is now a prisoner in the Abyss but for centuries he was the most powerful demon in this world. And his ego had no bounds. Ahriman would be second to no one and cursed Otto for this altar. Otto didn't really understand what was happening so he locked this altar away and never touched it again."

"Your teams and High Priest Othnial will see these so please provide them with copies of Jasmine's drawing. If anyone comes upon this they must call to us immediately because most of these are made to worship one of the Old Ones."

"Notice that now that you can see the walls, there are more of Otto's symbols here. Olin said they were used for marking territory and that is true but they can also be used for other things. Otto put his symbol on these walls as a source of power."

"Now, I want everyone to turn around and look at the markings above each doorframe. Jasmine we will need drawings of those also. That is very old magic. It is a curse for unwanted intruders."

"Angus, you and the others are lucky that that we watch over you. We disabled them the day that Tessa came in here. Again, you need to call to us when you see something like that."

"But, if you were to ask my opinion. When you plan to enter any area that you believe is controlled by a demon or dark lord you should call to us before you go in."

Tessa and Noah did not go into Langer because they were writing very detailed letters to Madeline and Javier about the visions Noah had seen. The letters were so long that they had to be divided and put into numbered envelopes because more than one Enrop had to carry them.

"We need Olin," announced Tessa as she and Noah entered the temporary office. "Actually why aren't all of you sleeping?"

"We are too excited too," said Ryan. "Besides all of the honors you can't believe how much money Mathas gave us. I am putting mine aside..." Ryan stopped talking and looked embarrassed.

"Ryan, you are turning red," teased Tessa. "What are you saving your money for?"

"Nyla," Noah said with a smile.

"Well, she is still young and we aren't ready but when we are I want to have the money for the ring and everything else. I mean she is a princess," Ryan said proudly.

"Ryan do you really think that Bella and Claudius are going to let you pay for anything?" asked Noah.

"I'm not their blood son."

"Neither is Thaos and he told us that he almost got into screaming matches with them and that was long before they adopted him. When he and Nikki got married they were just living in the castle; they weren't part of the family yet."

"You are probably right but I still want to be prepared," Ryan said.

"I've never had this much money in my whole life," said Elexas excitedly. "And this is just for the work we already did."

"What about you Olin?" asked Tessa. "You're pretty quiet."

"I have lots of money but...this just sounds too crazy. You'll laugh."

"Olin tell them," said Ryan.

"Don't laugh. I kind of feel like I have a home now." Everyone was touched by Olin's words and no one spoke for a moment.

"Well Olin you do," said Tessa. "Now we need to pick your brains since all of you are so damn smart. You heard us talk about the visions and dreams that Noah had in the meeting. Well, here are the notes and we are wondering if maybe you can help us figure them out."

After the group was done in The Rooster, Ruth told them to burn the building. A group of soldiers stayed at the shop to burn it while the rest of the group went to The Chicken and The Egg. Ruth walked into the shop first but moments later called the others in.

"Again you can pack up the clothing and items first. Everything except for the jewelry. Follow me." Ruth walked to a small glass display case. "Those are the necklaces that Drake saw the victims wearing in his vision. Those women were not taken against their wills. They were pawns of Otto's. There are other things in this display box that have the markings of the Master. The markings are all the same. Those items we will burn with the building. Everything else you can do with as you please."

It took longer for the soldiers and team members to empty out this shop. "Ruth, I certainly am not an expert on this," said Dominic. "But some of these paintings and statues look very expensive, as well as some of that jewelry. Would it be alright if we added these things to the auction for the Adam's Homes?"

Ruth smiled and everyone could feel the warmth. "I believe that would be a very good thing to do."

It took another half of an hour to empty the store. "Fennel, look at the walls. What do you see?" Ruth asked.

"There aren't any marks like at The Rooster. Why is that?"

"Juleta and Joanna surrendered this store to The Master. They didn't need symbols of power other than what was in that display case. Turner, I hope you are realizing what a dangerous game you and Tessa were playing. I know you were not familiar with us before but now you are. In the future you will call to us first before entering places like this."

"I understand," he said. "Just out of curiosity did you protect us before we joined all of you?"

"There were times," Ruth said and smiled. "Now, I am going to show all of you a very different type of altar and Jasmine, you will want to draw this too."

Ruth led the group to the back of the store where the changing areas had been. A door opened and she led them down a steep staircase. They descended into an old stone cellar and now they saw the magic symbols written on the walls.

There was a huge ornate fountain in the middle of the cellar. Rich carpets covered the stone floor. Ornate furniture was set on top of the carpets. "Everything down here will be burned," said Ruth. "It is all surrendered to the Master. That fountain is where the girls were cleansed and this room is where they were prepared to become sacrifices."

"If this is all surrendered to him, should we do like Bella and Isadore did in Otto's house?" asked Seth.

Ruth smiled. "You are good students but his presence left when I walked into the store. I have disempowered everything in here."

"Ruth, this is the first time an Angel has walked us through an area and explained it," said Nana. "This has almost been like a class. Should we assume we will see all of these things again?"

"As I said, you are good students. We should go now." As the group walked up the stairs the water in the fountain began to boil.

# Chapter XLIV
## Cons

The following morning Erebus and the Sanuri decided to attend Sudfad's morning meeting before leaving for Ryed. The reason for this short postponement was the magnitude of letters that had arrived from Langer.

As people were gathering in the study, loud voices were heard in the hallway. Hannah almost ran into the room and said excitedly, "Sudfad, Edward is planning on returning to Langer when Matthew and the others leave. He is not well enough to do this. He needs at least two more weeks to heal and you know he will start getting into fights as soon as he returns."

Hannah was angry and as she spoke she noticed that some of the men in the room were smiling at her. "Javier, don't you dare grin, you are in worse shape than he is. Sometimes the children are easier to take care of than all of you." She looked frustrated and as if she was about to cry.

Edward and Kate walked into the room while Hannah was talking. "Hannah, I will make sure he takes it easy for two more weeks," said Kate. "If he doesn't I will tie him to the bed."

Raul and Simon were both grinning and Raul handed Simon some money. "What are you two up to?" demanded Hannah.

"You forget that we lived with you for a long time," said Raul. "Hannah..."

Hannah glanced at Kate then looked at Raul and shook her head from side to side. He did not say another word.

"Hannah if you are pregnant you don't have to hide it from us," said Edward. "The world can't stop because we lost our baby but we appreciate your concern. We plan to start working on a family soon." Hannah didn't say anything.

Kate walked up to Hannah and hugged her. "Edward is right."

"Well, how did you all know?" asked Hannah. "I'm not really showing yet."

"Because you are a lot more emotional when you are pregnant," Simon said. "Although you aren't nearly as bad as Natasha or Annabelle." Calen laughed loudly at this comment. "I can't remember the last time I saw you mad."

Gabriel walked up to Hannah and put his arm around her. "Yes, we have been blessed again." People now walked up to the couple to congratulate them.

A few minutes later the meeting started. "We have been receiving letters all night," Sudfad said. "And the Enrops said the Angels were hastening their journeys, so I am very glad you are all here this morning. Are we missing anyone?"

"Nina fell and cut her knee so Renya is taking care of her now," said Nyla.

"Why aren't you in school?" asked Sudfad.

"Because Raphael planned all of our class schedules so we can come to the meetings," Saran said proudly. "So somedays our classes will run later."

"Very good idea Raphael," said Sudfad. "Girls, why don't you come up here and hand out this last stack of letters, some are for you." Nyla and Saran jumped out of their seats and each took a large stack of envelopes.

"I realize that some of these letters may be personal but the quantity makes me believe that most of them are business; so we will start the meeting after the letters are read."

Mathas' morning meeting started in much the same manner as Sudfad's. Letters were handed out and read before the meeting began. To everyone's surprise Queen Rosa was the first to speak.

"Dominic, I need you and your team to meet with me after this meeting. I am planning a celebration for High Priest Othnial and there are many things that I want to ask you. But first, do you want to have the celebration before the other priests come to escort him to Malga or after they get here?"

542

"You don't have to give me an answer right this moment but I would like one by the end of today."

"Of course," said Dominic. "And thank you. We will help you as much as we can."

"Now, I have taken the liberty of buying a few gifts from us. But Mathas stopped Tessa from going into Langer to get the gift she wanted."

Noah quickly turned and gave Tessa a stern look, "I told you not to sneak out without telling me."

"Noah, it is alright," said Rosa. "Tessa told me what she wanted and gave me the money. The gift is actually from all of you. I have it now if you would like to see it."

"Yes we would," said Fennel and walked to the front of the room. Rosa handed him a velvet pouch. "I will say that I really like it," she said. Fennel took a very ornate golden pocket watch from the pouch. "Read the inscription," Rosa said with a warm smile.

Fennel read it then turned and faced the group. "It's a beautiful watch and it says from your sons and has all of our names. Thank you Tessa and Rosa. Fennel kissed Rosa on the cheek. He walked to the table where his team was sitting and handed Dominic the watch then he walked around the table and kissed Tessa on the cheek.

"Tessa, this is beautiful," said Dominic emotionally and handed the watch to Lawrence. Seth, Lawrence and Noah were all as touched by the gift as were Fennel and Dominic.

"This is beautiful," said Jasmine. "But you shouldn't have to pay for it, we can all chip in."

"Yes, I was just going to say that," said Dominic.

"I don't want any money," said Tessa. "But I will think of another way you can pay me back," she said with a big grin.

"We've fallen for that before," said Garvis and chuckled. "You're better off giving her the money now."

"How do you always have so much money?" asked Noah.

"Well, King Mathas gave me the spending money for the mission."

"Is that what you used for the watch?" Noah asked.

"No. I used my own money. Noah, I make a good living as a con artist."

"I realize that but we spent most of the night trying to figure out those dreams I had. It just dawned on me that you could be in danger from the cons. What exactly do you do?" Turner sat back in his chair and laughed.

"Well, I do a lot of different things but I don't think everyone here wants to hear about them."

"Oh, I think we do," said Stephan with a huge grin.

"I really don't think you do want to know this because it isn't legal. But I only do cons on rich assholes. Excuse me Rosa, I shouldn't have said that in front of you."

"Actually I am intrigued. I have never met a con artist before," said Rosa. "I would like to hear this too."

"Why don't you show the others the watch and I will explain," said Turner. He walked to the front of the room. "All of you have probably heard that Madeline and Javier saved Tessa when she was a little girl. She was an orphan and they brought her back to where we were staying."

"Well, we couldn't tell her we were spies so we told her that we were con artists. Running a con is very much like running a mission."

"Stephan that night that we were playing cards and all of you were talking about that mission you were on in Ryed. Well, what you told us about Natasha; you could have been talking about Tessa. Tessa give everyone back their things."

Tessa laughed as did others as she handed them the things she had taken off them. "You are really good," said Ralf. "That was in my pocket."

"There isn't a safe the girl can't open," Turner continued. "In fact, I am looking forward to meeting Natasha because she and Tessa are made of the same cloth. Tessa has a very detailed mind so we often send her into an area to look around. Say for example if all of you wouldn't have known Otto so well, we would have found a way to be invited into his home; perhaps for a celebration. Tessa would look the place over while we distracted people."

"What would she be looking for?" asked Risa.

"If you really watch people they tend to do things the same way," explained Tessa. "So say I was in Otto's house, one thing I would look at is the way the house is decorated. Especially rich people will decorate their rooms in the same manners. Then I come to a room and something is different. For example: Otto had a secret door behind his desk at the bank. I didn't see that but when there are doors like that or where the entire wall moves, they can't have stuff on the wall because it will block the movement."

"So say I am walking through a house and the walls in every room are covered with things then there is one bare wall just glaring at me. That's the place I start searching. That's how Garvis and Louis found that secret floor in The Rooster because it was the only place that was cleared of things."

"Other examples are like a picture that doesn't look right where it is. Chances are good it is covering a safe. But I could go on all day with examples."

"That is why Turner and I were so insistent on going into all those shops because we have been trained to find things. If you really pay attention to people you can tell where they are hiding things on themselves and sometimes even what they are hiding."

"What Tessa has just found out is that a lot of the things or information that we had her get was for our roles as spies," said Bart. "But, she is very smart and studies many things like artwork. She does this in case she needs to carry on a conversation or we need to know what is the real deal and what is fake."

"So I do steal things," Tessa said. "And I am dating a priest, who would have imagined." The people roared with laughter.

Jasmine stood up. "The mission in Ryed was my first and it was horrible for everyone. Part of the reason is the culture there. No one trusts each other and everyone sells each other out. Even Gabriel and Natasha got conned. People we thought were good weren't and people we thought were bad weren't. It was very confusing."

"Natasha is a great pick pocket and she taught Rachel. Sometimes the things they stole were our only real clues. I don't know that much about cons but ask Stephan and Thaos, Natasha was one of the most valuable people we had. Tessa, I hope you stay on our team but whether you do or not I want you to teach me how to do those things. And some of the rest of you should learn too," Jasmine said as she looked at the people in the meeting.

Thaos stood up. "If Stephan and I have said it once, we've said it a dozen times that we wish we had Natasha working with us in Langer. Well now we do. I too, hope you stay and work with us Tessa. But I think Noah is on to something."

"The Angels told us that your group has bounties on them because they are so good at what they do and they have seen and heard things without realizing the significance. So I have a few questions. Can Madeline do the same things?"

"Yes and so can Javier," said Tessa. "We were what you call the front men in the operations."

"Gideon don't get mad because I am not calling Ashley a thief but she has skills and she is really bright too," Thaos continued. "All three of those women spent a great deal of time in Port Friada and I will bet in many instances they were at the same celebrations and things. I think they may have heard or seen something that is putting them in danger."

"Ashley and Madeline did know each other," said Gideon. "And I am not offended; that woman amazes me every day."

546

"Ashley and I know each other from Port Friada but not well. But I did go to her shop and see her in places," said Tessa. "We never worked a con that she was involved with."

"Tessa, I don't know if you know this," said Gideon. "But Ashley developed this underground system to help women and children escape from abusive men. She told me that most of these men were rich and powerful which is why she had to go to such elaborate means to protect them. I first wondered about that but she said there is a lot of money in that city. And it is also a haven to dark lords."

"She and Deborah helped Moses' wife to escape which is why he was attacking her home and shop, which is what Noah kept seeing in his visions. We are all so absorbed with this thing with Otto that we assumed Noah's dreams were related to that. I don't think so anymore."

"Can I say something?" asked Olin as he stood up. "Tessa and Noah talked to us for a long time yesterday while we tried to figure out those dreams. Since I have been around all of you, I have heard you mention some of the most notorious dark lords."

"But take it from me, the Insidiae, as a group, is all about power and money. Where there is money there is also the Insidiae. There are a lot more members there than any of you may realize. And not everyone wants to be noticed."

"I don't belong to that organization but I ran with some of the same crowds. There were a lot of people who were pissed at Dieter for making such a spectacle of himself. He had a huge compound surrounded by an army. There are a lot of people who are members of the Insidiae who appear to live ordinary lives. And with all the money in Langer, I will bet you have more members here than you think too."

"And after hearing what all of you have just said, I agree that something probably happened in Port Friada. Turner, can I ask who you used to spy for?"

"I don't think you are ready for that," Turner said. "And I am not saying that to be mean. I am saying that to protect you."

"Ryan do you know?" Olin asked.

"A little, not very much."

"I know that all of you don't really trust me and Elexas yet; and that is to be expected. But yesterday King Mathas made us the people who are sorting the information and trying to figure out threats. At least tell Ryan or we may miss something really important."

"The boy has a point," said Claudius.

Turner stood up again. "Besides Elexas and Olin how many in this room don't know about us?" Hands were raised. "If I tell you I can guarantee you won't believe me and secondly it will put you in danger. So decide if you want to hear this. Mathas, I don't think I should use up your meeting time to explain this."

"Actually, this might be the best time," said Sorren. "The Angels keep telling us that our enemies are uniting and it does seem like we find a lot of connections to things."

"If Turner does tell you, I promise you that you won't believe him," said Claudius. "But many of us in this room can verify that he is telling the truth."

"Tell your story," said Mathas. "Actually, I would like to hear it from your point of view."

"Bart, Garvis, Louis get up here," said Turner who was walking to the front of the room. "You too, Tally and Drake, you can talk about the mission you were on."

Tessa stood up and faced the room. "This is a great story," she said excitedly. "Turner told me when I first got here."

When Otto's son Jack was running for his life from the citizens of Langer, he kept screaming for the Master to help him. Then he disappeared from the eyes of those who would have hung him. But Jack did not get far. The Master was in no mood to help anyone.

He grabbed Jack and pulled him into the earth and left him there. Jack was buried alive but the ground above him showed no sign of disturbance.

Jack screamed hysterically but the people who had been chasing him could not hear him. The Master heard Jack's screams and laughed. Two days Jack screamed in the darkness of his cell. He could breathe but he could not move. He was filled with terror and during the moments when he was lucid he was making promises to the Master.

Jack was pushed out of his tomb as if the ground was spitting him out. He gasped for air, cried and laughed. So elated was he that he did not look at his surroundings. Jack thought at first that he had been returned to the same location that he was taken from but as he looked around nothing was familiar.

The Master did not directly speak to his minions. Instead he showed them visions of what he wanted. Since he owned their souls, their minds were easily manipulated. Jack expected to see a grand vision but he did not.

He knew the Master was not forgiving so Jack surmised that the Master was pleased with the promises he had made. But Jack had made so many as he pleaded for his life that he couldn't even remember what he said and now terror filled him again.

All of these thoughts and fears raced through Jack's mind in the first seconds after his release. Then suddenly he remembered what happened before his imprisonment. He remembered tying Olin to the altar and raising the sacrificial knife. He remembered calling out to the Master and in that same instant Olin yelled something but what was it? He called a name. He called 'Adam' and everything exploded.

Jack suddenly looked at his right arm as he remembered the excruciating pain as holy energy ran through him. Only Jack did not fully realize what had happened. He had no idea of who Adam was or why Olin would scream that name. Jack's arm no longer hurt because it was no longer his arm.

He stared with both horror and amazement at his forearm and hand which looked like they belonged to a beast. He quickly tore off his shirt. His arm above the elbow appeared the same. Jack had always been a muscular man and his upper arm was uninjured. But his forearm and hand were considerably larger than they used to be. They were covered with hair, long dark hair.

His fingers and hand moved normally. Jack bent down and picked up a handful of small stones. He picked them up one at a time to test the dexterity of his new fingers. Then he tightly closed his fist around the stones; when he opened his hand it was filled with sand. Jack smiled then laughed.

# Chapter XLV
## Letters and Gifts

The people in Mathas' meeting sat spellbound for hours as they listened to Turner and the five other men talk about the Kingdom of Inferus. Rosa rarely sat in on the meetings but once Turner started to speak she couldn't leave. What she was hearing was beyond her imagination.

When the men were done talking Claudius spoke. "Now, while you have those images in your mind of a distant world. A couple of months ago the Angels sent some of the team members here to save Javier because Andrac had put a bounty on his head and Hector's men were collecting it. So how do those two communicate?"

"And the Angels told us that Andrac and Gilder entered the Gefrey Games that Samael is sponsoring. Those are the types of things that Sorren was talking about when he said we are finding connections between things."

"Before Michael was killed, the group in Salar were reviewing lots of ancient manuscripts from various places and they found similar symbols on them. Even symbols from Inferus. Now honestly, I don't know if they have gone back to that since they returned home but it seems to some of us that the more we uncover the more questions we have."

"The next time we go to Salar do you think Sudfad would let me or us look at some of those things too?" asked Ryan. "This is fascinating."

"We have told him about the great job you have done here," said Sorren. "They would probably be happy for the help."

"How are you going to concentrate on the work?" Thaos asked Ryan and grinned.

"Nyla is taking a lot of classes, I could work while she is in school." Ryan said.

"I am teasing you but also asking a serious question," said Thaos. "Because none of us can believe the work you have done here. It's like you saw all the things we didn't and put them together. Of course this is just my opinion but when you are caught up here why don't we take you to Salar to help them? You don't have to wait until the next wedding. And Olin and Elexas, I am talking about you too."

"Artis and Ralph could run the shop," Ryan said as he looked at Claudius.

"Ryan, I know you are not a child but there have been several attacks on our people traveling back and forth between these cities. You can go but you aren't going in a carriage. We will send troops along."

"Claudius; Turner, Tessa and I are going to Salar to visit Madeline and Javier; they could come with us," said Noah.

"That would make me feel better," said Claudius. "And Ryan, I didn't mean to embarrass you. Olin and Elexas when I am talking about attacks, they are not minor raids. None of you should be traveling alone or in a small group."

"We understand," said Ryan. "If you are going to send troops with us then maybe Margarit and Amy can come along. Everyone keeps asking about them. Nyla said that Hannah is working on some special surprise with the head of the Cisero medical school for Margarit."

"Really?" said Rosa excitedly. "Mathas, I am writing to Hannah today. If that is true, I may go with them."

Mathas laughed and said, "Our daughter wants to become a physician and we are very happy about that."

"Noah, when are you planning on leaving?" asked Sorren.

"We don't have a date picked. We were waiting for this mission to end."

"Let's talk about this. Maybe more of us will go with you as long as we have a caravan going," said Sorren.

"Turner all of your men should go and meet the people in Salar," said Stephan. "And Renya throws the best celebrations you have ever been to. Maybe we'll come with you. And you know that Thaos will. His eight year old daughter has a seven year old boyfriend there and Thaos doesn't trust them." Everyone in the room broke out laughing.

"Would they let me come?" asked Olin.

"Son, as long as you don't sell your soul there won't be a problem," Sorren said. "I could tell you stories. In fact, if we all go, I will have time to."

"If all of you go you know Bella is going to want to go too," said Claudius. "I guess the real question is how long will it take Ryan, Olin and Elexas to go through all of that material? Or maybe they don't have to."

"Our team is helping them," said Dominic. "Because we all feel like we can't let it wait. And it might be good to see if what they have is connected at all to what we've been working on."

"Rosa, write to Sudfad and Renya too and tell them what we are discussing here," Mathas said and smiled at how excited Rosa was.

Sudfad's meeting ran into the afternoon because of all the information they received in the letters. The midday meal was served two hours later than usual and everyone in the meeting stayed at the castle for the meal which was served in the Great Hall.

The tables were set up as one long table. Raul laughed as he watched Nyla, Nina, Saran and Olivia all giggling and whispering. "What are all of you up to?" he asked and the girls laughed.

"Nyla doesn't know if she should show you something," said Saran. "It's not bad but she doesn't know if you will get mad."

Nyla took an envelope out of her pocket and handed it to Renya who was sitting across from her. "That's from Ryan. You can read it."

"The top of page two," Nina said and giggled.

"I am not sure if I am surprised by this," Renya said. "But we don't want any of you to feel like you can't tell us things."

"You aren't surprised?" asked Nyla. "I was." Then she looked at the rest of her family. "Uncle Mathas made Ryan the Minster of Information and is paying him a lot of money. And Ryan said he is saving it in case we want to get married some day. But he says I am too young now and we aren't ready."

Simon and Raul grinned when they saw the look on Sudfad's face. "Ryan is a very nice young man," said Renya. "And I think he is being smart and sensible."

"But I agree that you are too young and neither of you are ready for a step like that," said Sudfad. "But when you both are older if you still want to marry we will give our blessing."

"Really?" asked Nyla with surprise. "You know that I really like Ryan but with everything that has been going on I haven't thought about marriage."

"Good," said Sudfad with a grin and the others laughed.

"I'm marrying Milo," Nina announced and laughed.

"You can't!" snapped Petra. "Whoever heard of marrying a monkey?"

Nina was clearly enjoying making Petra mad. "I can too. Raul and Simon said we can be whatever we want and we can marry who we want," she said and laughed again.

"We did say that," said Simon and grinned. "Although we didn't have Milo in mind at the time."

Petra glared at Nina who was smiling at him. "Petra, I believe your little sister likes to tease you," Javier said. "I have it on good authority that she thinks Zack is really cute."

"Javier, you weren't supposed to tell!" Nina scolded then laughed loudly.

"I can see it is going to be very different raising daughters," Sudfad said to Renya and they both laughed.

Annabelle and Vitomas looked at each other then Annabelle said. "Every Tuesday morning Vitomas and I take a small boca into the city. We spend the morning shopping and talking with people then we go to the Dragon's Inn and Myla, the owner's wife, makes us special deserts. Madeline and Corsa we were wondering if you want to go with us tomorrow?"

"It is our time to escape from the children for a few hours," Vitomas said and laughed. "Sometimes we've been tempted to get a hotel room and just sleep."

"We would love to," said Madeline. "Thank you for asking us."

"They go by themselves," Raul said to Javier. "Every time we send soldiers with them the girls give them the slip."

"We enjoy talking to the people," Vitomas said. "And it's really different when the soldiers are around."

"Everyone knows they go into Salar on Tuesdays so people are waiting for them with gifts and flowers," Simon said to Javier. "And yes there have been problems too."

Corsa looked at Javier. "I'm not going to tell you that you shouldn't go. It is an excellent idea and I hope you all have fun. But you are all very intelligent women and understand the dangers of having behavior that is so predictable."

"Thank you Javier," said Raul then laughed when Vitomas scowled at him.

The Sanuri stood up at the table. "Erebus and I will be leaving within the hour if anyone has things they want to send along."

"I am sure that our families do," said Joshua. "I will go home and check. I already gave you everything that I was sending. And I wrote to Duncan about Risha. Erebus, he was fascinated with her story and might have some questions for you."

"I only wish I would have gotten to know her better," Erebus said. "I wasn't with her long and the situation was crazy but on some level I felt a bond with her."

"Others have said that too," said Joshua. "Her story was amazing but I wonder if there is more to it."

"What do you mean?" asked the Sanuri.

"She was only in our lives for a matter of hours but she touched so many of us. And Sanuri, you have to understand that when we first saw her we didn't know if she was a demon because of the way she looked. She turned out to be a hero."

Late that night two flocks of Enrops flew into Salar, one carried letters to Sudfad's castle and the other to Gabriel's home. Once again the birds said that the Angels were assisting their flights. The letters they carried told of the demise of Otto and Joanna and of Noah's visions.

Dagon and Koby created an area similar to what Raul and Simon had in the castle. It was a large room and the walls were becoming filled with charts and maps. They didn't create this room because they had doubts about the work of the Princes. They created it because every member of the team felt they were missing things that were right before their eyes. And they wanted to spend more time with the material.

It was another two days before Sudfad and Gabriel received the letters that told of Isabella's diaries. Sudfad never kept anything from Renya but these letters he did not want to show her.

Isabella had kept diaries her entire life. She constantly complained of her boredom and her jealousies of her brother and sisters until she fell in love with Josef. Two entire diaries we filled with her constant ramblings about her love for this young officer and the excitement about planning a royal wedding. The very week after the wedding Isabella's writings took such a drastic turn that the people reading them thought there must be a missing book.

Sorren, Angus, Claudius, Fahron and Mathas read the diaries first then gave them to the team members to study. Everyone was confused by the contrast in the writings. Some of the people wondered if two different people had written them.

Within a month after her wedding Isabella went to her first orgy that was set up by Otto. She was thrilled by breaking the rules of society as she wrote many times. The challenge of having two separate lives was exhilarating for her. She wrote in great detail about her affairs and interactions with others. And in these details the ruling members of the kingdom learned how she had betrayed her family and people over and over.

She talked about introducing Juleta to Otto. Even though Juleta was little more than a child, Isabella expressed her fear of the girl although she did not go into detail about why. Otto had asked for the introduction and Isabella was initially against it because she didn't want Juleta sharing in her new and exciting life. After this introduction there were pages of jealous tirades written in a diary. Isabella was insanely jealous over the attention that Otto was giving Juleta; attention she did not understand.

Mathas cried as he read about the depravities that his sister found thrilling. When the men were done reading about the life of the Princess not one of them believed she was a naïve fool. She was cold and calculating and very much aware of her betrayal and treason.

Although the diaries hurt and humiliated Mathas he gave them to the team members to read with the hopes that they could be more impartial and logical in their analysis. But many of the members were just as angered and disturbed by the writings. It was Olin and Elexas who found discrepancies. But they did not start to read the diaries for almost a week after the first letters were sent to Sudfad and Gabriel.

Sudfad showed the letters to Renya in private before sharing them with the rest of the family and team members. Renya wept bitterly as she read the many pages that described sides of her sister's personality that Renya never realized existed.

557

But by time she finished the letters, Renya was so repulsed and horrified that she emotionally released any bond that she had with Isabella. Renya now looked upon her baby sister as the monster others saw her to be.

Severe storms and two Huta attacks delayed the army of Patronus Priests who were escorting Padre Thomas and Padre Bartholomew in their journey to Langer.

This group expected an attack by the demon King of Stordt so they changed their route and traveled straight north from Nora. Which took them into the Rodite Forest and into the territory of the Giant Gants. The priests crossed into the Kingdom of Wetpr and stopped at the monastery at Philiste to have their wounded cared for.

It was at the monastery that they met the people of Olivia's village. Padre Thomas and Padre Bartholomew had received letters from both the Sanuri and Sudfad about Olivia and were excited to meet these unique people. When they resumed their journey the two old priests carried letters and gifts for Olivia.

High Priest Bernard was leading the small army and continuously sent messages to both King Sudfad and King Mathas. It was decided that Bernard would go to the castle of Sudfad to replenish supplies and to replace some of his more severely wounded men with priests from the Cicero Headquarters.

Renya as usual had an extravagant celebration for the men their first night at the castle. All of the priests from the Cicero Headquarters were present as were all of the Elods, who had recently moved into their own community south of the castle.

Gabriel, Raphael and Sudfad met with High Priest Bernard and shared much of the information they had received about the Master and Otto.

Olivia was still walking on crutches when she entered the Great Hall of Sudfad's castle with Emeral, Maxwell and Joao. "They are looking for me. I can hear their thoughts," she said excitedly.

"Stay here and I will get them," Maxwell said and disappeared into the crowded room. A couple of minutes later he returned with Padre Thomas and Padre Bartholomew.

"So you are Olivia," Padre Thomas said. "We have heard a great deal about you. You probably already know that your people are safe and very happy to hear that you are alive. They sent these for you." As he spoke, Padre Bartholomew showed Olivia a set of saddlebags.

"We need to find a place to sit down so she can go through these," said Emeral. "Please join us." Moments later Joao walked up to the group and led them to an empty table.

"I am so excited," Olivia kept repeating then she looked at the two priests. "Emeral and Maxwell adopted me and Joao is my boyfriend. I am very happy here but I do miss my friends also. I am glad they are all safe."

"What a wonderful experience that was to meet them," said Padre Bartholomew. "What wonderful gifts all of you have."

Olivia laughed and cried as she read her letters then passed them around the table for everyone to read. She saved the gifts for last. "My people are very poor so I expect that most of this is food," she said and opened a package that contained honey then another that contained cookies. She opened two packages that contained bread and cheese and another that contained candy.

She put all of these items in the middle of the table for everyone to try. "We raise bees and make a lot of things from the honey. That candy is made from honey you have to taste it," she said proudly. She pulled the last gift from the saddlebags. It was wrapped in a worn piece of material. "This has to be from our shaman," she gasped and unrolled a small scroll. "I have never seen this one before."

The scroll consisted of a small piece of leather that had drawings on it. She studied it for just a moment then turned white. "Oh my god, this is the location of the Originator. The shaman must have been afraid the demons would get it. But how do my people know about this? Maxwell take this and show the others. That has to be locked up."

Maxwell didn't say a word but grabbed the scroll and left the table. "Do you know about the Gefrey Games?" Emeral asked the priests.

"Yes," said Padre Thomas. "Sudfad and the Sanuri write to us every week."

"Armies of demons are looking for that information," Emeral said. "Thank The Great Ruler you got here safely."

"High Priest Bernard made a last minute change to our travel plans," said Padre Thomas. "On our original course we would not have gone near the monastery at Philiste. I can't believe that was an accident."

Maxwell quickly walked through the Great Hall and told people to meet him in Sudfad's study. Madeline was the first to enter the room where Sudfad, Gabriel and Raphael were meeting with High Priest Bernard.

"I am sorry to interrupt but this room will be filled soon," Madeline explained. "All I know is that one of the gifts that Olivia received from her people is really important. And Maxwell looked white as a sheet. I have never seen that man shaken by anything before."

Barely had Madeline finished speaking when all of the adults in Sudfad's family and the team members entered the study.

"Shut the door," Maxwell said to Jared who was the last to enter the room. It was obvious to all that Maxwell was not himself. "Miranda or any Angel please join us."

It was The Lion who appeared and his presence brought most of the people in the room to tears. "Thank you for coming," Maxwell said when he composed himself. "Is this what Olivia thinks it is?"

"Yes. That has been a secret of her people for years. And that is why their shaman told the villagers to move to the forest. He alone knew of the existence of that scroll. He prayed for guidance and gave it to the priests to bring here."

"It's a map to the location of the Originator," Maxwell burst out and handed the scroll to Sudfad.

"You will lock that away in the Holy Vault," said The Lion. "Do not destroy it for there will be a time when you will have need of it."

Sudfad's hands were shaking as he handed the small scroll to Gabriel. "How did her people get this?" asked Sudfad.

"By a divine accident," said The Lion. "That was originally drawn by one of the dark lords who attended the celebration where Emeric and Banaka would have turned this world over to that abomination. That is the same celebration where Adam and Ruth prevented Karzman from sacrificing Michael and the other villagers."

"When Adam took on the guise of Michael and fought that army of demons, the dark lords, witches and warlocks ran for their lives. This scroll was dropped and found by one of Olivia's villagers who gave it to their shaman. The shaman did not understand fully about the Originator but he could feel the presence of a great evil north of his lands."

"He prayed for guidance and kept the scroll hidden until it was time to turn it over to the priests. Ruth told you that Andrac is back on those lands because he could sense the power of Olivia's people. He also sensed this although he didn't understand what he was experiencing. The shaman heard Andrac's thoughts and told his people to move to the forest. You know the rest of the story."

"Do you want us to attack the Originator?" asked Simon.

"If you were to go there now it would be like a compass pointing the location out to the demons. That will go into the vault until we tell you it is time to bring it into the light."

# Chapter XLVI
## Discrepancies

"What time did you guys get here?" Ryan asked as he walked into the temporary office in Mathas' castle.

"We've been working all night," said Elexas. "Why are you here so early?"

"They are having that big celebration tonight for High Priest Othnial so Bella, Ingr and Nikki are helping. We've already been to the shop and set up the food. Bella wanted me to ask you if you two had clothes for tonight."

"You mean we are invited?" asked Olin.

"Sure you are. Bella said the Patronus priests are arriving late afternoon. We all have to be out front for some kind of ceremony. Then they all come into the castle and there is a, I forgot what she called it but there will be drinks and food in the Great Hall while everyone gets settled in their rooms. Then the big feast and celebration is after that. I brought my suit. You should dress up."

"I don't know if we have time to shop," said Olin. "And I haven't gone back to my room since you guys got me. I'm afraid to."

"Where is your room? Otto's house?"

"No, I have a room at the North Side Hotel."

"We can ask someone to take you there," said Ryan. "How about you Elexas?"

"Jasmine has been loaning me things. I should go shopping. But Ryan we have to talk about this first."

"It's too quiet," said Erebus. "I know we are being watched."

"I feel it too," said the Sanuri as he was fixing breakfast in the early morning hours. "I found it unusual that there were no border guards when we crossed into Stordt."

"And even though Sudfad has rights through this kingdom we usually have difficulty with the soldiers."

"Ruth told us that Sorphat was allowed to declare war on Stordt. I am wondering if he already won because we haven't seen any signs of battle."

"He sounds pretty shrewd. I wonder if he is watching to see where we go and what we do," said Erebus. "Maybe we should do something to draw him out in the open."

The Sanuri laughed and handed Erebus a plate of food. "And what are you thinking?"

"Actually, I was thinking we should pay a visit to the castle and ask him what he is up to. But then I remembered that you are probably one of the prizes in the Gefrey Games. Just so you know, I spent a lot of time in that castle. I know it like the back of my hand. I know all of the secret passageways."

"And you want to sneak in?"

"No, I am just telling you in case we ever need to get in there. I know the last king was a demon but he seemed to keep in the shadows. I would not expect that from Sorphat. If I was Sudfad, I would be really worried about having Sorphat rule the kingdom next to mine."

"Could it be worse than when Roch ruled this kingdom?"

"It certainly couldn't be better."

Ryan had left the office and now returned with Claudius, Thaos and Stephan.

"I just spoke with Mathas," said Claudius. "He wasn't going to have a meeting because of everything that is going on but he will have one now and you two will explain what you found. Then Stephan and Thaos will take Olin to his hotel and Nikki and Ingr will take Elexas shopping."

"I'm not going to run away," said Elexas.

"We aren't convinced that both of you aren't in danger," said Claudius. "We are doing this for your protection."

"Elexas, you know how much Nikki hates you," said Thaos. "She wouldn't be doing this unless she thought you were in serious danger."

"Why does Nikki hate you?" asked Olin.

"Because she tried to steal Thaos away," Ryan said.

"Elexas, I am going to give you a little fatherly advice," said Claudius. "Right now you are earning respect and a good salary. You have the chance to be part of something big and you are making friends. I don't know why you act the way you do sometimes but is it worth throwing all of this away to feed your ego?"

Elexas turned bright red. "Claudius, you are right. And I've never told anyone this before but sometimes I don't know why I act the way I do. That's why I don't know if I should go tonight."

"Go as my date," said Olin. "And we can keep each other in line."

"What are you afraid you'll do?" Stephan asked Olin.

"He drinks too much," Elexas said.

"So Ryan how does that make you feel that you are working with a drunk and a whore?" asked Olin.

"I think that's what you guys used to be," said Ryan. "Elexas hasn't done anything wrong since Dominic yelled at her and I've seen you have maybe two drinks ever. And that was the night that you found out the Master owned your soul. You've both been just fine so stop worrying so much."

Sudfad started his morning meeting early. "About an hour ago, I received an interesting letter. You know that some of the people from Langer are planning to come for a visit, among them Ryan, Elexas and Olin."

"Apparently these three are impressing everyone with the work they are doing. Dominic's team is helping them go through all of the papers and things that were taken during this last mission. And Turner told them all about Inferus."

"Ryan wants to make copies of all of their charts and maps and whatever else and bring them to us. He would like to put them up in an office and then start to go through some of our things. He believes it would be more efficient if the teams there and here were on the same page and I tend to agree."

"But, to do that right we should provide them with what we have. Which means we need to make copies. Do I have any volunteers?"

"Sudfad, we are all willing to help," said Bekka. "But we still have so much to go through. A lot of what we have needs to be translated."

Raphael stood up. "We have gone through all of Shanksaw's papers and Deckor's. They have been translated but even with that there is much we don't understand because they use symbols instead of names in the ledgers. The healers finished as much as they could with Juleta's books and feel there is one, possibly two more books that we need to get."

"The priests at Cicero are helping with the scrolls which so far have provided us with more of a historical prospective."

"The things that Madeline and Javier stole from Hector appear to be two spell books. Some papers listing supplies and a map that we don't know what it is."

"It will take us a long time to get through all of the scrolls in Erebus' library. So I would suggest that we make copies of what we have and our charts and maps. And organize the other materials by subject. I would like someone to make a list of all of the symbols we have discovered, so we can show Ryan and the others. We just have so much paperwork that it is easy to get lost in it. Olin was able to explain some of the symbols, I am hoping that he can help with more."

"Olin told Dominic's team that the Insidiae have a committee that approves symbols," said Thor. "They have to have a book on that. That's what we need to get our hands on. Because you can't tell me that every member memorizes that crap."

"Any idea of what something like that would look like?" asked Archetenus. "Because Erebus has several huge chests in his house that belonged to Meekos and Sophie. His library is so big he didn't even know he had that stuff. We've just been looking for information about the Second Sons but why don't some of you come with us after this meeting and look through the chests. They are all papers, books and scrolls."

"Vivian, Thor and I will come with you," said Joshua. "We are probably the most familiar with some of those symbols."

It was obvious to everyone in Mathas' study that Olin and Elexas were nervous about giving a presentation.

"Dominic asked Elexas and me to look at Isabella's diaries to see if there was anything all of you may have missed. We didn't find that but both Elexas and I have been to the same places, with the same people and we found things that didn't make sense."

"All of you mentioned about the change in the tones of the diaries after she got married and we saw that too. Sorry Elexas, I don't mean to insult you but even Elexas said how can you go from being so in love with someone to cold and heartless in three weeks."

"She doesn't write about anything of significance during those three weeks, which was strange because look at the detail before that. She would take a paragraph to describe her lunch. If you ask me that is what you have to look into because I am telling all of you right now that something happened during those weeks."

"What are you thinking?" asked Fahron.

"First, I would like to know a little more about her husband. Everyone says he was a great guy and didn't have a clue but there is something suspicious about all of that."

"For one, I am wondering if someone sold her soul. But there are a lot of things we could guess about."

"Another discrepancy is how she talks about Juleta. In her first diaries she not only sounds afraid but states she is scared of Juleta. Then later they are like quarreling sisters, which is what Elexas and I saw a lot."

"King Mathas, please don't get mad at me but I think Juleta either sold her soul or someone else did when she was really young. First, the things that Isabella writes about are not normal for a kid to do. Then Dominic said she tried to drown her baby sister. All of you suspect that she was a dark lord at a young age. Do you have any idea what it takes to become a dark lord? It's like getting a college degree. Uncle Otto got so frustrated with me because I wouldn't work at it that he gave me some basic powers because all of the men in the family had to be dark lords."

"The ceremony that he did lasted two entire days and I was probably the weakest dark lord in the world. Remember, when you said that he thought Tessa had to be a more powerful dark lord than me and all of you acted like that was something. Let me tell you it wouldn't take much."

"Claudius isn't even a dark lord and he beat the hell out of Uncle Otto. A kid could probably have beaten me in a fair fight."

"The reason I am going into all of this is, I don't know how to say it nicely. Mathas you are King, Sorren you are a chief, and the rest of you are ruling members. When anyone hears those titles they think power and all of you are powerful men."

"But I will bet that all of you have met men with important titles that really aren't powerful. When any of you hear the word dark lord you all give it power but there are incredible dark lords like the ones you have been fighting and mediocre and weak dark lords. I have never heard of a kid that could instill the kind of fear that Juleta did."

"And to become that powerful she needed a teacher and manuscripts. How did she get those things here? King Mathas, I may be out of line but you and Queen Rosa really seem like good parents."

"I can't imagined you ignored Juleta for the length of time it would take her to gain those powers. There is something very strange with both of those women."

"Then the part where Uncle Otto asked Isabella to bring Juleta to his party. Ok, he was a sex fiend but everyone that Elexas and I saw at those parties were adults or teenagers. Juleta was a kid. And the way that Isabella wrote that entry it made it sound like Otto was asking for an audience with someone important. Uncle Otto put on this show so the citizens thought he was a nice guy but he was and egotistical bastard. He bowed to the Master and no one else. Honestly none of this makes sense. And why would Isabella falsify diaries?"

"And there are other things too," said Elexas with embarrassment. "Olin's father and Otto were on the outs for a while so he didn't start going to the parties until a couple of years ago. I had been going to them for a long time. Remember I told you I was looking for a rich husband and as far as I was concerned the other women were my competition. I was going there with a purpose so I didn't get drunk or do drugs. I remember being at some of the same parties that Isabella talks about."

"Isabella and Juleta were already regulars at these parties when I started going and I was shocked to find out princesses were there. My first party Joanna brought me and I had to have sex with Otto which took about thirty minutes. Then I was allowed to go to the party. It was held at that old lodge that Deckor used to own."

"That building had a lot of rooms and they were all filled with people. I walked around and stared at everything. I had never seen clothing that nice or expensive jewels before. I opened the door to a room and saw Deckor on top of some woman. He turned and looked at me and I apologized and started to close the door. He told me to come in and join them. When he says that the woman looks around him to see me and it is Isabella. Ok, I am far from perfect but that was my first party and I was shocked."

"I closed the door and got about two steps when Juleta almost knocked me over. She burst into the room and started yelling. She told Isabella to get out and she did. Isabella was running down the hallway naked. I just got the hell out of there. Isabella was so much older than Juleta that I couldn't believe she would be ordered around like that. I mean they were in the middle of having sex."

"Isabella wrote about that party. She never mentioned Juleta interrupting her and Deckor; instead she wrote about the wonderful sexual encounter they had. I've screwed Deckor and let me tell you he wasn't that great. So why lie about that in a diary? I found probably two dozen similar things. The only reason I can see for lying is if she expected someone to read her diaries but then she locked them away in banks."

"Elexas are you sure about the dates?" asked Sorren.

"I don't know if I can say anything that will make all of you think worse of me than you already do. You act like it is a shock that I can work on charts. Sorren send someone to my home. Under the floorboard on the right side of my bed is my grand plan for finding a husband."

"I took notes and made charts and I have dates on things. Compare them to the dates in Isabella's diaries."

"Both of you are right that none of this makes sense," said Thaos. "But what are you thinking about all of this?"

"That's just it. We don't know. But it wasn't Uncle Otto who turned Juleta into whatever she was because believe me he wore stuff like that like they were medals. He would have been bragging forever. Honestly, I am beginning to wonder what Juleta was. I mean little kids don't just sell their souls. And just say someone sold her soul. Well, Uncle Otto sold Joanna's, Jack's and mine and let me tell you they weren't like that as kids. They had to work really hard to gain their powers. Juleta was something different."

"And all of this stuff with Isabella. Both Elexas and I wondered if she intended on planting those diaries for someone to read. But what would be the purpose? I mean she still confessed to a lot of bad stuff."

Tessa stood up. "First, I want to say that you both did a really good job. The other night Jasmine and Seth were telling me how Corsa was trying to get into Isabella's mind and she realized that both Isabella and Juleta acted like jerks to keep everyone away from them. They sound like really shrewd women. What if some of the things that we recovered were meant for us to find? Everyone got so pissed off and emotional reading those diaries that Dominic gave them to Elexas and Olin because they weren't emotionally attached to her."

"I can't prove what I am trying to say but I think that any new information we find on either of those women we look at first as if it was planted information. It's like they are dropping bread crumbs and we are following them."

"I agree with Tessa," said Turner. "Boy, if you didn't tell me that Angels were involved with the destruction of both of them, I would wonder if they were the real people."

"All of this crap is just getting more confusing," said Stephan and pounded his fist on the table.

"I have to admit that some of the things that both Olin and Elexas have said scare me," said Mathas. "All of our children are loving and wonderful people but Juleta seemed like an angry adult from the moment she could walk."

"I never thought to ask the Sanuri to look into her mind. Rosa and I just accepted that as her personality. Now, I am questioning so much. Is it possible that someone replaced our child or that she was really a demon in disguise? As crazy as that sounds it would answer the other questions."

"Elexas and Olin would you chart everything you said?" asked Claudius. "But it doesn't have to get done today. It's getting late and you both need clothes for later."

"Elexas, you aren't under arrest anymore," said Sorren. "You can go back to the village."

"I don't really want to, at least not yet. I am sure they all know I was arrested. But you should have someone get those papers from my house."

"Who are you talking to?" asked Noah as he walked into the room he shared with Tessa later that afternoon.

She laughed. "I was talking to Adam."

"Is he here?"

"No, well, I mean I know he can hear me. Now that I know he exists I just talk to him a lot. I suppose if he gets sick of it he can just tell me to shut up."

"So what do you say?"

"Well, just now I apologized for yelling at him all of the time."

"I'm surprised he doesn't shoot lightning bolts at you," Noah said and laughed.

"Where were you?"

"I started moving our things into the house and I wanted to find this. I'll understand if you don't want to wear it. I know you like fancy things but this is the only thing I have that was my mother's."

Tessa walked up to Noah as he took a necklace out of his pocket and handed it to her. It was a small golden locket on a golden chain. "Noah, this is beautiful. Is this your baby hair inside?"

"I think so, I don't really know. Teivel's soldiers burned our village after they killed everyone. This was the only thing I found in the ashes."

"Put it on me," Tessa said and held up her hair. "I love it and I am going to wear it always." She turned around and kissed him. You know I've been thinking. I don't think either of us are ready to get married but that doesn't mean we can't get engaged."

"No it doesn't," Noah said with a huge grin. "Tomorrow we go shopping for a ring."

Both Nikki and Ingr were surprised at the humbler side of Elexas they were seeing. The three women had spoken little as they rode into Langer. But once they started shopping the conversation became less strained.

"We should have just started here first," Nikki said as they entered Ashley's shop. "But I kind of wanted to see what the competition was selling."

"What do you mean?" asked Elexas.

"Besides that Ashley is our friend, Gladys is the manager here. Is this the first time you have been in the shop?" asked Ingr.

"Yes, it looked too expensive," Elexas said.

"Well, you have got to see this first," Ingr said and led Elexas to the room that held all of the Nordes arts and crafts. Elexas was shocked not only by the beautiful displays but by how many members of her tribe worked in the store. "Not only does Ashley sell our things here but she sent samples to two stores in Port Friada and they sell our work too. The tribe is making a lot of money now."

"This is amazing," Elexas said as she walked around the show room. "But everything looks so much better in here."

"I know," said Ingr. "I thought the same thing."

Nikki walked into the showroom with Ashley. "Ashley this is Elexas and Elexas this is Gideon's fiancé Ashley."

"I have heard a great deal about you," said Ashley.

"And probably none of it good," Elexas said. "This is a beautiful room you created."

"Actually Gideon and Claudius have been amazed at the great work you are doing with Ryan. Nikki told me you need a dress for tonight. I have a few things in mind. Why don't you come with me?"

"Honestly, I have never seen such beautiful things," Elexas said as Ashley showed her several dresses.

"Ashley designs a lot of the things here," Nikki said. "Elexas try on that dark green dress."

"I like that too," said Ashley. "But feel free to try all of these on."

"This is exciting," Elexas said as she took the dresses into the changing room.

"Stand back," Stephan said to Olin as they approached the door to his hotel room. The door was slightly ajar. "Miranda are there any living curses in there?" asked Stephan.

"No but it is wise to ask," said Miranda's voice.

Thaos kicked the door open with such force that it would slam into anyone who might be hiding behind it. "I wonder if they found what they were looking for," he said as the three men looked at the room.

All of Olin's belongings were thrown on the floor. The furniture was overturned and the mattress was lying half on the bedframe. Olin walked to the middle of the room and picked up a small suitcase. He took a pouch out of it and looked inside.

"Well, this doesn't make any sense. Look; my money is still here."

"Olin what else did you have in here?" asked Thaos as he walked around the room.

"My clothes."

"No books or papers?" asked Stephan.

"No. Really I have no idea why someone would break in here and not take my money."

"Well, let's pick your crap up and maybe you can tell if something is missing?" Thaos said.

"Ashley, why are you doing this?" asked Elexas.

"Because you have been so much help to us. Thaos said that the three of you sit up almost every night and work. We appreciate it."

"Thank you so much. I have never had such beautiful things," Elexas said and excitedly carried her gifts that Ashley had given to her.

"This doesn't make any sense," Olin said again. "All of my stuff is here."

"Olin do you have any idea why someone would do this?" asked Thaos. "Did Otto think you had something? To scare you? There has to be a reason."

"The only thing I can think of is after you guys grabbed me that Otto might have wanted his men to get anything that linked me to him."

"I don't know. I just don't think that is it," said Stephan. "Can't explain it."

# Chapter XLVII
## Monsters

High Priest Othnial was a humble man who was accustomed to a simple life. He was not prepared for the lavish ceremonies that Queen Rosa had organized to honor him and the priests who would escort him to Malga.

When the small army of Patronus priests entered the City of Langer they were met by an honor guard that led them to the castle. People stood on the streets and threw flowers as if this was a returning army of heroes.

Once these priests arrived at the castle there were a variety of acts and musicians in the courtyard. The priests were led to their rooms then they went to the Great Hall for a small reception. Only the team members and ruling families were in attendance. Two hours later a great multitude of guests started to arrive for the feast that was to be held in Othnial's honor.

High Priest Othnial, High Priest Bernard, Padre Thomas and Padre Bartholomew sat at the head table with the ruling families. After the feast Othnial was given his gifts. He was given gifts of honor which touched him greatly but it was the gift of love that brought him to tears. Dominic, Fennel, Noah, Lawrence and Seth gave him the golden watch. The old priest cried when he read the inscription as did many in attendance. These five young men hugged their mentor tightly as they did not know if they would see him again.

After Othnial returned to his seat, gifts were given to Bernard, Thomas and Bartholomew which surprised all of these men greatly.

Mathas, Sorren, Claudius and Fahron took the stage. Mathas read the names and honors as the ruling members presented the team members and others with medals and pouches of gold for their work on various missions. The audience applauded loudly after each person received recognition for their work.

King Mathas called out Drake and Tally's names twice before the men stood up from their table and walked to the front of the room. Many in the audience laughed at the shocked looks on the faces of the men.

Every person who received honors faced the King and ruling members then was told to turn around and face the audience. As with the other recipients, the audience started to applaud but stopped because of the looks on the faces of Drake and Tally. They were tough looking monsters of men. They carried themselves like professional fighters. The room became quiet as everyone stared at these men who looked as if they were about to cry.

"Tally and me are real honored and shocked to get these," Drake said haltingly. "But truth be told we don't deserve this none. We swore to protect Prince Michael and we didn't do our jobs. We will never rest until we find the bastards that had him killed."

"This is the first time that we have danced together," Tessa said. "You dance well."

Noah laughed. "The women on the Ryed mission taught us all. Teivel forbid music and dancing in the kingdom for longer than I can remember. Shortly after we joined up with Gabriel's team Micha and Bianca got married. It was spontaneous."

"I think Sorren pushed it so we could have a celebration because no one believed they would live through that mission. Gabriel's wife sent instruments along with some of the people and, now mind you a lot of the people didn't even know each other. But these strangers got together and played wonderful music. We didn't even know what to think; we were almost crying. Then all of these female Nordes warriors pulled us on the dance floor." Noah laughed.

"Those poor women, their feet must have been covered with bruises by the end of the night but they taught every one of us to dance. Now we dance whenever we can."

"When I hear any of you talk about Ryed I am just amazed that you came out of it the sane, wonderful guys that you are."

"I'm not so sure about sane or wonderful," he said and chuckled.

"You are. You are all heroes. Can I ask a personal question?"

"You can always ask me anything."

"I know how Seth and Jasmine met and Lawrence and Deborah. Those meetings were almost by accident. All of you are such handsome and good men, why didn't you, Fennel and Dominic date anyone?"

"I don't know if I have a good answer for you. It was really hard for us to get used to this new world. And we lost most of our friends, actually they were like our brothers in that last battle. Somehow it didn't seem right to be happy." Tessa hugged Noah tightly.

"You know one of the things that has surprised all of us," Noah said with a grin. "Is how quickly you became part of our group. Turner's guys all think of you as their little sister and Dominic and the others do now too."

"That is nice to hear because they all seem like my brothers. Maybe it's because we all grew up without families. The teams became our families. Being with all of you just seems really natural."

"You know after we talked about marriage the other day I have really been thinking about it. I mean I have been trying to picture what it would be like for us working on teams and being on missions together. I was trying to figure out if it could work."

"Sounds like you decided it would."

"Yes, but I really thought about it Noah. I was trying to imagine how we would handle that life and children. I even talked to Jasmine about it and she's had the same thoughts but then she told me about Gabriel's household. I mean Madeline had told me some but Jasmine and I really talked because she and Seth had the same concerns."

"While I think that is smart, I am surprised by it."

"Why? I am very detailed when I work on missions. I try to prepare for everything."

"Well, what did you come up with?"

Tessa gave Noah a coy smile, "I think that we should name our first son Asher." He stopped dancing and stared at her. "Oh no, you don't like that. I didn't mean to upset you," she said.

Noah took her into his arms and kissed her passionately, when the embrace was over they stood on the dance floor and smiled at each other for a few moments. "I don't know why you would think that would upset me. It made me very happy. I think we should tell Dominic and Fennel." Noah took Tessa's hand and led her off the dance floor.

"You look really nice," Olin said as he and Elexas danced. "You know you can talk to other guys. You don't have to stay with me."

"I guess I feel self-conscious. I didn't start off well with this group."

Olin laughed loudly. "Well, you didn't start off being a dark lord."

Elexas laughed too. "Yes, but you really proved yourself to them, I haven't yet. They trust you more than me."

"I don't know about that. When we went to my hotel room someone had busted everything up. They probably would have busted me up too if I would have been there. They didn't take my money so I don't know what they were after."

"You sound worried."

"I am. But I was going to say, I know this sounds so crazy. I hardly know these people but this is the only time in my life that I have ever felt safe. Or appreciated for that matter."

"I know, that is why I am afraid I am going to screw up. I wasn't kidding when I said sometimes I don't even know why I do things. That's why I got so scared when you didn't know Otto had sold your soul. I mean I do really mean things to people and I can't always tell you why."

"Elexas, I need you to be really straight with me and I won't tell anyone what you say."

"Alright, is something wrong?"

"Do you really want to stay and work with these people?"

"Yes, don't you?"

"I do but I don't think they realize how much danger they are in, which means that we are in danger too."

"So what are you thinking? Olin, you aren't thinking about running away are you?"

"No. I was thinking that you and me should let Gideon put us in a trance. He might make us remember things that could help. I mean, I was always drunk at those parties, I don't remember half of them and you were distracted a lot," Olin said with a grin.

"I am going to have to think about that because...well, I don't have anything to hide but that could be really embarrassing. If I agree, I don't want to do it in front of everyone."

"I really think we need to do this and I can't even tell you why. Come on."

Olin took Elexas' hand and led her to the head table. "Claudius, Gideon could we talk to you for a moment?" asked Olin.

"Bella this is Elexas and Olin and this is my beautiful wife Bella," Claudius said proudly.

"It is very nice to meet you," said Olin. "And I am sorry to interrupt your evening. We just wanted to ask a question."

Gideon started to make introductions when Ashley said, "I know Elexas; I haven't meet Olin yet but I have heard so much about you."

"Thank you, I think," Olin said and everyone grinned.

"Can I speak freely in front of your wives?"

"Our wives are warriors," Claudius said. "Is something wrong?"

"I don't know. Elexas and I were talking and we don't know if you realize how much danger all of you are in. And we want to help so we were thinking that Gideon should put us into a trance and help us remember things."

"I drink a lot, or at least I used to and I was drunk at most of those parties. And Elexas was busy a lot. But, she doesn't want to do it in front of everyone. What do you think?"

"I think it is a great idea," said Gideon. "Do you feel like you want to do it now?"

"No, we don't want to spoil the celebration. Maybe tomorrow if that is alright. I don't care if you do me in front of the group. But Elexas just wants a few people there; she's embarrassed."

"We understand," said Claudius. "Mathas isn't having a meeting in the morning because of all the guests. Perhaps we can get together then. Elexas do you mind if I am in the room?"

"No, you wouldn't be shocked at anything I might say. I really don't want to have to talk about sex in front of all of these priests. Tessa and Jasmine can be there too."

"What do you want help remembering?" asked Bella.

"Uncle Otto's parties were huge like this one. So there was a lot going on in every room. I heard how Gideon asked Noah to describe what he was seeing. And I think that Elexas and I probably saw and heard things that we don't really remember. It's worth a try."

"I agree," said Claudius. "And I think it is brave of both of you to do this."

"Claudius, tomorrow night bring these two kids home for dinner," Bella said.

"When she uses that tone of voice there is no arguing with her," Claudius said and winked.

"Should we dress up?" asked Elexas.

"No, it is family," Bella said.

After Olin and Elexas walked away Bella said, "Nikki won't like it but I will talk with her. I can't believe he was a dark lord. Those two look more lost then those pups the boys brought home."

The festivities ended at midnight since the priests planned to resume their journey after breakfast. Noah and Tessa barely got into their room before he started to make love to her. There was always a powerful electricity between them but this night it was greatly intensified.

All of the guests at the celebration spent the night at the castle. Gideon and Claudius met with Elexas and Olin in Mathas' study well before breakfast. "We don't have to start now," said Gideon but normally we have at least one person taking notes and since this is personal information we wanted to ask you who you wanted in here?"

"Jasmine said she would come," said Elexas. "Tessa and Noah are shopping for rings today. I really don't want Ryan here, he would never look at me the same again."

"I don't care," said Olin. "But is something else going on?"

"This is going to take some time," said Gideon. "Because we will be reviewing a lot of different events. I mean, I will be giving you breaks but we may need more than one person to take notes. And sometimes it helps to have people in the room who have some knowledge of the subject or person because they can bring up different questions."

"Besides Elexas, no one here has been to Uncle Otto's special parties. I don't know if some of you have been to his normal celebrations. Really, if you want to have the entire teams there when you do me that is fine. I really don't care," said Olin.

"Elexas does and I think we can all understand that. But now that you say that, it might take a long time. Can you put us both in trances and someone else ask one of us questions?"

"Actually, we were thinking about that too," said Claudius. "And one reason is that we can compare notes from the two interviews to help us ask questions. I am suggesting this so you don't have to go through this a second time. Elexas would you be embarrassed to have Sorren work with you?"

"Yes. Why don't you have Turner and his group work with me but I still want Jasmine there. I have to tell you I am kind of nervous."

"Elexas, I am not going to ask you questions about her sex life," said Gideon. "The only time that is relevant is if the person you were with said something or you overheard something. We are looking for information regarding the missions. We don't want to intrude in your personal affairs. Honestly, we think it is really brave for you and Olin to do this."

"Well, if that is true then I don't really care who is in there," she said with a look of relief.

"Once the two of you sit in on more of these you will understand why it helps to have other team members there," explained Gideon. "It was like when Dominic gave you the diaries to read. The two of you understood things that the rest of us didn't. We will never do these sessions to embarrass anyone."

"If you both don't care who is in here," said Claudius. "Gideon and I thought we would rearrange this room. As you can see there are drapes that can be pulled to divide the room. We will have people on both sides taking note and acting as messengers. What I mean by that is, telling us things to ask questions about or say getting you a glass of water."

Olin looked at Elexas who nodded to him. "That is fine. Did you want to start now?"

"We did want to get an early start," said Claudius. "We were thinking about working for a couple of hours then stopping so everyone can eat breakfast."

"Alright," said Olin.

"We asked the cooks to make coffee and biscuits," said Gideon. "You can go into the kitchen and grab something while we set up the room and get the others."

"Let's eat breakfast in the city," said Noah as they were getting dressed.

"Something is different about you; I can't put my finger on it," Tessa said.

"Ok, don't get mad but I thought of you as like a wild horse. I kept waiting for you to bolt and run away. And last night I realized that you have thought all of this over and you are ready for a committed relationship. I feel different. Kind of at ease."

"A wild horse huh?" she said with a smile and kissed him.

Dominic, Fennel, Seth and Lawrence wanted to spend their last few hours with Othnial so they did not attend the interviews although other members of their team did. Turner and his men attended as did Thaos and Stephan. Everyone in that family decided it would not be a good idea for Nikki and Ingr to attend since Elexas was already so nervous.

"I am going just to give that girl some moral support," said Ashley. "I wouldn't want to be in her shoes. I was scared to death when Gideon did that to me."

"I was thinking of going too," said Bella.

Both Thaos and Stephan said "No," in unison. And Bella looked shocked.

"Mother, the reason we are saying that is because you are the mother figure and you are already taking them under your wing," said Stephan with a big grin. "We aren't stupid, we can hear the wheels turning in your head. And I for one think that is a good thing but I think that if they see you there, they both will be too embarrassed to respond to you."

"I agree," said Ryan. "I don't want to go because I am their friend and I don't want them to feel embarrassed around me."

"Stephan is right," said Thaos. "When Claudius gave Elexas some fatherly advice I expected her to explode but she almost, I don't want to say seemed grateful but you get the idea."

"We were ready to string them both up because of the crimes they committed. They are adults and I am not excusing anything they have done. But you've got to wonder. Did they act like that because they are really bad or because they are so broken?"

"I understand what you are saying," Bella said. "And Nikki and Ingr, I know you hate her and you have reason but Thaos makes a good point too. Now might be the time to tell you that I invited them for dinner tonight." Nikki glared at Bella but didn't speak. "Nikki, you don't have to talk to her. But I would like a chance to size them up myself. And does it hurt anyone to be included in a family for one night?"

"Bella, you don't have to worry about us," said Ingr. "Actually, I would like to size them up too. I haven't really spoken to Olin and Elexas was acting really different yesterday."

"She has been called on the carpet a lot since we arrested her," said Stephan. "And let me tell you Turner and Dominic don't mince any words. But they are also good at giving praise when it is deserved. It's kind of like training the pups."

"And when exactly have you been involved with that?" asked Ingr sarcastically.

"I knew as soon as they brought those dogs home they would never help to train them," said Bella. "Thank goodness the kids are so good with animals." Both Stephan and Thaos laughed loudly.

Angus had planned to attend the interviews until he heard that Noah and Tessa were going shopping for rings. He believed that Tessa might still be a target and he knew the two were blinded by their emotions. Angus and some of his team members decided to go to Langer and watch over the couple.

Noah and Tessa met with Othnial before breakfast. He was overjoyed to learn of their engagement and blessed them both.

"You better make it back from this mission so you can christen our children," Noah said. "Tessa wants to name the first boy Asher."

A look of great sadness overtook Othnial's face and he hugged both Tessa and Noah. "You never got the chance to meet Asher," Othnial said to Tessa. "Ryed is a kingdom of great darkness and Asher was like a brilliant star in the sky. He touched everyone who met him and once you did, you could never forget him. This world would be a different place if there were more people like him."

"Then I hope our son takes after him," Tessa said with tears in her eyes.

When Elexas and Olin returned to the study they were each carrying a large tray filled with cups and sweet rolls. A cook walked behind them carrying two large pots of coffee. Risa and Mallory jumped out of their seats and cleared off a table.

"I didn't realize how many were here," said the cook. "I will be right back with more."

Ashley walked up to Elexas and Olin and said. "Gideon had to do this to me too and I was so nervous."

"Why?" asked Elexas as she and Olin were both surprised by Ashley's words.

"I met all of these people when they were on a mission in Port Friada and without going into everything the Angels told them I had things in my mind that I couldn't remember about the Insidiae. When I was little my father sold me to a dark lord; he was a monster and after I escaped I couldn't remember a lot."

"How did you get away from him?" asked Elexas.

"I killed him in his sleep." Both Elexas and Olin stared at Ashley because she seemed like such a gentle and refined woman to them.

Gideon waited until the cook had brought all of the refreshments into the room. He divided the people into two groups. Both Ashley and Jasmine sat near Elexas. Olin saw this and asked, "Can Ryan sit with me?"

"I'll get him," said Stephan and quickly left the room.

After Stephan returned with Ryan, Gideon first put Elexas into a trance then Olin. Gideon planned to interview Olin and Turner, Elexas. Bart and Mallory started out as the note takers.

Because they would be asking about events that occurred over years, Gideon asked the Angels to help them. Some people were surprised when Adam appeared in the room.

With Adam's guidance the interviews took on momentum. People periodically changed places with the note takers and Thaos and Stephan took over for Gideon and Turner to give them a break. Because Adam was helping them, Claudius decided that he would not stop the interviews for breakfast. He sent several people to the kitchen to get more food and coffee for the room. He didn't want the kitchen staff walking in on the questioning.

After the army of Patronus priests left the castle, Sorren and others entered Mathas' study to observe the interviews.

"I'll bet that some of the team members are watching us," Tessa said as she and Noah walked in the business district hand in hand.

"I would do the same."

"Look, Cyril is across the street. Let's go talk to him. Wait we should bring him something to eat." The couple turned around and walked into a small bakery. They came out with a huge pouch filled with baked goods, a pot of coffee and a cup.

Cyril grinned as they walked up to him. "Congratulations," he said.

"Thank you," said Noah. "She couldn't make up her mind what to get you so you have a variety."

"I will spread the kindness. Don't ask me any questions. Today is your day to enjoy. But your friends are here watching over you. You will find Angus in a tavern a block down. He is sitting in the window. Why don't you send him to me."

"Are you sure?" asked Tessa.

"Child, how many times in your life are you going to be shopping for wedding rings? Enjoy the moment."

Angus laughed when Noah and Tessa walked into the tavern and up to his table. "Cyril wants to talk to you," Noah said. "He didn't tell us what it was about."

"Where is he?"

"A block down on this side of the street," Tessa said.

Angus paid his bill and walked down the street to Cyril's corner. No matter how Angus dressed he could not disguise his bearing as a soldier and man of authority. He searched the faces of the people he passed. When he walked up to Cyril, he took money from his pocket and placed it in Cyril's overturned hat.

"Thank you kind sir," Cyril said. "Would you care for a baked good? Our friends have been most generous."

"No thank you," Angus said and paused. He looked around the streets. "I suddenly feel like I am being watched. Are you being watched?"

"Yes but it's not the eyes of heaven that you feel. All of you have been watched since you entered the city. The Master escaped Adam's attack but great damage was done. He is enraged and took his anger out on Jack, who he buried alive for days. Jack is back in this world but not as the same man."

"The most obvious difference is his right arm. Holy energy burned his arm as he was about to kill Olin. The Master could not be near anything touched by holiness and replaced the arm with that of a demon's. You will need to know this because that is how you will identify him. His appearance is greatly altered. He no longer has blonde hair and blue eyes. His eyes now are as black as his hair and soul."

"Jack made many promises to the Master to be released from his grave. The Master gave him considerably more power to fulfill these promises. But he is just one monster. Although Samael has postponed his Gefrey Games he made it known what he considered valuable entrance prizes. The Seven Sons and the Sanuri were among them but he was explicit that he wanted them alive."

"Many were angered when Michael was killed and a great deal of them monsters. No one has yet figured out who was behind the attacks but that individual basically defied Samael's orders. Now that being too is being hunted because Samael wants his head. The eyes you feel belong to many who have been sent to Langer to find the trail."

"Also, Otto had an extensive empire which Ryan and his friends are uncovering. An empire many would kill for. While the eyes you feel are enemies, for once they are not after you. Jack will try to keep his father's empire but he will need an army to do so."

   "Can you tell me who was behind the attacks?"

   "No, for several reasons. But, the man child you rescued is the only one who has realized the clues."

   "Are you talking about Olin?"

   "Yes, Bart showed him some symbols that he saw in tunnels under this city, and while Olin does not know who they belonged to he figured out what they were. Ask to see them when you return to the castle."

"Although Samael is in the midst of the worse battles of his life he is still paying attention to this world and he is not pleased with any of the humans who are vying for his favor."

"Which is why they are trying to please him by hunting down whoever was behind Michael's murder."

"Hector is in the city but has no intention of doing more than spying on all of you. He has changed the calling card of his men here. They no longer wear the black hats with red feathers. They all wear blue bandanas around their necks."

"Hector is very powerful but he has disappointed Samael and is putting his energies into getting back into the demon's graces. Samael killed Cabal without ever learning that the boy knew the existence of the Originator's cave. Until recently Karzman was the only other human with that knowledge. Karzman has not only disappointed Samael but greatly angered Sorphat so they are allowing him to slowly starve to death."

"When Erebus and Risha threw the powers of the World of Illusions back upon the demons many lost their masks. Karzman once again is a feeble old man but he has no village left to take care of him."

"Sorphat conquered Stordt with little bloodshed. He simply took Zieman's place and increased the pay of the humans who now work for him. He is enjoying this new existence. He is an old demon who does not make rash moves. Unless ordered by Samael, Sorphat will study many things before his takes action. Some may forget that he is a demon for a while because he wears the mask of a man. He never had the power before to change his appearance."

"Visterle is making a public mockery of Hecate's execution. He is having a stadium built on Sidus for the show. He has already sent out the invitations and his world will host a week of celebrations. Besides revenge he is trying to prove a point. Hecate is accused of turning against the Old Ones; that in any world is punishable by death."

"Toni lives, if that is what you can call her existence. Sorphat saved her from Raven's knife. What little spark of humanity existed in that woman has now been consumed by her demon lover. She can no longer think for herself. She is completely commanded by him."

"I am telling you this because Kate plans to hunt her. Tell Kate that Sorphat is not interested in Toni's former jealousies and has other things to contend with?"

"Are you saying that she is no longer a threat to them or her people?"

"They should be aware that she is alive. He took her mind. She doesn't remember any of those people. You know what to do with the information that I have given to you. But also send a letter to the Sanuri, he is traveling through Stordt and has questions."

"I too have some. You said until recently Karzman was the only one who knew the location of the cave of the Originator. Who else does?"

"King Mathas will soon receive a letter. The shaman who ministers to Olivia's people has been protecting an ancient map for years. That map was given to Olivia and is now locked in the Holy Vault. What are your other questions?"

"With everyone trying to please Samael are we kind of safe now?"

"No, the game board is temporarily changing and I want you to understand what you see."

# Chapter XLVIII
## Deal with the Devil

Angus found Noah and Tessa in a jewelry store. "Look!" Tessa said happily and showed Angus the ring on her hand. "Isn't it beautiful?"

"Yes it is," Angus said and smiled.

"She wanted a ruby," Noah said. "We haven't found wedding rings yet." Then he walked closer to Angus. "So, is Tessa in danger?"

"Actually he gave me a status report on all of our enemies. There is a lot of information. I wrote it down after he told me. When you are done, I'll ride back with you and tell you all about it."

With Adam's help the interviews went considerably more quickly than expected but they still lasted for seven hours. As soon as they were completed Adam left the room and everyone went to the Great Hall for a late lunch.

"Well, did you learn anything good?" asked Olin as he and Elexas walked to the Great Hall with Claudius and Gideon.

"We aren't sure yet," said Gideon. "But we got a lot of information. If you two are up to it why don't you read the notes after lunch? I prayed for help with the questions since we were covering years of information and the Angel Adam appeared and told us specific things to ask. He didn't explain any of it and he left as soon as we were done."

"Well, can you give us an idea of what we said?" asked Elexas nervously.

"First, neither of you said anything that you have to be embarrassed about," said Gideon. "But you both heard and saw things that you locked in your minds because they seemed suspicious to you."

"And some of it was things like the way a person acted, or hearing a partial conversation. We did get a list of people you saw at those parties. I think it was like pieces of a puzzle that we have to put together."

"Adam would not have been there if the information wasn't important," said Claudius.

"Where did Ryan go?" asked Olin.

"I'll have to check the office," said Claudius. "You said something and I can't even remember what it was but he got up and almost ran out of the room."

"Olin was talking about hearing Otto yelling that someone stole some things from his office," said Gideon. "And Elexas you had a lot of observations about Juleta and Isabella. We have a lot of notes and need to make copies of them. We aren't going to get all of this done today."

Claudius and Gideon told Olin and Elexas to sit at the table with their families. Moments later Turner walked up to them. "Garvis and I were making timelines of what you two said. We have to make better copies but we are going to hang them on the walls."

"Why?" asked Elexas.

"Because we all just got done reading Isabella's diaries and some of the stuff you two said, wasn't the same information. I am really wondering if those books were written to throw people off from something else."

Angus ended up shopping with Noah and Tessa. Their happiness was contagious. Shopping was never something Angus enjoyed but he was having fun with his friends. "So far, I have counted ten of Hector's men on the street," Angus whispered as they walked into another store. Cyril said they are wearing those blue bandanas now instead of the black hats."

"Why are they here?" asked Noah.

"That is part of what I have to tell you. Samael put the word out of what he wanted for entrance fees. And The Seven Sons and the Sanuri are on the list but he wants everyone alive. Apparently no one really knows who was behind the attacks on our people and Samael is taking it as a personal insult that someone had Michael killed. So all the guys who are trying to kiss up to him are looking for the same guys that we are."

"Well, isn't that a kicker," said Tessa and laughed.

"I'll tell you the rest when we are riding back. But I am starving. Want some lunch?" They walked into the dining room of the Excelsor Hotel and got a table near the window.

As they were looking at menus a man asked, "Mind if I join you?"

"Well, look who the cat dragged in," Tessa said sarcastically. "Please, have a seat. Should I make introductions?"

"I believe we all know each other," Hector said. "And I am just here to talk and have a drink. So you can put those weapons away." A waiter walked up to the table. "Put everything on my bill," said Hector. "We will start with a bottle of your finest wine."

"What are we celebrating?" asked Noah.

"You destroyed one of my rivals," Hector said. "Plus I have been watching all of you for a long time and you intrigue me. Not just you, your entire group. I couldn't figure out how you outsmart everyone then when Samael was having one of his temper tantrums he told me you have Angels on your side. I never knew they really existed."

"I am going to be honest Hector," Tessa said. "I didn't know they existed until a few weeks ago either. They are incredible. You should consider changing sides. Both Hector and Tessa laughed. "I am willing to bet you sat down here because you want to exchange information. So, what have you got that the Angels can't give to us?"

"Noah, your future wife is very smart but actually it is more than that. Noah don't look at me like that. I am telling the truth that I mean you no harm. I actually want to make a deal of sorts."

"We are listening," said Angus.

"I would like you to set up a meeting with me and Mathas or Claudius. They have no reason to trust me but as I said, I want to make a deal of sorts."

"You know we aren't going to let you near the King," said Angus. "Give us an idea of what you want."

"Oh my god," gasped Tessa. "I know why he is here. Adam just told me." Tessa stopped talking and just stared out the window.

"You might say that Adam is her guardian Angel," Noah said. Hector became pale at these words.

Tessa whispered to Hector, "You're in danger here and I am not taking about us or the Angels."

"I am always in danger. What did your Angel say?"

"Angus, Adam said for you to get Claudius, Thaos and Stephan and bring them here. Don't bring anyone else. He said we should meet in Hector's room which is 413. He wants us to help his parents."

Hector had been staring at Tessa while she spoke but Noah and Angus stared at him. As Hector listened to her he lost his cocky smile. It was clear to those at the table that Hector no longer felt that he had the upper hand.

"Did she get anything wrong?" asked Angus.

Hector did not answer Angus' question but leaned forward and said in a low voice, "I know you have no reason to believe me or to help me. But I will make it worth your effort. I did not come here to fight with any of you. Tessa's Angel must be able to tell if I am lying. I will explain more when we meet."

Angus slowly stood up. "If I come back here and you've hurt these two, I will tear you apart."

594

"Angus, I don't really understand what Adam showed me, but we are somehow keeping Hector safe right now," Tessa said then she looked at Hector. "I know you have all that dark lord crap but do you have weapons on you?"

"Of course. I have a dozen men outside of this restaurant..."

"Angus leave now," Tessa said. "Hector, we need to get to your room. Don't even think about arguing." The seriousness in Tessa's voice made the men do as she directed. Noah was searching the dining room with his eyes. Angus walked out of the door and mounted his horse. Several Ruala warriors were on rooftops watching him and followed him out of the city.

The three people at the table waited for several minutes then they stood up and walked up the front staircase. They didn't speak until they entered Hector's room, which they quickly searched.

"Why the hell is Adam protecting him?" asked Noah angrily. "The guy is practically a demon."

"I don't know but he wants us to talk to him," Tessa said. Then she walked up to Hector challengingly. "This better be good because you just wrecked the best day of my life buster." Both Hector and Noah laughed.

"I'll send you a wedding gift," Hector said kiddingly.

"Yeah, it will probably be demon snakes," Tessa said as she peeked out of one of the windows. "Hector can I ask you a personal question?"

"It has been a long time since someone has."

"We know your real identity and what you were like and what your life was like. Was it worth giving all that up to become a monster? We've heard that even the other dark lords and demons hate you. They hate you more than they did Juleta and everyone hated her. I grew up an orphan. I would have loved to have the life that you threw away."

"I can't argue with a thing you said and that is why I am here. But I am surprised at how much you know."

"Why? We are good at our jobs," Tessa said. "Noah, why are you being so quiet?"

"Hector, we counted at least ten of your men earlier," said Noah. "I don't see a one now. Mind telling us who is after you?"

"My men aren't wearing the black hats anymore."

"We know," said Noah. "Look for yourself if you don't believe me."

"Tessa did Adam tell you who is out there?" asked Noah.

"No, he just said that we needed to protect him until he talked to Claudius."

"Well, if we are going to die protecting some bastard, I would at least like to know who we are fighting. For all we know they could be good people," Noah said as he watched Hector peeking out the windows. "Do you see them?"

"No," Hector said angrily. "And I don't have people protecting me so don't worry about getting hurt."

"Angels don't lie," Tessa said. "We're doing this because Adam wants us to not because we care about what happens to you."

"Hector do you still have your powers?" asked Noah. "Because I heard you were the most powerful dark lord around. Why the hell are we protecting you?"

"Yes," growled Hector.

"Don't the hell growl at me," said Noah. "Are you sure?"

Tessa walked closer to Hector and said, "His eyes are black, so he must. Oh, I just realized what you guys are thinking."

"Yeah, that means whatever is coming for him must be stronger than him," Noah said. "Great!"

"Hector, Noah is studying to become a priest. Didn't you do that once?"

"Why are you asking me these questions?"

"Hey buster, you wrecked our day; now we are stuck up here with you. You can at least answer the questions." Hector didn't say anything.

"You know Thaos and Stephan are going to kill you for going after their wives and kids," said Noah.

"That wasn't me. That was all Juleta." Noah scowled at him. "Hey, I've done plenty against you guys. But that wasn't part of it."

"You had that damn kidnapping ring in Ganz," said Noah. "So don't try to sound like a good guy."

"I'm not. You're right but Juleta is the one who put all those bounties on them. Hell, she put bounties on me. All the men and demons she screwed and it was Stephan and Thaos she couldn't get over."

"Oh come on, she loved you," said Tessa. "She gave you everything."

"Let's just say that she had a different view of love then most people."

"When you are a demon or whatever can you even love someone?" asked Tessa.

"Stop with the questions will ya!" Noah laughed at Hector's frustration.

"Hector, Claudius and the others are coming. You seem off your game and I will bet it's because we aren't scared of you," said Noah. "If this is some kind of a trap for those men, you better hope your demons can save you."

Hector looked out of the windows and saw Ruala warriors on all of the roofs. "If there is a trap it isn't of my making," he said.

There was a pounding on the door. "It's Claudius." Tessa opened the door and Thaos ran inside and punched Hector who fell to the ground. He made no attempt to fight back. Noah quickly stepped between the men.

"Adam wants us to protect him until all of you talk; so save it," Noah said.

"Start talking," Claudius said angrily.

Hector stood up and rubbed his bleeding jaw. "We will probably kill each other someday but today I want a truce. Tessa, tell them what your Angel said so they believe what I am going to say."

"Angus told us," growled Claudius. "Just spit it out."

"That Angel was right I have a lot of enemies but that comes with the territory. I suspect you know I was transforming into a demon because Juleta screwed me up when she changed my looks. I paid a fortune for that transformation and Samael stopped it because he wanted me to bring him the Sanuri. That happened when all of you were in Ganz."

"I sent that army of demons to the monastery at Leven. Samael pulled me and Clev into his hell world to beat us up. He has this thing. It looks like a window and he can see into other worlds. He showed us an Angel and a handful of men fighting that army. You know my father wanted me to be a priest. Well, I never bought into any of that stuff. But I saw that Angel. And that is why I am here."

"Claudius, none of you ever change which is why you are so easy to set up." Claudius grabbed Stephan as he was about to strike Hector. "Stephan, I am actually saying that as a compliment. Just let me finish and then we can fight."

"You save everyone regardless of what kind of people they are. Hell, Tessa and Noah hate me and they are risking their lives to protect me. I know about Sarah and I have hidden my parents. They had no idea I was even alive. I faked my death so they wouldn't be harmed because of my choices. Well, Samael is all pissed off at me because I haven't brought him the Sanuri so he's blocking my transformation. I don't know what I will end up like because of what Juleta did but it is already affecting me."

"I have tried to protect Sarah's identity and my parents but if I become weak I can't. I am asking you to do that and I will make it worth your effort. Claudius, you know my parents; they are horrified by all of this. Mother can't stop crying. They just want to go home. But I have so many enemies now. I want you to ask your Angel to protect them."

"Are you shitting me!" yelled Stephan.

"Stephan be quiet," said Claudius. "I am listening."

"First, I got Juleta pregnant before I became a dark lord and before I really knew how crazy she was. Sarah won't suffer any of the side effects of my transformation."

"Is that even possible?" asked Claudius.

"Yes. Juleta had no idea what she was doing. She promised to create an army that was better and stronger than the Second Sons. She wanted to be a big shot in the Insidiae. Everyone she transformed is dead or dying. And I know because I have the ledger with their names and I am having them watched. I believe you have her other ledgers. But that is another matter. Two of the people had children and both of the children died with terrible deformities."

"Aren't there any cures?" asked Tessa.

"Trust me if there were I would be taking them. Why do you think that Noah asked me if I had my powers? He can sense a weakness and so can all of my enemies. I am not a good person, I am not your friend but I am telling you the truth and asking for a favor."

"And what do we get in exchange?" asked Stephan. "And it better not be money."

"First, you guys will save them just because they need saving. Remember, I grew up with all of you. But if you do this I will owe you greatly and I pay my debts. One of you reach into my right jacket pocket. This is not a trick."

Thaos removed a large bundle of papers. "Ask your Angel if I am telling you the truth. I have never put bounties on any of you that was all Juleta and actually I was amused at how you got around them. Thaos, those are all the bounties that existed on all of you. As you will read most aren't valid anymore because you beat them. Now look on page three and ask your Angel if I am lying."

"You paid off the bounties?" asked Thaos.

"I am asking you to protect my family so I am protecting yours. It is a fair deal but I am not done. In case, you haven't realized I have to be desperate to come to you. Keep reading. I have also pulled the bounties on your team members but Andrac still has some out on those Elods. Which brings us to the next thing."

"Some time ago Madeline and Javier stole some items that Juleta wanted me to get from Dieter. I know that those two work with you so I assume you have them. Hold the map up to a mirror and you will be able to read it. That is the northern tip of Marba."

"Dieter made a lot of money selling Second Sons to demons and he wanted to expand his business. Juleta was doing the transformations for the same reasons. She was always trying to get in good with the Master. When she learned that he was involved with the original plot of the Second Sons she got involved with Dieter. That map is where they are doing the experiments and those spell books were needed there."

"The experiments continue so I assume they found other spells. I am telling you this for a couple of reasons. I know you have saved some of the Second Sons but Andrac has learned about these experiments and he knows what Javier and Madeline stole from me. That is why he has bounties on them. He wants them alive so he can get those items. I don't know how much you know about Andrac but he makes Dieter look like one of you."

"Those are my friends you are talking about," said Tessa. "How do we get those bounties removed?"

"Well, you know he will kill them once he gets the things. So it is in their best interest to stay one step ahead of him. He's got a war going with that other sorcerer Gilder maybe you can play them off each other."

"If I pay you can you help?" Tessa asked.

"I know of Inferus but I don't have the ability to travel there. I see him when he wants to see me. And besides we are rivals now with the Gefrey Games. All of you probably think that I am crazy but that monster really is insane. He sent some men here to find out how Javier got away from us. They said he was cursed by an Angel and that he looks like the monster he is. They also told us that a bunch of their people disappeared the same day the Angel attacked Andrac. It's gotten to the point where I am just amused by what all of you are capable of doing."

"So are you still going after the Sanuri?" asked Noah.

"He saved my daughter. Do you really think I am that inept? Juleta put her in that monastery but she had that drunk Lazo help her. Well, he turns around and sells me the information. Sarah was better off with those priests. But then I find out that I am not the only one who Lazo sold that information to."

"I would send ravens to watch the area around the monastery. I don't know how he knew but the very same day that the Sanuri leaves with Sarah an army was riding to that monastery. You see dark lords can see through the eyes of ravens. I was about ready to send my men to intercept them when I saw them stop in their tracks. They must have seen something I didn't because after a couple of minutes they turned and rode out of there as fast as they could."

"Stephan, you are staring at me like you don't believe me. Well, I never thought you would settle down. You tell me that when you first held your babies that something didn't change in you. Sarah didn't ask to be born to monsters. She has a chance now and tell Mathas and Rosa that I am grateful and I will never interfere except to try and protect her. But I have one more thing for you and this may be why your Angel said I was in danger."

"I assume you know that Samael is or will be holding Gefrey Games as a means for others to bring him what he wants. Among lists of things, he wants The Seven Sons and the Sanuri. Samael wants to torture these men himself and he went crazy when Prince Michael was killed."

"For a long time the demon Ahriman wondered if Michael was one of The Seven Sons. He did not kill him because he believed that if he was; Michael would lead him to the other six. Ahriman owned the souls of the Grand Masters Emeric and Banaka."

"Emeric was the father of Karzman who was Michael's stepfather. And Teivel was another relative and the head lieutenant for those Grand Masters."

"Michael and his brothers destroyed Teivel and that same day Emeric and Banaka were destroyed. Ahriman was destroyed by an Angel but Samael had been a long time enemy and many believe he weakened Ahriman. Who would want to avenge all of these deaths? Not Karzman that fool is basically a pile of mush. See you are the good guys, you don't think about revenge. But on my side of the fence that is the first thing you think about."

"There were thirteen Grand Masters in Opots. There are eleven now and of those eleven only one was a friend of Emeric and Banaka. His name is Radnor. He hired the assassins who work for the Warlord Zourlock in Salszar. He avenged the deaths of his friends as well as taking a prize from Samael. I gave that information to Samael yesterday in hopes that he would stop blocking my transformation but the bastard is still playing hardball although I am not on his shit list anymore."

"You don't have the power to go after a Grand Master but Samael does. Your friend's death will be avenged. So do we have a deal?"

"Where can we find them?" asked Claudius.

"They are in Zorta. The last page of those papers will give you the information. I will owe you."

"Is there a way we can get in touch with you if something goes wrong?" asked Claudius.

"If there is a problem in Zorta leave a message with the bartender at the Lazy J Tavern. If it is here leave a message with the bartender at the Lady's Slipper."

"You're already having side effects aren't you?" asked Thaos. "That's why you had me grab those papers. Is your hand all messed up like that Zane concoction?"

"I would rather not answer that."

"So Hector, is the only reason you want to become a demon is so you won't have those problems? Because you are a good looking guy, why do you want to become a smelly demon?" asked Tessa.

Hector looked at Noah and shook his head. "She never stops does she?"

"Nope," Noah said with a grin.

"Ok don't tell me you ass," Tessa said. "But you know the Angels could heal you but you'd have to give up that darkness."

"You know I might really send you a wedding gift," Hector said and grinned.

"Better not be any damn demon snakes," said Tessa kiddingly.

"I don't know if he is going to live that long," said Thaos. "We were with that version of Zane in Zorta and Ganz. We saw what happened to him and it wasn't pretty. So is Clev taking over your empire if you don't get help?"

"Why do you want it?" Hector asked sarcastically.

"No, but I am wondering if we can do some more business like this. What else do you want?"

Hector got an evil smile. "I will think about it," he said.

"Adam," Tessa called out. "Are we done? What do you want us to do?" The men grinned when they saw the brief look of fear on Hector's face as he listened to Tessa. She was quiet and staring at the floor for several moments. "Can't you just say it because I don't understand what you are showing me?"

She continued to stare at the floor then at the men in the room then back at the floor. "Well, is this really Hector?"

"What is she saying?" asked Hector and Stephan held up his hand indicting that Hector should stop talking.

"I tried but he is a jerk," Tessa said as she continued to stare at the floor. Then she looked at Hector. "Ok, you haven't answered one damn question I've asked you but you better answer this one. Did Juleta make more of you?"

Hector looked shocked. "No."

"Are you sure?" asked Tessa. "Because Adam keeps showing me a whole bunch of guys that look like you and Thaos." Now Thaos too, lost the color in his face.

"Let me see your arm," said Stephan.

"Adam said he's the real one," Tessa said. "I keep seeing the same picture. So if she didn't create more of you does she have more children with you?"

"I never had sex with that crazy bitch," said Thaos.

"I stopped after she made me look like Thaos," Hector said. "Isn't your Angel explaining what he is showing you?"

"It's hard to explain," said Noah. "Sometimes they just show us clues."

"Adam, you are driving me nuts," said Tessa with frustration then she laughed. "Noah, he showed me lightning bolts."

"I keep seeing the same image. There is a group of men, I'd say like twenty and they all look like the two of you. Some have the eye patches and some don't. So would she be crazy enough to create an army of her lost loves and what would be the benefit?" No one spoke. "Hector, I know you kiss up to demons but when an Angel asks questions I would suggest you answer. So both of you spit it out!"

"They are both badass fighters and really intelligent men," Stephan said. "In a way they are like the good and bad version of the same person. Like looking in a mirror."

"Stephan, I don't understand what Adam is doing but you must have said the right answer because he is showing me something else. This is really frustrating. Usually he talks to me and I don't have to guess what pictures mean."

Tessa was staring at the floor as she spoke. "Oh my god! I think I know...Hector, you just told us that Andrac wants to get involved with those experiments. And Turner, he's an Elod, told us that the powers in that kingdom have been doing genetic experiments for centuries. Adam is showing me Andrac and making me feel like the two of you are in danger. Hector, I think you are one of the people that he wants to replace."

"Hector, I am going to tell you something and I want a straight answer. When you and others were hunting Javier, he couldn't figure out why. His wife came up with the idea that Isabella set him up and they searched his house. They found a leather pouch that had the same map you told us about and a bunch of papers that they can't read yet. Then we learned that Otto was frantic because someone had stolen some papers from him during one of his orgies. Can you explain any of that?"

"Let me think. Does anyone else besides me need a drink?" Hector asked.

"I'll pour," said Stephan.

"Wait!" shouted Tessa. "Ok, that whiskey is safe to drink but Hector don't drink that bottle of wine you ordered."

"Why in the world would your Angel be helping me?" Hector asked.

"That's a good question," said Noah.

"Do you have any idea what language those papers were written in?" Hector asked.

"No and a lot of our people are good with languages," said Claudius.

"That doesn't surprise me," Hector said. "I am just thinking out loud here. Otto has a big empire, not as big as mine but there are a lot of guys who wanted to overthrow him. The Master protected Otto because he was so loyal to him."

"And the Master was involved with the original plot of the Second Sons." Hector was quiet for a few moments. "Isabella was another crazy bitch. She couldn't get enough attention and would act out like a kid. I could see her stealing something and setting one of her boyfriends up. But if she took that pouch, I would really doubt she had any idea what that paperwork was. She probably had an opportunity and grabbed it. But how would others know about it?"

"I know that other gangs were after Javier too but I thought it was for the same bounties that we were trying to cash in on. So there are a couple of possibilities. One; that no one knows about those papers and everyone was just trying to cash in on the bounties that Andrac put out. Or two, that Isabella told someone or someone saw her take them and in that case your friend is in great danger."

"He doesn't have them anymore," Claudius said. "Do you think that Isabella was bright enough to know what she was doing?"

"She wasn't stupid but if something didn't center around her, she didn't pay attention to it. And I can't believe she was a good thief. I'd bet money that someone saw her or she acted so guilty that someone became suspicious."

"Were you the one sending letters to Otto and Joanna and signing them from Isabella?" asked Thaos. "You know she is dead, the Angels destroyed her after she sold her soul to Samael."

"I heard she was dead but I didn't know how she died," Hector said then grinned. "I didn't send those letters but I'll bet you a bottle of whiskey that whoever did was blackmailing those two. Do you know where the letters originated from?"

"Port Friada," said Thaos. "That's why we thought it was you."

"I haven't been there since all of you were. My compound is gone and my wanted poster is on every building in that city."

"Hector, you said you were transitioning into a demon," said Tessa. "And Samael stopped it. What happens to your body? And stop looking at me like I am crazy, I am asking for a reason."

"I can't describe it exactly but it's like your body gets torn apart and every little piece is changed by magic then you are put together again. Why?"

"Because someone got their hands on one of those little pieces and that is how they are going to make another you. Adam just showed me."

# Chapter XLIX
## Dinner

"So who betrayed you?" asked Thaos.

Although Hector looked angry he shrugged his shoulders and calmly said, "It's to be expected. Everyone has a price."

"No they don't," said Tessa sarcastically. "Great life you have." Hector shot her an angry look. "Adam isn't showing me anything else. I guess it's over."

"I assume you want us to get Clarence and Catherine as soon as possible," said Claudius. "Do they know about you now?"

"Yes they know more than they want to. But they don't know that they have a granddaughter. Tessa's Angel is right. I can feel...well let's just say trouble. I may be fighting my way out of the city. You were probably seen coming here, so maybe you should wait a couple of days. Mother really wants to go home but I don't know if that is a safe place for them."

"I assume you have them guarded where they are now. Are we going to have to fight to get them out?" asked Claudius.

"No. I will make arrangements. Where can I leave messages for you?"

"The desk in this hotel will work," said Thaos.

"Will Clarence and Catherine know why we are getting them?" Claudius asked.

"Yes. If I feel that you are in danger I may send some of my men with you."

"I think you will understand when I say that may not be a good situation," said Claudius. "We will protect them."

There was a knock at the door and Stephan opened it. Angus walked into the room. "Don't know what the hell is going on outside but there isn't a damn person on the streets except for us and a few of his men. Hector, I swear your men are disappearing. And it feels strange. The air I mean. Everything feels thick."

"There are demons out there but they aren't a threat to any of you," Hector said. "You should probably leave now."

"Do you need some help?" asked Stephan with a grin. "I never could turn down a good fight."

Hector laughed. "Like the old days. No, go home. You are giving me all the help I need."

"Hector, I've just got to ask. Would you do it all again?" asked Stephan.

"Hell ya," Hector said and flashed him a big grin.

The group walked out of Hector's room but stayed in the hallway. "Adam are we going to be fighting our way out of here?" Claudius asked.

"Hector is already gone," Adam's voice said in their ears. "There is less human in him than you think."

"So is saving his parents a trick?" asked Thaos.

"No, actually he told you the truth. He said he had to be desperate to come to you. I think you should think about that."

"Well, I am still starving," said Angus as they walked to the front lobby of the hotel. "Anyone want to eat?"

"I think we all could," said Stephan.

None of them talked about their encounter with Hector until after their food and drinks were served. "So does anyone else think that Adam was kind of doing a power play in there?" asked Noah.

"If you mean showing him that Angels exist? Yes," said Claudius. "But I think he was really telling Hector that Angels are with us. I think it was more of a protective thing."

"I thought Hector was an ass but in a way I kind of felt sorry for him until the end," said Tessa. "He really wants to be a monster."

"As soon as we get back, I will give a briefing and I want the rest of you to write down every detail of that meeting. And I mean even the things that don't seem important. Then we have to send letters. If Hector knows that Raul and Simon helped to kill Teivel so do others."

"He didn't mention Matthew," said Stephan. "I wonder why."

"Who knows," said Claudius and shook his head. "And I want to really look over those papers."

"When are we going after his parents?" asked Thaos.

"That one, I am going to ask Adam about," Claudius replied. "None of this feels right."

"What is going on?" asked Claudius as the group walked into Mathas' castle and saw that the Great Hall was filled with people who appeared to be cleaning and measuring things.

A housekeeper walked up to him, "Queen Rosa told us that Prince Matthew and Princess Angelina will be home tomorrow. They are traveling with General Bishop's army."

"Thank you," said Claudius. "Is Mathas in his study?"

"Yes, My Lord."

Claudius entered the study as the rest of his group went to the temporary office to work. Sorren and Fahron were in the room with the King. They were all waiting for Claudius to return and tell them about Hector. "So what the hell happened?" asked Sorren as he poured Claudius a glass of whiskey.

"You are never going to believe this. Angus was right. He really wants us to protect his family and Mathas that includes Sarah. You should bring Rosa in here and I will tell you everything. Mathas, it isn't bad," Claudius said as he watched the color drain from his friend's face.

"Actually he has known about her all along and has been watching over her. He wanted me to tell you that he is grateful you have her and that he will never interfere unless he needs to protect her."

"I'll get Rosa," Fahron said. "Sorren pour Mathas another drink."

Dominic's team was in the office working with Ryan, Olin and Elexas. When Noah, Tessa, Angus, Stephan and Thaos walked in. "Let me see the rings?" Jasmine said and jumped out of her chair. Tessa laughed as she proudly showed her engagement ring to everyone in the room.

"Elexas, Olin, Angus told us that you are having dinner with Claudius' family tonight and there are already some hard feelings," said Tessa. "Elexas, if you want to borrow some of my clothes you can and Noah and I bought these." Tessa took a pouch from Noah as she spoke. "It's always a good idea to bring gifts to the host and hostess so here is a bottle of whiskey for Claudius and some combs for Bella's hair. They are from both of you."

"Thank you," said Elexas. "I never even thought about that."

"Are you afraid we are going to screw things up?" Olin asked with a grin.

"Actually, I asked her to pick some things up," said Ryan. "Both of you are so self-conscious that I wanted you to start out on a good foot. Tessa how much do I owe you?"

"We'll pay for that," said Stephan. "And have we got things to tell you. We've been with Hector."

"Stephan, let me find Turner and the others before you start," said Tessa.

"They aren't here," Dominic said. "And that may be a situation for them. Turns out there is another group of Elod spies that work out of Castor."

"When news came out that Javier had been killed Turner sent that group a message that he was looking into the murder. But he hasn't contacted them since so their head guy came here looking for them."

"Garvis was in the city and ran into the guy and came back here and got Turner. So they might have a fight on their hands or we might get more people. From what Turner said it really could go either way. A bunch of the Ruala warriors are watching over them."

"Tessa do you know those guys?" asked Fennel.

"I might. Remember I didn't know they were spies or Elods until I got here for this mission. I know they would associate with other people who I thought were con artists so that could be them. But now that I think about it they really kept me away from those others."

"Let's get to work before we start forgetting things," said Angus. "I've already started the notes. I am going to copy down everything that is said while you brief the others, so let's start at the beginning. Noah or Tessa start."

Turner, Bart, Garvis and Louis were meeting with Abbott the leader of the Charto group in Castor, under the City of Langer. They were in an underground meeting room near the docks.

Abbott was a short man with a ruddy complexion which was bright red now as he tried to control his anger.

"So you are all a bunch of damn traitors!" Abbott said through clenched teeth.

"Didn't you hear what Turner said? Andrac has bounties on us all," said Louis. "It wasn't us who saved Javier and Madeline it was Gabriel's teams."

"Abbott, we were ready to kill the team members after we read that article in the paper," said Bart. "We did attack them and they wouldn't fight us. They said we should talk to Madeline. They didn't trust us enough to tell us that Javier was alive then."

"So we go to the King's castle expecting a battle. After Javier and Madeline both talked to us we called a temporary truce with the group since we were all looking for the guys who attacked Javier and the others."

"And just so you know, Javier was not dead but he had one foot in the grave when we saw him. Well, obviously none of us trusted each other. Those teams are professionals and they work as hard as we do. All of us were damn shocked that we could work together and it wasn't long before we all became friends. When we found out about the bounties on us, they offered to hire us and protect us. We didn't say yes at first. But Abbott they are good people; we've never worked for good people before."

"We were pissed at Javier and Madeline too, when they told us they hooked up with the teams. But I will tell you, bounties or not none of us would go back to working for Inferus. You can't believe the shit we've found out about the crap those sorcerers are pulling."

"We've already covered all of this a couple of times," said Turner with frustration. "Abbott, you can certainly go back and tell the bosses that we are traitors but they may have already figured that out. And while you're at it ask them why they have bounties on us."

"We're still doing the same kind of work but with people we actually trust and we are making a lot of money doing it. If any of you want to join us, fine. If they send you to attack us we will kill you. But we aren't the puppets of the Abuckto or the sorcerers any more. For the first time in our lives we are free men. And that is worth more than money."

"If you decide to just keep things the way they are and ever need our help just holler. But I was serious when I said you better damn well find out if you have bounties on you too."

After Stephan told the people in the office about their encounter with Hector, Tessa grabbed the small map they had taken from Endleson and brought it and a mirror to the table in the parlor. "Well damn," said Thaos.

"He was telling the truth but we can't carry mirrors with us. Jasmine think you can copy this so we can just read it normally?"

"Yes, but it will take a while and Seth will have to help me. Where is the big one that we got from Javier's house? We will need to see if there are any differences," Jasmine said.

"Mathas has that locked up," said Stephan. "And we may need to ask the Angels how to translate the papers with it."

"While we are on that subject, we have some things to show you," Ryan said. "When you came in here we were going over the notes from Olin's and Elexas' interviews. Dominic and Fennel started that timeline on the wall behind Lawrence. They did that because they realized that some of the things that Elexas and Olin were saying were different than Isabella's diaries. So that timeline is for the interviews. And Deborah and Lawrence are making a timeline from those diaries."

"When Olin was being interviewed he talked about being at a regular celebration that Otto held in his home. He said it was about six months ago. Olin said he was dancing when he saw a bunch of Otto's hired killers suddenly running around the house."

"Olin said that he walked down the hallway to Otto's study and the door was open. Olin didn't go into the room but listened from the hallway. He heard Otto yelling at Joanna and Jack about someone stealing some of his papers. Joanna asks where they were and Otto says in the safe. He said he walked into his study and the safe was open. His money was stolen as well as some papers."

"Olin said that Otto kept yelling, 'How the hell did someone get into the safe?' Olin said that Joanna kept telling her father to keep his voice down then asked him what was stolen. And Otto says in a lower voice, 'That leather wallet'. Joanna asks him what was in it but she must have remembered because before Otto could answer she starts yelling that the Master will kill them all. He said Joanne sounded terrified. He said that Jack didn't say much except to tell Joanna and Otto to 'Shut up.' Then someone shut the door to the study."

"Well, Elexas talked about that celebration too because she kind of snuck into it. She had never gone to any of the normal celebrations before but heard about it at one of the orgies. She remembered it because shortly after she arrived, Otto's men were searching people and Elexas was afraid she would get kicked out of the celebration. She flirted with the guy who was searching her and he told her that someone had stolen something from Otto."

"Sorren went to Elexas' house and got the paperwork she talked about. We have her chart on the wall to the right of the new timelines. And she put that on her chart and the date. Look at it, it was only five months ago. Isabella was a prisoner here so she couldn't have put that in Javier's house. Seth said he found it in a planter on the second floor balcony. Someone else set Javier up."

Soldiers escorted Claudius and his sons home. Also riding with them were Gideon, Ashley, Elexas and Olin. It was a two hour ride between castles so they had plenty of time to exchange the information of the day.

"Everything you said about Hector shocks me," said Ashley. "Well, except for the last thing he said. I never considered him having a soft side, or I guess a human side."

"This is changing the subject," Gideon said to Ryan, Olin and Elexas. "But all three of you did a really nice job figuring out when that paperwork was stolen from Otto. You should be proud of yourselves."

"Thank you but we have a lot more work to do," said Ryan. "When we left; the office was full of people going through things."

"Yeah, Turner and his boys came back just before we left," said Thaos. "There is another group of Charto spies who work in Castor and their leader had it out with Turner. Everyone was pissed off when they walked into the office. The leader of the other group is a guy named Abbott. He's going to go back to Inferus and report that Turner and everyone are traitors. But Bart said it doesn't matter because they already have bounties on their heads."

615

"What does Abbott look like?" asked Elexas.

"Don't know," said Thaos. "Turner and the guys were bitching so much about the crap he said that they didn't describe him. Why?"

"Because there was a guy named Abbott who was always at Uncle Otto's parties," said Olin. "It's not a name you hear every day. And he always stood out because his face is so red it looks like he has a rash."

"Does anyone have a piece of paper and pen?" asked Claudius as he stopped his horse.

"I do," said Ashley and took the items from her bag.

"How else would you describe this guy?" Claudius asked.

"Ask Elexas, he was always after her," said Olin. "The guy is short. Maybe three inches shorter than me with dark hair. I am not good at guessing people's ages but I would say he was in his late thirties."

"Early forties," said Elexas. "And no I never did anything with him because he made my skin crawl. Can't tell you why. But he was at that party when the papers were stolen because I danced with him."

"Anything else you can remember?" Claudius asked as he wrote down their words.

"He always wears a suit," said Elexas. "And he has a huge ruby and silver ring on his left hand."

Claudius handed the paper to Stephan. "Have a couple of the men take this back to Turner. Maybe send three or four; I don't want anyone traveling alone. They can stay at the castle once they get there."

"It smells great in here?" Stephan said as the group entered their castle.

"I am having a special meal fixed for our guests," Bella said as she walked up to them. Claudius, Ryan, Stephan and Thaos all kissed her on the cheek.

"Here," said Elexas and handed Bella a gift.

"This is for you," Olin said and handed Claudius a bottle of whiskey that he had just taken out of his saddlebags.

"Well thank you," said Bella. "That was very sweet. Oh, these are just lovely." Bella showed the combs to Ashley.

"So where are the girls and kids?" asked Stephan as he thought Nikki and Ingr might be mad because Elexas was with them.

Bella gave Stephan and Thaos such a disapproving look that they both broke out in laughter. "The children were out back when the pups chased a family of skunks. Nikki and Ingr are the only two who didn't get sprayed. They are giving everyone baths behind the house."

"Guess we should have brought some gifts," Thaos said with a grin.

"Our boys too?" asked Ashley.

"All of them," Bella said.

"I'm going out there," said Ashley.

"I will, you stay here," Gideon said.

"Let us know if it is safe to go out there," Stephan said kiddingly as he poured some glasses of whiskey.

Bella looked at Olin and Elexas and said, "Stephan and Thaos brought two puppies home and they haven't so much as lifted a finger to help with those dogs."

"I'd go out there but I am wearing Tessa's clothes," Elexas said.

"You are our guests if anyone should go out there it is those two," Bella said and glanced at her sons who laughed.

Thirty minutes later Gideon walked into the parlor holding two wet puppies. "Looks like you took a bath with them," Stephan said with a grin.

"You boys are going to have to sleep with one eye open tonight," Gideon said and laughed. "I'm putting the pups upstairs, the kids are next."

A few minutes later Amy, Cassidy, Logan and Marty ran into the parlor. "Mama is burning all our clothes," Amy announced.

"Tell them the rest," said Cassidy.

"You tell them," Amy said.

"Nikki and Ingr said that you two are next," Marty said as he looked at Thaos and Stephan and all of the children laughed, so did the adults.

"Yes, we may be going back to the office to work tonight," Stephan said with a grin.

"We told them what you said," Amy yelled when Nikki and Ingr walked into the parlor. Both women were soaking wet.

"I hope they believed you," Ingr said as she looked at Stephan and Thaos who were grinning at her.

"I'll make it up to you honey," Thaos said as he grinned. Nikki gave him an angry look and everyone in the room laughed again.

"You two are incorrigible," Ashley scolded. "Tell them now or they will be in a bad mood all night."

"Tell us what?" asked Ingr suspiciously.

"Ashley, you tell them; they won't believe us," said Thaos.

"I'm not telling them," Ashley said. "Bella, tell your boys to get over here."

Bella looked at Claudius who shrugged his shoulders. Ryan come up here and protect us," said Stephan with a huge grin.

"Like I could protect you from them," Ryan said and chuckled.

"Well, if we are going to do this now, I need to get something," Thaos said. "Amy come with me so your Mama doesn't hit me." Amy giggled and grabbed Thaos' hand.

"Stephan what is going on?" asked Ingr.

"You'll find out as soon as Thaos comes back."

"Ryan do you know?" asked Ingr.

"Yes but don't yell at me."

When Thaos and Amy walked back to the parlor, he handed Nikki and Ingr each a huge towel. "Here Mama; don't hit him," Amy said and giggled as she handed Nikki a small box.

"A ring," Nikki gasped.

"It's for your wedding and we all get to be in it," Amy said excitedly.

"Before any one yells," Stephan said. "Matthew and Angelina will be back tomorrow. Ingr and I were waiting for them to come home so we could have a second wedding. Then Thaos thought that sounded like fun, so he and Nikki are going to have a second wedding too. We are having a double wedding. It will be just close friends and family."

Nikki started to cry and Thaos put his arm around her and kissed the top of her head. "Ashley designed all of you dresses. We have dresses for both of you, Angelina, Amy, Mother, Gladys, Shara and Rosa. Gladys already made outfits for all the babies and we will get suits for the boys, Father and Sorren," Stephan continued. "So as soon as Mother can organize a gathering we will get married again." As Stephan spoke he walked up to Ingr and kissed her.

"You boys are making me very happy," Bella said.

"I already have my suit if anyone wants to see it," said Ryan. "They are going to wear their military uniforms."

"Yes Ryan, bring it down," said Bella.

"So are we out of the dog house?" Thaos asked Nikki who couldn't stop crying. She nodded.

"I'll think about it," Ingr said with a big smile and kissed Stephan.

# Chapter L
## Abbott

Turner, Bart, Louis and Garvis were in the office going through paperwork when a soldier walked into the room and handed Turner a note from Claudius.

"That bastard!" Turner spat. "Everybody listen to this. Thaos was telling the people going for their dinner about us and Abbott. Turns out both Olin and Elexas know him because he was always at Otto's parties, the orgies and the regular ones. He was at Otto's house the night those papers were stolen. Elexas remembers because she danced with him."

"Are they sure it's the same Abbott?" Bart asked as he jumped out of his chair and walked up to Turner to look at the note.

"Read their descriptions," Turner said. "Turns out he has had a thing for Elexas for a long time but she didn't want anything to do with him because he makes her skin crawl. We might just be using her to hang him."

"All the damn shit he said to us about being traitors," yelled Garvis. "He's got to be the one who planted those papers in Javier's house. I wonder if he is working for Andrac."

"Tessa, write to Madeline and Javier tonight. Here's the note. I have to talk to Elexas and Olin," Turner said.

"They're at Claudius'," said Dominic.

"I won't be able to wait until the morning," Turner said angrily. "I will damn explode by then."

"Well, then some of us are coming with you," said Fennel.

Nikki and Ingr were so happy about the second weddings their husbands had planned that they didn't mind having Elexas in their home. Elexas felt uncomfortable and was on her best behavior.

The family was sitting around the dining room table eating dessert when a housekeeper led Turner, Dominic, Fennel, Bart, Noah, Louis and Garvis into the dining room.

"We apologize for the intrusion," Turner said. "But that is the same Abbott, which means he is probably a spy for Andrac. We believe he is the one who stole Otto's papers. From what Hector told you today, Abbott probably stole them for Andrac but we don't know why he set Javier up. Can we speak with Elexas and Olin for a couple of minutes?"

"The girls were just going to put the babies to bed," said Bella. "You are welcome to sit down and have something to eat while you talk."

"I'll get more chairs," Stephan said.

"Children take your cake and eat it in the playroom," Bella said.

"Can we have some more?" asked Marty.

"Yes," Gideon said. "I'll help you carry it."

Claudius remained at the table while the rest of his family were either getting chairs or taking babies out of the room. Bella went to the kitchen to get food and settings for their guests. Turner didn't wait until everyone had returned before he started asking questions. Noah was taking notes. By the time all of the adult members of Claudius' family returned to the dining room Turner was convinced that Abbott was the connection between Hector and Andrac.

Elexas and Olin didn't know Abbott well but they had watched him. "Turner, I don't remember going to a party where I didn't see him," said Elexas.

"In fact, I thought he was one of Otto's hired men. Look at my chart in the office and if I was at a party so was he. You will have those dates. I couldn't stand him so I didn't talk to him much. I've danced with him a couple of times but that is it. He always made me feel really strange, I can't explain it."

"I only remember him because he is a strange looking man and he caught my attention," said Olin. "That and he does look like a professional. I would be amused watching him chase Elexas around. But at the orgies he was all over everyone."

"Elexas, in the note you said he made your skin crawl and just now you said he made you feel strange. Can you describe exactly how he made you feel? It's important and I will tell you why when you are done," Turner said.

Elexas was quiet for a few moments as she thought about her experiences with Abbott. "He was always touching me and his skin was almost slimy like he was sweating a lot. And when I said he made my skin crawl he did. The hair on my arms would stand up. I thought I was imagining that. He is repulsive so I would walk away from him as soon as I could. That's really all I can remember. That and he always wore a lot of fragrance."

"He's not an Elod," Louis said. "The sorcerers create their own demons. Gilder is much better at that than Andrac is and both sorcerers have their own brands, I guess you could call them. Everything you just described is common to the type of demons that Andrac creates but he must have used magic to give Abbott the appearance he has."

"If the other members of that team are real Elods they are in danger and so are Javier and Madeline," said Bart. "We need to take a trip to Castor."

"I know all of you guys are pissed," said Thaos. "But think about everything you have said. He came here to find out what happened to Otto and how much you know. I'll bet you anything he is still in Langer nosing around."

"He would be at the Catacombs," said Bart. "Thank you all for your hospitality."

"Wait," said Ingr as all of the men were standing up. "Can you kill him if he is a demon?"

"We can call to the Angels," said Dominic.

"Stephan, Thaos you should go with them," said Nikki.

"You don't have to tell us twice," Stephan said and kissed Ingr on the cheek.

"I am trying to decide if we should bring Elexas," said Turner.

"She doesn't want to go into that place," said Nikki. "She should stay here."

"Nikki, I won't go near Thaos," Elexas said with embarrassment.

"That's not why I said that. The Catacombs are the filthiest, most disgusting places. Trust me, you will be glad you didn't go."

"Boys, do you want me to wait until you come back to tell them the news?" asked Claudius.

"No, go ahead," said Stephan. "After today they can use as much good news as they can get."

"What are you talking about?" asked Bella.

"You are never going to believe this story," Claudius said. "We met with Hector."

Tessa was working in the temporary office. She had just given Enrops another letter for Madeline and Javier. The people in the office had worked out an efficient system. Every bedroom was filled with team members who were reading papers, books and scrolls. They would indicate significant passages and give them to Jasmine and Seth who organized the information then gave it to Lawrence and Deborah to write on the charts.

Crates of papers had been seized from Otto's home and office in addition to all of the paperwork taken from The Rooster. "Was anything taken from Joanna's shop?" asked Jasmine.

"No," said Lawrence. "And I was thinking about that. Did she and Jack have homes or live with Otto?"

"That is a good question for tomorrow's meeting," said Seth. "I want to run something past all of you. Every one listen up for a second."

"Olin told us that the really important information is written in languages that aren't easy to translate and so far everything we have found we can read. Of course we aren't done yet. But most of that stuff from Otto's house tells of his businesses, which you would expect but something doesn't make sense."

"His family has more money than we can imagine because they work for the Master and have for generations. Of course he is going to invest in businesses to make more money but he was a paranoid and powerful man. Wouldn't you think he would invest in things for protection, like armies and weapons? I think we are missing a lot of paperwork."

"Frankwich seems to be spending all of his money on weapons," said Sol. "What if those two were working together? We have been thinking that they were rivals."

"Has anyone searched the ships we got from Otto?" asked Nana.

"I am starting a list of all our questions for the meeting," Lawrence said.

"And there are still those businesses of Juleta's that he paid for," said Tessa. "He was smart. I'll bet he is hiding things in plain sight. When Claudius goes to Zorta they should look into those businesses."

"I suspect they will have their hands full" Adin said. "Maybe some of us should go ahead first."

"There is so damn much crap here," said Ralf with frustration. "And you know it's probably the tip of the mountain. I'm going to the kitchen and get us some food."

"Get some whiskey too," said Seth.

"And coffee," Jasmine added. "Ryan showed us that the real information is in the details so I expect we will be up all night."

"My Lady!" yelled Sauer.

"Please, I've told you all to call me Rosa. The titles we use in public. My, I didn't realize how much work you were doing in here. If you need anything for this area please let me know."

Sol stood up and pulled a chair out for the Queen. "As you know I don't usually go to the morning meetings. But Mathas often tells me what was covered. He told me about your suspicions that something happened to Isabella during the month after her wedding. I will admit I saw a change in her too. So I've been going through my things and I don't know if any of this will help you. You can use these as long as you like but they are family mementos so I don't want them destroyed."

Rosa had carried an armload of items into the office. She now sorted the items into piles. "This is a book I have been putting together for our family. I suppose in a way it is like a diary but I entered things like the first time one of the children walked. You know, special events for a family but they may not be interesting for anyone else. I plan to have copies of this made for each of the children someday." Rosa handed a huge leather bound book to Lawrence who was sitting next to her.

"This pouch is filled with letters that I haven't put into that book yet. As you can see I am behind. Now these are personal family letters so I trust you will honor that. I really don't know if there is any information in them but it is amazing what all of you have been putting together."

"Now, this book I put together when Mathas and I were planning our wedding. As you can see I am very sentimental. I also made one for Isabella when she and Joseph got married. I brought them both in case you needed to compare things." She opened one of the books.

"See I would put things on the pages then write information under them and maybe put art work, so these took me a while to do. I finished ours but I didn't finish Isabella's. But I have a lot of things just thrown in the back of that book, they aren't displayed. She changed so much that I lost interest in giving it to her then I forgot about it. I hope these things can help a little. I will keep looking."

"Thank you so much," said Lawrence. "And we will be very careful with them. We won't betray your trust."

"I would like to see some of the things you are doing in here," Rosa said as she stood up and walked to one of the walls.

"Lawrence or Deborah should explain those charts," said Jasmine. "We've divided the workload by duties and they are doing the charting."

"Are you sure you don't want more tables and chairs in here?" Rosa asked as she looked at the piles of papers sitting on the floors. "It's not like we don't have a castle full. You just tell me what you want and I'll have it moved here."

"Actually, book shelves would probably be the best," said Seth. "All of those things you are looking at we've already gone through and we have to keep it separate from the other stuff."

"Rosa, could we get some kind of baskets that will fit on the shelves so we can keep all of this organized?" asked Tessa.

"I'll have shelves moved in here tomorrow," Rosa said. "The baskets I will need to buy. Or I can give you money and you can get them."

"We'll get them," said Jasmine. "I already have something in mind."

Once Turner and his friends got to the Catacombs they split up. Turner and Thaos worked as a team. Bart and Stephan searched dens together. Louis worked with Dominic and Noah. And Garvis and Fennel worked together. This last pair went into the den run by Drake and Tally first and told them about Abbott.

"I've seen that guy in here," said Tally. "But not tonight. Angus sent us word about Hector's men changing their looks. Well, I haven't seen one in here all night; wearing either the hats or bandanas."

"He said he expected to fight his way out of the city," said Fennel. "So who knows what is going on."

Noah walked up the three men. "Bart and Stephan found him," Noah said in a low voice. Garvis and Fennel followed Noah out of the den. The men walked through the streets of the Catacombs without speaking. Turner and Thaos joined them. This group saw Dominic standing outside of a shartish den. The men all walked inside without saying a word to each other.

Bart, Louis and Stephan were inside of the den. "I've already called to Miranda," Stephan whispered. "He's not the only demon in here. This could be a setup."

"Guess we'll find out," said Turner and started to walk across the room. Abbott was lying on a mattress and smoking from an elaborate pipe. "We've got a few questions for you," Turner said and roughly grabbed Abbott and pulled him to his feet. Abbott was so high he started to laugh then got mad.

"What the hell is going on here Turner?" Abbott demanded.

"Just want to talk to you, that's all," Turner said as he looked around the room. "Want a drink?"

"Sure," Abbott said. "Have you guys ever tried this stuff, it's great."

"Maybe later," said Turner. "Come on."

Turner's group got the attention of everyone in the den but no one tried to stop them from leaving. As they got near the door guards Stephan said, "His wife sent us and she is really pissed." The two guards laughed loudly.

There were only a few entrances into the Catacombs and one of them was through the back door of Drake and Tally's den. Turner had to help Abbott walk as the group headed toward that den. Abbott kept laughing and talked constantly to the men.

Once inside of the den, Drake led them to a table near the back door. Tally brought over a bottle of whiskey then returned to the bar and grabbed two fists full of glasses. Turner sat on one side of Abbott and Thaos on the other. As soon as everyone started to drink, Thaos took his crystal necklace from his vest pocket and touched the crystal against Abbott's cheek. Abbott became enraged and dropped his human mask for just a moment.

"That's what we thought," said Turner.

"Wait," said Dominic. "Miranda can Andrac see through his eyes? She said no."

"What are you talking about?" asked Abbott harshly.

"Well, we know you are one of Andrac's creations," said Turner. "And my friend there was just talking to the Angel that put the curse on Andrac. So start talking or we play by different rules."

Abbott stared at the men. He no longer acted as if he was under the influence of the powerful drug shartish. Suddenly his skin began to smoke and he jumped up. Turner and Thaos pushed him back down on the chair.

"Was there ever a real Abbott?" asked Turner.

"No. I've been doing it since the beginning."

"Are the other guys on your team demons too?"

"No and they don't have a clue. How did you figure it out?"

"Because one of your girlfriends works with us," Stephan said sarcastically.

"Who?" demanded Abbott.

"We'll ask the questions," said Turner.

"Why did Andrac put you in the Charto? To spy on us?"

"Not as much. He wanted to know about people above ground. The dark lords in particular. Andrac believes you tell the Abuckto what you find. He wanted more information."

"Is that why you were always at Otto's parties?" Turner asked.

"Yes and your next question will be why Otto. I don't know. My assignment was to keep an eye on his family and Hector. Well, Hector is damn hard to spy on. He has layers of protection and his head lieutenant spotted me right away. And I don't know how but I got a major ass chewing from Andrac the next day. After that I got paranoid because that lieutenant is a human."

"I don't know if Otto ever suspected that I was a demon but he never let me close. So what is it? How can you guys tell?"

"Just answer the questions," said Thaos.

The group had previously decided that Turner would do the questioning. "So what did you learn about Otto?"

"That he serves something called the Master and he routinely grabs women to be sacrifices. His daughter is a witch and his son a dark lord."

"But it was Andre, the daughter's husband who I was able to get close to. That marriage was arranged and both he and Joanna were miserable. He was a dark lord but felt that he was the shit on everyone's shoes."

"He was the weak link and I got him drunk a lot. He's the one that got me into those parties. His last name is Wilchess. Sound familiar?"

"The shipping family in Port Friada?"

"Well, they do a lot more than make ships. They make weapons too. And the ships they build are built for war. He and I went to Port Friada and he took me on a tour of the Red Moon Shipyard and I've never seen anything like that. The ships have catapults on them."

"Is that the name of their company?" asked Noah.

"The company that makes the ships and weapons. He has another company called Jackson's; that is a line of merchant ships. No I don't know why it is named Jackson's but the mark on the ship is two black lines that look like lightning bolts."

"He also owns a huge farm outside of Port Friada and they produce a lot of the food that is sold in that city and shipped elsewhere."

"Is the food safe?" asked Thaos.

"Guess so."

"So back to Andre," said Turner. "By the way he is dead now."

"I wondered about that. I sent a message for him to meet me here. Andre was routinely kept out of the loop on things. The bastard once said that only Otto's wife knew less than he did."

"So for a long time I didn't get a lot other than access to Otto's parties. A couple of months ago he tells me that Otto, Joanna and Jack start having a lot of secret meetings and they are acting really paranoid. He didn't know why and it was pissing him off so he really started to spy on them."

"The guy was no fool, he even used magics but he thought that Otto was blocking him. Well, one day he barges in Otto's study because there was a meeting. Otto, Joanna and Jack all jumped out of their chairs and looked scared until they realized it was Andre. They all started yelling at him to leave and he did but he saw Otto trying to hide a large leather folder that was on his desk."

"Andre was really pissed. I asked him where the folder was hidden and he said Otto's safe. Well, about two weeks later there is this big celebration at Otto's house. I cracked the safe pretty damn easy and found the folder. I took some of the money to make it look good. I hid the crap on one of the balconies and went back inside because I knew Otto would have everyone searched when he discovered the theft. I was searched and spent some time at the party then left."

"So why did you plant the stuff at Javier's?"

"You have it?"

"Just answer the damn question."

"Because after I leave the party the carriage driver yells down that he thinks we are being followed. We were pretty close to one of Javier's houses so I had him stop there. The housekeeper let me in because she recognized me. Javier was home but it sounded like he was screwing somebody. So I walked into one of the other bedrooms and hid the papers on the balcony. I told the housekeeper that I left him a gift and not to say anything. He should really fire that housekeeper."

"Well sure enough, when I get outside some of Otto's guys are searching the carriage. They searched me again. I don't know why they didn't go up to Javier's house but they followed me home. I've been waiting until things settled down to get it. That is the reason I am in Langer."

"So you weren't trying to set Javier up?" asked Bart.

"Hell no, I was trying to save my ass. I only went to his place because it was close. I would have hidden it in any of your places if I had the opportunity. I stayed in Langer for two days and Otto's men followed me the whole time. So I went back to Castor and damn if they didn't follow me there. I heard Otto was dead that's why I came back now. And you guys verified that."

"Do you know what was in those papers?"

"No, I didn't have time to look."

"Does Andrac know?"

"I told him I stole them but Otto's men were on me all the time. I couldn't even get to Inferus so all he knows is they were important to Otto."

"And you told him where you hid them?"

"Of course."

"Is that why he put the bounties on everyone?"

"Listen, I didn't know anything about that until you guys told me. Don't look at me like that. He gives me orders; we don't socialize. And you know him, he always has a dozen irons in the fire. In fact, I am going to see if he has one on me just to make it all look good."

"He's trying to get in the Gefrey Games do you know why?"

"Hell, everyone is. That is all the talk in Castor. Samael is offering prizes you can't believe. I haven't seen the list myself but I heard that one of the prizes is a world."

"This one?" gasped Thaos.

"Probably not, you guys are too much trouble."

"Miranda has he been telling us the truth?" asked Stephan in a low voice. "She says yeah."

"Why haven't you lied to us?" asked Thaos.

"Have you seen Andrac since he tangled with her? He looks worse than any of his creations."

"How do you keep this appearance?" asked Turner.

"Magics but they are faulty. If I get emotional at all I lose it. And sometimes I just lose the face and I don't even know why. Andrac is doing a lot of experimentations. He is in his workroom all of the time when he isn't in this world trying to get in good with the demons."

"Is he going to know that you talked to us?" asked Thaos and handed Abbott a large pouch of gold coins.

"I don't know. I don't go back to Inferus often; I might just stay here. If he's got bounties on all of you, he will on me too otherwise everyone will know I am a spy."

"I'll tell you what," said Thaos. "We pay very well. You could make a really good living giving us information. But remember we work with Angels and if you lie we will know it."

Abbott felt the weight of the bag in his hand. "You know what Andrac will do to you," said Garvis. "If I were you I would take the deal. Even if you lose your appearance there are enough demons around here that you can blend in."

"You talked me into it," Abbott said. "I am going back to Castor and tell the others that I joined you. If that gets back to Andrac he may be too scared of your Angel to come after me. And that's a good group of guys, they deserve a chance."

"I've never heard a demon say something like that before," said Fennel.

"We aren't like the demons in your world. We were created from Elods."

"What!" shouted Stephan then looked around to see if he had drawn attention.

"That's what the sorcerers do," said Turner. "They turn their own people into monsters."

"Now I understand why Miranda didn't destroy you," said Dominic. "We've got to stop Andrac."

"That will not be easy to do," said Abbott. "How will I get messages to you?"

"See those two bartenders? They know us," said Thaos. "We are regulars and pay them well."

# Chapter LI
## The Chicken or The Egg

After Queen Rosa left the office, everyone put aside the papers they had been working on and poured over the items she had brought. "I can't believe she is letting us read these letters," said Tessa. "This one is from Renya. Both women are talking about being new mothers while Sudfad and Mathas are fighting wars. They both sound so lonely."

"I am going to start a timeline for Juleta," Lawrence said. "We may need it."

Abbott stayed and had a second drink with Turner and the others. After he left Stephan said out loud what they all were thinking. "What kind of a monster does that to his own people?"

"The kind that has unlimited power. No one will stop him," said Turner.

"Turner, I wasn't on that mission to get the Credo," said Dominic. "But do you think others would leave with us if we asked the Angels to send us back there?"

"It's hard to say. The Credo believe in The Great Ruler. A lot of Elods believe in the Abuckto and some of the Abuckto work with the sorcerers," said Turner.

"And the ones who don't are monsters themselves," said Bart.

"Hell, maybe we should go to Castor and tell those other guys to join us, If nothing else for their own safety," said Stephan.

"You have to remember that all Elods are taught fear and hatred from the moment they are born," said Louis. "While Inferus is bad, many of them believe that your world is worse. Let Abbott talk to them first. He has to be scared shitless of Andrac and he saw what Miranda did to him. I would trust that Abbott is going to work with us."

"You know that is why those of us who work here are a threat to Inferus because we know the truth. I wonder if that is why there are bounties on us," said Garvis. "After the Credo left, the Abuckto and sorcerers may be afraid that others will find a way out too."

Thaos and Stephan returned to Mathas' castle with Turner and the rest of that group. Bart and Fennel briefed the team members who were still up and working in the office, while Turner, Thaos, Dominic and Stephan briefed Mathas. Garvis and Louis wrote letters to Madeline and Javier. Noah went to the room that he shared with Tessa.

"Thaos when you and Stephan go to Salar take that folder with you," said Mathas. "I have it locked up. More of their people can read different languages, maybe one of them can translate those pages. I would really like to get that translated before Archetenus and Jared start their mission, since it concerns the Second Sons."

"I sure as hell hope they don't have to go to Marba," said Stephan. "They will never make it out alive."

"Would the Angels send them on a suicide mission?" asked Dominic.

Stephan shrugged his shoulders. "I would have thought they would have protected Michael. I mean after all he was one of The Seven Sons. The rest of us are just peons."

Noah walked into the office with a huge grin on his face. He winked at Fennel then he walked around the table to Tessa who was engrossed in reading a letter. He got down on one knee; that is when she realized he was in the room. She looked shocked and others in the room started to grin.

"Tessa, I love you will you marry me?" As he said these words he held up a small velvet box and opened it.

"Another ring," she gasped. "Noah..."

"Honey say yes or no then I will explain about the rings," Noah said.

"Yes, of course I will," Tessa said and threw her arms around his neck and kissed and hugged him. Everyone in the room applauded the couple. A few warriors yelled war cries. Noah and Tessa stopped kissing because they were laughing. "Noah, why did you get me another ring?"

"Because this is the one you kept looking at until you heard the price. Keep them both. You can wear one on each hand."

"Noah, this is too much."

"Tessa, the guy never spends any of the money he earns, I am sure he can afford those rings," said Fennel.

Noah stood up. "I know everyone is working but I have bottles of whiskey and wine in the hallway. I thought we could have a toast."

"You bet," said Bart. "Let me get Turner and the guys. They are going to want to toast this too."

The following morning King Mathas planned to have a short meeting since everyone in the household was preparing for the arrival of General Bishop's army, Matthew and Angelina.

Elexas and Olin had spent the night at Claudius' castle and traveled with him and Ryan back to the castle of Mathas.

"Why didn't you two make it home last night?" Claudius asked Stephan and Thaos when he saw them in the Great Hall waiting for the meeting to start. Both men were drinking coffee.

"Well, we have a lot to tell you about Abbott," Stephan said with a grin. "But once we got back here, Noah proposed to Tessa and well, one toast led to many bottles."

"Were you drinking all night?" Claudius asked as he realized how red Thaos' and Stephan's eyes were.

"Pretty much," said Thaos and chuckled. "And we weren't alone. I don't think I have ever seen Mathas put them back like that before."

"No one started out with the idea of getting drunk," Stephan said. "But I think with all that has been going on it was kind of a release. If you think we look bad, wait until you see Turner and his crew. Tessa is like their little sister, so this was a family event for them. And Dominic's team isn't in much better shape."

Claudius laughed and poured himself a cup of coffee. He looked around the almost empty room and saw that Ryan, Olin and Elexas had left. Claudius sat down next to his sons and said in a lower voice. "You are never going to believe last night."

"Before you start, where is Gideon? Is he alright?" asked Stephan.

"I'll get to that," Claudius said. "Well, you know how happy the women were after you told them about the second weddings you had planned. After all of you left I told them about our meeting with Hector. Of course they had a hard time believing all of that but they were really relieved that the bounties were canceled. So everyone was in a great mood. Nikki actually invited Elexas and Olin to the weddings. When she said this, Ingr swung around so fast that she started to fall out of her chair and we all had a good laugh."

"The women were all talking about the wedding when Gideon piped in. He's been frustrated that so many things have detained them from getting married that he practically ordered everyone to start working on their wedding arrangements which of course the women loved. So Gideon is with all of them today."

"Since you want a small group, your weddings are next week. Thought you might want to know that," Claudius said and grinned. "The following week we are taking care of Logan and Marty so Gideon can propose to Ashley in style. Then two weeks after that we are hosting their engagement party. Gideon can't stop grinning now and all the women are in a tizzy."

"Damn, we need to get suits made," Stephan said. "Father will you have time after the meeting?"

"I'm wearing my dress uniform but talk to Sorren," said Claudius. "And you need to get some for the boys. Gideon is wearing his dress uniform too."

"Wait a minute," said Thaos. "When are we going to get Hector's parents?"

"All night I kept thinking about him saying that he didn't know if their home was safe, so I am going to have it watched for a couple of days. I will leave him a message today," Claudius said.

The Sanuri and Erebus were always early risers but the previous night they had received a number of letters that kept them from sleeping. Unbeknown to anyone in Mathas' castle, the Angel Adam had assisted the Enrops in their flight so the Sanuri already had the letter that Noah wrote containing the information of their meeting with Hector.

The Sanuri was fixing breakfast over the campfire as Erebus reread the letters. "Although it is hard to believe, it does make some sense that Hector would not want to harm you. But he is going against Samael and Samael owns his soul, which means he can get into Hector's head. Surely Hector knows that so he must have some powerful magics to block that."

"I was thinking the same thing," said the Sanuri. "I am sure that Adam blocked that entire meeting in Langer. While I am sure that Hector was telling the truth about wanting to protect his family, he is also removing any weaknesses he has. I will bet he is going to war with a powerful demon."

"What do you mean weaknesses?"

"There must be a little humanity left in him. I think he would surrender his sword if Sarah or his parents were in eminent danger and he can't afford to do that now."

"Interesting. But what I keep going over is that he told them he had to be desperate to ask for their help. Do you believe that to be true?"

"I don't know. I think this journey is just starting to unfold for all of us."

High Priest Bernard was leading the small army that was escorting High Priest Othnial, Padre Thomas and Padre Bartholomew to the monastery at Malga. They could not travel through the Kingdom of Stordt because that would be considered an act of war. The plan was for them to travel south through Lentz then continue south through Zorta and into the Kingdom of Ganz.

They planned to continue traveling south until they reached the monastery at Leven. They would take rest there then travel west across that Kingdom of Ganz and into the Kingdom of Puntd. Malga was near the eastern border of Puntd. This was a long, arduous and dangerous journey for them all but Bernard was concerned for the priests he escorted. Othnial, Thomas and Bartholomew were old men, who should have been retired from their duties.

Bernard and the Patronus priests who he led all had great respect for these three older priests for undertaking such a labor some and dangerous mission. They knew Othnial, Thomas and Bartholomew believed they would not survive the mission but every Patronus priest in that army was determined to protect these men at all costs.

Kings Sudfad and Mathas, the Sanuri, Gabriel and Raphael had sent numerous letters to King Friada of Ganz, King Tobias of Puntd, the head priests of every monastery on the eastern coast of Opots and Commanding General Amundsen about Bernard's army. And every letter requested protection for the priests.

King Fahra of Zorta was left out of the correspondence since none of these men understood where his allegiance was. He had never directly attacked another kingdom but he gave shelter to those who had. Otto, Juleta, Zane and Hector had established businesses in that kingdom as had other criminals. The ruling members of Lentz knew they would need to send a team into Zorta to investigate that kingdom.

While many of the people who attended Mathas' morning meeting were suffering from the effects of drinking too much, they all sobered up when Turner explained how the sorcerers of Inferus would abduct their own people and experiment on them. He said the sorcerers could not create life but they wanted to create armies of powerful beings so they took living Elods and turned them into monsters.

Voice after angry voice in the room shouted that they had to stop the sorcerers from their diabolical ambitions. Turner explained the isolated culture of Inferus. He said that while the Credo wanted to escape that many Elods were loyal to the Abuckto and sorcerers simply out of fear of the unknown. He said another rescue mission would not be so easy.

Turner returned to his seat and Seth stood up. "Last night we made a list of questions but after hearing what Abbott said that answered some of them. Our first one is did Joanna and Jack live at Otto's house or have their own homes?"

"They lived in Otto's home," said Claudius. "Why?"

"So far all of the paperwork we have reviewed is Otto's normal business dealings. With him being a paranoid dark lord we figured he had to have a weapons company or something. Sounds like that was all under the Wilchess family operations. The second question is has anyone searched Otto's ships?" Seth asked.

"Gideon isn't here today," said Mathas. "He led the searches of those ships. Surprisingly they didn't find anything illegal or magical. They appeared to be normal trade ships which we have now added to our fleet."

"And this brings me to another subject," Mathas continued. "Gideon has talked more sailors from Ganz into coming here but we barely have enough to start a training program. One of the many buildings that is going up at the naval yard will be a school for training sailors. He has postponed putting up notices since all of the barracks he built are filled with homeless families."

"So, I've sent all of the carpenters from the castle and Fort Langer to help with the buildings."

"Gideon will be putting out notices which we will distribute throughout the kingdom and perhaps other kingdoms. Then he is going to hire men and start training them. It will be a long process. Not that you aren't all busy enough but if anyone wants to help him, he would appreciate that."

"I'll bet Artis and Ralph would teach some classes," Ryan said enthusiastically. "I'll ask them."

"Son, ask Gideon first," said Claudius. "But that is a great idea. And now I am going to change the subject. Hector wanted us to wait a few days before we left to get his parents. Edward will be here this afternoon and I want to talk to him about leading a group to Zorta ahead of us, to look into Juleta's businesses."

"He may not be in shape for that," said Angus. "I will go."

"We talked about that," said Mathas. "None of this is over in Langer and we would prefer for you to work here since you are up on everything. I've already asked Gabriel if your team can remain here and help us for a while. Half of Dominic's team is still healing from injuries and who knows what hell will break loose when we bring Hector's parents here. Also, we reported that Edward was dead, so I don't want him to be actively working in the city for a while."

"I understand," said Angus. "I would like to stay and see all of this through."

"And now for another matter," said Mathas. "Many of you may have noticed that Fahron has been absent from meetings. I know a lot of you visit Chaez and Lana and know they are healing just fine so Fahron is no longer staying home because of them. Fahron is on a special mission to answer questions that many of you have raised. And Angus, he may need your assistance which is another reason I want you to stay in Langer."

"I can't remember who in this group was the first to question how Isabella obtained military information that I sent by carrier to Josef. Fahron has been conducting an investigation into that and as you can imagine he doesn't want it to get out to the soldiers."

"He has tracked down most of the men who were assigned to deliver letters. He has investigated and interviewed them and so far he does not believe any of them were manipulated into giving Isabella information."

"He is still looking into the soldiers but now his investigation is leading him towards Josef. Olin, Ryan and Elexas came to me with a list of questions that I could not answer. The questions centered on what could have happened to Isabella in the month after her marriage that her personality would change so drastically and how someone as astute as Josef could be so blind to everything."

"With all of my heart I hope that Josef is not an accomplice in all of this. But if he is, he may know we will look into him. As you know he now works under King Tobias, who is my brother-in-law. Both Fahron and I have written extensively to Tobias and he now has assigned some members of the Guardians to spy on Josef."

"While Chaez and Lana are not up for a great deal of physical activity they are both sick of being in bed and begging for work. They are working on all of Fahron's notes."

"Angus, I would like you to be here for the celebration this afternoon and evening but starting tomorrow I would like you to work with Fahron and his children. Since you were a member of the Guardians as well as being an officer in the Military of Puntd you may see things that the others do not."

"Gladly," said Angus with enthusiasm.

There was great fanfare when General Bishop led his army to the King's castle. People lined the streets to welcome the troops home. Prince Matthew and Princess Angelina rode with the General.

Edward and Kate decided to dress in disguise since Mathas' didn't want people to know that Edward was alive.

The courtyard at Mathas' castle was filled with people, which included family members of the returning soldiers. Mathas had ordered every one of the team members to stop work and enjoy the festivities but Olin and Elexas felt out of place and returned to their office. Ryan was a rather shy man and never felt comfortable in crowds. He too, returned to the office after an hour.

Jasmine and Tessa saw Ryan leave the Great Hall and followed him into the office. They wanted to show him the items that Rosa had given them to review. Both of these women were fascinated with the intimate details of the Royal Family. By time they finished explaining what each item was, Elexas was just as enthusiastic about reading the letters and books.

Both Noah and Seth laughed when they walked into the office an hour later. "Why are you working?" asked Seth.

"We didn't intend to," said Jasmine. "But we just can't put these things down."

"Rosa must really trust us to let us read these things," Tessa said. "I mean these letters; I've actually cried reading a couple of them. She and Renya just pour their hearts out."

"There were horrible wars going on and Renya, Rosa, Bella and Isadore were all new wives and mothers. They were alone in those big castles. Renya talks about the castle being attacked while Sudfad is gone and Rosa can't understand why Renya helped to defend it. Well, now we know it is because she is a Keeper of The Scrolls. All of these women are so wealthy and gracious; you wouldn't believe how hard their lives were."

"And did anyone know that Mathas and Rosa had a baby before Juleta but he died almost right after he was born?"

"Tessa, let me see that letter," said Olin adamantly. "Everyone sort out the information from that time. This could be really important. Tessa does that letter say why the baby died?"

"No, but Rosa got sick about two weeks before she gave birth. She talks about having a high fever and awful nightmares," said Tessa. "Olin, your face just got white. What are you thinking?"

"Remember I am not an expert on any of this but I have heard all kinds of stories growing up about debts being paid with the soul of a new born baby. And then the next kid is Juleta who is like a demon incarnated. We really have to look into this."

"Surely you aren't saying that Mathas or Rosa had those kind of debts to pay?" asked Noah.

"No, but the demons and dark lords have been trying to figure out who The Seven Sons and the Keepers of the Scrolls were for centuries. Now it makes sense why everyone has been watching all of you."

"Who told you?" asked Noah.

"Mathas did the other night when the three of us were talking to him," Ryan said defensively. "I already knew and Olin suspected it. Mathas told us to help us with our work."

"I'm not going to yell at anyone," said Noah. "I just wondered."

"I didn't even know what any of that meant," Elexas said. "Mathas had to explain it. I'm really glad now that I am working with all of you."

"Olin, finish what you were thinking," said Noah.

"From what I've heard here, Ahriman certainly had his suspicions about who The Seven Sons and the Keepers of The Scrolls were. And the Master was involved with the Second Sons plot. You know the first King of Stordt who became a vessel for that Second Son seed had to kill, I think it was five of his new born sons. It would have been the Master who would have demanded that."

"Everything you are talking about was part of one of Gabriel's missions," said Noah. "We need to contact him too."

"Well, we aren't going to say a word about this until we have more to go on," said Tessa in a scolding tone.

"Rosa and Mathas have been through so much we can't bring them more pain unnecessarily. Olin just let me finish reading this letter then you can have it."

Both Noah and Seth sat down at the table. "What time frame are we looking for?" asked Seth.

"The baby died a year before Juleta was born," said Tessa. "Oh my god, Rosa is saying that her nightmares were about demons."

"Isabella was living in this castle at the time," said Ryan and walked up to one of the charts. She was thirteen when Juleta was born so that doesn't explain her strange behavior after her wedding."

"I am not sure that I can explain this well," Olin said. "But things with magics don't always happen right away. I mean, well, say the Master could put something into motion like the Second Sons; that took three generations. Juleta wasn't a Second Son but say Isabella was the weak link that helped some evil to get close to this family, well, if she sold her soul or something the Master could have planned for certain things to take place years later. That is just a vague example, I'm not saying any of that happened."

"But if something like that did," said Noah. "Are you saying the demon or whatever would need someone on the inside to help him?"

"With something like what I am suspecting, yes. Someone would have to bring him items depending on the spell. Like say, some of Rosa's hair."

"I just got chills," said Jasmine.

"Olin, you haven't looked this worried since the day we first got you," said Tessa. "Just tell us what you are thinking."

"I have no proof. But we keep going over and over trying to figure Juleta and Isabella out. I think this family is being used for some kind of a plot and...and it could be really bad."

They return from the wars
Changed within and without
Their families need healing
Their nightmares cry out

When the atrocities are committed
When the decisions are made
The consequences unequaled
The prices are paid

The families of warriors
Suffer in pain
For one that is lost
Is anything gained

The warriors, the heroes
Who die in the streets
Their comrades, their brethren
Forever to meet

If I had Wings
By Sandra J Yearman© 2008

# Glossary of Characters

**Aaron:** an escaped prisoner from Wetpr

**Aaryan:** a male Grand Master of the Insidiae

**Abaddon:** an ancient demon/one of the Old Ones

**Abbott:** an Elod/a member of the Charto/

**Abekk:** the ancient leader of the Clan of Elods, author of the Prophesy of Isto

**Abella:** daughter of Prince Lakin and Princess Zada/Ruala

**Abigail:** sister of Marie/ nurse for grandchildren of King Sudfad

**Abigale:** a waitress in Langer

**Abrass:** a demon from the World of Planteen

**Abraxas:** the demon that Hector sold his soul to

**Ackley:** hired fighter for Mayor Deckor of Langer

**Ackly:** an arms dealer in Ryed

**Ada:** demon midwife to Nada

**Adam James:** a notorious pirate

**Adam:** an emissary of The Great Ruler who takes on the disguise of a human man

**Adam:** Nordes child/brother of Celia

**Adi:** son of Elen and Batya/ Ruala

**Adin:** male Ruala warrior

**Adler:** a male Nordes warrior

**Adrone:** youngest son of Joshua and Iris/younger brother of Vivian/Clan of Gesmal

**Adwell:** Prince/ son of King Zachariah and Queen Noella of New Samona/husband of Nada/father of Misha/ Adwell was killed in battle leaving Nada to raise ten children/Ruala/

**Ael:** an ancient demon/ one of the Old Ones

**Aetes:** Shettee warrior

**Agnes:** owner of the Midnight Tavern in Stoba Lentz/wife of Bert

**Agnus:** a captain in the covert organization The Guardians

**Ahriman:** an ancient demon/ one of the Old Ones

**Aiden:** five year old Ruala boy/son of Artis and Jenna/nephew of Ratri

**Akasha:** former king of Ryed/grandfather of Nehmota

**Alex:** Nordes warrior/brother of Corsa, Kent and George

**Alexander:** former servant of King Roch's parents/ father of Annabelle

**Alexander:** one of the twin sons of Simon and Annabelle

**Alexandras:** King of Wetpr/brother of Jaretta/uncle of Sudfad and Roch

**Alexas Rose:** daughter of Matthew and Angelina

**Alexis:** son of Usman, the leader of the Valdore Tribe

**Alice:** and her husband find Jorge near death in Nora

**Alicia:** a female Nordes warrior

**Aloeus:** Shettee warrior

**Amelia:** baby Ruala girl

**Amiee:** sister of Marie/ nurse for grandchildren of King Sudfad

**Amper:** a Florine

**Amundsen:** Commanding General of Fort Friada in the Kingdom of Ganz

**Amy:** a young girl who was kidnapped by Sal

**Ana:** eleven year old Nordes girl/daughter of Edgar and Cora/younger sister of Batina

**Ana:** Princess/daughter of Zeman and Oda/niece of King Manu of New Samona/Ruala

**Anda:** one of Chief Romogi's three wives/Huta

**Andrac:** a powerful sorcerer and seer in the Kingdom of Inferus/Elod

**Andre Wilchess:** son of Chet and Darlene/ husband of Joanna Franks/ brother of Philip

**Andrea:** female Ruala warrior/ sister of Bekka

**Andres:** Princess of Ryed/daughter of Oren and Astrel/ has twin sister Jorga

**Andrew:** jeweler in Salar

**Andrus:** father of Rabi/Ruala

**Angelina:** daughter of Sorren, Chief of the Nordes Tribe/female warrior

**Anka:** Elod child

**Annabar:** daughter of King Sharonne

**Annabelle:** handmaid and best friend to Queen Vitomas of the Kingdom of Stordt

**Annie:** female Nordes warrior/ girlfriend of Terrance

**Anthony:** one of the twin sons of Simon and Annabelle

**April:** a young girl who was kidnapped by Sal

**Arca:** Enrop leader who protects King Mathas' family

**Archer:** Hector's true identity

**Arches:** a Patronus priest

**Archetenus The Brave:** Captain in the Taperian Army

**Argail:** a homeless mother

**Arianna:** daughter of Simon and Annabelle

**Ariel:** daughter of Raul and Vitomas

**Arland:** male Nordes Warrior

**Arlene:** housekeeper and cook for Erebus/wife of Theodore

**Arlene:** wife of Dixon/friend of Olivia

**Armstrong:** soldier and scout in the army of Wetpr

**Arthur Marcus:** father of Hannah

**Artis:** an old sailor from the Navy of Ganz

**Artis:** male Ruala warrior/oldest brother of Ratri/husband of Jenna

**Asgar:** an Old One on the planet Filsum

**Asher:** male Ruala warrior

**Asher:** youngest of three brothers who formed the Libertas in Ryed

**Ashlee:** young female Nordes warrior

**Asmodeus:** an ancient demon/ one of the Old Ones

**Astar:** General in the Military of Ryed who tries to take over the kingdom after the fall of Teivel

**Astrel:** former princess of Ryed/daughter of Akasha and Norah

**Atomos:** Elder of the Centras and Keeper of the Box of Itifer

**Augustus Endleson:** a wealthy businessman who owned part of the City of Nora

**Ava:** twin of Benjamin/daughter of Archetenus and Delilah

**Axel Sam:** a notorious pirate

**Azu:** a Florine

**Baal:** an ancient demon/ one of the Old Ones

**Babu:** Enrop

**Bac:** male Ruala warrior

**Bachnenus:** warrior guarding refugees/Shettee

**Baird:** an Elod/a member of the Charto/

**Bali:** Enrop leader of the flock that does battle at Juleta's castle

**Balin:** Prince of Norkv/son of Thaddius and Omara/grandson of Benjeman and Esther

**Balius:** Shettee warrior/brother of King Neputa

**Banacus:** General in the army of King Tobias of Puntd

**Banaka:** a female Grand Master of the Insidiae

**Barak:** Prince of Norkv/grandson of Benjeman and Esther

**Barak:** Prince/son of King Neputa and Queen Tiara/Shettee

**Barid:** Prince of Ogg

**Barid:** Prince of Ryed/son of Nehmota and Vasart

**Barnabas:** a member of the wealthy and elite in Ryed

**Bart:** male Elod/member of Javier's and Madeline's team

**Bart:** male Ruala warrior/ married to Bekka's sister Andrea

**Bartholomew:** alias used by Raphael in Ryed

**Baruk:** the leader of the Abuckto Sect in the Kingdom of Inferus/Elod

**Barush:** a major in the Military of Ryed

**Bastra:** Huta captain

**Batina:** young female Nordes warrior

**Batya:** wife of Elen/Ruala

**Beatrice Endleson:** wife of Augustus

**Beatrice:** an Elod healer

**Becca:** Princess of Norkv/daughter of Thaddius and Omara/granddaughter of Benjeman and Esther

**Behtay:** Princess/daughter of Segal and Cahina/niece of King Manu of New Samona/Ruala

**Bekka:** female Ruala warrior

**Bella:** wife of Claudius and mother of Stephan

**Benedict:** leader of the Credo in Inferus/father of Anka, Santi and Linus/husband of Cyrene/ Elod

**Benedict:** Prince of Norkv/son of Benjeman and Esther

**Benix:** boss of Ivan/ from the Kingdom of Inferus

**Benjamin:** twin of Ava/son of Archetenus and Delilah

**Benjeman:** vicious rebel leader who overthrew the government of Samona

**Benny:** adopted son of Fahron and Isadore

**Benson:** a Private in the Wetprian military

**Bentra:** an ancient demon/ one of the Old Ones

**Bert:** owner of the Midnight Tavern in Stoba Lentz/husband of Agnes

**Berta:** cook at Racing Horse Tavern

**Berta:** Queen of Stordt/wife of Micha/grandmother of Roch and Sudfad

**Bertha:** an elderly woman from Nora

**Bertuck:** the demon who Usman sold his soul

**Bethany:** female Ruala healer

**Betsy Sarbush:** wealthy socialite in the City of Langer in the Kingdom of Lentz

**Betty:** a woman from Nora

**Betu:** male Ruala warrior

**Bianca:** young female Nordes warrior

**Bill:** owner of a butcher shop in Stoba Lentz

**Bishop:** General in the Army of Lentz

**Black Jack:** a regular patron at the Ghost Ship Tavern in Port Friada

**Blackjack:** works for Hector

**Bode:** Shettee warrior

**Boris:** a general in the Military of Ryed

**Botis:** a demon

**Brandon:** Nordes child/son of Marsha and Kyle/nephew of Jasmine

**Bremmer:** an arms dealer in Ryed

**Brent:** a soldier from Lentz who fights in the Gefrey Games in Ryed

**Brik:** son of Prince Lakin and Princess Zada /Ruala

**Brina:** Princess of Norkv/daughter of Valor and Cai/granddaughter of Benjeman and Esther

**Brit:** male Nordes warrior

**Brock:** male Venator

**Bruce:** male Nordes warrior/eldest son of Edgar and Cora/older brother of Batina

**Bryce:** male Ruala warrior

**Burto:** high priest of the Abuckto in the Kingdom of Inferus

**Cabal:** son of Karzman and Nadia

**Cabot:** an Elod/a member of the Charto/

**Cacu:** Enrop leader that joined Raul and Simon on a mission

**Cade:** son of King Pergo and Queen Vinus/ Kingdom of Gandt

**Cadi:** daughter of Prince Hadar and Princess Paj/ granddaughter of Manu/Ruala

**Cadmus:** the demon that the Dura Tribe worships

**Cael:** Shettee boy who is adopted by Thedes and Ibula

**Cage:** male Ruala warrior

**Cahina:** Princess/ married to Segal son of King Zachariah and Queen Noella of New Samona/Ruala

**Cai:** Princess of Norkv/wife of Valor who was the son of Benjeman and Esther

**Cal:** male Nordes warrior

**Caleb:** son of Luca and Natalie

**Calen:** male Ruala warrior/cousin of Luca/son of Maxwell and Emeral/

**Calla:** female Ruala warrior

**Callie:** Nordes child/younger sister of Bianca/daughter of Tyler and Dora

**Calus:** a dark lord/member of the Insidiae

**Calvin:** a desk clerk at The Captain's Retreat Hotel in Port Friada

**Campbell:** one of the spies at the Castle at Wetpr

**Canton:** Cisero's second in command

**Captain Morgan:** Wetprian Military/Fort Serpha

**Cara:** Princess of Ogg

**Carl:** a drifter/travels with Zeke, Sam and Johnny

**Carlsman:** a Lieutenant in the Army of Lentz

**Carlson:** Sergeant in the Wetprian Army

**Carlton:** alias used by Archetenus in Ryed

**Carson Dormors:** a wealthy landowner in the Kingdom of Ganz

**Carson:** male Nordes warrior/ husband of Marlas/ father of Lana, Tanya, Norris, Terrance, Dalton, Lola and Curtis

**Carston:** member of the governing body of Nora

**Casey:** male Ruala warrior/father of Melanie/husband of Tasha

**Cass:** one of Hectors' men

**Cassandra:** female Ruala warrior

**Cassidy:** homeless boy

**Cates:** alias used by Sorren in Ryed

**Catherine:** second wife of Clarence/ stepmother of Archer

**Cedrick Teivel:** a ruthless, powerful man in the Kingdom of Ryed

**Celia:** Nordes child/sister of Adam

**Celo:** Prince of Ryed/son of Oren and Astrel

**Cere:** daughter of Tristt/Shettee

**Cerephus:** General in the Taperian Army

**Cerey:** orphan girl/sister of Nicholas/adopted daughter of Gabriel and Hannah

**Ceria:** Princess/daughter of Gunnel and Uma/niece of King Manu of New Samona/ sister of Elan/Ruala

**Chaez:** son of Fahron

**Chaladrone:** an ancient demon/ one of the Old Ones

**Chalice:** hired fighter for Dieter

**Chalta:** daughter of King Pergo and Queen Vinus/ Kingdom of Gandt

**Chance:** works with the Patronus

**Chara:** three year old Ruala girl/ daughter of Orin and Rene/niece of Ratri

**Charlene:** a woman from Nora

**Charles Moses:** a violent and abusive man

**Charles:** Father of Cassandra, Joao and Melinda

**Charles:** hired farmhand of Arthur Marcus

**Charter:** Colonel in the Military of Ryed

**Chasity:** missing sister of Joey and Tommy

**Chet Wilchess:** husband of Darlene/ father of Philip and Andre/rich businessman in Port Friada

**Chet:** owns a company of barges in the Village of New Flounder in the Kingdom of Zorta

**Chief Romogi:** leader of the Hutas/ Kingdom of Marba

**Christopher:** six year old boy who Luca saves from the Hutas/brother of Lila

**Ciao:** female Ruala warrior

**Cicely:** adopted daughter of Elan and Cassandra

**Cisero:** a member of the Insidiae

**Clair:** a woman from Nora

**Clair:** female Ruala warrior/mother of Ratri/wife of Joseph

**Clarence:** Father of Archer/ wealthy nobleman/ husband of Matilda then Catherine

**Claudius:** General in the Army of Lentz

**Clay:** the manager of the Teivel Manor Hotel in Ryed

**Clem:** a drunk who works odd jobs

**Cleo:** a man who works for Cicero/a vessel

**Cleta:** female Ruala warrior who fought in Ryed

**Clev:** Hector's head lieutenant

**Clifford:** a general in the Military of Ryed

**Cobren:** Prince of Norkv/son of Grace and Makalo/Grandson of Benjeman and Esther

**Cody:** orphan boy

**Collins:** Lieutenant in the Army of Ganz

**Compro:** Taperian soldier injured at Wall of Dorath

**Conrad:** father of Jasmine/husband of Leta/Nordes Tribe

**Cora:** mother of Batina/wife of Edgar/Nordes warrior

**Corina:** young female Nordes warrior

**Corsa:** female Nordes warrior/healer

**Corwin:** son of King Fahra and Queen Sitha of Zorta

**Crater:** a Sergeant in the Wetprian army

**Crater:** a soldier in the army of Wetpr

**Crispus:** a guard at King Roch's castle

**Crocell:** a demon

**Cronn:** a demon

**Cronos:** Shettee warrior

**Crystal Jillian:** daughter of Raphael and Vivian/ sister of Robert

**Curtis:** male Ruala warrior who fought in Ryed

**Curtis:** Nordes child/youngest brother of Lana and Tanya

**Cyrene:** wife of Benedict/mother of Anka, Santi and Linus/Elod

**Cyril:** a street preacher

**Daceron:** a demon from the world of Balterak in the Mensor Galaxy

**Dack:** male Ruala warrior

**Dacron:** former prince of Ryed/is murdered by his younger brother Nehmota for the throne

**Dael:** an ancient demon/ one of the Old Ones

**Dafney:** a witch

**Dagon:** a male Ruala warrior

**Dagor:** son of King Fahra and Queen Sitha of Zorta

**Dai:** son of Gael, grandson of Manu/Ruala

**Daisy:** a young woman from Langer

**Daisy:** nine year old Nordes girl/ daughter of Edgar and Cora/younger sister of Batina

**Dalton:** male Nordes warrior/brother of Lana and Tanya

**Damas:** an ancient demon/ one of the Old Ones

**Danar:** a man created to be a vessel for demons

**Daniel:** an emissary of The Great Ruler who takes on the disguise of a human man

**Danilla:** mother of King Mathas

**Dano:** seven year old Nordes boy/son of Edgar and Cora/youngest brother of Batina

**Darius:** Prince of Samona/son of Thomas and Rewel/brother of Varden

**Darla:** young female Nordes warrior

**Darlah:** sister of Marie/ nurse for grandchildren of King Sudfad

**Darlene Wilchess**: wife of Chet/mother of Philip and Andre/ socialite

**Dax:** a male Nordes warrior

**Dea:** Nordes warrior/mother of Adam and Celia/wife of Vilem

**Deborah:** a servant of Charles Moses

**Deckor:** mayor of Langer, the capital city of the Kingdom of Lentz

**Delilah:** wife of Dieter

**Delilia:** Queen of New Samona/mother of Ibula, Lakin, Gael and Hadar/ wife of King Manu/Ruala

**Demanko:** a demon

**Demetries:** a demon

**Denise Froush:** wife of Martin who is a wealthy ship builder in Port Friada

**Denks:** a soldier in the army of Wetpr

**Denton:** one of the spies at the Castle in Wetpr

**Derek:** friend of Thaos

**Derlock:** Huta warrior

**Desavo:** the demon who leads the Armada of the dead

**Diana:** a Venator/sister of Thor

**Dieter:** member of the Insidiae

**Dillion:** hired killer who works for Otto Franks

**Dillion:** one of Karzman's hired fighters

**Dion:** Princess of Samona/wife of Yorggi who was the son of Thomas and Rewel/brother of Varden

**Dirk:** Nordes Tribe/father of Corsa, Alex, Kent and George/fisherman

**Dixon:** a Taperian soldier

**Dixon:** Chief Seaman of the Falcon

**Dixon:** husband of Arlene/friend of Olivia

**Dominic Petlov:** was the senior High Priest at the monastery at Malga before he was murdered

**Dominic:** oldest of three brothers who formed the Libertas in Ryed

**Dora:** Nordes warrior/mother of Bianca/wife of Tyler

**Dorack:** an Elod man

**Dorme:** Prince of Ogg

**Doros:** works for High Priest Meekos

**Douma:** King of Ogg

**Dr. Theodore Jackson:** head of the medical school at Cicero College in Salar

**Drake:** worked for Karzman

**Dresden:** a Sergeant in the Wetprian army

**Duncan:** Chief of the Clan of Gesmal in Ryed/ husband of Liza

**Duran:** father of Nikki/Nordes Tribe

**Durst:** Colonel in the Military of Wetpr

**Dymas:** Shettee warrior

**Eachann:** Shettee warrior

**Edgar:** father of Batina/husband of Cora/Nordes warrior

**Edith:** wife of Lloyd a banker in Nora

**Edna:** a Nordes healer

**Eilig:** male Ruala warrior

**Elan:** male Ruala warrior/son of Gunnel and Uma/

**Eldridge:** works with the Patronus

**Elen:** son of Andrus and Naomi/ brother of Rabi/ Ruala

**Elexas:** a female Nordes warrior

**Elizabeth:** wife of Wickfield

**Ella:** female Ruala warrior/mother of Bekka/wife of Sam

**Elliot:** a hired fighter who works for King Friada of the Kingdom of Ganz

**Eloise:** a store clerk in Salar

**Eloise:** female Ruala warrior/oldest sister of Bekka/wife of Tony

**Elsa:** female Ruala warrior/mother of Mia/wife of Tyron

**Emeral:** mother of Calen/Ruala

**Emeric:** a male Grand Master of the Insidiae

**Emily:** sister of Angus

**Emma:** daughter of Luca and Lila

**Emmet:** worker for Gabriel

**Emon:** a male Grand Master of the Insidiae

**Enzo:** male Ruala warrior

**Erebus:** sorcerer from Ryed

**Eric:** a male Nordes warrior

**Erwat:** a member of the Half-Man's Tribe who helps the Clan of Gesmal

**Esser:** Prince/son of Segal and Cahina/nephew of King Manu of New Samona/Ruala

**Esteban:** a member of the Insidiae

**Esther:** Queen of New Norkv/wife of rebel leader Benjeman

**Ethan:** a male Ruala warrior

**Everite:** a Major in the Wetprian Army

**Fabron:** Prince of Ogg

**Fadil:** a male Grand Master of the Insidiae

**Fahra:** King of Zorta

**Fahron:** General in the Army of Lentz

**Fairoot:** demon/ lieutenant for Salzar

**Fala:** female Ruala warrior

**Farnsworth:** General in charge of building Fort Serpha in Wetpr

**Fatima:** Prince of Ryed/ son of Oren and Astrel

**Fatronas:** an ancient demon/one of the Old Ones

**Felistine:** a member of the wealthy and elite in Ryed

**Fengu:** Enrop leader who helps Gabriel and his group against Omnibus

**Fennel:** one of three brothers who formed the Libertas in Ryed

**Ferguson:** a Sergeant in the Army of Lentz

**Fiona:** mother of Nadia/grandmother of Michael

**Fraisier:** a businessman and member of the Insidiae in Nora

**Frank:** a villager in Telmark

**Frankie:** Nordes child/younger brother of Jasmine/son of Conrad and Leta

**Frankwich:** husband of Matilda/father of Olin/warlock

**Fred Stapleton:** a farmer in Wetpr

**Fred:** a bartender at The Treasure Chest Tavern in Port Friada

**Friada:** King of the Kingdom of Ganz

**Gabi:** an Enrop

**Gabriella:** sister of Marie/nurse to grandchildren of King Sudfad

**Gad:** male Ruala warrior

**Gael:** Prince/son of King Manu and Queen Delilia/Ruala

**Gala:** a healer from the Kingdom of Stordt

**Galen:** male Nordes warrior

**Garvis:** male Elod/member of Javier's and Madeline's team

**Geobel:** General in the Military of Ryed who tries to take over the kingdom after the fall of Teivel

**Geof Thurstand:** ship owner/husband of Linda

**Geoff:** Prince of Lentz/son of Princess Isabella and Captain Josef

**Geoff:** Prince of Norkv/son of Benedict and Sasaha/grandson of Benjeman and Esther

**Georganson:** an arms dealer in Ryed

**George:** an advisor for King Fahra of Zorta

**George:** middle son of Chief Duncan and Liza of the Clan of Gesmal in Ryed

**George:** Nordes warrior/brother of Corsa, Kent and Alex

**Gideon:** Admiral in the Navy of Ganz

**Gilder:** a dark lord from the Kingdom of Inferus

**Giles:** hired fighter for Mayor Deckor of Langer

**Gilmore:** a Wetprian soldier

**Giovani:** Rachel's older half-brother

**Gita:** wife of Hadi/ Ruala

**Gladys**: member of Nordes Tribe/ mother of Nikki

**Glenda:** great, great, great grandmother of Gala/ a healer from the Kingdom of Stordt

**Grace:** Princess of New Norkv/daughter of Benjeman and Esther

**Gracie:** cook for the Arthur Marcus family

**Grady:** worker for Gabriel

**Grant:** a male Nordes warrior

**Great Ruler:** God

**Gregory Bancar:** a wealthy landowner in the Kingdom of Wetpr and member of the Insidiae

**Greta:** older Ruala woman/friend of Emeral's

**Greta:** wife of Hugo/mother of Sasha/ sister-in-law of Sorren

**Gunnel:** Prince/ son of King Zachariah and Queen Noella of New Samona/husband of Uma/father of Elan/Ruala

**Gunter:** Seaman in the Navy of Lentz

**Gus:** husband of Penelope/ killed for trying to help Nadia and Michael escape from Karzman

**Gus:** owner of Racing Horse Tavern

**Haas:** a Lieutenant in the Wetprian military

**Hadar:** Prince/son of King Manu and Queen Delilia/Ruala

**Hadi:** son of Andrus and Naomi/ brother of Rabi/ Ruala

**Hadi:** son of Andrus and Naomi/brother of Rabi/Ruala

**Hadu:** female Ruala warrior

**Halsal:** Sergeant in the Military of Lentz

**Hamon:** one of the members of the Nordes Tribe who was injured in an attack at Snakes Crossing

**Hamond:** General of the Taperian Army who declares himself king

**Hanger:** one of the spies at the Castle at Wetpr

**Hangered:** Wetprian soldier

**Hank:** low level criminal

**Hannah:** physician in Nora/ Roch murdered her sister

**Haris:** an assassin

**Harlow:** an investigative reporter for The Port Friada Gazette

**Harold:** husband of Berta/part owner of the Racing Horse Tavern

**Harold:** owner of the general store in Nora

**Harriet Marcus:** mother of Hannah and Laurabelle/wife of Arthur

**Harris:** male Ruala warrior who fought in Ryed

**Harrison:** Lieutenant in the Military of Lentz

**Harvard:** President of the Port Friada Bank

**Hatus:** General in the Army of Lentz/on loan to Sudfad

**Hazel:** housekeeper at Erebus' mansion in Salar

**Hector:** fighter hired by Juleta

**Hector:** Prince of Samona/son of Varden

**Henry:** and his wife Alice find Jorge in Nora

**Henry:** husband of Noreen/father of Jacob

**Hermanas:** second in command to Archetenus at Wall of Dorath

**High Priest Aaron:** member of the Patronus

**High Priest Alfonso:** a member of the Patronus

**High Priest Amos:** a member of the Patronus

**High Priest Barnabas:** most Senior High Priest of the monastery at Leven

**High Priest Bernard:** a member of the Patronus

**High Priest Caleb:** member of the Patronus

**High Priest Ephraim:** a member of the Patronus

**High Priest Frederick:** a member of the Patronus

**High Priest Gabriel:** member of the Patronus/demon hunter

**High Priest Gideon:** a member of the Patronus

**High Priest Gregory:** member of the Patronus

**High Priest Henrich:** a member of the Patronus Priests

**High Priest Ira:** a member of the Patronus Priests

**High Priest Joseph:** member of the Patronus, in charge of the Cicero Headquarters

**High Priest Josiah:** member of the Patronus

**High Priest Maddox:** a member of the Patronus Priests

**High Priest Meekos:** priest at the monastery at Malga

**High Priest Nicholas:** most Senior High Priest of the monastery at Philiste and most Senior High Priest of the Patronus

**High Priest Norbert:** Senior High Priest at the monastery at Casum in NW Wetpr

**High Priest Othnial:** Senior High Priest of the monastery in Rubar in the Kingdom of Ryed

**High Priest Paulas:** member of the Patronus

**High Priest Phanuel:** member of the Patronus

**High Priest Philetus:** member of the Patronus in charge of Malga Headquarters

**High Priest Pravis:** priest at the monastery at Malga

**High Priest Raphael:** a leader of the Patronus

**High Priest Rueben:** member of the Patronus in charge of Nora Headquarters

**High Priest Silas:** a member of the Patronus

**High Priest Tenebrae:** priest at the monastery at Malga

**High Priest Timothy:** was murdered by Meekos, Pravis and Tenebrae

**High Priest Tyrus:** a member of the Patronus

**High Priest Uriel:** member of the Patronus

**High Priest Vincent:** assigned to the monastery at Malga before he was murdered

**High Priest Zophar:** priest at monastery at Malga/ trained as a healer

**Hilgra:** a witch

**Hobart:** a man who works for demons

**Horace:** father of Rachel and Zach/husband of Zelda/freedom fighter in Ryed

**Hores:** son of Chief Romogi and Anda, Kingdom of Marba/Huta

**Hors:** a clerk at The Rooster

**Horta:** Prince/son of Gunnel and Uma/nephew of King Manu of New Samona/brother of Elan/Ruala

**Howie:** one of Deckor's hired fighters

**Hugh:** Manager of The Rooster

**Hugo:** younger brother of Sorren/father of Sasha/husband of Greta

**Hunter:** Prince of Samona/son of Varden

**Hunter:** son of Natalie and Troy/Clan of Gesmal

**Ian Maxwell Luca:** son of Koby and Bekka

**Ian:** husband of Mia/ brother in law of Calen/ Ruala

**Ibula:** warrior princess and healer of the Ruala Tribe/daughter of King Manu and Queen Delilia/

**Iden:** warrior guarding refugees/Shettee

**Igor:** brother of King Sharonne

**Ike Ferguson:** elderly neighbor of Gabriel and Hannah

**Imad:** a male Grand Master of the Insidiae

**Ina:** daughter of Mia and Ian/ Ruala

**Ingr:** female warrior of Nordes Tribe

**Inon:** one of Cisero's men/a vessel

**Ipos:** an ancient demon/ one of the Old Ones

**Iris:** mother of Vivian/wife of Joshua/Clan of Gesmal in Ryed

**Irit:** daughter of Hadi and Gita/ Ruala

**Isabella:** Princess of Lentz, sister of Mathas, Renya and Tasha, married to Captain Josef

**Isadore:** wife of Fahron

**Isla:** daughter of Prince Lakin and Princess Zada/Ruala

**Isla:** female warrior of Nordes Tribe

**Ivan:** boss of Javier and Madeline/from the Kingdom of Inferus

**Ivan:** youngest son of Chief Duncan and Liza of the Clan of Gesmal in Ryed

**Iverson:** hired killer/foreman

**Jace:** husband of Oda/ brother in law of Calen/Ruala

**Jack Franks:** son of Otto and Ruthie/old money in Langer

**Jack:** member of governing body of Nora

**Jackson:** a private in the Army of Lentz

**Jackson:** an escaped prisoner from Wetpr

**Jackson:** Corporal in the Army of Lentz

**Jackson:** one of Deckor's hired fighters

**Jackwitz:** Sergeant in the Military of Lentz

**Jacob:** boy who Angelina found in the woods

**Jacot:** son of Prince Lakin and Princess Zada/ grandson of King Manu/Ruala

**Jaden:** Sergeant in the Army of Lentz

**Jago:** son of Elen and Batya/ Ruala

**Jake:** hired fighter for Mayor Deckor of Langer

**Jake:** works for Talverson Transport Company in Port Friada

**Jakiv:** Prince/son of Segal and Cahina/nephew of King Manu of New Samona/Ruala

**Jama:** Enrop leader who protects Chief Sorren's family

**James:** Taperian soldier

**Jana:** female Ruala warrior

**Janja:** Princess/daughter of Gunnel and Uma/niece of King Manu of New Samona/ sister of Elan/Ruala

**Janson:** Wetprian soldier

**Jared:** hired fighter

**Jaretta:** King of Stordt/husband of Queen Lillian/ father of Roch and Sudfad

**Jarrod:** works for Pravis/leads attack on castle in Wetpr

**Jarvis:** a farmer who is killed by escaped prisoners

**Jasmine:** young female Nordes warrior

**Jason:** male Nordes warrior

**Jasper:** a large white dog that Gabriel brings home

**Jasper:** Prince of Lentz/son of Princess Isabella and Captain Josef

**Jatu:** Enrop leader who protects Fahron's family

**Javier:** a spy from the Kingdom of Inferus/brother of Madeline

**Jeb:** friend of Thaos

**Jeb**: one of Cisero's men

**Jela:** Queen of Samona/wife of Varden

**Jenna:** female Ruala warrior/married to Ratri's oldest brother Artis

**Jenny:** secretary of Mayor Deckor

**Jeremy:** cousin of Andrew the jeweler in Salar

**Jerik:** a male Grand Master of the Insidiae

**Jess:** a soldier of Wetpr

**Jillian:** Queen of Ogg/wife of King Douma

**Jinn:** an ancient demon/ one of the Old Ones

**Joanna Franks:** daughter of Otto and Ruthie/old money in Langer

**Joao:** male Ruala warrior

**Joe:** works for Hector

**Joey:** adopted son of Elan and Cassandra

**Johnny:** a drifter/travels with Zeke, Sam and Carl

**Jonas:** Captain in the Taperian Army

**Jonathan Gabriel Maxwell:** son of Calen and Natasha

**Jonathon Blackmoore**: a physician who attended college with Hannah

**Jonathon:** a waiter at the Calla Lily Restaurant in Teivel Ryed

**Jordy:** male Nordes warrior

**Jorga:** Princess of Ryed/daughter of Oren and Astrel/ has twin sister Andres

**Jorge:** a cook who is kidnapped from Endleson Hotel in Nora

**Josef:** Captain in the Lentz military/ married to Princess Isabella, sister of King Mathas

**Joseph:** male Ruala warrior/father of Ratri/husband of Clair

**Joseph:** nine year old Ruala boy/son of Artis and Jenna/nephew of Ratri

**Josh:** Nordes warrior/husband of Stella

**Joshua:** father of Vivian/husband of Iris/Clan of Gesmal in Ryed

**Josie:** an escaped prisoner from Wetpr

**Juleta:** cousin to Raul and Simon/daughter and oldest child of King Mathas and Queen Rosa

**Julie:** a young woman from Langer

**Kadin:** a member of Valdore Tribe

669

**Kagen:** a man who kidnaps and exploits children

**Kalee:** female Ruala warrior/married to Ratri's older brother Quinn

**Kantof:** hired killer/foreman

**Karin:** wife of Mayor Deckor of Langer

**Karl:** two year old Ruala boy/son of Artis and Jenna/nephew of Ratri

**Karta:** male Ruala warrior

**Karzman:** leader of Kozach Tribe/ stepfather of Michael

**Kasper:** Prince/son of Zeman and Oda/nephew of King Manu of New Samona/Ruala

**Kata:** Princess/daughter of Gunnel and Uma/niece of King Manu of New Samona/ sister of Elan/Ruala

**Kate:** a Venator from the Clan of Gesmal

**Kent:** Nordes warrior/brother of Corsa, Alex and George

**Khryriss:** an ancient demon/ one of the Old Ones

**Kiana:** Princess/daughter of Gunnel and Uma/niece of King Manu of New Samona/ sister of Elan/Ruala

**Kinsman:** a warrior from the Valdore Tribe

**Klass:** Lieutenant in the Wetprian Army

**Koby:** male Ruala warrior

**Koh:** son of Prince Gael and Princess Mada/grandson of King Manu/Ruala

**Kora:** Princess/ married to Raphael son of King Zachariah and Queen Noella of New Samona/ mother of Luca/ Raphael and Kora were killed in battle when Luca was a small boy/Ruala

**Korbin:** one of Teivel's lieutenants

**Korth:** son of Tristt/Shettee

**Kraus:** hired fighter and intended vessel, works for Dieter

**Kretcher:** Commanding General of Fort Polta in Wetpr

**Krister:** Princess of Samoan/daughter of Thomas and Rewel

**Kyle:** Nordes warrior/older brother of Jasmine/son of Conrad and Leta/husband of Marsha/father of Brandon

**Kyra:** young sister of Marie/ friend of Petra

**Laban:** Prince of Samona/son of Yorggi and Dion/grandson of Thomas and Rewel

**Lael:** daughter of Nina and Rhea/ Ruala

**Lakin:** Prince/son of King Manu and Queen Delilia/husband of Zada/Ruala

**Lala:** Princess/daughter of Adwell and Nada/niece of King Manu of New Samona/ sister of Misha/Ruala

**Lana:** female Nordes warrior/older sister of Tanya/

**Lana:** female warrior of the Nordes Tribe

**Lana:** Princess/daughter of Segal and Cahina/niece of King Manu of New Samona/Ruala

**Lance:** a gang leader in Langer

**Lance:** Nordes warrior/older brother of Jasmine/son of Conrad and Leta

**Lani:** daughter of Mia and Ian/Ruala

**Lara:** one of Usman's wives

**Larson:** a fighter hired by Juleta

**Laurabelle:** Hannah's sister who was murdered by Roch

**Laurel:** Annabelle's mother and former servant of King Roch's parents

**Lawrence:** a member of the Libertas

**Lawrence:** father of Dack/husband of Rose/Ruala

**Lazo:** fighter hired by Juleta

**Lea:** Princess/daughter of Adwell and Nada/niece of King Manu of New Samona/ sister of Misha/Ruala

**Leith:** four year old Ruala boy/son of Quin and Kalee/nephew of Ratri

**Leo:** Prince of Samona/son of Darius and Rebek/grandson of Thomas and Rewel

**Leon:** Captain in the Military of Ryed/ a member of Teivel's inner circle

**Leta:** mother of Jasmine/wife of Conrad/Nordes Tribe

**Lieutenant Strater:** Wetprian Military/Fort Serpha

**Lieutenant Tarp:** Lieutenant in the Wetprian Army

**Lila:** seventeen year old girl who Luca saves from the Hutas/sister of Christopher

**Lilian:** female warrior of the Nordes Tribe

**Lillian:** Queen of Stordt/wife of Jaretta/ mother of Roch and Sudfad

**Lily:** daughter of Calen and Natasha/Ruala and human

**Linda Thurstand:** wife of Geof/lover of Mayor Deckor

**Linus:** Elod child

**Liza:** wife of Duncan the Chief of the Clan of Gesmal in Ryed

**Lloyd:** banker in Nora

**Loftus:** Commanding General of Fort Styls

**Logan:** boy stolen by Hector's human trafficking ring

**Lola:** female Nordes warrior/sister of Lana and Tanya

**Lordes:** Seaman in the Navy of Lentz

**Louie:** works for Talverson Transport Company in Port Friada

**Louis:** male Elod/member of Javier's and Madeline's team

**Luca:** male Ruala warrior

**Lucene:** male Nordes warrior/oldest son of Hugo and Greta/older brother of Sasha

**Lucifer:** an ancient demon/ one of the Old Ones

**Lucile:** a member of the wealthy and elite in Ryed

**Lucky:** Sally's puppy

**Lucy:** one of the housekeepers in King Mathas' castle

**Lulu:** female dog adopted by Gabriel's household

**Luque:** Prince/son of Segal and Cahina/nephew of King Manu of New Samona/Ruala

**Mab:** a female Grand Master of the Insidiae

**Mable:** a servant in the castle of King Nehmota of Ryed

**Mabon:** warrior guarding refugees/Shettee

**Mada:** Princess /wife of Prince Gael/Ruala

**Madam Bular:** owner of a dress shop in Port Friada

**Madeline:** a friend of Princess Isabella

**Madix:** General in the Army of Ryed/member of Teivel's first inner circle

**Maggie:** elderly store owner in Salar

**Maggie:** Mayer Tetly's wife

**Mahon:** son of King Neputa

**Makalo:** Prince of Norkv/husband of Grace who was the daughter of Benjeman and Esther

**Malana:** daughter of King Neputa

**Malard:** Captain in the military of Wetpr

**Mali:** Princess of Norkv/daughter of Makalo and Grace/granddaughter of Benjeman and Esther

**Maligma:** an ancient demon/ one of the Old Ones

**Malik:** member of the Insidiae

**Mallory:** female Venator

**Malus:** sorcerer from Ryed

**Mandrake:** Taperian soldier

**Manhure:** Sergeant in the Army of Lentz

**Manu:** King of New Samona/The Chief of the Grand Council made up of Rualas and Shettees/ father of Ibula, Lakin, Gael and Hadar/husband of Delilia

**Manutu:** King of the Gants

673

**Marcia:** friend of Hannah's/ Roch's men murdered her family

**Marcus Stephan:** son of Stephan and Ingr

**Margarit:** daughter of King Mathas and Queen Rosa of the Kingdom of Lentz/ cousin of Raul and Simon

**Margerie:** female cook of King Mathas and Queen Rosa

**Margo:** a young girl who was kidnapped by Sal

**Margolia:** girl from Nora who was sacrificed to a demon

**Marie:** a cook for King Sudfad and Queen Renya

**Marina:** female Ruala healer

**Markus:** a soldier in the Army of Wetpr

**Marla:** High Priest Meekos' housekeeper

**Marlas:** female Nordes warrior/ wife of Carson/ mother of Lana, Tanya, Norris, Terrance, Dalton, Lola and Curtis

**Marsha Jarvis:** a sixteen year old girl who is raped and killed by Timothy

**Marsha:** wife of Charles Moses

**Marsha:** Nordes warrior/wife of Kyle/mother of Brandon/sister-in-law of Jasmine

**Marshal:** Captain in the Military of Lenz

**Marshal:** Major in Army of Lentz

**Martha:** a cook for Cerephus

**Martha:** hotel owner in Telmark

**Martin Froush:** wealthy ship builder in Port Friada/husband of Denise

**Martin:** a member of the Libertas

**Martiz:** a ghost

**Marty:** boy stolen by Hector's human trafficking ring

**Mary:** Jared's young wife who was brutally murdered by Hutas

**Mata:** Igor's wife

**Mateo:** Chief Healer of the Ruala Tribe

**Mathas Sorren:** son of Matthew and Angelina

**Mathas:** King of Lentz/ brother to Queen Renya

**Matilda Frankwich:** wife of Frankwich/mother of Olin

**Matilda:** first wife of Clarence/ mother of Archer

**Matilda:** one of Usman's wives

**Mattel:** hired killer/foreman

**Matthew:** son of King Mathas and Queen Rosa of the Kingdom of Lentz/ cousin of Raul and Simon

**Matty T:** son of Stephan and Ingr

**Max:** one of Hector's men

**Maximus Bartholomew Joshua:** twin son of Misha and Diana/brother of Thor Adwell Gabriel

**Maxwell:** father of Calen/ Ruala

**Maxwell:** infant son of Nina and Rhea/grandson of elder Maxwell/Ruala

**Maynard:** an Elod healer

**McAvoy:** Sergeant in the Army of Wetpr/stationed at Fort Serpha

**Melanie:** female Ruala warrior/daughter of Casey and Tasha

**Melina:** mother of Thaos

**Melinda:** grandmother of Misha

**Melinda:** older sister of Cassandra and Joao

**Mia:** daughter of Maxwell and Emeral/ Ruala

**Mia:** female Ruala warrior/daughter of Tyron and Elsa

**Mica:** Princess of Norkv/daughter of Benedict and Sasaha/granddaughter of Benjeman and Esther

**Micha:** oldest son of Joshua and Iris/older brother of Vivian/Clan of Gesmal

**Micha:** son of King Sharonne/ grandfather of Sudfad and Roch

**Michael:** ancient king of Wetpr/father of Queen Sumona

**Michael:** son of Sudfad and Nadia

**Milo:** abused monkey

**Milo**: male Ruala warrior

**Miranda:** daughter of Raul and Vitomas

**Miranda:** emissary of The Great Ruler who takes on the disguise of a human seer

**Miriam:** a friend of Hannah's/works at Endleson Hotel in Nora

**Misha:** male Ruala warrior/lieutenant

**Molach:** a member of the Insidiae

**Moloch:** an ancient demon/one of the Old Ones

**Moraine:** Captain in the Navy of Lentz

**Morgan:** Sergeant in the Wetprian Army

**Morris:** member of governing body of Nora

**Morton:** Cedrick Teivel's original name

**Muhar:** Shettee warrior

**Murdock:** Major in the Wetprian Army

**Murphy:** Lieutenant in the Army of Wetpr/stationed at Fort Serpha

**Myla:** wife of Rex, the owner of the Dragons Inn in Salar

**Naal:** warrior guarding refugees/Shettee

**Nabi:** male Ruala warrior

**Nada:** Princess/ married to Adwell son of King Zachariah and Queen Noella of New Samona/ mother of Misha/ Adwell was killed in battle leaving Nada to raise ten children/Ruala

**Nadene:** a member of the wealthy and elite in Ryed

**Nadia:** wife of Karzman/mother of Michael

**Nami:** mother of Frankwich/ a witch

**Nana:** female Ruala warrior

**Naomi:** mother of Corsa, Alex, Kent and George/wife of Dirk/Nordes Tribe

**Naomi:** mother of Rabi/ Ruala

**Napo:** Enrop leader who protects Claudius' family

**Nash:** a soldier of Lentz

**Natalie:** female Venator/wife of Troy/mother of Hunter

**Natasha:** sister of High Priest Gabriel

**Nathaniel:** Sorren's oldest son/ Nordes Tribe

**Nebula:** son of Chief Romogi and Anda/ Kingdom of Marba/Huta

**Ned:** Patronus priest

**Negal:** a demon

**Nehmota:** King of Ryed

**Nelpus:** Shettee warrior

**Neputa:** leader of the Shettee Tribe when it was conquered by the Hutas

**Nestor:** a demon that specializes in procuring things for a price

**Nethers:** one of Karzman's hired killers

**Nica:** Enrop leader who protects Sudfad's family

**Nicholas:** orphan boy /brother of Cerey

**Nicolas:** Prince of Puntd/son of King Tobias and Queen Tasha

**Nieatzae:** an ancient demon/ one of the Old Ones

**Nigel:** Chief Seaman in the Navy of Lentz

**Nikki:** female warrior of Nordes Tribe

**Nina:** daughter of Maxwell and Emeral/Ruala

**Nina:** youngest daughter of Karzman and Nadia

**Nita:** Princess/daughter of Adwell and Nada/niece of King Manu of New Samona/ sister of Misha/has twin brother Waed/Ruala

**Noah:** a member of the Libertas

**Nobel:** former prince of Ryed/son of Akasha and Norah/father of Nehmota

**Noel:** a cook at the Teivel Manor Hotel

**Noella:** the first Queen of New Samona/wife of King Zachariah/mother of seven sons/Ruala

**Norah:** former queen of Ryed/grandmother of Nehmota

**Norbert Franks:** father of Otto and Frankwich/husband of Tomina/old money in Langer

**Noreen:** mother of Jacob/ wife of Henry

**Norge:** Private in the Wetprian Army

**Norris:** hired fighter and intended vessel, works for Dieter

**Norris:** male Nordes warrior/ oldest brother of Lana and Tanya

**Novack:** Corporal in the Wetprian Army

**Nyla:** oldest daughter of Karzman and Nadia

**Oda:** daughter of Maxwell and Emeral/ Ruala

**Oda:** Princess/ married to Zeman son of King Zachariah and Queen Noella of New Samona/Ruala

**Odam:** male Ruala warrior

**Odell:** one of the spies at the Castle at Wetpr

**Olin Frankwich:** son of Frankwich and Matilda/dark lord

**Olin:** Patronus priest

**Oliver:** a member of the Libertas

**Olivia:** young girl who can hear people's thoughts

**Omar:** Prince/son of Zeman and Oda/nephew of King Manu of New Samona/Ruala

**Omara:** Queen of Norkv/wife of Thaddius who was son of Benjeman and Esther

**Omnibus:** an ancient demon/ one of the Old Ones

**Omoria:** former queen of Ryed/wife of Nobel/mother of Nehmota

**Opago:** an ancient demon/ one of the Old Ones

**Oran:** son of Visterle and Nada/twin brother of Verto

**Orcus:** Shettee warrior/brother of King Neputa

**Oren:** former prince of Gandt who marries princess Astrel of Ryed

**Oriah:** name used by the Grand Master Banaka

**Orin:** male Ruala warrior/older brother of Ratri/husband of Rene

**Otis:** Nordes Warrior/first adopted father of Benny

**Ottillia:** Princess of Lenz/daughter of Princess Isabella and Captain Josef

**Otto Franks:** husband of Ruthie/father of Jack and Joanna/old money in Langer

**Otu:** son of Hecate and Sampson

**Padre Augustus:** a member of the Patronus

**Padre Bartholomew:** survives the massacre at the monastery at Avaide

**Padre Bishop:** assigned to the monastery at Leven

**Padre Cornelius:** a member of the Patronus

**Padre Darius:** a member of the Patronus

**Padre Dibon:** a priest at the monastery at Malga

**Padre Dominick:** priest at monastery at Malga

**Padre Edgar:** member of the Patronus

**Padre Edward:** a member of the Patronus

**Padre Finn:** Patronus priest assigned to the Cicero HQ

**Padre Francis:** priest at monastery at Malga

**Padre Joram:** member of the Patronus

**Padre Lucas:** a member of the Patronus

**Padre Markle:** a Patronus priest

**Padre Nebat:** alias for Dominic leader of the Libertas

**Padre Octavos:** runs orphanage in Salar

**Padre Philip:** a member of the Patronus

**Padre Philip:** a priest at the monastery at Malga

**Padre Simpson:** priest at the monastery at Malga

**Padre Sorben:** a member of the Patronus

**Padre Sornce:** Patronus priest assigned to the Cicero HQ

**Padre Stephens:** priest at monastery at Malga

**Padre Thomas:** priest at the monastery at Malga

**Padre Tobias:** a member of the Patronus

**Padre Xavier:** priest at monastery at Malga

**Paj:** Princess/wife of Prince Hadar/Ruala

**Pallas:** Shettee warrior

**Parker:** a banker in Port Friada

**Pata:** daughter of Chief Romogi and Trina/Huta

**Paterson:** a Private in the Wetprian military

**Patrick:** owns a company of mercenaries/ a member of the wealthy and elite in Ryed

**Patris:** six year old Nordes girl/daughter of Hugo and Greta/younger sister of Sasha

**Paul:** third son of Joshua and Iris/younger brother of Vivian/Clan of Gesmal

**Paulas:** a man who works for Cicero/a vessel

**Paulas:** Sergeant under Archetenus in Taperian Army

**Paullo:** works for High Priest Meekos

**Paxel:** Major in the Military of Lentz

**Pearl:** eldest daughter of King Tobias and Queen Tasha of Puntd

**Penelope:** wife of Gus/ killed for trying to help Nadia and Michael escape from Karzman

**Pergo:** King of the Kingdom of Gandt

**Peter:** Sorren's second son/Nordes Tribe

**Peters:** member of the governing body of Nora

**Petorus:** an ancient demon/one of the Old Ones

**Petra:** peasant boy from Ort who saves Padre Bartholomew

**Phifer:** nine year old Nordes boy/ son of Hugo and Greta/younger brother of Sasha

**Philip Wilchess:** son of Chet and Darlene/ brother of Andre

**Philip:** Prince of Puntd/ son of King Tobias and Queen Tasha

**Phillip:** Court Physician to the Royal Family of Wetpr

**Polgate:** one of the men who kidnapped Petra

**Potomas:** warrior guarding refugees/Shettee

**Powell:** a lieutenant in the Military of Lentz/stationed at Fahron's castle.

**Prescott:** a hired killer

**Quin:** male Ruala warrior/older brother of Ratri/husband of Kalee

**Quinn:** an Elod/a member of the Charto/

**Rabi:** male Ruala warrior

**Rachel:** member of the freedom fighters in Ryed

**Radnor:** a male Grand Master of the Insidiae

**Rael:** Prince of old Samona/husband of Krister who was the daughter of Thomas and Rewel

**Rafa:** an Enrop

**Rahi:** a female Grand Master of the Insidiae

**Rakio:** Prince/son of Adwell and Nada/nephew of King Manu of New Samona/brother of Misha/Ruala

**Rako:** a male Ruala warrior

**Ralf:** male Ruala warrior

**Ralph:** an old sailor from the Navy of Ganz

**Randolph:** a manager of The Rooster

**Raphael:** Prince/ son of King Zachariah and Queen Noella of New Samona/husband of Kora/Ruala/father of Luca/ Raphael and Kora were killed in battle when Luca was a small boy/Ruala

**Ratri:** male Ruala warrior

**Raul:** Prince/son of King Sudfad and Queen Renya of the Kingdom of Wetpr

**Raum:** an ancient demon/ one of the Old Ones

**Raven:** female Nordes warrior/healer

**Rebek:** Princess of Samona/wife of Darius, who was the son of Thomas and Rewel

**Rebke:** six year old Ruala girl/ daughter of Orin and Rene/niece of Ratri

**Reed:** male Nordes warrior

**Reese:** a male Ruala warrior

**Remi:** an Enrop

**Rene:** female Ruala warrior/married to Ratri's older brother Orin

**Renya:** Queen of Wetpr/ wife of Sudfad

**Rewel:** Queen of Samona/wife of Thomas/mother of Varden

**Rex:** a notorious pick pocket in Port Friada

**Rex:** owner of the Dragons Inn in Salar/husband of Myla

**Rhea:** husband of Nina/ brother in law of Calen/ Ruala

**Richard:** third husband of Madeline

**Ridon:** General in the military of Wetpr

**Riftca:** male Ruala warrior

**Riker:** a scout in the Wetprian military

**Riley:** an abused dog that Luca saves

**Risa:** female Ruala warrior

**Risha:** a witch who deals with potions

**River:** one of Karzman's soldiers who he murdered

**Roch:** King of the Kingdom of Stordt/brother of King Sudfad

**Rogers:** one of the men who kidnapped Petra

**Rolif:** son of Chief Romogi and Silva/ Kingdom of Marba/Huta

**Romale:** member of the Insidiae

**Romos:** an elder of the Centras

**Rosa:** Queen of Lentz/wife of King Mathas

**Rosalie:** a dressmaker in Nora/wife of Peters

**Rose:** mother of Dack/wife of Lawrence/Ruala

**Roy:** owner of the Pirates Flag Tavern in Langer

**Ruth:** emissary of The Great Ruler who takes on the guise of a frail old woman

**Ruthie Franks:** wife of Otto/mother of Jack and Joanna/old money in Langer

**Ryan:** grandson of Jeb/friend of Thaos

**Rybkin:** Warlock who worked for the dictator Teivel

**Sabot:** member of the Insidiae

**Sahil:** a male Ruala warrior

**Sal:** a murderous pedophile/also goes by the name Tyrone

**Sally:** a young girl who was kidnapped by Sal

**Salzar:** powerful demon on Sidus

**Sam Endleson:** an investigator

**Sam:** a drifter/travels with Zeke, Carl and Johnny

**Sam:** male Ruala warrior/father of Bekka/husband of Ella

**Sam:** Patronus priest

**Samael:** a demon as powerful as Ahriman who rules the hell world Xibalba

**Samara:** wife of Tristt/Shettee

**Samat:** son of Chief Romogi and Silva/ Kingdom of Marba/Huta

**Samos:** Prince of Norkv/son of Thaddius

**Sampson:** oldest son of Chief Duncan and Liza of the Clan of Gesmal in Ryed

**Sampson:** Sergeant in the Taperian Army

**Samuel:** a high priest at the monastery at Malga who was murdered

**Samuel:** Prince of the original Samona/grandson of Thomas and Rewel

**Samuel:** second son of Raul and Vitomas

**Santi:** Elod child

**Sanuri:** a holy man/emissary of The Great Ruler/warrior

**Sar:** an Enrop

**Sar:** male Ruala warrior

**Sara:** daughter of Usman

**Sara:** female Nordes warrior/ girlfriend of Norris

**Sarah:** baby granddaughter of Mathas and Rosa

**Sarah:** housekeeper for Claudius and Bella

**Saran:** daughter of Karzman and Nadia

**Sargei:** a Venator/ husband of Risha

**Sasaha:** Princess of the original Samona/granddaughter of Thomas and Rewel

**Sasha:** young female Nordes warrior

**Sasha:** female warrior of the Nordes Tribe/wife of Galen

**Satan:** an ancient demon/ one of the Old Ones

**Satter:** male Ruala warrior

**Sattleman:** a Sergeant in the Wetprian army

**Sauer:** male Ruala warrior

**Sauer:** Nordes warrior/older brother of Bianca/son of Tyler and Dora

**Saunders:** a Taperian soldier

**Saxton:** powerful lieutenant who works for Teivel the dictator of Ryed

**Schroeder:** man who works for Insidiae leader Dieter

**Schuester:** Commander of a special unit of Teivel's government/identifies betrayers

**Sean:** one of Karzman's hired killers

**Segal:** Prince/ son of King Zachariah and Queen Noella of New Samona/husband of Cahina/Ruala

**Seguna:** former princess of Ryed/daughter of Akasha and Norah/ committed suicide

**Selen:** house keeper for Juleta

**Seth:** a member of the Libertas

**Sez:** male Ruala warrior

**Shadow Men:** a spirit army of Venatores

**Shanksaw:** mercenary

**Shara:** wife of Sorren/Nordes Tribe

**Shard:** Captain in the Military of Ryed/ a member of Teivel's inner circle

**Sharon:** one of Mayor Deckor's lovers

**Sharonne:** King of Stordt; great, great, grandfather of King Roch and King Sudfad

**Sheba:** a female Nordes warrior

**Shon:** son of King Fahra and Queen Sitha

**Shone:** Princess/daughter of Zeman and Oda/niece of King Manu of New Samona/Ruala

**Sicily Bella:** daughter of Stephan and Ingr

**Sila:** Princess of Ogg

**Silva:** one of Chief Romogi's three wives/Huta

**Simmons:** Commanding General of Fort Nir

**Simon:** adopted son of King Sudfad and Queen Renya of the Kingdom of Wetpr

**Sinclair:** King of Lentz/father of King Mathas

**Sirius:** works for High Priest Meekos

**Sitha:** Queen of Zorta

**Smoking Joe:** a regular patron at the Ghost Ship Tavern

**Sol:** male Ruala warrior

**Sonja:** female warrior of the Nordes Tribe

**Sophie:** cook and servant of King Roch

**Sorphat:** demon/ a lieutenant of Samael's

**Sorren:** leader of the Nordes Tribe

**Soto:** male Ruala warrior who leads first death squad for criminals

**Spencer:** an Elod/a member of the Charto/

**Spooner:** an architect in Lentz

**Sporos:** priest turned demon

**Stafus:** a powerful sorcerer who first broke the code to one of the demonic languages

**Stella:** Nordes warrior/wife of Josh

**Stephan:** Captain in Army of Lentz/son of Claudius and Bella

**Stiller:** a fighter hired by Juleta

**Stolas:** an ancient demon/one of the Old Ones

**Stone:** an alias used by Dominic during the mission in Ryed with Gabriel's team

**Stone:** hired fighter and intended vessel, works for Dieter

**Strait:** Lieutenant in the Army of Ganz

**Stranton:** Colonel in the Military of Wetpr

**Strauss:** Lieutenant in the Military of Lentz

**Sudfad:** King of the Kingdom of Wetpr and brother to King Roch of Stordt

**Sudfad:** little Sudfad is grandson of King Sudfad

**Sumona:** Queen of Wetpr/wife of Alexandras/aunt of Roch and Sudfad

**Suzette:** a clerk at The Chicken and The Egg

**Sven:** male Nordes warrior

**Swenson:** one of Shanksaw's hired men

**Syrius:** a Bakken hired by Juleta

**Tabeth:** daughter of Fahron

**Tabith:** son of Tristt/Shettee

**Tabitha:** Princess of Lentz/daughter of Princess Isabella and Captain Josef of Lentz

**Tadeo:** Prince/son of Adwell and Nada/nephew of King Manu of New Samona/brother of Misha/Ruala

**Tafer:** a warlord who drove the Hutas out of the Kingdom of Norkv after years of wars and rebellions

**Tahira:** a female Grand Master of the Insidiae

**Tahira:** Princess of Samona/granddaughter of Thomas and Rewel

**Taj:** a Florine

**Tal:** son of Oda and Jace/ Ruala

**Tally:** worked for Karzman

**Talmai:** Shettee boy who Thedes and Ibula adopt

**Talon:** a male Ruala warrior

**Tambor:** male Ruala warrior

**Tamour:** General in the Army of Lentz/on loan to Sudfad

**Tanner:** a Lieutenant in the Wetprian army

**Tanner:** a Sergeant in the Army of Lentz

**Tanner:** one of Deckor's hired fighters

**Tanya:** a female Nordes warrior/younger sister of Lana

**Tapster:** a demon who works for Meekos

**Tarig:** a lieutenant in the Huta army

**Tarin:** son of King Neputa and Queen Tiara/Shettee

**Tarla Grey:** wealthy socialite in the City of Langer in the Kingdom of Lentz

**Taron:** Prince/son of Adwell and Nada/nephew of King Manu of New Samona/brother of Misha/Ruala

**Tasha:** female Ruala warrior/mother of Melanie/wife of Casey

**Tasha:** Queen of Puntd/ married to Tobias/ sister of Renya and Mathas

**Tate:** a Lieutenant in the Wetprian Army

**Tatterd:** a Sergeant in the Wetprian military

**Tavin:** son of Prince Lakin and Princess Zada/Ruala

**Ted:** one of Juleta's hired men

**Ted:** one of Karzman's hired fighters

**Teddy:** male Nordes warrior/son of Edgar and Cora/ older brother of Batina

**Teddy:** owner of a general store in Stoba Lentz

**Teddy:** works for Hector

**Tega:** housekeeper for the cabins of the captains of the Taperian Army

**Tegman:** soldier of Wetpr

**Tehtfote:** a Lieutenant for Dieter

**Temark:** villager of Neva

**Teresa:** the manager at The Chicken and The Egg

**Terrance:** male Nordes warrior/ older brother of Lana and Tanya

**Tessa Demat:** a con artist

**Tetly:** a mayoral candidate in Langer/ Kingdom of Lentz

**Tetro:** Huta warrior who was a captive in Ogg

**Thadddius:** Prince of the new Kingdom of Norkv/son of Benjeman

**Thaddies:** member of Nordes Tribe/ father of Ingr

**Thanatoes:** an ancient demon/ one of the Old Ones

**Thaos:** a hired fighter

**Thatcher:** Prince/son of Zeman and Oda/nephew of King Manu of New Samona/Ruala

**Thatus:** Taperian soldier

**The Lion:** emissary of The Great Ruler who takes on the appearance of a lion when he is in the world of man

**The Master:** a monster beyond comprehension

**The Originator:** the original darkness/father of demons

**Thedes:** warrior guarding refugees/Shettee

**Theodore:** handyman for Erebus/husband of Arlene

**Theodore:** the physician at Fort Stanus in the Kingdom of Wetpr

**Thomas:** King of the original Kingdom of Samona/father of Varden

**Thomas:** second son of Joshua and Iris/older brother of Vivian/Clan of Gesmal

**Thomas:** the young husband of Zoya who was murdered in Taperia

**Thompson:** Wetprian soldier

**Thor Adwell Gabriel:** twin son of Misha and Diana/brother of Maximus Bartholomew Joshua

**Thor:** a Venator/brother of Diana

**Thot:** an emissary of The Great Ruler

**Thronson:** one of Meekos hired killers

**Tiara:** Queen of Shettee Tribe when it was conquered by Hutas/wife of Neputa

**Timothy:** son of Fahron

**Tina:** Mother of Cassandra, Joao and Melinda

**Tito:** member of Valdore Tribe

**Titus Derek:** son of Thaos and Nikki

**Titus:** a lieutenant in the Taperian Army

**Tobankto:** an Old One from the World of Filsum

**Tobart:** a member of the Nordes Tribe

**Tobey:** a carriage driver in Ryed who helps Gabriel's team

**Tobias:** King of Puntd.

**Tom:** a homeless family man

**Tomas:** works for High Priest Pravis

**Tome:** a businessman and member of the Insidiae in Nora

**Tomi:** son of Usman the leader of the Valdore Tribe

**Tomina Franks:** wife of Norbert/mother of Otto/old money in Langer

**Tommy:** adopted son of Elan and Cassandra

**Toni:** young female Nordes warrior

**Tony:** a male Ruala warrior

**Tony:** male Ruala warrior/ married to Bekka's oldest sister Eloise

**Toomback:** Huta warrior

**Torance:** father of Thaos

**Torin:** oldest son of Karzman and Nadia

**Trace:** male Ruala warrior

**Trace:** one of Karzman's hired fighters

**Tratz:** one of the men who kidnapped Petra

**Travor:** Taperian warrior who was injured at the Wall of Dorath

**Tresdor:** nephew of Usman

**Tresdore:** son of King Sharonne

**Trevor:** Prince/son of Zeman and Oda/nephew of King Manu of New Samona/Ruala

**Tria:** daughter of Oda and Jace/Ruala

**Trina:** an Elod healer

**Trina:** one of Chief Romogi's three wives/Huta

**Trina:** Princess/daughter of Zeman and Oda/niece of King Manu of New Samona/Ruala

**Trist:** a male Ruala warrior

**Tristt the Horrible:** Shettee warrior

**Tritor:** a powerful demon of Sidus and ex-lover of Hecate

**Troy:** male Venator/husband of Natalie/father of Hunter

**Tye:** Prince of Norkv/son of Princess Grace and Prince Makalo

**Tyler:** Nordes warrior/father of Bianca/husband of Dora

**Tyron:** male Ruala warrior/father of Mia/husband of Elsa

**Tyson:** Wetprian soldier

**Ulger:** a demon

**Uma:** Princess/ married to Gunnel son of King Zachariah and Queen Noella of New Samona/mother of Elan/Ruala

**Umar:** Prince/son of Adwell and Nada/nephew of King Manu of New Samona/brother of Misha/Ruala

**Uri:** an Enrop

**Uri:** son of Nina and Rhea/ Ruala

**Usman:** leader of the Valdore Tribe

**Valdus:** name used by the Grand Master Emeric

**Valerie:** young female Nordes warrior

**Valor:** Prince of the new Kingdom of Norkv/son of Benjeman and Esther

**Vandrew:** Petra's male tutor

**Vania:** Princess of Samona/daughter of Yorggi and Dion/granddaughter of Thomas and Rewel

**Varden:** last king of Samona/he and his family were murdered by rebels

**Vardin:** one of the men who kidnapped Petra

**Vasart:** Queen of Ryed/ wife of Nehmota

**Verto:** son of Visterle and Nada/twin brother of Oran

**Viktor:** an ancient priest in Ryed who tried to stop the Insidiae

**Vilem:** Nordes warrior/father of Adam and Celia/husband of Dea

**Vinca:** Queen of Stordt, wife of Sharonne

**Vincent:** Prince of Ryed/son of Nehmota and Vasart

**Vincente:** a captain in the covert organization The Guardians

**Vinus:** Queen of the Kingdom of Gandt

**Visterle:** a powerful demon

**Vitomas:** Queen of Stordt

**Vivian:** a demon hunter from the Clan of Gesmal

**Voltar:** Prince of Samona/son of Darius and Rebek/grandson of Thomas and Rewel/later becomes King of Wetpr

**Voss:** one of Karzman's hired killers

**Vuall:** a demon

**Waed:** Prince/son of Adwell and Nada/nephew of King Manu of New Samona/brother of Misha/has twin sister Nita/Ruala

**Wainburst:** Commanding Admiral of the Navy of the Kingdom of Ganz

**Wallis:** member of governing body of Nora

**Wanda Ferguson:** elderly neighbor of Gabriel and Hannah

**Watkin:** an Elod/a member of the Charto/

**Wickfield:** editor of the most powerful newspaper in the Kingdom of Lentz

**Wilard:** Captain at Fort Polta

**William:** son of Jared and Zoya

**Willis:** son of King Pergo and Queen Vinus/ Kingdom of Gandt

**Xeni:** a female Grand Master of the Insidiae

**Yara:** daughter of Nina and Rhea/Ruala

**Yorggi:** Prince of Samona/son of Thomas and Rewel/brother of Varden

**Yori:** son of Usman the leader of the Valdore Tribe

**Yuri:** Prince/son of Adwell and Nada/nephew of King Manu of New Samona/brother of Misha/Ruala

**Zac:** one of the men who kidnapped Petra

**Zachariah:** first King of New Samona/husband of Queen Noella/father of seven sons/Ruala

**Zack:** eight year old brother of Rachel

**Zada:** Princess/wife of Prince Lakin/Ruala

**Zadok:** a male Grand Master of the Insidiae

**Zander:** a male Nordes warrior

**Zane:** one of Juleta's husbands

**Zede:** an ancient demon/ one of the Old Ones

**Zehmann:** an ancient demon/ one of the Old Ones

**Zeke:** a drifter/travels with Sam, Carl and Johnny

**Zelda:** mother of Rachel and Zack

**Zeman:** Prince/ son of King Zachariah and Queen Noella of New Samona/husband of Oda/Ruala

**Zieman:** a demon

**Zorda:** Taperian soldier injured in battle at the Wall of Dorath

**Zortus:** demon/lieutenant of Visterle

**Zourlock:** a notorious warlord from the Continent of Salszar

**Zoya:** a seer from Taperia

# Glossary of Terms

**Aboultis:** the calling cards of demons

**Abrax:** the planet that orbits closest to the three suns/ uninhabited

**Abuckto:** a sub race of superior intelligence in the Kingdom of Inferus

**Abyss:** a vast void used to imprison demons

**Acura:** the whispering shadows/are in the inner circle of demons that directly serve the Old Ones

**Adros:** one of five solar systems in the Mensor Galaxy

**Alferto:** a type of grain that is common in Opots

**Altar of Kenar:** the special altar mandated for the Blood Moon Ceremonies

**Amark:** ancient language of The Great Ruler

**Amper Tree:** special wood/forests of these trees are found in the lands of the Valdore Tribe

**Amulth:** means filth in the language of demons/these monsters are made out of the waste of tortured souls from the hell dimensions

**Anewa:** one of seven continents in the World of Nunc

**Aplewort:** an herb when mixed with water purges poisons from a body

**Asherane:** ancient tribe that lived in the northern regions of the Kingdom of Lentz

**Ashta**: a common herb/when the dried leaves are boiled they give off a pleasant scent

**Astras:** the ancient underground city of the Centras

**Astrum**: the solar system that consists of three suns that form a triangle and seven planets

**Backor:** one of the eight worlds in the Naz Solar System in the Mensor Galaxy

**Balterak:** one of the eight worlds in the Naz Solar System in the Mensor Galaxy

**Beltrad:** a species of lower level demons

**Blood rings:** Large red rubies set in silver with markings of the Old Ones

**Boca:** a covered wagon pulled by horses

**Box of Itifer:** a gift to the world of man from The Great Ruler; this gift affects the balance of creation

**Bozie:** a game of skill played by the Nordes Tribe

**Calphy:** an ancient art form from Ryed

**Cava plant:** a poisonous plant that grows freely near bodies of water

**Centras:** ancient race of creatures who have the responsibility of protecting the Holy Box of Itifer

**Cerfic:** an ancient language widely spoken among many kingdoms/a language of the masses not royalty

**Chalice of Ascension:** a gift from The Great Ruler, this gift contains unimaginable powers

**Charto:** the most radical political faction in the Kingdom of Inferus

**Cheyweg:** the ancient language of the Village of Tameric in the Kingdom of Marba

**Cicero College:** in Wetpr, outside of Salar, where Raul, Simon and Hannah attended college

**Clan of Gesmal:** a tribe of demon hunters who live in the southern region of the Kingdom of Ryed

**Code of Denark:** the ancient code hidden within the Cerfic language

**Credo:** a secret group in Inferus who worship The Great Ruler

**Crystal pillars:** in the Ice Caves of Mordv/are blessed by The Great Ruler and filled with spiritual life force

**Cyrus cloth:** an ancient cloth made in Ryed

**Czarsta:** one of seven continents in the World of Nunc

**Daliosis Demons:** an ancient species of demon that lives underground in lairs

**Danger Card:** Elod slang for a person's trigger

**Demalogs:**  an inferior species of demons

**Demosa:**  a slow acting poison from the cava plant

**Diamond of Cazo:**  a gift from The Great Ruler, this gift can unleash powers from the center of the world

**Dirtx:**  one of the eight worlds in the Naz Solar System in the Mensor Galaxy

**Discedo Sect:**  a radical sect of the Insidiae

**Durisks:**  large demonic birds/their elongated beaks contain rows of fangs

**Ekel Beast:**  similar to a deer

**Elods:**  a race of people who live in the center of the World of Nunc in the Kingdom of Inferus

**Engas:**  a wild cat that inhabits the Vandrew Mountains

**Engor:**  a small pack animal that lives in trees

**Enot:**  a demonic unit of measurement comparable to 1.5 inches

**Enrop:**  a large species of bird that can speak many human languages

**Epocos:**  one of the original tribes in the Kingdom of Ryed

**Eto:**  a sub race of beings in the Kingdom of Inferus. They are all seductresses

**Farduth:**  a Shettee necklace that symbolizes a male has completed his rite of passage to become a warrior

**Filsum:**  the sixth planet in the Astrum Solar System/ two moons

**Florines:**  a brightly colored species of bird that lives in the Kingdom of Inferus

**Frebre:**  one of five solar systems in the Mensor Galaxy

**Fuln:**  one of the eight worlds in the Naz Solar System in the Mensor Galaxy

**Gafet:**  an ancient Shettee weapon

**Gafferd:**  a type of demon created by the dark lord Gilder of the Kingdom of Inferus

**Gamay:** an ancient language that was once popular in the lower kingdoms of Opots

**Gants:** large apelike creatures/Watchers of the Caves of Muldun

**Gartose:** demons that resemble huge cats but with wings and protruding teeth

**Gate of Isula:** the only opening in the great Wall of Dorath

**Gefrey Games:** games of sport where men fight each other and great beasts to the death

**Grand Masters:** the first people to call to the demons and invite them into this world

**Great Ruler:** God

**Half-Mans:** a tribe of creatures that are partially human and partially nature. They are three feet tall and walk on two legs but can change their coloring to match their environment.

**Hall of Antiquities:** a giant hall located in the monastery at Malga/ a sanctuary for holy items and manuscripts

**Hall of Light:** the Great Hall in the Ice Caves of Mordv

**Halrut:** an herb commonly found in the Kingdom of Stordt/used to help people sleep/

**Hells Wrath:** the ship that Tessa Demat travels in from Port Friada to Langer

**Hengers:** giant blue eagles/ birds of war

**Highland Pass:** the only passage through the Rosu Mountain Range

**Holy Scrolls:** gifts given to each kingdom by The Great Ruler, these gifts contain powers, wisdom and immortality

**Holy Vault:** a secret vault under the King's study in the castle in Wetpr designed to protect holy objects

**Horn of Asher:** a horn used by the Patronus warrior priests to signal each other

**Horn of Cass:** a horn used by the Wetprian soldiers to signal each other

**Horn of Cornwell:** a horn used by Dieter's men to signal each other

**Horn of Eel:** a horn used by the Ruala warriors to communicate with each other

**Horn of Esker:** a horn used by the Valdore Tribe to communicate with each other

**Horn of Ire:** a horn carried by the Taperian soldiers to communicate with each other

**Horn of Shana:** a horn carried by the soldiers of Lentz to communicate with each other

**Horn of Tula:** a horn used by the members of the Nordes Tribe for communication

**Horn of Vamont:** a horn used by the Kozach Tribe for communication

**Horn of Xepoltr:** a horn used by the Shettee warriors to communicate

**Huta:** a race of humans that is driven by hatred and ideas of racial superiority who live in the Kingdom of Marba

**Insidiae:** means conspirators/a highly organized secret group of humans who have sold their souls to demons

**Irtma:** one of the eight worlds in the Naz Solar System in the Mensor Galaxy

**Jacar:** giant leech-like creatures

**Jacept Plant:** a plant that a powerful poison is made from

**Jaze:** one of the eight worlds in the Naz Solar System in the Mensor Galaxy

**Juntos:** Talismans of black magic that Karzman would use to terrorize and weaken his opponents

**Kafer:** a small crescent shaped knife carried by the Beltrad

**Keepers of the Scrolls:** the Royal Family of the Kingdom of Wetpr entered into a covenant with The Great Ruler to protect his gifts until a time when they can be safely given back to the world of man

**Keno:** a demonic unit of measurement comparable to 13 inches

**Kier:** one of five solar systems in the Mensor Galaxy

**Kinsman:** the capital city of the planet Sidus

**Kozach:** a tribe that lives in the far north central regions of the Kingdom of Wetpr

**Lafz:** one of five solar systems in the Mensor Galaxy

**Lamsman:** an ankle bracelet worn by Venatores/stones in the bracelet signify great feats they had to accomplish to become a demon hunter

**Learning Center:** the first of its kind/a complex educational facility that is open to multiple peoples and guards the students and staff from terrorists

**Leaves of the Talamar plant:** used for food and medicine but also used in black magics to alter people's senses and to create illusions of the mind-in small quantities/ in large quantities can effect time/

**Libertas:** the name of a group of freedom fighters in northern Ryed

**Linges plant:** a plant that grows in damp, swampy regions in Opots/the white berries are used to make the drug Melanwhop

**Lithanize:** an ancient language common to the southern kingdoms of Opots.

**Lynswood:** an herb that reveals tracks that are concealed by black magic

**Mark of Satan:** a coiled red snake with green eyes and a yellow tongue

**Matu potage:** a food staple of the Shettee Tribe

**Mayka:** one of seven continents in the World of Nunc

**Melanwhop:** a drug made from the linges plant, causes lethargy and apathy

**Mensor Galaxy:** is 20,000 light years from the Astrum Solar System/this galaxy contains five solar systems: Adros, Kier, Lafz, Frebre and Naz

**Menzine:** a species of giant snake in the Kingdom of Inferus

**Mordov:** the special place in hell for hypocrites

**Motfer:** the land of the dead

**Muysack:** a huge flying beast from hell

**Naz:** one of five solar systems in the Mensor Galaxy/this solar system has eight worlds: Balterak, Nords, Jaze, Fuln, Backor, Dirtx, Irtma, Puner

**Nefandus:** a secret sect within the Insidiae

**Nordes:** a tribe of fiercely trained warriors who live in the northern region of the Kingdom of Lentz

**Nords:** one of the eight worlds in the Naz Solar System in the Mensor Galaxy

**Nunc:** the world where this story takes place/third planet from the three suns

**Old Ones:** the original demons that came to the World of Nunc

**Opatu bread:** a food staple of the Shettee Tribe

**Opots:** one of seven continents in the World of Nunc/the continent where this story takes place

**Oran:** a tobisk that is filled with a mixture of ramni oil, buruto powder and meno salts, designed to explode on impact

**Orantho:** the seventh planet in the Astrum Solar System/inhabited/four moons/ large planet/many hell worlds

**Patronus:** an elite group of men who serve as the protectors of the church

**Pfison screen:** a type of demonic cloaking devise/it is sensitive and has to be calibrated for the specific individuals it is intended for

**Planteen:** the fourth planet in the Astrum Solar System/inhabited/two moons

**Plyogram:** a drawing containing pictures within pictures to hide secret messages.

**Porto:** one of seven continents in the World of Nunc

**Prophesy of Isto:** an ancient prophesy of the Elods

**Prophesy of Izera**: Predicts the downfall of the Teivel regime

**Prophesy of the Blood Moon:** a demonic prophesy that predicts the doors to hell being opened.

**Propilatry:** a powerful form of demonic curse

**Prostras:** an ancient tribe that once inhabited the Ice Caves of Mordv

**Puner:** one of the eight worlds in the Naz Solar System in the Mensor Galaxy

**Raftifa:** ancient bat-like creatures that devour human flesh

**Rappal demon:** a lower level demon with slimy skin and an unusual smell

**Ravens:** messengers used by the dark lords

**Recupero:** a sect within the Insidiae that worships the demon Omnibus

**Rites of Purification:** an ancient ritual to close the windows of the demons

**Rogetts:** a tribe of humans that have digressed into murderous mutant monsters

**Rualas:** an ancient tribe of warriors said to be half human and half bird

**Ryisone**: a sedative

**Salszar:** one of seven continents in the World of Nunc

**Salts of Envoy:** a sleeping potion

**Schumack roots**: used for food and medicine but also used in black magics to alter people's senses and to create illusions of the mind-in small quantities/ in large quantities can effect time/

**Scio:** a crystal ball

**Scroll of Imari:** a gift of The Great Ruler, a scroll that unleashes the power of The Box of Itifer

**Seal of Natun:** a gift from The Holy Ruler that can open doors to other worlds

**Second Sons:** men bred to become vessels for demons

**Serpents of Satan:** can only be called forth by dark lords and demons, large red snakes with green eyes and yellow tongues

**Seven Sons Prophesy:** an ancient prophesy about seven sons who stand up against the demons and dark lords

**Shadow Men:** creature that can only be seen when illuminated at night

**Shaker Winds:** incredible storms that form when the currents and winds of three oceans converge

**Shamac:** the most commonly spoken language in the Continent of Opots

**Shesone:** an ancient fighting style of the Shettee Tribe

**Shettee:** an ancient tribe of warriors said to be half human and half lion

**Sidus:** the fifth planet in the Astrum Solar System/inhabited/red fog surrounds the planet

**Solv:** a specific prison within the Abyss

**Song of the Second Son:** an ancient prophesy about an evil that is passed between second son's of a family resulting in a monster that brings terror and darkness to the world of man

**Stratas:** Creatures bred by the Elods

**Sundra Templer:** a gift from The Great Ruler that was stolen by dark lords/an orb with extraordinary powers that can be used in multiple ways such as transporting humans through other worlds

**Tabutu:** an ancient form of fighting developed by the Asherane Tribe of the Kingdom of Lentz

**Tagnit Trilogy:** a group of three spell books that are so powerful they have living powers

**Talisman:** an object with magical or supernatural meaning

**Talmuth:** giant red dragon-like creatures

**Talus paper:** a strong but almost transparent paper

**Taluth:** a light weight metal used to make the ancient Shettee weapons called the Gafets

**Tameric:** the place where Karzman claims he came from although it does not exist on any map of Opots/also the name of the collective hell worlds of Nunc

**Tangers:** large wild, grazing animals that travel in herds

**Tansof:** one of seven continents in the World of Nunc

**Tarus demon**: huge, power creatures that walk on two legs but have the head, neck and shoulders of an ox

**Telgras:** a hell beast that looks like it is half wolf and half panther

**Teragon:** death terror/a monster created as a result of diabolical acts

**Terbot bear:** a bear that roams in the northern regions of the continent of Opots

**Tervator:** fourteen foot monster that walks like a man with long dark hair over its entire body and bull-like horns protruding from its head

**Texts of Semalia:** ancient texts about demonic language and rituals

**The Boldface:** Admiral Gideon's ship

**The Book of Horror:** a book that is worshipped by demons/contains prophesies

**The Celebration of Days:** an annual celebration of the Centras

**The Dead Runner**: ship of the notorious pirate Axel Sam

**The Hall of Knowledge:** the primary meeting room in the Temple of the Abuckto in the Kingdom of Inferus

**The Hall of Understanding:** the building in Astras where the history of the Centras is documented in drawings

**The Hunters:** another name for the Shettee Tribe

**The Lion:** a very powerful messenger of The Great Ruler assumes the form of a lion when he walks in the worlds of man

**The Tempest:** a clandestine organization made up of witches and warlocks

**The Thirteenth Color:** not seen in the world of man it is the color of horror/hell

**Thresiose:** a knife used in demonic ceremonies

**Timbar:** ghost dragons/ demons that can fly

**Tinchure water:** an herbal pain remedy used by the Nordes Tribe

**Tincture of the Redeti Plant:** Hutas dip the tips of their weapons in this insect infested liquid. The insects lay eggs inside of the victim. When the eggs are mature and hatch, two inch worm-like creatures are produced and will eat the organs of the victim causing a long and painful death

**Tobisks:** sphere shaped objects, metal and hollow inside that are designed to be launched from a Trebuchet

**Tramor:** a flying monster in the Kingdom of Inferus

**Traxsor:** the second planet in the Astrum Solar System

**Trebuchets:** wooden machines used to catapult objects

**Trimoth:** a game of skill, strength and speed

**Triolie:** a Nordes gambling game

**Twanize:** a language common to the Continent of Porto

**Tygrus:** a ship that docked in Port Friada

**Unholy altar:** altar used to worship demons

**Valdees:** the tribe that lives in the underwater Kingdom of Ogg

**Valdore:** a tribe of merciless separatists who live in the extreme northern regions of the Kingdom of Lentz

**Velvadera:** purgatory

**Venator:** means hunter in the old language

**Venom of the Atha serpent:** one of the poisons that Hutas put on their arrows

**Vessel of Darkness:** a human created from darkness to hold the essence of a powerful demon

**Vue:** a flute-like instrument used in the Kingdom of Inferus

**Wall of Dorath:** a giant wall that separates the Kingdoms of Norkv and Xepoltr from the Kingdom of Marba

**Willimonns:** small furry creatures that are hunted for food and sport

**Xelope:** the oneness of spirit with all that lives

**Yellow Jay:** a bird native to Opots

**Yellow Mandeze**: a song bird common to Opots

**Zehno demon:** thin, creature with long red and blue plumes on the back of its head with large eyes and round mouths

**Zendoti:** demons that are distinguished by the geometrically shaped tuffs of hair that protrude from their heads

# Glossary of Maps

**The maps are displayed in order of relevance**

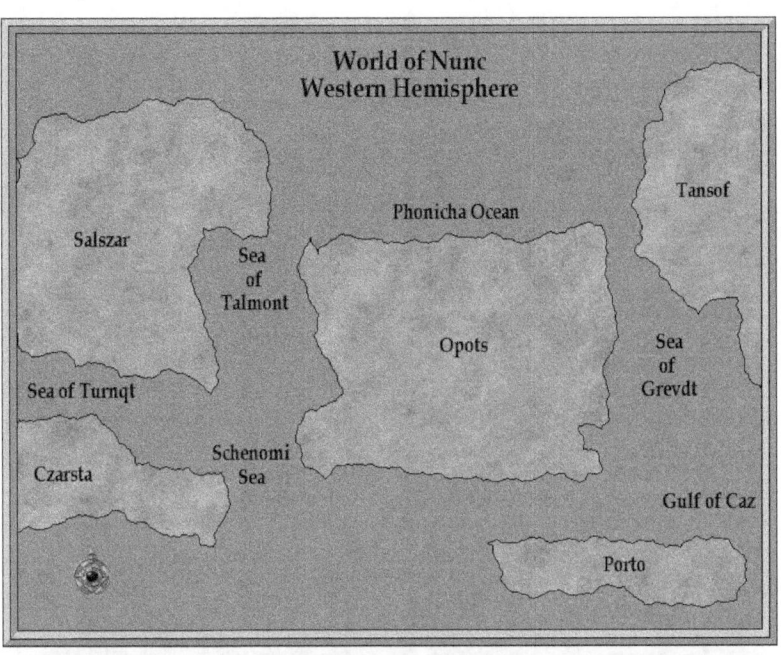

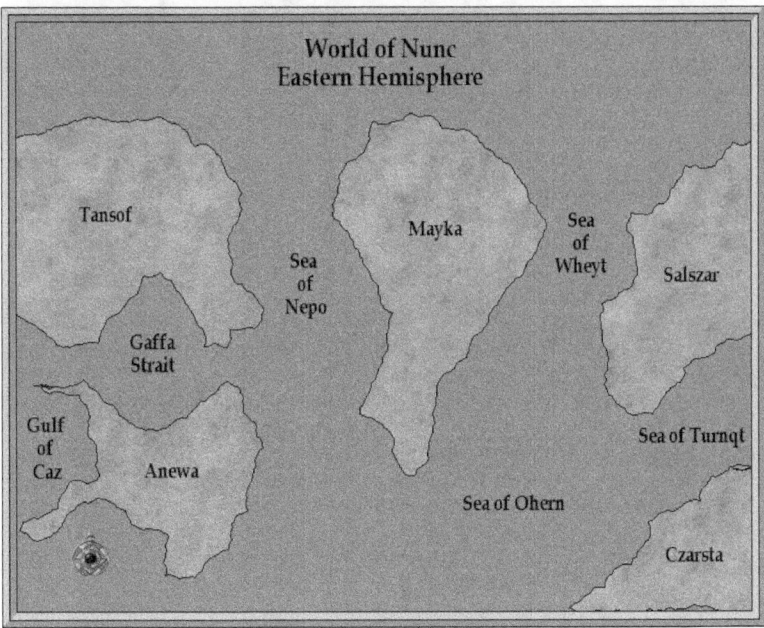

707

# Continent of Opots
## With new forts

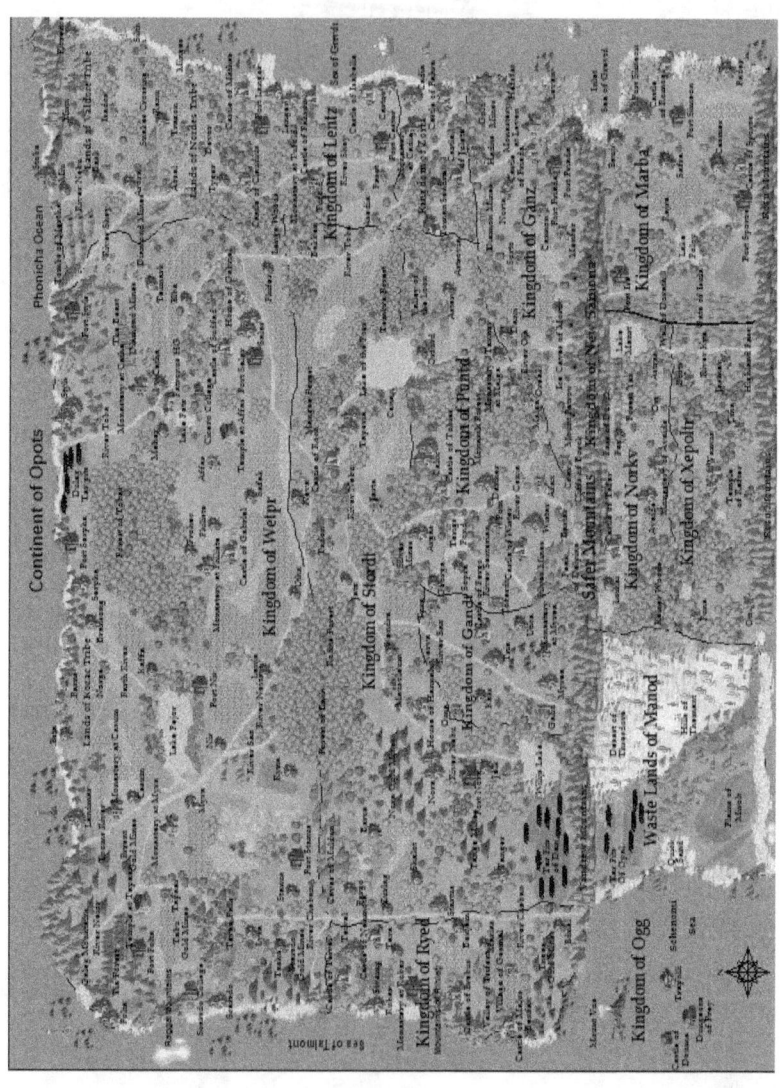

## Western Stordt
## With Fort Nora

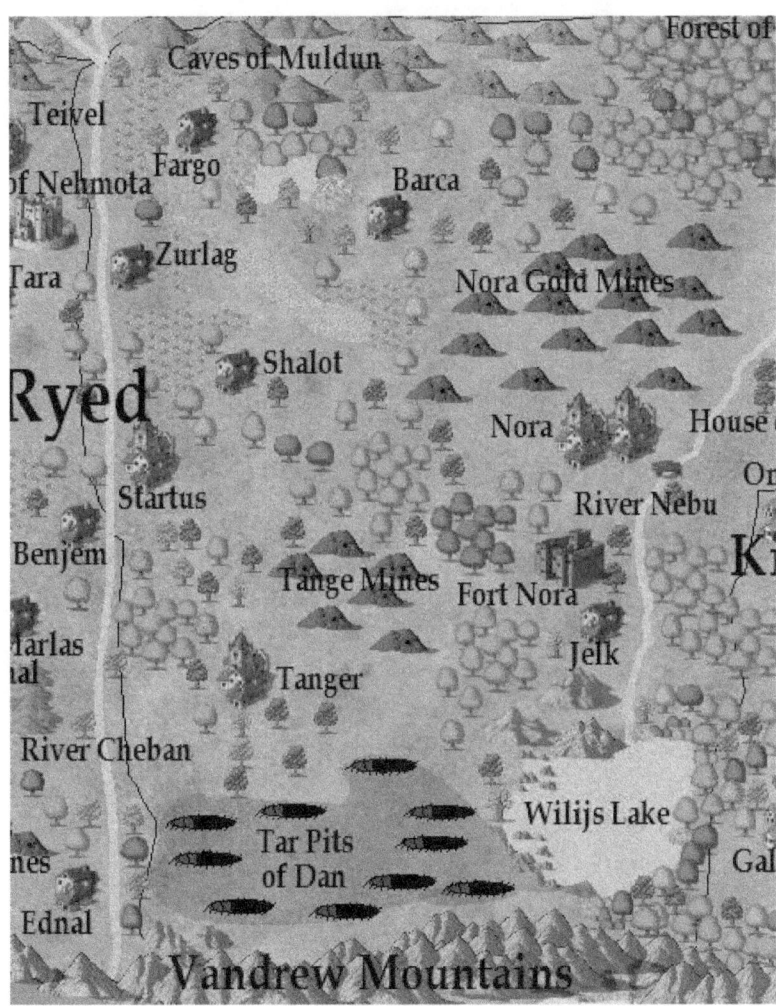

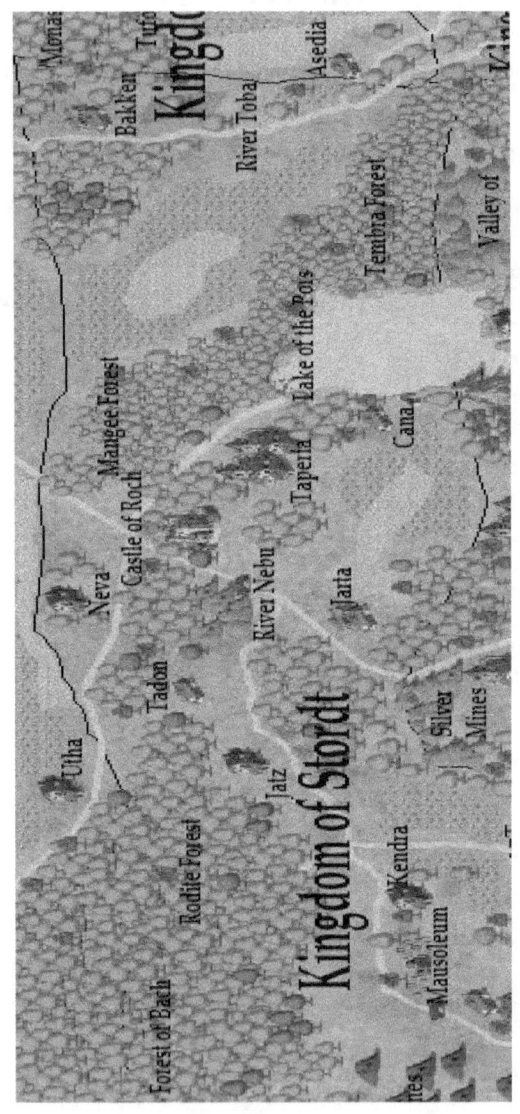

## Western Wetpr
## With Fort Stanus

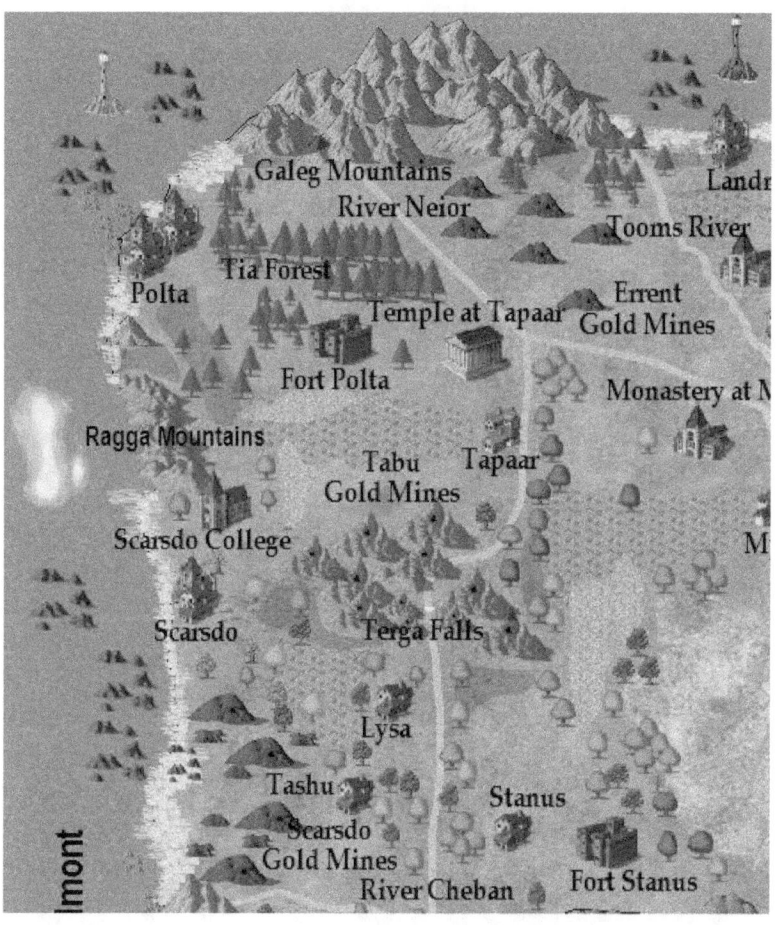

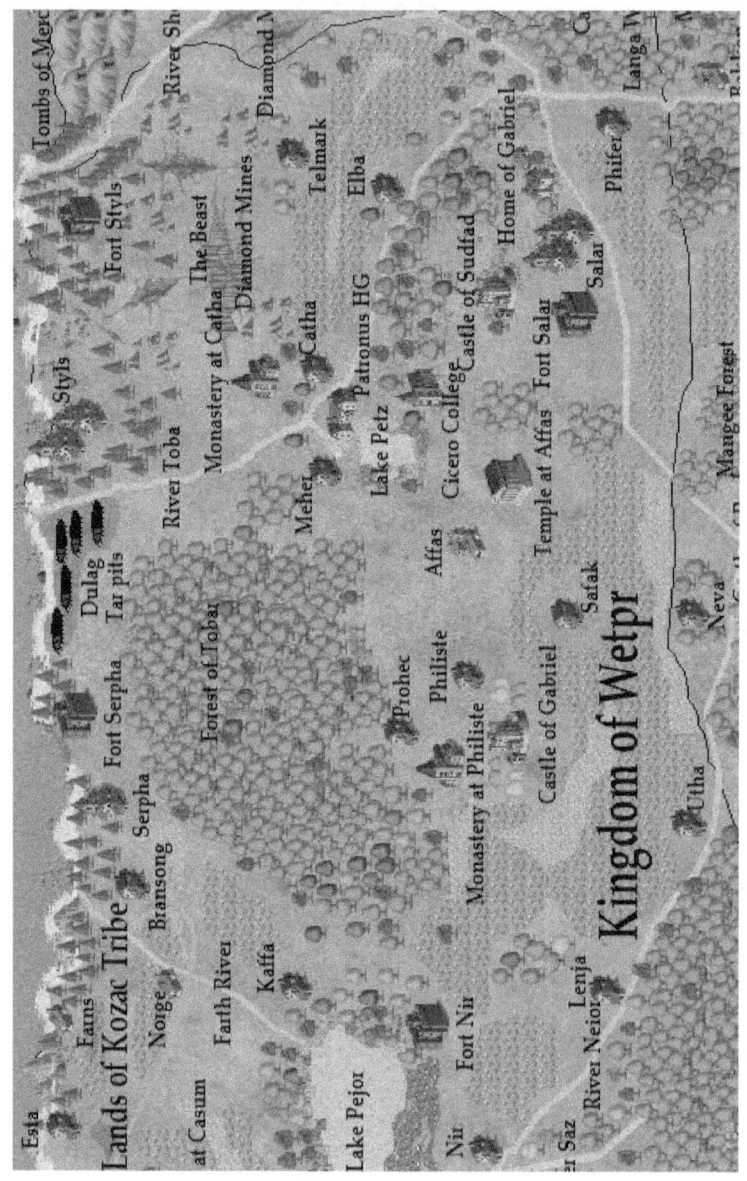

## Marba

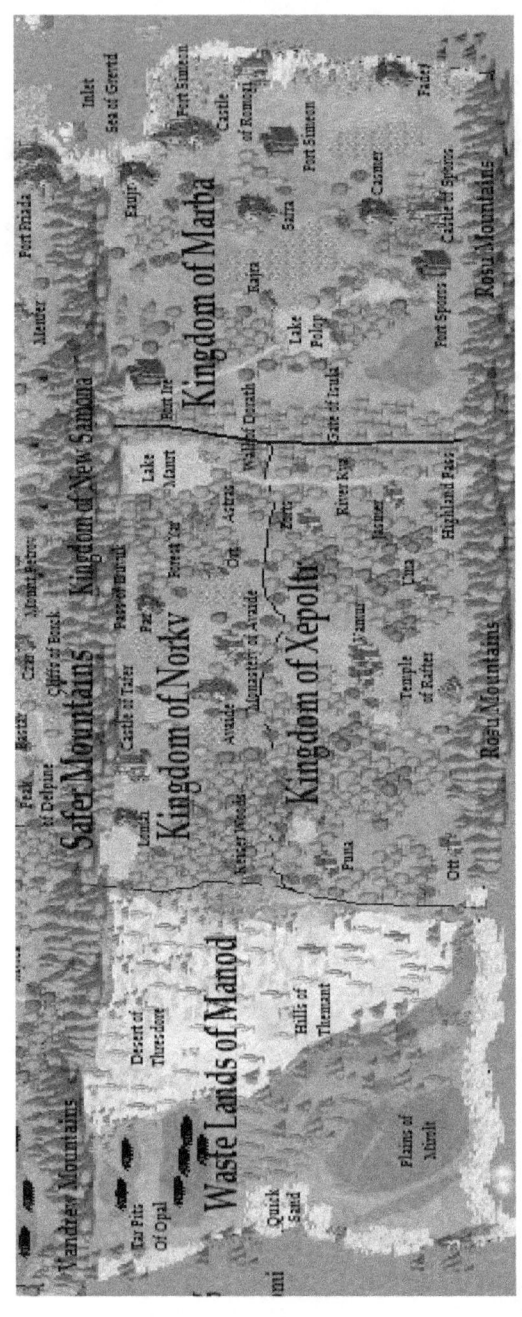

# New Samona
## Ice Caves of Mordv

# Astrum Solar System

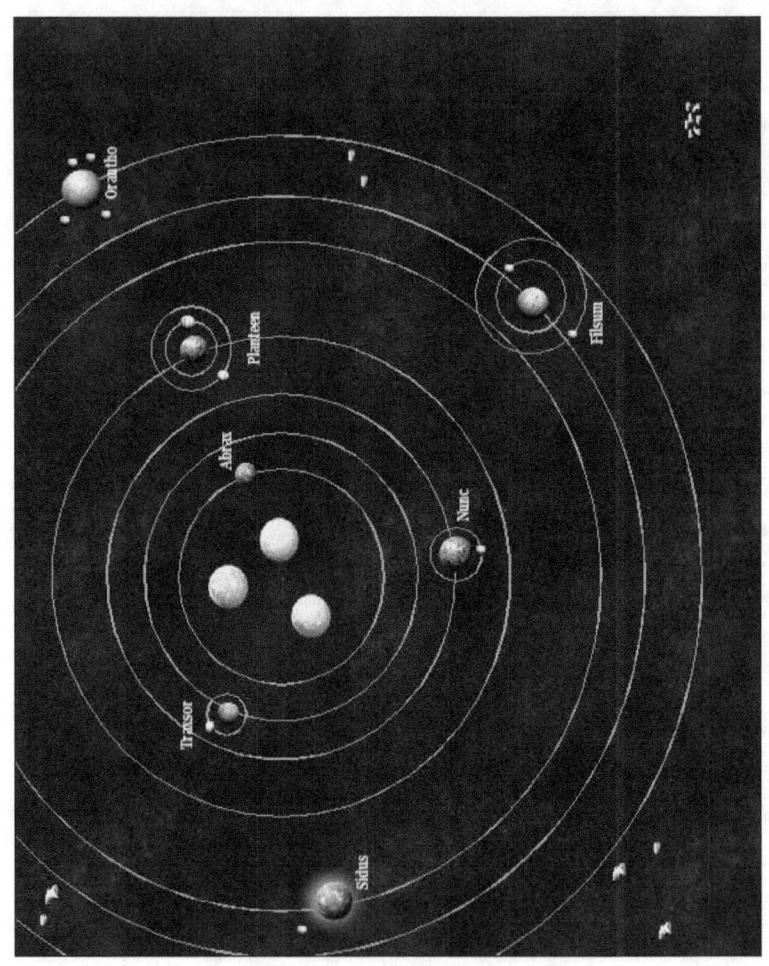

www.ingramcontent.com/pod-product-compliance
Lightning Source LLC
Chambersburg PA
CBHW052338020726
47503CB00001B/13